Flirtation Point Publishing
Emma Kate
www.authoremmakate.com

Cover Design by Emily Wittig
Editing by Kelly Siskind
Copy Editing by Claudette Cruz, the Editing Sweetheart
Proofreading by Judy's Proofreading

Ebook ISBN: 979-8-9908678-0-2
Paperback ISBN: 979-8-9908678-1-9

Contents

1. Bryn   1

2. Jameson   10

3. Bryn   19

4. Jameson   26

5. Bryn   32

6. Jameson   40

7. Bryn   48

8. Jameson   57

9. Bryn   64

10. Jameson   70

11. Bryn   81

12. Jameson   91

13. Bryn   99

14.	Jameson	106
15.	Bryn	110
16.	Jameson	117
17.	Bryn	126
18.	Jameson	136
19.	Bryn	146
20.	Jameson	156
21.	Bryn	164
22.	Jameson	174
23.	Bryn	182
24.	Bryn	188
25.	Bryn	196
26.	Jameson	199
27.	Jameson	209
28.	Bryn	214
29.	Bryn	220
30.	Jameson	222
31.	Bryn	233
32.	Jameson	243
33.	Bryn	249
34.	Bryn	251
35.	Jameson	259
36.	Bryn	269

37. Jameson   274

38. Jameson   277

39. Bryn   283

40. Jameson   290

41. Bryn   297

42. Jameson   307

43. Bryn   314

44. Jameson   323

45. Bryn   335

46. Bryn   340

47. Jameson   350

48. Jameson   356

49. Epilogue   363

Acknowledgments   369

About the author   371

To the readers who just want ten minutes to sit in silence and read their book. To the ones who cannot possibly make one more decision today. To the ones who want to escape into a world where a happily ever after is guaranteed.

***

Welcome to Wild Bluffs.

Chapter One

Bryn

"Take any longer and our balls are going to turn blue," my sister Kelsey yells from the next tee box, where she and her friends are waiting for me. I heft the golf bag onto my shoulders, and the straps immediately dig into my skin. Relishing the warm sun on my face, I make my way over to the group. The course looks exactly the same as when I used to caddie here as a teen. Luckily, today I'm carrying my own bag rather than schlepping around someone else's.

Developed in an old cow pasture, Wild Bluffs Country Club was built on the sand dunes that surround Wild Bluffs, Colorado. With its golf holes enveloped by a natural grass rough, you have a hard time finding golf balls if your shot isn't straight down the fairway.

I spent many an hour searching for members' lost balls, working to get a better tip as a teen. Even at that age, I knew college wasn't going to pay for itself.

Today is different, though. We're here for the 32nd birthday party of my oldest sister, Kelsey. The music is blaring—spurred by our mutual friend Becca's recent breakup—and our group is the only one still out on the course. The rest of Kelsey's friends, along with a couple of groups of golfers who flew in for a weekend of fun, gave up after nine holes and headed to the bar for food and drinks.

"When you see my face, hope it gives you hell," I sing along under my breath, loving that Becca is fueling her angst with 2000s pop.

I adjust my stance and take a few practice swings before putting down my Titleist 4 golf ball on the tee. Closing my eyes, I inhale deeply and then launch the ball through the air. It soars but slices right into the rough between our hole and the one next to it.

I swear under my breath. The sun is too bright to follow the ball. It's definitely somewhere between the second or third yucca clump, right?

Why did I let Kels talk me into a bottle of wine each last night? It wasn't even her birthday yet.

Making my way through the sandhills, I search for my ball with my 7-iron, hoping to get out of the weeds before finding any rattlesnakes. Spotting a Titleist approximately where mine landed, I quickly hit it back into the fairway where the other girls had all managed to find their tee-shots.

As I follow its trajectory, I suddenly hear the thud of a bag being set down and somehow know it wasn't my ball that just flew off.

Oops.

Turning around, I see a dark-haired man standing there, looking in disbelief at the ground. I slowly approach him and see my Titleist 4 golf ball lying next to his feet, complete with the small penis Izzy drew on it this morning.

"So you know how to mark a ball, you just don't know how to *use* the mark to identify your ball?"

Looking into his face, I can't help but cringe a bit at the bitterness in his voice, despite being pleasantly surprised by the fact that I am actually looking up at a man for a change, a rarity at five feet, ten inches.

"Oh. Shoot. I'm playing a Titleist 4 too, and I wasn't paying enough attention, I guess. Yours was right over there." Recognizing how ridiculous I look pointing at the spot he had clearly just seen me hitting from, I quickly lower my arm and glance at his face again.

In addition to being tall, this man is all kinds of eye candy. He clearly hits the gym on a regular basis, if how tight his white, collared shirt is pulling across his chest is any indication. His dark brown hair matches a thick beard.

Don't I know him from somewhere? I'm usually pretty good at matching faces with names, and there is something about his dark green eyes that seems familiar. Maybe the facial hair is throwing me off.

Would it be inappropriate to ask if he has a beard all the time?

He crosses his arms, the movement drawing my attention to his defined biceps. "Sure, well, a lot of good that does me. It's still a stroke. Maybe pay more attention next time you and your sorority sisters decide to use Daddy's golf membership, okay?"

Definitely an inappropriate time to ask about the beard, then.

"Excuse me?" I feel my eyebrows shoot up under my baseball cap. "First, you've got to be joking about it being a stroke. You are out here"—I look around—"alone? You get to decide what number you write on your scorecard. Second, fuck you. This is my sister's membership, you arrogant prick."

I turn to point at Izzy, an almost six-foot-tall brunette decked out in Wild Bluffs Country Club attire, nicely proving my point.

The fact that she decided to curtsy with her hot-pink golf skort after her shot does not help my case, but, in her defense, it was a pretty damn good shot.

He pulls his baseball cap off and runs his hand through his hair, a gesture I find irritatingly handsome. "Ahh, yes. A real credit to the sport of golf, that one."

"Again, fuck you. Just play my ball. It will be easy for everyone to identify as yours."

Arms crossed warily across his chest, he shoots me a confused look. "...because you're such a dick?"

Continuing to search his face to figure out who this man is, I'm surprised when I see an almost smile pulling at the corner of his mouth.

"Original. I've never been called a dick before."

Despite his gruff attitude, I feel a pull to keep talking to this man. Okay, yes. By *pull*, I mean a purely physical attraction that is entirely due to his large frame and handsome smile now on display.

"Well, welcome to Wild Bluffs. Home of the honest."

"Wow. What a tagline. I'm surprised they've managed to keep its existence a secret from the world for as long as they have."

I laugh, my annoyance morphing into something else. He's got a sense of humor and can at least keep up with me in a verbal sparring session.

"Oh, the town hired the same PR team that helps keep Atlantis's location a mystery. It's a bit pricey but clearly worth every penny."

He chuckles, leaning casually on his golf club while we banter back and forth.

"Do you think they'd let me in on the secret?"

"Not a chance. It's not for the likes of you."

"Oh really? And just how is that decided?" he asks.

"Multiple rounds of interviews, an IQ test, and an intense psychological evaluation. Unfortunately, I don't think you're going to make the cut," I tease.

"How will I ever recover?"

"I'd suggest therapy, which you can clearly pay for if you're a member here, but I'm not sure it will help. If you can't pass the test, you can't pass the test."

"Of course you'd go there. Whatever." His face changes abruptly, his eyebrows pulling together into a deep crease. He swings his bag onto his shoulders, making me realize again how tall he is. I watch him stomp away, leaving me and my penis ball behind to recover from that emotional roller coaster of a conversation.

***

The back nine flies by in a flurry of stories and laughter. By the time we reach the eighteenth hole, the sun is starting to set, staining the sky with its own watercolor painting of pink and purple.

Becca leads us back toward the clubhouse, talking excitedly about her new plan to stay single for a while.

"Taking a couple months off from the dating scene will allow me to find my sshpecial sshomeone," she slurs slightly at the end, clearly in need of some hydration and likely some food to soak up the booze from today. "You agree, don't you, Bryn? It's working for you, right?"

Before I can answer, Kelsey grins over at us, clearly ready for some mind ninjaing, a side effect of her days with the Marines and now at her cybersecurity firm.

"I don't know if three years can actually be considered 'a couple months,' Becca."

Becca looks at me, her warm green eyes widening at the revelation.

"You haven't had sex in YEARS?" she practically yells.

I grab her elbow as she loses her footing and her bag starts to tip her backward.

"Jesus, Becca, could you say it a little louder? I don't think all the old men in the locker room heard you," I angrily whisper back.

"One"—Becca holds up her finger—"you know most of those men are not that old and would totally be doable at this point. You're twenty-eight. Also, three years is a long, long time to go without...ya know...*companionship*."

I sigh deeply, hoping she'll get distracted if I just stay silent.

"Bryn." She grabs my face so I have to look at her.

I spot Izzy and Kelsey over her right shoulder, waving to the rest of the birthday party already encircling the firepit but clearly planning to stay and enjoy the show.

Just great. The last thing I want is for my sisters to start thinking they need to meddle in my love life. Like I don't get enough of that from my mom, and apparently now Becca.

"Peter was a dick," she continues at a more reasonable volume. "It wasn't fair that he put all the blame on you when you guys broke it off. Relationships are two-sided. He expected a lot from you he wasn't willing to give in return."

Goodness, I'm tearing up a little bit, which I most definitely do not want to do.

Unluckily for me, Becca isn't done. "It's not a good enough reason to go without S. E. X. for"—she drops her voice to a whisper—"three whole years."

"I promise it has nothing to do with asshole Peter. Have you met the men who are on dating apps these days? None of them have been worth a second date, let alone actually sleeping with. Plus, there is no need to worry, Beccs. I can take care of myself, if you know what I mean?" I say with a wink, hoping I can get out of sharing that it has been a hell of a lot longer than three years—twenty-eight, to be exact.

True to Becca form, she turns bright red and starts giggling. She's been this way forever. She so badly does not want to be a prude, but she most definitely is, at least at heart.

Not that I have a leg to stand on, of course.

Becca turns and starts toward the fire, muttering something about needing some damn s'mores in her life if she isn't going to be getting any action, and I can't help but roll my eyes.

My sister Izzy hangs back, the only one who knows about my un-popped cherry. "You could tell them, you know. I don't think they'd make you being a twenty-eight-year-old virgin into as big of a deal as you seem to think they would."

"But they would make it into *a* deal. Which is the exact opposite of what I want. You know I don't care about being a virgin. If I did, I wouldn't be one. It just hasn't happened. And it's not like I'm lying to them."

Izzy gives my shoulder a squeeze, prompting me to continue before she offers me sympathy I most certainly do not want. "They've literally never asked me if I've had sex with someone. Plus, all the men I've gone out with in the last three years have been complete skeazeballs. I wouldn't have slept with them even if it weren't my first time."

"While it was pretty obvious from the fact that you were best friends with all the guys in high school that you were a virgin then, we all assumed you and Peter had sex. You dated for *three years* and never once complained that *he* was the one holding out."

"Meh. The effort of fighting him on a decree from his mother did not seem to be worth the reward."

She grimaces. "It's like he gets worse every time I hear about him."

"You know, he wasn't a bad guy. He was actually a good boyfriend the majority of the time. He just had mommy issues."

"And, apparently, performance issues."

"I want to deny it, but in hindsight, it does feel like there could've been a bit more spark."

"A lot more spark, Sis. A lot more spark," Izzy says as we make our way after our friends.

CHAPTER TWO

JAMESON

AFTER I FINISH THE back nine, I head to the weight room for my second workout of the day.

Yes, I may have gained a few too many pounds in the last year. Yes, it may have been equally due to stress eating chocolate chip cookies and sad beer drinking.

After a month of two-a-days in the gym and walking at least thirty-six holes a day, I'm finally back in shape. Okay, fine, it probably doesn't hurt that I've also cut back to a few beers a week rather than the few beers an hour I was consuming before.

But it's mostly the extra workouts.

I finish the final set of my core round, wishing I were back home in my gym with extra fans and air-conditioning rather than sweating my ass off in this little one the course keeps open for nonlocals like me who stay the night in their guesthouses and hotel rooms.

As I start the short trip back to my hotel room in the building just next to the putting green, I notice a group of women sitting around the fire. They're cute, but as one catches my eye, I quickly turn my face away, hoping she doesn't recognize me.

The girl from this afternoon wasn't with them. Maybe she went home? Why do I feel a little sad about that? I mentally shake my head. I've learned my lesson about getting involved with women like her.

After closing the door to my room behind me, I lie down on my bed, letting the air-conditioning cool my sweat. The extra endorphins from my workout didn't even last all two minutes of my walk back, and the scorecard sitting on my desk sapped what little joy remained in me as I walked in.

I bury my face in my pillow and let out a deep sigh.

Ugh. I suck at golf.

My phone rings, and I barely register it's Erica, the head of the public relations team handling my downhill spiral, before I answer it.

"Hi, Erica."

"Just calling to check in on my favorite golfer."

"I can't possibly be your favorite golfer, Erica. Tell me what's really up."

"I just wanted to let you know that my team has been in contact with all your current sponsors, and things are starting to settle down now that you're out of the spotlight. I think we're going to be able to keep them all."

Thank God. While I wouldn't be hard up for cash or anything like that if I lost those deals, I'm not sure my ego can handle any more losses this year. I've always been the go-to golfer for sponsorship deals and ad campaigns, and the fact that I've lost that status hurts far more than I ever expected it to.

"Thanks, Erica. That's great news. Any news of the couple of new ones you were chasing?"

"Nothing yet, Jameo," she says, underemphasizing the "O" in my nickname so it comes out as "Jame-ah" instead of "Jame-oh," like it does for everyone else. "Just focus on your game. Don't get drunk. Don't hit on random women. You know what? Let's just say no women whatsoever."

"Of course. I haven't done anything but golf and exercise since I got here."

"That's what I like to hear."

We make small talk for another minute before Erica has to go. As I hang up my phone, I think about how stupid I've been the last year. Sure, I was hurting, but I made some bad decisions that almost cost me the profession I love and a lot of money in winnings and sponsorships.

But I'm totally focused now. I've barely looked at a woman since arriving at Wild Bluffs until today, and she only serves to remind me what terrible taste I have in women.

With that thought, I roll off the side of the bed and make my way slowly toward the shower, legs burning from the extra eighteen I got in today after the first two rounds ended poorly.

The water pounds down on me like a hundred tiny punches but doesn't put a dent in the feeling of defeat that has settled into my bones. I stand in the shower, my six-foot-four frame slumped as I let the hot water run over me, trying to wash away the disappointment of failing to score more than five under par yet again during my third round.

The round started out fine. And then it had been rough—the trudging through cacti and yuccas to find my balls in the, well, *rough*. That is the essence of golf: the more time you spend in the rough, the rougher the round becomes.

And the hot-as-hell girl who stole my ball and called me a dick before casually mentioning I'm rich? Why is it that women can't help but focus on my money?

Been there, done that. It is the one mistake I'm not interested in making again.

As soon as a woman mentions me being rich, I'm out.

Not that my dick seems to remember the last part.

"Damn it, Jameo," I mutter to myself as I lean against the tiled wall. "Get your head in the game." But the image of her smirking at me from under the brim of her cap refuses to leave. If it weren't for my self-imposed celibacy and her clear interest in me being "rich," she'd be my usual kryptonite, all tanned legs and a fiery mouth.

Just what I need to screw up my already precarious career.

Unfortunately, my brain and my anatomy down south don't seem to agree on what our focus is in Wild Bluffs.

Knowing my head is unlikely to win this battle, I let my mind wander back to the girl from this afternoon. Down her long legs and back up to her adorable smirk, my hand and thoughts wandering into carnal territory. I'm just about to give in to the urge—it's been a hot second since that specific club of mine has gotten any play—when the sound of an incoming text pierces the steamy air.

That, of course, will be Lila, my younger sister and—jeez, I'm lame—my best friend. Unfortunately, and unbeknown to her, she has always had a disturbing habit of interrupting my most private moments. And getting a text while thinking about getting myself off in the shower is actually very low on the list of embarrassing moments she's intruded on.

In high school, as I was losing my virginity, I heard my sister's pipsqueak friends *giggling* about Lila playing seven minutes in Heaven...as I was about to come inside a girl for the first time.

Needless to say, it was not my best showing, and no one had a happy ending, least of all Bryan Godsey, the sixteen-year-old I found behind a tree with my thirteen-year-old sister. He was so scared, he may have left with a bit of pee running down his leg. He should feel lucky it was me rather than my dad who heard her friends.

It wasn't until college that I met Sarah, who fortunately hadn't heard the story of me leaving my date unsatisfied in a field. Unfortunately, Lila called halfway through, and my phone played the "Cheetah Girls, Cheetah Sisters" song she had picked out as her ringtone until I finally found the Decline button through my horny haze. Luckily, Sarah was willing to try again after I figured out how to silence my phone.

I have, thankfully, gotten better since then, although my sister's bad timing remains the same.

Knowing the moment is gone—shit, how pathetic am I that I can't even romance myself these days?—I sigh and turn off the water.

I grab one of the white, fluffy towels from the rack, sling it around my waist, and sit on the edge of my room's extra bed.

Hey, Jameo, how's the golf thing going?

I can't help but smile at her nonchalant way of referring to my career.

Could be better.

How's grad school treating you? Need more cash for textbooks or late-night pizza?

Haha. I asked for pizza ONE TIME. And I was drunk and very hungry, in my defense.

Plus, you've paid for enough. I told you my internship should be enough to cover tuition this semester.

My heart tightens at the memory of the first time she had to ask me for help with her tuition and how embarrassed she had been. If I hadn't been such a self-centered ass, I would've known the small college fund our parents had saved wouldn't be enough to cover all four years of an engineering degree plus a master's degree. Especially with no sports scholarship like I had.

I'm happy to help you. You get paid shit at your internship, and you should be having fun.

Like you're having fun right now? When was the last time you saw any of your friends?

You know being seen with me right now is a black mark on someone's image, right?

That's what private clubs are for. I thought that's why you were out in the middle of nowhere at the only fancy golf course on the planet where you might accidentally step in cow shit.

Plus, JT reached out to me. You've ignored all his texts and calls. FOR A MONTH.

How did he get your number? I swear to God, if he was hitting on you, I'll shove my driver so far up his ass, it tees up his eyes.

I'm actually very certain Lila and JT haven't been talking about anything other than how pathetic I am. They actively hate each other with a passion so strong, I can rarely be in the same area as both my favorite people at once. My parents set up two tables at Thanksgiving, supposedly because there are so many of us, but really so JT can come without having to fight with Lila the entire time. Still, it's nice to remind her every once in a while that she's too good for every man ever.

Super gross, oddly specific visual, bud. Plus, who I text is not your concern.

You avoiding the world for the last month, on the other hand, is my concern. I know you haven't seen your BEST friend. Have you talked to anyone?

I would gladly endure the required brain bleach to even know you'd had a one-night stand at this point.

I sigh, running a hand through my wet hair.

I talked to a hot girl just this afternoon, in fact.

Not *not* true.

Ooh. Tell me everything.

Actually, on second thought, don't. Go find her. Kiss her. Hold her hand. TALK TO HER. And then never tell me what happens.

(…)

Lila

UGH. You are so infuriating. You need a rebound. It has been a year since you broke up with she-who-will-not-be-named. YOU NEED TO GET LAID. I have it on good authority it has been A YEAR. That's too long for anyone, including yours truly.

Me

Jesus, Lila, TMI.

Lila may be twenty-four and completing her master's in engineering next spring, but I do not need to think about her getting laid. And as much as I want to deny it, I also know she's right. It has been a long time since I've felt any interest in anyone—until that infuriating girl today.

Fuck. No, not the girl today. That zing I felt in my chest was pure anger at her comment, nothing else. No sparks.

Me

And just who is this "good authority"?? Stop talking to JT!

Lila

Gotta run to class. Love you!

"All right, Sis," I say out loud, grabbing my keys and wallet. "You win. I'll go to the bar tonight and see what happens."

Let's just hope the woman from today isn't there. I'm not sure how long my body will let me stay away from her, even knowing she is just after my money.

Chapter Three

Bryn

"BRYN, THERE HE IS. You have to go apologize for calling him a stupid dick."

Izzy shoves my arm, forcing me to stop inhaling my french fries and focus on the spot where a freshly showered "Dick" has just walked through the door into the club's restaurant and bar area.

I thought golf-attire Dick was handsome, but he is nothing compared to the version walking in front of me in slacks and a white button-down shirt. His dark hair is just long enough to need to be brushed back from his face, and his eyes are a piercing green that is noticeable even from twenty feet away. The man has a presence that can't be denied, and, based on the number of people staring at him when he walks in, I'm not the only one who feels that way.

It's unfortunate he was so hot and cold this afternoon. After our rocky start, there had been a minute there when I thought he might be worth getting to know.

"I didn't call him stupid. I implied he wouldn't pass some made-up test to get into Wild Bluffs. Or a secret society. Maybe Atlantis?" I groan. "And I'm honestly not sure if I was insulting his character, IQ, or his psychological state. All were included in the test."

Izzy blinks a couple of times, clearly trying to work through what I just told her. I drop my head into my hands. "You know things just come out of my mouth without me knowing what I'm saying!"

I quickly glance up, eyeing his table, and again feel the twinge that comes with knowing I'm forgetting something.

"Do you recognize him, Iz? Is he from Wild Bluffs?"

Not many of the locals are members out here, with the club primarily catering to out-of-town big shots who fly into the small airport in town on their private planes, but enough are members to warrant the question. While unlikely that I wouldn't recognize a local, I've been out of high school long enough that it's possible I don't know everyone in town anymore.

"Hmm..." She turns, giving him a long once-over. "No. Definitely not a local. But he does seem familiar. I think it's the beard that's throwing me off."

This is what I love about Iz: though she is very different from me in temperament—the sweet to my sour, if you will—we always seem to be on the same wavelength.

"That's what I was thinking too."

Taking a bite of my cheeseburger, I watch as Dick looks over the menu at his table. Seeing him sitting there all alone, I do feel a bit bad about what I said earlier. Even though he *is* a dick, clearly something I said hit a nerve with him in a way that I really hadn't meant it to.

"Wait." Becca leans over me, craning her neck to get a better look. "That's Dick? He *is* hot."

"I told you he was. You're the one who chose to give me a five-minute lecture on how you and I do not see attractiveness the same way. Then you ate my s'more."

Becca takes a drink of her margarita, shrugging as she puts it down. "I was drunk then."

"And you're not now?"

"That's beside the point. Now I'm feeling just the right amount of buzz to go introduce myself to Hottie McHotterpants."

Izzy rolls her eyes. "You would. I could be hammered and would still never be drunk enough to go introduce myself to a complete stranger. People are the worst."

Pinching her cheek, I smile. "Yes, Iz, it's one of the things we love about you. And, while you aren't wrong, I luckily did not inherit the anxiety and overactive imagination genes that burden you with expecting to become a pariah following each of your social interactions."

She rolls her eyes at me, self-aware enough to not argue the point.

Mentally squaring my shoulders, I push away from the table. "I'm going to go say sorry."

Becca widens her eyes at me, clearly surprised by my decision. Izzy, on the other hand, wears a slightly smug smile. Damn. She does know me too well. Actually, she might've just reverse-psychologized me into this whole thing.

As I make my way across the room, I notice a deep furrow between Dick's eyebrows.

Looking up, his eyes land on me, and his frown deepens. He can't still be mad, can he?

Shoot, deciding to apologize may have been a mistake.

Maybe I could detour to the bar? No, I would definitely look like a crazy person after pulling the necessary ninety-degree turn it would take to get there. I quickly run through any other possible escape routes and realize there's no bailing on this plan at this point.

Shit, shit, shit.

With that helpful thought, I stop just shy of Dick's table, forcing a slight smile on my face.

"Hi!" I squeak out in a voice much higher than normal. Clearing my throat, I try again. "I mean, hey, sorry to bother you, but I just wanted to apologize for earlier. I definitely shouldn't have said what I did earlier. I'm sure you could pass the Wild Bluffs/Atlantis test."

He looks me up and down, taking in my bright orange golf shorts that I still haven't changed out of. Shoot, I probably smell. Can I casually smell myself without him noticing? As I tilt my head down and start to breathe in, I think better of it and return my head to its full upright position. Flight attendants everywhere would be proud.

"You," he starts, his bearded jaw tightening, "think apologizing to me for saying I can't pass some imaginary test will make me give you the time of day?"

What the actual fuck?

"I'm actually not looking for any time out of any of your days, thanks. I felt bad because you seemed way more offended about not being let into an imaginary secret group than the average person does. But I don't know anything about you, so I figured that maybe it was some random sore spot because at your dental practice back home you have a hygienist who won't let you into her secret club, and it's demoralizing, and you're beginning to question your intelligence and self-worth, and you just can't take it anymore. So I wanted to say sorry."

Dick stares at me for a moment, confusion prominent on his face before his frown turns into a smirk. "No worries." Running a hand through his hair, he takes a deep breath. "I may have misread the situation and reacted a bit aggressively. I was also in the middle of a shit round in what is turning out to be an overall shitty year. Not that that's a good excuse for acting the way I did, so I'm sorry too."

I turn to go but am pulled back when he releases a deep chuckle and asks, "You think I'm a dentist? Who is being bullied by his hygienist?"

"Well, I mean, not necessarily a dentist. My dad is a dentist, so it just popped into my head. My mom is his hygienist. Though, to my knowledge, she doesn't bully him. Or lead a secret society...or lost city."

His eyes twinkle a bit at my story. "Ah, well, that clears up so many things."

I notice his waiter, Tony, hovering a few steps away, clearly waiting to take the man's order.

"Well, I'll leave you to it. But yeah. Again, I'm sorry for"—I wrack my brain trying to remember what I did to make him angry—"whatever I did, I guess."

I nod at Tony. "Hey, Tony, how's your mom?"

"She's doing all right. Hip is getting stronger every day. Started being able to walk up and down stairs again."

I smile, thinking of his mom, Brenda, and her love of puns.

"Hip, hip, hooray!" I chuckle at my own joke. "Glad to hear it. Well, I may have accidentally hit this guy's ball today and then insulted him through unknown means." Tony, whose sister I was friends with growing up and therefore knows about my lack of filter, laughs. "So can you put his drinks tonight on my tab?"

Tony glances between us, his eyebrows furrowing. "You want me to put Mr. Walker on your tab?"

I nod. "Yeah. Just this once." But that name releases the memory that has been bouncing around my head. I turn, squinting at the man in question, trying to see past his annoyingly attractive beard. I stare harder at the dangerous cut of his jaw as my pulse kicks up.

"Wait. Did you just say Walker? As in Jameson Walker? The professional golfer?"

I start laughing. I can't help myself. I called him a dentist when, in fact, he is one of the top golfers on the PGA Tour. Or at least he was until this last season when he became notorious for how quickly he fell. No wonder I thought I recognized him.

He dips his chin in acknowledgment.

"Oh God." I continue chuckling. "I take it back, then. If I've learned anything from Nike and Titleist, it's that I should not be seen sponsoring this guy."

I slap my hand over my mouth. "And now I've insulted you again, the one thing that I came over to fix. Classic me, really," I say, wishing I could find a rock to hide under forever. "I'm double sorry. Tony, keep his drinks on my tab, and I'll go ahead and leave you alone so you have a chance at having any sort of a good night."

I quickly walk back to our long table on the other side of the dining room, strangely aware of his eyes following me.

Is it possible to die of mortification? Maybe I can get some version of a shock collar that zaps me *before* I say things like that? I still have no idea what I did to offend him in the first place, but I guess, on the positive side of things, I do know what I said to offend him the second time.

Utterly embarrassed, I slouch down in my seat next to Becca, who is basically bouncing in her seat at this point.

"Guess what Kelli told us when she came over to take our order?! 'Dick' is actually Jameson Walker. Like, *that* Jameson Walker."

"Yeah." I bang my head against the back of the tall seat. "I found that out. It would've been helpful if Kelli could've shared that information about five minutes ago, before I completely made a fool of myself."

CHAPTER FOUR

JAMESON

I WATCH THE WOMAN walk away, her long, brown ponytail swishing in time to her steps, her ass like a beacon in a pair of bright orange shorts.

With a concentrated effort, I pull my eyes back to my menu, pretending to study it as I mentally work through what just happened.

She didn't know who I was. And, even once she did know, she didn't try to stay, arrange to meet up later, or, hell, flirt with me. She insulted me. Again.

Who does that? Shit. I don't even know her name.

"Tony," I say, turning to look at my tall waiter. "Who was that?"

"Oh, that's Bryn Harper. She's a local."

"A local, huh? How many locals are members out here, anyway?"

Tony shifts on his feet before answering. "I'm not exactly sure, Mr. Walker. I could go find the manager if you'd like me to." Taking a deep breath, he continues, "Though you should know Bryn is here as her sister's guest. They're celebrating their other sister's birthday, and I would really hate for the manager to get them in trouble. My sister is around their age, so I've known them my whole life. They're good people. Bryn just doesn't have a filter. She wasn't trying to be mean." Then he adds, as if an afterthought, "Sir."

"Shit. No. That's not why I was asking. I don't want to get her in trouble," I say as I run my hand down my face. "I may have even deserved it. I was just curious how many people from Wild Bluffs were members out here... Oh, and really, Tony, you don't have to call me sir."

Tony glances down at his order pad. "I don't know the exact number, but there are a few. Maybe ten local members. The Harper girls grew up caddying out here, and Bryn even played out here during a few tournaments in high school."

Thinking of the end of her swing that I saw today as she hit my ball, I can believe that. She clearly isn't new to the game.

"Thanks, Tony. That's more than I anticipated. I suppose I should probably let you get back to your job. I'll take the burger with avocado and sweet potato fries on the side. Hold the bun. And a whiskey on the rocks. Blanton's if you've got it, please."

"You've got it, Mr. Walker."

As I wait for my dinner, I catch tidbits of the conversation floating over from the birthday party in the corner. Apparently, one of the women just went through a bad breakup and is taking a hiatus from the dating scene. Here's hoping that goes better for her than it has been going for me.

Tony drops off my whiskey, two fingers in a glass tumbler with the Wild Bluffs Country Club logo etched on the front. With a name like Jameson Walker, I had no choice but to love whiskey. So, even though I've curbed my drinking in the past few months, I still allow myself one a day to sip on while I relax over my dinner.

Taking in the oaky scents, I'm transported to the back deck of my house overlooking the beach in Florida. I can hear the waves crashing and see the dark greens and purples that fill the sky as the sun sinks lower. Then I hear the memory of her voice—Alexis, talking on her phone—and I shake my head, forcing myself back to the present.

I'm going to have to sell that house. It's got too many memories of Alexis, and thinking about her will only piss me off. I've gone down this road enough times in the past year. Her memory will only lead to me ordering another round, and then another, and likely another, until I'm so drunk, I can't stop thinking about the woman who broke me.

Somehow, more whiskey always seems like the perfect plan to make me forget and only manages to make me remember more.

I hate that gold digger. And most of all, I hate that I was ever stupid enough to love her.

Luckily, Tony drops off my burger, bullying me out of my dark memories. He sets down a milkshake next to my plate and glances over his shoulder.

The entire birthday party is watching me with smiles on their faces.

"Bryn's sister Izzy," Tony says, gesturing her way, "wanted me to make sure you got this to make up for Bryn."

The girl in question waves, making it blatantly obvious they were listening to every word. "To make up for Bryn being a complete twat-waffle, Tony!" Izzy's eyes spark with mischief as she yells it across the dining area. "If you're going to relay the message, at least do it correctly!"

Turning bright red, Tony nods before replying, "Right, for that. Somehow, Iz is embarrassed by Bryn's actions, but not by yelling *twat-waffle* across a dining room."

The whole table breaks into laughter, some of them falling over onto the others, they are laughing so hard.

I pick up the milkshake, salute the table with it, and take a long pull from the straw.

Coughing, I look up at Tony through watering eyes.

"What...the hell...is that?"

This, for some reason, makes the women laugh even harder, their cackles reverberating off the walls of the dining area.

With a small smile, Tony points to the chalkboard behind the bar. "It's a peanut butter whiskey milkshake, Mr. Walker. It's one of our specials tonight."

Grabbing two more of the milkshakes off the counter, he walks over to the only other table left in the dining room and sets them down in front of two gentlemen.

Bryn's sister Izzy gets up from the table and walks over to the two men, quietly apologizing for the disturbance. The men both laugh and soon she's sitting at the table, telling them about some business she owns.

These women are funnier than the ones I'm used to meeting at golf courses, although that may be because the only women who I interact with while golfing apart from my sister and mom are either reporters or fans. All the women I've dated lately have definitely fallen into the fan group, and, if I'm being honest, the hero worship is getting to be a bit old. It's been a long time since a woman other than my sister told me something that wasn't exactly what she thought I wanted to hear.

I take another drink of the peanut butter concoction and find it's surprisingly good once you know to expect the booze. I nod toward the table of women once more, most of whom have gone back to chatting and eating, and dig into my burger.

As I finish my meal, I realize it's just me and a few of the birthday party women left in the room. One of which is the girl in the orange shorts, Bryn. It looks like it's just her and her sister and one other girl at the table. As they get up to leave, Bryn's light brown eyes land on mine, and her mouth twists into a small smile. Damn, it's a nice smile.

Without thinking, I stand up and quickly cover the space between my table and theirs. "Big plans for the evening, ladies?"

The three glance at one another conspiratorially, then Izzy finally nods, and Bryn smiles a bit sheepishly. "Indeed, Mr. Walker. Tonight is the drunken drive contest."

Laughing, I reply, "You know you're not supposed to drink and drive, right?"

"Ooo, the famous Jameson Walker wit. Finally, it comes out. I was starting to think those gossip rags were filled with lies!" Bryn clutches at her chest dramatically, making my smile widen.

"Well, they say you shouldn't believe everything you read, but I personally have never bought into that. The gossip columns should be considered absolute fact."

She lifts her right eyebrow at my sarcasm, clearly enjoying the banter as much as I am. "As the only one here with any firsthand knowledge, we will have to take your word for it. Don't have too much fun tonight...Mr. Walker."

"Please, call me Jameson."

The three girls smile, the third clearly the other sister based on the similarity in the gesture, and they turn to leave. Bryn calls over her shoulder, "Well, don't have too much fun tonight, *Jameson*. And if you happen to see someone streaking outside your window this evening, maybe don't call the manager, huh?"

With a wink, she lets the door close behind her, leaving me standing there wondering how the hell my night made such a 180 and why I didn't want it to end. And why I'm suddenly thinking about sleeping with my blinds open tonight.

CHAPTER FIVE

BRYN

"OKAY, LADIES," KELSEY SAYS to the group of women who have reconvened on the driving range after dispersing post-dinner. "The game is simple. You want to get your ball past your yardage marker. Each time you do, it's one point. Every time you fall short of the fifty-yard marker, you have to take a shot. If you whiff it, Becca, you have to do two shots." We all laugh as Becca groans. "As in an actual round of golf, we've handicapped everyone into skills-based groups. Group one, as the newbies, you have to get your drive past the 150-yard marker. Group two, 175. And you lucky bitches in group three with me, we've got to get it past that pretty blue 200-yard marker. Whoever has the most points at the end wins. Whoever has the least amount of points"—we all turn to look at Becca, who never golfs—"streaks. Everybody understand?"

We all nod, laughing at the look of sheer terror on Becca's face.

I move my bag to where Kelsey indicated group three would be, pulling out my driver and stowing the head cover in the side pocket of my black and red golf bag. Lifting the club above my head, I take a few seconds to stretch out my back, knowing this game has forced me to use my heating pad to soothe an injury more than once before. No matter how many times I tell myself to just swing easy, there is something about drive contests that makes me take the hardest swing I can.

Kelsey clears her throat, drawing our attention back to her. "Before we start, everyone has to take one shot. We've got two shot options—whiskey or tequila. Just grab the one you want."

Throwing my arm around Izzy's shoulder, I ask, "What's your poison for the evening?"

"Whiskey, definitely whiskey. I already had two milkshakes with it. I can't switch it up now."

I laugh, tightening my hold into a one-armed hug before I let her go so we can each grab a shot glass. Noting the height of the caramel-colored liquid in the glass, I'm pleased to note they are at most half-shots. We are not twenty-one anymore and have had a long day of sun and booze.

At Kelsey's signal, we all clink glasses and toss back a shot, the burn setting my throat on fire before it travels down to warm my belly.

As the birthday girl, Kelsey hits first in our group. She flies it over the 175 marker, but it sticks and doesn't make it past our line.

I grab my driver, ready to take my turn. I step up to the tee, taking a deep breath to calm my nerves. I feel the club connect with the ball, the sound ringing in my ears as it soars through the air. The ball lands just a few yards short of the blue 200-yard marker, and I let out a sigh of frustration. I knew I should have swung easier.

Kelsey pats me on the back, a smirk on her face. "Not bad for a first shot, but I know you can do better."

I grin at her, feeling good from the amount of liquor we've had today and the thrill of the game. "Still tied with you, aren't I?"

We all take turns teeing off and occasionally throwing back shots, though no one is really holding anyone to the shot rules at this point. We've definitely had enough to drink today.

The newbie group has dissolved into a fit of giggles, Kelsey's friend Skye deciding to forgo even attempting to hit the ball. She takes a sip from a shot glass each turn instead. Becca is still valiantly giving it her all in group two, but she misses the ball more often than she makes contact with it. Her lack of skills has led to more shots than if she had just accepted her fate and followed Skye's example.

As the game goes on, the sun begins to set, and the sky turns a deep shade of orange and pink. The air grows cooler, and I pull my sweater tighter around me. The whiskey has gone straight to my head, and I'm feeling a warm, happy level of intoxication. I've managed to rack up a few points, but Kelsey has managed to keep pace. Iz hit a decent shot last round, so she's not going to be streaking tonight, but she's definitely out of the running for first.

"Last shot, ladies," Kelsey calls out, holding up a bottle of tequila. "Becca and Skye, you better start stretching. I think you've got a sprint across the putting green in your future."

We all laugh, including Becca and Skye. They both knew this was their likely fate. Plus, they are both bombshells who run on a regular basis, so they've got nothing to worry about showing off to any lucky old men who happen to glance out the window of their cottage.

Groaning inwardly at the thought of more shots, I set up for my final drive. Even though the ground has become a bit wobbly and I'm having a bit of trouble getting the ball to stay on my tee, I can't resist the challenge.

I line up my shot, trying to steady my hands. I take a deep breath and swing. This time, I feel the ball connect solidly with the club, and I watch in amazement as it sails past the blue marker, landing almost at the edge of the range.

"Yes!" I shout, pumping my fist in the air. I turn to Kelsey, grinning from ear to ear. "Beat that."

Kelsey looks at me with a smirk. "Oh, I intend to," she says, grabbing her driver and setting up her shot.

I watch her take her backswing, the club moving gracefully through the air. She connects with the ball, and it rockets off the tee, soaring high into the air. We all watch in amazement as it lands past the 200-yard marker, rolling to a stop just a few yards short of 215.

I stare at her in disbelief, impressed despite myself. "How the hell did you do that?"

Kelsey grins, taking a victory shot of tequila. "It's all in the hips," she says with a cocky grin.

I roll my eyes, laughing. "Well, I guess that means we tie, then."

Kelsey nods, looking pleased with herself. I almost always win when we play. "Looks like it. Becca and Skye, you ready to run?"

We all head over to the putting green, Becca and Skye already stripping down to their underwear in anticipation of their impending streak. Izzy hands me a beer, and I gladly accept, taking a long sip. The sun has set entirely now, leaving us in darkness, except for the lights that illuminate the range and putting green.

Becca and Skye take off across the green, their arms outside like airplanes, asses shining in the moonlight like they don't have a care in the world.

We all laugh and shush each other, drunkenly trying to be quiet as our friends dash back toward us. Becca and Skye return, their faces flushed with adrenaline and the cold air. Kelsey hands them their clothes, and they quickly get dressed, still giggling and out of breath.

As we pack up our golf clubs and make our way back to our cottages, I can't help but feel grateful for the fun evening we've had.

I feel more content and happier than I have in a long time, the buzz of the whiskey and beer still coursing through me. Tomorrow, we'll all be nursing hangovers, but it will be worth it for the memories we've made tonight.

I look up at the sky, with its bright stars and glowing moon, and take a deep breath of the fresh, crisp air. This is what life is all about. Moments like these, surrounded by good friends, my sisters, and laughter, making memories that will last a lifetime. It makes me sad to know I've missed out on so much of it, traveling all the time for work.

Izzy and I stay up, sitting outside our rooms on the dark blue Adirondack chairs and chatting about Izzy's company and my work building out Hungry Guy's loyalty program. There is a full moon out, lighting up the course and the cottages, offering the perfect view of the stretch of tall prairie I've come to see as beautiful.

As we talk, I feel a sense of ease wash over me. Izzy is a good listener. Like I always do when we're together, I find myself opening up to her. It's not a coincidence that she is the only one who knows I'm a virgin. I trust her to not make a big deal about it. The whiskey has loosened the tight knot in my throat, allowing me to finally talk about the things that have been weighing on me.

"I'm worried I'm not focused enough on my job. I think freaking Kyle might end up getting the promotion instead of me."

"Bryn, you are the most focused person I know. In fact, some people might argue you could be a little less focused on your job."

"Yeah, but being successful at my job is important to me. You know what happened last time I tried to split my focus." I shift my eyes away from her dark ones, scouring the ground for something, anything to avoid my sister's all-knowing gaze.

She takes another pull from her beer. "But you *are* successful. You make more money than you could possibly know what to spend it on. Are you really happy with just you and your dog?"

I sigh, leaning back into the Adirondack chair. She's right, I do want more than just me and Jack, who happens to be the best rescue mutt and most loyal friend a girl could ask for, but there's so much I still want to do with my life, so much I still have to prove. And I can't do that if I'm not 100% dedicated to my job.

"Hey, Jack is a good companion. Plus, you know it's about more than that. I have to prove to myself, to everyone, that I can be good at something."

"Bryn." Iz sighs, the softness in her voice painful on my ears. "Any-one who has spent more than one minute with you knows you are amazing at a lot of things. You're a great friend. You're smart. You're funny. You're kicking ass at your job."

"Tell that to Peter. Tell that to Bryn of three years ago who was about to get fired!"

"You were on airplanes multiple times a week, trying to get to all the functions Peter needed you at and all the places work needed you. No one could have been successful with that schedule."

"Momma Easley sure seemed to think I should've been able to do it," I say.

"Momma Easley hasn't had a job or a husband in the last two decades. I don't think she's a real reliable judge on the subject."

"But she was right. I couldn't juggle my career ambitions with a relationship then, and I don't know why I would think I could do it now. I just need to focus on my job. When Tara leaves in three to five years and I'm promoted to head of North America, then I'll make time for non-work things. Until then, I need to be one hundred percent focused on work."

"Honestly?" She hugs herself, pulling her hands into her dark blue sweatshirt. "I wish you were a little less focused on work. Then I'd at least get to see my best friend every once in a while."

I stare at the grass stain on my golf shoe, not sure what to say. "You...you know I love you, Iz. I wish I saw you more too."

"I know, B. I know." She then smirks at me and, with all the gumption of an older sister, says, "I also know there's a certain pro golfer around here who also wishes he could see more of you..."

"Iz! That is not true!" I run my hand down my very sweaty golf tank seductively. "I mean, he would, obviously, be lucky to get a piece of this, but there's no chance that man feels anything for me other than mild irritation. Plus, don't forget, he was a dick. I don't need that in my life."

"Pshh. You might not need him in your life, but I can think of somewhere else you need that beautiful man."

"Izzy!"

"What?" Her eyes are twinkling now. I swear to God, they are actually twinkling with mischief. "You know it's true. He would undoubtedly be the best lay you ever have. Actually, on second thought, don't do it. If you lose your virginity to the man, the myth, the legend that is Jameson Walker, it will destroy your chances of ever being fully satisfied with anyone else."

With that, she finishes her beer, pulling her knees under her large sweatshirt before saying, "You know what? It's cold as balls out here. I'm going to bed."

She wanders off to our room, muttering something about hoping *Friends* is on, since hotel reruns are the best.

Finishing my beer, I pick up my golf bag and head back to the driving range. I need to get a certain professional golfer out of my head before he becomes a distraction. I've already unsuccessfully been down that road before.

CHAPTER SIX

JAMESON

I'VE BEEN TRYING TO fall back asleep for the last hour after being unceremoniously awoken by what could only be described as jungle noises. I swear a pack of hyenas was chasing after Pumba out there. Once fully awake, though, I recognized the sounds for what they truly were: feminine giggles and a few snorts. Not noises commonly heard on golf courses, particularly not the high-end country clubs I tend to frequent.

My mind quickly placed the blame on the sisters from earlier in the night. Clearly, Bryn and her friends were getting into some late-night shenanigans on the putting green.

It wasn't until I was pulling out my portable sound machine, the little box I take with me everywhere, that I remembered Bryn mentioning about the possibility of someone "streaking outside my window." I had to force myself to climb back in bed rather than open the window for a peek, mentally chastising myself for the image I couldn't seem to shake: Bryn running across the putting green, nothing on but a baseball cap.

I'm not sure why the cap was still on, but damn, her smile peeking out from under it was almost as distracting as her bouncing tits as she ran across my mind. Since then, I've tried all the breathing exercises I know, watched two reruns of *Friends*, and scrolled social media. I still can't sleep.

Finally giving it up for a lost cause, I let out a frustrated sigh and decide to hit the driving range. The moon is still high in the sky, casting an eerie glow over the golf course. As I walk, the cool night air washes over me, clearing my head.

I'm so lost in thought that I almost don't notice her. Bryn, still in her golf attire from the day, has her back to me, practicing with one of her irons.

I stand there, stuck in place by the round curve of her ass, the smooth flow of her backswing.

As she turns her head to follow her shot, I notice the glint of white AirPods sticking out of her ears. No wonder she didn't hear my clubs rattling as I climbed up the slight hill to the practice area.

Unsure what to do, I awkwardly stand there watching as she tees up another ball. She bends over to place it on the tee, and I can't help but feel a zing of attraction.

Suddenly, she stiffens, then whips around to stare at me.

"Oh my God." She waves her hand around, gesturing in my direction. "You scared the crap out of me."

"Sorry," I say, cringing at being caught staring. "Can't sleep."

"Yeah?" she asks, a faint smile on her lips. "You too?"

I nod. "I may have been woken up by what I can only assume was the aftermath of a drunk driving game."

She grimaces. "We really should get a better name for it. For the record, I don't think drunk driving is a laughing matter. My college roommate's parents were killed in a drunk driving accident. It's just"—she looks at the starry sky like it might provide her with the answer—"alliteration, I guess."

I continue to stare at her, not sure what the appropriate response is.

"Anyway," she continues, clearly picking up that I'm not going to bail her out, "I'm sorry about the noise earlier. There were a lot of shots involved, and we got a bit overly rowdy."

"It's all right," I say, clearing my throat to hide the excitement in my voice at the chance to talk to her. "I needed to get out and clear my head anyway." I don't mention that she's part of the reason I need to clear my head. Despite having committed to being off women, this one intrigues me. She's witty, even when she shouldn't be. She is kind to waiters to the point where they stand up for her. She is clearly close with her sisters, a trait that I'd never considered before but now seems important to me. And she apologized before she even knew who I was. She's snarky and fun but has a good heart.

And for some reason, I can't stop thinking about her.

She nods, turning back to face the range. "Yeah, same here. Golf is always my go-to for that."

I take the spot on the range a couple down from her, watching as she lines up her next shot. "You're pretty good," I say, trying to start a conversation. "Did you play in college?"

She shrugs, taking her swing. "No. I thought about it, but I had a full-ride academic scholarship, and golf requires a ton of time off campus. But it's not like I'm telling you anything you don't know."

I chuckle. "I do know a thing or two about how much time golf can take up. But a full-ride academic scholarship—that's pretty impressive. What do you do now?"

"I'm the director of technology at Hungry Guy." She pulls out her phone as she says it, almost like it's reminding her of all the work she still needs to get done.

"I fucking love Hungry Guy. They have the best bacon burgers." I don't mention that before I came to Wild Bluffs, I rarely treated myself to eating out. Before I started my spiral, I was on a strict diet from my nutritionist. I know a lot of people consider golf a "hobby sport," but diet and exercise are now key parts of almost all professional golfers' routines.

She rolls her eyes. "Obviously. But…" She leans in a bit. "The insider secret is the truffle fries. I would give up my dog for those."

I laugh. "I'll have to try them next time. So, director of technology—that sounds pretty important. What does that entail, exactly?"

Bryn takes a deep breath, clearly ready to give her elevator pitch. "Basically, I oversee all the tech aspects, from the in-store purchasing systems to the app to the website to the databases. My team and I work to make sure everything is running smoothly and efficiently, and that we're constantly innovating and improving."

Impressed, I nod. "That sounds like a lot of responsibility."

"It is, but I love it. Plus, it allows me to travel and live the digital nomad lifestyle, exploring new places both for fun and to visit restaurants or specific team locations."

I can't help but admire her passion for her job, and the way her eyes light up as she talks about it. It's a trait I find incredibly attractive in a woman, since I've always been all-in on profession. Though, after the year I've had, I've lost some of the excitement I once had, and I worry I won't be able to get it back.

"That's really cool," I say, genuinely enjoying our conversation. "You must have seen some amazing places."

"I have. It's actually pretty crazy when you consider the fact that I almost gave it all up a few years ago."

"You did?" I ask, curious why she would give up something that seems to bring her so much joy. "Why?"

"Oh, normal life things," she says, clearly avoiding giving me a real answer. "You know how it goes."

I don't know. But we also just met, so it doesn't feel right to pry. We stand in silence for a moment, watching as the range lights dance across the grass. There's a comfortable ease between us, a sense of mutual respect I haven't felt with anyone in a long time. I want to take the opportunity to get to know her better, to find out what makes her tick.

"You know," I say, breaking the silence, "I think we got off on the wrong foot. I was a bit of a jerk earlier..."

Bryn waves me off, her expression thoughtful. "It's all right," she says finally. "I suppose someone as famous as you probably should assume the worst in people at first. And I've been known to rub people the wrong way." Her mouth tenses at the sides as she says this final part.

Turning back to her tee box, she grabs another iron and starts hitting balls. Taking the hint, I do the same.

We fall into a comfortable silence, both of us hitting ball after ball. Every so often, I catch myself staring and have to physically force my head back down to the ball.

She does have a great swing.

And a great ass.

As the night wears on, I can feel the exhaustion setting in. I'm not sure how much longer I can keep up with this, but I don't want to leave Bryn just yet. It's as if something is keeping us both here, refusing to let us part.

Finally, after what feels like hours, though a look at my Rolex informs me it has only been forty-five minutes, Bryn turns to me with a smile. "I think I'm ready to call it a night," she says, lifting her cap and wiping the sweat from her forehead. "Thanks for the company."

I nod, feeling a sudden pang of disappointment that our conversation has to end. I wonder if they're leaving tomorrow. "Yeah, I should probably try to get some sleep too."

As she starts to walk away, I consider asking her to join me for a round tomorrow but quickly shut that down. I may have been wrong about her this afternoon, but that doesn't mean she wouldn't stomp all over my heart and then ask me to pay to have her shoes cleaned before she leaves.

Dragging my hand down my face, I turn to follow her back in the direction of the clubhouse and rooms.

Bryn stops in her tracks, her back still turned to me. I can't tell if she's waiting for me or doing something on her phone.

Finally, she turns back around, biting the right side of her bottom lip between her teeth. "Any chance you want to get a quick nine in tomorrow morning? Our tee time isn't until eleven oh eight, and I know I'll be up well before that. We could probably play the back nine if we tee off at eight."

Shocked, I stare at her face, trying to figure out what her angle is.

"You know what," Bryn says awkwardly, clearly uncomfortable with my silence, "that was silly of me to ask. Of course you want time to work on your game alone. I mean, why else would you be out in the middle of nowhere, and with your game as bad as it's been lately—" She winces. "That's not what I meant! I mean, I'm sure you know it hasn't been great, but it definitely hasn't been that bad, and who am I to talk, anyway? You're still way better than me. Anyway. I'll just...go." She whirls around and hurries off.

Ouch. Not going to lie, hearing that rambling evaluation of my game stings. Even if it's technically true. I don't know what I'm supposed to say. I'd love to have some company out on the course, but I heard Erica loud and clear—no distractions. I also don't know if my ego can take another round of feedback from this woman.

I take a deep breath, trying to get a handle on my emotions as she reaches the bottom of the hill.

"I'd love to play a quick nine with you," I shout after her. She stops but doesn't turn around. I hustle to catch up. "But just to be clear, I'm not looking for any kind of a relationship right now. I just want to play some golf and have a good time."

Bryn turns to look at me quizzically, and I wonder if I said something wrong. Finally, her face relaxes into a smile. "Me too," she says, her eyes meeting mine. "Just some golf and company. That's all I'm looking for."

I nod, feeling a weight lifted off my chest. "Sounds perfect."

We make plans to meet at the clubhouse at 7:30 the next morning, both of us eager to get some rest before our early tee time.

As we part ways, I can't help but feel something fluttering to life inside of me. Unfortunately, I can't tell if it's my body telling me it's excited or that I'm in danger and should be running as far as I can in the other direction.

Chapter Seven

Bryn

The next morning, I'm up bright and early, eager to hit the links with Jameson. Our exchange last night was fun and easy until the end. I'm not sure why an invitation to golf together made him shut down so quickly. It's not like I asked him to have my babies. Or even out to dinner. But I heard him loud and clear: he's not looking for anything romantic. Same, bud. Same.

I dig through my suitcase, wishing I would've brought a cuter bra than the thick-strapped sports bra I prefer to golf in, and then mentally chastising myself for the thought. It's just golf. Neither of us is looking for anything close to a romantic relationship. We're both focused on our careers. And, even if we were, I'm not the type of girl who needs to worry about her bra on the first date. Not that this is a date.

I shoot off a quick text to Izzy and Kelsey, letting them know I'll meet them for brunch at 10:00 or a little after, and then head out.

When I get out to the clubhouse, Jameson is already there waiting for me. He looks even better in the morning light, a light blue polo and dark blue shorts making his green eyes fade toward blue. The whole ensemble reminds me of the edge of the ocean when the blues of the deep sea slowly shift into the teals and aquas of the coast.

"You sure you're awake enough to golf?" Jameson asks, a smirk tugging at his lips. "You don't look too well rested."

"Wow," I say, fluttering my eyelashes. "What did I do to deserve such a compliment this morning? I knew I was looking good, but nothing confirms it like someone telling you that you look tired," I say sarcastically.

"Ah, yes. It's almost as endearing as someone pointing out how shitty you've been at your job lately."

I snort out a laugh, remembering my attempt to cover my awkward backtrack last night. "Feedback is a gift, Jameson, so, you're welcome."

We both pick up our bags from where the pro shop left them by the putting green and walk toward the first tee.

"So," I ask, "I'm thinking we play a quarter a hole? But I get a stroke a hole, for the obvious reasons."

"Oh really? You've been telling me since the minute I met you how terrible my game is, and you still think you need a stroke a hole to have a chance?"

"To be fair to me, I didn't even know who you were when I first met you. And, while it pains me to admit this out loud"—I put my hand on my heart to show how sincere I am—"I do believe you may, possibly, be a better golfer than me."

His shoulders shake as he laughs. "Fine, I'll give you one stroke a hole. But I'm not playing for quarters." He looks at me with one eyebrow raised. "What are you, eighty? Only old men play for quarters."

I laugh because that is, without a doubt, correct. "I may not be an eighty-year-old man myself. Though, again, please feel free to stop complimenting my appearance at any time. I'm not sure my ego can handle all the praise. But I did grow up playing with my dad and grandpa and their friends, so I have a deep appreciation for the need to have a quarter bag with me any time I'm on a golf course."

He laughs a deep rumble that sends shivers down my spine. "How about this, we'll play for something else. How about a drink once we get back? Loser buys?"

I don't typically start drinking before noon, but it feels safer than offering up something like a meal, which he may (again) misconstrue as me trying to ask him on a date.

"Deal."

It's clear that Jameson and I are both competitive when it comes to golf, but as the round goes on, it becomes obvious that Jameson is—and I recognize my own ridiculousness at this thought—very, *very* good. He's clearly a professional who does this day in and day out. On every hole, he out-drives me by at least twenty yards, even though he's playing from the tips and I'm playing from the women's tees. He also makes putts that would make even the most experienced golfer jealous. It's a huge turn-on. Apparently, I have some sort of putting kink I wasn't aware of until now.

"Dang," I say. "You read that green like a book."

"Thank you," he replies, taking the compliment smoothly. "It helps when I have such a talented player putting before me. It lets me get a good feel for what the green is doing."

"Sheesh. You sure know how to make a girl blush. I bet you tell that to all the women you golf with."

"You look good when you blush."

If my cheeks weren't on fire, they are now.

"And, no," he continues like he wasn't just blatantly flirting with me. I'd been suspicious before, but now I know he is. "My sister is the only woman I golf with, and I would never say something like that to her. If you think my ego is big, just wait until you meet my pint-sized sister who thinks she can take on the world."

"It's always the short ones you have to look out for," I joke. "Unfortunately, I'm about to be in California working a lot with a couple other trips thrown in here and there, so I don't know that I'll get to meet her." I stop short, realizing I likely read too much into his turn of phrase.

Silence hangs heavy between us until he coughs gently and says, "That's too bad. She would really like you."

He sets up for his next drive, and I quietly hang back by the walking path so I can watch his swing from the best vantage point. His shorts hug his ass as he moves, the power building in his body and flowing through to the ball as he swivels his hips and connects. Never in my life have I wished for a photographic memory more. Not only because it's a lesson in technique, but because—damn. The man is a snapshot of power. His ball lands perfectly, smack-dab in the middle of the fairway. I catch the small smile that escapes from his lips before he catches himself and settles his features back into a look of professional disinterest. But that little glimpse into his happiness is infectious, and I can feel my spirit lifting with each shot he hits.

I'm surprised by how well he's doing. I know he's good. I know he's a pro. But I wasn't exaggerating when I said his game has been shit lately. I don't watch golf religiously like my dad does, but I keep up with sports news enough to know that in Jameson's last tournament, he got multiple triple bogeys. He played so bad, it made the news.

His time off and his new workout regimen have apparently paid off. He is hitting his drives solidly, his iron game is strong, and his putts have been on point. I'm honestly surprised I ran into him in the rough yesterday. He hasn't missed the fairway all morning.

I'm also surprised by how much fun we're having together. We've chatted throughout the round, the conversation flowing smoothly despite the regular quiet pauses necessitated by the game of golf.

Jameson has been fun, even a little flirty, which is a bit of a shock after yesterday.

By the time we reach our seventh hole, I'm feeling less confident that I can pull off a win despite the stroke a hole he's giving me. He tees off and hits an impressive drive while I hit a much shorter one. I would love to say that his shirt hugging his biceps tightly or the lazy smiles he's been sending my way are distracting me, but I'm having a very solid round. One of the best I've had in a while.

We continue to play, with him leading most of the time but me managing to stay respectably close. We reach the final hole with him narrowly ahead by a respectable three strokes. As someone who is undoubtedly a sore loser, I focus in, knowing I'm going to need to both play the best hole of my life and for Jameson to fall apart for me to have a chance.

As we step up to the tee box, Jameson turns to me with a sly grin on his face. "You know, I'm feeling generous today. How about we make this hole winner takes all?"

Do I want to win? Hell yes. Do I want to win because we changed the game in my favor at the last minute? Never.

"No way. I don't need you to make this easier on me. We had a deal, and a stroke a hole was fair. I don't want your charity." I gesture to the men's tee box. "I've seen you fall apart on eighteen before, I've still got a chance."

He shrugs. "Okay, but don't come crying to me when you're the one buying our drinks."

Damn it. Now I have to double down on this. "Tell you what, Jameson, how about this—we'll make a side bet. Loser of this hole has to do whatever the winner wants."

Jameson raises an eyebrow. "Anything? You know I'm a man in my midthirties, right? I've already thought of ten things I could ask of you that would make every girl at your sister's birthday party blush. Even the streakers."

My body lights up at the thought, but I nod anyway. "Anything. Plus, who's to say I haven't thought of eleven things to ask of you?" I most certainly have not, but he doesn't need to know that.

His grin turns devilish. "You're on."

We both tee off, and I manage to hit a decent drive, but Jameson hits one of his best all day. We both make it to the green in regulation, but I'm on the fringe while he has a short putt. My heart is pounding as I line up my shot. Taking a deep breath, I tap the ball, playing the downhill.

My line is good, and as the ball slowly trickles toward the cup, it looks like I might actually win the hole. We stand there watching as the ball slows before the cup, before finally stopping just short of the hole.

"No!" I yell, completely disregarding any course noise regulations. There is a reason I like playing in the middle of nowhere. "Ugh. I can't believe I nancied it."

"That's tough," Jameson says, casually leaning on his putter. "Too bad you didn't put a little more oomph behind that one. You had the line. Now watch and learn how you make a putt."

With that, he taps his ball forward, easily sinking it in the hole. Then he turns to me, grinning wickedly. "Looks like you owe me a drink and some sort of favor."

I'm suddenly incredibly nervous. What have I gotten myself into? But I never renege on a bet. When I was eight and my dad bet me he could catch more fish than me, and I lost, I didn't run and hide—I ate the whole freshwater mussel, even if it took me way more tries than anyone wanted to witness.

"I guess I do. Just let me know when you want me to come back out and give you some golf lessons," I say, trying to sound confident.

"Oh, really?" He smirks. "You think you've got something you can teach me about golf?"

How had I not noticed his lips before? They are just on the masculine side of plump, his bottom one a pillow I could easily sink into. Forcefully dragging my eyes away from his full mouth, I pause for a second, trying to remember what we were talking about before I was distracted by his stupid, handsome face.

"Umm…" *What were we talking about? Oh! Right. Bantering. It's always banter.* "Yes, as a matter of fact, I know I've got something to teach you about golf. For my remedial course, I always start with a lesson I feel would be particularly useful to you: how to avoid snowmen on a scorecard."

I shoot him a playful wink, letting him know I'm joking about his recent triple bogies, which are typically eights on the score card, rather than trying to rub it in his face.

He chuckles a deep, short-lived rumble as we reach our golf bags. "Damn, Bryn, you really know how to kick a guy when he's down."

"Thank you. It's a skill of mine," I reply as we both pick up our bags and head toward the clubhouse.

"You know," he continues, "that's a lot of shade coming from someone who just lost."

"It may not have been my best showing."

"So you're saying you'll do better next time?"

"Oh, I have no doubt I'll come out with the *W* for sure."

"Very confident, considering our respective professions. No matter what the last year may suggest, I *am* a professional golfer."

"You are?!" I let out a mock gasp. "Someone should tell that to your game."

"God, you're insufferable. It's like you don't remember losing our bet three minutes ago or that you now owe me *anything*."

The way he emphasizes the word *anything* makes my insides tingle. This has been fun. Jameson is surprisingly easy to be around. I know this isn't a date. Neither of us want it to be a date. But, if it *were* a date, it would be the best date I've ever been on. Not that I'll be admitting that to him...or to myself.

I mentally slap myself, reminding my hormones *this is not a date* one last time before saying, "Luckily, I also have a credit card that is very good at buying whiskey, and, regardless of what you might think, I am an absolute delight to be around, so it's not as big of a loss as you might think."

He looks over at me, the sun and his baseball hat casting his eyes into a dark shadow. "I'll be the judge of that."

Chapter Eight

Jameson

Playing nine with Bryn has been so much more fun than I expected. I can't remember the last time I truly enjoyed being out and playing. As we walk up the hill that leads from hole nine's green to the clubhouse, I'm racking my brain for ways to ask her to casually hang out again. I don't want more. I *can't* have more, but I would like to hang out again.

"Bryn!"

We both turn, noticing the whole birthday party crew making their way to the restaurant. They are a rainbow of golf skorts and collared tops, clearly abiding by the dress code today—no hint of the chaos and rule-breaking that leaked into my room through the windows last night.

"Oh, hi, Jameson," says Bryn's brunette sister. "Fancy seeing you here."

Bryn's eyebrow rises as she says, "I told you this morning we were going to get in a quick nine."

"Huh. Must've slipped my mind." She's giving off real cat-who-ate-the-canary vibes. "Anyway. Jameson, you should join us for brunch!"

There is a chorus of "Yes!" and "Definitely!" and somehow, despite being raised with a sister who was constantly trying to convince me to do things with her, I am no match for their sheer energy and unwillingness to take no for an answer.

I agree to tag along, mostly because I'm hungry and want to eat—it certainly has nothing to do with not being ready to say goodbye to Bryn.

We sit down, and the table orders a round of mimosas. "Oh, Jameson will take one too," Bryn says to the waitress.

"No, that's—" I begin.

"I'm buying, remember?"

I nod to the waitress but turn back to Bryn, saying, "You promised me whiskey. What kind of bald-faced liar are you?"

"The kind that doesn't believe in drinking whiskey before noon. Come on, mimosas are tasty. Way better with brunch."

We all order, the women appearing to be carb loading after their drinking last night. I glance at Bryn as she inhales the second half of her breakfast burrito. I'm eating my usual four-egg omelet, but watching Bryn devour her choice is making me hungry, and not just for food.

She splashes more Cholula onto her burrito and brings it to her lips. I follow the movement with my eyes, taking her in. She is undoubtedly beautiful. Between her smiling eyes and tanned legs, she's got the girl-next-door look down pat. If only she had a pair of glasses on, she'd be the main character of any '90s rom-com. And, unlike any other girl I've met since I joined the tour, she hasn't once tried to kiss my ass or get me to pay for something. Except quarters.

Suddenly, she halts her progress and looks at me, crinkling her forehead.

"What?" she asks around a mouthful of sausage and egg. When I don't reply, she turns her head fully and stares at me. "You're staring at me."

"You're staring at me."

Another eye roll. "That's because I asked you a question. One that you still haven't answered, in fact."

I break my gaze away from her and glance around the table, pretending to be interested in the conversations going on around us. But my mind is focused solely on Bryn—on the way her eyes sparkle in the sunlight filtering in through the large windows, on the way her lips curve into a smile as she takes another bite.

I can't help but feel a pull toward her, a magnetic attraction that's been building ever since we met. Fuck. She's the first girl I've ever actually enjoyed golfing with. Well, other than Lila, but she doesn't count.

Unfortunately, I know I shouldn't act on it. My agent and publicist would kill me if they knew I am sitting at this table full of tipsy women right now. I'm supposed to be getting my head on straight. I'm supposed to avoid dating around. Plus, Bryn said she's leaving soon. I feel another pang in my chest, a twin to the one I felt when she mentioned leaving earlier.

Maybe I should see if she wants to hang out again before she goes. Golf again. Go back to my room and—Nope. Not even thinking about that. That is *not* something we can do. I'm smart enough to know that once I take that step with Bryn, I'll never be able to go back.

Taking a deep breath, I turn my attention back to Bryn. "I'm sorry, what was the question?"

She rolls her eyes again, but there's a hint of amusement in the action. "I asked if you were going to finish your omelet or just stare at me while I eat my burrito."

I glance down at my half-eaten omelet. I clear my throat, feeling a wave of heat move up my neck and across my face. "I was just..." I pause, trying to figure out how to explain myself.

"Just what?" Bryn presses, her gaze intent on mine.

"It's nothing," I say, unsure if I should broach the subject of casually hanging out more or not.

"Come on," she says playfully, not letting the subject go. "Is it the fact that you've never seen a girl eat this much in one sitting before? Because I promise I can, and have, eaten far more than this."

Damn, she's cute. And she has the best sense of humor now that I know what to expect. I don't want this to be the last time I see her. Sitting this close is making it harder to deny my attraction to her.

I take a deep breath and lean closer. "One, I have a sister who could, if not keep up, at least give you a run for your money, but no." I pause, lowering my voice to a whisper, "I was thinking how sexy you look when you eat."

Bryn's eyes widen for a moment, but then she laughs, a sound that's like music to my ears. "Is that so?" she teases, reaching out to grab the hot sauce again but this time brushing against my hand in the process.

"Yeah," I joke quietly, feeling a rush of heat spread through me. "I've always had a thing for women who could shove a whole burrito in their mouth. It bodes well for me." I punctuate the suggestive comment with a wink, deciding to see where this flirting goes.

"Oh my God." Izzy leans across her, laughing. Unfortunately, I may have forgotten we were at a table with other people.

"Did you just compare your penis to that burrito? Because both *wow* and just *no*." She cringes. "I appreciate the level of confidence, no matter how misguided, but no woman, or man for that matter, wants that. There is such a thing as too big. And a breakfast burrito that took up an entire plate definitely falls into that category."

Bryn glares at her sister. "Iz, mind your own damn business. We aren't even talking about burrito dicks."

Izzy throws her hands up in mock surrender. "Sorry for trying to prevent a potential disaster over here. I'm just looking out for your well-being."

Bryn shakes her head, her eyes sparkling with amusement. "Yeah, well, I think I can handle myself just fine, thank you very much."

I lean back in my chair, grinning at the playful banter between the sisters. From a distance, they appear to be almost carbon copies of each other except for a couple of inches in height. Now that I'm next to them both, though, I notice the subtle differences. They're both beautiful, but damn if Bryn's ever-changing eyes and strong angles of her face do it more for me than her sister's softer features ever could.

Bryn's cheeks are flushed a light pink with embarrassment, but she doesn't let it show as she turns back to me.

"I'm glad we got that cleared up," she says, glancing down at her burrito before picking it up again and making eye contact as she takes an even larger bite. "I wouldn't want any misunderstandings."

"Neither would I." I chuckle, feeling a warmth spread through my chest.

For a few moments, we eat in comfortable silence, the noise of the table fading away as I focus on Bryn.

"So, what's the plan for the day?" she asks the table.

Her other sister, the one who doesn't look as much like Bryn due to her shorter stature, blonde hair, and blue eyes, replies, "Golf. Our tee time is in...oh, shoot. Ten minutes."

The women at the table all finish shoveling food and coffee into their mouths and a few start to make their way toward the doors leading to the course.

I'm not sure what to do. I know I can't ask Bryn out, but I *want* to hang out with her again. How do you ask a girl you find unbelievably attractive to be friends? Do I even want that?

Four years ago, I would've already made my intentions with Bryn very clear. I was in it to find someone to be with forever, but I wasn't opposed to having a bit of fun along the way. I never misled a woman into thinking they were the one for me, but I was always at least open to the possibility. My schedule rarely accommodated anything more than a date or two with a woman before one of the two of us moved on physically or emotionally.

As the final women start to leave the table, Bryn starts to stand as well. I hesitate, still unsure if I should say anything. Luckily, she beats me to it.

"Do you want to play with me—I mean—us this afternoon?" she asks, her uncertainty apparent in the way her eyes are focusing on everything but me.

I feel a surge of excitement at getting to spend more time with Bryn before I remember I have a call with my agent, and I have to get in a grueling session in the weight room today.

"I would love to, but unfortunately—"

"Oh, no worries. I get it. Two ass-kickings in one day is too many for one man to handle, anyway. Anyone would be intimidated." She turns to leave but throws one final, half-hearted smile over her shoulder. "See ya around, Jameo."

Chapter Nine

Bryn

"Bryn!"

"What?!" I turn back toward the fairway where my sisters and Becca have all stopped to look at me.

They look like they just stepped out of a candy shop. As usual, Iz is in all pink from her hat to her skort. Kelsey, the more restrained of the bunch, is in a pair of black shorts and a light blue shirt. Becca, the real wild card, since she doesn't play golf, is in black yoga pants she is passing off as appropriate golf attire. As her collared shirt is Barbie pink, I can only assume she borrowed it from Izzy.

"Your ball is way back there!" Kelsey shouts while shielding her eyes from the sun so she can see me.

My head falls back. Ugh. Could this round get any worse? How did I possibly have the shortest drive of the group *and* end up in the rough?

My game this afternoon has been complete and utter shit. Luckily, I'm not the only one feeling the grueling combination of heat, booze, and a walking-only golf course.

The little hairs around my face have started to curl with the heat, and my baseball hat is soaked through around the band. I've added my sunglasses because the sun decided it needed to shine as bright as possible today. Real asshole vibes, the sun.

It does not escape my notice that my game was great this morning with Jameson. The weather was perfect, and I was having fun. And, while I hate to admit it was anything other than coincidence, it may be the lack of a tall, muscular man that has turned my afternoon into a raging dumpster fire. Either that or Mother Earth suddenly developed a vendetta against eastern Colorado.

As I make my way through the rough for what feels like the millionth time, I can't help but think about my encounter with Jameson yesterday. God, he was such a dick. But last night and today? Definitely not a dick. Though I'm not opposed to getting acquainted with—

Okay, I may be a bit distracted by my thoughts of Jameson. The man is hot. I need not offer excuses as to why my brain wants to focus on him at the most inopportune times. But just because a hot, successful, *professional golfer* hung out with me this morning does not mean that I need to lose this round to my sisters. Sisters who will never let me live it down.

I sullenly walk back to where they said my ball was, finding it next to yet another yucca. I swear there are a million of them on this hole itself. As I punch my ball back out into the fairway, my mind drifts back to my final conversation with Jameson at brunch. I thought we'd both had fun this morning, so it stung a bit when he said no. It's not like he can have anything else he's doing today—he's literally in the middle of nowhere so he can work on his golf game.

As much as I hate to admit it, I wanted to keep spending time with him. He is so fun to heckle, and after that first time, he has taken my sarcasm and joking well, something that can't be said for all the men I've encountered in my life. It was definitely one of the reasons Peter's mom didn't like me. The number of times he reminded me to "tone the sarcasm down" before we met with his mom should've really clued me in to the fact that she wasn't my biggest fan.

But after the day I had with Jameson, I really thought that, even if we were both very clear about the fact that we aren't looking for something serious, we were at least becoming friends.

Kelsey walks over to me on the green after tapping in a three-footer. "Are you okay? You've been a bit in your head this morning."

I give her a smile that quickly turns into a grimace. "Totally. Just had one too many shots last night, I guess."

"Same. Why did we think that golfing after a night like last night would be a good idea? It's really the last thing I want to do."

Izzy joins us as we pick up our bags, saying, "We should've opted for a hot tub morning, though the extra dehydration may not be what we are looking for.

"Well, there is a handsome lad currently in residence that I wouldn't mind seeing in a swimming suit." Izzy waggles her eyebrows at me, and I pretend to gag.

"Eww, Iz. Why would you call him a lad? It makes him seem like a twelve-year-old Scottish boy," I joke, hoping to distract her.

"Atch, well, the lad may be a bit more o' a man than a wee laddie o' twelve," she replies in a truly terrible accent. "I, for one, would be much more likely to want to see what's under his kilt, at least..." At that, Izzy falls into a fit of giggles, pulling laughter out of the rest of us.

When she finally gathers her breath, she says, "Okay, fair. *Lad* may not be the right word for it, but you know I'm re-reading *Outlander* again. It just happens."

And it does. Every time Izzy re-reads that series, she starts using random Scottish words.

Becca picks back up the conversation before I can get Izzy going on one of her *Outlander* dissertations. "But really, Bryn, when are you going to tell us about how you ended up playing a round of golf with not only a professional golfer, but one you actively insulted yesterday?"

Avoiding the question, I set up on the tee box of hole seven, a short par three that requires a good tee shot or your ball will be lost forever.

They all remain quiet as I swing, but the silence is short-lived.

"Soo...are you really not going to tell us? Because this is possibly the most exciting thing to have happened to you in a long while, and you're being oddly quiet about it."

"What are you talking about? I have exciting things happen to me all the time. Just last month, I had another girl all up in my lady-business."

I see the look of surprise flash across Kelsey's face before Izzy grins, saying, "Gyno appointments don't count as exciting, Bryn. In fact, if that's the first thing that popped into your mind when forced to come up with something exciting, I'm concerned about you and the status of your life."

"Oh, like you have any more excitement happening? You live in Wild Bluffs. Nothing exciting ever happens here," I shoot back, knowing my sisters live just as work-centric lives as I do, even if they do it from our small town.

"I actually do have a very exciting life, thank you," she says, flipping her ponytail over her shoulder. "Okay, I get it. You don't want to wax poetic about the beautiful man you hung out with all morning. Let's start simple... When did you decide you don't hate the guy? We were literally calling him Dick this time yesterday."

Ignoring the question, I hit my ball, watching my shot settle a good six feet away from the hole.

Knowing I'm going to be forced to answer eventually, I take a deep breath and tell my sisters and Becca about my trip with Jameson to the practice green last night, asking him to play this morning, and then asking him to come play with us this afternoon.

"I mean, I get it, honestly. Not only would it require spending his afternoon with you assholes"—I smirk at my sisters—"but also, it's probably for the best. What would be the point of spending more time together? I mean, we head back to Wild Bluffs tonight, and I'm definitely not telling Mom and Dad that I'm going to miss dinner tonight because I'm going to stay out here to have a one-night stand with a professional golfer. Can you imagine?"

From the looks on my sisters' faces, it's clear they feel equally as horrified as I do at the thought, but surprisingly, Becca seems to be considering it. "Is a one-night stand actually in the cards? You could tell them you're staying the night at my place. It wouldn't be the first time that we stay up drinking and you decide to crash with me rather than going back. It could work."

"I appreciate the offer, Becca. And, honestly, I don't know. Everything I know about his reputation suggests he'd be on board for a hookup, but he definitely wasn't putting out those vibes...except for that one exchange at breakfast, I suppose. Doesn't matter. As previously mentioned, the man shot me down. After I instigated every single one of our interactions, he finally manned up enough to say no to spending time with me. I'm totally fine with it." I may not be *totally* fine with it, but I recognize it's silly to be upset about a guy I met less than a day ago.

"I know you're fine, but we saw you guys together, and I guess I just don't agree he's not interested. I don't know why he didn't say yes, but I do think there is a chance there is more to the story than him just not wanting to spend time with you."

My heart perks up at her statement, but I quiet it back down. Neither Jameson nor I are interested in a relationship.

"We were both clear we aren't interested in a relationship. As crazy as this whole thing was, I think it's over. Honestly, I'd be surprised if I ever see him again."

Even though I don't want to, even though I know how ridiculous it is, I can't help but keep an eye out the rest of the round, hoping to catch a glimpse of his black hat and green eyes.

CHAPTER TEN

JAMESON

I SHOVE THE BENCH press back up, wiping the sweat off my forehead as I reach for my vibrating phone.

"Hey, Jon," I say, answering my agent's call.

"Jameson. How are you doing?" he asks.

I consider how much has changed since I came to Wild Bluffs. I've stopped drinking to excess. I'm in the best shape I've ever been in physically. I no longer have a 125-pound succubus slowly eating away at my soul—something she continued to do long after she left me.

"Doing well. How about you?"

"Oh, going good. Just calling to check to see how you're doing. How's the weather out there in Wild Bluffs?"

"Can't complain," I say, grabbing a swig from my water bottle.

"Sure. That's great."

Jon's not someone who calls just to chat, so I know he's tiptoeing around something. I decide to give him an out and casually demand, "What's up, Jon?"

"How's your game? What kind of scores are you getting?" There it is. As much as I appreciate the work Jon does, how much he's looked out for me in the past, at the end of the day, he's only calling to see how his most lucrative client is performing on the course.

All things considered, my game should be better than it was last year. Unfortunately, the majority of my practice scores have been crap.

"Yeah. It's...fine," I reply.

"Have you talked to Dr. Sandra since you've been out there?"

"Yep, still meeting with her once a week virtually."

Here's the thing about the last year of my life and the truly embarrassing golf performance—it's all in my head. Ask any professional athlete why their game is shit, and unless they've had an injury, the answer is mental. I regularly see Dr. Sandra, one of the best sports psychologists in the game, but somehow, even she can't get me figured out.

Jon and I discuss increasing my hours with Dr. Sandra, switching to someone new, and the potential of moving to a new course for the rest of my time before the season starts. I assure him I'm moving in the right direction, but I can tell he's not buying it any more than I am.

Just as he's about to sign off, he sighs deeply before saying, "Jameo, you've got to be laser-focused on your game this season. If you don't get your shit together, we may have to start talking retirement."

I barely register saying goodbye and starting my workout again. I'm on autopilot. Retire? At my age? The perk of being a golfer rather than any other professional athlete is that you can have a career span decades. Look at Arnold Palmer. He played in his last Masters at seventy-four.

Being a professional golfer is amazing, but it does lack some of the fringe benefits that are afforded to other professional athletes. Not counting a few outliers—of which I used to be one—people don't know us, which means we are less likely to get endorsement deals. Our body types tend to skew toward the less muscular end of the professional athlete bell curve, really losing some of the sex god status other professionals get. I mean, have you ever read a romance novel with a golfer as the main character?

My sister, Lila, has loved sports romance novels since the inappropriate age of fifteen. I have had to sit through her rants about how there are series geared toward puck bunnies and cleat chasers, but where are the ones for gallery girls and golf groupies?

If I gave one shit about romance, I might be inclined to at least appreciate her annoyance on my behalf. As it is, I'm mostly just confused about why my smart sister would choose to waste her brain space with that unrealistic nonsense.

Romance books aside, I used to be at the top of the pile in the golf world. I was good-looking, bringing in big endorsements, and had a gorgeous girl on my arm. Too bad her heart was as black as mud, and when she left me, I was too depressed to do anything but drink, gain weight, and play like shit.

And now I might have to think about retirement? Fuck that.

If my round this morning is any indication, I'm on my way back. I may have had a terrible year, but I'm turning it around.

I'm halfway through the core portion of my workout when the door to the weight room opens and Bryn's friend walks in, pulling at the bottom of her skirt—obviously working hard to avoid meeting my eyes. I pause my music and pull out an earbud.

"I'm really not interested." Groupies. It's always best to set them straight up front so they don't think they have a chance. If you're a nice guy, they think they can change your mind.

She blinks at me a couple of times before a slow smile crosses her face. "Oh my God. You really are a dick. To be clear, guy-I-could-not-care-less-about, I was never here for you. I'm here because I'm a good friend, but I've changed my mind."

She turns to leave, pushing down on the handle to exit the workout room, when it hits me. If she's not here about herself, then she must be here about...Bryn? Shit. I can't believe I just jumped straight to a groupie assumption. What is wrong with me?

"Wait!" I scramble off the floor, my arms still a little rubbery from the chest work I did today.

She doesn't, however, choose to wait. And, as I chase her out the door, I run face-first into something solid.

"Oh, shit. I'm sorry. I wasn't—JT? What are you doing here?"

My best friend for the last ten years looks me up and down, rubbing his shoulder where we just collided. "Jameo, you look good, man."

I shoot him a wink. "Thanks, bud. It's all for you."

He laughs, taking in the space around us. "Not a bad little setup you've got here. Think there will be enough room for both of us to work out in that tiny-ass gym?"

"Working out together? Damn, it's like a flashback to our first year on the tour."

JT flips his cap backward—a nervous tic of his that everyone and his mother knows about—and nods.

Then I remember why I was in a hurry. "Shit, JT, did you see a blonde woman leave?"

"A blonde woman? Jesus, man, Alexis hasn't been here, has she?"

"Fuck, do you think I'm that big of an idiot? No, that parasite of a human has not been here. It was a different girl."

JT's blue eyes brighten at that information. "Ooo. A different girl, huh? Wait until I tell Lila about this. Maybe she'll finally get off my jock about helping you move on."

I push out of the building, searching the grounds for Bryn's friend, only to catch a glimpse of blonde as she drives by in a dark blue Mazda. Wait, was she giving me the finger?

"Was that girl who just flipped you the bird the one we are looking for?" JT watches the cloud of dust that encapsulates the car as she leaves.

"Yeah, she was." I nod, searching the rest of the mostly empty parking lot for any sign of Bryn or her sisters. "Though it is definitely not what you think. Come on, let me buy you a drink at the bar, and you can tell me why you are here and why the fuck you are texting with my little sister."

***

The bar area and the restaurant around it are quiet as JT and I sit down to order our beers. I can't get that girl's taillights out of my head. Why was she leaving? Isn't the party here for another night?

Shit, did Bryn ever actually tell me when she was leaving? I figured this morning when I told her I couldn't play that we'd have time to set something else up, or for me to at least get her number for when she's back in town.

I drag my hands through my hair, staring at the table the girls were at last night, hoping maybe I can will her back into existence. JT tips back in his chair next to me, his golden curls everyone loves so much bouncing cheerfully as he watches the football game on the big screen above the bar. Unsurprisingly, he hasn't told me what he's doing here or why he's been texting my little sister. This charade, the one where we both pretend we are the silent, brooding type, unwilling to break the silence first, is a key part of our friendship.

The game switches to commercials as the bartender sets down our Stellas with a smile. "Thanks, Aubrey."

"No problem, Mr. Walker." Seeming to note our silence, she heads back into the kitchen.

Watching her leave, JT turns to me. "So you're not fucking the bartender, though she apparently would be willing if asked…"

I sigh, mentally preparing myself for the come-to-Jesus JT clearly needs to have with me. I'm getting better at spotting them. "Why are you here, JT?"

He takes a long drink. "Isn't it obvious?"

"No, it's obviously not obvious, or I wouldn't be asking. So why did you fly your happy ass all the way from California? It can't just be for the sake of my bubbly personality."

I decide to wait for him to say what he needs to say, so I turn in my seat, slowly perusing the course through the windows. Shit. The girls must really be gone. It hasn't been anywhere near this quiet and still since they arrived.

JT's eyes follow mine, scanning the area. "So, despite seeing the girl drive away, you're still looking for someone? Interesting. I haven't seen you this distracted by something that wasn't in the bottom of a bottle for a while now."

"Nope, not searching for anyone. Just trying to figure out why you're here, and why you are speaking to my little sister when the two of you can't stand each other."

It's true. In addition to the chaos they've caused at Thanksgiving with refusing to sit at the same table as one another, JT and Lila's hatred of each other has been a thorn in my side for the last few years. Ever since Lila turned eighteen, it's like she and JT can't handle being in the same vicinity as one another. I don't even bother inviting them out for drinks at the same time anymore, which really sucks, since they are two of my best, and only, friends.

"Oh, trust me, I still can't stand Lila. Unfortunately, she is apparently worried enough about you to break the long-term silent treatment she has been giving me since she hit puberty and is instead texting me daily to ask me when I'm going to"—he makes those annoying little quote things with his fingers—"grow a pair and come talk to you."

I turn to face him fully. "And why does Lila think you need to come talk to me?"

He sighs heavily. "Damnit, Jameo, you know why she thinks I need to come talk to you. The same reason I agreed with her enough to fly to the middle of nowhere to actually talk to you. You've had a shit year and followed it up by isolating yourself in the middle of godforsaken Kansas out here—"

"We're in Colorado, man. Check a map."

"Oh, okay, well, a very flat, no-mountains-in-sight Colorado doesn't really count as Colorado. It might as well be Kansas."

"I think you should ask the staff about it. I know for a fact that they *love* when people tell them about how this isn't really Colorado," I deadpan.

He rolls his eyes, pushing a hand through his hair before putting his hat back on. "Jameo, chasing after a random townie today was the first time I've seen a spark of life in your eyes in over a year. So yes, I'm worried about you. Your sister is really worried about you. She called me. On the phone. Your basically gen Z sister put a phone to her ear and actually talked on it, *to me*, to convince me this was a trip that I had to make. Turns out she's been talking to your parents and Jon, and they all decided I was the only one you wouldn't just kick out the minute I walked through the door. So cut the shit and tell me how you are really doing."

Well, crap. I know the last year has sucked, and I have been failing on the course and off it, but damn, when he puts it that way... I hadn't realized how worried everyone was about me. I can't, however, stop the hurt that builds up in my chest. "What the hell? You all are talking about me now? What, do you have a meeting once a week to talk about how big of a fuckup I am and then vote on who has to come hang out with the poor loser?"

"Jameson, cut the shit." The deep blue of his eyes burns as he glares at me. "You know that's not how it is. We all love you, and we're all worried as shit that you're losing yourself in the pool of darkness Alexis threw you into."

He's not wrong. Not that I expected him to be. JT has been my best friend for a long time, and while being in the same sport naturally makes us competitors, it's never felt that way. He's a smart, truly good-hearted guy. No one, apart from Lila, has ever had anything but good things to say about him. Even the press can't seem to find anything to dig in to other than his truly terrible decision to continue to be my friend last year.

"Fuck, man, I know," I say. "I just—Fuck. Misplaced anger, I think is what my therapist would call it. I'm really glad you're here. And I'm doing pretty well. I played the best round of golf in a while this morning. I'm finally getting my swing back. I'm not drowning myself in booze every night. I'm going to be back this year."

He looks me up and down. "You do look like you've been hitting the gym fairly consistently. Or...have you just been chasing after a lot of women in cars? I suppose there's more than one way to get back in shape."

"Didn't you hear? That's how women want to be picked up. Chasing after their cars is the new foreplay. Just you wait, she'll be back to find me later."

JT raises his eyebrows, clearly amused. "Damn, things have changed. Here I thought it gave off desperate-stalker vibes."

I chuckle, relaxing back into my chair and finishing my Stella in a long drink. "Honestly, I'm doing okay. There are days when everything still feels so out of control that I can't mentally get myself where I need to be with my game, but for the first time in a while, I'm feeling like there might be a light at the end of the tunnel."

"And does this light have anything to do with the blonde we were chasing out of the workout room?"

I pull on the bill of my cap, annoyed with myself for how poorly I behaved during that interaction. "No, but also yes. That girl—whose name I'm not even sure I've been told—is the friend of the girl who I golfed with today. And, shit, I think *she* might have something to do with me finding my love for the game again."

"Why were you chasing her, then?" JT asks. "Like a complete stalker, might I add."

"Yes, yes, you've mentioned the stalker part. I may have incorrectly assumed she was interrupting my workout to suggest a booty call. The evidence now suggests she was there to talk to me about her friend, Bryn—the girl I golfed with this morning. When Bryn asked me to golf with them again this afternoon, I turned her down. Which is likely for the best, but I'm not so sure now."

"When are you going to stop assuming that every girl just wants to use you and walk away?" he asks, a slight grimace spreading across his face.

"It's not the walking away that I'm worried about. It's falling in love only to find out that all they wanted was my money, my name, my fame, but never me." I take a deep breath. "But blondie wanted none of those things. And I don't understand it, but I can't stop thinking about the sarcastic girl who ruthlessly ragged on me, even while I was handing her her ass on the course. The one who never once seemed to care about who I am or the size of my bank account."

"So why are we sitting in the bar, not out on the course with her?"

"I'm pretty sure she's gone. And honestly, I'm not interested in finding someone to be serious with, and neither is she. But she definitely felt like the type of girl I could be serious with."

"Then why were you chasing after the friend?"

"Fuck if I know."

But maybe, just maybe, I do know. I'm just scared of what it would mean for my plan to only focus on my game.

Chapter Eleven

Bryn

You'll never guess who came to the office today…

Okay, it's not any fun if you don't play along.

…

GUESS!

Okay, okay, jeez. Uhm, Janice, HRH Queen of Wild Bluffs?

Don't even joke about that. I can't handle the gossip queen in my office on a Monday morning. There is not enough coffee in the world to have prepared me for that.

Leave it to Izzy to draw this out. She knows how busy I am during the week, but no, she still insists on texting me right during the middle of a meeting with one of our development teams and then has the gall to be annoyed that I waited until the meeting was over to respond. You would think running a management consultancy firm with Becca would keep her busy, but apparently she's looking to gossip this morning.

Turns out, I don't care who came to your office today. *peace emoji*

As expected, seconds later my phone's screen lights up with an incoming from Izzy.

"Oh, hey, Iz," I say as the connection finalizes. "To what do I owe the pleasure?"

"You are a pain in my ass. You know that, right? Why can you never play along?!" She's glaring at the screen, but her smile is trying to fight its way out.

"Izzy, just tell her already!" I hear Becca's voice from somewhere close to the phone.

I roll my eyes. Clearly, a lot of work is getting done at Flat Roads Consulting today. "Hey, Becca."

Her face pops into the frame as Izzy flips her phone's camera around.

I wave and then the video is switched back to Izzy. "How was Sunday night dinner, Iz? Did Mom lecture you on your current marital status again?"

"Ugh. Yes. Luckily, Kelsey didn't ditch me like you did, so we at least got to share the burden of not providing grandchildren." She shrugs. It's a lecture we've all heard about a million times now, so it's not one we take too seriously. "But, really, that is not why we called. I've got two words for you—Jameson Walker."

"Umm." I search her eyes through the screen, hoping for some more context. "I'm going to need more than just a name."

Both Izzy and Becca are in the video now. "Jameson 'The Dick' Walker was just in my office," Becca says somewhat grumpily.

The Dick. It makes him sound like he's got some super dick and as such is the only thing that can define him. It's like being "The Arm," except instead of being a pitcher with a kickass fastball, he's a man with an incredibly talented dick.

"Technically, he was in both of our offices, since it's an open floor plan. And"—she flicks Becca's arm, causing the phone to jiggle nauseatingly—"if you want to be even more specific, he was here to find me, so I'd say he was in *my* office."

I glance at my watch, realizing I've got three minutes until I need to be on my next meeting, a virtual one with our team in Vancouver. "I've got two minutes. I need one of you to tell me why the hell Jameo was in your office and why it matters to me."

I get the same pitying look from both of them at the last comment as we all realize why it would matter to me. I may or may not have been in a pissy mood since they last saw me, due to the man.

"Okay, I can do this. Two minutes." Izzy rolls her neck like she's getting ready for a fight. "Jameson stopped by here approximately an hour ago looking for you. Apparently, he asked Tony for your number, since you seemed to know him, but he said he wasn't allowed to give out members' or their guests' numbers per club rules. He did, however, mention my bio is on the club's membership page, and it lists me as the owner of Flat Roads Consulting. He also happened to share the fact that we have an office in town. So Jameson and—honestly, it was crazy—Jameson came in with *JT Johnson*, Bryn. Two professional golfers were in our office at the same time. It was..."

"Guys!" I'm dying over here. "Please, for the love of God, tell me what happened."

They both laugh. "Well, the gist of it is that he asked for your phone number, I typed it into his phone for him, and now the ball is in his court. Do you think he'll call you?"

Holy cow. Jameson Walker asked for my number. He went out of his way to find someone who had my number, and now he's going to reach out to me. I might actually see the man again. The thought has me both nauseous and giddy.

I hear my phone buzz with a work message. "Shit, I have to go. I will talk to you both later."

"You have to tell us as soon as—" I cut Becca off, pounding the red End button while simultaneously pulling up my laptop.

As I settle into my chair, my mind keeps going back to Jameson. I don't know why I'm so flustered about this. I'm a successful, attractive woman, and men asking for my number isn't anything new. But there's something about Jameson that's different. Yes, he's obviously very good-looking. He's got those moss-green eyes which, I will admit, made me just a bit weak in the knees when I stared at them a little too long. And, yes, he has clearly been spending some time in the weight room. It's hard to miss an ass like that when he's on the tee box in front of you.

But it's something more. He took my normal sass and threw it right back at me. There is also something strangely appealing about the way he dominated me on the golf course. Pulled zero punches for my sake, and I appreciate that.

Whatever it is, I can't stop thinking about him. I know nothing can come from it, but something inside of me is begging me to at least give it a try.

My meeting goes on for what feels like hours, and I'm barely paying attention. Every time my phone buzzes, I hope it's Jameson, but it's just more work messages and a constant barrage of texts from Izzy and Becca asking for updates. By the time the meeting is finally over, it's already late afternoon. *This.* This is why I can't let myself fall for a guy. I need to be focused on my career right now, not wondering if someone is going to text me or not.

As I walk toward the elevators, I'm stopped by Kyle Davis, the director of marketing. "Bryn, can I see you in my office for a minute? I need a number of changes to the app to be made before a big marketing push rolls out next week," he says, straightening his perfectly tailored suit sleeves.

Kyle is one of the few individuals at this company I truly cannot stand. I may go as far as to call him my nemesis. It's not just his douchey face or the fact that he seems to have everyone fooled by his polished demeanor and weasel smile. No, I hate him because he frequently claims my ideas as his own and then still has the nerve to treat me like he is my boss rather than at the exact same level as me. Someday, when Tara retires as the head of the North America region, we are going to have a battle royale to determine who actually is the boss of the other. A battle I cannot—I will not—lose.

An hour later, I'm finally able to go home. As I leave Kyle's office, ready to dump a cup of coffee straight in his arrogant face, I look down at my phone and see there's a voicemail from an unknown number. Ugh. I have spotty service in the office, and my calls occasionally get sent straight to voicemail.

As I go to pull up the message, my phone vibrates with a text coming in.

Unknown Number

> Hey, Bryn, this is Jameson Walker. I hope you don't mind, I got your number from your sister today. I just wanted to say I had a lot of fun with you this weekend. Please disregard the voicemail I just left. I'm very aware that no one actually calls people anymore. It was a weird thing to do.

I laugh as I read the message, glad he gave me an out with the voicemail. There was zero chance that I was going to call him back.

I save his number in my phone and make my way down to the street. On the short walk to my hotel, I stop by one of my favorite restaurants to grab my takeout order.

Me

Hmm…Jameson Walker, you say. That name seems familiar for some reason. Are you the guy at the airport who asked for my number after trying to airdrop me a dick pic?

Jameson

Bold. Please tell me that did not actually happen to you.

Me

Just one of the small perks of flying the friendly skies as much as I do. I'm constantly inundated with the best the country has to offer in terms of humans, germs, and dicks.

Jameson

What a privileged life you live.

I wander into my hotel room, setting my takeout dinner on the little desk while pulling off my shoes. I decline yet another FaceTime from my sister, enjoying my conversation with Jameson too much to talk to Izzy right now. Plus, it's fun to make her wait.

I text him back, thinking about how easy it is to talk to him. Jameson is funnier than I anticipated. I didn't expect his humor on the course to be quite as…intelligent? I am well aware there are many smart professional athletes, but I guess I played the odds and assumed he wasn't.

I'm also resisting the urge to Google Jameson. One, because I don't want to be tempted to creepily stare at the pictures of him all night long. And two, because I'm not sure I want to know everything the internet has to say about him. I might—okay, I definitely will—at some point give in to the temptation, but now, when things just seem easy and fun, I'm probably better off not knowing.

My FaceTime rings again, and I give in, swiping to answer my sister's call.

"You're a real dick, you know?" She's glaring at me, her eyes tiny slits behind her glasses.

I point to my chest. "Me? Your favorite sister?"

"I'm officially handing the title to Kelsey. You know what you did."

I sit in silence, knowing it'll just irritate her more.

She finally breaks. "Ugh! You really are the worst. Tell me! Did he text you?"

I do my best to look confused. "Who?"

"I hate you. Did Jameson Walker, the professional golfer you hung out with this weekend who also came into my office today to ask for your phone number, contact you in any way, shape, or form?"

"Thank you for clarifying. I am *wildly* popular, so can't be expected to remember whose calls you believe I'm waiting on."

She blinks rapidly at me, something she only does when signaling her annoyance.

"Tell me, Bryn, or I will get Kelsey to have her team hack your stupid phone. And while they are in there, I will make them change your autocorrect so that every time you write 'meeting,' it changes to 'hookup.'"

"Jesus, Iz, that's oddly specific." I think about the implications of such a switch. "And, upon further reflection, would completely unhinge my work messages. I'm also like ninety-nine percent certain Kelsey's team can't, technically or legally, do that."

"I will kill you."

"Fine!" I smile at her. "You're so testy today. Yes, he randomly called and left me a voicemail while I was still at the office, but then he immediately followed it up with a text, so I've decided to forgive him for such a ridiculous notion."

Izzy crinkles her nose. "Can you imagine if you would've had to call him back? It would've been the beginning of the end right there."

"I know. I truly don't think I would've done it. I mean, I would've responded...just via text."

She laughs. "Obviously. No way you're not responding when Jameson Walker calls. That man is beautiful."

"I don't know if I would go with beautiful. Definitely handsome, but I think he might be a bit too rugged to be in the beautiful classification."

"You're not wrong. His friend JT, though? He—and can we just spend one more moment reflecting on the two hot, professional golfers in my office today?—is beautiful with his blond hair and blue eyes." She gets a dreamy look in her eyes but shakes it away. "Anyway, did he ask you out?!"

"Yes, in the first ten text messages he, like any other normal, red-blooded male, poetically asked me out on a date with a horse-drawn carriage and a pathway of rose petals," I reply sarcastically.

"Ew, that sounds like a terrible first date. I hope he has something better planned."

"I would truly hate being taken on that date."

"I know. So, are you going to drop the cherry bomb on him before you go out?"

"Can we please not call losing my virginity that? And no, I'm not going to tell him. He, like all other people, will just assume that I've had sex. I'm twenty-eight and not actually all that awkward."

"Or you could tell him so you don't start your relationship off with a lie..."

"You're the worst. I regret telling *you* about still being a virgin. Plus, I gotta go. I need to eat this beef lo mein that is currently getting cold."

Plus, I have someone waiting for a text back from me.

Chapter Twelve

Jameson

The last week has been one of the best in a long while. Not only has it been a good time having JT hanging out and playing rounds with me out at Wild Bluffs, I also fill most of my spare minutes texting Bryn.

She has quickly become the first person I think about when I wake up in the morning and the last person I think about before I go to bed at night. This week she is in California, so I'm generally in bed before she is, and I may or may not have fallen asleep the past four nights before saying goodbye. Waking up to her text from the night before—her *Good night, Jameo*—sure as hell starts my day off on a good note. JT has been quick to point out my good mood every morning when I'm not quite as surly at breakfast.

Today, I'm nursing my daily cup of coffee when JT walks into the restaurant. Even though I'm enjoying his company, I wonder again why exactly he is here. I know he said Lila has been pestering him to come, but from the way he has lingered, his happy smile and good-natured jokes just a little slower than usual, I'm beginning to wonder if it's not something more—something going on in his world.

He sits down, gesturing to the waitress to bring him his usual cup of coffee as well. "Morning, Jameo. Weather looks good today. Thinking we get in another thirty-six holes?"

I nod. "Yup. Sounds good. Want to hit up the gym before, or after?" It's early September, and the mornings are still cool. It keeps us from getting too warm while we play, but we're quickly approaching the time of year when it will be too cold to get out in the mornings. The staff won't let you out on the course if there is still frost coating the grass.

"This afternoon sounds good. Or, you know, I could get us an airplane out of here this afternoon. We could head to, say, California, for the weekend?"

I shoot a glare at him, though inside I feel a spark catch. "California, huh? And what, exactly, would we do there?"

JT's eyes light up into his usual good-natured smirk. "Oh, I'm sure we can find something."

***

"I'm glad we were able to get in a quick round and a workout this morning," JT says, navigating his rented dark blue Ford F150 down the road away from the course.

"Yeah. I am definitely not in a place where I should be skipping training. Especially not for an impromptu trip to California."

"Sam says we should land just before dinnertime," JT replies, referencing his virtual assistant who handled our last-minute plane request like a pro.

I glance down at my phone again as JT pulls into the private airfield. Surprisingly large for a town the size of Wild Bluffs, the airport is the only one in the area for private jets to land and refuel. It's definitely not going to be a cheap trip for the weekend, but what's the point in being this rich if you never spend it?

"Did you ask her out?"

I snap my head up from my phone and shoot JT a glare.

He rolls his eyes as he pulls into a parking spot. "What? Are we going to pretend like we aren't going to California so you can go on a date with Bryn?"

"We are not going out on a...date." I nearly choke on the word as it comes out of my mouth. Nope. Dating implies way too much. "I'm not even allowed to date right now."

He grabs his bag out of the back, his eyebrows pulling together as he looks at me, the question clear in his eyes even before he voices it. "Okay. Not a date. But definitely flying halfway across the country so you can hang out with a girl. A girl who you've been talking to nonstop. A girl who makes you happier than you've been in a long time." He nods like that isn't the most ridiculous thing he's ever said. "Got it."

I scratch my hands through my hair. "Never mind. We should just stay here. She hasn't even responded. I haven't asked her anything yet." I start moving back toward the car, even though I know from our numerous texts exchanged that Bryn has a bunch of big meetings taking place this week—it's one of the main reasons she's working in the California office rather than remotely from Wild Bluffs. "This was a mistake. I most definitely should not be thinking about starting anything with anyone."

"Jesus, Jameson. You can't be serious. Of course we are going. Not only are the pilots already here with the plane refueled and ready to go, but we also both know this is what you need. You need to get Alexis out of your system."

"She *is* out," I growl.

He looks me up and down, noting my hair sticking out from pulling my hands through it. "Clearly."

With that, he picks up his bags and heads to the plane, leaving me with no option but to follow. As I finally settle down in a seat across from JT in the back, he says, "She's not worth it, you know." JT is rarely serious, but I can tell he is now.

"What do you mean?"

"Alexis. She was never worth the effort you put into her." He pauses, clearly thinking. "But that doesn't mean no one is. I'm not saying it's Bryn, though I hope I get to meet her this weekend so I can have an opinion on the subject, but even if it isn't, you need to stop letting Alexis ruin your life. She used you when you were together, and from the looks of it, she still has her claws in you."

As I go to respond, my phone lights up with a text.

Bryn

> Big plans for dinner at the hotel.

"Sounds like she's free tonight. Want to come to dinner and meet her?"

JT shakes his head. "No way I'm crashing your first date." He must note the panic that shoots through me. "Oh, excuse me, your first casual hangout that is certainly not a date with a woman you definitely like."

As I feel the plane start to move beneath us, I still don't text her back, unsure of what to say.

"Just see if she wants to grab dinner together. It doesn't have to be a thing."

Me

> I am actually going to be in LA tonight. Want to grab dinner?

I wait a minute, but she doesn't respond. Fine. I'm already in, might as well commit.

Me

> I'm on the plane, but text me back where and when you want to meet. I promise it'll just be fun.

Knowing the Wi-Fi is shit and tends to kill my battery, I turn off the phone and tuck it into the front pocket of my black backpack at my feet. I look over at JT, who is reading a book he'd pulled out. I'm about to ask him why the dust cover is removed when I note the darkness is back in his eyes, so I decide to leave it alone.

As I sat there watching Colorado disappear below me, the movement of the plane must have lulled me to sleep, because the next thing I know, the jolt of the wheels touching down at Van Nuys Airport is waking me up.

I glance around, notice JT on his phone, and quickly grab mine out. After what feels like forever for it to turn on, I text myself to forcefully push my messages through.

Disappointment crashes through me when only mine arrives. I am about to demand the pilots take me directly back to Colorado when my phone vibrates with an incoming message.

Thank fuck. It's from Bryn.

Bryn

> Oo. I can't wait to hear about what could've brought you last minute to California. I can only assume it's for your big break into the porn industry. Meet you at The Grill at 7:30? I got us a table under my name.

I smile, unnervingly pleased with the fact that I get to see her tonight. It also did not escape me that she thinks porn could be a future for me. It's not in my immediate plans, but I don't hate hearing that she thinks it's an option for me.

Me

> Sounds perfect. I'll see you there. I'll be the one with the porn 'stache.

***

"Jameson Walker, you are a bald-faced liar."

She's already sitting on one side of a deep booth. The traffic to get here caused the trip to take longer than expected. I ended up sending my bags with JT so I could get here close to 7:30 p.m. At 7:40, I know

I'm late. At least I had the foresight to text Bryn to let her know I was behind schedule when it became clear my Uber would not make it in time.

"I told you I would be late," I defend myself as I slide into the opposite side of the booth.

"That is not what I am talking about," she says, pulling her best stern-librarian face. "You said you would be rocking a porn 'stache, and I was very much looking forward to seeing it."

A deep chuckle rumbles out of me as I take in Bryn sitting across from me. Her hair is down, the light brown shining from the light above the table. She's got on a deep navy shirt, and her eyes seem blue, different from the light brown I remember from last time.

"Your eyes are different."

"What?"

WHAT? Why in the name of all things holy is that what decided to come out of my mouth?

"Uhm." Shit. No going back now. "Your eyes. They are blue tonight. I didn't think they were blue last time."

She laughs, a real, joyful laugh that leaves me no option but to laugh along with her.

It takes her longer to calm herself than expected, but when she does, the smile is still spread across her beautiful face as she says, "I've never had someone point it out in quite that way, but, yeah, I have hazel eyes. They fluctuate at will, generally depending on what I'm wearing." She looks down at herself. "So it makes sense that they look blue, given I'm wearing a blue shirt."

"Hazel, huh? Who knew there was a word for color-changing eyes?"

"Most people, actually. I'm pretty sure it's a well-known eye color."

"Is it, though?" I scratch my chin. "I'm definitely above average as a person, and I didn't know about them."

Smirking, she throws it right back at me. "Might suggest your assessment of your intelligence is incorrect."

"Oh, please." I wave my hand down my front. "I am anything but average."

"Sure, you might be physically above average; the 'professional athlete' title suggested that would likely be the case. But, if the rumors surrounding the professional sports world are to be believed, you likely aren't even smart enough to tie your shoes without repeating the story about the bunny going in a hole."

Her lips are tight and her eyes are gleaming, holding in the smile and pride she feels from her comeback, and it makes that little ember that sparked to life on the plane burst into a small fire.

"Oh, trust me, I'm quite able to get things into holes without the help of any kind of rhymes."

Chapter Thirteen

Bryn

My cheeks are starting to strain from how much I've smiled tonight. And I'm certainly not going to need to get in any sort of an ab workout tomorrow with how much I've laughed—shit, I might be able to skip abs all week at this rate.

We're almost done with our entrees, and I can honestly say this is the best date I've ever been on. Or, at least, it would be if it were a date. *Which it's totally not, because neither of us date!* Gah! Why do I have to keep reminding myself of this?

As the waitress brings out the dessert menu, I glance at Jameo. He's concentrating on the options, and I take the chance to look him over. His beard, which he—thank God—did not shave down into a mustache, is thick and dark. His hair is styled slightly. He's paired dark jeans and a white long-sleeved button-up, transforming him into the type of man you only see in commercials. He may be the most handsome man I've ever met in person.

He catches me staring, and I quickly glance back down at my menu, asking, "So, are you going to get anything?"

"Actually…" He looks a bit nervous, and I wonder if he's about to blow me off again. "I was thinking we could walk a few blocks and see if we can find some ice cream." He runs his finger down the side of the menu as he continues, barely taking a breath. "I mean, I know this dinner invite came at the last minute, so maybe you've got something else planned, but I could definitely use a walk. I know you really like ice cream, so maybe we could get some."

He glances up at me, and I nod. "Sure. I'd love that."

Jameson stands up. "I'm going to run to the bathroom really quickly, then."

The waiter brings the check while Jameson is in the bathroom, and, as I know this isn't a date, I just go ahead and throw my credit card down. I am fully aware that my bank account can handle the $220 charge better than I could emotionally handle the awkwardness of figuring out who pays.

I'm filling in the receipt as Jameson comes back, and with a quick flourish, I finish signing my name and stand up to go.

Looking confused, he asks, "Did you pay?"

"Yup." I shrug, grabbing my phone off the table.

"Shit. Bryn, I didn't mean to make you pay. I asked you out. I definitely intended on paying." His eyes look a bit frantic, so I instinctively reach out and put my hand on his arm— a gesture we both follow with our eyes, unsure what to do next. Then, as if he's made a decision, he turns on his heel, tucking my hand into the crook of his arm, and starts walking to the door.

Neither of us say a word as we navigate through the tables scattered around the restaurant. Jameson drops my hand as he pushes through the door, holding it open for me.

The weather outside is still warm, though the heat from the day is being swept away by the cool evening breeze common this time of year.

I take off toward the direction of the ocean, guessing ice cream will be that way, but not really caring if it takes us a while to find some. Jameson keeps pace with me easily. He keeps opening his mouth like he's about to start talking before giving his head a slight shake and continuing forward.

I give him some time, finding the whole thing slightly amusing. Usually, I'm the one who is unsure of what to say.

We walk in companionable silence, our hands brushing against each other every few steps. I know I could take a step away from him at any time, but the zing that passes up my arm and into my core each time it happens is making me a little bit giddy. You'd think I'd had a bottle of champagne with my steak tonight—rather than the Guinness I'd sipped on—with how light and bubbly I'm feeling.

Jameson stops suddenly, turning to look directly at me. "Thank you for dinner."

He is so serious. I feel like I'm missing something—something important. So I pause for a second, searching for the answers in the dark green depths of his eyes, noting how the streetlights are making gold flecks ignite within them.

"Of course. I'm truly happy to buy you dinner. I'm having so much fun tonight. And…" I trail off as I look at him. Whatever. Might as well say it. "Honestly? I get it. It's hard to tell who likes you for you versus those who are just using you for fame or money. I don't ever want you to question that about me." I look into his serious eyes again. "I like hanging out with you, and I'd rather be clear that I'm not interested in your money than get a free dinner. Though"—I shrug—"I do really like free things."

He laughs. "Who doesn't? It's why swag exists. No one needs another branded ChapStick, but we sure as shit are all going to take it when offered."

He grows serious again. "But thanks, Bryn. It means a lot to me to hear you say that. You're not wrong; it hasn't always been easy to know who is in it for the wrong reasons." He starts walking again, grabbing my hand to pull me along with him.

We wander through the streets of LA, not trying particularly hard to find an ice cream place, and, in fact, deciding to continue on past a few of them under the guise of "walking off dinner."

While strolling through town is a good way to burn off the ribeye I took down at dinner, I, at least, am not in it for the extra steps. The feel of his large, strong hand in mine is everything I never knew I wanted, so I do my fair share of turning down the shops as we get to them, intent on stretching out our time together for as long as I can.

Finally, Jameson lets out a loud, impossible-to-ignore yawn.

I laugh. "Next shop. We're definitely going in."

We walk a few more minutes before begrudgingly—at least on my part—entering the next ice cream store we come to. It's one we passed an hour earlier—turns out we had been walking in a large circle the entire time, but neither of us is acknowledging that fact or what it could mean.

As we finish our ice cream, a woman checks out, and as she turns to leave, she does a double take. She gazes at Jameson for a moment longer before finally making her way toward us. I watch her confident steps—something I could never pull off in the four-inch heels and pencil skirt she has on—unsure how to handle this. Jameson's back is to her, so he has no idea she's approaching.

"Jameson, hi."

He swings his head around at the sound of her voice, glancing at me with wide eyes before standing up to give her a hug.

"Erica. How's my favorite publicist?"

"Flattery will get you nowhere. Last I heard, you were hunkered down in Colorado." She pointedly looks at me. "What brings you to California?"

"Oh, um." He turns to look at me. "This is Bryn."

"Hi, Bryn," she says, her tone almost frigid.

"Hi." I offer a small wave.

"Well, this is...cute. Jameson, you and I will need to discuss some things later, but I had better get going." She shoots Jameson a look that I've only seen on my mom's face before and pushes through the doors into the California air.

"Erica is my publicist."

"I gathered that," I say, tucking back into my ice cream.

"I just want you to know she's not someone...else."

"Duly noted. You might owe her an apology, though. She had a you're-in-trouble look on her face."

"Yeah." He lets out a heavy breath. "I'm sure I'll be getting some texts shortly."

I do feel bad he's in trouble. Judging by her face, it feels like I might be the cause of it.

"I'm sorry if I had something to do with it."

"Ehh. Normal professional golfer stuff."

"Oh, dear." I put on my best Mrs. Doubtfire voice. "Not *professional golfer* stuff. How positively brutal."

"You're a dork," he jokes.

"True."

We finish our ice cream, and after about five more yawns from Jameson, we both call Ubers to take us back to our respective hotels. My driver arrives before his—five-star Uber rating for the win!—and with the click of a button on his phone, he jumps in with me, claiming it's unsafe for me to ride home without him.

Pleased with a chance to extend the night just a bit longer, I latch on to the excuse, sharing a conspiratorial wink with Gemini, the petite twentysomething in the driver's seat. As we ride along, Jameson reaches over and takes my hand again, unaware of the way it makes my heart beat double time in my chest.

We arrive at my hotel much quicker than I would've liked, and I begrudgingly wish Jameson good night. He squeezes my hand, thanking me again for dinner. We both sit there awkwardly for a moment before Gemini clears her throat in the front, breaking me out of my trance.

I push out of the car, taking a few steps toward the front entrance before turning back to wave as Jameson pulls away. The glow from his phone is lighting up his face inside the car, and as soon as I enter my hotel, his text buzzes on my phone.

Jameson

Thanks again for dinner. I had a great time.

Me

Me too. And anytime. Truly.

CHAPTER FOURTEEN

JAMESON

I PUSH INTO THE suite JT and I decided to share, kicking off my shoes by the door. I walk into the living space to find JT sprawled on the couch, his phone in one hand.

"How was the date?"

"It was...fun?"

"Why are you phrasing it like a question?"

"I dunno. I guess I've just never really had that much fun out with a woman before." I sink on the couch next to him. "Plus, she bought dinner. So I kinda feel like a jackass about making her pay for our first date."

"I'm sorry, I think I'm behind. I called it a date to see if I could get you spun up. You've now called it a date twice, and I'm pretty sure you're being serious."

I let out a groan, dropping my head to the back of the couch. "Fuck. I don't know what to do."

"You mean about the fact that you went on a date with someone after so vehemently stating it wasn't a date? Is that what you mean?"

"When did you learn the word *vehemently*?" I ask.

"Oh, likely around the same time you were out on a *date*. I thought you weren't allowed to date."

"Yeah. Erica and Jon have both been all over me about focusing on golf." I pick at a nonexistent stain on my shirt. "And I must've really pissed some god off, because we ran into Erica while getting *ice cream*—I don't think I've ever seen her eat sugar before."

"Do you think she's tracking your phone?"

It's not impossible, but it does seem pretty unlikely, even if I could've used a babysitter a time or two in the last year.

"Nah." I consider it some more. "I don't think so, at least."

"Did she yell at you?"

"No. She's much too aware of my public image for that. She did send me a text message on my way home, though."

"And? What did it say?"

I pull my phone out of my pocket, reading the message aloud, "Jameson Walker. I'm having a hard enough time convincing your current sponsors not to drop you, let alone find you a new one. You can't be seen dating random women."

To be fair to Erica, the photos of me leaving the bars, clearly inebriated, with a different woman every night kept her busy for months last fall. I'm not sure how much money we ended up paying to keep the worst ones from hitting the gossip sites—it was worth it to keep my sponsors happy.

"Not great," JT replies. "So what are you going to do?"

"I don't know." I shrug. "Fuck. Just keep texting with Bryn? Erica can't get mad about that. Plus, it's not like we're in the same place that often. Maybe it won't be that bad."

"Really? You came in here looking like you were a kid who just found out they were going to Disney World. You think you'd be happy with just being her casual friend?"

I understand why he's questioning this. Jameson of twenty-four hours ago wanted nothing to do with dating anyone, but that Jameson hadn't realized the joy, the contentment, the peace that I experienced this past week were just a sliver of what it is like being fully in Bryn's presence. No, I don't want to just be texting buddies with her. I want her to be mine. I need her to be mine. And making someone yours requires dating—or kidnapping, I suppose.

"Do you think Erica will mind more if I date her or if I kidnap her?" I question.

"It alarms me how serious you look when asking that."

We both sit there, lost in thought, my stomach twisting itself into tighter and tighter knots with each passing minute. Finally, I can't take it anymore. "Ugh, fuck this. I don't know what to do."

"Well..." JT draws out.

"Do you have an idea?" I ask desperately.

He gives me side-eye that I fully deserve. "Erica's text said not to *date around*. Not to be casually dating. What if you didn't?"

"How does rephrasing the question help us?"

"I mean, don't date her casually. Date her seriously. Go to full-on-relationship status."

"It might be coming on a little too strong to ask her to be my girlfriend after one not-date."

"Or you sack up and just explain it to her," he says. "Explain you're basically on probation with your sponsors and your PR team and that, if you guys want to casually date, you need to look like you're seriously dating."

"How did I reach this point in my life?"

"A string of bad decisions," he says with a smile that makes me want to break his perfect teeth. "But I do think this can work."

"I don't know. I guess I'm going to sleep on it. Maybe a better plan will come to me in my dreams." I stand up from the couch and head to my room.

"Good luck with that," JT says, raising his hand in a half-assed wave.

Chapter Fifteen

Bryn

Thanks again for last night. I had a really good time.

I've been in the office since 5:30 this morning, trying to track down one of our development team leads in London.

I hate being in the office on the weekends. I'm not someone who loves to work just for the sake of being busy. I like being good at my job, I like getting things done, but I hate working more than necessary. Unfortunately, it's currently necessary for me to spend a lot of time at the office. Some of it is getting in-person face time with the teams who are pushing extra hard on this new campaign. I also have so much work to do that forcing myself to go into the office every day I'm in California is the only way I'm going to get it done.

Me

I did too. What are you up to today? After establishing your trip isn't your foray into the porn industry, we didn't ever actually talk about what you are doing out here.

Jameson

Would you believe me if I told you I had meetings with my agent and a couple of potential sponsors?

Me

I would have believed you if you had simply told me you had meetings with your agent and a couple of sponsors. Now that you asked it as a question? Most certainly not.

Jameson

I knew it was a mistake as soon as I sent it. Let me try again.

I had a last-minute meeting come up with my agent and a couple of potential sponsors.

Me

Too late. I know it's a lie now.

I shake my head, laughing. This side of Jameo is so much fun. He's not just the witty, sarcastic guy from the golf course. He's also kinda a goofball who has, surprisingly, been very open. I was expecting him to be a bit more of a player based on the way he's been portrayed in the media. That worry was actually one of the main reasons why I'd so readily agreed I wasn't looking for anything serious.

Jameson

> I actually had a few hours open up today. Want to grab some brunch or something?

I'm surprised by the invitation but remind myself that he's likely just bored.

My phone buzzes with yet another incoming message.

Kelsey

> Iz told me you had a date last night with Jameson Walker.

> I'm not trying to tell you what to do, but I'd be careful. He seemed to be dating around a lot this time last year.

Me

> Thanks for the warning, but we are keeping it super casual.

Kelsey

> I don't think you know what super casual dating actually looks like. How many days last week did you text him?

Me

> I want to say all of them, but it feels like the wrong answer…

Kelsey

Just be careful. You're a person. It's very possible he's texting other women too.

Me

Is that a general feeling or one based on cyber hacking?

Kelsey

zipped lips emoji

Nah. I wouldn't waste the resources on that. He's a professional athlete. I'm just playing the odds.

Even my ex, Peter, for all his flaws, had been loyal to the very end. Or, at least, he hadn't cheated on me. I'm not sure it counts as loyalty, since he never once sided with me or stood up for me to his mom. It's what, in the end, had been our downfall. Eleanor—or Mrs. Easley, she insisted I call her—never liked me. I wasn't at Peter's beck and call, didn't quit my job to move to the same city as him, and wore my hair in a messy bun far too frequently to be good enough for her baby.

Peter never seemed to care about those things, and, considering he was the son of a billionaire, was surprisingly low-maintenance himself. But, as it turns out, his expectations of me were to be more. To be like his mom.

Even with his mom regularly trying to undermine me, I thought Peter and I were the real deal. Then things started to go south. His usual disappointment when I couldn't make one of the many events he was attending each week started morphing into frustration. He started actively siding with his mom, saying things like, "I know your work is important to you, but I can't be in a relationship with someone who cares more about their job than me. I need you here. I need you at these events with me."

I tried explaining I was committing as much time as I could to being with him. That I was the one who was always flying to see him, even though airplanes work both ways (and one of us had access to a private jet). That my job wasn't more important than him, but it was important. I told him about all the work meetings I'd joined from the car rather than in person so that I could make it to a gala or charity event with him.

He just didn't understand that I couldn't dedicate every minute of my time to us...to him.

A couple weeks later, as I left work right at closing time yet again to sprint to the airport, I ran into my then boss's boss, Tara. She let me know that, while I was still performing *fine* at my job, I was starting to be overlooked when management was discussing up-and-comers. I needed to focus if I wanted to be on the leadership team someday.

When I finally opened the door to Peter's apartment—four hours late because I missed my flight—I heard him say my name and walked toward his kitchen to find him. Realizing he was on the phone, I slowed down, unabashedly listening in on his side of the conversation.

"No, Mom, I knew Bryn wasn't going to be able to be at the event tonight. I told you she's having a hard time at work and really needed to stay there for a last-minute meeting with her boss." I tried to slow my breath, hoping he wouldn't hear me and censor his thoughts.

"Yes. Yes, I know. We both know how important it is that she comes," he said, followed by a creak as he stood from a chair. "She just can't do both things." He started pacing. "Mom, she just can't excel at her job and as a girlfriend. It would be hard for anyone." More pacing. "I don't know, Mom, I guess maybe she just can't juggle both."

I could picture him, running his hand along the back of his neck like he does when he's frustrated. It was a gesture I'd seen frequently lately.

"Maybe, Mom. I mean, I loved Bryn." He sighed after he said that, and I felt the *d* on the end of the word *love* like it was a knife thrown straight at my heart. "You're right. Maybe we just aren't a good fit anymore."

All I heard was yet another person saying I wasn't good enough on that same day.

We broke up that night, and I flew back to Wild Bluffs knowing the only way I could ever be enough was to focus 100% of my energy on my job.

So what am I doing now, letting myself develop an interest in a professional athlete?

I have three minutes before the team leader said he could meet, so I quickly dial Izzy.

She answers with a yawn, asking, "Why are you calling me so early?"

"Am I ridiculous for going out with Jameson Walker?"

"Why would you be? And are you *going out* with him?"

"He's a professional athlete. He's likely not just going out with me."

I turn around, startled by the masculine "knock, knock" behind me. Ugh. Why does it have to be Kyle? Gosh, I hope he didn't hear anything.

"Is he, though?" Iz asks in my ear.

"I gotta go, Izzy," I say, hanging up before she can say goodbye.

I straighten my back, refusing to seem any more rushed by Kyle's unexpected appearance.

"What do you need?" I ask, not at all pleased that I get to see him on the weekends as well now.

"Just wanted to see how things were going with the development team. You know marketing is waiting on that update."

Marketing doesn't actually need to know about the update. It has almost zero impact on anything they are doing. This is just typical Kyle, needing to be in the know about everything while doing absolutely nothing.

"I actually have a call with them right now," I say, swiveling my chair back to face my computer. "Bye, Kyle."

Chapter Sixteen

Jameson

After getting in a morning workout with JT at the hotel fitness center, I'm in an Uber on my way to pick Bryn up. She's already been to work this morning, which was crazy to learn. Bryn insisted she could just meet me at the restaurant for brunch, but I was just as insistent that I pick her up after she had a chance to drop her stuff off at her hotel. Because I still believe a guy should pick a girl up for a date. And this *is* a date. Even if Bryn doesn't know it yet. Even if I was adamantly opposed to dating just twenty-four hours ago. Now all I have to do is convince her to date me seriously. While keeping it appropriately casual for our first official date. Fuck.

The black car I'm in rolls to a stop in the Marriott roundabout, and I see Bryn sitting out front wearing a pair of black joggers and one of those baggy cut-off shirts that seem to be so popular these days. I've never really thought about how hot workout clothes could be—*athleisure,* as the kids are calling it these days—but damn. I really want to cuddle with her.

I can imagine it now. A cool autumn day at a cabin in the mountains, lazily sprawled out on the couch, binge-watching a show together while she snuggles up into me. I shake my head and throw open my door, hurrying around to catch Bryn before she lets herself into the other side.

"Hey!"

"Morning, Jameo. What brings you to this side of LA?" she jokes.

I pull her into a hug because…well…I want to hug her. "I've got a hot date I'm here to pick up." Then, looking behind her, I say, "Have you seen Mila Kunis anywhere? I swear she said she was staying at this hotel."

"Thank God." Bryn whacks my arm good-naturedly. "I was worried you thought this was a date. Which would be highly out of character for the man who was a complete dick to me and then went out of his way to make it very, very clear that he was not interested in dating."

Well, shit. I feel my shoulders slump slightly as I close her door and walk around to my side of the car. That's true. I was a dick. And I did make it clear I wasn't interested in dating. But, on the other hand, I'm now very interested in dating Bryn. How the hell do I explain that to her? I have no idea.

Taking a steadying breath, one I've worked on with my sports psychologist regularly over the years, I slide in next to Bryn. She's staring out the window, and I sit silently next to her, trying to figure out what I'm supposed to do. I can't spend the rest of the day pretending this isn't a date in my mind. Even if I wasn't in a situation forcing me to make it official, I would still want this to be a date. This is the most uncomfortable I've ever been around her.

It's clear she can feel it too, her shoulders climbing higher with each passing minute. Finally, she turns to look at me. "I thought you didn't want it to be a date. That's why I said it. You told me you weren't looking to date. I wanted to make it clear I knew that." She rolls her shoulders down her back, clearly unsure.

I drop my head back on the headrest before quickly pulling it forward again. I know I have to explain. "I get it." I pause and glance into her eyes—gray today. "The problem is that I meant it when I said I wasn't looking to date. It's just—"

She cuts in. "I—"

"No, please, let me get this out. I wasn't looking to date anyone. I'm pretty fucked up from a past relationship, and yeah, I don't want to enter into the dating scene. Don't want to do the apps, the blind dates, the awkward double dates with friends of friends." I run my hand through my hair. "But I do want to date you. I know I joked around about Mila Kunis, and honestly, I stand by that—she's hot. But I was actually hoping today could be a real date." Noting her slightly confused look, I add awkwardly, "With you."

The driver—like the saint that quiet Uber drivers are—makes a show of pulling out a pair of earbuds and putting them in. I guess this is getting too personal for him.

Bryn, on the other hand, is chuckling and has a genuine, full grin making the whole back seat of this car light up like it's Christmastime. "Thanks for clarifying. Here I thought that whole speech was just to let me know that you're interested in Mila Kunis if she and Kutcher ever break up," she teases. "Hmm...so is this you officially asking me out?"

I tap my lip with my finger, pretending to ponder the question. "*Official* makes it sound so...official. But, since you're really pressuring me into things here, I guess I'll go with the audible and say, yeah, I'm officially asking you out. Will you go on a date with me?"

"Gosh. You're asking me out and using football terminology. It's really throwing me for a loop here." Her eyes are dancing.

"Okay, fine," I say. "Will you do exactly what you planned to do with me today but call it a date?"

"And who, exactly, do you imagine I'm going to be sharing this 'official date' news with?" she asks.

"Well, this is where things do get a bit more complicated." I pause, not quite sure what to say. "It's just that, my PR team and sponsors"—I'm basically whispering now, just in case the Uber driver didn't actually turn on their headphones—"well, they were pretty upset with me last year. I totally get it. I was in a bad spot, and I did a lot of things I shouldn't have, including being photographed with a lot of different women. So I've been warned, a lot, that I can't be seen dating casually...which I definitely should've thought of yesterday before we went to dinner in California of all places. I was just so excited at the thought of getting to see you, I didn't really think about it." I guess word vomit is a thing I'm doing now.

"So we can't date?" she asks, her brow drawn in confusion. "I thought you wanted me to call this a date?"

"Right. I do. I definitely want to date you in a non-weird, normally paced way, where we don't have a conversation about being official or dating seriously or anything until at least date three or four." I take a deep breath, winded from saying so much at once. "But, I'm me. Which makes things more difficult. So, to casually date me, I kinda need you to officially date me. Like exclusive, boyfriend/girlfriend date."

"You're asking me to be your girlfriend?"

Why do her questions feel like a tiny jab to my gut each time? I should've known the casual/committed relationship was a terrible plan. JT and I most certainly cannot be trusted to handle a situation like this. I should've called Lila.

"Yes. But I don't want to rush it. I want us to date like we would've. Just call it something more official-sounding if asked."

"But you do *want* to date me? This isn't some media thing where you need a fake girlfriend?"

"No. Basically everyone who works for me would prefer I have no girlfriend. But I want to get to know you. I'm not willing to give this up before we even get a chance to try." I shrug. "So officially dating is the best I can do."

She nods. "Officially dating. Noted. Will you expect me to be at all your things? I'm sure you're super busy with tournaments and galas and whatnot, and I am swamped with work, and, even if I tried, I can't make everything. Or really most things."

"Nope. You're welcome to join but not expected to at all. I don't think I would ever expect that of my girlfriend, but definitely not my officially casual one."

"And it's exclusive. No dating anyone else?"

"No. Is that a problem for you?" Why am I suddenly jealous of the faceless man I'm imagining taking Bryn out for dinner? If I weren't in this situation, I would've never asked her to be exclusive at this point.

She scoffs. "Definitely not. But are you sure it's not a problem for *you*?"

"Definitely not," I parrot her answer. "I haven't talked to another woman since I met you, and after last night, it's literally the last thing from my mind."

My heart double taps at the sweet pink color rising to her cheeks. "Okay. Well, as long as you understand I may not be around a lot and that my work is really important to me, I think I can make officially dating work." She looks down at herself. "Though I wish you would've told me earlier. When I got back from the office, I changed three times and, after giving myself a firm talk about how I should not get dressed up for two friends hanging out, I finally decided on this. I may have actually said out loud at one point, 'This is not a date. You do not have to wear real pants.'"

I chuckle and take the opportunity to really check her out, something I had been trying my hardest to avoid since the full-body ogle I snuck in earlier.

"Work-of-art status, I know," she says. "I feel the messy bun really pulls together the whole twentysomething look I was going for." She says it with confidence, but I can tell from the shift in her eyes that she's feeling unsure of herself.

"You are gorgeous, Bryn. You looked beautiful last night, and you look even hotter today." I slowly peruse her body one last time, not even trying to hide the lust I'm sure is in my eyes. She should know how hot I think she is.

Her cheeks flush, and she bites her lip.

"Damn, Jameo. Really coming on strong. Message received. You think I'm gorgeous. You want to date meee." She says the last in a singsong voice, clearly quoting someone, though it's completely lost on me. I raise my eyebrows in silent question.

"*Miss Congeniality*?" she says with an exasperated huff.

"Oh." I scratch my beard. "The one with Sandra Bullock as the FBI agent?"

"Mmmhmm. The same movie that made it so I can't say Texas without pronouncing it Tex-ass. It's actually pretty good."

"I do think I've seen it once, maybe with my sister. It clearly wasn't that memorable." Thinking about my Netflix and Chill fantasy from earlier, I add, "But I'd definitely be interested in giving it a try if you want to watch it together sometime."

She smiles, glancing out the front windshield as the car nears our brunch spot. "Sure. That sounds like fun. I love watching movies, though it does annoy my sisters how often I quote them."

I pause before opening my door. "So, you're like a *real* fan of movies, then?"

She shakes her head noncommittally. "Eh. I'm definitely a fan, but it's more that my brain has just decided movie quotes are important enough to remember. Most of my classes from grad school? Completely forgotten. Random line from a movie I watched once in eighth grade? Holds a prominent place in my long-term memory."

I laugh as I open my door and climb out. Bryn slides across the seat, choosing to exit onto the sidewalk rather than braving the LA traffic whizzing by on her side of the car.

Glancing at the brunch spot a few paces away, I take note of the people milling about, drinking coffee from paper cups and playing cornhole. Kids are running around, their parents clearly too tired to even pretend this is abnormal behavior for a Saturday morning.

Bryn notes my glance and shrugs. "Saturday-morning brunch. I've never understood why more places don't have reservations available. It's like if, as a society, we've decided brunch is better if we have to suffer a bit before we get in."

"Well, sure. For dinner, the masses have already suffered through a whole day of work or of chasing their offspring around the house or to various activities. Your penance has been paid. Breakfast, you're up early, so that's punishment enough. Brunch, though? You need to sacrifice something before you get to it. Clearly they should've gone with firstborns, but people get so touchy about sacrificing children these days."

She laughs, and I smile back, enjoying the simplicity of being with someone who gets my sense of humor.

"You know," I say, hating what's about to come out of my mouth but knowing I need to offer it, "I could probably go throw my name around and get us in right away."

"Nah." She shakes her head as she moves toward the door. "I'll put our name in. You stay incognito. Plus, I'm happy to just hang out with you while we wait."

I smile and tug on the baseball hat I've been carrying in my pocket, watching her long legs disappear into the restaurant. And damn if it doesn't make me just a little hard, something I know is inappropriate brunch talk, but, frankly, can't be helped.

Chapter Seventeen

Bryn

One of the hardest decisions in life is if I should get something sweet or something savory when I'm brunching. Izzy would tell you to get both. I, like the sane person I am, feel mixing sweet and savory ruins them both, so I opt for the breakfast sandwich. It was delicious and messy, and I am now licking egg yolk off my fingers. "So, it was terrible?" Jameson asks as we both rise from our booth.

"Oh yeah. Hated every bite."

Jameson holds the door for me as we exit, his eyes narrowing on something behind me.

I'm surprised when I feel the pressure of his big hand on my lower back, a little more forceful than expected as he shepherds me forward. Jameson starts lengthening his stride, almost like he's running away.

"Excuse me, sir!" a voice sounds from behind us.

Jameson sighs, and I note the defeated lowering of his shoulders before he is smiling and turning around. I follow suit, and we come face-to-face with a man and his teenage son, both of whom appear to be big Jameson Walker fans. Thank goodness we made it far enough away from the waiting crowd that we don't draw more attention.

"Excuse me, sir," the dad says again. "Could my son get a picture with you?"

"Are you sure you want one with me, man?" Jameson jokes with the kid who now looks embarrassed at the whole spectacle. "Last year wasn't my best showing."

"Uhm." The boy turns a brighter shade of red before starting again, "You've always been my favorite golfer. I follow JT on social media just in case you happen to be in one of his stories. I know this year will be better for you."

Jameson laughs, and I mentally make a note to start following JT. *That won't be too weird, right?*

The dad pulls out his phone, and I jump in, offering to take the picture so both father and son can be in the photo.

"Oh!" The man seems to notice me for the first time. "That would be wonderful."

They all pose for the picture before shaking hands with Jameson and heading back in to—assumedly—finish eating the breakfast they just abandoned.

I don't think either of us have a plan as to where we were headed, but it seems prudent to leave before anyone notices Jameson being noticed.

"I'm sorry about that, Bryn. I'd like to say that won't happen again, but it almost certainly will."

"It's fine. I understand," I say.

"I know it can be a lot to handle. I love my fans, but it's hard sometimes not getting to be a normal guy." He looks at me intently. "But I want you to know that you do not have to take the pictures."

"I know," I say. Because I do. "I was happy to help so the dad could be in the picture too."

"Truly, Bryn. You're not my personal photographer. I know that. Fans will understand it too. I don't want you to feel—"

"Jameson," I cut him off, recognizing he might continue to belabor the point if I don't stop him. "I hear you. I understand. I did not feel like you or anyone else expected me to take the picture. I was happy to help out so that kid and his dad could share in the memory."

We walk a bit more before I say, "Actually, if you saw the pictures I took, you would feel much more comfortable about it all. I've never really seemed to understand the appropriate angles to hold a phone to make anyone look their best. Fingers crossed they don't submit that one to the press. You undoubtedly have both eyes crossed and are in the middle of a sneeze."

"Luckily, I haven't sneezed once today."

"That, my guy, is just how impressive my skills are," I joke.

We walk around the neighborhood, burning off some of our breakfast before ordering another Uber and heading to Venice Beach. Though neither of us brought swimming suits, we walk along the shoreline, Jameo with his hat pulled low and a pair of sunglasses on like the incognito celebrity that he is. The good part about LA is that, while most people assume a person in a hat AND sunglasses on a partially sunny day is some version of a celebrity, there are so many of them around that no one really seems to care.

I know I should be in the office, working, but I just can't seem to convince myself that spending more time on my computer is a better alternative to spending time with Jameson. I just hope Kyle isn't there anymore. The last thing I need is him gloating on Monday about all the hours he put in this weekend, even if I'm very aware of the fact that he doesn't accomplish anything close to what I do in any given day.

After about an hour of walking, I'm starting to feel sweaty despite the cool ocean breeze. I'm not sure how to navigate the awkwardness of not wanting to say goodbye but also wanting to find some air-conditioning. I'm about to pull the trigger and just ask if we should call it a day or find something else to do, when I see a sign for a movie theater ahead.

"Ooo! Let's go to a movie," I basically shout, grabbing on to the excuse to prolong our time together.

Jameson is surprisingly easy to convince, and I wonder if he loves movies as much as I do or if he is also looking for a way to keep our date going.

After an awkward conversation where we feel out each other's movie preferences, we end up at the newest Marvel movie. Jameson heads to the booth to pay, but I insist I use my monthly movie passes. So he buys the snacks—popcorn, Milk Duds, and Cherry Coke—just like Izzy and I always get when we go to the movies together.

Two hours later, we stroll out of the theater, trash in hand, eyes blinking as they adjust to the bright light of day.

"Look, it's one thing to want to split the cost of our dates fifty-fifty, which I do find insulting to my manhood no matter how progressive you want me to pretend to be, but to make me have to buy that trash snack combination? Who eats Milk Duds and popcorn *at the same time?*" Jameson teases.

I shoot him a fake glare. "If you had just *tried* them, you would have a leg to stand on. But no, poor Jameo couldn't bear the thought of combining two 'totally different snacks.' And you really missed out. What makes the two such a beautiful combo is that the stickiness of the Milk Duds counteracts the popcorn getting stuck in your teeth and vice versa. Somehow, two things that normally stick around in your mouth for days both go in together and, voilà, perfection." To be clear, it's not the same sweet and savory combination I was hating on when deciding what to order earlier. The way I do movie theater popcorn with the perfect amount of butter is most certainly sweet.

I glance at him, noting how he is subtly trying to remove popcorn from his teeth with his tongue. "You are going to be stuck eating soggy popcorn as it drops out of your teeth crevices for the rest of the night." I pause, knowing I should stop rambling about snacks—and crevices—but then can't help myself. I continue, "And the Milk Duds today were fresh. Easy to chew. It was bliss in my mouth."

His eyes darken at my last comment, and I mentally cringe. Did not mean to put a somewhat sexually charged statement out into the night. And honestly, is it sexually charged? I'm still a little confused by Jameson's quick bounce from not dating to I-need-this-to-be-a-date to getting turned on by a statement.

"Hmm. Bliss in your mouth." He stares at my lips for a moment. "That checks out. I promise next time you offer something that is bliss in your mouth, I will definitely be in."

We both stop and stare at each other, his eyes growing wider, before I burst out laughing, and he quickly follows suit. He gasps out, "Oh fuck. I went for it with the first innuendo, but the second one, it was unintentional. It just happened. God, it was so good."

"Damn it, Jameo. I am never going to be able to look at Milk Duds the same way." I playfully swat his arm, and he grabs my hand, keeping hold of it as we continue down the road.

"Good. Glad to know my dick in your mouth is now going to be all you can think about while enjoying your favorite snack at the movies." My eyes widen in shock as he taps his chin, pretending to think. "You know, you might even say that my cock *is* your favorite snack now."

A double puff of air bursts from me, not quite a laugh, but what my sisters have deemed "the least girly giggle in the world."

"Jesus H. Christ, Jameson." I look around at the crowded sidewalk. "You can't say shit like that. Particularly since—" Crap. Why do I let these things come out of my mouth? Dang it. I wonder if I should somehow use this opening to tell him I'm a virgin. *No, not dropping that bomb...but maybe just like, casually let him know without actually telling him?*

"Particularly since...what?" He squeezes my hand reassuringly.

I internally roll my eyes at my inability to control my mouth. Oh well, I'm in it now. "Particularly since your cock has never been in my mouth." The merriment from his eyes is gone and it's all dark smolder now. *Don't focus on his sex-eyes right now, Bryn. Keep going!* "I'm definitely not willing to pass the favorite-snack award on without any sort of evidence."

"Evidence, huh?" He clears his throat, but his voice still comes out a bit raspy.

I smirk, loving that he is so affected by our conversation, but at the same time, definitely not ready to put my money where my mouth is on this one. And, since Jameson has made it clear this is a date, I know I need to make a few things clear. I mentally face-palm. This is going to be so awkward.

"Yup." I pull Jameson to a stop in an alcove near the bratwurst stand we have been making our way to for a quick dinner. We—okay, *I*—have already gorged myself on movie snacks and don't want too much more. Jameson, though, insists that dinner must take place, as it's a key element to a real date.

"Look, I—" I roll my shoulders, preparing myself for the awkwardness that is undoubtedly about to come out of my mouth—"I would've told you this before today, but, while I'm really glad this is a date, I definitely didn't come into it thinking it was a date." *FUUUCK. Why am I so bad at this?*

Jameson rubs his thumb over the back of my hand, a slight frown of confusion on his face. "Okay. I know. But it is a date, right?"

"Yup. Totally a date." I nod. "We are dating." He starts to say something, but I hold up a hand. "And, as I would've usually mentioned to a guy—via a well-thought-out text, I might add..." I look into his eyes then, making sure he knows I'm blaming him for not letting me do this via text as I would've preferred. "I'm a little old school and don't believe in sleeping with someone or, I suppose, welcoming their cock into my mouth."

His thumb stops moving. "Wait, you don't...you're like...you're waiting until...marriage?"

Oh no. *This*. This is why I need to be able to send this via text, so I can proofread! "Shit. No." I can feel the look of slight terror on my face. "That's not what I meant. I didn't finish my thought. Got distracted by including the part about your penis, which felt...big." I smirk.

He chuckles, dropping my hand to run his through his hair. "Bryn, can you please tell me what you're trying to tell me? Because I'm both very confused and slightly turned on right now, and I'm not sure how to handle that."

"Oh." My cheeks burn with embarrassment for making this so f-ing hard. "I was just trying to say that I need to take this slow. Not wait-until-we-are-married slow." My eyes widen. "No, no! Not that I'm saying we are going to get married. Ugh. I promise I am not a stage-five clinger. Shit." I cover my face with my hands. "I just want to take things slow and see how they go. If that's not cool with you, I totally get it, and we can go back to friends. Or"—and I will fully admit I'm rambling now—"since we aren't actually friends, just maybe friendly acquaintances who may or may not be dating. But if you're interested in someone...easier? And I don't mean that in a bad way. To each their own. Different strokes for different folks and all." The amusement is back in his dark green eyes, his hands stuck casually in his pockets while he takes in this embarrassing monologue. "So I guess what I'm trying to say—in an obviously very clear way—is that if you're looking for someone to sleep with tonight, we can definitely call off this whole dating thing. I can even be your wingwoman for the night. Help you find someone else."

He's scowling now. "You...you want to help set me up with someone else?"

Fuck. I definitely do not want to help him find some other girl. "Um. No. That was an insincere offer. I was just trying to give you an out."

"Why would I want an out? I was the one who wanted this to be a real date."

I nod. "True, but you wouldn't be the first guy who decided to take me up on the offer of an easy out when he found out that I wanted to take things slow. Honestly, you'd be the fifth, though most of those guys were from dating apps, which are their own circle of hell."

He grabs my hand again and starts walking us toward the brat cart on the corner. "Okay, well, those guys are shitty humans, and I am not one of them. I promise I have no expectations, though definitely have some aspirations, about a future sex life. I want to date you, whatever that looks like for us."

I smile, still embarrassed, but so pleased by his answer.

An hour later, the Uber pulls back into my hotel. Jameson opens his door and hops out, sticking his head back in to ask the Uber to wait a minute while he says goodbye.

"Thanks for a great day, Jameo."

"Best *date* I've had in a long time, Bryn." He smiles at me sweetly and grabs my arm, tugging me into a hug.

He feels so good wrapped around me. I bask in his warmth and strong arms, subtly breathing in his cologne—some manly scent that reminds me of rainy days and trees.

I tilt my head back, a grin splitting my face as he reaches out and runs his thumb tenderly down my jaw. He leans in, his dark gaze focused on my lips, but stops before he kisses me, giving me the option of going the last few centimeters or not.

But it's not really an option. Not when I feel so right in his arms, when his smile makes me light up from within. He may be asking for permission, but there is no way I'm not granting it.

I tilt my head up a little further and lean into his kiss, a jolt of desire pulsing through me as our lips meet and his hand moves to the small of my back, lightly stroking the skin right above the waistband of my joggers.

I pull away slowly, noting the lust in Jameo's eyes and the grin spreading across his face.

I smile back and head toward the door to the hotel, turning back to offer a small wave. "Night, Jameo."

Chapter Eighteen

Jameson

Alexis and I dated for two years, and, honestly, I always thought we were happy. I thought we were in love. I enjoyed our time together. We had fun. We had amazing sex. That's why, when she suggested she move in after dating for only six months, I thought, why not? She was always over at my house anyway. Might as well give her a key.

The relationship my parents have has always seemed like the ideal. It's what I always wanted, at least before Alexis messed with my head. I wanted happy. I wanted content. I wanted Friday nights watching TV together while joking around and commiserating about our jobs.

Turns out, you can't just jump straight in with nothing but fun times and good sex to act as your foundation. Sure, it's a start, but pretty early on, that has to develop into trust, support, and love.

As luck would have it, Alexis was terrible at all three of those things. And the part that really gets me is that I should've known. I should've seen the signs—I should've listened when my family and friends blatantly *pointed out the signs.*

Like when my sister pointed out that Alexis always traveled with me to the fancy PR or charity events I had around the country but she would never travel with me for work. Never walked the courses while I played, claiming I needed the focus. Then, if I pushed her on it, she would distract me with sex, and I'd go without her.

Or, as my dad often mentioned, we didn't actually act like we were in a relationship. When we were together, we were usually in bed, and when we were apart, well, we didn't really talk much. Sure, we would text sometimes, call each other here and there, and even both got off while on FaceTime together after a couple of my bigger tournament wins, but when I was gone, we didn't talk regularly. Early on, I tried calling her while I was away, but she'd always decline my call and shoot me a quick text about how busy she was working. Working a remote marketing job that I now question if it even actually existed.

Which is why I'm shocked that, three weeks after getting her number, Bryn is still the first person I text in the morning and the last one I talk to at night. She's been traveling for work for an extended time, so I haven't been able to take her out again. Now, she's coming back to Wild Bluffs this afternoon, and I'm like a puppy sitting by the door, waiting for her to get home.

After our date, I sat in the back of my Uber to my hotel rocking a halfie *from a kiss.* A fucking kiss and I was at half-mast and also completely unsure what to do next. The date had been—shit, it had been better than I ever imagined. I'd just been on the best date of my life. Never once did I feel like I was arm candy or like she was using my name or my fame to get ahead. In fact, it had been clear she was going out of her way not to.

But, sitting there in the back of that car, my insecurities had started to worm their way in. Because here's the problem, I never thought Alexis was using me either. Sure, my family and friends noticed, but not right away. In the beginning, she seemed genuine, and everyone liked her. It's not like she was walking around, shouting "I'm dating this guy for his money! I'm actually going to use his connections to meet other famous athletes and then fuck them on our kitchen table!" I'm pretty sure she even offered to pay on our first date. I hadn't let her, of course, but she had offered.

So I sat there on my way home from the date, staring out the car window, torn between liking Bryn so much that a simple goodnight kiss made me horny and wanting to have nothing to do with another relationship ever again. I typed out a text asking her to fly back with me the next day and quickly deleted it. The next one I drafted thanked her for the date and suggested we get together at some nonspecific time in the future. It also got deleted. About three more failed attempts later, I had one composed that essentially told her I'd had a momentary lapse in judgment when I asked her to call it a date and to lose my number. At which point, I had given up and called my sister.

Apparently, she had already gotten wind of the fact that I flew to LA with JT, no doubt from the man himself, and was literally shrieking with glee when I told her I'd been on a date with Bryn. Her joy quickly turned to annoyance, though, when I explained my predicament. Her exact words when I asked her what I should do were

"Sack the fuck up and stop thinking that every woman is out to take advantage of you just because Alexis was."

It was hard to disagree with her assessment, so as I made my way into my hotel that night, I listened to her advice and sent Bryn a text telling her just how much fun I had with her. Her response had been equally as enthusiastic.

Now I'm parked in front of Bryn's sister's house, waiting for Bryn to get back so we can go out for dinner. To be fair to me, she said she was going to get home five minutes ago. I hadn't wanted to look too eager, so I arrived two minutes ago—literally the longest I could convince myself to wait to see her.

Apparently, there was a tractor slowing down traffic on the highway outside of town, causing her to arrive later than anticipated. Bryn flies commercial, so she had to make the two-hour drive from the commercial airport. The 120 minutes since she messaged me that her plane had landed and she was on her way have felt like the longest of my life. Even longer than the time I had to wait out a rain delay to finish the last two holes of the Masters and claim my first Green Jacket.

Noticing Bryn's car pull into the driveway, I climb out of my truck, shoving my hands in my jeans pockets and strolling toward her parked Tesla.

She climbs out of the car, and I can't help but blatantly check out her long legs and perfect round ass as she bends over to grab her suitcase out of the back seat.

"Here, let me take that in for you."

She whirls, pulling out a headphone I hadn't noticed. "Shit, Jameo. What are you doing lurking out here?"

I love that she calls me Jameo.

I extend my hand, offering to pull her suitcase in for her. She rolls her eyes. "I got it. I'm fully capable of carrying my own suitcase."

Shrugging, I put my hand back in my pocket, unsure if giving her a hug is appropriate at this point in the night. She's not particularly putting off hugging vibes at the moment.

"Okay. Though I can also carry a suitcase. Just for the record."

"Yeah, yeah, yeah. You're very strong. We all know. No need to flash your arm porn around."

As she makes her way inside, I follow like the helpless puppy I've already established I am.

While she's setting down her suitcase to love on the actual dog inside the house, I look around. It's a fairly modern-looking home, a mixture of grays and blacks.

Bryn grins up at me from where she is squatting on the floor, her black work pants covered in dog hair. "This is Jack."

I come closer, letting the dog sniff my hand before I pet his neck a couple times. "Hiya, Jack." Looking over at Bryn, I ask, "How old is he?"

"Almost eight," she says. "I got him in college. I don't take him when I travel, so I end up leaving him here or with my parents a lot."

"Makes sense why he's so excited to see you, then. I understand the feeling myself." I feel my cheeks heat up with the admission.

She stands up, turning around with a teasing glint in her eyes. "Ah, Jameo, did you miss me?"

The dog's tail wags vigorously, and I nod at it. "If I had a tail, it would be doing exactly the same thing."

Bryn's chuckle reverberates through my soul as she moves deeper into the house. "Are you okay to hang out here for a few minutes? I need to shower and change real quick to get the airplane off me."

I look around the living room, taking in the two gray couches that face the large flat-screen TV on the wall. "Of course. Sorry, I should've asked if you would need a few minutes once you got home to get ready."

"Not a problem. I was excited to see you too. Plus, I promise I'll be quick in there." She hands me a remote for the TV and starts to walk toward the stairs to the second floor. She stops, quickly turning around and giving me a tight hug. "It's good to see you. I'm looking forward to tonight."

She tries to pull away, but I hold on to her, not ready for the contact to be over. "Same."

I finally let her go, knowing from our many conversations the past few weeks that she's a bit of a germaphobe who most definitely wants to get the airplane off her. I really should've thought of that before I showed up right as she was getting home.

As she walks up the stairs, I call out, "Let me know if you need any help in there."

I listen to her laugh in response as I flop down on the couch. The TV has just switched on when I hear a door behind me open.

"What does she need help with?"

I whip my head around, surprised to find that we aren't alone in the house, though I don't know why I made that assumption. "Oh, uhm," I fumble out.

Kelsey just stares at me, a semi-bored look on her face.

"She's just taking a quick shower before we head out for dinner," I say.

She snickers in amusement as she sits down on the other couch. "Oh, and you thought she might need help with that, huh? Very chivalrous of you to offer."

I clear my throat. "Just, uh, just trying to..." I trail off, noticing her almost silent laughter. "Dang. You Harper sisters sure know how to keep a guy on his toes."

"We do appreciate a good verbal spar for sure. Plus, Bryn essentially uses this place as an Airbnb. The least I can get out of it is the opportunity to embarrass her dates every once in a while."

I look at her, feeling the scowl pull on my face. "Dates, huh?" I hadn't actually meant to ask it, but now I can't take it back, mainly because I really want to know the answer.

"Oh no, I'm not having that conversation with you. Though"—she looks up the stairs toward Bryn's room—"I will say you have absolutely nothing to worry about."

I nod and turn my attention back to the TV. "Anything you want to watch?"

"Nah, I'm fine with whatever."

I put on the news, unsure what else to watch with a woman who is basically a complete stranger.

"I heard you're going to start playing in PGA events again next weekend." She's back to looking at me intently.

I'm somewhat surprised Bryn mentioned it to her, not that it's a secret. My publicist made the announcement last week, and I told Bryn the night before the news broke, just so she wouldn't be surprised. I had, instead, been the one who had been surprised by her response. She was totally unfazed, suggesting I send her the dates for the events I plan to attend, and she'll see if she can end up in any of the same cities for work while I'm there.

It was easy. Normal. Unfortunately, with the way the Tour schedule works with the important events only being open to golfers with high enough standings, I need to get back in some tournaments to be in the top 50. If I get enough points, I will have a guaranteed spot and won't have to spend every weekend of the year traveling. It will require a hard last few months of the year, but it's doable. If I play like I was a year and a half ago—winning over a quarter of the tournaments I played in, and placing in the top 10 in all but one—I'll have that guaranteed spot.

I'm not sure what Kelsey is looking for, so I stick with a simple, "I am."

She raises an eyebrow. "You think you're ready to be back?"

The balls on the Harper sisters. "I do. I've been playing really well the last few weeks."

She nods. "That's what I hear."

I don't love that Bryn appears to be passing all my news straight to her sister, but I guess I can't blame her. Now that I'm out of my pit of despair and back to communicating with my family and friends on a regular basis, I've talked to both my sister and JT about Bryn.

Kelsey continues, "In small towns, nothing is a secret. Sure, at clubs like Wild Bluffs, they make sure everyone knows to keep your information out of the press and to toe the official no-comment party line, but that doesn't ever actually translate to town gossip. The town has never been more knowledgeable about your golf game. You could say we're all invested now."

She must be able to see the confusion on my face, because she continues, "Bryn hasn't been back to Wild Bluffs since you announced your return, and I would hate for her to find out something like that from town. Which she will the minute you guys get to dinner."

Ahh. So Kelsey didn't hear it from Bryn. I suppose it's nice that she's trying to help me out. "Bryn was the first person I told after confirming everything with my team."

"Really?" she asks, raising one eyebrow. "She didn't mention it to me."

Luckily, I don't have to respond, as we both turn at the sound of Bryn's feet coming down the stairs, Jack following after her.

I stand up and take her in. She's in light jeans with a dark gray sweater that hugs her full tits perfectly. "Damn. You look great." I look at my watch. "And done in less than fifteen minutes. Very impressive."

She smiles and grabs my hand, pulling me out the door. "Yes, I'm very impressive all around. You'll see. I'm also starving and was unaware I left you down here with ninja-mode Kelsey." She shoots a glare over her shoulder at her sister, who wiggles her fingers in farewell.

We take my pickup the few minutes to Main Street, and when we pull up in front of the restaurant, she turns to look at me fully instead of getting out of the vehicle. "I heard Kelsey warning you about this before, but I feel like I need to give you one last chance to back out. As soon as we go in there and people see us together, the rumors will start. By tomorrow morning, the town will all know we are dating, and half of them will have already picked out our wedding colors." She blushes as she says the last part, and I'm thrown back to our last date when she made her "taking it slow" speech that was equal parts unnecessary, awkward, and hilarious.

"Oh. Well, I mean, I think it's kinda late to be worried about us being in public together after California. I don't think any pictures will end up coming out from that, but we did decide to be casually official, right? It'll be okay if the press gets a hold of this?"

She shrugs. "Oh, I wasn't thinking about the press. Paparazzi are truly nothing compared to small-town gossip. I know you're a big, famous golfer and all, but in this case, this is about me, not you. It has been...a while since I went on a date in Wild Bluffs, so I'm sure the tongues will be wagging." She looks over at my slightly shocked expression. "If it makes you feel better, the fact that you're a professional athlete will definitely *add* to the drama level."

"I'm not—" I start, then decide better of what I was going to say. "I mean, okay. Anything specific I need to be prepared for?"

She taps a finger to her chin, highlighting the small dimple there. "I would like to say your media training should have prepared you for this, but I'm honestly not sure. Just don't give more information than necessary. And, whatever you do, do not, under any circumstances, tell a lie. Those people can sniff out lies like hunting dogs after a rabbit."

Why am I more nervous about this than my first ever press conference? Maybe I should've called Erica for some talking points. Oh well, it'll be worth it. "Got it," I say, pushing open the door. Though, honestly, I'm not sure I do got it.

CHAPTER NINETEEN

BRYN

Despite what I said to Jameo in the pickup, it feels like a risk coming to dinner at The Cattlemens together. Not because of the national press or seeing my name in the gossip columns, but because this town is hard up for entertainment and this will be the biggest story of the fucking year. I meant it when I said this is not about Jameson. This is about me. These people are going to flip about *me* being on a date with anyone, let alone Jameson Walker. To be fair to them, I haven't gone out in Wild Bluffs since my junior prom, but still. Get a life.

The two-story restaurant is the best place for dinner and also happens to contain the only bar in the town proper. The bar itself is on the second story of the old brick building on Main Street. The first floor is reserved for a medium-sized event space. They have concerts come through regularly, somehow managing to book fairly big-name bands as they are passing through on their way to larger cities.

It's Friday night, and the place is packed with locals, just like I knew it would be. We walk up the wide staircase, and I only allow myself to stare at Jameson's ass for the first half of the climb. I'd like to send whoever bought him those jeans a thank-you card. Truly, between his butt and his strong thighs, I'm not sure which looks better from this angle.

We reach the main part of the dining area, and like a scene out of the movies, every face turns toward us as we walk behind our waitress to our table. I suppress a strong eye roll as I wave good-naturedly at the people we pass. I've never been as popular with the town.

Luckily, once we get settled, people calm down and go back to dinner, though I know the flow of information has begun. In fact, I get an almost immediate text from Izzy telling me she's already received two texts from her friends about me dating a professional golfer.

Small towns. You gotta love them, but damn are they a pain in the ass sometimes.

I show the text to Jameo, and he chuckles, his dark green eyes lighting up with humor.

"Damn, that's more impressive than the gossip magazines, and they get paid to publish that shit."

I hold my arms out wide. "Welcome to Wild Bluffs, Jameson Walker."

We both order burgers, a staple at Cattlemens. I opt for a hard cider on ice, while Jameson orders a single whiskey.

"So tell me about this big news your boss dropped on you today," Jameson says.

"Okay. Well, remember how I told you I'm trying to bulk up my portfolio at work so that when my boss, Tara, retires in, like, five years, I'll be well-positioned for the promotion?"

He nods, hopefully remembering the conversation we had last week about my job.

"Well, turns out her husband recently had a health scare, and it was a wake-up call for them both. So she's retiring. In May."

"Wow. That's big news for you."

"Yep. And to make matters more intense, Tara pulled me aside to let me know that the decision is between me and freaking Kyle."

"And Kyle is the guy from marketing that you hate, right?"

I could probably use a filter. "Um, *hate* is maybe a strong word. But definitely dislike." I take a long sip of my drink. "Okay, definitely dislike so much, I can barely stand to be in the same company as the man, let alone on the same team, so, maybe hate? But whichever one of us gets the promotion, we'll be the other one's boss."

"And you'll spend your days plotting ways to make Kyle cry?"

"Yep. Like sending him notifications at five on a Friday that he has to change the entire scope of a marketing campaign before Monday morning."

"You'll make such a good boss," he teases.

"The problem is, if Kyle wins, he'll do worse. I can't lose."

Jameson shrugs. "So don't lose."

"I'm not planning on it. But I'm going to have to work my ass off on this new campaign for delivery orders that is being rolled out as a joint marketing and technology project. It's releasing early next year, and, since Kyle and I are both on it, it will no doubt be the main data point they use to decide who gets the promotion."

"Sounds tough. But, also, you're amazing. I'm sure you've got it in the bag."

"I appreciate that. I also just want to make sure you know that this means I'm going to be even busier than before. I mean nights, weekends, the whole shebang."

"It's okay, Bryn. Trust me. I understand what it takes to get to the top. I'd never try to get in the way of that. I will take whatever time you have to give me and love every second of it, but I'm not going to get upset about you being dedicated to something. I'm sure I will be just as busy, if not busier than you are, during that time."

Well, the man talks a damn good game. And it's seemed to be true so far. Maybe, just maybe, he actually means it.

We switch to small talk as we wait for our drinks, chatting about my flight and his golf rounds today. JT ended up staying in California rather than flying back to Colorado, so Jameson's been on his own again at the course.

Our waitress brings out our beverages, and I take a deep drink of my cider before asking Jameson, "So, how are you feeling about the tournament next weekend?"

He shrugs, the fabric of his button-up pulling across his broad shoulders and distracting me from the beginning of his response. "...but yeah, my game hasn't felt this good in a long time. I'm ready. I'm not saying I will win this weekend, but I sure as hell could, which is more confidence than I've felt in a while."

"That's really great, I'm not sure if I can be your official casual girlfriend if you play like you did last year. I have *standards*, Jameson," I tease.

He coughs, the whiskey he had been attempting to drink running into a surprised chuckle on the way out. I watch his throat work as he clears it before asking, "So...you won't go out with me again unless I win?"

Oh no. I know this is sensitive territory for him. I still don't know the whole story, but I do know he is very worried about being wanted just for his status. Unfortunately, I am not good at sensitive territory, so I pause, trying to take my time before responding.

"Well..." I tilt my head, pretending to consider it. "I definitely don't care if you win or if you lose. You could be the manager at the public course in town, for all I care about that side of it. It's the triple bogeys that I can't be associated with. Snowmen are an embarrassment that I cannot, in any way, have connected with my name."

This time his chuckle turns into a full laugh, and I blush, feeling the eyes in the room find us again.

Laughter subsiding, Jameson looks at me, his eyes turning a darker shade. "Somehow, that's one of the nicest things I've ever been told."

I give myself a mental high five for not completely messing things up with my response before turning my attention back to the handsome man in front of me. "I'm worried you might need better friends if that's one of the nicest things you've ever been told."

He shakes his head noncommittally before digging back into his burger. Which is how the rest of the dinner goes. Laughter and conversation intermittently broken up by one or the other of us shoveling food into our mouths.

After a pretty perfect dinner, Jameson grabs the bill, shooting me a glare as I try to reach for it too. "You're not paying for dinner again, Bryn. This has nothing to do with how much money either of us makes. It has nothing to do with feminism." He shrugs, a smirk pulling at his lips. "It does have a little to do with making sure this town doesn't think I'm a cheap ass who doesn't pay for his date. But mostly, it has to do with me wanting to treat you. These past few weeks have been just what I needed, so let me buy you a cheeseburger and beer, okay?"

"Fine, but I'm buying ice cream."

I mentally face-palm. Good gracious, could I be any worse at accepting it when people are nice to me?

Jameson chuckles again, clearly amused. "We'll see, B. We'll see."

"B, huh? Are we doing nicknames now?"

"You've literally called me Jameo since the day I met you. You didn't even know me and were calling me Jameo."

"Wait, your name isn't Jameo?" I ask, feigning confusion.

He shoots a glare at me as he calculates the tip before signing it with a flourish. "Has anyone ever told you that you're a pain in the ass?"

"I can't confirm nor deny, but most certainly cannot deny it."

"Come on, *B*, let's go get ice cream," he says, standing.

He waits patiently as I extricate myself from the booth. Why do they make these benches this deep, anyway?

Jameson grabs my hand, and I blush as I take note of all the eyes that are glued to our intertwined fingers. As he leads me out of the restaurant, I notice two familiar faces and pull Jameo away from the stairs, nodding my head toward the bar.

He looks confused for a second before recognition flashes across his face.

"Oh, hey, Izzy. Fancy seeing you here," I drawl, stopping in front of my sister and our friend, who are attempting to look casual at the bar.

Izzy's cheeks burn as she pulls an innocent smile. "Oh! Hey! Hi, Jameson. Good to see you. So funny running into you guys."

He mirrors the little wave she gave him. "Hey, Izzy...and Becca, right?" Jameson waves awkwardly at Becca.

She, unexpectedly, returns his greeting with a glare. "Yup, Becca."

Well, that was...cold. I look between the two of them, confused, but clearly neither has any plans to say anything else.

"Okaaaay. Well, just wanted to make sure you both got a be-hind-the-scenes look at our date, since it is certainly not a coincidence you're here."

Izzy tries to look confused but gives up. "I was getting play-by-play updates about it, anyway! At least now I'm here, my phone has stopped blowing up with details about what you're wearing, what you ordered, and the town's take on how interested each of you is in each other."

Jameson seems to choke. "I'm sorry, what?"

"Ugh. This town." I grab his hand and start pulling him away, but he stops me with ease, hauling us back toward my sister.

"What's the verdict?" he asks her gruffly.

"Huh?" Iz and I both reply at the same time.

Jameo looks directly at my sister. "How interested is she in me?"

Izzy's laugh booms across the bar, Becca's lighter laugh joining hers as both women throw their heads back in glee. For Jameson's sake, I hope this doesn't work out between us. He will never, ever live that question down.

Unfortunately, Jameson doesn't seem to find it as funny as the rest of us do. He's growing noticeably more irritated as Izzy and Becca continue laughing, his hand growing tighter on mine.

After what feels like days, Izzy finally gets herself under control. "I can't believe you asked that. You know normal people would just wonder about it but never actually ask, right?"

I'm going to kill my sister. I will murder her and bury her in the middle of a cow pasture where no one will ever find her body.

Jameson clenches his jaw. "Yeah, well, I've learned external people can sometimes have more clarity into this type of thing."

I'm not sure how to feel about that. I mean, I'm not saying it's untrue, but it feels like he's really focusing on the wrong thing here. I told him the town would talk about us. Who cares what they think about our date? I mean, was he not having as good of a time as I was? He sure seemed like he was enjoying it.

Izzy looks back and forth between us, trying to figure out what to do. I just shrug my shoulders—she got herself into this mess.

Surprisingly, Becca breaks the silence by saying, "You really know how to make friends and win people over, don't you, Jameson?"

I'm 100% asking him why Becca seems to hate him when we get outside. She rarely has one unkind thing to say to people, and she's already been bitchy to him twice. It is basically unheard of for her.

He looks at her and shrugs, his dark eyebrow rising in challenge. Dick, the guy I met at the course, seems to be making an appearance for the first time since that fateful day.

I pull on his arm, trying to get him to leave with me as I say, "Okay, well, this has been...fucking awkward, but we've got to go—"

"No." He looks at me. "I'd like to hear what this town thinks about us."

I look up at him. At his expressionless face. How did our date turn into this? "Why? Why would you possibly care what the town thinks of us? Why would you want Izzy to tell you what these random people think instead of just asking me how I feel about you?" I glance back at my sister, silently promising death with my eyes.

He grunts out something that sounds a lot like "Just do" as his hand tightens on mine.

What an absolute dumpster fire.

I turn toward my sister, who is still watching us, though Becca has turned her attention to the TV above the bar.

"Okaaay. Can you tell him what they said, Iz?" I ask.

She looks back and forth between us again and finally just passes her phone to Jameson. "There are a couple group chats in there that capture most of it."

He drops my hand to take her phone and scrolls through each of them. Yup. Still scrolling as I awkwardly stand there, feeling like everyone is talking about me, but I'm the only one who doesn't get to know what they are saying.

As he reads, his shoulders relax, his face turning from the unfeeling mask he had been wearing back into a light smile.

He hands the phone back to Izzy, says a gruff "Thanks," and reaches for my hand again.

We head for the exit, and I flip my sister off over my shoulder as I leave. Unfortunately, it does nothing to ease the uncertainty and hurt swirling in my chest.

What was that about?

Chapter Twenty

Jameson

When I was twelve, my sister got some huge pink Barbie mansion that took up half of our living room. It had been a gift from my aunt—my dad's sister who never had any girls of her own so always went all out on Lila. One day, my friends and I were fucking around playing football inside when I tackled my friend Brian directly into the dollhouse. The pink construction crumbled, completely wrecking the toy.

Lila cried for hours because she was sad, but also because she was so angry. It was the first time she had ever truly been mad at me for something I did that I couldn't quickly make right.

I apologized over and over, but finally my dad took me aside and told me that I had two options: I could move on, and risk Lila never forgiving me, or I could make it right. But making it right would require sacrificing something on my part. I honestly considered just letting Lila get over it. I knew she would forgive me eventually. But I also knew I wasn't likely to forgive myself for risking it.

So Dad let me do extra chores all summer, and it was all I did. It was the first time I realized I was exceptionally good at blocking out the rest of the world when I was focused on something important to me. I barely spent any time on anything that wasn't earning money for the dollhouse. Two months later, I bought Lila a replacement Barbie house. It wasn't quite as big as the first one, but it was the best I could do with the money I'd earned.

As the ice that filled my veins at the thought of the town knowing something I didn't about the relationship between me and Bryn slowly melts, I recognize there is now frost coming from Bryn's direction. Fuck. A replacement Barbie house may not be enough in this situation.

We both climb into the car, and she squeezes her hands together in her lap, turning her whole body away from me.

"I shouldn't have asked to read your sister's text messages," I say, trying to break the tension.

"It's fine."

I've heard that from my mom's and Lila's mouths enough times to know that it's not fine.

"Look, Bryn, I didn't mean to hurt your feelings."

"It's fine."

I hate the dejected tone in her voice. I throw the pickup into reverse as I say, "It's not fine. You're upset. And I don't like seeing you this way. Can you please talk to me?"

I can see her staring out the window from the corner of my eye as I make my way slowly back to her sister's house.

Finally, she says, "You essentially read the Wild Bluffs version of the *National Enquirer* to decide if I'm interested in you instead of just manning up and asking me yourself. I was having a great time. The last few weeks have been great. And you decided you needed to see other people's opinions of us?"

When I don't say anything, she continues, "What would you have done if Izzy's random high school friend who I haven't seen in five years had said she didn't think I was good enough for you? Would you have just ended things with me on the spot? Do you care that much about what other people think of us eating dinner together?"

"Dating," I growl.

"What?" She's still upset, but at least now she's distracted.

"We aren't just eating dinner together, we're dating."

"Yes. Casually officially dating. I know." She sighs. "Look, my ex ended things between us after *three years* because of what other people thought about me, and it's definitely a sore spot for me now."

Oh, shoot. I really hadn't thought about how it was going to make Bryn feel. I roll to a stop in front of Kelsey's house and quickly grab Bryn's hand as she reaches for the car door. Barbie house time, I guess.

"Please just let me explain? And, after I explain, can we please circle back to the casually officially dating?"

I can see the war happening in her head, but finally she sighs and says, "Of course."

"My ex-girlfriend, Alexis, was..." Shit. How do I explain how taken in I was by her? How I loved her and she was fucking other guys for a year before I caught her?

Bryn's still staring at me, a downcast look on her face, so I force myself to continue. "She was using me. The whole time. She moved in with me. She bought a fuckton of clothes and shoes and all kinds of other shit using my money. She used my name to make connections and get invited to the most important events everywhere."

I drag my hand through my hair, feeling that same sense of bone-deep despair that I always do thinking about it, but Bryn squeezes my other hand briefly, just letting me know she's still there.

I glance at her, and she shoots me a grimace. "Well, Alexis sounds like a shitty person."

"Yeah. Turns out she was. She was also fucking every B-list celebrity she could find when I was away at tournaments."

"So a shitty person and, clearly, a certifiable idiot if she was willing to risk being with you to sleep with, who? Jonas Charmon?"

A small chuckle escapes me at Bryn's mention of one of the other golfers on the tour. A good guy, but he never seems to be in the top 10 and only makes the cut about a third of the time.

Sighing, I shake my head. "I don't think Jonas was ever one of her targets. From what I put together after—when I obsessed over it all—it was mostly high-risk, high-return guys. Ones who aren't famous now but definitely could be in the future. I found out because I came home half a day early from a training session with my coach and walked in on her and Newson, the backup quarterback for the Dolphins, going at it on our kitchen island. *My* kitchen island."

"That sucks, Jameo. I'm really sorry that happened to you. And, honestly, it explains a lot about your golf game last year." She looks down at her hands. "But I still don't really understand why you cared so much tonight. Do you think I'm cheating on you? Can you not tell how much I like you?"

"Bryn, I'm...sorry." I know it's not enough, but I don't know what to say.

She looks up at me, and I see the tears starting to form in her eyes. "Do you know how humiliating it was to stand there with you while you read through my sister's texts about what the town thinks of us? Not because it was funny, but because you actually wanted to know. You *needed* to know what they thought about us."

"I know. I'm sorry. I didn't mean to embarrass you in front of your friends. It wasn't my intention. It's just that"—I take a deep breath—"the worst part about the Alexis thing is that my family and friends told me. They obviously didn't know she was cheating on me, but they knew she wasn't good for me. They could see the way that she used me without actually caring about me as a person."

Her thumb is stroking mine now, a warm, comforting presence that encourages me to continue. "When I told Lila about a purse Alexis had given herself 'as a gift from me for being gone so often,' she lost her fucking shit and blatantly told me to break it off. But it seemed fair to me. I was gone"—I look at Bryn, making sure she hears this part—"I *am* gone all the time. So I ignored Lila. A few months later, I was home visiting my parents, a trip Alexis was supposed to be on with me but had canceled at the last minute, and my mom pulled me aside and gave me a whole speech about what love really is and how sometimes people just aren't a good fit for one another." I sigh, still ashamed when I recall how I treated my mom during that conversation. "I got mad and stormed out."

I glance outside, watching a leaf blow across the street. Bryn sits there in a friendly silence, giving me the space to say what I need to say.

"So anyway, they all knew she was wrong for me. Even fucking JT—who knows absolutely nothing about women and relationships—knew she was a terrible girlfriend. But not me. I couldn't see it. I was so blind that I thought I fucking loved her." I look at Bryn again, trying to gauge how she's taking all this. It definitely doesn't paint me in the best light, but hopefully it helps her understand why I couldn't walk away tonight.

"And so tonight you saw an opportunity to double-check. To see if everyone else could tell something about us that you were missing," she says.

"I am sorry, B. I couldn't not see what these people who have known you your whole life had to say about us together. I saw how annoyed you were, and it only made me feel more compelled to see what they had to say. Like you knew it would say something bad and so you didn't want me to read it. But"—I flash her an embarrassed smile—"turns out, you may have been trying to save me from reading everyone's assumptions about how big my dick is and if I'm boring in bed or not."

She lets out a quiet laugh. "There is a strong division in this town about whether professional golfers are as boring in bed as their sport is. And, if you consider the average age of a professional golfer, I'm on Team Boring...on average."

I smirk at her. "Oh, I assure you, I'm well above average. In all aforementioned measures."

She blushes, her cheeks turning a light shade of pink, and I pull her knuckles to my mouth, giving her hand a quick kiss. "Can you please forgive me for tonight? I promise, if I ever want to know what you are thinking or how you are feeling in the future, I'll ask you first."

She purses her lips, considering it. "Fine. I forgive you, as long as you promise never to trust gossip over me again."

"Promise," I say.

"Then it's a deal." She nods, letting go of my hand and opening the door before gracefully hopping down from the pickup.

I jump out my side and race around to meet her at the sidewalk. She raises one eyebrow and asks, "Oh, are you inviting yourself in now?"

I grab her hand and smile down at her. "We can hang out on the porch if you want, but yeah, I'm not ready for tonight to be over. Plus, I still want to have a conversation about the casual part of our casual official dating."

"Yes?" she asks suspiciously as we walk toward the swing and sit down.

"I think we should drop it. This doesn't feel casual to me."

"It doesn't feel very casual to me either," she says.

"So officially dating?"

"Officially dating," she confirms. "You can change your Facebook status and everything."

I can see the smile pulling at the corner of her mouth before she finally gives in and lets it spread into a full grin. And, fuck, she's so beautiful. I discreetly stick my other hand in my pocket, rearranging myself to hide the effect of her smile, her willingness to hear me out, to forgive me for being a dick.

I am *officially* dating the most amazing woman on the planet.

CHAPTER TWENTY-ONE

BRYN

I'M FINISHING UP A Taylor Swift–themed Peloton cycling class at my hotel in Vegas, thankful the gym in my hotel is empty at six in the morning because I am belting out the lyrics to "Blank Space" as Ally Love kicks my ass.

I've been in Las Vegas this week for a tech conference, which happens to align with Jameson's first tournament back this weekend, also in Sin City. A happy coincidence—or at least, that's what I told Jameson as we sat on Kelsey's back porch last weekend after our fight. In reality, it had taken some finagling on my part to get a last-minute ticket to this conference. One of my work friends ended up letting me take her spot, with the requirement that I bring her along to one of Jameson's tournaments in the future.

I'd told Jameson that I wouldn't be able to make his first day of play, both because I hadn't decided if I wanted to skip the conference to watch his first round, and because it felt like I might be a distraction.

And Lord knows Jameson has had enough girlfriend-based drama impacting his golf game to last him a lifetime.

After working through Jameson's insecurities last Friday, we hung out all weekend, watching TV, playing a few rounds of golf, and eating essentially every meal together. We never spent the night with each other, but the days inevitably ended with a long make-out session and some light dry humping. I mean, the man is freaking hot, and his kisses make me feel like my body is on fire. There was no way I was going to be able to resist grinding against his seemingly ever-present erection, especially when his hands would wander under my shirt to play with my nipples.

And...now I'm getting turned on in the gym, which is so much worse than singing.

I unclip from the bike and grab my water bottle, then head to my room to shower before leaving for the day.

I throw on a pair of cute but classic black golf shorts and a royal-blue collared shirt before heading out to the course. Jameson's tee time is at 9:40 this morning, and I still have to pick up the VIP pass he held for me at Will Call. I offered to pay for my own tickets, especially since I wasn't sure if I could make it today, but Jameo insisted. He actually seemed so genuinely excited about me coming to watch him that it made me want to go over to Alexis's apartment, knock on the door, and when she opens it, wham! I'll cunt punch her. When she's crying "why?" I'll say "you know why!"

Okay, I'm not Lake Bell in *What Happens in Vegas,* but I am in Vegas, and Alexis deserves it. She really did a number on the guy's self-confidence, and I think she deserves to be punished for that, though maybe losing him is punishment enough.

When it turned out I could make it today, I decided not to tell him I would be watching. I really don't want to fuck with his head by being there, but I do want to support him. So I'm going to spend my morning following his group and then let him know when we meet up for dinner that my schedule changed, so I was there.

Vegas traffic is at least somewhat manageable in the mornings, the denizens of the Strip still sleeping off their hangovers from the night before, so I opt to Uber to the course rather than taking the shuttle. When I arrive, I'm pleasantly surprised with how busy the course is for a Thursday. From watching golf with my dad growing up, I know the first day of play typically has far fewer spectators than the final rounds on Saturday and Sunday.

I pick up my pass from Will Call and head into the course, searching for some much-needed coffee. Caffeine in hand, I make my way to the number 1 tee box to wait for Jameson's group. I'm here a bit early, so I get to see the two groups in front of him tee off as well.

While I wait, the crowd grows noticeably larger. Almost all the conversations around me have turned into speculation around Jameson Walker's return. The man and his wife next to me are currently discussing what a terrible season Jameson had last year. The husband, a real finance-bro type, thinks Jameson is done—can't bounce back from a year like that. The wife, a petite blonde rocking a golf dress, is totally on Jameson's side. The husband claims she is biased because she is "swayed by his rugged good looks." I both want to laugh and to casually mention that he's dating someone, a surprising urge to claim him as my man.

I do neither, the conversations around me stopping as Jameson walks out with the rest of his group. He looks good. The royal-blue polo with the Titleist logo on the front pulls against his broad shoulders, highlighting his toned arms. I glance down at my own and am somewhat embarrassed to realize we match. His dark hair peeks out from under his black cap with a Nike swoosh, both of his main sponsors having ultimately decided against suspending his contracts.

Jameo is the second to tee off, smacking a drive straight down the fairway at least thirty yards farther than the others in his group. Apparently, the majority of the crowd is here to see Jameson's group, because we move as a herd down the fairway, leaving behind just a few stragglers to watch the next group tee off.

***

As Jameson taps a five-foot putt in on hole thirteen, the petite, dark-haired woman who joined our group last hole starts clapping louder than everyone else. She's not clapping loud enough to get kicked out, but it is distracting enough that she could definitely draw Jameson's attention.

Curious, I slow down a bit as we walk to the next tee box, letting her catch up to me. As she passes, I smile at her good-naturedly and ask, "Big fan of Jameson Walker, huh?"

"The biggest." She smiles back. "I'm so glad that he's finally back on the Tour again, though I'm not sure I can handle another year like the last one he had."

I chuckle. "It was not a great year to be a Jameson Walker fan. At least his friend JT Johnson did pretty well. Are you a fan of JT too?"

She cuts her dark green eyes to me. "No. Definitely not a JT fan."

"Oh." I really have no idea what to say in response. I wasn't aware people felt so strongly about golfers. "Okay."

We walk in companionable silence next to each other for the rest of the hole, the only two women in the entire group of thirty following Jameo who don't seem to be here with our boyfriends or husbands. I know I should be jealous of this cute, twentysomething girl who I could fit in my pocket, but for some reason, I'm not. After he shared the shit Alexis put him through, I'm confident this woman could throw herself at him and he still wouldn't cheat on me. Plus, she hasn't checked out his ass once—a feat for any hot-blooded individual with an interest in men—so he might not be her type either.

As the players and their caddies analyze the green, she sticks her hand out. "I'm Lila."

I stare at her for a second before it clicks. She's *Lila*. No wonder there isn't one ounce of interest when she looks at Jameson—they are related.

"You're Jameo's sister."

She looks me up and down. "And you are a superfan who not only knows his sister's name but also casually calls him Jameo. I am usually better at spotting you all."

As she turns to go with a grimace that is likely supposed to be a smile, I reach out to stop her. "Oh, shit. No! I'm not a superfan. I mean, I am a fan, but I'm not a stalker or anything." I smile. "I'm Bryn." Unfortunately, that doesn't seem to do anything for her. Shit. Jameson has told me all about Lila and her grad school. Has he not told his family about us? I assumed he had, but I definitely don't want to be the one to break the news.

I'm also actively trying not to think about all of the reasons that Jameson might have chosen not to tell his family about me. A few may be sneaking through my guards, though, since I'm currently thinking *am I not good enough for him to tell his family about?* And *what if they don't like me?*

Unsure what to do, I shoot Lila an uncertain smile and say, "Well, it was nice to meet you. I really promise I'm not a stalker." I nod and take a couple steps away, turning back to watch the men on the green.

Lila, however, does not seem to be done with our conversation. She moves closer, a quizzical look on her face. "You thought I would know who you are."

"Uhm," I glance back up at Jameo on the green, as if catching a glimpse of his face will make it clear what I should tell his little sister. "I met Jameson at Wild Bluffs a few weeks ago. We'v—"

"You're BRYN!" she all but shrieks, drawing a number of stern looks from the people around us. She pulls me into a hug, her petite frame comically small against my height. "Oh my goodness! I was so sure you were a stalker, I didn't even pay attention to what name you told me."

I smile and hug her back awkwardly. "Yup. Not a stalker. But I wasn't really sure what to do with *you*, Miss Superfan."

Her green eyes twinkling, Jameson's sister replies, "Oh, you'll get used to the superfans. You think the women are going to be the awkward part, but they aren't. It's the men, and not the gay men, the straight men. They fawn over my brother like he's the second coming or something. I've never known what to do with that level of adoration for a man who I know still wants to eat cereal for most meals."

She nods to a guy in green who has been walking along with Jameo's group the whole time. "That's a man-crush for sure. I'd say there is a seventy-five percent chance Jameo is his favorite athlete, not just golfer."

I watch the man in green as we all follow along with the golfers to hole fourteen. He does seem to be a superfan, but then again, I thought Lila was a superfan two minutes ago too.

"Wait." I stop and look at her. "Why aren't you in school? It's Thursday."

She rolls her eyes and then starts walking again. "Why aren't you at work?"

"Uhm, I'm playing hooky from the last day of a tech conference."

"I'm playing hooky from the last day of classes this week."

As it would be very hypocritical of me to say anything else about her presence, I opt to turn my attention back to the golf. When Jameson birdies the next hole, Lila starts her obnoxiously loud clapping again.

I grab at her hands. "Lila, what are you doing? Shut the fuck up," I hiss.

But it's too late. Jameson hears her and, as if he knows it is his sister, his eyes find hers, his smile slowly spreading across his face.

Lila tips her head toward me. "It's my way of letting him know I'm here," she says. Jameson follows her movement, and after a momentary look of confusion, his eyes widen in surprise and recognition. As he turns to walk toward the next hole, I see the pleased grin he tries to hide from me and the rest of the crowd.

***

"I'm supposed to be here!" I joke. "You're the one who showed up unannounced in a completely different state!"

Lila and I are in the lobby of Jameson's hotel, both of us sipping on our third Coors Light of the afternoon. We've been here for the last hour, waiting for Jameson to get done with all the post-round nonsense that he has to get through—the interviews, a call with his swing coach, changing, getting pounded by the hot water of his shower as he...

I jerk my head back to Lila—the sister of the guy I was just picturing taking a hot, steamy shower. *Why did I not decide to share a hotel with him on this trip?*

"What?" I ask, clearly having zoned out there for a minute.

Lila's easygoing laugh is so much like Jameson's that it's a bit disconcerting at first.

"I said, my last class for the week ended early this morning. Then I basically sprinted through the entire airport to make my flight. I knew my parents weren't able to make it out for the beginning of Jameo's tournament, and I didn't want him to feel like he was alone. If I had known you were going to be here..."

"You what? Wouldn't have decided to come to Vegas for a weekend?"

She smirks. "Hell no. I would've skipped my class this morning so there would've been no doubt that I was going to make it."

I laugh and take a drink of my beer.

Lila stares at me for a moment before saying, "He's a good guy, you know."

"Who? Jameo?"

"No, Prince Harry." She rolls her eyes. "Of course Jameo."

"Why am I not surprised that you are still talking about me," his deep voice rumbles from behind me, his arm wrapping around my shoulders as I turn toward him.

Lila jumps off her barstool and throws her arms around her brother, giving him a tight hug that he returns. His eyes, though, stay locked on mine, a promising smile glinting within them.

Unaware of the heated look passing between us, Lila answers Jameson's original question. "Because you're egotistical, so you always think people are talking about you, or at the very least thinking about you."

Lila breaks their hug, settling back on her stool. I stand up, turning to give Jameson a quick hug, but he pulls me in deeper, kissing my forehead softly before squeezing me again.

A smile spreads across my face as I hold him tighter. "Not a bad round today, Jameson."

His voice is soft as he says, "I thought you weren't going to be able to make it until tomorrow."

"I didn't want to be a distraction for your first round back."

Lila fakes a cough, breaking us out of our awkwardly long hug, and says, "So, where are you taking us for dinner tonight?"

CHAPTER TWENTY-TWO

JAMESON

Dinner with Lila and Bryn on the deck of Picasso, overlooking the fountains at the Bellagio, is a blur. They fully carry the conversation, talking about Lila finishing up her grad classes at the end of the year and what she plans to do after. At one point, Bryn suggests Lila consider working at her sister's firm, not the consulting one I walked into on Main Street to beg for Bryn's number, but the security firm Kelsey runs out of Wild Bluffs.

I, on the other hand, spend the entire time replaying the moment when Lila pointed Bryn out to me. It's not surprising I hadn't noticed her. I tend to focus solely on my game when I'm playing, and even if I didn't, she had her hat pulled low over her eyes, clearly trying to go unnoticed.

It means so much to me that she came to watch me play, that she supported me and hadn't even wanted the credit for it. She was there completely for me.

Why having my girlfriend support me at my first tournament back is such a shock is something I clearly will need to work through at a later date, but for now, all I feel is a fucking adrenaline rush. I'm horny as shit, and I've never wanted to push my sister into a fountain as much as I do right now just to get her out of the way.

I pay for dinner, though Bryn does offer to split it with me, telling me she could talk to Lila about working for her and charge it as a business expense, but I, of course, decline.

Lila, like the brat she is, smiles innocently back at me when I raise my eyebrow, silently asking her if she is going to offer to pay.

However, she earns back a few points in my book when she fakes a yawn and says, "Welp, I'm tired. I'm going to head back to my room." Neither Bryn nor I protest, though I know I should offer to walk her to her hotel, or even know which hotel she's staying at.

Bryn and I linger at the front of the restaurant, and I grab her hand, pulling her into a kiss the moment Lila disappears from sight. Bryn parts her lips for me, and our tongues dance while my hands slide lower, my thumbs brushing the top of her ass before I force myself to slowly slide them back up her sides.

Bryn pulls back, breaking our kiss. "Your room is here, right?"

I nod, clearing my throat before grabbing her hand and pulling her toward the elevator. "Want to come up?"

"Well, it's that or climb you in the middle of a crowded casino hallway."

"Bryn." I reach down and adjust my now present erection. "You can't say shit like that when we are still in public."

She pulls away, a look of panic in her eyes. "Oh, sorry. I didn't think about the possibility of paparazzi. I'm new to this whole—"

I push her against the wall of the elevator as it closes, bracing my arms on either side of her head before attacking her lips with mine.

The elevator slows, and I gently grab her face in mine, forcing her to look at me. "I don't give one single fuck who sees us together. I do—because of my fragile ego—care about coming in my jeans in public from the image of you climbing me."

Her gaze travels to my tented pants, her eyes darkening before moving to the door that's now opening behind me.

"Come on, Jameo." She heads out of the elevator, her hand lightly brushing against the bulge in my pants as she passes by.

I let out a hiss, taking a deep breath and reminding myself I'm not a fourteen-year-old boy who loses control just because a girl touches his crotchal region.

Clearly realizing she doesn't know where my room is, Bryn is waiting outside of the elevator for me. I grab her hand before tugging her down the hall toward my room.

"Whoa there, tiger. No need to run."

I look back at her over my shoulder, and what she sees in my eyes must assure her otherwise, because she picks up her pace as well, letting out a breathy laugh.

Stopping at my door, I pull my key card out of my wallet, tapping the reader and pushing through the door into my room. The two minutes it took to get here was too long. Too long without tasting her mouth or feeling her pressed up against me.

As soon as we make it inside, I slam my mouth down on hers, leaning her against the closed door. She groans, her fingers pulling at my hair as she pulls my head down, deepening the kiss.

She tastes delicious, and I can't stop myself from grabbing her ass and pulling her to me, my cock desperately in need of her heat, her friction. Bryn wraps her legs around me, and I press her back into the door so I can free one of my hands.

I rub my thumb over the round peak of her nipple that is trying to pop through the thick fabric of her bra and dress. She arches her back, pressing herself into my hand. *Fuck, she has great tits.*

"Thank you." She laughs as she breaks the kiss.

"Huh?" I blink, trying to force blood back into my brain.

"You said I had great tits. I said thank you." She drops her legs, and I lower her to the ground as she grips her own breasts. "They're larger than I would like them to be. Back problems and all that."

"Uhm." I stare at the deep V of cleavage as if in a trance, trying to figure out how my thoughts are now escaping my head as words. She chuckles.

"That...that sucks. Back problems." I drag my hand down my face. "I hear you. But, fuck. I think they are perfect."

With that, I step back toward her, one hand sliding around the back of her neck to bring her mouth to mine, the other going right to the perfect tit in question, a heavy handful that I want nothing more than to lavish with kisses and bites before sucking what is sure to be a perfect nipple into my mouth.

Bryn groans and, reaching down, starts giving my dick the attention it has been demanding. The pressure from the heel of her hand as it rubs against my zipper feels so good.

It ends too soon, but Bryn reaches for my belt buckle, undoing it before starting to work on my zipper. I take the hint and unbutton the top of my shirt before pulling it over my head.

I hear Bryn's intake of breath as she sees my bare chest for the first time. I pause for a moment, taking in her hooded eyes as they follow the light V that I've worked so hard for down to the briefs sticking out from my unzipped jeans. She wets her lips, and my dick jolts like he was the one that just got licked by her pink tongue.

She notes the movement, a daring smile igniting in her eyes as they meet mine.

I reach out, grabbing her hands and pulling them over her head. I pin them against the wall with one hand, my other sliding down her back, where I snag the zipper of her dress, slowly dragging it down. I place kisses down the side of her neck, and she tilts her head, giving me access to every inch.

Unable to wait any longer, I run my fingers along the bottom of her dress, feeling her shudder as my fingers touch the sensitive inside of her thighs. Grabbing the fabric, I pull it up and over her head, tossing it to the ground as I take in her curvy body still covered by a simple black bra and underwear. Shaking my head, I look into her eyes, noting a hint of self-consciousness, before stalking back forward to claim her mouth with mine.

Our tongues tangle as I make quick work of her bra, throwing it on the floor to join the rest of our clothes. My thumbs find her nipples, and I slowly rub them back and forth before gently pinching them between my fingers.

She tilts her head, letting out a soft moan, and I take advantage of her arched back to bring her nipple into my mouth, sucking. She pushes her hips into mine, and I can feel the wet heat of her through our underwear.

I release her nipple with a "pop" while giving her the friction she wants from my dick. "B, are you already wet for me?"

She nods, a moment of insecurity evident on her face.

I nuzzle into her neck, kissing the soft skin there while trying to re-assure her of just how attractive I find her arousal. "That is so fucking hot."

Emboldened by my praise, she tugs on my jeans, pulling them down as she pushes me backward until my calves hit the bed. I sit, quickly kicking my jeans off and pulling Bryn between my legs.

She flashes me a lopsided smile, the left side of her lips tugging up before she runs her hands down my shoulders, bringing her mouth back to mine as she climbs on top of my lap, our underwear the only thing between us. The heat from her mouth vanishes then, only to reappear moments later on my neck.

I tilt my head, releasing a groan as she nips at the column of my throat.

Bryn's exploration moves lower, and I lean back, bracing my arms on the bed as I watch her kiss her way down my stomach. As she reaches the waistband of my briefs, her eyes find mine again before she starts to tug them down. I shift my weight backward, lifting my hips to help her.

As my dick pops free, she pauses, kissing the head before dropping to her knees between my legs.

"Fuuuck, Bryn." I groan, the remaining blood in my body rushing to my erection at the soft feel of her lips against my skin.

She smiles up at me as her tongue darts out, licking her lips before she bites the bottom one.

I stroke my thumb across her cheek, forcing her chin up so she makes eye contact with me. As much as it pains me, I want to make sure she comes before me. It's just good manners.

"There is literally nothing that I want more in my life than to have your mouth on me, but I want to make sure you get what you need first."

She rolls her eyes, scoffing slightly. "Such a gentleman. But let's pretend that I know what I want, and what I want is to make you feel good."

"B—"

"Jameo."

I stare at her. She stares back.

Then she breaks into a wicked grin, leans down, and licks up the entire length of my shaft, swirling her tongue along the tip before continuing like she hadn't just almost made me come from one lick. "Can't you just let someone do something for you?" she asks when she comes up for breath. "You had your first tournament back today. You still have three more days of golf to play. So, yes, I'm going to give you a blow job. You're going to sit back and take it like a good boy."

"Damn, B, that's—" I'm cut off from telling her just how sexy that little monologue was by her pulling my cock deep into the back of her throat. She sucks her cheeks in as she grips the base, sliding me in and out of her warm, wet mouth.

She keeps up the pace, and I use the opportunity to explore her with my eyes, the minutes passing as I watch her sweet mouth take me deeper and deeper.

As she pumps me, she runs her tongue up along the underside of my dick, hitting a sensitive vein there that makes my hips thrust against her.

She chuckles, the vibrations causing me to pump even faster, encouraging her to speed her hand as well. Her other hand cups my balls, lightly massaging them as she continues to pull me deeper into her mouth.

Sooner than I'd like to admit, I'm on the edge, unable to pull myself back. I'm not sure I'll ever be able to pull myself back when it comes to Bryn. "Fuck," I grit out. "Fuck, I'm going to… I'm about to…"

She pulls her mouth off me with one last flick of her tongue, her hands continuing to work my shaft and balls in sync.

"Fuuck." With a groan, my orgasm hits, ropes of cum covering Bryn's hand. Being with Bryn? It's the best I've ever had.

CHAPTER TWENTY-THREE

BRYN

Holy shit. Watching that man lose control was literally the sexiest thing I've ever seen in my life. Knowing I caused him to become unleashed like that...wow. I'm so turned on right now. Luckily, I brought a toy from home to help me with that once I'm back in my room.

Jameson grabs a towel from the bathroom, cleaning himself off my hand before pulling me to his chest in a deep kiss.

Wait. He's not...going to sleep? I don't know why I assumed he would want to make this quick so he could get a good night's rest. I mean, besides the fact that he is a professional golfer in the middle of his first tournament back.

He moves his mouth over mine, nipping at my lower lip before angling my head to the side and diving in deeper. As his hand starts to work down to the top of my panties, I push back.

"Oh, it's okay, Jameo. I'm good. I'll just—"

"Are you kidding me, B? You just gave me the best blow job of my life. You expect me to not return the favor?" he asks.

He looks me directly in the eyes before continuing. "And that's not even the right way to say it. It's not a favor for you. I fucking want to eat your pretty pussy. I *need* to know what you taste like."

I'm pretty sure my arousal is so strong at this point that he can probably taste it just by taking a deep breath, but I don't think that's the answer he's looking for.

"Look," I say. "I really appreciate the offer. I've just never really liked guys going down on me. I don't know why, but it just doesn't do it for me."

His heavily lidded eyes meet mine again, and I see the competitor in him flare to life. The pull of the man who has risen to the top of his professional sport.

"Oh, Bryn," he groans. "You're telling me I can be the first person to taste your orgasm on my lips while I fuck you with my tongue?"

I back away, overwhelmed by the battle in my brain between overwhelming desire and the memories of Peter between my legs, his tongue doing nothing for me as he worked and worked. We both eventually agreed it was just better if we used a toy on the rare occasion we decided to do anything other than a make-out session with heavy dry humping.

"Uhm. No?" I say, looking everywhere but at his face. "I'm saying you could spend the rest of the night trying, and we'd both just end up frustrated."

Jameson closes the gap between us in one long step, reaching up to cup my face and force my eyes to his. "Challenge fucking accepted, B."

With that, he lifts me off my feet, throwing me down on the edge of the bed. He kisses his way down my stomach, stopping only to pull my drenched underwear off.

"Fuck," he groans, his tongue darting out to taste me. One of his big hands slides to my breast, kneading, while the other slides down my seam, splitting me open before him.

I'm so aroused, so absolutely turned on from this man, that a spark of hope ignites inside of me. Maybe oral will actually work this time.

"You've got the prettiest fucking pussy I've ever seen," Jameson says before his tongue hits my clit, and holy cow. It is not the same. As he continues to work his mouth over that sensitive bud, sucking and teasing, he slowly slides his finger into me. The slow pace is in direct contrast to the pulsing vibrations, which somehow makes them both feel more intense.

"Holy...shit," I moan, digging my hands into his hair to urge him on.

He pauses, angling his head up just enough to send me the smuggest smirk I've ever seen. Fortunately for him, there is no way I can form a coherent thought right now, let alone a witty reply.

I whimper, needing friction, and he responds by slipping another finger inside of me. His two fingers are bigger than anything I've ever had in me before, so I gasp at the stretching sensation at the same time that he mumbles, "So tight."

He continues to work my clit as I ride his face, his fingers following the speed I'm setting with my hips. He's really good at this, and surprisingly willing to keep at it for more than the five minutes I've ever been willing to try before.

He starts toying with my nipple, and I can feel the orgasm start to crest, and he must too because he pulls away long enough to say, "Fuck yeah." I squirm in agitation, not quite able to get where I need to go.

As if he senses the fear of failure in me, he nips my clit at the same time he curls his fingers inside of me, brushing just the right spot. One, two, three strokes of my inner wall and...holy shit! I'm coming! My back bows off the bed, my thighs trapping his head in a vise. He strokes me through the aftershocks as he laps up my orgasm, drinking me in like he's been lost in the desert without water for days.

"Wow," I say when I'm finally coherent enough to think straight. "That was...wow."

I look down at Jameson, who is kneeling between my legs, looking mighty proud of himself.

"I'm not going to lie, B. It's a goddamn privilege to know that I'm the only man who has ever seen that before." He runs his hand through his hair. "That was...amazing."

You could say that again. It *was* amazing. Not just because I actually came for the first time that way, but because...wow. I didn't even know I had that many nerve endings.

"Thanks, Jameo."

He climbs over my body, leaning in to kiss me gently. I feel like I should be disgusted by the taste of my pleasure in his mouth, but I can't help but love everything about this moment. It's bliss.

"The pleasure is truly all mine."

I give him another kiss before heading into the bathroom to clean up. Once I've run a warm washcloth over myself, I wander past the bed, searching for my discarded clothes. As much as I would love to cuddle into that man's chest and never let him go, I know he needs to focus on his golf.

"You're not leaving, are you?" he asks, a note of desperation in his voice.

"Yes. You cannot tell me that sleeping in the same bed as someone for the first time ever is going to *help* your golf game tomorrow." I wink at him, trying to be clear that I would stay, but I know I shouldn't.

"Come on, B. I want to sleep with you tonight."

There's something in his tone that makes me think he might mean more than just lying in bed next to each other. But after what we just did, how do I explain why I'm not ready to have full-on sex with him when I was more than happy to have his cock in my mouth less than an hour ago? I swivel the ring on my finger, staring at him as I try to explain without also springing the virgin thing on him. "I really like you, Jameo, but..."

I see his face become guarded—right, almost no good statement ever begins that way—and I try again.

"I just, I told you that I..." I bite my lip, trying to decide how to say it. How much to say.

Luckily, realization seems to wash over him, his body transforming with his understanding.

"I need you to talk to me. To cuddle with me." He stands up, pulling me into a hug. "You told me you want to take it slow. I respect that. As much as I can't wait to have sex with you, I *can* wait. For you."

"I didn't bring any clothes with me."

"You can sleep in some of mine."

"I'm worried you'll sleep poorly, and I'll be to blame if you don't play well."

"I promise I'm going to sleep better with you here, but if it makes *you* feel better, you can take the pull-out couch." He lets go and heads to his suitcase. "Plus, if I can't play well after sleeping with the most amazing girl in the world, I should probably reconsider my profession."

He offers me a clean tee out of his bag, but I don't want some freshly washed shirt. Instead, I grab his white undershirt off the floor and head back to the bathroom with it. "Okay," I say, embracing the happiness I'm feeling right now. "I'll stay. Of course I will." I peek back out of the door. "For you, of course."

"Of course," he deadpans. "There should be a new toothbrush in there with the other stuff from the hotel," he calls after me, as if reading my thoughts about exactly how disgusting my breath was going to be in the morning.

A few minutes later, Jameson and I are both ready for bed, and I cautiously crawl in next to him. I lie on the far side of the bed, trying to be as unobtrusive as possible without actually having to sleep on the couch.

Jameo is having none of it, though. He wraps his arms around me, pulling me to him until my head nestles in the nook of his shoulder. Unable to resist, I sigh deeply, sinking into his warmth. With a contented sigh, Jameson kisses the top of my head and whispers, "Sweet dreams, beautiful."

CHAPTER TWENTY-FOUR

BRYN

"Oh...my...God," Becca deadpans.

"Wow there, Janice. No need to go all *Friends* on us," I say, propping my feet up on the extra desk they have in their office space.

Izzy shoots my white sneakers a disapproving look. "More details, Bryn. You can't just casually drop that you ended up just 'staying with Jameo' and not give us more details."

I most certainly can. In fact, I have no plans on telling them about how, after waking up to Jameson's alarm clock on Friday morning, we'd taken turns eating each other for breakfast. Or how, after he knew he made the final group on Saturday, we'd been twenty minutes late meeting Lila and JT for dinner because we'd been so wrapped up in celebrating. Or how on Sunday, after he'd gotten second, he'd all but begged me to take the next few days off so I could come to his house in Florida with him to relax before his tournament this weekend.

Izzy continues, "Also, there are these newfangled things the kids are using these days called cell phones. You could, and I'm just spitballing here, text us this news so we aren't getting it *a week* later. Or, and this is getting really crazy, you could pick up the phone and call us. God, what I wouldn't give to have been on the receiving end of a FaceTime from you in Jameson Walker's bathroom."

I snap my eyes up to meet Izzy's, my focus fully on her now. "Why am I FaceTiming you from the bathroom in this situation? We've been over this more times than I feel is appropriate for people our age, Iz. You *cannot* FaceTime people in the bathroom."

She pulls her long brown hair, which is so similar to mine, back into a bun at the nape of her neck. "First, it's called *Face*Time. I don't know why you can't see my face while I'm peeing. It's not like I do it if I'm going number two. Second, because you clearly need to be in a room where the door can close so you can tell us all the dirty details while Jameson is in a post-sex coma on the bed."

"Do you have a third, or are we just making lists out of two things these days?"

She flips me off, directing her other middle finger at Becca when she starts laughing too.

"It felt like news that could keep, especially since I spent the whole weekend at the course, where phones are very frowned upon."

Becca looks up from her computer, swiveling in her chair to give me her full attention. "Honestly, Bryn, I can't believe you're dating Jameson Walker. Partly because he looked fucking hot as he tapped in that last putt to get second this weekend, but also because he is a dick.

Like a certifiable douche canoe. You of all people tend to avoid dating anyone with dick tendencies."

"Why do you hate him so much, Becca? I mean, I know I started the Dick thing that weekend, but you never get on board with me hating people." A flashback from that awful end to our night at Cattlemens floats through my memory. "You were even rude to him that weekend at the bar."

Izzy's head tilts to the side. "That's true. You were. And even when he came into the office to get Bryn's number, you were pumped about meeting JT and were super friendly to him but barely even looked at Jameson. Did he do something to you?"

Shit. Did he?

Sighing, Becca rolls her eyes before she says, "No. But also, not no." Izzy and I both continue to stare at her, waiting.

Finally, I crack. "Care to expand, Becca?" I ask, somewhat more harshly than absolutely necessary, but gosh. If he did something that would make Becca of all people this mad at him, I need to know now before I fall even further for the guy.

"Ugh! Fine." She throws up her hands dramatically. "If you must know, before I left the course that first weekend, I went to find him to talk some sense into him about how awesome you are. I found him in the workout room, and he, like the Dick he is, assumed I was there to hit on him and basically told me to go fuck myself before I ever even had a chance to say anything."

That doesn't sound like the Jameson I know now, but it definitely is par for the course for the guy who had his heart ripped out by his girlfriend, had his career take a huge hit because he couldn't get his head on straight, and was licking his wounds at the most remote private golf course he could find.

Izzy looks at me, her eyes wide, questioning what she should do.

"He never mentioned it to me," I say. "But, to be fair to him, I saw the way women will just hit on him wherever he goes. I'm not saying he was right to treat you like that, Becca, but I can see how that would quickly become his go-to response. I'll make sure he apologizes next time he sees you."

"I don't need an apology."

I drop my feet to the ground and lean forward, my elbows on my knees. "Clearly, you do. You've been holding on to this for a while now."

"Well, I'm not a floozy!"

Izzy and I both start, taken aback by the outburst. "Of course you're not. What's going on with you?"

Becca's cheeks turn pink, and she focuses back on her computer screen. "Nothing. I just don't like that I was trying to do something kind, and he just assumed the worst in me."

"Okaaay. Well, I'll make sure he understands how rude he was." I shoot my sister a look, but she just shrugs. I guess she doesn't know what's going on with Becca either.

Taking the hint, Izzy changes the subject. "So, Bryn, have you decided what you're going to do for Thanksgiving this year?"

"You mean after you all decided to go to Europe for the week, knowing I can't be out of the country on fucking Black Friday?"

"Yep. That's exactly what I mean. Did you find any time during your sex dungeon weekend to ask Jameson what he is going to be up to?"

I throw a pen at her head. "What the fuck is wrong with you? How do you hear that we spent the weekend together in a suite at a Vegas hotel and somehow that gets changed to a sex dungeon? Jeez Louise. And no, I did not casually drop the fact that I'm without Thanksgiving plans because my family are assholes who couldn't travel to Scotland literally any other week of the year."

She, too, turns back to her computer. "Testy, testy. Seems to me like a normal thing to mention to your boyfriend—sex dungeon or not."

"Ugh. You are the worst," I say, before opening my laptop, tucking my AirPods into my ears, and getting back to work.

Two hours later, my phone rings with a FaceTime call from Jameo. After he came in second to JT last Sunday, our celebration had gotten cut short by my flight to Vancouver for work. Despite his repeated requests for me to ditch work and come to Florida with him, I was needed in Canada, and there was no way I could miss out on that prime work opportunity to go play hooky with him, no matter how much I wanted to.

I was surprised when, ten minutes after arriving at my hotel in Vancouver, Jameo called me via FaceTime. He was waiting for one of his private pilots to arrive to prepare the plane and fly him to his house. We spent over an hour talking about everything, from our histories, to his tournament, to what his schedule looks like for the next few months.

Because he needs to get more FedEx Cup points, the end of his year is busy. But, according to Jameson, that shouldn't keep us from having a normal relationship where you talk every day and know what's going on in each other's lives, so we've both made an effort this week to stay in pretty regular communication. We typically text off and on throughout the day, and then we FaceTime at night.

Today was the first day of his tournament in Houston, and, according to my ESPN alert, he finished his round about an hour ago.

"Hey, Jameo," I answer, raising my phone so he can see my face.

I see both Becca's and Izzy's heads lift, unabashedly eavesdropping on our call.

"Hey, B. How's Wild Bluffs?"

I turn the camera around, giving him a view of the whole office. "Terrible company, but otherwise not so bad."

Izzy butts in, "You are welcome to stop treating our office like your personal WeWork any time you want. It really won't hurt our feelings."

"Hey, Izzy. Hi, Becca." Jameson waves from my phone screen.

Iz holds up two fingers, flashing him a peace sign, while Becca opts for a one-fingered salute—the middle-finger kind.

I turn Jameson back around before telling him, "Becca is still upset about how big of a dick you were to her when she tried to talk to you out at the golf course."

Becca throws a pen of her own at me. "I told you I didn't need you to mention it to him!"

Looking apologetic, Jameson asks me to turn him back around before saying, "I'm glad she did mention it, though, Becca. I should've apologized to you when I came to ask for Bryn's number. I was a complete dick. Sorry."

Shrugging, she replies, "It's really not a big deal. But for the record, I was definitely not hitting on you."

Turning him to face me again, I say, "Well, that was fun."

"Hey, Jameo," Izzy yells from across the room. "We were just talking about you." I can tell she's scheming something by the evil glint to her eye, and I most certainly don't want to stick around to find out what it is. I stand, shoving my laptop back into my bag.

"All good things, I hope?" he yells back.

I'm almost out the door but don't make it out in time before Izzy responds, "Just wondering what you were up to for Thanksgiving, since B is home alone and all."

He watches my face closely as I push my way out the door, shooting Iz the bird over my shoulder. "Why didn't you tell me that you were home alone for Thanksgiving? Where will your family be?"

"They are all going on a weeklong vacation to Scotland and Ireland. However, I have to be around on Black Friday because it's a huge day for our online platform, so it doesn't make sense for me to go with them."

"But why didn't you tell me?"

"I'm sure you've got plans, and I didn't want you to feel obligated to invite me out of pity."

"B, I want to spend every spare second I can with you. No oblig-ation. Please, come to Ohio with me to do Thanksgiving with my family. JT comes every year, so it's not even like it's just family or something. If anything, you should do it out of pity for me—dealing with JT and Lila together requires all the pity."

I bite my bottom lip, thinking. "I'd have to fly out that night so I can be at headquarters all day on Friday."

"Done. We always eat around one, anyway. Please? Just come."

I smile. "Fine. I'd actually really like that."

CHAPTER TWENTY-FIVE

BRYN

izzy

Did you drop the cherry bomb yet?

Me

No.

Kinda?

We did stuff! Sexy stuff!

And, update on Peter. He was not great at some things. Plus, I told Jameson I like to take things slow when we were in California!

Izzy

shocked face No way. I love this for you.

Also, it's possible he has a different definition of slow.

Me

It's possible he will never know, and he
will solve the problem for me. *winky face*
winky face

Izzy

Still on Team Tell Him.

Me

Still on Team It Seems Easier Not To…

There is a "knock, knock" from outside the room I've been holed up in since arriving back in California three days ago, and I internally groan.

"You could just actually knock, Kyle. Then you wouldn't need to say it."

"Just dropping by to see how your day is going. I've been slammed with the marketing side of things, and I have a plan for the commercials that is going to be amazing. It's going to blow your mind."

I eye my plastic fork from lunch, weighing the pros and cons of stabbing myself in the eye with it. On the plus side, it would get me out of this conversation. "Okay. Great. The tech will be ready, so I'm glad we will have people who are excited and ready to use it."

"I can't tell you about it just yet—trying to keep it hush-hush until the deal is done—but I know you're going to be floored when you hear about it," he continues as if I hadn't spoken at all.

"Okay, well...sounds good." Then, because I can't help myself, I add, "I'm sure your team came up with something great."

A dark glint flashes in his eyes before he suppresses it with a forced chuckle. "No, Bryn. This idea was mine. All mine."

With a final chuckle, he pushes out of the glass door, and I'm struck by just how similar he is to a Bond villain. Does that mean he just revealed an evil plan to me?

Chapter Twenty-Six

Jameson

I SWING OPEN THE door to my parents' house at nine on Thanksgiving morning. Bryn couldn't catch a flight from California to Ohio after work last night, so she flew in early this morning. I offered to pick her up from the airport, but she insisted on Ubering so I could spend more time with my family.

Seeing her standing there with a bottle of wine in one hand, I'm hit with just how much I've missed her. The smile that lights up her face when she sees me makes me think maybe she has missed me too. She looks gorgeous in a sweater dress that hugs her body, emphasizing her athletic figure. A deep V down the middle emphasizes her full chest, and it takes effort to pull my gaze away.

"Hey, B. You look great today." I pull her into a quick hug complete with a forehead kiss before grabbing the bottle of wine out of her grip and sliding my hand into its place.

She tightens her hold on my hand as I move us toward the sounds of the kitchen. "Thanks for inviting me. I really appreciate it," she says, though her voice carries a note of worry.

I stop in the hallway just before the kitchen. "Are you okay?"

"Just nervous about meeting your family."

Pulling her into another hug, I reassure her quietly, "They're going to love you. Lila already does. She was pumped when I told her you were coming."

"I just know how much their opinion of me means to you." She looks up at me, her face creased in concern. "I'm worried I'm going to mess it up. I'm more of an acquired taste for a lot of people."

"Jameson!" My mother's voice carries from in the kitchen. "Is that Bryn?"

I give Bryn a playful nudge. "Showtime."

As we turn the corner to my parents' kitchen, I watch Bryn take in everything. My mom, wearing a bright red apron over her sweater and dark jeans, measuring ingredients into her big mixer. My dad, dressed in a button-up and jeans, posted up at the end of the long white island, helping skin potatoes. The long dining room table is decorated with a fall-themed tablecloth and a centerpiece of orange and red flowers coming out of a pumpkin.

When I first started winning big in the pros, I tried to buy my parents a new house. They refused. A couple of years later, when I bought my place in Florida, I offered to buy them a second home next to me so we could see each other more. My mom suggested I could fly to Ohio if I wanted to see them more. Then, two Christmases ago, after getting off yet another call with my dad complaining about how long it was taking the plumber to fix yet another broken appliance, I renovated their kitchen for them. Learning from my past mistakes, I had already paid for the kitchen by the time I told them, so there was no way for them to tell me no.

"Mom, Dad, this is Bryn."

She smiles nervously, giving them a small wave as my dad goes to stand up. "Oh, no need to get up. It's nice to meet you both."

My dad, of course, doesn't listen, and, pulling Bryn into a hug, says, "We are so glad you could make it."

Mom doesn't leave whatever she's mixing but offers Bryn a large, genuine smile instead. "So nice to meet you. We've heard a lot about you"—she shoots me a stern look—"from Lila."

Bryn chuckles as Lila yells from upstairs, "I still maintain you're way too good for him!" We can hear her feet pound down the steps, and suddenly, she's in the kitchen too.

"Wow, Lila, you look great. Those boots are...well, let's just say there's no chance I would ever be able to walk in those," Bryn compliments Lila, drawing the rest of our attention to her black dress and some sort of break-your-ankle heeled boots.

Mom, Dad, and I share a confused look before Dad asks, "What are you so dressed up for, sweetheart?"

She looks down at herself, the color rising in her cheeks. "Just didn't want Bryn to feel overdressed." We all look at Bryn now, her casual sweater dress and short little boot things. It's nothing compared to Lila's outfit.

"Ahh..." Bryn looks between us all. "Well, thanks. That's super nice of you. I do hate being overdressed. Or underdressed. I basically forced

Jameo to show me pictures of all the Thanksgivings he had on his phone so that I could decide what to wear."

We stand there in awkward silence for a moment before it's broken up by the doorbell.

"Honey, that should be JT," my mom says. "Can you go get the door?"

I look at Bryn, unsure if I should leave her alone, but she just smiles, indicating with her head that I should go. As I leave the kitchen, I hear her turn on the sink to wash her hands and then ask my mom, "What can I do to help, Mrs. Walker?"

Pulling open the door for the second time this morning, I smile at my old friend. "Hey, man. How was the flight in?"

"Fucking brutal. Remind me again why we do this in Ohio." JT rubs his hands together, a California boy through and through.

I grab his jacket, throw it onto the coat rack, and smugly mention, "You know, Bryn didn't even wear a coat. Some people don't think midfifties is that cold."

He stares down the hallway toward the kitchen. "Is Lila home?"

"Um, yes. Have you ever known Lila to miss a family Thanksgiving?"

"Right." He clears his throat. "Yup. That makes sense."

"Why are you being so weird right now? Is this about Bryn being here? You know I trust her. You don't have to be 'on' today just because she's around," I reassure him as we walk toward the kitchen.

"Right. Of course. I'm not worried a—" He cuts off, staring at my sister as she stands at the island, helping my dad with the potatoes.

"I know. Completely ridiculous outfit to wear today. She claims she didn't want Bryn to feel overdressed." I roll my eyes, making my way over to Bryn, who is helping shape the bread dough into crescent shapes for the dinner rolls.

Coming up behind her, I lean my head over her shoulder, wrapping my arms around her waist.

"Did you just smell me?"

"Shhh…" I whisper into her ear. "I'm just making sure you don't stink after that plane ride."

She shoves me away, and I throw up my hands, a huge smile plastered on my face. "I'm trying to *help*, Bryn!"

"Go away, you pest." My mom flings a dish towel at me before moving to the other side of the island and pulling JT into a hug.

Bryn watches JT, a smile that I will later have to remember to ask her about pulling at her lips.

The whirlwind that is preparing Thanksgiving dinner ramps up, JT and I setting the table and helping mash the potatoes, Bryn and Lila chatting while decorating sugar cookies for dessert, and all the while, my dad pouring generous glasses of wine for everyone.

By the time we sit down to eat hours later, we are all buzzed. My parents are each at one of the heads of the table, with Bryn and I on one side, and Lila and JT on the other.

"JT, move your fucking arm. Jesus, Bryn's not going to be invited back if it means I have to sit next to this giant oaf. What happened to the second table we had out last year?" Lila asks.

"Just because you're the size of a five-year-old doesn't make me a giant, pipsqueak."

"I'm five foot four, you baboon. The average five-year-old is like four feet tall. How you ever graduated from Cal State is truly beyond me. Do they just hand out degrees? We all know it can't be because they give golfers special treatment like the real athletes."

I glare at my sister across the table. "Nice. Why don't you keep me out of your little lovers' spat that you have going on."

Both their faces turn bright red, but Bryn cuts in before either can yell at me for that last little jab. "Were there more people here last year if you needed two tables?"

"Yeah, where is everyone this year?" JT asks.

My mom shakes her head. "Oh, my brother Mark moved to Arizona this past winter, and my sister Karen and her kids are at her husband's family's place in Michigan."

"We're glad you're here, though, Bryn," my dad offers from the end of the table. "It's great to actually have one of Jameson's girlfriends join for a family event." He coughs then, clearly catching the glare his wife is sending his way. "Lori, could you pass me the potatoes, please? That gravy is delicious."

As my mom hands the dish down our side of the table, I catch Bryn glancing between Lila and JT, clearly unfazed by my dad's comment. "What?"

She shakes her head. "Nothing." She offers me a smile before turning to my mom. "The turkey is delicious, Mrs. Walker."

"Thank you. I've never been a huge turkey fan, but I feel it's a necessary part of the Thanksgiving tradition," my mom replies before asking, "Have you heard from your family? How are they enjoying their trip? And, remind me, you have two sisters, right?"

"Yep. Yes. I'm the youngest of three girls, which likely explains why my dad is going bald. I talked to them during my ride from the airport, and they are having a great time. My mom is in love with the little Highland cows over there, and my dad and sisters are essentially drinking their way through the country between the distilleries and pubs."

I jump in, "B, show my mom the picture of the cow and her calf that your mom sent you. She'll love it."

Mom smiles sweetly, clearly pleased that I know this information even though I haven't been in the same town as Bryn since Vegas. She takes the phone Bryn offers her, chuckling at the fuzzy momma cow and baby on the screen.

"They are adorable. I remember when Jameson convinced us to go to Scotland with him for some tournament a few years ago. Steve and I rented a car and drove up to the Highlands. It was a magical place; it almost made me believe in things like fairies and the Loch Ness monster."

"If you go with him to Scotland this year, Bryn, you should definitely make the drive," my dad says from the end of the table.

Bryn's face turns red. "Oh, um, I'm not sure if...but yeah...if that..." She looks at me, her eyes beseeching me to say something.

Unsure what to do to help the awkward situation my dad unknowingly just put us in, I jump in anyway. "That tournament isn't until next summer, Dad. Plus, I'm sure it would be difficult for Bryn to take that much time away from her job."

"What is it you do again?" JT thankfully asks. "Something with technology, right?"

Lila rolls her eyes, but Bryn shoots him a grateful smile before answering, "Yup. I'm the director of technology for Hungry Guy."

I finish the food on my plate and reach my hand over, resting it on Bryn's thigh as my mom says, "I love Hungry Guy. I must admit, I'm not sure I understand what your job is, though it sounds important."

Bryn slides her hand into mine, our fingers lacing before she replies, "It sounds more important than it is. I'm the person who is in charge of making sure everything, from our app to our back-end customer management system, is working correctly and everything is talking to each other."

Just then, my phone starts ringing. I pull it out of my pocket, planning to decline the call, but notice it's Jon, my agent. It's not like him to call on holidays unless it's something urgent.

"It's Jon," I say to the table. "I'll take this and be right back."

I slide into my parents' office, shutting the door behind me as I answer the phone. "Hey, Jon. What's up?"

"Jameson. Happy Thanksgiving, man. Sorry to disturb your home time, but I had some exciting news that is very time sensitive. Erica and her team have finally gotten a deal offer for you."

I raise my fist in silent victory, unable to contain how excited I am to be turning my life around.

"Now, they came in with a real lowball offer, but both Erica and I think it's something you should take. I know your game is coming around, but we're both worried that, if you don't start getting your face back out there, it won't matter how well you play this year; it'll be lost in terms of sponsorships."

"Okay, I hear you. I don't love taking lowball deals when they still take the same amount of my time, but I hear you. We've got to start somewhere. What is it?" I ask.

"Well, this is where things get a bit more complicated due to your relationship with Bryn."

Jon and Erica had been annoyed when I told them Bryn was my girlfriend. They saw the logic in us moving straight into officially dating, but both made it clear they felt not dating at all would've been the better answer. I think they are starting to come around after my performance in Vegas.

"What do you mean? What does Bryn have to do with it?"

"It's Hungry Guy. They want you to be part of a big commercial campaign they are pushing out in conjunction with some update to their online ordering system."

Bryn. That's what Bryn is working on all the time. This is Bryn's big project. The one that, if it does well, she'll get the promotion she's been vying for for years.

"Jameson?" Jon asks in a tone that makes it clear it's not the first time he's tried to pull me back into the conversation.

"Yeah." I run my hands through my hair. "She's mentioned it before."

"Well, they seem convinced that you'll take this lowball offer. That could just be because they follow the news and know you're not in high demand right now, but...I feel I need to ask, has Bryn mentioned it to you? Tried to talk to you about it, even casually?"

"No. She hasn't mentioned anything about me working on it. I need...fuck. I need to talk to Bryn."

"Okay, Jameo. But don't take too long. It is a time-bound offer."

Chapter Twenty-Seven

Jameson

I turn the corner from the hallway, trying to hide my confusion and failing miserably as I have to force myself to unclench my jaw and focus on the words coming at me.

"What did Jon want, dear?" Mom asks.

"Uhm. There is a time-sensitive commercial deal he wanted to get in front of me." I take a deep breath, moving to sit back down next to Bryn. I don't think she is behind this. We've come a long way in the trust department in such a short amount of time, though I do know how important this campaign is to her. That fact is the little worm that just keeps niggling the back of my brain. The only reason I can't fully say I trust she isn't behind this.

"Oh, well, that's a good sign. I know you've been feeling a bit down about your future sponsorship prospects. I told you it would all turn around."

"Who's it with?" asks Lila.

"Uhm." I consider telling them all right then and there, just so I can better gauge Bryn's face, but it doesn't feel right. "A restaurant chain."

I watch Bryn's face intently as I announce it, but there's nothing suspicious about her tilted head and slightly raised eyebrows. She seems genuinely interested.

"Actually, I've really been hoping to show Bryn the backyard. Do you all mind if we head outside for a bit before dessert?" I ask.

There are nods and sures from the table, and I unconsciously grab Bryn's hand as she stands from the table. I consider dropping it, but I somehow need her reassuring touch even when it's her I need the reassurance from. Fuck, I hate this. I hate that Alexis is still making me question myself. I hate that if this were happening four years ago, I would've given Bryn the benefit of the doubt.

I lead her to my parents' porch swing, sitting down before dropping her hand.

"It's Hungry Guy."

She has a blank look on her face as she asks me, "What's Hungry Guy?"

"The commercial deal. It's with Hungry Guy." The color starts to drain from her slack face as I continue, "And, based on the details Jon provided during the call, it's *your* campaign. The one that's so important for you for the promotion."

She's still just staring at me, and I'm starting to feel like she didn't know about this at all.

"The 'online ordering system' one?" she asks.

"Yup."

She rubs her temples, her breathing picking up. "What the actual hell?"

"Look, I'm sorry, but I have to ask: Did you know about this?" She's back to staring at me with a blank expression, so I continue, "Because they came in with a really low offer. And it's not that I wouldn't want to help you out, but I just... I would've wanted to talk about it before you—" I cut off as she stands, a look of pure fury on her face.

"Goddamn Kyle."

"What?" I ask, feeling even more confused than I did before.

"It had to be Kyle." She's pacing the porch in front of me now, two steps one direction, two steps back.

"So you didn't know?" I ask. "I recognize I'm likely not focused on the correct portion of this conversation, but I could just really use your confirmation on this."

She sits down heavily next to me, her hand finding mine. "I'm sorry, Jameson. I jumped right into focusing on me and what this means for my job." She looks me square in the eye. "No, I did not know until this very conversation."

"Right," I say. "I want to believe you. I *do* believe you. But I also have put my trust in the wrong person before, so this feels...scary."

She sighs. "I understand, Jameson. I guess the silver lining is that I can say, without a doubt, that this is actually going to completely derail my promotion plans." Her eyes are scanning the ground in front of her, clearly trying to solve a problem I haven't even begun to understand yet.

"What do you mean? You bringing in a professional golfer to the campaign can only help you, right?"

She scoffs. "You'd think. Unfortunately, no. Hungry Guy had a problem a few years ago with a campaign director sleeping with one of the actresses and getting her crazy-good terms on the agreements. Ever since then, they've had a strict policy about fraternizing with our large-dollar contracts. If you take the deal, I'll have to report our relationship to HR and will be replaced on the team."

"Well, shit." It's not the most eloquent, but it's all I can think to say. She's been working so hard on this. "I'm sorry I even had a little bit of doubt."

"It's not your fault, Jameson. I understand why you would ask. It's not like you knew that this would all but guarantee Kyle getting the promotion."

"What if I just say no? Turn down the offer?" I ask, back on Team Bryn.

"No—"

"I don't need the money," I cut in. "Sponsorships at this point are just a way for me to feel like I'm back on top again. That people believe in me."

Her lip quirks up at the side, a sad smile that I can't help but lean over and kiss lightly.

"I don't think that will work," she says once I pull away.

"Why not?"

"Clearly, someone—who am I kidding?—clearly, *Kyle* knows about us. You're an amazing golfer, and you're going to be highly sought after again very soon, but—and please don't take this wrong—it's too much of a coincidence for this to just be about you."

If I ever meet Kyle, I'm going to break his fucking nose. "So Kyle is a douche who happens to know about us and made a play to get you kicked off the project. Luckily, he underestimated how much I care about you. I would gladly give up a quarter million dollars for you to get this promotion."

Her nose crinkles in displeasure. "That's all they offered you? Don't you normally get, like...twice that much?"

I shrug. "I said it was a lowball offer. I truly am happy to give it up."

She leans her head on my shoulder, and I wrap my arm around her. "Unfortunately, I don't think that will help my case. If you don't do it, then I'm the person who wasn't willing to put the company ahead of herself. The one who convinced her boyfriend not to do a campaign—for a steal, might I add—all so she could stay on the team. That won't look good when considering who to give a promotion to either."

"Well...fuck," I say, pulling her more closely into my side.

"Yeah, you're telling me."

I slowly stroke my finger up and down her arm. "I can take a couple of days, do you want me to wait? See if you can figure something out?"

"Maybe? I don't know," she says, her voice trembling. "Actually"—she sits up abruptly—"I might have a plan."

CHAPTER TWENTY-EIGHT

BRYN

"So I DO NEED you to wait to accept until at least tomorrow. Monday would be best."

Jameson nods. "Okay, I can definitely do that. I don't even really want to accept it anymore."

"No, you've got to." *Oh, shit.* "I mean, you obviously don't *have* to. It's just the only way that my plan works. You should do whatever is right for you and your career."

"B, I'm in. Whatever this plan is."

I outline my plan. I know I can't fight the fraternization rule. It's too risky, especially with how high-profile of a guy Jameson is. I might not be getting what I want, but maybe I can take Kyle down with me.

When I finish, we nestle on the porch swing together, Jameson throwing his arm around my shoulders again as I lean into him. "I mean, it's not as diabolical as him somehow getting you to recuse yourself from the promotion project, but I like it," he says, giving the side of my head a kiss.

We sit there in silence for a few minutes before I say, "I really enjoyed celebrating with your family today. Thanks again for inviting me."

"Of course. I'm so glad you could make it. Usually, it's just me stuck playing peacekeeper between Lila and JT."

I slide my hand into his. "You think that they hate each other...?" I don't want to give anyone's secrets away, but it sure seems like there is something more going on there.

He scoffs. "Oh, yes. Most definitely. Deep animosity between those two."

"Hmm," I reply.

His hands are warm in mine, his thumb slowly rubbing circles on the inside of my wrist as he says, "You know, I was thinking during dinner that maybe it's time for me to sell my Florida house."

"Really? Why?"

He kisses my forehead, my absolute favorite gesture. It's just so...selfless. "It's full of bad memories. And Florida made sense when I bought the place, but now it's just"—he pauses, staring out into the yard—"a long way from all the people I love."

"I kinda forget that you actually live in Florida. I always think of you like me, a bit of a nomad who just travels around, no permanent residence."

"It's not wrong. I may have had a house in Florida, but it was never really a home. It was basically an Airbnb I paid a lot of money to store my stuff at. But I also don't really think of you as a nomad. Sure, you don't have a house or an apartment, but you have a home. Your life is in Wild Bluffs."

That's true. My life is in Wild Bluffs. My sisters are there. My parents are there. But there has always been something that has held me back from pulling the trigger on making it permanent.

"Sure," I say. "For now, at least."

"Do you ever think about settling down? Buying a house in Wild Bluffs?"

I'm not opposed to settling down. If I had a reason to slow down my travel schedule, I would, but up until this point, I haven't had a good reason to. And I don't want to put the pressure of being my reason to put down roots on Jameo. He has to travel just as much as I do, if not more.

So I hedge, replying, "I'm not opposed to it. It's just never made sense with my life so far."

We sit in companionable silence for a bit before I ask, "Will you buy a new house? Or try out the nomad life for a while?"

He shrugs his strong shoulders. "I'm not sure yet. How would you feel if I just fly to wherever you are between my tournaments?"

I think about the flight schedule, airport drop-offs, and logistics of it all before finally answering, "Chaotic?"

He laughs. "I'm kidding. I'm not actually planning on following you around the country every week. But I would love to get to see you more. And it doesn't make sense for me to be flying back and forth to Florida when I hate it there, anyway."

"I would love to see you more too." With that, I lean in, kissing the strong column of his neck. He reaches up, his thumb stroking my cheek as he moves my mouth to his and immediately deepens the kiss.

Our tongues tangle, and a spark ignites deep in my core, sending a shiver down my spine.

"Shit. Are you cold?"

"No." I kiss him again. "Definitely not cold."

A smug smile crosses his face, and he leans in, kissing me again before moving down, peppering my neck with hot kisses. I groan, unable to stop myself.

Making his way back up my neck, he leans into my ear, whispering softly, "You're so sexy." He glances down, swallowing deeply as he stares at my cleavage. "This dress makes your chest look fucking amazing." As if he's unable to resist himself, his hand reaches up, the back of his fingers tracing the side of my breast. His eyes shutter, and his mouth captures mine again.

My senses are overloaded by the taste of his tongue, the warmth of his body pushing me backward on the swing, the strength of his arm keeping me upright. His other hand traces the curve of my side, touching me everywhere.

And suddenly, he's gone.

"Lila!" he groans, his eyes locked on the door over my shoulder. "Why are you always such a cockblock?"

Mortified at being caught making out like a couple of teenagers, I make sure the girls are where they are supposed to be in my top and discreetly tug the bottom of my dress down off my upper thighs.

Lila crosses her arms. "Mom was going to come get you guys for dessert, but I, being the kind, benevolent, *helpful* sister that I am, offered to do it instead. Next time I'll just let Mom catch the two of you playing tonsil hockey."

"Thanks, Lila. I don't know if I could've ever shown my face in your house again if your mom had caught us," I say, grimacing at the thought of Lori catching us.

"Well, I can see how you thought no one would see you out here. It's *clearly* a very secluded spot."

I feel the heat rise to my cheeks again. "Feedback noted."

"Come on, Bryn, let's head in. Jameson"—she covers her eyes as I catch sight of the noticeable bulge in his jeans—"clearly needs a minute to get himself composed."

I shoot a look at Jameson, as if to say "Well, turns out it *could* get more awkward."

He just closes his eyes and shakes his head, his chest lifting with a deep breath.

"You know, that is actually fairly mild for the various positions I've interrupted my brother in." Lila leads me inside, happy to carry on a one-sided conversation. "He always wanted to be invisible as a kid, and I sometimes wonder if he doesn't think he actually is when he's getting busy. It's like it's always a surprise to him that our family might actually, ya know, move around the house and, *gasp*, be able to see him groping his girlfriend."

I continue to follow her back into the dining room. "That seems...awkward for you."

"Oh, it is. But I've decided to just move past it. I just hope he never returns the favor someday and catches me with someone. That seems much worse."

Someone coughs from the table, and we both stop talking to stare at JT as he chokes on his water.

"Are you okay?" I ask.

He waves his hand, signaling he's fine, and Lila just rolls her eyes as she flounces over and plops herself in the seat next to him.

"Come on there, big boy. I know it seems hard at first, but drinking water isn't so hard. I believe in you."

He lifts his middle finger as he takes a couple gulps of air.

"Worried about getting caught with someone, Lila?" he questions when he can breathe again.

"I would only worry about getting caught with someone if I were ashamed to be with them, JT," she fires back.

They both sit there, glaring at each other well past the normal mark.

"Well..." I drawl. "This has been...awkward. I'm going to go...somewhere else." I stand back up, heading for the kitchen to see if I can help Lori bring the cookies in for dessert before I have to leave for my flight in an hour.

Chapter Twenty-Nine

BRYN

"I KNOW, IT REALLY has been a whirlwind romance." I think about Jameson kissing me before I sprinted from the car, late for my flight home last night, and I feel a real smile crowd the fake one off my face.

"He's truly the best. I'm just so glad I could convince him to take the lowball offer the marketing team put in front of him." This is the fifth time today that I've had a conversation like this one, all strategically with or within the earshot of the company gossips.

As soon as my plane landed last night, I emailed the head of the Human Resources department, letting her know I needed to come in and speak with her first thing this morning. No way am I going to let Kyle win on a technicality. Then I got to work spreading the news. To be clear, I'm not lying; I really was the one who convinced Jameson to take the offer. Now, would I normally be so vocal about it? No, most certainly not. But fuck you, Kyle. Jameson is fully on board with the plan, so I have absolutely zero qualms about stealing Kyle's thunder.

Since Jameson hasn't officially accepted the offer yet, Kyle hadn't said anything to claim this victory as his. So, when I arrived at the office hours early this morning, it was only my version of the story that got spread. And, while today is a chaotic day at work, I've made sure to share my version of the story whenever possible.

Jameson's chuckle reverberates from where I hold the phone to my ear. I had been updating him on Operation Fuck You, Kyle when Alex, the company's biggest gossip, strolled by the bench where I'm eating my lunch. Luckily, I was prepared to get right to the good part.

"You're conniving," Jameson whispers in my ear.

"I know. It *is* hard to have to give up my place on the team, but it's what's best for the company!" I reply.

"Is it weird that I'm getting turned on right now?"

"Trust me, he's hotter in person. There's no doubt he's going to make this campaign an absolute success, which is why it's so ridiculous that Kyle thought he could get him for half of his usual rate. Thank God I was there to save the day."

"Yeah, you and that fuckable mouth."

"Well, anyway, I better let you go," I say with forced cheerfulness, my legs clenching together at the thought of his cock in my mouth. "I'm sure you've got...*things* to take care of."

I chuckle at his deep groan, hanging up the phone before either of us say something that will make it very clear I'm not casually talking to a work colleague.

Chapter Thirty

Jameson

I'VE SPENT THE LAST two weeks fully focused on my game. The tournament in the Bahamas last weekend was the last one until after the holidays, and I had to do well to guarantee a spot in the tournaments in the new year.

After spending a week practicing with my coach and JT down in the Bahamas before the tournament started, I was on top of my game all four days. It felt great to get my groove back, especially after I sank a chip on Sunday that clinched the win for me. I'm riding a high from the win for sure.

The only thing bringing me down is that Bryn's not here. I know other athletes, "real athletes" as Lila would call them, who brag about or bemoan the post-game adrenaline that essentially begs your body to find someone to fuck and fuck hard.

It's not quite as aggressive for golfers. Games are slower paced, and your adrenaline isn't getting pumped through you from beginning to end. But, let me assure you, when you're tied going into eighteen on Sunday and have to chip in your ball from ten yards off the green, your adrenal glands get the fuck to work.

And when your girl isn't there to celebrate with you...well, it's not preferable. Luckily, Bryn was watching from her hotel in Canada and FaceTimed me as soon as I hit the locker room.

I can still hear the way her voice dropped when my face filled her screen, her breath catching as she said, "Hey, sexy."

Refusing to hang up with her beautiful face and miss out on the intoxicating effects of her presence, I took her with me during my entire post-round routine. Yes, even the press conference and the following interview with ESPN. Did Bryn spend almost an hour staring at the darkness of my pocket? Yes, yes she did. And, in hindsight, I see how she could've just watched me on TV and then called me back as soon as I was done, but I asked her to stay, and she did.

As I left the course, Bryn's face remained on my phone, held directly in front of mine as my driver for the weekend headed to the hotel. She entertained me with her thoughts about the round, what I did well, what she thinks I could do better, Izzy's thoughts on the various players' attire. We talk essentially every night now, and we never miss a night before one of my rounds. I'm not superstitious enough to say she's my good luck charm, but I do believe in routine, and lying in bed, talking with Bryn the night before a round, is by far the best part of my new routine.

Hell, she's the best part of my life right now, something I've never felt about a woman before. Even when things with Alexis were good, golf was always my highlight. I lived for the tournaments, for spending time out on the course in Florida, working with my coach or my caddie. Now, I still enjoy playing, but I can't wait to be done so I can talk to Bryn, even if it's just sending her a text because I know she's in meetings all day.

I don't love her, of course not. It's way too early to be throwing around phrases like that, but damn, it might be close. I've never felt like this with anyone else. It's like my life is the tide, and she is the moon. No matter how far away she is, without even trying, she impacts every move I make, every thought I think.

Which is how I came to be in Denver this weekend, standing in the concourse at the DIA arrivals to surprise Bryn with a weekend together.

Bryn

Just landed! How goes the time with Ryan?

Ryan, who's been my caddie for the last four years, and I have been in Arizona the last two days, playing golf from sunup to sundown. We were supposed to be there all this weekend as well, but when Ryan mentioned he might be coming down with a cold this morning, I jumped at the excuse to cancel the rest of the trip. Health is very important. And fuck, do I need to see my girl.

Me

Call me when you get to the main terminal.
I have something I want to show you.

Bryn

Is it going to be a dick pic? You know how I feel about airport dick pics.

Me

I said call. Obviously I would just send you that as a picture, hence the name dick PIC.

Wait, are you saying you'd be up for dick FaceTimes if they aren't in the airport?

BRYN! Inquiring minds need to know the answer.

And now I have a half-stiffy thinking about us using FaceTime for sexy time.

Update, it's now a full-on erection.

My phone buzzes, Bryn's FaceTime coming through.

"Hey, babe!" My smile is so large, my cheeks can barely hold on to it.

"Hey, sexy—where are you?" I hear her voice, both over my earbuds and from the group just getting off the escalator in front of me.

I pull my hat down, confirming I'm as incognito as possible, and shout, "Bryn!"

I see her then, pulling her navy-blue carry-on behind her as she scans the room. I start making my way toward her, reminding myself not to run. "Bryn!"

She sees me, and fuck if her smile doesn't make me light up like a goddamn suburban house at Christmastime. I reach her in three more steps and pull her into a tight hug, kissing the top of her head before nuzzling her fully against my body.

"Hey, Jameo," she whispers into my chest. "I missed you."

I tighten my arms around her, not able to let her go yet. "I missed you, too, baby."

After far too short of a time, in my opinion, she pulls back, flashing me another brilliant smile. "What are you doing here? You're supposed to be in Arizona."

I shrug, pulling her in again for a chaste kiss on the lips, ever aware that someone could recognize me at any time. "I missed you."

"So you're here for the...night?"

"Nope. The whole weekend. If you're good with it, I actually got us a room at The Brown Palace downtown, thinking maybe we could spend the weekend together?"

"That sounds amazing. Let me just shoot Kelsey a text to make sure she's good to watch Jack for a few more days, but I'm sure Izzy or my dad can always go grab him if not."

We make our way out of the airport, walking in the below-freezing temperatures to reach her car in the outdoor parking lot.

"When am I going to get to meet your parents, anyway?" I ask.

She pops her shoulders. "Whenever you want to. You'll like them. They're genuinely fun people to be around. A lot like your folks, actually."

"Maybe next week?"

"I'm sure they're around." We take a few more steps before she stops. "Wait, are you saying you'll be in Wild Bluffs next week?"

I take advantage of the stop to pull her into a deeper kiss, reveling in her warmth. Finally, I pull away, saying, "Yep. The realtor thought it would be best if I was out of my house completely so he could stage it, so I figured I might as well grab a room out at WBCC. I'm actually planning on basing out of there until after the New Year."

She laughs, jumping into my arms and pressing her mouth against mine. I catch her, wrapping my arms around her hips, and pull her tighter to me. "So you're not annoyed that I'm going to be around for a month?"

Pulling back, she wraps my face in her ice-cold hands. "I truly think the only way it could be better was if I had my own place so we could stay together."

Her eyes widen as if that was a confession she hadn't been prepared to make. I lean down, softly biting her lower lip, before I lean back so I can look into her eyes. "You could stay with me. Waking up next to you for a month sounds...fucking amazing, B."

She slides down out of my arms, leading me again to wherever she parked her car.

"Why don't you park in the covered parking?" I ask when it's clear she's not ready to respond to my invite to essentially live with me for a month—an invite I had not been planning to make, but one I in no way regret.

"Have you seen how much it costs to park in covered parking?! My car is just fine out here, thank you," she says, pulling out a travel-sized hand sanitizer and squeezing a dollop onto her palm.

I honestly have no idea how much it costs to park at an airport, in covered parking or not, so I choose to remain silent.

"There it is." She points to the black Tesla along the back row of the airport parking lot.

"Lucky you were able to find a spot so close," I say sarcastically.

I swear I can hear her eyes roll as we both climb into the car.

"It appears I may have done something to upset the parking gods. Perhaps a ritualistic sacrifice is in order." She looks me up and down. "Eh, probably not their first choice, but you'll do."

I pretend to be offended. "I'll do?!" I throw my arms up. "The parking gods would be lucky to receive such a fine specimen as a sacrifice."

She chuckles.

"Plus, it's not like we've got a virgin readily available to sacrifice. Those are hard to come by these days."

When she doesn't laugh or play along, I turn from the window to look at her. Her knuckles are white, she's gripping the wheel so hard, and she's working her bottom lip with her teeth.

"What just happened, B?" I reach over and rest my hand on her thigh, giving it a light squeeze.

She glances at me out of the corner of her eye. "There's..." She bangs her head against the headrest. "Ugh. There's something I probably need to tell you."

Fuck. Fuckity fuck. This definitely does not seem good.

I clear that thought, trying to dislodge the huge lump of fear that landed in my brain. "Um. Okay. You can tell me anything."

That sounded...good. Normal. That's a normal response, right?

Bryn keeps her eyes focused on the road, slowing the car as we wait to merge onto the highway. I give her space to think, trying to tell my pounding heart that it's not going to be something bad. She's not going to confess to cheating on me. She hasn't been banging random Canadian hockey players all week.

"I'm..." She massages the middle of her forehead with one hand. "Fuck it. I'm a virgin."

She finally turns her head to look at me, but I'm actually in shock. She's a virgin? How? She's twenty-eight. She has had past boyfriends. Sure, we haven't gotten into our past dating lives or our sex partner count, but...we've fooled around. How has this not come up? Wait, do I actually care?

"So...yup. I could be the sacrifice if we decide that's the route we need to take. Actually, if you're going to just continue to sit there with that stunned look on your face, just do me a favor and kill me now. No sacrificial altar needed."

Damn it, I'm not handling this right.

"B. I don't care. I mean, I do care. But it also doesn't change anything."

Her eyes dart my way again, and I can see the lights reflecting off the tears pooling along her lower eyelids.

"Fuck, baby. Don't cry. I'm sorry. I know I'm not saying the right thing. I'm just surprised, is all. You're a smoke show and are so confident both in life and in the bedroom. It just seems...out of character, I guess."

She finally releases the steering wheel with her right hand to wipe at her eyes, and I reach out and grab it, pulling it to my lips before setting it in my lap.

"Can I—can I ask some clarifying questions?"

"Clarifying questions? What is this? An interview?"

"B..."

"Fine. Ask your questions."

"Are you saving yourself for marriage?"

She shakes her head, letting out a wet laugh. "No."

"Then, why...?"

She shrugs. "It just kinda happened. I was friends with all the guys in my 200-person high school, so no way was I ever going to hook up with one of them. Then, in college, I dated a little bit, but I was so focused on doing well and keeping my scholarship that I wasn't willing to risk even the tiny percentage of a chance of getting pregnant unless I was in a fully committed relationship. And I never was. After college, I dated Peter and, well, he did believe in waiting until marriage—or, his mom believed in waiting until marriage, and he could never disappoint her—so we did other things, but never did go all the way."

"And since then?" he asks.

"And since then, I'm sorta back to where I was in high school. All the single guys in Wild Bluffs are the same dorks I went to high school with. I've been on a few dates with randos from an app when I'm traveling for work, but I've never liked anyone enough to see them more than a couple of times...before you."

She's biting her lip again, and fuck if I don't want to make her pull over so I can just hold her. Let her know that this doesn't change anything.

I'm not sure what to say, so I just go with the first thing that comes to mind. "Makes sense."

She rolls her eyes, dislodging a few of the remaining tears. I reach over, carefully wiping them off her cheeks as she continues to navigate us to our hotel.

"I'm not sure I'm allowed to ask this, but...does that mean you do like me enough to consider it?"

She sniffs. "Always fishing for compliments..."

I chuckle as she continues, "I mean, yeah. And, for the record, I had considered—planned on, really—not telling you. It's never been a big deal to me, and I didn't want it to be for us. But Izzy has been on me to tell you, and then it felt like a sign when virgins randomly came up in conversation."

"You weren't going to tell me you were a virgin? You were just going to...going to..."

"Have sex with you like a normal person? Yes, that was my plan. It's not like I'm unaware of how it works."

My dick, with its selective hearing, is only picking up on the fact that she was planning on having sex with us and is now hard as a rock.

"Yeah," I reply. "But it just feels like I should've known. So I could make it...special?"

"So you're saying that, had I not been a virgin, your performance would've been average at best? But now that you know you're my first, you feel you need to put some effort into it?"

I shake my head. "Nope. Of course not. I have no doubt in my mind that every time I fuck you, every thrust, every moan out of your mouth, will be fucking perfection. I just could've"—I run my hand through my hair—"gotten flowers or something?"

She laughs. At least she's enjoying how awkward I'm making this. "Oh, really, is that what you got when you lost your virginity?"

I chuckle too. "Nope. Gave myself a nice high five for a job well done. Though, in hindsight, it wasn't deserved. It was awkward, with a lot of fumbling around."

"Well, I promise to let you give me a high five after you fuck me for the first time, but I expect you to keep the awkward fumbling to a minimum." And with that, she focuses back on the road, successfully navigating us around the streets of downtown to our hotel like she didn't just drop a huge bomb and then asked me not to act like nothing had changed.

CHAPTER THIRTY-ONE

BRYN

THAT WENT...WELL. BETTER THAN expected. He didn't throw himself out of the car, roll into the landing, and jump back up, sprinting in the opposite direction. Not that I really thought he would do that...probably.

We've reached the point in our relationship that, even before he surprised me with a weekend at one of the nicest hotels in Denver, having sex is definitely on the table. A place I desperately want it to be.

I pull my car into the parking lot across from the hotel and hit the button to turn it off. I'm pulling my bag out of the back seat when I notice Jameson hasn't moved. I stick my head in through the back door and ask, "You okay in there?"

He nods a couple times before replying, "Yup." He looks at the dark parking lot. "Wait. Why are we parked here?"

"Oh, instead of dying of mortification, I thought it'd be easier to just have us murdered. This seemed like a good spot. Now grab my computer bag. They aren't going to try to kill you if you don't look like you have something worth stealing."

His look clearly says "That's not funny," but regardless of what he thinks, I know I'm hilarious.

I roll my eyes and grab the bag instead. "Come on, princess. The hotel is across the street."

"Why would you not use valet parking?"

I look between the hotel half a block away and his face. "Because we are basically at the hotel now and it will cost half of what it does to valet."

I grab his hand and start pulling him toward the hotel.

"Yeah, but I'm supposed to be treating you this weekend." He shoots me a glare. "*Princess,* I can afford valet."

"So can I. It just seems silly to waste money on it, no matter how much you make, when there is a perfectly good parking lot right here."

"Will we also be getting dinner from the 7-Eleven I can see down the block?"

I flip my hair over my shoulder. "No, you may treat me to fine dining. Though, shit. I only have my work clothes, which are basically all dirty and are definitely all too casual for someplace nice... Oh! I know. We can just go to the Ship Tavern. It's a more casual place inside The Brown Palace that I went to a few times for special occasions during college."

I look down at my attire. "This should be fine for that. Maybe tomorrow we can hit up the 16th Street Mall so I'll have something for dinner then. Unless, of course"—I squeeze his hand—"you're reconsidering the weekend?" The note of uncertainty that laces the question detracts from the calm exterior I'm trying to put on.

He stops, turning me to face him as we approach the hotel. "Definitely not reconsidering anything, B. Just got caught a little off guard, is all, and now I'm unsure if saying 'who needs clothes, we can order room service all weekend' like I want to is pushing you into something you don't want."

"You know," I say as I start walking into the revolving door, "I've always been a fan of room service."

Jameson catches back up to me once we enter the lobby, the sound of his steps echoing off the marble floors. The atrium lobby, with balconies surrounded by railings rising eight floors aboveground, is a flashback to a historic time of lavish parties and decadence. A grand piano sits on one side, a pianist softly playing elevator music. All around, people are chatting on plush chairs and sofas or enjoying happy hour at the small tables spread throughout the place.

"Here, let me take the bags," he offers, reaching for my backpack.

I let him take it, handing him my suitcase as well. "About time you started acting like a gentleman. What would Lori say?"

He leans into my side, his warm breath tickling my ear as he whispers, "I have no plans on acting like a gentleman tonight, and let's just go ahead and leave my mom as far away from here as possible, okay?"

I huff out a laugh, my blood pressure spiking from his nearness and the promise in his statement.

Jameson leads us to the elevators, telling me he checked in before coming to meet me at the airport. We ride to the top, and I follow Jameson to our room. He opens the door, pushing it open to reveal the extravagant suite he booked for us. I look at him, surprise in my eyes, and he smiles, clearly pleased with himself.

"This is...wow."

"Cathy informs me this is the Beatles Suite."

I haven't had a chance to meet Cathy, Jameson's virtual assistant, yet, but she does a damn good job of keeping Jameson and his life in order.

I point to the picture of the four band members hanging on the wall. "Ahh, that would explain the picture." I turn and look at the glowing box next to the door. "And the jukebox."

Throwing my coat in a corner, I plop down on the couch, turning on the TV. "Oo, I hope *Friends* is on."

"You have an addiction, you know."

I glare at him. "I only watch it when I'm in hotels!"

"You're in hotels more than I am, which is saying something with how much I have to travel for golf, so saying you only watch it in your hotel room is basically like saying you watch it all the time."

I shrug, finding an episode on the menu. "It's like comfort food but for my eyes and ears."

Jameson joins me on the couch, resting his crossed feet on the white oval coffee table and throwing his arm over my shoulders. I snuggle into him, sighing as I rest my arm across his strong stomach.

"This is amazing. I'm glad you're here."

He kisses the top of my head, and butterflies take off inside my core. "There's literally nowhere I'd rather be."

We sit like that, cuddling, until the end of the episode, when my stomach decides to make its displeasure known. At the rumble that emanates from it, Jameson raises an eyebrow. "Starving?"

"Well, I was promised room service..."

He reaches for the phone. "That you were." Jameson orders us both cheeseburgers and fries from the hotel's kitchen, throwing in a milkshake for us both to share as an afterthought. He hangs up, sitting back on the couch, and letting me know it's going to be about an hour until the food arrives.

"You know what else you owe me?"

He scrunches his brow, thinking. "No. What else do I owe you?"

"A high five," I say as I rise from the couch, moving to straddle his lap. Kissing him softly, I weave my hands through his hair.

"B," he groans, breaking the kiss. "I'm going to ask you this one time and then we will move on from it, together, no matter the answer. Are you sure this, now, with me, is what you want?"

I nod, but he reaches out, forcing my chin up so I'm looking in his eyes. "Is this what you want?"

"Yes." I swallow hard. "I want this. Now. With you. I haven't been saving myself for you, just to be clear, but somehow, God, or Zeus, or the Supreme Ruler knew that this—us—was going to be worth the wait."

A dangerous smile tugs at his lips. "Good."

Releasing a dark chuckle of my own, I press myself against him, sparks igniting at each point of contact. I can feel the heat emanating from his body against mine and I arch into him, eager for more. He wraps his arms around me, gripping my ass like it's the only thing keeping him tethered to the earth.

The movement brings us fully together, the size of his arousal apparent. I knew, logically, how big he was since Vegas, but seeing it again? *Jesus Christ. This...might hurt.* My eyes roll back as his bulge comes in contact with my swollen clit, unable to stop the guttural moan that escapes my lips. He consumes the sound as I roll my hips against the contact of his erection, my mind floating away as my body demands I do it again and again.

"Fuck, B." He raises his lustful eyes to mine, almost black with need. "I'm trying to go slow over here."

I blink once, bringing myself back into my body. "Not me." I disentangle myself from him and stand, pulling my shirt over my head. I nod toward the bedroom, but the look in his eyes tells me he's about to protest.

"Please?"

With a feral surge, he picks me up, and I wrap my legs around him. He walks us into the next room, gripping my thighs like I'm the only thing holding him back from going over the edge. Once we are inside, he presses me against the wall, and I arch my back as his hand works the clasp of my bra. When it pops open, I slip my arms out, and he buries his face in my chest.

"I fucking love your tits. They're perfect."

My head drops back to the wall as I continue to roll my hips, seeking the contact I so desperately need. He tortures me, taking his time, kissing every inch of my boobs as he pinches and rolls my nipples until

I'm on fire. I need him to touch me. To ease the aching need between my legs.

I drop my feet to the ground, reaching forward and pulling his shirt off before attacking his belt buckle like its existence is personally offensive to me.

Pushing my trembling fingers to the side, Jameson undoes his pants with controlled ease, freeing his straining cock. I lick my lips as he throws them on top of my shirt and bra, a move that makes his dick jump in his briefs.

He stalks toward me, his eyes threatening dark things, and I smirk, daring him to fulfill that promise, to fuck me hard and rough.

When he reaches my side, he whispers in my ear, "This time, and this time only, I will be gentle. After that, I will take you up on the offer that smile just made."

Pulling me to him, he palms my ass, his hands so big, they fit perfectly. He kisses me, his lips a hot brand on my mouth, my jaw, my neck. I groan, my hips seeking the contact that this position denies me.

"Get on the bed, B."

I nod and practically sprint to the bed, sitting on the edge of it. Jameson, on the other hand, takes his time, devouring me with his eyes as he stands there, too far from the bed for me to reach.

"Good girl."

My body is on fire, and only he can control the burn. I take matters into my own hands, lifting my hips to push my jeans to the ground. He licks his lips, watching my thong-clad pussy as it lifts and drops back to the mattress.

"Jesus," he sighs, and my head falls back to the mattress as my hand moves to my breast, kneading and pinching. It's not like I've never done this for myself. And at this point, I am too far gone. I can't stop. If he is going to torture me, I'll just do it myself.

Suddenly, Jameson is there, hovering over me, his hand replacing mine as he pinches and rolls my nipple. "So sexy," he hums against my lips before he devours them again.

He kisses down my body until he reaches my black thong. His eyes flick back up to my face, and I give him a small nod before he turns his attention back to my underwear, giving them a gentle tug and pulling them down my legs. His briefs quickly follow.

Buzz, buzz. "Jesus fucking Christ," Jameo mutters, searching for his phone. *Buzz, buzz.* When he finds it, he takes one look at the screen and angrily holds the side button, turning it completely off. "Fucking Lila has the goddamn worst timing in the fucking world." Then he turns his full attention back to me.

Jameson stands at the end of the bed, taking in the sight of me laid bare in front of him while I do the same, admiring his broad shoulders, his strong abs, and his thick dick standing proudly at attention. Noticing the direction of my attention, he grips the base of his cock, giving it a soft tug, his head falling back in pleasure.

Seeing him like this, the last remaining thread of my control snaps, and I close my eyes, my hand snaking between my legs, applying the pressure I so desperately need.

"Bryn." His voice is like steel, cutting through the fog of my arousal.

"Hmm?" I murmur.

"That. Is. Mine."

Wetness coats my fingers at his claim, and I look up to find him hovering over my pussy. Grabbing my hand, he brings my fingers into his mouth, sucking my slick off with a groan.

Then he pins my hands by my hips as he nudges my knees apart with his legs. Sinking onto his haunches, he buries his head in my pussy, his tongue flicking my aching clit.

I gasp, the tight pressure of my orgasm flickering to life at the base of my core.

He licks my pussy, his tongue savoring my taste before plunging it into me, his middle finger circling my clit, coaxing a whimper from my lips. I ride his face as the mounting orgasm builds, and hearing my moans, he slips two fingers inside of me, curling them forward to stroke my core until I'm trembling with pleasure, gripping handfuls of the comforter beneath us.

"I'm about to—" I thrash my head to the side, trying to piece my fracturing mind back together to remember what words are. "Come," I grit out as, suddenly, he's gone.

I lift my head, watching from under hooded eyes as he finds his wallet and pulls out a condom. I reach down, my finger finding my clit as Jameo rips the top off with his teeth.

"Tell me," he hisses as he rolls the condom down his thick shaft, "if I go too fast."

I nod, and he lowers himself slowly over me, his thick shoulders bulging as he strains with the effort of it.

"Fuck me, Jameo," I whine.

"B, I... I'm not sure I can go slow."

"I don't"—I thrust my hips up, connecting with his straining erection—"want slow." I bite his lower lip, tasting a hint of blood as I pull away.

He lets out a huff of air as his hips lower, so fucking slowly, toward the molten lava center of my core.

I wiggle, trying to push myself up higher, but he clicks his tongue. "Slowly, B."

"Ugghhh—" My protest is cut off by the feel of his thick length sliding home, filling me.

He pauses, giving me a second to adjust to his size before slowly continuing in, inch by inch. As he makes one final push that leaves him fully seated inside me, he hits a spot deep inside me that makes my pussy clench around him.

"Oh, fuck, B. Oh, fuck."

Jameson starts moving, pumping in and out of me in a rhythm that tightens the coil inside me with each movement. As he thrusts, his hot lips find mine, his kisses promising an ecstasy beyond any I've felt before.

Before I know it, my orgasm has built back to its peak, my legs shaking with the need to jump headfirst over the ledge.

I break the connection between our lips, panting, "Jameo. I'm—I'm there. I'm..."

He grips my ass, increasing his speed as he grunts, "Just...about...there."

The change in angle causes him to hit that spot inside me, and I fall over the edge, a moan bursting from my lips as I clench around his hard length still pumping in and out of me.

CHAPTER THIRTY-TWO

JAMESON

"Fuuuuck." Her pussy was tight before, but now, as her walls squeeze around me, the wetness of her orgasm coating my dick, I can't hold myself back. I pump in and out, my hips out of control as my own orgasm builds to unbelievable heights at the base of my spine.

I grip her ass, my fingers digging into her round perfection, as I angle her just right, hitting the exact tempo I've been craving.

My vision goes black as I come, my guttural roar filling the room.

I ride out what might be the strongest orgasm of my life, my hips continuing to pump until every last drop is spent. I drop my forehead to Bryn's, shifting my weight to my elbows as I breathe in her scent.

Her shuddering breath rumbles through me, jarring me back to my senses.

That was fucking perfection. I may truly be ruined for the rest of my life after that. If that is what she was like her first time...*oh, shit. That was her first time.*

"Oh my God. Bryn. Are you...?" I search for the answer to my unspoken question in her eyes. "Was that...okay?"

I'm so fucked. My dick springs back to attention, already ready to see what she's like now that she's gotten the first time out of her way. Or maybe that was beginner's luck. That has to be it. There is no possible way she can rock my world at that level repeatedly. I've been with plenty of women to know that's not a reasonable expectation to have.

She raises her eyebrow. "Is 'okay' how you would describe it?"

I love how feisty she is. I can assure you I was not that confident after losing my virginity, but she...she *should* be confident. That was amazing.

Shoving against my shoulder, she pushes me onto my back, slipping her leg over my waist to straddle me. Leaning forward, she pins my hands next to my head with hers and asks again, "Was that just okay for you?"

"Fuck, no." I strain upward and nip her lower lip. "That was"—I search for the words to describe how absolutely life-changing the last hour had been—"mind-blowing."

Her hot breath tickling my ear, she whispers, "Yeah, well, I'm inclined to agree. I'm not some blushing fifteen-year-old girl who has never had an orgasm before. I know what I like, and—not to inflate that already enormous ego of yours—but you delivered exactly that."

I know she told me not to let it inflate my ego, but, yeah, there's no way I'm not going to consider that the greatest compliment I've ever been given. Might even request it on my gravestone.

Realizing I'm still wearing the used condom, I roll Bryn off me and stand to go clean up. "I'm just going to take care of..." I gesture down at my still-hard penis. Then I look at her, an uncomfortable realization about virgins crossing my mind. "Wait, do you need to clean up? Is there"—I look at the white comforter and then back to her face, feeling my own cheeks heat—"blood?"

Smooth, Jameo. Real smooth. The women in my life would be so disappointed at how poorly I just handled that. Thank God they will never know.

"Oh, for Pete's sake," she scoffs. "Jesus, Jameo, this isn't the 1800s. As both a past athlete and a regular tampon-wearer, I have no doubt my hymen and I went our separate ways many, many years ago." She smirks at me as I walk away. "So don't try to get any of those cows you paid for me back from my father."

"I don't think that's how dowries worked," I comment over my shoulder as I head into the bathroom.

She throws one of the square blue pillows at my head. "You're right. Somehow, women were so worthless that their fathers had to *pay* for someone to marry them."

I tie the condom and throw it in the trash, letting the water heat before wetting a towel and bringing it out to Bryn.

"You know, I'd consider it...for the right number of cows, of course," I say, leaning in to kiss her.

Fuck, did I just offer to marry her for cows?

She smacks my ass, laughing, before pulling me back down until I'm fully covering her body with mine, exploring my mouth with hers.

We lie in bed, alternating between exploring each other's bodies and catching each other up on the little things until there is a knock at the door, our food finally arriving from room service.

We both jump up, grabbing robes from the closet before I yell, "Come in!"

Bryn heads into the bathroom to see to her needs as I head out into the living area, directing the dark-haired waitress where to leave our food tray. I slip her a generous tip, thanking her as she leaves.

As the door closes, Bryn slips into the living room, her hands tucked deep into the pockets of her robe. Settling down on the couch, she pulls her knees up next to her, resting her head back and closing her eyes.

"Dinner?" I ask.

"Always." She drops onto the couch, leaning over the coffee table where I've set up her meal.

We both dig in, eating in a comfortable silence while Monica and Chandler bicker about something in the background.

"So, you doing okay?" I ask around the bacon burger in my mouth.

Dipping a fry into our shared milkshake, she nods. "Yep. And truly, Jameo, you don't need to worry about me. Like I said, I wasn't even going to tell you about it until it happened to come up in conversation. If we could act like we've both slept with someone before, that would be great." She holds up a hand, emphasizing her point. "And I promise I'm not about to become a stage-five, virgin clinger."

I squint my eyes at her before guessing, "*Wedding Crashers*?"

"M-hm."

"Your extraordinary ability to quote movies aside, I feel like there are a couple of things to unpack in there."

"Can we not?"

I shake my head. "No, I feel we must. First, if you wouldn't have told me, I would've been really fucking offended. Honestly, I'm pretty offended that you continue to tell me that you weren't going to. You should be able to trust me, B. With anything." When she starts to cut in, I hold up two fingers. "Second, you haven't slept with someone before, so, no, we aren't going to act like it was just another hookup. I'm going to make sure you know that it was special. I am not taking it lightly that I was the one you decided was important enough to take that step with. Plus, it wasn't just sleeping with someone for me. It was sleeping with you for the first time, and that makes it really fucking special in my book. And third—" I hold up a third finger as Bryn leans back and groans, "Jesus."

"And third," I continue, "please be a clinger. Maybe not stage five, but, like, maybe stage two?"

She scrunches up her nose. "That was surprisingly sweet. And you're right, it would've been shitty of me not to tell you, but, honestly, it was always about me not feeling like it was a big deal, not about me not trusting you." She chews her food for a few seconds before adding, "It was pretty fucking great, wasn't it? That wasn't just because I don't have any other experience to compare it with?"

"Honestly?"

"No, please lie to me," she jokes before widening her eyes, a hint of fear seeping through. "Actually, maybe do lie to me."

"It was without a doubt the best sex I've ever had."

She blinks. "I'm not sure if it was a lie or not."

"Definitely not a lie."

She smirks, turning back to her dinner.

"You know," I say, "I wasn't joking earlier. When we're in Wild Bluffs, you should stay out with me instead of Kelsey."

She finishes chewing, contemplating her answer with an angle of her head. "Doesn't that feel like... Like actual clinger status? I'm 1000 percent in on this relationship, but we see each other one or two days every couple of weeks right now. Being on top of each other—"

I raise my eyebrows, causing her to roll her eyes.

"Not like that, you horndog," she teases. "Don't you think it would be a little too much too soon? I work from home. I'm around *all the time*. And you live in a hotel room. Where would I even take my work calls?"

I consider it. I really want to spend all my time with Bryn, but she's probably right. Moving into a hotel room together doesn't actually make sense.

"Okay, it might be a bit too much while I'm staying at the golf course. But can I still see you as much as humanly possible?"

A smile blooms on her face as she takes one last bite of her burger. "Deal. Now, are you ready for round two, or do you need a longer break, old man?"

"We are basically the same age!" I laugh before pulling her onto my lap and bringing her mouth down to meet mine.

CHAPTER THIRTY-THREE

BRYN

Me

> I think I may be addicted.

> To his penis.

> And his fingers.

> His tongue too.

Izzy

> Ugh. Now I'm jealous. And a bit turned on.

Me

> On that note, I'm out.

Chapter Thirty-Four

BRYN

"Have you figured out how you're going to steal that promotion from that asshat Kyle, Bryn?" Izzy asks from the kitchen.

"Isabel!" my mom chides.

"No. Not yet," I reply glumly. "I've got a few ideas of upgrades I can propose, but the best one would take a level of financing and outside coordination that I just don't have access to."

"I still think it's a brilliant idea," Izzy says. "I hate having to re-enter my specific order on all the different apps each time I try to get food. It would be so much more convenient if there was one that just knows what I want at each place. It's not like people actually change up their fast-food orders. At least, people who aren't psychopaths."

It's the last Sunday in December, and Jameson and I are over at my parents' for our weekly family dinner. Kelsey and Izzy are helping Mom in the kitchen while Jameson and I set the table. Dad has been keeping us all entertained by sharing random facts from that day's newspaper.

Sunday-night dinners with the family are part of the new routine Jameson and I have fallen into since we returned to Wild Bluffs tired, and, at least in my case, extremely sore from our weekend together in Denver. The man's body is addictive.

After we finished dinner that first night in Denver, we started round two out on the couch, which ended with me riding his face, his tongue wringing a level of pleasure out of me that I hadn't known existed. I, being the considerate partner that I am, had returned the favor by dropping to my knees and sucking him off right there in the living room.

After another round in the shower where he took me hard and fast from behind, we climbed into bed, and I slowly rode him, barely moving my hips until we both saw stars.

I'd woken up both mornings in Denver to his hard cock poking me in the back as he cuddled me from behind. I didn't care that he was sleeping, I was happy to indulge the silent demand from his erection—it *is* my favorite body part of his, after all.

Once back in Wild Bluffs, we spent as much time together as possible. Jameson joined Kelsey and me to watch whatever sporting event happened to be on most nights before we snuck up to my room to fool around or out to the golf course to spend the night in his room.

I would come back to Kelsey's or go to Izzy's office to work for the day. Jameo quickly learned he could buy my friends' and family's affection by bringing in lunch or cookies to wherever I was working that day. Needless to say, I've not been as productive in the last month as I would've liked, especially with the promotion growing ever closer.

Today is the first day Jameson has been back in town since the holidays, and we are enjoying the last bit of time we have together before he heads to Hawaii for the first tournament of the new year. I've already told my parents we have to head out right after dinner to head to a New Year's Eve party at the country club. They don't need to know that I have no intention of actually attending the party besides the obligatory stop-in from the celebrity-in-residence.

"Jameson!" my mom calls from where she stands, glaring at the top of her cupboards. "Could you come help me get down that bowl?"

Putting the last fork down on the table, Jameson heads toward my mom with casual steps. "Sure thing, Mrs. Harper."

Mom rolls her eyes good-naturedly. "Jen, Jameson. You can call me Jen."

Dad, the pain in the ass that he is, gruffly calls out, "Feel free to still call me Mr. Harper, young man."

I flip my dad the bird and he chuckles before putting his readers back on, hiding the twinkle in his eye. He leans down to rub their dog, JoJo, behind the ears before resuming his reading.

My parents were decently strict growing up. We always had curfews on the earlier side, and we were only allowed to go on group dates until we turned 16. But now that we're all grown, they've really relaxed. They're more like trusted advisers at this point than authority figures.

Jameson catches my exchange with my dad and shoots me a wink. "Yessir, Mr. Harper. I'd never dream of calling you anything else...sir."

My dad flashes me a "God save me from these people" look that I've seen him wear a thousand times before. It wasn't easy for him, being the only man in a house of women. It was especially hard when my sisters and I were seventeen, fifteen, and thirteen. I'm still traumatized by the fights we got into.

As we all sit down for dinner, Izzy asks, "So, Jameson, are you planning on playing in most of the Tour's events this year? Or will you be taking some of the tournaments off?"

He looks at me before replying, "I'll be at all of them at least through the Masters in April. After that, I'm hoping to be able to cut back to about two a month, but a lot of that will depend on how I'm doing."

Mom looks back and forth between me and Jameson. "That sounds like it might be...difficult."

She is not wrong. We've fallen into a rhythm of fun, fucking, and friendship. It has been amazing, but, as Jameson loaded up his suitcase to head to his parents' house for Christmas, it also hit me that it wasn't real life. At least, not what our real life would look like.

Jameson's career essentially has him on the road every weekend from January through August, and I travel almost every other week for my job. In a moment of minor freakout, I had texted Izzy and Becca about what to do, and their insightful guidance had been, to quote Becca, "Keep riding that train to pound town until something forces you to jump off."

And honestly, I'd taken her up on that advice. Jameson and I FaceTimed multiple times a day while he was with his family for Christmas, at least one of which led to us locking ourselves away to have phone sex. Making him come in person is a thrill, but watching him stroke his strong hand over his thick length while he watches me pleasure myself...damn. It made me glad my vibrator is rechargeable.

"Ahh." He runs a hand through his hair, clearly not missing her implied concern. "It will be busy, but I'm really looking forward to the couple that Bryn is going to get to join me at."

She turns her concern toward me. "Well, that's nice. Where will you be joining him? Anywhere fun?"

I twirl my spaghetti around my fork before replying, "Mom, he's a golfer. The only places they play are fun. It has to be warm and have enough rich people to warrant a fancy golf course. Professional golfers are kinda entitled babies who can't stand to be cold."

Jameson's hand finds my leg, squeezing tightly.

I cut my eyes toward him. "What?! It's true!" I can't keep my straight face and let out a laugh. "Fine," I acquiesce. "Jameson is not necessarily a baby when it comes to cold. But you should meet his friend JT. He rolled into Thanksgiving like it was the middle of a blizzard in northern Canada or something."

Izzy, clearly picking up on my distraction technique, pulls the conversation back to me with an evil grin on her face. Okay, maybe it isn't actually an evil grin, but I feel it is implied as she asks, "So how many of his tournaments are you going to get to go to, Bryn?"

"About one a month lines up with my schedule."

"Oh." My mom's voice echoes some of the devastation I'm doing my best not to acknowledge. "Well, that will be nice. And you all seem to enjoy talking on the phone, so I'm sure that will help."

Jameo squeezes my leg again, lighter this time, just letting me know he sees me. "I haven't had a chance to share this with Bryn yet, but I'm also hoping to rent one of the smaller cottages out at the country club for the foreseeable future as well. I got an offer on my house in Florida this afternoon, and it would be nice to have a home base to come back to in between everything."

I feel the side of my lip curling up into a small smile, hope filling my chest. Maybe, just maybe, we can make this thing work. The last month has been amazing, but dating a professional athlete of any kind is hard, and golfers travel more than most, with tournaments taking them across not just the United States but the world.

I reach down, giving Jameson's hand a tight squeeze of my own, noticing the pleased smile that lights up his face.

"That's great news," my mom responds when it's clear I'm not going to say anything about his announcement. "Please know we're always around if you need anything." She pauses before continuing, "I guess I didn't know you had listed your house in Florida."

"Yeah," Jameson responds. "I decided about a month ago that it was time for me to let it go. It just wasn't the right fit for me anymore."

"Are you looking to buy somewhere else?" Kelsey asks from her seat at the end of the table.

Jameson's eyes stray to mine before snapping back ahead. "I'm not sure yet. It feels like my life is a bit in flux right now, so I don't really plan on buying anything new until I know where I want to be."

"Ah, the nomadic lifestyle," my dad chimes in. "Sure is popular these days."

I reply cheekily, "All the cool kids are doing it, Dad. I actually peer-pressured Jameo into it by threatening him with a swirly."

"I think that's just called assault at that point, B, not peer pressure," Jameson jokes.

"Well," Kelsey says. "Bullying aside, I'm glad you've got a place at the club. I can't house any more wandering travelers. One nomad just dropping by my house whenever it pleases her is enough for me."

"Rude, Kelsey. I thought I was your favorite roommate."

"Nope. I just keep you around for Jack," she shoots back.

"It's tough when you lose out to a guy who drinks water from the toilet, but I respect your decision. He *is* cooler than me."

After dinner wraps up and we have to leave to head to WBCC, we give out hugs to my family, wishing them a happy New Year. Jameson hugs them all except my dad. As they shake hands, Izzy pulls me into a tight hug, whispering in my ear, "Never let the fear of striking out keep you from playing the game."

"Did you just quote *A Cinderella Story* to me?"

"Yup. Felt it applied. And, it turns out, it's actually a Babe Ruth quote." She glances over my shoulder at Jameo. "I'm just saying. I've never seen you as...grounded...as you've been the past month. Don't give up on that just because it's not going to be easy."

"Izzy, I'm not—"

She holds up her hands in defense. "I'm just saying, Bryn. Do with it what you will."

As we head for my car, I grab Jameson's hand, a slight skip in my step. Izzy is right. This might be hard, but we can definitely do it. And being with Jameson is worth it—he's worth the travel, the time apart, everything. I just hope he feels the same way about me.

CHAPTER THIRTY-FIVE

JAMESON

I NORMALLY AM NOT a huge fan of New Year's Eve, but this year, it feels like I really am starting a new chapter of my life. Last year started out as a total shit show, but if next year is anything like these last few months have been, it's going to be great.

Bryn drives to the front of the club and starts to pull into the normal parking lot. "Oh, not here," I say. "I've got the new cottage at the end of the road here. They said they'd leave it unlocked for me with the keys in it."

"Oh, yeah," she says. "I guess I didn't realize that you'd already started renting it. I can't believe you didn't tell me you were planning to move out here."

I shrug. "I just called about it earlier today." Which is true. But Bryn had been right a month ago when she said that we couldn't live together in a hotel room. And, in reality, our lives both have enough hotel rooms in them that we don't need to come home and spend time in another one, so I've been spending a lot of time thinking about how to have a home that works for the both of us. Because I want to make a home with Bryn someday.

"How do you feel about your house selling?" she asks. "I know it held a lot of not-great memories for you..."

Yeah, it did hold a lot of memories of Alexis, which, even the ones that were good when we made them, have been tarnished after finding out about how she used me for my money, my status, my connections, and then still had the fucking balls to cheat on me. Thank God Bryn has never shown one sign of being interested in money or status.

The truth is, though, that I've barely once thought about Alexis since Bryn entered my life. It's not like I've forgiven her or anything as asinine as that, but I just don't care. She may have actually done me a favor by wrecking my life, because if I hadn't been at rock bottom, I sure as shit wouldn't have been in the middle of nowhere, Colorado. And I would've never met Bryn, which is turning out to be one of the very best things to ever happen to me.

"Honestly, B, it feels good. Like a weight lifted." I lift her hand in mine and kiss the back as she pulls into the driveway of my home for the foreseeable future. "And it will free up some of my time so I can be here with you. Win-win."

She squeezes my hand. "I'm glad you'll be around more too. I'm...nervous, I guess is the right word, about you going back on the Tour. I just got so spoiled having you around and being able to base your schedule off mine that I'm worried what's going to happen now that we're both going to be super busy."

"I know." I unbuckle and lean forward to kiss her head. "I don't love it, either, but it's part of the sport. It's part of who I am. And I truly think we can do it." I pause, taking in the concern in her eyes that she rarely lets show about anything. "Plus, we already know we're both good at phone sex. So at least we have that going for us," I joke.

She chuckles, a sound that has my dick standing at attention just as much as the memory of her panting, back arching off the bed as she makes herself come as I watch from my phone.

"Is there an actual term for having sex over FaceTime?" she asks as we walk to the cottage. "Video sex? FaceTime sex? I feel like 'phone sex' seems like we're in *American Pie 2,* having sex over the landline."

"SextyTime?" I offer as I push open the front door.

"Wow, Jameo. This place is great." Bryn takes in the large, open living room, dining room, and kitchen space before wandering into the kitchen to open the fridge. "Look at that, they even stocked some basic food in here."

"Yeah, I asked Mary when I called if she could have someone grab the essentials for me. I'm not planning on doing too much cooking, but they'll keep me stocked with the basics and throw out anything that goes bad while I'm out of town."

"You are so bougie sometimes," she mocks. "Can't even throw away your own rotten milk, huh?"

I grab her in a hug, silencing her tirade with a deep kiss. Backing her up to the couch, I run my thumb down her cheek, reveling in the feel of her soft skin. Before we hit the edge, I turn us, sit down, and pull her onto my lap in one smooth motion. The feel of her weight on my cock is exactly what I've been needing.

As much as I enjoy spending time with Bryn and her family, arriving back after a week away and heading straight to dinner was not ideal. I had to keep thinking about my grandma and her friends at the nursing home to keep from pulling Bryn into a hallway closet and having my way with her—or at least from having a noticeable boner in front of her parents.

She leans in, peppering my neck with hot, open-mouthed kisses. I grip her muscular ass, pulling her forward to create the friction my dick is demanding as I use my other hand to slowly circle her nipple through her shirt.

"Ugh, fuck, Jameo. That feels so good," she groans softly.

My name on her lips almost sends me over the edge. I capture her lips with mine, and she parts them, granting my tongue access to her hot mouth.

Unable to resist, I slide my hand to the edge of her jeans, lightly skimming her exposed skin there before sliding my hand inside her panties, parting her seam with my fingers.

"Fuck, baby. You this wet for me?"

Her half-hooded eyes catch mine, a firestorm of lust flashing through them.

"M-hmm." She buries her head in my shoulder as I press my fingers inside her. "Only for you, Jameo."

For as much as my girl likes to give me shit and keep me on my toes, I fucking love when she opens up like this, completely unguarded. I just lov—nope. I shake my head.

"What? What's wrong?" she asks, disoriented by my abrupt stop and headshake.

Pulling my focus back, I kiss her neck slowly, leaving little bites as I make my way down to her collar. I pull her shirt and bra off, exposing a dark pink, pebbled nipple. "Not one thing, baby."

I flatten my tongue, lapping at her peak while my fingers continue to pump in and out of her tight pussy, but my mind isn't in it.

Fuck, I don't think I'm ready to be in love again. Though, now that I'm with Bryn, I'm starting to realize that what I felt with Alexis likely wasn't love. It was lust and convenience.

But with Bryn, it's...it's definitely too soon for that. But, damn it, I'm pretty sure I do love her. Her smile brightens up my day more than any sunrise ever could, even when it's just over the phone, separated by thousands of miles. Hell, my heart goes all Grinch on me and grows three sizes every time her name pops up on my phone with a text or a call.

"Jameo." She cups my jaw, tilting my head up until I'm looking in her ever-changing eyes.

"Hmm?" I ask, trying to remember if we were talking about something.

Her eyes slowly move back and forth between mine, trying to find an answer there. "Where did you go?"

"Nowhere, I j—"

"Don't. If you don't want to tell me, fine. But don't lie to me about it. Trust me, after the last month, I know what it feels like to have your full attention, and that was not it."

I drop my forehead to hers, staring directly into her wary gaze. "You're right. I'm sorry. I got in my own head about us, you."

"Anything you want to share with the class?" she asks.

I run my fingers through her hair. "All good things, I promise." I catch the end of one light brown strand, slowly rubbing it between my finger and thumb. I kiss the side of her mouth. "I was just thinking about how much I like you. How much I like being with you."

"Mmm," she breathes. "Well, the feeling is mutual."

Realizing the party has already started, we quickly change into our semiformal attire. I'm sitting on the edge of the bed, pulling on my shoes, when she exits the bathroom fifteen minutes later. Her dark blue dress hugs her curves, highlighting her fantastic chest. My eyes trace the deep V, following it past her tight stomach and the curves of her hips to the pair of nude heels extending her legs. My cock jumps at the sight, and she smirks, noting as I adjust myself.

I take her beautiful face in my hands, noting the light spattering of makeup she threw on her eyes and her lips before kissing her deeply, her mouth opening on a sigh to welcome me in.

I step back, rubbing my jaw. "You look amazing."

"You don't look so bad yourself."

We shrug into our coats and head toward the main building. As we walk along the dirt path, I tuck her into my side, my arm around her shoulder. I tell myself it's to keep her warm, but the truth is, I can't stand to have her any farther away than that. I need her next to me.

The sounds of a crowd reach us almost as soon as we leave our building. When I asked the staff at WBCC if they'd be able to accommodate me this winter, they were happy to oblige. Since the course is officially closed, it's an easy, steady source of income to have me in the house. That said, they had asked one thing in return—to come to the event tonight, which a number of their bigwig members and potential members were in town for.

Knowing that Bryn will hate being pulled into my public-life persona any sooner than necessary, I drop my arm from her shoulders as we near the building, my stomach dropping with it. I feel like a piece of me is missing when she's not right there with me.

We hand off our coats as we enter, and I note the number of men who check out Bryn as she turns to face the room. I can't blame them, even if the unease I feel in my gut is almost certainly a flare of jealousy. I quell my need to pull her into my arms and claim her with my body in front of the entire crowd, but it flares again as she waves at a man across the room.

Suddenly, my view is obstructed by Conrad Ferguson, the elusive owner of Wild Bluffs Country Club.

"Jameson, how are you, man?"

Conrad and I met a few years ago at a fundraiser event and had hit it off right away. At the time, he was the newest partner in a VC, and I had a few major wins under my belt.

We kept in touch sporadically, getting together whenever our various professional obligations landed us in the same city. Unsurprisingly, based on how sharp he is, Conrad excelled over the last few years, and he and two of his brothers are now a huge deal in the business world. We actually spent a weekend at Pebble Beach, discussing if golf courses were good investments or not. Many struggled and went under during the last recession, but some of them are extremely profitable. Conrad decided to pursue it as a line of investments for his firm, and he now owns eight courses across the world. When I was in need of a place to escape last summer, he had offered up Wild Bluffs Country Club.

He reached out a couple times over the past nine months, but I've always declined anything more than a drink at the clubhouse. I was in a shit headspace and was avoiding everyone, including the people trying to pull me out of the darkness.

"Conrad." We shake hands. "Doing well. Can't thank you enough for suggesting this place to me last summer."

"Rumor on the street is that you're becoming a long-term renter."

"Yeah. I got an offer on my house in Florida and need somewhere to land. Don't worry, though, I'll make sure to be gone before the course gets busy and you need that cottage again."

He just shrugs. "You know you're welcome to stay as long as you'd like."

Bryn reaches out, squeezing my arm to let me know she is headed to the bar.

"Oh." Conrad looks between us. "I didn't realize you'd brought someone with you tonight, Jameson."

Shoot. How could I have forgotten? "Conrad Ferguson, meet Bryn Harper. Conrad owns the club. Bryn is from Wild Bluffs."

She nods her head. "I grew up in Wild Bluffs, but now I actually live all over the place. I'm director of technology for Hungry Guy."

Conrad chuckles. "I love Hungry Guy. I've actually been trying to acquire them for a while, but the owners aren't ready to sell. It's one of the reasons I'm here in town."

"Good luck with that," Bryn replies. "They love running the company. It's not about money for them at this point, so I'm not sure what you will use to convince them."

Conrad shrugs. "Ah, well, I do like a challenge."

"Then you've come to the right place," Bryn replies as Conrad's assistant taps on his arm.

"Well, it was nice meeting you, Bryn. Jameo, let's get together soon. Maybe when you're in New York for the tournament in February?"

"That'd be great. It's been way too long, man."

We slap backs in a quick hug before Bryn and I head to the bar.

We both order drinks, grabbing seats at the bar while we wait. Bryn smiles at the man next to her before leaning a bit closer to me and asking softly, "Is there a reason you introduced me as 'from Wild Bluffs'?"

"What do you mean?"

"I just found it...odd, I guess, that you introduced me to that guy as 'this is Bryn. She's from Wild Bluffs,' like I'm some acquaintance from town. I was just wondering if there is a reason he shouldn't know we are dating."

I notice the slight droop to her shoulders, the hint of uncertainty in her now blue eyes. I grab her hand, swiveling around on my stool so I can pull her up to stand between my thighs. I kiss her. "Never. I would never want to keep the fact that I'm dating you from someone."

"Good." Her warm mouth melts on mine for a second before she pulls back, sliding one of the thin blue straps of her dress back onto her shoulder.

I pull her forehead to mine, staring straight into her eyes, not caring that we are likely making a bit of a scene. "I mean it, B. I'm sorry. I truly meant nothing by it." I look around the room for Conrad. "Come on. Let's go talk to him again. I'll make sure I introduce you as my truly fantastic, amazingly sexy girlfriend."

She giggles but shakes her head. "No. That's okay. It just hurt my feelings a little, I guess, so I thought I should do the mature thing and let you know."

"Well, I'm glad you told me. I promise I'll learn from my mistake." I kiss her one last time and pass her the drink she ordered before we head out into the crowd, ready for mingling.

Chapter Thirty-Six

BRYN

"I've got to go, Izzy. I'm going to be late for my flight," I say as I hastily pack my laptop into my backpack.

"Ugh. Fine. I still can't believe you're going to see him instead of me. You haven't been home in three weeks either. Some of us want to see you."

"I know. I know. But you know how important it is that I'm at headquarters right now. Luckily, Jameson's tournament is in California too."

I scan the office I've been using one last time, confirming I've got all my chargers and other paraphernalia. "Love you, bye, Iz."

"Love you, bye."

I'm standing in the lobby of our floor, waiting for the elevator, when I hear a sound that makes my ears bleed—okay, I guess Kyle's voice isn't quite that bad.

"Leaving early?" he asks.

I look at my watch. "It's five o'clock, Kyle. It's the end of the workday. I understand you don't have a life, but some of the rest of us do."

He offers what I'm sure is supposed to be a charming smile, but he just looks constipated to me. "Unfortunately, neither of our teams is getting to go home tonight. The big bosses are coming in for a last-minute meeting this weekend. Apparently, they've called a last-minute leadership team meeting."

"Okay, but neither of us are on the leadership team...yet," I say.

"Well, they did mention that we should come. Of course, I'm sure they would understand that you can't be here. I know you all are buddies since you all came from Wild Bluffs. I'm sure they will give you a pass for missing this meeting, just like they give you so much more flexibility than the rest of us."

I scowl at him, mentally trying to figure out how I can still see Jameson while also being in this meeting. No way am I going to let Kyle be in that meeting without me. It would all but guarantee him Tara's seat next time.

"When are the meetings?" I ask, ignoring his dig at me.

"All day tomorrow and Sunday. Drinks tonight at eight at the bar around the corner."

Why? Why does it have to be this weekend?

"Great," I say as I move into the waiting elevator. "I'll see you at eight."

"Bummer about your weekend plans. I guess sometimes your work has to be your life too," Kyle says as the doors close.

The entire elevator ride down to the first floor, I consider how I'm going to break the news to Jameson. This is the first weekend we were supposed to be able to get together. The first. God, how is this going to work if we can't even manage to see each other once a month? I can't miss these meetings. And Jameson obviously can't miss his tournament. He made the cut today and scored well enough that he's actually in the running for placing in the top 10.

When I get outside, I nervously pace back and forth, my finger hovering over the button to call Jameson. He's going to be so disappointed. Hell, *I'm* so disappointed. I like Jameson. So much. But how is this ever supposed to work if we can't ever be together? Neither of us is at a place in our career where we are willing to settle for anything less than the best, but I really thought that we'd be able to see each other at least once a month.

I mean, we'd planned. We'd actually sat down with his tour schedule and my work calendar and found dates that would work for us to get together. Who's to say this won't keep happening? That we won't continue to have one conflict after another arise and, soon, we realize it's been months since we've seen each other. Can a relationship survive that? Should we just call it quits now, no matter how much we like each other? At least it would save us from the heartache later.

I don't know what to do, but I do know there is only one person who can make me feel better right now, so I FaceTime Jameson.

"Hey, B. You on the way to the airport?"

"No, I'm...shit. There's a last-minute leadership meeting at work this weekend. Kyle and I both got the invite, and I obviously can't not go, especially since he's going. But even if he weren't, it's a big deal that

I got invited, but it's also the first weekend that we were going to be able to be together." I sniffle, my image in the upper right-hand corner of the screen staring back at me with a red nose and tear-rimmed eyes. "I'm so sorry, Jameson. I really wanted to be there."

I can see he's upset by the news, but he tries to play it off, likely knowing I already feel terrible enough without having the guilt of a sad man on my hands. "That's...it's...it'll be okay. We're supposed to be together in New York in two weeks. It won't be so bad."

"Yes it will." I sigh. "It *will* be terrible."

"Yeah, it will be terrible, but we can still talk every night. We'll make it work."

"Will we? I'm so worried about what this means for us. I mean, what if something happens, and I can't go to New York? What if my job just keeps getting in the way?"

"Hey. This isn't just about your job. I also have a kinda important job that makes me travel occasionally," he jokes, pulling a snotty chuckle out of me. "I've got to work this weekend too. I understand how important your job is to you, and I know that you need to be there. We will see each other soon."

A sound behind him pulls his attention away from the phone, and after agreeing to something they said, he turns his attention back to me. "I've got to go do another set of interviews, but we'll talk tonight, okay?"

"Okay," I sniffle.

He hangs up just as I remember the cocktail hour tonight. "Wait!" I say, but he's already gone.

Great. Now I've not only ruined our first chance to see each other since the Tour started, I also am going to be late for our first call after that.

I shoot him a quick text to let him know as I'm walking back into work, a thick weight sitting in my stomach. How are we going to make this work?

Chapter Thirty-Seven

Jameson

I know Bryn is questioning how this is going to work. I heard it in her voice last night, and I felt it deep in my bones with every text we exchanged.

To help us both feel better, I rush ordered her a new vibrator as a gift. And guess what just popped up on my screen? A delivery notice. Less than twenty-four hours for the delivery to reach her. Pretty impressive.

I FaceTime B, instructing her to head down to her hotel lobby to pick up a gift.

"Oo, did you order me dinner?" she asks. "You know, we ate with the leadership team, but I was so nervous, I barely touched my food."

"No, though now I wish I *had* ordered you food. I'm sorry you're hungry."

She talks to the front desk manager, who hands her a nondescript cardboard box. "What is it?" she asks, trying to tear it open as she walks.

"Um, you may want to get back to your room before you open it."

"Jesus, Jameo," she says, pulling out her new, dark purple, 12-speed present as soon as she walks into her room.

"Get naked. Let's try it out," I suggest.

She quickly pulls off her jeans and sweater, crawling on top of her bed. After setting up her phone next to her so I can see her from head to about mid-thigh, she looks at me, her eyes dark pools of lust staring at me from the other side of the screen.

"I see the On/Off button, but what controls the rest of it?" she asks.

"Me," I say, pulling up the remote app for her new vibrator. Tech these days. So fucking cool.

Her eyes flutter closed as the vibrations start, her husky voice demanding, "Why aren't you naked?"

Needing no more prompting, I quickly pull my shirt over my head and drop it and my pants to the ground. I lie on my hotel bed, keeping my phone in one hand so I can control her vibe with the app.

"Tell me what to do," she pleads breathily.

I'm more than happy to oblige. "Tease yourself with the toy, baby. Circle around your clit, coming closer, but don't touch it yet." She does as I instructed, her other hand coming up to grip her breast. "That's it. Play with your nipple. Roll it between your fingers. That's a good fucking girl, B."

My hand moves up and down my shaft, increasing in tempo to the breathy moans that slip through her open lips.

I increase the speed of the vibrations as B, without waiting for me, moves the head of the toy to her clit, her back arching in pleasure.

I watch, enthralled, as she loses control, her orgasm moving through her, and I follow, my release hot on my stomach.

"You're amazing, Bryn," I say as she turns over to bring her phone closer.

"We're going to be okay, right?" she asks, uncertainty pushing through her post-orgasm haze.

"We're going to be better than okay."

Her eyes crinkle in a grin as she lets out a yawn. She had a full day of important meetings, and I'm sure tomorrow will be just as bad. "Will you stay on and fall asleep with me?" she asks.

"Of course, sweetheart. I'm not going anywhere." *Ever.* I add that last part in my head, the certainty of us—of Bryn and I—cementing itself in my mind and my heart.

I know it's going to take work. Relationships aren't ever easy, and relationships where both people travel are more complicated than most. But this is worth it. Bryn is worth it.

Chapter Thirty-Eight

Jameson

"Hey, babe," I say as Bryn arrives at the restaurant, her suitcase in tow, after a delayed flight.

"Hey," she sighs, leaning into the kiss I place gently on her forehead.

It has been five weeks since I last saw Bryn in person, and it has been absolutely brutal. Despite texting every day and having SextyTime at least three times a week, it's like a piece of me is missing. I'm also horny as hell.

Turns out, after you've been inside Bryn, your cock raises its standards, and it's no longer content with your hand. Which is why my shower getting ready for our date tonight took twice as long as normal. It wasn't until I had replayed an entire FaceTime sex session with Bryn that I had been able to ease some of the tension building in my body like a Diet Coke bottle that just had a Mentos dropped in.

"You ready for the best dinner of your life?" I ask.

"I have been looking forward to it for weeks," she responds, lacing her fingers in mine.

We head into the restaurant, asking the hostess to hold on to Bryn's suitcase before following our server to a dimly lit booth with dark wood seats.

Dinner is amazing. We order way too much food, but eat it family-style, both of us grabbing rolls and slices of fish off the various platters spread in front of us.

The Hungry Guy commercial shoot took place yesterday and today here in New York, and, knowing how many questions Bryn has already texted me about it, I jump into giving her all the details.

"Kyle is an idiot. He kept trying to tell me what to do with my face." She snorts a laugh. "I'm not kidding. I was this close to punching him square in the nose." I hold my chopstick tips half an inch apart to demonstrate just how much I hate the guy.

Honestly, Kyle does seem like a self-centered asshole, but my hatred is 100% on Bryn's behalf rather than from my own experience. The shoot was actually very professional, and both Jon and Erica were impressed by how smoothly it all ran. That said, when Kyle sauntered over to introduce himself, it took all my self-control to not sucker punch him right there for the shit he pulled on Bryn.

She drops her head into the heels of her hands, massaging her temples. "I can't believe that douche canoe is going to be my boss. I truly believe I need to start looking at other jobs. I cannot work for him."

"Have you talked to Tara? What does she have to say about it all? They have to realize how unfair it is to promote him just because he got you kicked off a project," I say.

"I did get to talk to Tara. The good news is that she, at least, recognizes how unfair it all is. Unfortunately, one of the men on the leadership team is a big Kyle stan. So, the compromise is that we will both pitch via projects in a couple of months. Since Kyle is spending all of his time on this one, he gets to pitch it and talk about what he would do differently next time. I have to use something else."

"Can you pitch the MyUsual app you've been talking about? I know your sister is all about being able to easily place her custom orders everywhere."

"A low-key version of that is what I'm hoping for. It's basically just going to be a feature on our app that lets you save your usual and then, when you log in, the landing screen will push a pop-up asking if you want to order it. I'm worried it's not going to be enough, though."

We continue eating, chatting about other jobs she might consider, but I know Bryn loves Hungry Guy. She would hate to have to leave the company she's put so much of her soul into the last few years.

"Do you want the last tuna?" Bryn asks, pointing with her chopsticks to the last piece of yellowfin tuna sashimi on the white platter, the last man standing from our feast.

"All yours," I reply. "I'm actually going to use the restroom before we head out." I stand up, pulling my wallet out of the pocket. "Here's my card, can you ask for the check?"

"Of course."

I weave my way between tables, heading to the restrooms in the back of the building.

"Hey, Jameo." My head snaps to the left, recognizing that voice from my nightmares. I gape at Alexis, standing there in front of the bathrooms in a shiny silver dress and her made-up face pulled into a phony smile. How have I never noticed how fake she is before?

"Alexis," I say, moving to walk around her toward the bathroom. What are the odds?

She moves in front of me, her hand lightly touching my chest. "I miss you."

I shake her hand off me, my heart pounding as hatred rages through my veins at the gall of this fucking woman.

"I don't miss you, Alexis. You cheated on me. I'd actually be shocked if you ever liked me at all."

"Come on, baby, you know that's not true. We were in love. It's why the breakup was so unbearable...for both of us," she says, batting her thickly coated eyelashes at me.

I go to step around her again but she moves with me. "That wasn't love, Alexis. It was roommates who had sex." I glare at her. "Plus, I'm dating someone new now."

"Oh really?" Alexis's gaze searches the dining area. "Is that right? A new girlfriend?" She finds Bryn, the one woman sitting alone, and her mouth becomes an evil slash. "And look at that, she clearly needs your money. Looks like a match made in heaven."

That does it. "Fuck off, Alexis," I say, moving around her. "Not everyone is a moneygrubbing whore like you. Bryn is smart and funny and doesn't give one shit about my wallet or how famous I am. She is a better person than you could ever imagine being, and she makes me happier than I've ever been before."

Alexis doesn't even flinch. "Oh, please, Jameson. We both knew what we were getting into with that relationship. It was clear from the beginning. I was good for you and your career. So what if I entertained myself with other guys when you were gone?"

Is she kidding me? How can she possibly think I knew what I was getting into or that it was okay for her to "entertain herself with other guys" while I was gone? *Fuck that.*

"We were not on the same page. There is no way you thought I was okay with you fucking every athlete you could find *in our fucking bed*, Alexis. You are a piece-of-trash human, and even though I should've seen it earlier, I could not be happier now that you're out of my life."

She glares at me, venom seeping from every pore. "You wouldn't know a good thing if it smacked you straight in the dick, Jameo. I guarantee you that girl is after your money or your fame, just you wait. No one puts themselves through a golfer's schedule if all they are looking for is love. If you haven't figured it out yet, it's likely just because she's good at playing the game. Good at hiding her intentions while playing the loving girl next door. Trust me, she'll fuck you over worse than I did." With that, Alexis stalks back toward the dining area, her heels clacking with each step.

Alexis is wrong. That's not Bryn at all. She is sexy and smart and has never cared about my wallet or my fame.

When I get back to the table, Bryn is focused on the check, calculating the tip. "I added a twenty percent tip, hope that's okay. It felt like anything lower would be bad for your image, but I also didn't want to spend more if that's not what you normally give."

"I usually go a little higher, but I'll throw out some cash as well." I pull a couple bills out of my wallet and put them down on the table. "Let's go."

Bryn looks up at me, confusion pulling at her features. "You okay?"

"Yeah." I grab the pen, signing the credit card receipt without sitting down. Alexis is wrong about Bryn, but that doesn't mean I want to stay in this building with my ex any longer than necessary. I definitely don't want to give Alexis a chance to spew her hateful comments toward Bryn directly.

I grab Bryn's hand, tugging her out of the booth. "Ready?"

"Sure. Let's blow this popsicle stand."

CHAPTER THIRTY-NINE

BRYN

Jameson pulls me from the restaurant, his mood drastically altered from when he left to go to the bathroom. Hopefully the sushi isn't hitting wrong. I've got plans for tonight that do not include my boyfriend spending time intimately getting to know the toilet in our hotel room.

Once we are out on the sidewalk, I catch up with Jameson's long stride and ask, "What's going on, Jameo? You feeling okay?"

"Yeah, I"—he runs his hand not holding mine down his jaw—"I ran into Alexis outside of the bathrooms."

I pull him to a stop, moving us out of the way of the other people walking by. "You ran into Alexis?" I mentally scan through the people I had seen in the restaurant. It hadn't been a large place, but it had been divided into two rooms. I don't recall seeing anyone who looked like they might be Jameson's ex, but in all reality, I hadn't really been looking.

He nods.

"Did you guys...talk?" Obviously they did. He wouldn't be this upset from just seeing her, but I also don't know how to tactfully handle this conversation. Dealing with exes is not something I've had to do before, since Peter had never had a serious girlfriend before me.

He nods again. "Yeah. I mean, sorta. Basically, she just told me she missed me and how we both knew that we had an open relationship—which, for the record, we both did not fucking know that—and how good she was for me."

Alexis is clearly even more screwed up in the head than I originally thought. I mean, it's one thing for her to have convinced herself that she was good for Jameson. I mean, they were dating when his career really took off, but to have convinced herself that Jameson knew she was sleeping with all those other guys? He's still scarred from finding out about it.

"What did you say to her?" I ask, my voice trembling enough to give away my unease. Logically, I know Jameson would never get back with Alexis, but deep down, in the part of my soul where logic holds no sway, I can still hear Peter's last words to me, telling me I would never be good enough for him. I may be falling for this man, but could he ever, truly, feel the same way about me? The girl who builds walls with her words and sarcasm, terrified of anyone ever tearing them down, more afraid that the prize inside isn't actually worth anyone ever trying.

Jameson leans down, rubbing his thumb along my cheek before giving me a light kiss. "I told her I was dating someone else who was better than she could ever hope to be." His dark green eyes find mine, softening. "And you are. I am so lucky to have you in my life. I—I love you, Bryn."

Smiling almost bashfully, he leans in to kiss me again, but I pull away, not willing to go one more second without saying it back, without expressing what I feel in every fiber of my being, with every beat of my racing heart.

Looking into the face that I've come to know, to adore, so much, I smile back, saying softly, "I love you too."

His eyes flare before he presses his lips to mine in a deep kiss. The world around us seems to disappear, leaving only the two of us standing there on the bustling sidewalk. It's a kiss filled with intensity, a silent affirmation of the connection that has grown between us.

As our tongues slowly untangle and our mouths finally break apart, Jameson keeps his forehead pressed against mine, his breath coming out in warm puffs against my lips. "I've never felt like this about any-one, Bryn," he whispers, his voice tinged with a mix of vulnerability and adoration.

I search his face, seeing the truth in his words. "I haven't either," I admit, my heart swelling with the honesty of the moment. Jameson has brought a depth of emotion into my life that I never knew was possible, and I can't imagine a future without him by my side.

He smiles, a genuine, heartwarming smile that makes my knees go weak. "We're doing this, then," he says, his fingers brushing through my hair. "I don't say those words lightly. I want you. I want us. I know it's too soon to talk about forever, but I need you to know that's where I see this going."

"You see this as forever?" I ask, somewhat afraid to know his answer. I know I love him, but talking about forever? It's too soon. I was together with Peter for three years, and we only said we loved each other the last year we were dating. But I do love Jameo. I'm sure about that. But loving someone isn't the same as marrying them. As committing to them for the rest of my life. It's too fast. Right?

He takes in my face, the uncertainty that I must be doing a poor job of hiding, and his beautiful smile drops, just a little. "Yeah, I do. Bryn, you are the most interesting woman I've ever been with. Every time you talk, I want to get out a pen and take notes. I'm enthralled by the way your mind works. You are strong and sassy and unbelievably sexy. You make me want to be a better man just so I can deserve to be with a woman like you. I want you to be my everything." He runs his thumb along my cheek again, calming me with his body and his words. "But I also know that you're not—we're not there yet. I know this is still fresh and maybe I shouldn't have mentioned forever, but that's how I feel. And when have either of us ever held back what we truly think or feel?" I chuckle at that as he continues, "So I'm not going to be sorry for it or start censoring myself. But I will wait."

He kisses my brow and offers me a tentative kiss. "I promise there is no ring in my pocket that I'm about to spring on you, but there is also no doubt in my mind that one day I will be down on my knee asking you to make me the happiest man in the world."

Running my thumbs under my eyes to catch the tears that sprang free at the beauty of his words, I smile a watery smile, grateful for how well he knows me. That, even if I'm uncertain, he can be confident enough for the both of us.

"Thank you. That's…I appreciate it, Jameo. And I love you even more for being willing to believe enough for the both of us."

I want to tell him that, despite his best efforts, I may not be good enough to fit into his life, good enough for him to want me on my bad days, the days when my hair isn't washed and I'm in the same sweats I wore yesterday. He'll figure it out eventually, just like everyone else has, and then he'll move on. At least this way, if I keep silent, I'll get a few more months, maybe even a year or two, of loving him. So I fall back on my handy-dandy self-defense mechanism, using humor to avoid deep conversations. "But the dick that I met on that fateful day on the golf course? He would've definitely scowled at you and threatened to kick your ass for saying something so sappy."

"Yeah, well, that guy thought he was nursing a broken heart, so he didn't have much sympathy for sappiness." He glances down, thinking, before starting again in a quiet voice, "Turns out, it might've been a bruised ego more than a broken heart. Plus, deep down inside, even that dick was looking for someone to love him."

I grin, thinking of that fateful encounter at Wild Bluffs Country Club. "Well, it's a good thing we both have a penchant for wild roughs and clearly marked balls, then, isn't it?"

He nods in agreement, saying, "Who knew such a shitty string of bad shots could lead to something so wonderful?"

And with that, I tug on his hand, anxious to get back to our hotel. The lady at the front desk frowns as Jameson all but drags me through the lobby, my wink and wave only pulling the scowl deeper.

The door to the hotel elevator barely closes before Jameson's mouth is on mine, his hands taunting me as they run up and down the sides of my waist, tickling the sensitive skin there.

Once we're back in the privacy of our room, Jameson pulls me into his arms, his lips capturing mine in a slow, lingering kiss. It's a kiss that speaks of longing and desire, a promise of what's to come. Our hands roam each other's bodies, his finding and exploring every sensitive place on my body, the ones that have been begging for his attention since I saw him last.

Jameson's touch is electric, setting my skin ablaze with sensation. He kisses a trail down my neck, leaving a trail of fire in his wake. I arch into him, my fingers tracing the contours of his muscular back, reveling in the warmth of his skin against mine.

As we move to the bed, Jameson's eyes never leave mine, filled with a hunger that matches my own. We sink into the soft sheets, our bodies entwined in a dance of desire and need. The world outside disappears, leaving only the two of us.

Our entwining is slow and deliberate, each pump of his hips a slow agony I never want to end. Every touch, every kiss, every whispered word is a declaration of our love for each other. The room is filled with the sound of our sighs and moans, a symphony of passion that would've made me blush a few short months ago.

"I love you, B."

It's so soft, I'm not sure I would've heard it if his mouth hadn't been hovering over my ear, but the tender, hopeful way he says it breaks down all my barriers, filling my heart with nothing but love for him.

Jameson's lips find mine once more as we move together, our bodies becoming one in a slow, sensual rhythm.

As we reach the pinnacle of our pleasure, our bodies tremble together, and I'm overwhelmed by the depth of our connection. Jameson's whispered words of love in my ear send me over the edge, and I cling to him, lost in the ecstasy of my release.

Afterwards, we lie in each other's arms, our bodies tangled together in the aftermath of our lovemaking. It's a contented silence that speaks volumes.

Jameson leans down to place a gentle kiss on my forehead, his fingers tracing lazy circles on my back. "I meant what I said earlier, Bryn," he murmurs, his voice filled with sincerity. "I love you more than anything."

I smile, my heart overflowing with love for the man beside me. "And I love you, Jameson, more than I ever thought possible."

In that moment, my ear above his slowly pounding heart and my hand softly tracing the grooves of his abs, I realize that I've finally found what I've been looking for—someone who will love me for me, no changes necessary.

As we drift off to sleep, his strong arms keeping me warm, I know I will forever be wild about this man.

Chapter Forty

Jameson

STANDING ON THE LUSH green fairway of the eighteenth hole at the course for the Phoenix Open, the Arizona sun casting a warm, golden glow over me, I focus on the path between my ball and the cup. The few fans who came to watch the practice round get slightly less rowdy as I prepare to take my final shot of the day. I putt in for par, ending another solid round. I offer the fans a slight wave, pulling off my ball cap to shake JT's hand as we finish the round. While I'm finally back on top of my game, JT has been playing terribly lately. Though he typically remains his cheerful self, I can tell his mind has been elsewhere. Distracted.

"Tough round," I say to JT as we make our way toward the club-house.

"Not for you. You've been playing great." He sighs, flipping his cap around backwards. He looks like shit.

"You okay? You know you can talk to me about anything, right?"

"It's…" He shakes his head. "Nothing, man. I've just got to get my head on straight."

I offer a shrug. "Been there. Let me know if you need to head to Wild Bluffs. You know I'll come with you."

"How is Bryn these days?"

It's been two long weeks since I last saw Bryn heading into the airport terminal in New York City. Two weeks since we said goodbye with a fiery kiss that left me breathless and craving more. Two weeks of practicing my swing, playing PGA tournaments every weekend, and losing myself in the sound of her voice or her face on my phone screen every night.

I played well those two weeks, moved up the rankings, and even managed to snag a few new endorsement deals. My agent and publicist couldn't be happier with my progress. But even as I've been racking up wins and endorsements, I can't escape the feeling that something's missing. Or rather, someone.

"She's good. She's been in Wild Bluffs the last few weeks, so she keeps sending me ridiculous updates about the people in town. While she was walking Jack the other day, the local busybody stopped her to let her know that if I'm good enough for Levi's, I'm good enough for her. Who knew doing a jeans commercial could have so much sway over other people's opinion of my character?"

He chuckles good-naturedly. "I've heard about the magical power of a man in dark jeans, I just never knew it had that kind of power."

"What about you?" I ask. "Are you planning to use your jean magic to woo any lucky Phoenix women this weekend? Is"—I pause, trying to remember the name of the woman JT tends to meet up with when he's in Arizona—"Halley going to join us for drinks tonight?"

"Hailey. And...I don't know." He glances around as if the entryway to the clubhouse might have the answer he needs. Unfortunately, it seems like the perfectly manicured lawn is of no help. "I just, I guess seeing you so happy with Bryn makes me want more than just a casual hookup, you know?"

I pause as we walk into the locker room. "Am I your relationship role model now?" My shock at the thought mirrors his own. "Fuck, that can't be a good sign. Clear doom approaching."

JT scoffs, pulling off his shoes as he sits down on the padded bench that runs in front of the three walls of lockers. "I hope not," he says on a sigh. "It does feel that way right now, though."

I take in my usually sunny friend, realizing his slightly gaunt face, the defeated set of his shoulders—that was me last year. That was me before I met Bryn and was brought back to life by her sharp wit and even sharper sense of loyalty.

I turn to my buddy and promise, "You'll find her someday, man. You'll find the girl who makes you happy, who reignites your sunshine."

I turn to pull my jacket off, so my ears are covered, but I swear I hear him reply under his breath, "What if I already have?"

"What?" I ask, but it's clear he wasn't talking to me, and now he's staring at his phone.

"Jameo." JT's glance slides up from his phone. "Have you checked your phone yet? Jon sent me a text asking to have you call him." Sometimes, it's helpful sharing an agent with your best friend.

I pull out my own phone and curse. I've got five missed calls from Erica and three from Jon. I push on the button to return Jon's call.

"Jameson, we have a situation," Jon says, answering on the first ring. "I'm going to add in Erica."

"Hey, Jon," Erica says as she answers.

"Erica, I've got Jameson on the line as well."

I take a deep breath, trying to calm the nerves that have suddenly flared up. "What's going on, Erica?"

"There's an article that is just about to come out, and it's not good," she replies, her voice tense.

My heart sinks. I've had my fair share of negative press in the past, but I thought I was past this. "Send it to me," I say, my voice low and steady.

"Jameo," Jon cuts in. "You need to be prepared. This article isn't just about you. It's about Bryn."

"What do you mean? Bryn who? My Bryn? Bryn Harper?" My voice rises with each ridiculous question out of my mouth. JT is looking at me with raised eyebrows. "Why would anyone want to write an article about Bryn?"

"I've been on the phone with the newspaper since they sent a request for comment this morning," Erica replies smoothly. "Apparently, everything in the story has been confirmed, so they are running it, no matter what pressure I put on them."

I growl into the phone, "Can one of you forward me the goddamn article so I can see what the fuck we are talking about?" I know Jon and Erica are on my side, but I'm about to lose my mind if they don't tell me what's happening.

"It's coming through now," Erica responds as my phone buzzes.

I put them both on speakerphone and open the link Erica sent me. It's an article for a gossip magazine, but one that has enough legitimate information that it won't be dismissed out of hand. The headline reads "Is Business Professional the New Black Dress? One Woman's Unusual Path to Fame and Fortune." I run my hand through my hair, letting loose a deep sign. My stomach churns as I scroll through the article, my eyes narrowing in disbelief.

The story starts out explaining how Bryn and I have been spotted at various events, and our relationship was confirmed a few months ago. It includes a picture of Bryn and Lila watching me play at Las Vegas. It outlines my current commercial deal with Hungry Guy, suggesting there are "speculations about her motives and the potential deals that took place to land someone like Jameson Walker at that price." They quote an anonymous source saying that Bryn was an integral part in making that deal happen. The article then details Bryn's previous relationship with Peter, who it turns out is Peter Easley, the son of a billionaire shipping mogul. They've even dug up photos of her with her billionaire ex, looking all smiles and expensive clothes at some big event. The next section shows her shaking hands with Conrad Ferguson outside some restaurant. It speculates that Conrad is her next conquest in a line of men she's used to propel herself to the top.

It ends with a quote from a woman about seeing Bryn and Conrad together and how devastating it will be for me to have this happen again.

I can't believe what I'm seeing.

Fury bubbles up inside me, and I clench my phone so hard that it creaks in my grip. How could I have missed the signs? I should've seen this coming.

"Fuck," I sigh, not caring that another group of golfers is nearby, having just finished their own rounds.

I bang my head against the side of my locker, trying to keep myself under control. To maintain my focus. I can feel JT's eyes on me, but I don't care. All I can think about is Bryn.

Erica's voice comes through my phone again, but it sounds distant, like it's coming from another world. She's probably saying something about damage control, since the article is coming out online in less than an hour, but right now, I can't bring myself to care.

I drag my hand through my hair. "Look, this is what I pay you a shitload of money to deal with. So please, just deal with it. I can't let this derail this tournament."

"We'll see what we can do," Jon says before ending the call.

I turn, throwing my phone back into my locker with more heat than I intended. The screen shatters, a broken spiderweb covering the image of Bryn and me from my lock screen before the whole thing turns black. "Oh, Jesus fuck," I mumble, reaching back in to grab the destroyed device, desperate to turn it back on.

When the screen refuses to light up for even a second, I hang my head between my legs and take a deep breath, trying to calm myself. But the anger lingers, festering like an open wound. How could I have been so blind, so naïve? I should've known better, should've seen this coming.

"You okay, man?" JT asks, concern etching his surfer-boy features.

"Yeah...no...I don't know." I rub my eyes, rallying my energy to get off this bench and go back to my hotel room. "I've got to get my head on straight before tomorrow."

As I stand, I ask JT, "Did you know that Bryn's ex-boyfriend was Peter Easley, like the son of the billionaire Easley? Or that she was meeting with Conrad Ferguson?" God. I should've listened to my own warning when I told JT that doom was approaching. It had all been too...easy. Smooth. That's not how life is.

Luckily, I can already feel my brain blurring the edges, forcing me to focus on the goal that is right in front of me—golf.

His face grows more concerned at my question. "Um, no. But it's not like we are that close. We only hang out if you are there too. I'm sure she...well, I'd think she..." He trails off, clearly unsure if he's willing to stand up for Bryn.

"Yeah," I say, sliding into that tunnel vision of focus that has pushed me into the upper echelons of the golf world.

I walk away from the clubhouse and slide into my waiting car before sinking back into my seat. As I stare out my window, my mind is fully on my game, on what I need to change for tomorrow, except for the one thought that breaks through any time I lower my mental shields: *She's not going to get away with this.*

CHAPTER FORTY-ONE

BRYN

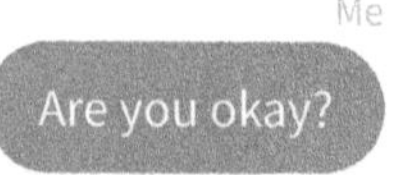

Jameson finished his practice round over an hour ago and I still haven't heard from him. Considering I had an early-morning meeting, it's likely the longest we've gone without talking since we started dating. We didn't specifically agree to talk tonight, but it's still unusual for him to not respond within an hour of me sending a text when he isn't playing.

Now, I'm sitting in Kelsey's kitchen, pounding a burrito bowl with extra hot sauce, replaying every minute of the meeting I had last week with Conrad Ferguson and his brother, trying to figure out where I went wrong.

Me

> That big plan I had to try to save my promotion…didn't work.

Izzy

> Ugh. I'm sorry. You seemed so confident in it.

I had felt good about it. I had absolutely crushed my presentation on MyUsual. It had been surprising enough when Conrad's assistant had invited me to New York for a meeting after I intentionally left Jameson's name and our meeting at the New Year's party out of my initial correspondence, but apparently, Conrad's memory is in fine form, and he was able to put two and two together when he saw my name and "Hungry Guy" in the proposal.

Me

> They claim it's just not the right partnership for them. The main investor called me himself this morning to let me down, so at least it wasn't an assistant brush-off?

Izzy

> And this investor is…

Me

> You know I can't tell you. If I hadn't told you about the meeting before I read the over-the-top NDA, I wouldn't even be telling you this now.

It is too. I wasn't even allowed to tell people that I went to New York for the meeting. I feel bad not looping Jameson in, especially since he was the one who introduced me to Conrad, but I've also never had a legal document make me anxious like the Ferguson Brothers Investment Firm's NDA. That thing is intense.

I guess that's the silver lining of them turning down my proposal to partner with Hungry Guy as investors in the multi-restaurant app that makes ordering your usual quick and easy.

I jump as a knock sounds on the door, a rare sound in my small town. Most people just walk right in.

"Come in," I yell, making my way to the door.

My mom and Janice breeze in, letting in the cold of late February before Mom closes the door with a bang behind her.

She holds up a carton of ice cream, saying, "We came to see how you are doing."

"How I'm doing?" I ask, unsure what she means.

"Yes." She thrusts the ice cream at me before bustling over to the cupboard, grabbing two cups of water. "Janice just told me at coffee about the article. We came right here."

I stop trying to open the ice cream long enough to shoot my mom a confused glance. "What article?"

Janice and my mom both go completely still, causing me to pause as well. "What article?" I repeat.

Tentatively, Janice starts to explain, "Well, Bryn, it's..."

A loud bang echoes overhead, and Kelsey's footsteps pound down the stairs, the sound so much louder than expected for someone as petite as my oldest sister.

"Bryn, did you see—" She halts mid-sentence, taking in our mom and Janice. "I assume you're here about the article?"

Mom nods, adding, "She hasn't seen it yet. We were just starting to tell her—"

"Here." Kelsey doesn't wait for Mom to finish, shoving her phone into my hand instead.

As I read, I feel the color drain from my face and the tears that start to leak from my eyes. "This isn't..."

Kelsey scoffs. "Of course it's not true, Bryn. Anyone who knows you knows that."

I sit down, picking at plastic still encircling the top of my pity ice cream. "Jameson hasn't talked to me since his practice round ended. Do you think he saw this and..."

And what? Just decided to completely ghost his girlfriend? Jameson wouldn't do that. He loves me. He would let me explain. He wouldn't just blindly believe the lies spewed by a toxic article that was about as click-baity as any I'd ever seen.

But for all the growth that Jameson has made in the last few months, he is also still healing from the wounds Alexis left behind.

Still fears, more than anything, people using him for his money and connections—exactly what the article implies I am doing.

"No. Of course not, honey. He wouldn't believe those lies about you." Mom runs her hand through my hair, but I pull away, unable to believe this is happening.

Their kindness in the wake of my humiliation is making my skin crawl, the weight of their sympathetic stares crushing my lungs until there is no room for breath. I know they mean well, but I need them to leave.

"Right. Yeah. I'm sure it's just a misunderstanding." I get up, herding the busybodies toward the door. "I appreciate you both coming by, but I'm sure it will all turn out the way it's supposed to." Catching my mom's look of uncertainty, I give her a hug and say, "Truly, Mom, I'm fine. It was obviously a shock, but I'm fine now. And Kelsey is here, should I decide I need moral support."

We both look back at Kelsey, who is puttering around the kitchen, making dinner for herself, and Mom raises her eyebrow as if to ask "You think she's going to offer you moral support?" But I just roll my eyes and close the door, wishing I were in bed.

I head back into the kitchen and grab my phone off the kitchen counter where I left it sitting next to my unfinished burrito bowl and melting ice cream. I consider finishing them both, but the burrito half I ate is already like a stone sitting in my stomach, growing heavier with each thought running through my head. I don't know how my meeting with Conrad was leaked, but it doesn't matter. What matters is that Jameson is going to see me using him to access money and men to get ahead—just like Alexis.

***

I sigh, tucking my hands into the oversized sweatshirt I threw on after barely making it through the end of my workday today. I quickly shut down any talk about the article itself, though a few colleagues tried to offer their words of support or anger at such blatant lies. I'm sure a few of them think it is true—the ones who know how badly I want this promotion, the ones who heard me taking credit for bringing Jameson on to the commercial campaign.

Kyle made sure to comment on the article, sweetly noting that he hoped it wouldn't impact my presentation next week. As if I didn't have enough to worry about.

I sent Jameson another text, asking for the chance to explain. Then, hours later, when I knew he had to be back at his hotel for the night, I sent him another. I called. FaceTimed. But everything went straight to voicemail.

Izzy and Becca barge in, bringing with them the faint, almost metallic smell that always accompanies cold days, bearing a pizza from Wild Crusts, the one pizza place in town.

Plopping down next to me and shoving her legs under my blanket, Izzy leans her head on my shoulder, a position we've sat in so many times throughout our lives, before saying, "Who would've thought that you would ever be interesting enough to get a gossip article written about you?!"

Becca glares at my sister over the slice of pizza she just stuck in her mouth as I huff out a laugh. "Have you heard from Jameson yet?" she asks cautiously.

"No. Not a text, not a call, not even a 'fuck off' to let me know where I stand." I burrow deeper into the couch, wishing I could avoid this day. This hurt.

"What a dick," my sister grumbles, reaching forward to grab a slice of pizza for herself.

"Iz…" Becca shoots my sister a warning look, almost like she'd already told her to be on her best behavior. My sister is kind—and sarcastic, yes—but she feels deeply. And when someone hurts someone she loves, she can be brutal, holding grudges far past the point when others have let go.

Shrugging, Izzy says, "How could he not respond? It's his fault—his fame—that made that article even exist. No one would write an article about Bryn if she weren't dating Jameson. If I were him, I would be here, begging for Bryn's forgiveness."

"He's in the middle of a golf tournament, Izzy. The Waste Management Phoenix Open is this week. He can't just drop out so he can fly here. This is his career," I say.

"He can pick up a fucking phone and call someone." Her dark eyes flash with rage. "Or he could extend you the same courtesy that you do any human and answer his phone when it rings. Respond to one text."

I glance between the two of them. "I take it Kelsey has been keeping you up to date on the situation?"

"Mom called after she left this afternoon, and, yeah, Kelsey has been begrudgingly answering our texts about you today."

As if summoned, Kelsey strolls into the room before curling up on the couch next to Becca. "It's been very annoying. Almost as annoying as having a random pizza party at my house at ten on a Wednesday night."

Becca rolls her eyes at the end of Kelsey's tirade before bringing the conversation back to Jameson again. "All I'm saying is that there could be an explanation for why he hasn't responded. Maybe his phone is dead."

"And the entire Phoenix area is out of chargers?" Kelsey asks before leaning forward to grab her own slice of pizza.

"Okay, maybe someone stole his phone."

Izzy raises an eyebrow. "At the exact same time an article comes out about his girlfriend?"

"Coincidences do happen!"

"It doesn't matter," I say. "This was bound to happen eventually." At their confused faces, I shrug. "Well, not this exactly, but Jameson deciding that I'm not worth it. With Peter, I was too focused on my job. Now, with Jameson, it's happening again. My job is coming between us. Is it such a flaw to want to be good at what I do?"

"Bryn—" Becca starts, but I shake my head.

"Look, I'm not going to pretend that this isn't bringing up some shit from when Peter broke up with me. I also know that there are things I'm amazing at. I'm good at my job. I'm a fun, interesting person. But I'm not great at relationships, especially relationships where I'm supposed to act like I think the other person is the lead character, and I'm just there to support them. Look what happened in January. The first time we were supposed to get together, I had to cancel because of work." I take a deep breath, trying to push down the sob threatening to burst from me. "Jameson is great, and I'm great, but I'm not the right fit for him. This would end eventually, and I guess it just seems like I should take the easy out now before I get in too deep."

"So you're just going to dump him?" Kelsey asks, flicking through something on her phone.

Becca shoots Kelsey a glare, but she simply shrugs a shoulder, as if to say "We were all thinking it."

"Do you even have to dump someone who ghosts you?" Izzy asks.

"Jesus, Izzy." Becca throws up her hands, clearly annoyed by us all at this point.

"Honestly—" I pause, considering if this truly is what I want before I start again. "I don't think Jameson is ghosting me. I have no idea what the fuck is going on, but"—I shrug—"I don't think he's ghosting me. But I also think this is a sign that we aren't supposed to be together. And it feels like I should listen to that sign."

"I could text his sister, I suppose," Kelsey says.

"Oh my God, Kelsey. How did you not think of this earlier?" Izzy asks.

"Well, I have her number because I'm trying to convince her to come work for me once she graduates. She's interviewed, and I've offered her the job, but she's not sure she wants to move to Wild Bluffs, and I need someone who is at least nearby to meet occasionally. It felt weird to then text her about her brother ghosting my sister."

"He's not ghosting her!" Becca explodes.

"I mean, he may not be intentionally ghosting her, but at this point, I think we can all agree she is experiencing ghosting," Kelsey lobs back.

Izzy pulls out her phone, raising it to eye level to unlock it. "Give me her number. I'll text her."

We all sit in silence, waiting as Izzy's fingers fly over her screen. "There. Now we wait, I guess."

CHAPTER FORTY-TWO

JAMESON

I ENTER MY HOTEL lobby, the air-conditioning blasting me in the face as soon as I walk through the automated doors. I am contemplating if I want to eat, shower again, or use the lobby phone to fire every person in my employ. I mean, how hard is it to get someone a new phone?

I was laser-focused on my game today, but somehow, everything just felt wrong—off. There was a niggling in the back of my mind, like when you forgot to pack your toothbrush for a trip, that just wouldn't leave me alone. My game suffered because of it.

I usually love the chaos and apparent middle finger the spectators give the rules of golf at the Waste Management, but today it was overwhelming to have drunk spectators jeering when my ball came up two inches short on yet another putt. It's not a hole that I can't come back from, but it's a clear deviation from the exceptional rounds I've been playing lately.

I'm almost to the elevator when I notice JT and Lila sitting next to each other in the lobby, intently focused on their phones.

"Uh, hey, guys," I say, sticking my hands into my pockets as I look back and forth between the two of them. "What's up?"

Lila jumps up off the deep, leather couch. "Hey, Jameo. I've got a new phone for you."

I pull the bag out of her hands, too focused on opening the box inside to pull her into the hug she was clearly aiming for.

"Good to see you too," she drawls, folding her arms across her chest and sticking out her hip in a posture of frustration that I've been immune to for about ten years now.

I vaguely catch JT offering to give her a hug instead, but all my attention is on the phone screen lighting up with a white apple. I blink at Lila.

"It's brand new."

"No shit, Jameo. You broke your old phone."

"I mean, none of my stuff has been transferred over," I say.

JT looks between my sister and me and, apparently, decides to jump into the mix. "Just log in to your account. All your old stuff will be there."

I tug off my cap and run my hand through my hair before slumping heavily into the couch, my head cradled between my hands. "I don't know my login information," I admit. "Cathy always has to do it for me."

Lila drops onto the couch next to me, pulling me into a hug. "Not something we should probably admit to other people, bro. You're a grown-ass man. Learn your login information."

I let my head rest on her shoulder for a minute before she suggests, "Let's go get a beer. We'll get it figured out. Maybe it's your birthday? The name of your favorite pet? Cathy's favorite pet?"

I ride the seven minutes to the bar in silence, spinning the blank phone in my hands as I plot the various texts I need to send and calls I need to make when I get access to my contact list. My brain has apparently decided to let me focus on something other than golf, and now I'm overwhelmed with the number of calls I need to make, but can't until Jon gets a hold of Cathy and passes my login information over to JT.

Of all the weeks for Cathy to take a vacation. Okay, this may be on me for relying a little too heavily on my assistant for the last five years.

Finally, Lila and I slide into a booth in the back of an upscale bar, and JT makes his way toward us with three Corona Lights. They both look at me, and the sympathy on their faces makes me lose it.

"Can you believe that article?" I ask. "I should've seen something like this coming."

I take a long pull of the beer, needing it to take the edge off just a bit more than I need to forgo drinking before the round tomorrow.

"Has Jon gotten back to you, man?" I ask JT. "I need to get access to my contacts so I can start making calls. She will regret this decision. And that stupid Kyle too."

Lila looks like she's about to fight me on it, but instead, she pulls out her phone. "I can text her sisters. They've sent me a few texts, trying to figure out why you went radio silent. I didn't know at first, but then I talked to Mom, and once I knew, I let them know your phone broke, but…" She pauses and looks at me again. "I can't believe you, Jameo. This isn't her fault. You have to know that."

I look at my sister in confusion. "What are you talking about, Lila? What sisters?"

She and JT exchange another look. "Kelsey and Izzy. Kelsey had my number because she interviewed me for a job with her company. She gave it to Izzy, and Izzy texted me, asking why you decided to ghost Bryn when you would be a dick not to know that Bryn isn't like that—I'm paraphrasing, of course. But I was in class and then I didn't know, and so anyway, when I finally heard from Mom that your phone broke, I put two and two together, but I was already on the plane when I hung up with Mom. When we landed, I texted Izzy, but I haven't heard back since I got here."

"I didn't ghost—" I start, but JT cuts me off.

"I know you're upset about the article, and, yeah"—he looks at Lila, and she gives a subtle nod—"yeah, it's a bit weird that she didn't mention that she dated a fucking billionaire before you or that she met with Conrad, but I truly don't think she's using you. Bryn seems to genuinely care about you, and it seems like she makes you really happy."

Lila jumps in then. "At least talk to her before you jump to any conclusions."

"You guys think…" I trail off, trying to put all the puzzle pieces together. "You think I'm mad at Bryn? Why?"

They exchange a puzzled look, so I continue, "I know Bryn isn't anything that article made her out to be. She's smart and funny and makes my life twenty times better than it ever was."

JT raises an eyebrow. "Then who have you been ranting about?"

I gape at the two of them, shocked to realize that they both thought I was talking about Bryn, the love of my goddamn life, for fuck's sake. "Alexis," I bite out. "You read the part about my past, didn't you? Almost no one knows she cheated on me. She has to be one of the sources. And I'd bet a lot of money that Bryn's coworker Kyle is the insider at Hungry Guy."

I see the comprehension flit across both their faces, but Lila's is quickly offset by a look of horror. "Jameo, she thinks you ghosted her. Bryn thinks you're mad at her. Have you talked to her at all since the article was released?"

Shaking my head, I reply, "No. My phone is broken, remember? Is it surprising that I don't have her phone number memorized? It's saved in my goddamn phone. Plus, I'm in the middle of a tournament. She knows how focused I get when things aren't going well." I look between the two of them, their worry seeping into me from across the table. "Bryn has to know I don't believe that about her, that I don't think that article is true. Right? I mean, everyone knows how focused I get, right?"

Shit. It never even occurred to me that Bryn would think that I was mad at her. My stomach sinks as I realize that I've barely even stopped to think about Bryn at all since this started. I let myself focus so much on my career that I forgot about the most important person in my life.

"I don't know, Jameo. She didn't know your phone broke. She just knew that an article saying she was using you came out and then you went radio silent." I can feel Lila's judgment as she looks at me. "I mean, did you even try? Did you try looking up her work number on her website? Or asking Mom to have me reach out?"

I drop my head into my hands, taking a deep breath. "Fuck. No. I mean, I obviously wanted to talk to her, but I've been focused on my game. And on getting a new phone. I didn't even consider the website. Or her sister's website." Now that Lila has suggested reaching out in a different way, I feel like a complete and utter moron. A failure. I'm not even sure I deserve Bryn after this.

"Shit, the club would've given it to me..." I continue.

Glancing at the troubled faces of two of my favorite people in the whole world, I can't help but feel like the best thing in my life is slipping through my fingers. I've let Bryn down. She deserves better than this, and I'll do whatever it takes to make things right. I know one thing for sure: I won't let this article destroy what Bryn and I have. I'll fight to prove that I know she's not the person they're making her out to be. Because deep down, I know Bryn is worth every challenge and every sacrifice. She's the one who has stolen my heart, and I'm not about to let her go without a fight.

"Can you find out where she is, Lila? I need to get to her. I need to explain. Or at least get her number? So I can call her?"

Lila nods, her fingers flying over her phone.

"I can't believe I was so focused on a stupid game that I didn't realize how much she must be hurting," I say. "And if she forgives me, I will spend the rest of my life trying to be the type of guy that does deserve her."

JT's surprise is clear as he asks, "The rest of your life?"

I feel no hesitation at the answer, even giving it to my perpetually single best friend. I want to spend forever with Bryn. She may be as snarky and nomadic as they come, but she's also fierce and smart and makes my heart feel like it's finally home.

"Yeah. I'm not saying I'm ready to propose or anything, but yeah. There is no doubt in my mind that Bryn is my forever. She's my endgame. Now, I just need to convince her."

CHAPTER FORTY-THREE

BRYN

"I HATE HIKING. I can't believe this is what you decided to do. We could've gone and gotten ice cream. Everyone knows this is the ideal ice cream situation," Izzy says, pulling out her water bottle for a drink now that she's caught up with us.

Kelsey is mumbling at her phone as she holds it over her head, searching for a signal she hasn't been able to find for the last three hours.

"Do you have service, Iz?" Kelsey asks, ignoring Izzy's displeasure.

Digging into her pocket, Izzy pulls out her phone and checks it. "Nope. I don't think I've had it the entire time we've been on this trail. Another point in the ice cream column, if you ask me." She plops down on the bench, ready to take a break of her own. Kelsey and I both share a look, ready to get back on the trail, but we've heard Izzy rant enough times about how, as the slowest hiker, she shouldn't be the one who is forced to skip a break. We can either walk slower with her or take longer breaks. We've opted for the longer breaks.

Here's the thing. When I was fourteen, Izzy was sixteen, and Kelsey was eighteen, I would've traded my sisters for just about anyone or anything. Three teenage girls in a household meant a constant roller coaster of emotions and hormones, with recurrent battles involving stolen clothes and psychological manipulation. Kelsey has never been too forthcoming about if she had to undergo torture training in the Marines, but I firmly believe she would've been the top of her class, based on the shit we put each other through growing up.

Now that we are older, though, my sisters are my best friends. I genuinely like them, and we have the added bonus of having so much in common. Weird cousin is up to his shenanigans? My sisters know all the players in the story and can dissect it with me. My boss at work is up to her shit again? My sisters have been living through the saga with me. Ran into the boy I kissed in high school? My sisters can update me on not only his life but those of his siblings *and* his parents.

They get me.

Which is why I am now sitting on a rock, halfway through a seven-mile hike. Kelsey and I end up hiking in the mountains quite a bit, but Iz has never developed a love for it. The fact that she is here is actually a testament to how much she loves me.

After Lila responded following her night class and was unable to explain why her brother had gone radio silent on me, Izzy suggested at the unreasonable hour of three in the morning that we drive down to Arizona and ask him ourselves. I protested, saying if he didn't want to see me, I wasn't going to chase after him. Plus, it was *three in the morning*, so why were we even awake to talk about this? Kelsey jumped in to point out that, even if all I wanted to do was break up with him, I still needed to talk to him to do that.

I tried to argue, but the look on both their faces made it quite clear this wasn't an argument I was going to win. Becca had a meeting she couldn't miss the next day, but the Harper sisters had poured coffee down our throats and jumped in the car.

After driving for twelve hours, we passed out in our hotel room before waking up to watch Jameson's last few holes. It wasn't until we watched him walk off the course that I realized we had no idea where he was staying. No way of finding him now that we were here. I had scrambled, yelling at my sisters that we needed to get in the car right then, but Kelsey had pointed out how futile it would be—he would be gone by the time we could drive out to the course.

Despite not seeing him, I know Jameson has seen the article. If playing his worst round in months wasn't indication enough, the dark circles standing out prominently against his wan skin on the television screen certainly suggest he's seen the article and is not okay.

Despite my sisters trying to remain positive, my mind continued to wander, flipping between possible conversations I could have with Jameson and ones I'd already had with Peter. I thought focusing on my work would allow me to be successful. Now I'm being punished for focusing too much on it. For being too good at what I do.

So we went hiking.

"Time to turn around?" Iz asks, screwing the lid back on her water bottle.

Kelsey looks at me, but all I can muster is a shrug. "Sure."

As we start back down the brown, dusty trail, Kelsey takes the lead, navigating through the desert landscape awash in hues of brown and green. As I follow the path, reminding myself to go around the boulders and sagebrush, Iz slings her arm through mine, laying her head on my shoulder briefly. "What are you going to say to him when we find him?"

"I think at this point we have to accept it's an *if* we find him, not *when.*"

"Nah," she says, letting go of my arm to make her way around a suitcase-sized rock in the middle of the trail. "We'll find him. All else fails, we can always stake out the tournament tomorrow."

"If he doesn't drop out. He played like shit today. It's possible he won't be playing tomorrow."

"Then we will find him at his place at the club," Izzy responds, her confidence starting to annoy me.

"Why would he go back to Wild Bluffs?" I ask. "He rented there to be close to me, something he clearly doesn't want to be anymore."

Iz shrugs. "He came to Wild Bluffs before he even knew you existed. Sometimes, the wide-open spaces are what we need to settle ourselves. To see the full picture of our life and realize where we want to go."

"Maybe I should've stayed home, then," I respond. "I could use some clarity about what to do."

And I could. I know I'm not a good fit for Jameson. I know he deserves someone better than me. And, fuck, I also deserve more than someone who goes this long without reaching out. Without making sure I'm okay after that article was released.

Even as I think it, my heart tightens in protest. I know Jameson didn't ghost me. I may not be right for him, but he's a good guy. He wouldn't do this.

Eventually, Izzy falls back behind, stopping to take a close-up of a lizard along the path, a photo that I'm sure will never make it off her phone because, as much as she loves taking the pictures, they are actually very mediocre, and Izzy has no use for them.

I, unfortunately, have no such distraction. Instead, my mind focuses in stark clarity on my current situation. I'm in love with a man who I will never be good enough for. Once he finally calls me—and let's be honest, I know he's going to call me at some point and explain why he's been out of touch for days—I'm going to have to break both of our hearts.

He may be the one person in this world who makes me feel like I'm worth it, and if he were any other guy, we could make it work, but I can't do famous. I won't quit my job so I can spend my days supporting my husband, and if I miraculously win this promotion, I'm going to have to be at headquarters much more frequently. And, while I know Jameson would never ask me to give that up for him, I also know how naïve that truly is. He is going to get back to the top of the golf world. He is going to have major deals and win all the big tournaments. He is on the road constantly. I'm going to be working all the time. What kind of relationship is that?

But even the thought of losing him is sending shockwaves of grief into my heart. It's like Jameson currently fills each groove, each capillary, and the thought of removing him is enough to trigger a full eruption of heartbreak.

The sight of the parking lot ahead of me pulls me from my melancholy, and my heart is shocked into action by the buzzing coming from Kelsey's pocket.

"Finally," she grouses, pulling out her phone as we reach the flat expanse of trail leading to our car.

Glancing back to find Izzy, who, despite her stops, managed to stay fairly close behind us, I ask Kelsey the question I'm not sure I want to know the answer to. "Did Lila get back to you?"

Kelsey doesn't stop or turn around to answer me, and I'm about to ask again when she turns, shouting over her shoulder, "Hurry up, Iz. I know where Jameson is!"

"Where is he?" I ask, doing a shit job of hiding the desperation in my voice.

Kelsey is already on the move again, making her way quickly down to my car. "Some bar I guess."

"Do you"—I start but can't seem to finish the sentence, to get the question out that will make this all real.

"Know where it is?" she finishes for me, and I can sense the unseen eyebrow raise that accompanied the question. "Lila is there with him now and sent me a pin. It's about thirty minutes away."

Izzy catches up to us, panting slightly from her jog to catch up. "I hate hiking. Walking I can get behind, but why do we need to make it harder by adding the constant uphill climb?"

"Because without the climb, you never get to see the view from the top. There's no reward for all your work," I respond with the answer I give her every time she asks this question.

"So where is he?" Izzy asks, draining the last of her water bottle before pulling open the car door and sliding into the back seat.

Kelsey sinks into the passenger seat and finishes sending a message on her phone before answering, "Some bar in town. Bryn, I just texted you the address so you can have the car direct you."

I pull up her message and select the bar as our destination before putting the car into gear and maneuvering around a rusty pickup that had parked far too close to my Tesla for my liking.

Following the directions to get back to the main highway takes the majority of my attention, but as I merge into traffic, I can feel the pressure of the upcoming conversation building, not just within me, but in my sisters too.

Izzy breaks the silence, leaning forward so her head is between the seats, asking the question that has been floating through my head since the article was released, "What are you going to do?" She pauses but continues before I can answer, "I mean, what are you going to say when you see him?" She flops back into her seat. "Ugh. Why am *I* nervous?"

Kelsey shoots our sister a look of exasperation before turning to me. "She may be overly dramatizing this, but she is right. You need a plan."

"What do you mean?" I ask, glancing over my shoulder before switching lanes.

"What are you going to say to Jameson when you see him? Are you dumping him? Are you questioning him about how that article came to exist? Are you begging him to stay with you? Are you poisoning his drink?"

"Ew. I'm obviously not begging him to stay with me. The rest are all still on the table," I joke.

"Good." I catch Izzy nodding from the corner of my eye. "I'm personally in favor of junk punching him and walking away. Though, I could be persuaded that you should start by asking him where the fuck he's been the last day and then moving to junk punching if the answer doesn't meet a certain set of standards."

I roll my eyes. "Oh, and who will be evaluating said answers?" I tease. "And while we are on the subject, should we be developing a rubric to ensure it's fair?" My sister loves a good evaluative process—it's one of her primary roles in the firm she and Becca own.

"We all know Kelsey is basically a human lie detector after all her military training. I suggest she be the primary, but you should probably be the one asking the questions to make sure we keep him as off-balance as possible."

I'm not actually sure if she's joking or not. I think she is, but there is enough of an edge to her voice that she might be serious. Fortunately, I'm saved from responding by Kelsey.

"They don't just train all military personnel in interrogation, Iz. You've got to stop telling people things like that. I had someone call me the other day to ask if I could help them break into their ex-husband's house to hotwire his car and interrogate his new wife about the whereabouts of a very expensive necklace. I literally hung up on her. It was so outrageous."

"Or that's just your cover so we won't know it was you when the news reports an eerily similar story," Iz shoots back.

"Regardless." I jump in. "I'm going to talk to him alone, so no ninja skills needed by Kelsey." Catching my sister's scowl from the back seat, I add with a smirk, "Though I'm sure she would've loved to have a warm-up before her interrogation of Wife Number Two next week."

CHAPTER FORTY-FOUR

JAMESON

I'VE BEEN TO THE bathroom six times since Lila told me Bryn was in Arizona and on her way here right now. It can't be good news that she decided to drive all the way to Arizona yesterday.

After I'd been to the bathroom twice in ten minutes, Lila politely inquired as to the state of my GI health. The two middle fingers I shot her way did nothing to deter JT from asking me the next time if he needed to go buy me some Tums. At this point, I'm not even going into the stalls. It's just direction for the pacing currently sandwiching my self-reflection time.

I am a fucking idiot. Each time I look into the mirror, each step I take along my well-worn path to the bathroom, each beat of my heart, reminds me of this indisputable fact.

I am a fucking idiot who may have lost the love of his life.

The girl of my dreams.

My happily ever after.

And while I would understand if Bryn decides to dump my ass after the way I left her on her own after the article came out, my heart would never be the same. I know for a fact that Bryn is it for me. And now that I've had her, now that I know what love truly feels like, I know I can't settle for anything less than what I have with Bryn.

Which is why I can't get my feet or my brain to settle down. As I stare at myself in the bathroom mirror, my hands braced on either side of the white porcelain sink, I know I'm at a crossroads. Bryn is going to walk in any minute now, and she holds my happiness in the palm of her hand. I'm not sure how, after everything with Alexis, I ended up handing my heart over so easily, but with Bryn, it's always been that easy. It's been the type of love I saw with my parents. The support. The holding hands. The casual acts of love and kindness that build into a great love story.

Shit. She could walk through those doors any minute now. I give myself one last look in the mirror, one final word of warning—*Don't fucking mess this up, Jameo*—and head back out into the bar.

JT and Lila are at the table, arguing about something, likely me, based on the way they stop talking every time I get back to the table. I don't even bother asking again what they were talking about.

I sink down on the dark faux leather booth, making sure I keep an eye on the door.

"How long until they are here?" I ask, running my hand through my already disheveled hair.

Lila makes a show of checking her watch, the bright face lighting up as she flicks her wrist over. "Any time now. Like I told you when you asked two minutes ago before you stomped off to do God knows what in the bathroom."

She's trying to distract me. I know she is. But dammit, I can't help but take the bait. "What, exactly, do you think I'm getting up to in there, Lila? Do you have some nefarious bathroom exploits you'd like to share with the class?"

JT snort-coughs so hard that liquid flies from his mouth (maybe nose, but I'm a good friend, so I'm choosing to overlook that possibility). Lila watches, a devious glint in her eye. One I know well from growing up together. "Actually," she starts. "Now that you mention it, there was this time in a hotel room, and the counter top was juuuust—"

"Jesus Christ, Lila," I cut in, passing a wad of napkins to JT, who is about to die next to me. "I obviously don't want to know the details of your sex life. In my mind, you are and will forever be an asexual blob."

"Oh, really?" she asks, looking at me. Then she turns her full attention to the poor man next to me who seems to be sending his drink out all the wrong . "What about you, JT? Do you see me as an asexual blob?"

But I don't hear his answer because at that moment, the air shifts, and a pull from deep inside me draws my attention to the door opening at the front of the bar and the beautiful woman walking inside, flanked by her two sisters. I would know the lines of that face anywhere. That body that could make stronger men than me weak at the knees. The lips that turn into a smile that, when earned, is one of the very best rewards in the world.

I'm out of my seat before the door finishes closing behind her, forcing myself not to run or create a scene in my haste to reach her. Not to scoop her into my arms, throw her over my shoulder, and keep her locked up until she agrees to forgive me. Instead, I meet her halfway to our table and, when I see the look of hurt and confusion on her face, pull her into a deep hug. Her face presses up against my chest, and, for one heart-stopping moment, she doesn't return the hug. But then she's sliding her arms around my waist and leaning into me, and a small ember of hope lights in my chest as I breathe in her scent.

I know that ember could end up burning me, though. Forgiveness is not something I've earned at this point. I know that. It's very possible Bryn will still decide this isn't worth it. I'm not worth it.

Over her sister's shoulder, Kelsey raises her eyebrow at me, and I catch Izzy as she whispers behind her hand, "Did he just sniff her hair?" I honestly can't care what they think right now. I close my eyes and inhale deeply again, resting my cheek on the hair that I did, in fact, just sniff. I've got Bryn in my arms, and I will do everything in my power to keep her here.

"Hi, baby," I whisper into the top of her head. Her shoulders start shaking, and I am shocked when I pull her back and see the tears streaming down her face.

"Fuck," I breathe, knowing that Bryn is not someone who cries often, who abhors the thought of crying in public. Pulling her back into my arms, I look to her sisters. *Am I going to lose her? Is it this bad?* I try to telegraph with my eyes.

Kelsey's eyes are skeptical and seem to be saying "Of course it is, you dumbass." Izzy, I'm having a hard time deciphering her look, but it seems to be a combination of "go fuck yourself" and "I'm rooting for you two kids." *That's not confusing at all.*

Someone clears their throat next to me, and a look from JT, who is now standing next to me in the middle of the bar, reminds me that I'm not alone. That I am a public figure standing in a public place, holding a crying woman. A woman who has received more press this week than she's ever wanted in her entire life. A woman I left alone, like the fucking idiot I am, to deal with it herself.

I start to turn us back to the table, but Kelsey stops me.

"Bryn has her car key." She looks between us. "But maybe you should be the one to drive her car."

"I don't... I don't feel great about leaving you all," I start, but Izzy shakes her head.

"We'll hang out here for a while and then catch an Uber to our hotel. I don't think the conversation you all need to have is really one you want to have here, and—" Izzy glares at me as she adds, "I don't want Bryn to be stuck somewhere without her car."

"Iz."

Bryn's first word since getting here throws me off guard. It's not that I had forgotten about her. It was more that she had become a part of me, sunken into my soul like the snow melting into the earth, becoming one, in the minutes I had held her.

"It's just being smart, B. Don't give me that look."

I swear I can feel Bryn's eye roll.

"Are you—" I start but have to swallow the lump rising in my throat before I can finish. "Are you okay with going back to my hotel with me?" She moves back slightly, and I look down at Bryn just as she looks up at me. Her eyes are a deep blue today, a color I've never seen before, and it makes me wonder what other colors they can be. What other colors I will miss seeing, miss loving, if I lose her?

And in that moment I know, without a doubt, I will do whatever it takes to keep her. I will give up the spotlight, I will give up golf, I will give up every dollar I've ever made if it means I get to spend my life with this woman.

She nods, a tentative smile tugging at the corner of her mouth.

The emotions I've been trying to contain since she walked through the door are back, and I try not to let them overwhelm me, to let them overwhelm her. So I give her a smile and wrap my hand around hers, tugging her back toward the front.

"Thank you both for getting her to me," I tell her sisters as I walk by.

"Don't make us regret it," Izzy responds.

"I won't."

As I pull open the door and tug Bryn through, I watch our sisters and JT all head back to the booth, shooting us furtive glances as they go.

With some guidance from Bryn, we find the car, and, as soon as I close Bryn's door, I hustle around to the other side, sliding in and grabbing her hand. She doesn't pull away, which I take as a good sign. I want to have this conversation now. I want to apologize. I want to beg until she forgives me. But I also know the parking lot is not the right place.

Navigating through the quiet streets, I rub my left thumb back and forth on the seam of the steering wheel, my pace increasing with each passing moment. Bryn's silence weighs heavily in the car, a tangible reminder of the chasm that has grown between us. The city sights flicker past, casting fleeting shadows on her face as she stares out the window, lost in her thoughts. The tension builds until I finally can't take it anymore.

"I'm so sorry, Bryn," I say, my voice thick with emotion.

"What happened, Jameo?" Her voice is soft, laced with a mixture of curiosity and pain.

"It's fucking Alexis," I begin, my frustration bubbling to the surface. "Of course it is. She—"

"No," Bryn interjects, her tone gentle yet firm. "I'm not talking about the article. I—" She pauses, drawing in a deep breath. "I know you broke your phone, but why did you go radio silent on me? You could've reached out some other way."

Her question hangs in the air, heavy with accusation and hurt. I swallow hard, grappling with the shame swirling inside me.

"Bryn," I begin, my voice hoarse with emotion. "After I found out about the article, I... I was mad. I could tell based on some of the comments that Alexis was one of the sources. And then my phone... I smashed it in a fit of rage. But you're right, I should've figured out a way. I should've had my parents call Lila and have her drive to Wild Bluffs to find you. I should've found your sister's number online. I should've called Hungry Guy and had them leave you a message. I should've borrowed JT's phone and emailed your work email. Anything to let you know you're not alone. I'm so sorry, Bryn."

She nods, turning her face toward the window again, pulling herself together as we pull up outside of my hotel. I park in the lot and meet her behind the car, grabbing her hand before she has the chance to walk away.

"Where's Jack?" I ask, trying like hell to make this feel normal. I know the minute we are in my room I will be groveling with everything I have, but for now, I just need to feel the comfort, the spark of hope that I didn't ruin this.

"Mom and Dad have him. He likes it there best anyway, despite JoJo antagonizing him constantly."

The half-hearted smile she gives me makes it clear that even the image of her dog getting annoyed by her parents' black Lab isn't enough to bring a real smile to her face.

I force a smile back, and we ride the elevator in silence before getting out on the sixth floor and making our way to my room, where I key us in, my hand noticeably shaky.

Bryn enters and walks across the room to stare out my floor-to-ceiling windows. "Everyone told me you were ghosting me." The hurt in her voice as she says it breaks my heart.

"I wasn't—"

"I know. I told them you wouldn't ever do that to me. You're not that type of guy. But the silence, it hurt."

"I just... I knew I needed to focus on my game. It was stupid and selfish, and I can't believe how insensitive I was. I never meant for you to feel alone or to hurt you. I just couldn't get a phone, so I tried not to let it distract me."

Bryn's gaze softens. "I understand your need to focus. And I'd like to say that any other day I wouldn't have minded, but the truth is I want to hear from you. Going a day without hearing from you would've been brutal, even without the article."

I nod, my heart aching at the pain I have caused her. "I feel the same way."

At her skeptical eyebrow raise, I continue, "I know it doesn't make sense, but I do! I wanted to talk to you. I kept reaching for my phone to text you. It's like I was having imaginary conversations with you, so it was like you were there. But I'm not making excuses. I didn't mean to, but I was so focused on what I needed that I shut you out when you needed me the most, and I can't... I can't forgive myself for that."

Tears well in Bryn's eyes, shimmering in the bright light of the room. "Jameo," she murmurs, her voice trembling with emotion. "I understand why you did what you did. And I appreciate that you weren't trying to hurt me. But...but I can't shake this feeling that I'm not... I'm not right for you. That we aren't right for each other."

"That's not true, Bryn. We are. We are perfect for each other." I gently wipe a tear that escaped and is now running down the side of her face.

"I called in sick today. I needed to see you so bad that I called in sick the last workday before my big presentation," she says.

I hadn't even thought about the fact that today is a workday for Bryn. I knew her presentation was Monday, but the timing of this is the worst. It's truly like all the stars are aligning against us. But fuck the stars, I won't let them ruin what I have with Bryn.

"I'm sorry, Bryn. I'm so sorry."

"I know. I appreciate that. But it's not just about missing work today. It's about our lives not actually lining up. It's not likely, but I might get this promotion—"

"You will," I cut in.

She shoots me an exasperated look and continues, "And I'll be less nomadic. I'll likely have to move to California full-time."

"They have golf courses there," I say.

"I won't be able to come to your tournaments. I'll have to actually build time into my schedule to come and visit my family instead of just crashing at their houses."

"I'll meet you there."

"You'll realize I can't be a good girlfriend and good at my job."

Her words cut through me like a knife, slicing through the facade I have carefully constructed around my heart. "I don't believe that for a second. You're already the best girlfriend, and you're great at your job."

"Peter," she starts, and I release a growl at the name of her ex on her lips. She puts her hand on my chest as she continues, "Peter and his family never thought I was good enough for them. Mrs. Easley couldn't stand the way I would show up in my work clothes, hair pulled back in a casual bun, talking about my job instead of Peter's. It was like everything I was proud of about myself, everything I liked about myself, was wrong. I tried to be in both places. I tried to be both women. I tried to excel at my job and be there for Peter, but it didn't work. I wasn't enough. I failed at both things."

My heart breaks for my usually confident girlfriend, and I want to pummel the man who made her think she was less than the absolutely perfect woman that she is. "Love, that's such—"

"Look, I like who I am. I'm proud of who I am and what I've accomplished so far in my life. Would I like to lose five pounds and stop cussing around the kids in town? Sure. But who doesn't have one or two things to work on? What I don't like, what I can't force myself into again, is a life where I feel like I'm failing for being that person. I love you, Jameson, but I can't be the girlfriend you need me to be."

"I don't want you to be that person, Bryn!" I shout before catching myself and bringing my voice back to a normal range. "I love how much you love your career. I would never ask you to change that. I love how laid-back you are. I love your body and your potty mouth. I love that you would rather wear jeans than a dress. And I don't give a fuck how you wear your hair as long as I can wrap it around my hand when I'm fucking you from behind."

Her eyes flare at that last statement, and, as much as I want to bend her over the desk in the corner and do just that—I can already feel the silky hairs pulling across my knuckles—I know she doesn't quite believe me yet.

I hate where this is going. I can see her steeling herself to break both of our hearts.

"Jameo, I—"

"Don't," I all but beg. "Please don't, Bryn."

The tears are back, spilling down her cheeks, leaving trails as they fall.

I continue, "Don't make any decisions right now. I know the last couple of days have been brutal. I know you have the most important presentation of your life on Monday. Just focus on that. I will text you and call you every day and won't even expect you to respond or pick up the phone. You focus on your presentation. Then we can talk more about us. About our future. Because if I have anything to say about it, we *will* have a future, Bryn."

"I don't know, Jameson. It feels like putting off the inevitable."

"It's not, Bryn. Please just try. For me?"

I need her to agree. I need to have a chance to make this right. To make it up to her. To show her that our love is stronger than she thinks it is right now. I completely understand why she is uncertain, but I'm confident enough for the both of us. I broke her Barbie house, but I'm going to make it right.

Before she can answer, I play my trump card. "You still owe me. From our first round together. I won. I won one thing of my choosing. I'm choosing this. I'm choosing us."

"Okay," she breathes, looking shocked that I remembered our bet from so long ago. "Okay. But I'm going to... I'm going to head out for tonight."

I nod, pulling her into one last hug before letting her go with a kiss to the forehead. I know I have to let her go, but watching that door shut behind her is the hardest thing I've ever done.

CHAPTER FORTY-FIVE

BRYN

I make sure my phone is on silent before sliding it into the pocket of my black work backpack that's currently stuck between my feet. True to his word, Jameson has texted me multiple times every day. I've responded each time but haven't worked up the courage to answer any of his calls. He continues to leave me voicemail messages, just short recordings telling me about his day, or something he loves about me. They're actually very sweet.

I know I need to make a decision about what I'm going to do, but it feels like I need all the information. I want this promotion so bad, but I also know it means Jameson and I are likely over. It's a real lose-lose.

Or win-win, I suppose. If I embrace either having Kyle as my boss or being jobless. The stress of it all has been threatening to overwhelm me since I walked out of Jameson's hotel three days ago.

Luckily, today is the day. Promotion presentations are happening in just under thirty minutes. After Conrad and his brothers passed on partnering with Hungry Guy (and therefore, me) on the app, I had to go with my second option. It's a solid upgrade, one that would use register data and in-store cameras to estimate wait times at each of our locations, but after the success of Kyle's campaign, I'm worried it's not going to be enough.

I want to bitch and moan about Kyle, but the truth is I got out-maneuvered. It may have been completely underhanded the way Kyle managed to get me kicked off our joint campaign, but I should've seen it coming. He was playing chess while I was playing checkers. I was distracted by my relationship with Jameson. And now I have to face the music. Or, in this case, the horrible sound that will be Kyle's name getting announced for the promotion.

They decided to tell us today who will be promoted so Tara can have a few months to fully train her replacement.

Kyle strides in, his scuff-less loafers coming into view as I sit, staring at my hands. "That article last week," he says in greeting. "So crazy. How are you holding up? Everything still okay with you and Jameson?"

The words seem kind, but the self-satisfied glint in his eyes tells me that he is enjoying the fact that I was knocked off my game last week. And, because I'm catching on to his scheming, I'm pretty sure he's bringing it up now just to try to throw me off my game before we go present.

No way am I going to let him get to me. "I'm fine. And yeah, things are fine with Jameson. He thinks it was probably his ex."

"Oh, yes. I'm sure it was Alexis," he says in a tone just as Tara opens the door and calls us in.

Three hours later, we all exit the conference room.

I didn't get the promotion.

They gave it to Kyle because his project was better. Not because his presentation was better or because he leads better, but because the project that we started together and I had to recuse myself from was better than the one that I had a couple of weeks and no team to put together.

Tara tried to stand up for me, to argue it wasn't fair, but it was clear the boys' club who all came up through the marketing department wanted Kyle. So they made it happen. It feels both better and much worse knowing their decision actually had nothing to do with me—I could've had the best idea and the best presentation and they would've given the job to Kyle regardless.

It makes my decision to quit that much easier. I'll write it on my flight home tonight, and I'll be gone in two weeks. What will I do after it? I don't know.

We're walking down the hallway as a group, me trying to burn a hole in Kyle's back with my eyes, when Kyle's comment about Alexis from earlier flies into my consciousness.

I slow down. "Hey, Kyle," I say.

He slows down as well, and now we're walking side by side at the back of the group. "How'd you know Jameson's ex-girlfriend's name is Alexis?"

It's like the one question unleashes the evil cartoon character in him. His eyes darken, his lips curl into a smirk, and I swear two animal henchmen pop into existence at his side. "Oh. Did I forget to mention that, when doing my due diligence before asking Jameson to be part of the commercial, I actually ended up having a lovely chat with Alexis? Just wanted to make sure there weren't any skeletons in the closet that I should know about."

I stop completely, turning to face this man who has been manipulating a game I didn't even know we were playing. To say I'm shocked doesn't even begin to cover it.

Kyle, on the other hand, is clearly enjoying this. "And, when it was looking like Tara might be able to convince one of the other leaders to vote in your favor, I thought it might be a good idea to reach back out. It was remarkable how quickly she agreed to being a source for the article. It's almost like she wants Jameson back or something... I know which of you I'd choose if I were him."

The gall of this man. Not only is he standing there admitting to being the impetus behind an article that not only screwed me over but didn't look great for Hungry Guy either, but he's also trying to make me jealous of Alexis of all people.

"And Conrad? How did you know about that?"

"The benefit of being the best is that you work with the best. The journalist I reached out to actually dug that portion up on his own. You know, while we're on the subject, I do have questions about that. I'm not sure how you managed to connect with one of the top investors in the world, but, since I'm your boss now, I'm going to need you to pass that relationship over to me."

A laugh escapes me. "Wow. You are making this so much easier for me." I start walking again, this time changing direction toward the elevators.

Confusion pulling at his brows, he catches up to me quickly. I can tell he doesn't want to look stupid by asking, but his curiosity finally wins out. "What did I make easier for you?" he asks.

"This," I say, striding into the elevator as it opens. "Bye, Kyle. Good luck trying to fill my position and take on a new one of your own. I bet it takes"—I tap my chin, pretending to think—"less than three months for them to realize that you don't actually know how to do your job and you just take credit for everyone else's work."

I stick my hand out, holding the elevator from closing. "I won't be here when that happens, but I look forward to watching you fail from afar."

As the doors slide closed in front of his shocked face, I wiggle my fingers in a wave. "Toodle-oo, Kyle."

CHAPTER FORTY-SIX

BRYN

"So it didn't matter how your presentation went?" Izzy asks.

"That's what he-who-shall-not-be-named implied," I reply over the Bluetooth as I drive toward Wild Bluffs. "But, I mean, he's also a source in that highly inaccurate article, so I wouldn't say he's the most reliable."

"I honestly can't believe he was in cahoots with Alexis. What a wild pairing."

"Somehow, that doesn't even crack the top three most outrageous revelations of my day."

"Your upcoming fun-employment throwing you off, huh?"

I sigh. After taking the first ten minutes of my flight home to write and send the world's most generic resignation letter, I spent the rest of the time thinking about what comes next. Really trying to figure out what matters to me. I've used my job as a barometer for my success for so long, I don't know what to do now that I don't have it.

I've reconsidered my resignation about every thirty minutes at this point, but every time, I remember Kyle would be my boss, and I'm glad I pushed Send while the anger was still controlling my actions.

I'm also glad I didn't pitch my original idea. I'm sure Kyle would've stolen it and somehow his team would've turned it into something great. He would've been praised, and I would've been unemployed. About as far from the professional trajectory I had planned for myself as possible, watching as my idea was taken and turned into something that paled in comparison to what it could be.

I realized something else while on that flight, emotionally spiraling through every decision that led me to this point: I want to be with Jameson. Does it hurt that he didn't try harder to reach out to me when that article came out? Yes. Of course it does. It's also understandable that, after the year he had following his break with Alexis, he forced himself to focus on his game. He's not holding it against me that I haven't been the chattiest the last few days. While it hurt, I am a grown-ass woman, and the further I've gotten from the hurt, the more I realize I get to decide if I let this one mistake ruin something that has the potential to be amazing.

I have no doubt he would've called me if he wouldn't have broken his phone, though I might insist he memorize my cell number just in case. To be fair, maybe I should memorize his as well—I've broken a phone or two in my day, and they aren't as easy to replace in Wild Bluffs as they are in a city.

At the end of the day, I still love him. He's still the person I want to call to talk through what my next step should be. I feel grounded when I'm with him, like my soul recognizes it's home when it's near him.

A text from the man himself came through as I was deplaning, letting me know he was in Wild Bluffs and he wanted to have dinner with me tonight to celebrate my victory. I'm so overwhelmed by everything I learned today that I simply agreed, not bothering to correct him about the whole "winning" portion of the message.

While I find it a bit odd that he just went for the dinner invite after the weirdness between us the last three days, you've got to respect the man's focus. I said I'd make a decision about us after the presentation, and here we are. After the presentation.

To be clear, I'm not complaining. I want to see him.

I just don't know that I'd have that level of confidence. Definitely not today, when I not only lost the promotion I'd been going for and ended up unemployed instead, but I also learned it had nothing to do with my presentation or proposal. Kyle had already won when we walked into that room.

I pull into the parking lot at the club and jump out of my car with much more pep than I would've anticipated, considering the day I had. It's like my body knows it's about to see Jameson and has decided to say F-you to my overthinking brain and just be happy. Bold move, body, but I guess we will see where it takes us at this point.

I finish up my call with Izzy, promising to text her later with updates. The wind that hit me as I stepped out of my car is chilly, a spring wind that was likely warm earlier but lost its heat as the sun went down. Following the path of stairs made of old railroad ties at a jog,

I don't stay cold long. Instead, I'm slightly winded by the time I push open the doors to the restaurant.

I scan past a few tables of men before my brain realizes that one pair of men is standing up to welcome me. My eyes immediately go to Jameson, and I drink him in like I've just played thirty-six holes of golf in midsummer, in 100-degree heat.

It's not until I'm about to throw myself into his arms, my body having crossed the large expanse of floor separating us before my mind could issue the command, that I realize Conrad Ferguson is with him.

I pull up short, but Jameson doesn't. He wraps me in a hug right there in front of everyone, dragging me to his chest, his chin on the top of my head. I burrow into him, the weight of the day lifting off me with each second I'm in his arms. After watching for what was likely an inappropriate amount of time for a public hug, Conrad coughs lightly, breaking Jameson and me apart.

I'm not sure why Conrad is here, and it's throwing me off my game. I was ready to make up with Jameson, maybe eat a little food, say what we need to say, and then head back to his room. I'm ready to jump into the WAG lifestyle, following Jameson wherever he goes. It'll give me something to do. Hopefully I can be successful at that, at least.

"Hey, Conrad," I say. "Good to see you...again?" I'm not sure how much I can say at this point. Somehow, the Conrad portion of the article never made it into the list of things that Jameson and I talked about in Arizona, and I'm definitely not going to break that NDA with the man right there.

"Bryn." Conrad extends his hand, and I shake it. "Good to see you too." He moves to sit back down, so Jameson and I both follow suit, Jameson helping me with my chair.

"Just to clear the air, I've filled Jameson in on our conversation last week. I apologize if our NDA caused any issues between the two of you."

I shrug. "Surprisingly, it never even surfaced as an issue. But I do appreciate you sharing what you could with Jameson. It definitely will make things easier going forward, although I'm not sure it was worth the trip all the way to Wild Bluffs just to clear that up."

"Ah, I'm not actually here for that. Jameson and I have talked on the phone a few times in the past couple of days. I informed him about our meeting and the unfortunate timing of your article on Saturday."

"Oh." I don't know what else to say. I'm clearly missing something, and the stress of the day is starting to catch up with me.

Jameson, seeing my confusion, says, "It seems that Conrad and his brothers have a couple of big deals in the works that are going to make waves, so there have frequently been photographers stationed outside of their office. Bad luck, I guess."

"I am sorry it ended up that way, Bryn. We didn't know they were paying us any more attention than usual, though I'm inclined to believe it has more to do with my younger brother's most recent breakup with yet another actress than our actual business. Unfortunately, it seems when your job is to photograph semi-famous people, you can sell to business sites or gossip columns. I suppose you have to respect a diversified income stream."

"Well, I appreciate the apology." I take a drink of the water our waitress brought, pretending to read the menu before ordering my usual burger and fries. The men both order as well, which answers my question about if Conrad is joining us for dinner or not.

Once the waitress leaves, I turn back to Conrad. "So, if you don't mind me asking, what brings you to Wild Bluffs?"

"Ah," Conrad replies. "I think that portion of this story belongs to Jameson. And while he tells it, I'm going to hit up the bar for a drink." He asks what we want and wanders off toward the bar, clearly trying to give us some privacy.

Jameson clears his throat, fiddling with the napkin in his lap before bringing his eyes up to meet mine. "I felt terrible after you left my hotel room. I could feel you slipping away, and I knew it was entirely my fault. You deserve more than the man I was the past week. You deserve someone who never stops focusing on you. But *I* can be that someone. I know I can. Yes, my job makes it harder, but I'm willing to do what I need to in order to make this work."

It's everything I want to hear from him, but also so unnecessary now. I've all but resigned myself to just designing my life around his. "Jameson, I really appreciate that. And I forgive you. I do." I plaster on a fake smile as I add, "But, good news! I didn't get the promotion, and so I submitted my letter of resignation on the plane. I'm totally free to just follow you around the country. If you want me to, of course. I definitely don't have to. I'm sure I can find something else to do until I find another job. Oh! And it turns out Kyle and Alexis were behind the article the whole time." I say it all in one breath, so it takes him a minute to parse it all out.

"You want to follow me around the country?"

Not the part of the statement I thought he'd latch on to, but okay.

"Yes! It'd be lots of fun. I have enough savings to last a while. Especially if you're okay with me staying with you."

Jameson rubs the back of his neck. "You, the most driven person I know, want to be a WAG who hangs out at all the tournaments?"

My spine hits the back of my seat as I slump a bit. "You say it like it's a bad thing. Lots of women do it."

He nods, reaching out his hand to grab mine from where I'm holding it across my stomach. "Yes. And if that's what you really want, I would of course love that. But I think you may want to hear what Conrad has to say first."

"Conrad?" I ask. "Why?"

"Like he mentioned, we've talked a lot the past few days. Please don't be mad at me, but I didn't know that you'd already talked to Conrad about your MyUsual idea. So, when I was trying to think of ways to let you know that I support your career, I realized I could use my connections to help. So I called Conrad. Unfortunately, he told me the same thing he told you, that his firm wasn't interested in partnering with Hungry Guy on it."

I nod, not that surprised that we both thought of Conrad. It still doesn't explain why he's here, though.

"I thought I failed," he continues, running his hand through his hair. "I didn't know how to prove to you that you could do it both. That you could be successful in your career and be with me. Because I know you can." He lifts my hand, kissing my knuckles. My heart expands at the words, even as a small part of my brain argues that it can't be true. Giving that part of my brain the middle finger, I convince myself to believe Jameson, this man who has never asked me to be anyone except who I am.

"But then Lila helped me out. And so I called Conrad back."

At this point, he finds Conrad at the bar, clearly waiting for a signal that it's safe to return to the table. Jameson gestures with his head, and Conrad makes his way back with our drinks.

"Is she caught up?"

"Ready for your part of the performance," Jameson jokes.

Conrad relaxes back in his chair, one ankle crossing the other knee. "I'm sure Jameson mentioned that he also reached out on behalf of your MyUsual concept."

He pauses, and I nod my agreement before he continues, "After explaining to him the same things I told you about why Hungry Guy isn't the right partner for us for that app, he called back with a different idea—that the Ferguson Brothers Investment Firm develop the app ourselves and bring in all the major restaurant chains as partners."

"Oh. I...that's..." I stumble over my words, unsure what to say. Is he offering to buy the idea from me? Just telling me that they are going to take it? I don't think they can do it without paying me something. I did get some level of protection from the NDA.

Conrad, sensing my confusion, continues, "I liked the idea, so I discussed it with my brothers, and we came back to Jameson with the dollar amount we thought we could buy it for. Jameson, however, thought that you'd prefer something other than the quick buyout, so I went back to my brothers, and what I'm here today to offer you is a director-level position with Ferguson Brothers Investment Firm.

It's a fully remote position that reports directly to me. You'd manage the development of the MyUsual app, and then, once that is running, you'd be responsible for building a portfolio of similar products."

I feel my mouth drop open, and my chest tightens. Is he for real?

"I can send you the contract with all the information, but not knowing your current salary, I think the amount we are offering should be about twice as much as what Hungry Guy offers their directors."

"Oh, I—" Jameson shakes his head, silently trying to communicate that I shouldn't tell Conrad that I quit today, but I don't want to start off by lying to my boss.

I look Conrad in the eye and say, "Thank you so much for the offer. It truly sounds like everything I could have dreamed of. And I know this isn't the best tactic, but I want to be honest with you. I quit Hungry Guy today. Turns out, they promoted the guy who leaked the article about Jameson and me to the press. Doubling my current salary of zero dollars shouldn't be too hard."

Conrad laughs. "Okay, first professional development day will be spent working on your negotiation skills. I actually know a former hostage negotiator who can do wonders for you."

"I also want to make sure you're not doing this because of Jameson. I can find another job on my own. I'm—" Conrad holds up his hand.

"Let me stop you right there. I do not hire people just because of who they know. I looked into your work at Hungry Guy. I even talked to your boss, Tara. I believe you are the right fit for our company. Jameson might've been the one who suggested the idea, but I would've never agreed to it if I didn't want you for your own skills and experience."

I smile, appeased by his statement. "I'll definitely need to look over the job offer, but this sounds amazing." I exchange an updated email address with Conrad, and he promises to send over the offer first thing in the morning.

Our food arrives and we fall into casual conversation, the men carrying the bulk of the conversation while my brain tries to process everything that has happened today.

I can't believe I started my morning thinking I was going to get a promotion at Hungry Guy, have to move permanently to California, and lose Jameson in the process. Now, I'm employed by one of the top investment firms in the country, am free to work from wherever, and it's all because of Jameson. Because he believes in me and supports what's important to me. Because now that I've had the chance to think about it, I know I would've never been happy just following him around. I need the challenge of work. I like the mental stimulation of my job.

But I also want to be with Jameson.

And somehow, the man managed to coordinate the perfect opportunity for me to do both.

CHAPTER FORTY-SEVEN
JAMESON

"I NEVER THOUGHT THAT dinner would end," I say, pulling Bryn back to the house I'm renting as fast as I can. Would it be too much to just fireman-carry her?

"I can't believe you did that for me," she says, practically jogging to keep up with me.

"I would do anything for you."

"I'm beginning to understand that."

"Trust me, by the time I'm done with you, you will believe it with your whole entire being."

I push the door open, pulling her into the living room and dragging her body against mine. Leaning in, I press my lips gently against hers, savoring the taste of her, the warmth of her against my skin. Our kiss is tender yet fervent, a silent plea for forgiveness, for redemption in each other's arms.

My fingers tangle in her hair, pulling her closer as I deepen the kiss, pouring all of my love and longing into the moment.

I pull away, breathless and dizzy with emotion, and look into Bryn's eyes, seeing the depth of her love reflected back at me. "I love you, Bryn," I whisper, my voice raw with emotion. "More than anything in this world. More than golf, more than money, more than anything. If having you means I need to give everything else up, I will. You just say the word and I'll quit and become your personal assistant or dog walker or anything that would allow me to be in your life forever."

She smiles at me, and I know it's going to be okay. I know I haven't lost the woman who makes me whole. I wasn't sure this whole plan was going to work, and my assistant and I were both working overtime all weekend to make it happen, but seeing the smile on Bryn's face tonight made it all worth it. Especially after hearing how shitty of a day she had. I can't focus on Kyle and Alexis's betrayal now, but I mentally file it away in a "Future Revenge" folder of my brain. No one fucks with Bryn and gets away with it.

"I love you, too, Jameo," Bryn murmurs, her voice barely a whisper. "More than you'll ever know. But please don't become my assistant. You would be truly terrible at it. Maybe stick to your golf hobby for now."

I laugh, a deep, throaty sound that vibrates through my soul. Her eyes scan my face, darkening at whatever lust she must see there. Bryn places a hand on my chest, pushing me back gently until my legs bump against the couch, forcing me to sit. Taking the hint, I grip her hips, thumbs stroking the curve of her side as she moves her thighs to either side of my legs.

She lowers tauntingly slow onto my lap, and I reach out, guiding her hips until her core is directly over my straining erection still held captive by my pants. Bryn leans back slightly as I continue to guide her up and down, running her center along my length.

She crashes her mouth to mine and I tangle one of my hands in her hair, pulling slightly.

"Fuck," I moan. "I was so sure I'd never have the chance to do this again."

"I know. I know. And I'm sorry. I didn't want to end this. I was just scared. I was so scared I would just end up letting you down, or that I'd get lost in the process of keeping you."

Just as I feel her start to tense, I stand and carry Bryn to my bed. She flops back on the mattress and I reach out, grabbing the waistband of her pants and slowly pulling them down. Her body relaxes, her head tilting back as she lets out a contented sigh.

I chuckle softly before lightly stroking her seam with the knuckle of my index finger.

"Bryn," I sigh, her name a prayer and a curse on my lips. "You are so fucking wet." Then, unable to hold myself back anymore, I drop to my knees, my head bowed in front of her hips. She jolts, her hands squeezing the comforter as I start slowly torturing her with my tongue, running it along her slit before circling the bundle of nerves begging for my attention. I play with her, coming close but never giving her the pressure I know she needs. Circling and circling before backing off again to drive my tongue into her, deeper with each pass.

"Please?" She's begging now, and I'm helpless to do anything but give in.

Her head slowly lifts, and she's so far gone in her desire that all I can see is the deep black of her exploded pupils. This might be my favorite eye color of hers.

I watch her take a deep breath and shut her eyes briefly before I slowly spread her folds with one hand, my tongue flicking her hard nub.

She groans, her head thrashing from side to side. My other hand traces up her side, sliding under her shirt and bra before cupping her breast. I squeeze her perky nipple at the same time I suck her clit into my mouth. She breaks, and everything in my body wants to break with her, but I hold back, focusing all my pent-up energy on worshiping Bryn's body.

"So fucking perfect."

She sits up, pulling her shirt and bra off and tossing them to the side before standing and pulling me up with her. I quickly unzip my pants before reaching an arm over my head and pulling my shirt off in one smooth movement.

She takes in my body, and I take in hers. As I scan her inch by inch, every cell in my body thrums with excitement. I tug down my briefs to free my straining dick.

Bryn swallows hard at the sight, her gaze laser-focused on the glint of precum that has escaped the slit at the end.

Bryn takes control, pushing me back down onto the bed, before opening my nightstand and pulling out a condom. She leans over, giving my leaking head a quick kiss and sweep of her tongue, unleashing a deep groan from my chest. With a chuckle, she rolls the condom on before slowly lowering herself onto my length. She repeats my torturous move from earlier, slowly moving up and down, up and down.

As my control weakens, she increases her tempo, grinding on me with each slam of our connected bodies. She leans forward and my hands grip her hips, moving us even faster.

"Good girl, B," I whisper in her ear, groaning slightly. "Just like that. You are perfect. You are perfect for me."

The praise rockets her back to the edge, and I follow. The pleasure is looming right there, just waiting. We are both on edge, and our pace is no longer rhythmic but rather the impatient pounding of two people who cannot, no matter how hard they try, ever get quite as close as they want to be. Two people whose souls are entwined at such a molecular level that their bodies will never be able to match that level of intimacy.

Bryn's breath is coming out in ragged gulps, thighs clenching as she tries to keep up with the grueling pace I am demanding of her. Recognizing the strain on her face, I flip us over, and I lap at her nipple while I pound into her.

"I'm about to..." I groan.

"Do it," she urges.

I shake my head. "Not without you." I snake my hand between us and find her clit with my thumb, applying just the right pressure to send her falling again, the clenching of her walls bringing me with her.

I watch, eyes half closed, as she finishes, the tight muscles of my ass flexing as I slowly rock in and out of her. A slow trickle of our combined fluids makes its way further down her body with each movement.

"Stay with me?" I ask, not even trying to mask the vulnerability I'm feeling.

"There's nowhere else I'd rather be."

With everything I've ever wanted right there in front of me, I give the love of my life a quick kiss before heading to the bathroom to take care of things. Her eyes are closed when I return to the room, so I lift the covers and nestle in behind her, pulling her ass until it fits perfectly in the crook of my hips. I nuzzle her ear, listening to her deep breathing as I fall into the deep sleep that only home can bring.

CHAPTER FORTY-EIGHT

JAMESON

Bryn is snuggled into my side, her head resting on my chest. A drop of drool is dangling from the corner of her lip, and while I know she would be disgusted by this fact, I actually find it particularly adorable. I love her all soft with sleep. Unable to help myself, I lean down and gently kiss her forehead.

Her eyes crack open and a soft smile pulls at her lips before she snuggles in deeper and falls back asleep. Unfortunately, a buzz from her phone brings her back to consciousness. She sits up, wiping the spit from her mouth with the back of her hand.

"Good morning, sunshine," I tease.

"Coffee?" she asks groggily.

"I figured we would go into town and get some."

"Wait!" She jumps from the bed and starts throwing clothes at me. "You are late! You've got to get to the course."

I catch the bra she just threw at my face, lifting my eyebrows in question. "It's Tuesday."

"Oh, shit. The last five days have been so insane. I don't know what town I'm in, let alone what day it is."

"Your phone has been buzzing. If I had to guess, your sisters have lots of questions." She catches her bra as I throw it back to her and rolls her eyes good-naturedly. I continue, "Plus, your stomach has been growling for the last thirty minutes. It's probably about time we get you fed."

"I am starving, and I will not be a good person in about ten minutes if I don't get some caffeine in my system." She scrolls through her phone. "Kelsey just texted me. She and Izzy are demanding we join them in town for breakfast. Want to join?"

"Definitely," I say, pressing a kiss to her forehead as I make my way into the bathroom. "I just need to make you come two, maybe three, times in the shower, and then we will be right there."

Thirty minutes later, I climb into the passenger side of Bryn's Tesla, my cock twitching at the sight of her ass in a pair of yoga pants. *Down, boy,* I think, reminding my dick that it already got to find release in that gorgeous pussy once that morning as payback for the feast I consumed when she first joined me in the shower. Unfortunately, the image of her bent over, the water pounding her from above as I pounded her from behind, has the opposite effect.

"We are going to be eating in town…with my sisters," Bryn says, pulling me from my fantasy.

"Yeah?" I say, confused.

"It's probably inappropriate for you to have a raging boner." She glances away from the road to stare at the bulge in my pants, and I don't fail to notice the way she bites her lower lip as she tears her gaze away.

"Well, you should've thought of that before you wore those pants," I say.

"Ah, yes. It's clearly on me for wearing tight clothing. I forgot that we were living in the 1900s and men cannot be held responsible for their actions when they see the shape of a woman's legs."

"Keep me out of this," I joke. "This is between you and my dick. He's the one who clearly doesn't realize he's being inappropriate."

Bryn nods thoughtfully. "Noted. I will make sure to have words with him later. Really punish him for his actions."

"Fuck, Bryn," I say as I adjust myself. "I thought we were trying to avoid me having a raging boner when we see your sisters."

She giggles, and it's one of the most magical sounds in the world. I don't think I've stopped smiling since Bryn walked into the restaurant, and I swear I feel the muscles in my cheeks burn from overexertion. I can't prove it, but it feels likely I even smiled the whole time we slept, my arms holding her tight.

***

I grab Bryn's hand as soon as she's out of the car, and we walk into the coffee shop to find all three of our sisters sitting at a table in the back. I do a double take when I see Lila sitting there, but Izzy jumps in before I can ask anything.

"Look who finally deigned to grace us with their presence. Did you two kiss and make up?"

"Based on the looks on their faces and the amount of time it took them to get here," Lila responds, "I'm guessing they did more than kiss."

"Lila!" I groan, and the admonishment is echoed by Bryn and at least one of her sisters.

"No one wants to think about that. We are literally all related here," Izzy says.

I kiss Bryn's head. "Well, we aren't *all* related yet."

Bryn whips her head to me, and I smile innocently. I know it's too soon, but there is no doubt in my mind that someday we actually will all be related.

Izzy rolls her eyes. "You know what I meant."

Lila looks at Kelsey and asks, "Do you think us being related will impact if I can work with you?"

"You're going to work with Kelsey?" I ask.

"Yup. Agreed to it yesterday while you two were off making up. It's why I'm here. Did you not find it odd that I'm in Wild Bluffs? I don't live here...yet."

"I did find it a little strange, yeah. But you all didn't give me the opportunity to ask." I pull her into a hug. "That's awesome. I can't wait for you to be out in Wild Bluffs." And it's true. I can't wait. Having Lila and Bryn in the same town will make it a home for me. Maybe I should even consider buying a house here rather than just renting the place at WBCC.

"It will be great to get to see you more," Lila says.

We chat as we eat, the sisters all sipping on varying types of lattes. Bryn updates us on everything that has happened since we were all together in Arizona. It feels like a lifetime ago, and in some ways, maybe it was. That us, the ones who were faced with insecurities pushing us apart—it's not who we are anymore.

After Bryn tells the whole story, the sisters stare at her in amazement.

"That is...wild," Kelsey says, shaking her head.

Lila looks at me. "So what are you going to do about Alexis and Kyle? Because I've got a plan for Alexis. I've been thinking about it *for years*. I think the first step is to trash her in the media, make her essentially toxic. That will cause her to lose all the public figures she's fucking." She continues, clearly mistakenly taking everyone's stunned silence as a good thing, "Then I need to figure out some way to fuck with her appearance. Maybe pay her hairstylist to, like, buzz her head or convince her to eat an extra thousand calories a day. Then, once we destroy those two things, all that's left is—"

Bryn bursts out laughing at that point, and Lila stops talking long enough to notice that the other two women have looks ranging from shock to horror on their faces.

"Well," I offer. "I think it could work."

Bryn laughs. "First of all, this isn't *Mean Girls*. You're not going to trick Alexis into eating an extra thousand calories a day, you fucking psycho. Second, I think we should consider just letting her wallow in her self-hatred."

"Ugh." Lila sighs. "That sounds so boring."

"She's clearly a miserable human being who hates herself so much that she not only can't stand other people being happy, but she actively self-sabotages her own happiness. You're never going to 'punish' that out of her. She's already punishing herself every day. Why else would anyone ever cheat on Jameson?" Bryn asks. "Plus, I think she might've actually believed what she said in the article, and if that's the case, I just feel...bad for her."

Bryn's sisters both nod their consent as well.

"I don't know," I say. "I do think Lila is onto something here. I think we need to do something to Kyle and Alexis. No one should be able to pull that shit on us and get away with it. I'm not sure I'm in for Lila's plan, but we've got to do something."

"You do not," says Kelsey. "You and Bryn staying together is a bigger 'fuck you' to Alexis than anything else you could ever do. And Kyle and, frankly, all of Hungry Guy are going to realize they lost as soon as the news breaks about Bryn getting hired by Conrad." She thinks for a moment. "I do have some thoughts—hypothetical, of course—about how you could fuck with their social media accounts should you ever decide the high road is not the way you want to go."

"Kelsey!" Bryn exclaims, but Izzy just leans across the table to give Kelsey a high five, which she returns begrudgingly.

I think about what Bryn said, about Alexis being the one with issues, not us. Of how much I love Bryn and the joy that I have found because Alexis cheated on me. I think about how much stronger Bryn and I are going to be now that we know we can make it through this, because it certainly won't be the last gossip that is published about me. And I realize that I don't need revenge. I don't need to make Alexis or

Kyle pay in order to move on. Because in the arms of the woman I love, I have found my redemption, my salvation, my home.

"Fine." I grab Bryn's hand, rubbing my thumb across hers as I absorb her calm.

"But, shit," I say, looking at Kelsey. "I have a bad feeling about you and Lila working together." And, terrifyingly, all four of them laugh.

CHAPTER FORTY-NINE
EPILOGUE

Bryn

1 YEAR LATER

I'm standing at the edge of the eighteenth green at Augusta, holding my breath as Jameson's group hits their approach shots. I'm standing next to Izzy and Kelsey, all of us in sundresses with our hair pulled back. Jameson is tied coming into this last hole at the Masters, the Super Bowl of the pro golf world, and the tension in the stands is palpable. It all comes down to this hole—a Masters fan's dream come true.

Izzy is keeping up a steady stream of chatter which she is all but whispering into my ear. "I can't believe you and Jameson finally moved in together. I mean, I thought you would have moved in like a year ago, but at the same time, I understand not wanting to move into a cottage on the course with him. Not that you didn't basically live there when you guys were in town, but still! And then the freakin' builders are taking so long to finish everything. I can't believe how long building a new house takes in the middle of nowhere."

She has a point. It has taken forever for our house to get built. When Jameson announced last summer that he was going to build us a house in Wild Bluffs, I initially balked. It's not that I didn't want to move in with him, it's just that I wanted to be an equal partner in it. After explaining that to Jameson, we worked out a deal. Instead of him financing the house himself, we went through the local bank to get a loan, one that includes both of us. It took some finagling, but I was even able to come up with half of the down payment.

As much as Jameson loves spoiling me, I think it feels better to both of us that the house is truly *ours*. We've both been heavily involved in each step of the process. As hard as it is to coordinate, we both joined the meetings with the architect and interior designer, constantly reassuring each other that, as painful as this process might be, it will all be worth it when it's our home. And, if we were going to go through the pain of building it, we should at least make it something that we both want to grow old in.

We are set to move into the sprawling house on the edge of hole two at Wild Bluffs Country Club in six months. It can't get here soon enough.

"Becca hasn't returned his call. Can you imagine not calling a man like him back?" Izzy is still rambling as Jameson crests the top of the green, chatting with his caddy, a look of ease on his face despite the pressure of the situation.

Jameson has played so well in the last year after all of the nonsense with Alexis, Kyle, and the article, that we know there is a good chance he will take home the Green Jacket today. I've been in PR training the last year, and Jameson and I have slowly become more and more public with our relationship based on the guidance of Erica and her team. We still are careful about doing anything that might even hint at scandal, but it has been such a relief to be able to be seen together at his tournaments.

After the article about me last year, I was worried about stoking the fire by doing anything too "couply" when there was the possibility of press nearby. Jameson was, as I've come to expect, completely understanding of my unease, though it was hard for both of us to limit our interactions, especially when Jameson had a particularly good or bad round. A year later, Jameson has done a world of good for my self-esteem. I occasionally still hear Tara's or Peter's or his mom's voice telling me I can't do it all, but now Jameson's voice follows it, telling me I'm everything he's ever wanted.

To be fair, we are also old news now, so no one cares enough to publish an article about us if I give him a hug after a round.

Jameson lines up his shot, and, as he waits for his opponent to putt, his eyes find me in the crowd. I give him an inconspicuous wave and wink, and he unsuccessfully tries to hide his smile before turning his attention back to his putt.

The other golfer's putt leaves him about two feet from the hole, an almost guaranteed make. I grab Izzy's hand, forcing my eyes to stay open instead of closing under the pressure of this shot that Jameson has to make to win. I watch him step up to the ball, his black shirt pulling just right across the thick muscles of his chest and arms, and send it toward the hole.

"Shit, shit, shit, shit, shit," Kelsey chants almost silently next to me as the ball slowly rolls across the green grass before finally making its way into the cup.

The crowd goes wild as Jameson throws his hands into the air, celebrating his victory. Despite the media representative from the course hovering nearby, I am tempted to duck under the barrier rope and run to celebrate with Jameson. Emily, the name of my representative/bodyguard, shoots me a look that clearly says "don't even fucking think about it." Succumbing to her peer pressure, I stay on the appropriate side of the boundary and jump up and down with my sisters while the golfers remove their hats to shake hands.

Scottie Nyram, last year's winner, approaches with Jameson's Green Jacket, and I stop bouncing so I can take in the sight of Jameson slipping his arms into the grass-green symbol of success at golf.

As the crowd roars, Jameson finds me again, and I can't help but lose my breath at how handsome he looks, standing on the green of one of the most beautiful golf courses in the world, a smile on his face, sporting a Green Jacket with the middle of the three buttons done. He turns to wave to the audience, and I'm struck by how nice the center-vent in the back looks pulling just right over the man's strong ass. Damn, the adrenaline from the day has really turned straight into desire.

Finally, Emily nods to us, and we intercept Jameson on his way to the clubhouse. I throw my arms around his neck and kiss him deeply.

At a pointed cough from fun-killer Emily, I pull back and whisper against his lips, "I'm so proud of you, baby."

His eyes crinkle in pleasure just for me, and he kisses my cheek before putting back on his professional smile for the waiting reporters.

"Go on," I say. "Your adoring public awaits."

I watch as the love of my life answers interview question after interview question, and, each time he is asked what caused the turnaround, how he went from rock bottom to the very top, he smiles and says, "I hit a ball into the rough and walked away with a whole new perspective on life."

Finally, when all the interviews are done and Jameson walks out of the locker room, I wrap my arms around the man of my dreams, the one I will love wildly, forever.

Want to know what happens with that Green Jacket when Bryn and Jameson get back home?

Use the QR code below to find out in Bryn and Jameson's bonus scene!

Ready to return to Wild Bluffs?
Don't miss JT and Lila's story coming January 2025!
Follow me on Instagram @authoremmakate or join my newsletter at www.authoremmakate.com to stay up to date on all the latest Wild Bluffs news!

Acknowledgments

Writing and publishing my first book has been a terrifying and exhilarating experience. As such, I have needed A LOT of support along the way.

My husband encouraged my writing career even before I was writing. Most certainly before it was a career. If not for his unwavering support, I'm not sure I would've found the courage to make it to "The End." He was the first to read this novel (when it was in much worse shape, might I add), and he balanced enthusiasm with constructive feedback like a professional. He is proof that love, caring gestures, and support continue long past the words "and they lived happy ever after."

My younger sister has been on this journey with me since the day I bought my first Kindle. Not only do we make up an informal book club boasting only two members, but because of our similar reading interests, we've spent countless hours dissecting stories and learning what makes a novel great. I have no doubt that Bryn and Jameson would not exist without her inspiration.

A heartfelt thanks to Kelly for taking the time to help me mold my ramblings into the love story that it is today. And to Claudia and Judy, for making sure the story could shine without all my typos and missing commas.

Finally to my family, thank you for putting up with my late-night writing sessions, for being my biggest cheerleaders, and for supporting me as I embark on this new adventure. It's clear awesomeness is genetic. ;)

About the Author

Emma Kate is an author of rom-coms and contemporary romances. She lives in a small Colorado town with her rancher husband, three kids, a dog, and a whole lot of cows. When she's not writing or reading, she can be found chasing after her kids, eating ice cream or cookies, or binge-watching sitcoms.

www.ingramcontent.com/pod-product-compliance
Lightning Source LLC
Chambersburg PA
CBHW070558300726
48975CB00006B/1628

I dedicate this book to Ortie.

The love of my life.

A Novel by

JOHN LAWRENCE

AN AMERICAN HERO

DEWPOINT
PUBLISHING

The idea for this story came to me in the early 1990's, just after the Gulf War, but it was developed over the course of 30 years. The concept was simple in my mind at first. But I soon discovered how truly difficult it would be to tell the story of this fictional family. Like my own family we are very close, and by close, I mean even to this day I speak to my brother at least once a day no matter how many states away we live. I guess to me family is everything. My wife is my biggest advocate she is my other half, my partner in crime, my biggest fan. I rely on her for pretty much everything in my life. She is the rock in our family, and the love of my life. Without her encouragement and that of my entire family, I don't think I would have been able to sit down and write this story. My loved ones would have never thought I could write a book. Especially historical fiction.

Growing up with a single father was an adventure. My father was a ferocious reader, but I did not take after him in that arena. I am dyslexic and I have a hard time reading anything, especially books. Over the years I have developed a method to focus on words and so I could speed up my reading ability. But this means I have only read a few books throughout my life. When audible books came on the scene that opened a new opportunity for me to read the same books my father would talk about. But taking on a challenge like this one I would have certain roadblocks in my way. For starters I couldn't really get a critique partner or collaborator. That would mean I would have to read and critique their work as they would read and critique mine. That would have been a one-way Street for them since it would have taken me a long time to read their work. while they can read and critique mine on a much quicker scale. This makes me a poor candidate to be someone's critique partner. Out of thousands of roadblocks in my way this was the biggest by far.

So why even take on a project like this, you may ask. If I'm being honest with myself, I would have to admit, it probably comes back to my father the ferocious reader. I think my father would have loved reading this story. This story would not leave me alone, every year that passed that I did not start this project, well It was like a ghost haunting me in my quiet times, in my sleep like something prompted me, poking me, almost daring me to start this project. I must admit though since it took a while for me to do this project. I was able to come up with more content and more ideas for the development of the story. Developing awesome characters in this story and what they go through is one of my proudest accomplishments in my writing career. They have really come to life for me, and I can't wait to see what they do in my next book.

Writing and publishing a book is much like eating an elephant the only way you can do it is one bite at a time. There are literally dozens of people that I would like to thank starting with my family, friends, beta readers, editors, cover designer, formator, and the list goes on and on. But above all I thank my creator for giving me this story to tell. For giving me the courage and the knowledge to complete this project.

The Gulf War was a human and environmental disaster. It's my belief that the Gulf War was set in motion years before when Iraq started borrowing money to finance its war with Iran. Iraq kept accusing Kuwait of exceeding its oil production to lower the cost of fossil fuels which in turn was making oil too cheap. Iraq claimed that it could not pay it's debt with Kuwait with the price of oil being forced lower by Kuwait. Iraq continues to accuse Kuwait of cheapening oil and calling it an act of war against Iraq. Iraq also claimed that Kuwait was part of its rightful territory based off the Ottoman empire's Province of Basra, something that

Iraq tried to make claim to the Kuwait territory. The ruling family al-Sabah had agreed to let the UK handle foreign affairs in 1899. The UK drew border lines between Kuwait and Iraq in 1922. This made Iraq almost landlocked.

After accusing Kuwait of slant-drilling across the border into Iraq's Rumaila oil field. Saddam demanded $10 billion in restitution during diplomatic negotiations in Baghdad. When Kuwait offered only 500 million diplomatic talks broke down and on August 2nd, 1990, Iraq annexed Kuwait. The condemnation and reaction around the world were swift and immediate against Iraq and Saddam Hussein.

The United States and 35 other countries around the world formed a coalition to stand up against what Iraq had done. The invasion of a lightly defended country was not going to stand. The small country of Kuwait almost ceased to exist but if it were not for the coalition of countries that came together to stand against a tyrant. The United States was the first to jump into action. George HW Bush needed to prevent Saddam Hussein and Iraq from invading the next country Saudi Arabia which would give them control of most oil reserves in the world. The "wholly defensive" mission to prevent Iraq from invading Saudi Arabia went under the name of Operation Desert Shield on August 7, 1990. King Fahd of Saudi Arabia requested U.S. Military assistance.

At this time the world's eyes and attention turned towards the United Nations Security council.

At the United Nations several UN resolutions were passed and adopted, it was clear that Iraq needed to leave Kuwait immediately or face expulsion by force. The date was set, January 15,1990. UN resolution 678 deadline came and went and on the 16th the Gulf War began with an extensive aerial bombardment. 42 consecutive days of bombing had begun. The coalition flew 100,000 sorties and dropped over 88,500 tons of bombs.

Saddam Hussein answered back by launching scud missile attacks on Israel and Saudi Arabia he threatened the world by using chemical weapons. This created a lot of fear and anxiety. There were even some deaths recorded from improper use of gas masks and of Atropine an anti-chemical drug. Families put on their chemical masks every time the air raids sounded. The use of chemical weapons, and the threat of them, outraged the entire world. The U.S. and its allies knew this was going to be one of the biggest and deadliest battles. The United States rapidly deployed the patriot missile air defense artillery battalion into Israel and Saudi Arabia. This was successful in knocking down some of Saddam Hussein's scud missiles making them ineffective. Iraq fired more than 80 scud missiles at Israel and Saudi Arabia killing 31 people. The largest death toll was 28 U.S. soldiers in the barracks Khobar city, just outside Dhahran. The U.S. patriot missile system engaged approximately 45 scud missiles, but results later revealed success rate was only about half hit their target.

The United States estimated 10,000 Americans

would be killed in the first week of the Gulf War and up to 30,000 casualties would be expected if the war lasted 20 days. But on the 29th of January 1991, Saddam Hussein ordered the invasion of Khafji inside Saudi Arabia. Khafji was lightly defended, and Iraq despite heavy artillery efforts by US military, had captured the small town quickly. This infuriated the king of Saudi Arabia. He ordered Saudi and Qatar forces along with assistance from the US marine and air units to recapture the city. In less than 48 hours the Saudi Arabian military along with Qatar and the US. had retaken control of the town of Khafji.

The battle for Khafji however was more significant than most realized. It showed that the Iraqi army had no fight left in them. The 400 Iraqis captured at the battle of Khafji suffered dehydrated and battle fatigue. There was no way they could continue a long insurgency in their condition. What coalition generals realized from the battle of Khafji is that the air campaign and artillery strike's were having more effect than they could have ever hoped for, taking the battle right out of the soul of the soldier.

Operation desert storm started February 24th, 1991, and by the 28th it was a massive win for the U.S. and its allies. The country of Kuwait was liberated, and the United Nations resolutions were enforced. Sometimes I think we forget what it would have been like to be a US marine stationed in Saudi Arabia prior to the war. Hearing some of the casualty predictions that were coming out of the Pentagon during that time. Most of the young men and women in our military during that time in our country had only the Vietnam conflict to use as a reference. How brave our military men and women are astonishes me. I do not want to go into deep details about the Gulf War in this book but just to show some of the evil that families may have gone through.

Kuwait is a very special place and I hope to visit one day. I am so glad it is free from the grip of Iraq. The Kuwaiti people have a very special place in my heart. Alongside US military and co-alition soldiers that fought and sacrificed to stand up against a bully. I feel we need more of that currently. Otherwise, I think history will continue to repeat itself. The reference material I used in this book have been Wikipedia and Google searches on Gulf War, Timeline Gulf War, Battle of Khafji. I dedicate this book to the men and women who suffered and died during this conflict. I hope the memory of them will continue through their family and loved ones. I know there must be a million stories about the Gulf War that could be told. I hope I've inspired those that really have lived through it to write it down. If someone like me can write a book with all my obstacles in my life. I hope that inspires them to right a nonfiction account of what they went through.

CHAPTER 1

The immense noise from the Sikorsky helicopter blades beating the air into submission across the desert floor as we flew low increased the pain in my arm. I sat on the floor of the helicopter with my elbow resting on the seat. Corporal Brown was sitting directly across from me in the same position. We both stared at each other as the medics worked on our lieutenant's partially severed leg. Lieutenant Kleinsmith had two rounds hit his upper leg and another through the palm of his hand. I caught one in the shoulder, but they said it was just a simple flesh wound. The pain was getting harder and harder to ignore even if it was just a flesh wound.

The bandage on Corporal Brown's head was full of blood and starting to drip down his neck. He had lost an ear.

"Reem, is that the gulf?" he asked.

I looked out through the open door of the helicopter where Corporal Brown was pointing. Our elevation was just high enough to see the curve of the Persian Gulf. I knew my homeland of Kuwait was just over the horizon. I turned to Corporal Brown and answered, "Yes." My attention went back to the view. I hope my family's okay, I thought to myself. "I hope they're still alive," I said.

Corporal Brown looked at me with encouraging eyes.

"What was it like growing up in Kuwait?" he shouted over the noise of the medics and helicopter.

"It was normal like anywhere else. Our family is close, so we do a lot of things together. My brother Rico and I had a sibling rivalry going on as young kids, but we grew out of that by Junior High. We're very close now," I explained, shouting.

"This rivalry between you and your brother, what was that like?" Corporal Brown asked. I considered him for a moment; his current condition and that bandage doing little to staunch the blood. The dripping of blood had now formed a trickle and become thick and aromatic.

My thoughts turned to the end of my fifth grade and my mother. Everything around me faded away.

"Mom, I've been playing kickball all year with my friends and not once have I been able to beat Rico. It pisses me off!" I said out of frustration.

"Reem! Language!" Mom quickly snapped. She was washing dishes in a sink that was big enough to take a bath in.

"You just need to spend more time kicking the ball hard," she said.

My mother had never been afraid of hard work. She grew up in Quebec and was the middle child of five kids. She had three brothers and one sister. Grandma Green would come to visit and would always repeat the same thing when we asked about our mom growing up. She would say, "Your mom was the biggest tomboy in our family." She would always follow that up with "Susie Q was the best at whatever she put her mind to. If there was something she didn't know how to do, she would work, day and night until she was the best at it."

I guessed Mom's tomboy days were behind her; she had been fixing up the family home by remodeling each room one at a time. Now she was driving us crazy with art projects. She'd discovered painting and made weird-looking figurines that kept showing up in each of our rooms.

Mom shut off the water and asked Bella, our maid, to take over for her. She took me by the hand and sat me down in the living room. She loved the new cushions she'd got after remodeling – blue and gold, with some fancy design on both sides. Our home was a typical, one- story marble palace; from the outside you could see part of the carport but not the entrance. We had a grand foyer as you came in the front and an open-floor plan which caught you by surprise as you passed the foyer. You could see my mom's Canadian style all over our house. She had a Kuwait and Canada flag sewn together and framed on the wall in the foyer for starters, and of course the teapots she came home with from each trip back home. We had no couches or chairs in the living room, just cushions and a nice rug that dad's side of the family had given them as a wedding gift. It was this room where we'd bring most of our guests. The family room just off the kitchen had sofas and chairs in it, with a console TV.

"What's the matter, son? You're making such a big deal out of this game. It's just a game." Mom pushed my hair back off my forehead.

I sat up very straight and turned to the side.

"This year, Mr. Polson is having a championship game between the fifth grade and the sixth-grade classes. Mom, that's less than a month away! Rico is so competitive I don't see how I can beat him!" I repeated the same motion, pushing my hair off my forehead.

"Okay, let's go, son!" Mom said abruptly.

She got up in one fluid motion and motioned to me to follow her. She walked into the kitchen, grabbed her car keys, and asked Bella to let my dad know we would be back. Out in the garage, she grabbed a ball from the closet where we kept all our sporting gear.

"Is this the ball you guys use?" she asked.

"Yes!" I replied.

She threw the ball in the back seat along with seven or eight red cones we would use for football, and drove to the nearest park, about a mile and a half from the house. Mom put the red cones in the chain link fence with the bases hanging out, then had me stand the distance a pitcher's mound would be from them and use the cones as targets. I immediately got the idea.

"Reem, I want you to come here every day after school. Set the cones up in seven different areas and practice for three hours a day. If you do this, I guarantee you will beat your brother Rico," Mom said.

She was teaching me how hard work and practice always pays off. That's how Mom used to beat her brothers. Mom was tall for a lady, with blonde hair and piercing blue eyes. People could tell right away that she was a foreigner because of her eyes and the confidence she carried.

So, I took my mom's advice. I started practicing that day, kicking the ball to red cones in different areas of the chain-link fence. When my leg started hurting, I would switch to the other. It felt good. I like the fact that with practice, I could give myself a chance at beating Rico at a sport. I told my sister June that I was helping a friend learn how to speak French after school. I didn't want June to leak it back to my brother Rico, as I'd lose the element of surprise. June was in second grade and wouldn't be able to keep a secret, I thought. By the end of the second week, I'd become ten times better at kicking that ball. It didn't matter where you were on the field, if there was a gap, I could kick the ball there. When it was time for recess, I would take my friends on the playground to play kickball with them. They were extremely impressed with how good I had become. I didn't have to worry about Rico because we had different recess periods since he was in the sixth grade, and I was in the fifth. Rico felt that he should be in the seventh grade, but his birthday landed on the cut-off, putting him into school late. This of course also made him bigger than all the sixth graders. We would see each other occasionally, mainly at lunchtime and the last class of the day. Our classrooms faced each other across the quad. We would walk to the front of the school together, where Bella would pick us up and take us home.

I didn't think we were wealthy because most of the kids at our school had cars that would take them home too. It wasn't until I was about twelve and a half years old that I discovered we might be wealthier than most people. Staying overnight with friends and seeing how they lived was eye-opening to me.

Dad was preparing to go on another business trip, and Mom was picking out what color she wanted to paint the sunroom in the back of our house. I interrupted their conversation to let my mom know, I was ready for the big game the next day.

"I'm ready, Mom! Mom, I'm ready!" I declared.

I pulled on her blouse to get her attention. My parents stop talking and looked at me, puzzled.

"Ready for what, sweetheart?" Mom asked, looking back at my dad. He just shrugged and raised his hands.

"He's your son," Dad said.

Anytime we were terrible as kids, dad would say "They're your kids" and mom would say "No, they're your kids." We all thought this was funny because when we did well, it was always "That's my girl" or "That's my boy."

"The big game! The kickball game is tomorrow, and I'm ready. I can't wait!"

"You'll do good, son. Get plenty of rest, and hydrate, so you don't get cramps," Mom said with a smile.

That morning I must have gotten ready in record time. All I could think about was the opportunity to beat Rico and rub his nose in it.

At the end of the second period, Mr. Polson gathered the fifth graders and the six graders together on the playground. We had just come from our classrooms where we'd been signing each other's yearbooks and turning in all our study materials.

"I want the fifth graders to line up on my left, and I want the six graders to line up on my right. Come on, guys, I don't have all day!" Mr. Polson said with a clap of his hands.

He looked eager to get the game started. After yelling at us for a while, we all finally settled down and picked captains for each team. Of course, they chose Rico for the sixth graders. The fifth graders chose Mohammad, which was fine with me as we'd been playing during recess every day. He could see the strides I'd been making by practicing after school and set me to go fourth, in the cleanup position. Nothing does more for your confidence than giving you that kind of responsibility. I had to admit it felt good. We finally hit the field. The fifth graders were up first, and of course Rico decided that he would be on the pitching mound for the sixth graders. We only got one player on first base; a very athletic boy named Raza. It was finally my turn, with two outs and a runner on first. Rico rolled the ball so fast and hard it was difficult to judge the speed. I'd been practicing with the ball just at a standstill and not being thrown towards me. I'd soon realized that during our recess, weeks before the game. So, I had Mohammed practice with me, throwing the ball and trying to spin it quickly. I was ready for whatever Rico threw at me.

The look on my brother Rico's face when I kicked the ball over his head and into the outfield was something I'll never forget. I scored not only Raza, who was on first base, but also myself. The rest of the game continued much about the same. The fifth graders destroyed the sixth graders.

I would like to say that I enjoyed rubbing Rico's nose in it, but something weird happened that afternoon. Rico seemed to be more excited than I was, regarding how well I played that day. Even when we got home, Rico ran into the kitchen where our mom was on the phone with Grandma Green. Rico wouldn't shut up about how awesome of a game I had. It was then I realized that my brother was proud of me. Something changed between Rico and I that day. I felt Rico respected me as an equal and not just his little brother.

That evening I went into my mother's art room where she was painting a new picture of two camels. I sat down on a cushion next to her.

"Well, you had a good day today, didn't you?" Mom said.

I could tell she was proud of me.

"I guess... It's just weird because it seemed like Rico was proud of me. Just when I was going to rub his nose in it. Every time he beats me at a sport, he always rubs my nose in it," I said.

"Honey, he's your big brother... Of course, he's going to be proud of you. Siblings always have rivalries together, but family is family. He will always be your big brother and have your back. That's what I think you're feeling and seeing with Rico."

I still had a look of confusion on my face.

"If you say so, Mom."

I must have looked deflated. Mom put down her brushes and sat on the cushion next to me. Her blue eyes looked over the top of her glasses.

"Reem, I want you to listen to what I'm going to say."

She looked at me with love in her eyes. "Life can be hard and scary at times. It's a big world out there. No matter where life takes you. No matter how far you go, your family will always be there for you."

She put her hand on my cheek. "When your father and I met in college, we knew it would be hard for me to leave my family. To go across the world to a place I'd never seen before. But I didn't hesitate to go because I knew your father would always protect me. There was comfort in knowing I always had my mom and Dad, my brothers and sister. I think it was harder on your father bringing me home to meet his family." Mom gave a little laugh. "He had to explain to all of them that we were to be married. I was a foreigner; we knew this would be hard. Your father and I were in love, and we wanted to start a family together. I look at you, Reem, and I am so proud of you, son."

She stood up, walked over to her easel, and picked up her brushes.

"Remember son, our family is everything. No matter how competitive you get with your brother, he will always be there for you," she said with the most loving smile on her face.

For some reason, what my mother told me always stuck with me. Maybe it was the way she looked at me or the smile she gave me, but I realized that Rico and I were brothers first and rivalries are not that important. Coming to that realization allowed me to look at Rico with more love and affection. I became a fan of his, cheering for him throughout the rest of our lives.

CHAPTER 2

The kickball game and the school year quickly vanished as my summer vacation started. June was driving us all crazy, preparing for our trip to the United States. Our Dad had some business to conduct in California so he and my mother decided to make a family vacation out of it. They wanted to take us to Disneyland. Our mother had been there before as a child, but this would be the first time for the rest of us. June kept spouting off with useless facts about America and California. "Did you know that California became a state in 1850? It was the 31st state of the union in America…"

Back then June loved to carry a purse that Mom had bought her from her Avon representative. Inside, she carried a bottle of Sweet Honesty perfume and a copy of *Reader's Digest*. As time passed the contents of her purse would also include lip gloss (that she told Dad was Chapstick) and a brush for her long black hair. June was a ferocious reader. Books and magazines would always be about her person on any given day. She loved reading anything that had a good story. Mom would encourage June to read as much as she wanted if she looked up and interacted with the world occasionally.

My brother Rico, on the other hand, some would say that he was too big for his age. In fact, some teachers mistook Rico for a senior in his first year of high school. By now it wasn't just the advantage of having started school later, Rico's natural, physical maturity gave him more self-confidence (a byproduct of his good fortune), which made him appear older than he was. He could also grow a beard faster than some of the teachers, which again was misleading. I always liked mentioning this to people when I described my older brother. Rico would inherit the bulk of our father's wealth, so Dad wanted him to take over the family seat. Kuwait had nationalized the oil production in our country and our family had a seat on Kuwaiti's Advisory Council. Dad thought he would have to give up his position after marrying our Mom, as she wasn't from Kuwait. However, it seemed that with some consideration he had been allowed to keep the advisory seat in our family.

"Can you believe it? We're going to see the Pacific Ocean, and you can travel to any of the different states in America without stopping," June said.

She was bugging Dad this time as we started out for the airport.

"Yes, I know honey, I've been there before, remember," Dad said.

Dad had a look of annoyance on him.

"Not to California! You only went to New York, Washington DC, and Texas," June said.

"California is a whole different state. It's way different than the other ones you've been to, Dad."

Dad smiled at June and patted her on the shoulder. "You're right, dear."

Kuwait is nestled at the end of the Persian Gulf with Saudi Arabia to the southwest and Iraq to the northwest. The city itself pushes out east into the Persian Gulf. My dad was born and raised in Kuwait City. He attended engineering school in Canada, which was where he and my mom met. After my dad had completed college, he'd developed a very sophisticated valve for oil distribution and became a treasured member of the oil giant, British Petroleum. Kuwait nationalized its oil industry in the '60s. This move put my dad into the Kuwaiti government almost overnight. The Emir needed technical help at OPEC (the Organization of the Petroleum Exporting Countries), so Dad became a technical staff member. We were so proud of him. He went on trips with high government officials all the time and I liked telling my friends that he was important.

Dad was only going to be able to spend a couple of days with us at Disneyland. He had some business in Washington DC, and he was of course taking Rico with him. I was jealous because I wanted to go too.

"You're too young, Reem, you'll just be in the way," Rico said, as if he was so much older than me.

Mom convinced me that it would be more fun with her and with Grandma and Grandpa Green.

We arrived in California early in the morning at the executive terminal, Los Angeles International Airport. The place looked futuristic, with blue and silver décor. There were pictures of new and old airplanes all over the very tall walls. I'd slept well on the plane, so I was up and alert, looking out the car window on the way to our hotel. I remember watching the sun coming up over Los Angeles. I had never seen anything like this place in my life. I could be an alien visiting a new planet, I thought to myself. June was so keyed up on the trip, she had not slept, so she was out by the time we arrived at the hotel.

"June, wake up, sweetheart. We're almost there." June had fallen asleep on Mom's lap, and she was now gently shaking her. Rico and I instantly started hitting June and mocking Mom.

"Wake up, sweetheart. Time to get up, you little spoiled baby," Rico said. I started shaking June and was laughing.

"Come on, sweetie pie," I teased.

"Leave me alone! Mom!" June started her fake crying.

Before Mom could snap at us, our father gave Rico and me a look. It's hard to describe "The Look" if you don't have a father. All I can say is it's the point past yelling or threats of physical punishment, and just before getting hit. Rico and I sat up straight and looked forward in all of two seconds and Dad went back to reading his book. The car pulled up to the hotel's porte-cochère. As we exited the limousine, I could hear Mom whisper to Dad, "I wish I could give that look."

Dad chuckled. "You have a look, but it only works on me. The boys know you wouldn't kill them, but with me, they're not so sure," he replied with a laugh.

Dad got out and walked to the back of the car with Mom. I was trying to beat Rico into the lobby of the Disneyland hotel. That was when we both saw a very familiar face, our dad's secretary, BJ. When I was little, I thought he was part of the family because I couldn't remember a time he wasn't with my dad. BJ was from India – his real name was Balaji Anand, but everybody called him BJ. He stood about 6 foot 3, slim build with a unibrow. BJ would tell Rico and me stories when we were younger about how he was really an assassin for the king of India. In reality BJ had studied business in England and met my dad through a professor. BJ had gone to work for my father right out of college.

BJ's familiar smile was a welcome sight to all of us. He had come out a couple of days earlier to make some arrangements for my dad.

"How are you, my friend," Dad asked while giving BJ a quick hug in the lobby of the hotel.

"I'm good, Ahmed, thank you. All the arrangements are confirmed. Here are your keys and passes. We have all three presidential suites. The Greens are set to arrive later this evening, and arrangements have been made for them to be picked up at the airport and brought here."

This, of course, pleased my mom. As the bellman passed us with our luggage, he motioned to BJ, and BJ nodded his head to confirm the room location. Dad was going over the package that BJ had handed him.

"Dinner is at six, as we discussed. The hotel will provide dinner in the residence and there are a lot of food options here so…"

Dad cut BJ off. "We got it from here, BJ. We're going to rest for a bit, and Sue will take the kids swimming later. She can order lunch at the pool."

"Very well, sir, just give me a call if you need anything."

Dad was right; after resting in the hotel room for a while, we had a fantastic lunch out at the pool. I had something called a turkey club with fries. Mom had a southwest chicken wrap with Dad. Rico and June ate pizza.

"Rico, June, hurry up! I want to get going," Mom yelled for them to get out of the pool.

Rico and June loved swimming. Rico liked playing Marco Polo because he cheated. Mom wanted to go shopping before Grandma arrived, and before we had dinner in the residence.

Our grandparents' flight was delayed by an hour. Dad had wanted them to fly by private plane, but Grandpa had insisted on flying TWA. By the time we were eating dinner, I was so hungry.

"Reem, slow down. No one is going to steal your plate," Grandma said.

"Don't you feed these children, Susie Q?"

Mom looked at Grandma and rolled her eyes.

"Mom, you know these boys can eat their fair share. It's June I have trouble getting to eat."

In the morning, Uncle Jim and Aunt Carol arrived with my cousin Robert. Robert was my Uncle Dennis's only child and Uncle Dennis was the oldest of Mom's brothers. As Uncle Dennis had to work and wouldn't be joining us until the next day, Uncle Jim who was the youngest of my mom's brothers had decided to come with Robert a day earlier.

Aunt Carol was incredibly beautiful. She had long black hair and brown eyes, but it was always her happy and cheerful personality that made you want to be around her. Man, was I in love with Aunt Carol. She always favored me; I think maybe because she too was the middle child in her family. She used to whisper to me when she thought no one was looking, "I love you forever, Reem. You're my favorite," and she'd always give me a big hug and a squeeze.

June and I got into an argument my senior year of high school. "Aunt Carol loves me more. I'm her favorite, she told me so," June said. I told her that Aunt Carol loved me forever; she always said I was her favorite. June and I looked at each other, and as we added up 2+2, we realized the obvious. After confirmation from Rico, we concluded that Aunt Carol was telling us all the same thing.

The park opened early in the morning, so we took the Monorail from our hotel into the park. I think we ended up in Tomorrowland. Mom and Dad gave us some tickets for the rides and a map to use. We were all to meet back at the food court in two hours. June stayed with Mom and Dad. Rico and I went with my cousin Robert, who was my age. We wanted to go on the brand-new ride called Space Mountain. The line was going to be awfully long, so we rushed to get there.

"This line will take forever," Robert said.

He was looking very distraught. The line did look longer than I'd imagined, but at least it was moving. After about an hour waiting in line, we finally got to the opening of the building. We realized that the line continued inside for a while, and I was starting to get worried that we wouldn't make the two-hour deadline to be back at the food court.

"It's nice and cool inside here," Robert said.

He seemed to be more excited the closer he got to the end of the line.

"Why? Was it getting too hot outside for you?" I asked.

"I've started getting a sunburn standing out there for an hour," Robert said.

Rico and I looked at each other. We both busted out laughing.

"You cannot be serious. It's August, do you have any idea how hot it is in Kuwait right now?" Rico said with a half-laugh.

"I know you two live on the surface of the sun, but us Canadians are more of the winter weather type," Robert replied.

After the ride was over, we all three ran back towards the food court, in Tomorrowland. Laughing and talking about how awesome the roller coaster was. Robert stopped abruptly and yelled.

"LOOK, LOOK WHO THAT IS!"

Rico and I stopped immediately and looked in Robert's direction. We didn't recognize anybody. The crowd was thick and there were a lot of people.

Robert said with a look of confusion, "I think that was Telly Savalas, the actor."

Rico and I had no idea who he was talking about and continued running towards the food court. When we arrived, everybody was there. Mom looked like she had been crying. Our dad had his arm around her and was consoling her. Dad looked sad but not overly sad.

"Boys, come here!" Uncle Jim said.

My uncle Jim had us huddle around. He explained that they had just found out that Elvis Presley had died. Mom loved Elvis. Mom and my Aunt Carol went back to the hotel room to watch TV and listen to Elvis's songs. My dad and Uncle Jim kept us kids going all day at the park. We had so much fun. There was no Mom to yell at us, "Slow down! Tie your shoes! Don't eat sweets before dinner!"

Dad and Uncle Jim let us do anything we wanted. Rico and I loved playing on Tom Sawyer's Island. We must have gone on all the rides at least twice by the time the fireworks started that night. We arrived back at the hotel after midnight. I could see Mom was feeling a lot better, smiling and laughing with Aunt Carol and Grandma. Mom promised to hang out with us all the next day at the park. Dad and Uncle Jim stood there with bags of Mickey Mouse ears, pop guns, huge colored lollipops, T-shirts, and sweat-shirts, and all the other souvenirs they'd bought for us.

"Good lord, Ahmed, did you have to buy them everything in the park?" Mom said.

Dad collapsed on the couch, still holding all the bags. He was exhausted.

"Go get ready for bed, boys, I'll be in to check on you in a minute," my Mom commanded.

I was out before my head hit the pillow. The next day was much the same. Mom was having a great time with Grandma and Aunt Carol shopping for all things Mickey Mouse, and Dad was spending time with the boys. He even went on a few rides with me. Rico and Robert seemed to be in competition with each other over everything. Who could get into the next line faster, who was braver putting their hands in the air during the ride. I didn't care – I was having a fun time with my dad.

CHAPTER 3

When Dad woke me up, I could tell he was running late. The hotel suite was a mess, with all the food trays and empty glasses and Disneyland paraphernalia strung out on the chairs and tables. Mom and the girls had already left. I could smell the scent of hair spray in the air.

"Come on, Reem, get ready. You're coming with me today," Dad said.

"Uncle Jim and Rico left already?" I asked as I got up and headed to the bathroom to get ready.

"You were hard to wake up this morning, so I told Jim to leave you with me today. I want to spend some one-on-one time with you," he said.

We met BJ in the lobby, and he had the car waiting for us. Dad told BJ that we would be okay for the rest of the day. BJ had a lot of his own family in town, and Dad wanted him to spend as much time as he could with them. We drove to Los Angeles Airport and picked up my Uncle Dennis. The car was big and had that fresh car smell. Dad let me play with all the switches and buttons in the back for a while until I overdid it.

Uncle Dennis was waiting in the passenger pickup area. I got out and gave him a big hug. Dad had me get in the front passenger seat with the driver so they could talk in private. Uncle Dennis looked like a cop, with his buzz cut black hair and a suit and tie that seemed out of style. By the time we were entering the driveway into the USC campus, I could hear Dad and Uncle Dennis talking loudly. So much for privacy, I thought.

"She loves you and just wanted to help you, Dennis! We're family, and there's nothing wrong with giving money to help each other out."

"She thinks I can't take care of myself! Susan has always interfered in my business to make me look bad in front of our parents! I'm a doctor! I make a good living, Ahmed! If she thinks…"

"Dennis, it's not like that! She's living on the other side of the world! I have her doing as much as I can with the house and her arts and crafts. Susan is just heartbroken, being so far away from her family. The kids and I keep her going, but when she heard about you going through your divorce, it killed her not to be there for you."

"So she pays off my student debt? She's gone too far, Ahmed. How would you feel if that were you?"

"Look, Dennis, I just needed to talk to you first, so the two of you don't get into some big family rift, and don't speak for years. No one is more understanding than me when it comes to money. Susan wants to feel like she's there for you when you need her."

Dad and Uncle Dennis were still talking as we walked into the lobby of a campus building.

Then Uncle Dennis turned around and stood in front of me, smiling and with a gleam in his eyes. Like a lightbulb had just turned on.

"Okay, Ahmed! We don't want a rift in the family. I'll pay for Reem's college education. If that's okay with you…"

Dad looked shocked. "But I have Reem's college fund already in place for him."

Uncle Dennis looked incredibly pleased with himself.

"Do you see how it feels, Ahmed? I'm sure you could use the money somewhere else."

"Dennis, do you have any idea what my net worth is?" Dad whispered.

Uncle Dennis shrugged. "I don't care."

Dad took out a memo pad from his coat and started writing.

"I'm going to write a number in US dollars," Dad said.

Dad palmed the paper in his hand and showed it to Uncle Dennis.

Uncle Dennis took a step back.

"Bullshit! Really?"

Dad nodded, but Uncle Dennis didn't relent.

"If you want to keep the peace between my sister and me, you'll have to take the money. That way, I'll feel that I'm there for you and Susan. That's my final offer. Or I'll call Susan out on this bullshit."

Dad looked defeated.

"Okay, Dennis, you can pay for Reem's education, but Susan can't ever know about it. I mean it, Dennis! If she finds out, all bets are off."

Dad was in the process of swearing me to secrecy about what I'd overheard when an impeccably dressed lady interrupted us.

"Sir. They are ready for you."

Dad kissed me on the top of my head and walked into the classroom where a lot of engineering students and faculty where waiting. I was right behind him with Uncle Dennis. I could hear someone giving my dad an introduction.

"Mr. Al Saba has traveled from the Persian Gulf to be here with us today, so let's give him a warm…"

Uncle Dennis grabbed me by the arm and stopped me from going into the classroom.

"Hey Reem, you want to check out the campus with me instead of listening to your dad's speech?"

"Yeah, but my dad wants me to …"

I looked up at Dad, and he was motioning for me to go with Uncle Dennis.

"It's okay, son, have fun. I'll be about two or three hours."

Dad started to wave to all the people in the classroom as the double doors slammed shut.

Uncle Dennis and I found the campus dining hall – he was starving after his long flight. I was trying to take it all in. The campus was very well-manicured, but it was the architecture of all the buildings I fell in love with. I hadn't seen buildings and architecture like this before. It was summer classes, and Dad was giving his time to lecture the engineering students who'd graduated a few months ago. The campus was something right out of a movie, I thought.

"Uncle Dennis, can I tell you a secret?" I asked.

Uncle Dennis leaned over and was giving me his ear while stuffing a bit of salad in his mouth.

"I'm going to go to school here. I love this place," I said.

Uncle Dennis raised his eyebrow.

"Oh. What are you going to be studying here?"

He had to cover his mouth as he chewed his food.

"Architecture!" I declared with a smile on my face.

Uncle Dennis started laughing. "You know, USC has one of the best programs in the world for Architecture. Are you sure your dad will be onboard? I think he wants you to go to school in Kuwait."

I looked at my uncle.

"Every time we travel somewhere, I love the different types of architecture I've seen. Even at Disneyland, I can't stop looking at all the wild designs in the park. I know what I'm going to be!"

At that moment, the tumblers of the universe and fate had clicked into motion. Just saying it out loud made me feel that it was going to be a certainty. I would be an architect. And I would design buildings that would outlast me and my children. Let Rico try to top that while he was in our dad's world of oil production and distribution, I thought to myself.

Uncle Dennis laughed. "Do you want to go check out the USC School of Architecture? It's not far from here."

I couldn't even say the words. The excitement took hold of me like something I'd never felt. Uncle Dennis could see the excitement in my eyes.

"Come on, Reem, you'll love this. Just don't let

your mom know I encouraged you to go here," Uncle Dennis said.

We walked over to Harris Hall. Uncle Dennis had me stay outside as he walked in. Summer classes were in session, but we had the run of the place. There weren't a lot of students or faculty around, so I just took it all in. It smelled like summer grass and trees. The flowers in the flowerbeds were in a design spelling USC. I couldn't get over all the vegetation on campus and in California. It was like the first-time Mom had taken us to Canada. I hadn't wanted to go home. Kuwait had trees and flowers, but nothing like Canada's. Standing in an actual forest, just a small hike from my grandparents' house, had been like being in the best playground for a kid from the Persian Gulf.

Outside there was a square-shaped water fountain with a sculpture in it. I sat down and put my hand in the water. It was beautiful and refreshing. It had a blue-green bottom with the smell of moisture on concrete. My uncle Dennis was walking toward me with a younger man. He was short, chubby, and looked like he was homeless. He had a backpack on that looked like all his worldly possessions were in it. It looked heavy and very used. The closer he got, I could see that he had dark skin and was wearing eyeglasses that didn't fit his face.

"Reem, I want you to meet Juan Gonzales. He's a student here studying for his BA in Architecture. I was telling Juan that you want to attend the Architectural program here at USC."

He had a very devious look on him.

"So, Juan, tell us a little bit more about yourself

and why you chose to go to USC," Uncle Dennis asked.

He moved out of Juan's path so he could sit next to me on the side of the fountain. Juan grabbed the strap on his right shoulder, and with one fluid motion, his backpack hit the ground at the same time he sat down.

"Sorry, that was so heavy I had to take it off," Juan said.

He looked relieved to sit down.

"You have a lot of books in there?" I inquired.

"No, just some supplies I got for a model I'm scaling up for a project. So, you're thinking about coming to USC?"

He was rubbing his left shoulder with his hand.

"I want to be an architect!" I sat up straighter.

"Well, you have a few years to prepare for it, being as young as you are. It's not easy to get in at USC. We're one of the top ten architectural programs. I'm from Mexico City and I worked hard to get a scholarship to USC, so I had to study my butt off. My dad has an import/export business and helps with what he can. But the competition is intense."

He opened his bag and took out a pen and notepad.

"Your uncle wants me to give you a road map on how to get into the program. He said that you don't need a scholarship. That will be so much easier. I competed for so many scholarships during my senior year of high school, but I started preparing for them in my freshman year."

He started going over the list of things I would need to do academically and with all my SAT scores.

Uncle Dennis told me to stay there and that he would be right back. I assumed he was going to check on my dad's speech. It was at this point I could see two or three hundred-dollar bills in Juan's shirt pocket. Juan looked to see where I was looking. He smiled at me.

"Your uncle must care a lot about your education," he said.

We both started laughing.

I can see that Juan was a nerd, but boy did he earn whatever Uncle Dennis gave him. The road map was so detailed. Juan even took me inside to meet some professors. I was so impressed that a kid like myself was taken seriously. I was incredibly young, but that didn't matter to them. They loved talking to me about all the different majors I should investigate. By the time uncle Dennis came back for me, I had all the information I needed to set a goal for my future. Juan and I exchanged home addresses so we could keep in touch with one another.

When we got back Dad was shaking hands and saying goodbye to all the remaining students in the room when he turned to me.

"Did you have a nice tour of the campus?" he asked.

I had a death grip on the road map and some literature Juan had given me.

"I did… How was your speech?"

I wanted to change the subject away from the campus "tour." I wasn't sure what my uncle had said to him.

"The speech was good, but I've done that one a hundred times. Today was more of a chance to network with new engineers," Dad said.

Dad was putting away his notes and an engineering drawing into a cylindrical cardboard tube. Then he noticed I was confused about what he meant.

"Every year, we have a new class of engineers that have graduated with their degrees," he explained, "and we all like to get together and exchange information. We call it networking."

I just nodded and gave him a thumbs up.

Uncle Dennis put his hand on Dad's back.

"Do you need any help? I want to go see Robert now," Uncle Dennis said.

Dad smiled at Uncle Dennis as he grabbed the handle of a new USC tote bag. Dad had been given a lot of USC swag for speaking at these events. It was common to see Dad come home with free stuff.

"Dennis, that boy of yours is with his cousin, and I'm pretty sure he isn't even thinking about you," Dad said, with a smile on his face.

I opened the exit doors for my dad and Uncle Dennis. Dad and I looked at each other and started laughing. Robert was an only child, and happy to be with other kids (boys) his age. He'd been bouncing off of every wall in the hotel the first night.

Dad was laughing so hard he could hardly get the words out as we left the building.

"I think Jim and Carol are reconsidering having kids at all," he said.

"I warned them he'd be a handful, but Carol insisted on bringing him," Uncle Dennis said.

Uncle Dennis started laughing at the thought of his little brother having kids.

That day was the best. Not because I went with my dad. But because I felt like for the first time, Dad and Uncle Dennis looked at me as a young man and not a baby. Having them to myself was the best feeling ever. They made me feel like one of the guys.

CHAPTER 4

BJ came busting into our hotel room early in the morning. He opened the curtains, letting the morning sunlight envelop the room. I had to pull the covers over my head, not to go blind. The pain from the light and waking up so early made me want to hit someone. We had all stayed up late the night before, talking and enjoying our time together.

"Your dad's almost ready, Rico. Time to get going, your royal highness," BJ said.

Rico got up and started to get ready. He was excited to go with our dad, but he was going to miss out on a lot of places. The beach, Knott's Berry Farm, Hollywood, and Griffith Observatory were all on the schedule for the next three days. After I got up and got ready, I raced down to the hotel restaurant for breakfast.

"Reem, sit over by your cousin Robert," Mom demanded. I could see she was upset over something.

"Where are Dad and BJ?" I asked Rico across the table from me. Rico and Dad should have left by now, I thought to myself.

"I think our waiter said something to Grandma that pissed off my dad and yours," Robert said under his breath so no one could hear him.

"The waiter sees your Arab clothing and just assumes you're all Iranians," Aunt Carol said.

"I don't care what that asshole thinks. There's no reason he should have said that to Grandma," Mom said.

Rico and I were both shocked to hear Mom use a bad word like that. We all sat there uncomfortably for a while, until my dad and BJ came back to the table.

"The hotel manager is taking care of the issue," BJ said with a tone of anger in his voice. I started to feel everyone's eyes in the restaurant looking at us. Everyone hates us, I thought to myself. I didn't like this feeling that people didn't want us eating there.

"Mom, what did the waiter say to you again?" Dad asked Grandma.

"The boy said very sarcastically that there is no curry or baklava on the menu today. I don't care if he was just trying to be funny. I don't want anyone to spit on my food just because my grandchildren are wearing Arab clothes," Grandma said. Grandpa was looking at his newspaper and wasn't wearing his hearing aids, so I doubted he knew what was going on.

"The hotel manager has agreed to serve us," Uncle Dennis said as he came back to the table. Mr.

McNabb the hotel manager was nice and insisted on serving as our waiter, so Dad and Uncle Dennis felt comfortable staying and eating there. The morning's conversation didn't change, however. All the adults talked about was how people looked at us, which made me feel even more self-conscious.

After all the goodbyes, kisses, and hugs from dad, Rico, and BJ, we set out for the beach. Mom was a little quiet at first but only due to Dad's departure. My parents didn't like to be apart. Uncle Jim and Uncle Dennis had Mom laughing and thinking about other things in no time. The smell of the ocean air filled the car as we got closer to the beach. Robert was sitting next to me in the back of the station wagon BJ had arranged for us. We'd reached Huntington city limits and Mom and Uncle Jim were saying they were hungry.

"Look, there's a Bob's Big Boy. Let's get a hamburger," Uncle Jim said.

He drove the big station wagon into the parking lot.

"Oh, come on, we're never going to get to the beach," Robert blurted out of frustration.

Uncle Dennis reached his hand back to Robert and grabbed his right arm.

"Be patient. We have all day to spend at the beach, son!" he said.

I could see that Uncle Dennis didn't like the way Robert was acting around us. I thought he was acting spoiled because Grandma was there.

"The boy is just excited to be here, son. Don't be mad at him," Grandma said, sticking up for Robert.

"Okay, Mom." Uncle Dennis just looked at Robert with eyes of "I'll kill you later."

I could feel the humidity of the ocean as I breathed in and out. I knew we were awfully close to the beach now. No one had eaten that much at breakfast because of the stupid waiter. And now that it was almost lunchtime, I had to admit I was getting a little hungry also. The hamburger place was on Beach Boulevard and was so good. I had a big boy hamburger with a chocolate shake. Robert, the one who couldn't wait to get to the beach, ate the most. He had a burger, fries, salad, and a shake. Uncle Jim also stopped at a 76-gas station and bought two truck-size inner tubes. The gas station attendant inflated the inner tubes and strapped them to the roof of our station wagon. I'd been right, the beach was remarkably close. Just a couple of miles down on Beach Boulevard, I could see the ocean. The beach was so big and clean. We parked and got out. Robert and I wanted to start running to the water, but Mom made us wait for everyone.

"You two stay with your Uncle Jim and don't talk back," she said.

I could hear the worry in my mom's voice. Mom and Grandma didn't want us to run ahead, and out of sight. So, we helped Uncle Dennis and Uncle Jim with the inner tubes and blankets. Mom had two umbrellas, and Grandma had June and an ice chest. We picked out a spot in front of the ocean and back far enough so Mom and Grandma could see us play. This was way different from the beaches back home. It's hard to describe the differences in the water and sand. The Pacific Ocean has so much more life in it.

June had been noticeably quiet all day. Mom said

she wasn't feeling good and kept her close to her and Grandma. She did get in the water after a while and played in the sand, while Uncle Jim taught me how to body surf. The waves were quite big and sometimes the wave would hold me under after crashing down on top of me. I was fearless and loved the exhilaration of the waves. I could see the relief in my mom's face every time I came up out of the water. Uncle Jim was particularly good at bodysurfing. I was having so much fun, I didn't want the day to end.

Grandpa stayed behind that day because he was moving us to a new hotel. He also needed to buy parts from a couple of distributors and ship them back home. Grandpa Green owns an excavation company and owns a lot of heavy equipment. He said that I could drive one next time we went to visit. Canada was very cold and snowy. That was all I could remember about our visit to Quebec. I was about seven or eight and had never felt cold like that. It cut right through me, my hands and feet never got warm that trip, and I also caught the flu. Dad said when we were younger, we visited during the summer and loved it. But I was too young to remember.

The ride to the new hotel was longer. We were all so tired from the sun and water, but I wanted to go back the next day. I needed to think of a good reason not to go to Knott's Berry Farm tomorrow. We arrived at the new hotel after about an hour of driving. Grandpa Green was outside the hotel waiting for us.

"Hey, there you all are. Did you have fun, Reem?" Grandpa asked.

Grandpa was happy to see us all in one piece and helped us to our new hotel rooms. This place was way more luxurious than the Disneyland Hotel. I could tell by the quality of the furniture, carpet, and the overall layout of the room. It smelled like lavender but not overbearingly so. The main living room was large and more spacious. We had what looked like a glass and steel dining room table with huge centerpieces on one side of the room separated by an L-shaped pony wall – separating the dining area and living area. Uncle Jim helped me put my things in my room.

"What a day, huh kid," he said.

He liked to call me "kid" sometimes. I think it was because he was the youngest, and it made him feel older. Standing there in shorts and a Hawaiian shirt, he was newly married and only twenty-six. I looked at him and said to myself, now is my chance to ask him.

"Uncle Jim, tomorrow we're going to stand in long lines and it's going to be in the '90s again. I'd rather go to the beach again."

Uncle Jim looked surprised.

"Are you kidding me, Reem! That's what I want to do!"

Uncle Jim walked out of my room and into the living room quickly.

"Hey, Sue! We're going back to the beach tomorrow. Reem doesn't want to go to Knott's Berry Farm," he announced.

I peeked around the corner of my room and down the hallway. I could see my mom standing in the living room looking down the hall at me.

"It's okay, Reem, if you want to go back to the beach you can," she said, with a smile.

Uncle Jim was loud. Mom always said Uncle Jim was like a bull in a china shop. Robert came out of the bathroom with a look of surprise on his face.

"We can go back to the beach tomorrow?" he asked.

"Yep! Sue told me that she just wanted you and Reem to have fun. We thought you'd like to go to Knott's, so I wasn't allowed to say anything. But Reem just said he wanted to go back to the beach instead," Uncle Jim said.

He put his arm around Robert and leaned on him with a smile on his face. Mom walked over to me and kissed my cheek.

"Is that what you want to do, son?" she asked.

I nodded. Yes.

"Okay!" Mom clapped her hands together.

"Tomorrow it's the boys on the beach all day, and the girls will go shopping and sightseeing. Dad, you can come with us if you don't want to go to the beach," Mom said.

Grandpa just chuckled as he was bending over to pick up the TV clicker.

"No way in hades am I going shopping or to the beach. I'm staying right here and taking advantage of my son-in-law's presidential suite. So, you can tell Alibaba I'm going to use all the room service in this hotel," Grandpa said.

Grandpa had a lot of names for my dad, like Alibaba, Lawrence of Arabia, Shabu, Mr. Oil King, and my favorite, Sim Sola Bim. Yep, my grandpa was a racist. He didn't like blacks or Mexicans either.

"Frances Benjamin Green, you will do no such thing!" Grandma snapped at him.

You knew if Grandma called you by your full name you were in trouble. Grandpa was a veteran of WWII. He'd served in the Canadian 3rd Infantry, and would tell us the coolest stories about D-Day and Juno Beach in Normandy. The stories always started off with, "Did I ever tell you about the time I killed more Germans in one day then I had bullets in my rifle?" or "Did I ever tell you about the time I threw a grenade over the enemies' front line and into their command bunker?" Grandpa liked telling us his war stories but in the middle of telling them a memory would pop up in his mind and by the end of the story he'd get sad, to the point you could tell he wished that he hadn't brought it up.

"It's okay, Mom, as long as Dad is happy and busy, he won't be in anyone's way," Mom said.

Grandpa was already deep into the news and wasn't listening to either of them at this point. He probably couldn't hear anything, as he wasn't in the habit of wearing his hearing aids.

"Grandpa is so cool. He doesn't give a shit."

Fear came quickly over my body as I realized I'd said that out loud. My mom's eyes were big, and Uncle Jim and Uncle Dennis started laughing uncontrollably. My fear left me slowly as I could see my mom was trying not to laugh with her brothers.

"Reem, do you want me to tell your dad what you just said?" she asked.

"Oh, Sue, leave the boy alone. You know he's right; dad doesn't give a shit!" Uncle Dennis said, laughingly.

That night we ate Italian in the residence because that was what Grandpa wanted. I loved hanging out with Grandpa Green. We'd sit and watch old westerns and cop shows. He also had the best bedtime stories about Sally, Dick, Stuffy, and George the Ant. Sally and Dick were brother and sister, Stuffy was Dick's Teddy bear and George the Ant could make Stuffy come alive using magic. In these stories, they would all go on incredible adventures together.

CHAPTER 5

Griffith Park was next on the schedule for us but first we took Grandma and Grandpa Green to the airport. Grandpa had to get back home to bid a job. After that, our day started with a beautiful drive through Beverly Hills. We had an excellent breakfast at a bistro on Rodeo Drive. My mom and Aunt Carol were hoping to see a movie star.

"What if we ran into Johnny Carson?" Aunt Carol said.

"Or how about Goldie Hawn?" my mom added.

Hollywood was not what I expected. The place looked dirty, and the people were too. Other than the tourists, everyone looked like they needed a bath. We checked out the Walk of Fame and the Chinese Theater. Mom and June liked the hand and footprints. I thought they were kind of cool.

The observatory was so much fun. The view from the grounds was like being on top of a tall building. You could see most of L.A.

Inside the planetarium was a huge swinging ball that knocked down pellets to show the earth's rotation. I was checking out the electricity exhibits when June started bugging me.

"Reem, look, the theater has a show that's going to start soon. Come with me? Mom is busy with Uncle Dennis," she said.

I liked the idea of sitting. My feet and legs were killing me from walking on the sand and swimming for two days. My muscles weren't used to all this, and it was taking its toll on my body.

"Okay, June," I said. "Mom, I'm going to take June with me, okay?"

Mom looked in our direction as I pointed to the theater entrance. Mom raised her hand to say okay.

"How did you know the movie was getting ready to start, June?" I asked.

June and I were looking for a good seat to watch the movie, but the chairs were in an oval that confused us.

"Reem, we passed by the sign that had all the showtimes on it. It was right in front of you," June said.

June was brilliant and observant. She read everything, it seemed. We found seats in the middle of the dome. June was happy and a little excited. She sat on my right and held my hand. I could feel her little hand, squeezing mine with excitement as the lights dimmed and the music came on. The narrator's voice was loud.

"The Cosmos!" the narrator's voice said as the movie began. It made me feel small and insignificant looking at images of the entire galaxy. A few minutes went by when I realized I didn't have June's hand anymore. We both were looking almost straight up at the ceiling, so holding her hand had been helping me not get so dizzy from the flashing lights. I looked over to see June looking down at her feet. As I put my hand on her left shoulder to see if she was okay, I could immediately see that something was very wrong. She had saliva coming out of her mouth.

"June, what's wrong!? June, what's wrong!?"

I started yelling. June began to lift out of her seat about halfway with her back towards me. Her body lunged back at me violently. The back of June's head hit my bottom lip and knocked me to the ground with June on top of me. June's body was so stiff, like all her muscles were flexing all at once. It sounded like she was trying to cough through her nose. I could hear a girl's voice screaming.

"UNCLE DENNIS!! UNCLE DENNIS!!"

I realized that it was me yelling for my Uncle Dennis. The projectionist had stopped the film, and the lights had come on. The weird sound June was making from her nose or mouth was getting louder. Everything just stopped, and it felt like everything was in slow-motion. Someone had pulled June off me. I didn't see who because everything was blurry. I had too many tears in my eyes. My entire body was shaking with fear for my sister. The auditorium doors opened as I wiped away the tears so I could see. One of the ushers was holding June in his arms. He was the same person that had helped an elderly couple with their seats before the show started. I could hear my Uncle Dennis's voice yelling, "MOVE, I'M A DOCTOR!!"

At the same time, I could hear my mom yelling for my sister and me. Uncle Dennis had descended upon June like a superhero. Things were coming more into focus for me, but the hell I was in and the fear I was going through were still very much real.

"I got you, sweetheart. Uncle Dennis is here, so is Mommy," Uncle Dennis said calmly.

Uncle Dennis had one hand underneath June, and with the other, he pulled out a handkerchief and put a corner of it in her mouth.

"Sue, give her some space!" he snapped at Mom.

Mom was yelling June's name and asking what was wrong with her.

"She's having a seizure! Now everybody, get back!" Uncle Dennis demanded. He went back to whispering to June. "It's okay, sweetheart. I'm here. You'll be okay."

"Sir, the paramedics are on their way," one of the employees said to Uncle Dennis.

My mom and I looked up at each other. I could see the same fear and confusion in her face that I had. Uncle Jim and Robert came running in and past the employees that were trying to keep us secluded. Uncle Jim grabbed me from behind with his right arm and squeezed me hard. I put my hand on his arm. I was still crying.

"She's going to be okay, son," Uncle Jim said. "Robert, go get your Aunt Carol. I think she went to the gift shop earlier."

Robert took off like a man on a mission. It was just then I heard June crying. My whole body started to shake and cry again, I think with relief.

Mom and Uncle Dennis were talking about something. I couldn't hear what they were saying. Every second seemed to be an hour. Then Uncle Jim let go of me.

"Over here! Over here!" he yelled.

He was waving at three firemen. Why did they call the firemen? I thought to myself. What the hell was a fireman going to do for my little sister? We need medical help!

Two of the firemen had bags over their shoulders and tackleboxes in each hand. The third fireman had just a big green tank. Uncle Dennis was still holding on to June with one arm. She was limp as a doll. The first two firemen took off their coats and placed them on the ground. Uncle Dennis lowered June onto them.

"Start an IV. I'll get her vitals. You're a doctor?" asked the small fireman.

"Yes, I'm a trauma surgeon in Quebec! And her uncle!" Uncle Dennis replied.

The fireman started working on June's IV, and Uncle Jim started pulling me away. I fought him at first, but then I saw my Aunt Carol by the doorway. I ran over to her and wrapped my arms around her. My mom was in no condition to hold me. Two more firemen came into the auditorium with a gurney.

"Is June going to be alright?" I kept asking my Aunt Carol.

"She's going to be fine, sweetheart. They're taking good care of her."

As fast as the gurney disappeared in the sea of firemen's bodies, it suddenly reappeared, jumping up with June on it. The firemen had put something on June's face, so it was hard to see her. The big green tank was lying down by her feet as they rushed her out of the auditorium.

It was how small she looked on the gurney that made me start crying again. She's so little and help-less, I thought to myself, I love her so much.

We all ran to the station wagon in the parking lot: Uncle Dennis and Mom rode with June in the back of the ambulance.

"Where the hell is this guy, I don't see a pink Cadillac! Who in the hell drives a pink Cadillac?!" Uncle Jim said.

I could tell Uncle Jim was pissed off, but only because he was scared for June, as we all were. My Aunt Carol was so upset she didn't even snap at Uncle Jim for cussing in front of us. I think she was just as scared and frustrated as he was. One of the staff members at the planetarium agreed to have us follow him to the hospital. We had no way of knowing how to get there. The hospital was close to where we were, but Uncle Jim didn't trust the map he had.

"Over there, look, Jim! It's a Mary Kay car, that's got to be him," Aunt Carol said with excitement in her voice.

Sure enough, there was a 1977 Cadillac Coupe Deville. It looked like someone had painted it with Pepto Bismol. We followed the staff member for a few miles. The pink Cadillac with the Mary Kay sticker in the back window took a right-hand turn into the parking lot of the hospital. You could see the building from a few blocks away.

"This must be the hospital," Uncle Jim said.

My cousin Robert and I sat in the back. We were very quiet the whole way. You could tell I'd been crying a lot; Robert just looked confused. We both knew this was profoundly serious, but I don't think Robert knew how to feel about it. I just kept staring straight ahead at that Mary Kay sticker on the car in front of us.

"Reem, sweetheart, come here, I have to talk to you," Aunt Carol said.

My Aunt Carol had the passenger door open and her feet outside the car, but she was still sitting. I came over to the front passenger side of the station wagon, and she put her arm around me.

"Sweetie, I know you're scared, we all are, but when we're in there let's try to all hold it together for your mom," she said.

Uncle Jim had walked around to our side of the station wagon. He bent down on one knee to be at the same height as I was.

"Reem, I have to pick up your dad and Rico in two hours at the airport. Did you want to come with me to meet them?" he asked.

"No, I just want to be with June," I said as Aunt Carol was wiping my face with her handkerchief.

We got inside the hospital and discovered that we were in the wrong place. The young girl at the info desk informed us we needed to go to the emergency room, which was on the other side of the hospital.

"Damn it, Jim!"

My Aunt Carol had grabbed my hand, and we were walking very quickly down a long hallway towards the emergency room side of the hospital.

"Well, how in the hell was I supposed to know?"

The stress was getting to them.

We found my mom in the emergency waiting room with a clipboard and pen in one hand, and a bag of June's clothes in the other. She was sitting halfway off her chair, staring at the bag of clothes. June had had on a pair of white Capri pants, a pink and white blouse and a canary yellow sweater. Mom was losing it, sitting there by herself, tears streaming down her face. Aunt Carol grabbed the bag and clipboard out of Mom's hands as Uncle Jim picked her up in an embrace.

"She's going to be alright, Suzy Q. She's strong and tough like you," Uncle Jim whispered, with his forehead touching hers.

Mom was the toughest person I knew when it came to cuts, bumps, and broken arms but this was different. She looked utterly devastated.

"June had two more seizures in the ambulance," Mom said, with a low tone in her voice, huddled together in an embrace with Uncle Jim and Aunt Carol.

Mom was wearing a yellow and white summer dress. Mom and June liked to match one another. I had my hands around her waist and was hugging her from behind.

"I'm going to call the airline; do you need anything?" Uncle Jim asked.

Mom shook her head no and sat back down. I sat down next to her while Uncle Jim was at the bank of payphones in the corner of the waiting room.

"Reem, what happed in the theater? I mean, did she say anything to you. Son?"

I think Mom was trying not to place any blame.

"We just sat in our chairs and started watching the movie. I didn't feel June's hand anymore, so I looked over at her. MOM, she didn't look right, Mom…"

I started to cry again, reliving that horrible moment.

Mom grabbed me by my shoulder and pulled me into her embrace.

"Shh, it's okay, son. I know, I know."

Uncle Jim put down the phone and walked over to the reception desk. After about a two- or three-minute conversation with the receptionist, he waved us over to him. Mom quickly shot up and out of her chair, grabbing the clipboard from Aunt Carol. She had hoped for news from the receptionist, but from here it looked like she was just giving back the forms. The receptionist had us follow her back to a private meditation room. It looked like a place where you got terrible news. A room where no one could see you fall apart when you learned your loved one had died. It had an altar in the back where you could kneel and pray, bench seating with cushions and Bibles.

"I don't like this room. It gives me the creeps," I confessed.

I could feel my fear turning into anger as Uncle Jim walked over to me and sat down.

"Reem, remember what we talked about outside? Keep it together for your mother, son."

After about an hour of waiting, the doctor came into the room and sat down next to my mom. He was a small Asian man with a stiff white lab coat which made soft scratchy noises anytime he moved his arms about. I didn't know what it was exactly, but that scratchy noise was calming. His smile and demeanor exuded confidence, which was a much welcome addition to the quiet, uncertain room it had been.

"I'm Dr. Joy. I'm a specialist here at Valley Children's Hospital. I'm the resident professor of neurosurgery, neurology, and otolaryngology for pediatrics. Your daughter June was brought to my attention from Dr. Christianson in the emergency room. June was exhibiting signs of an epileptic seizure. We have ordered a battery of tests including a CT scan which requires your signature for consent."

The way the doctor spoke to Mom and all of us made me feel good. Dr. Joy seemed to be very smart. June would love him.

"Is she going to be okay?" I blurted out. Mom and Aunt Carol didn't snap at me for being abrupt or rude. They wanted to know too; Dr. Joy turned to face me. He looked straight into my eyes.

"Since June has not regained consciousness yet, we're still in the question phase of our diagnosis. Currently, we're all asking questions and waiting for answers. We hope to know more after we do a CT scan. June is in good hands," he said.

"When can I go back and be with her again?" Mom asked.

She handed back the pen and consent form to Dr. Joy. Dr. Joy stood up and put the pen back into his lab coat pocket.

"The hospital has extended a professional courtesy to your brother. You can come back now until we take her to radiology for the CT," he replied.

"Thank you so much, Dr. Joy."

Mom got up and gathered her things so that she could go back to see June.

"June is in good hands, Mrs. Al-Saba. I'm an expert in my field. We will get to the bottom of this."

Dr. Joy's confidence was very reassuring to us. By looking at him, you would think he would have a heavy Asian accent, but his command of the English language was easy to understand, even for me. Uncle

Jim and Robert left to wait at the airport for my dad and Rico. Dad was scheduled to be back in California that afternoon and was already in the air when June got sick. Uncle Jim said that he would call me from an airport payphone. So I had to listen for a page at the hospital. He instructed that he would give me the payphone number he was calling from while he waited for my dad. This way I could call him if there was any news about June. Aunt Carol and I sat in that meditation room awaiting news from Mom or word from Uncle Dennis.

"Why don't you like this room, Reem?" Aunt Carol asked.

She was playing with my hair as I laid my head on her arm.

"This place is full of sadness; where those in their desperate hours come. Just look at that altar over there. And there's like a Bible on almost every bench. I feel like I'm in a church."

I said it with a look of disgust or disdain on my face.

"Reem, this should be a place of comfort and solitude. Where someone can go to be closer to God and ask for help." Aunt Carol softly placed her hand on my head.

"You know, Aunt Carol, we're not deeply religious in my family. Ever since the death of Uncle Yousef, dad has had a problem with organized religion."

Uncle Yousef was my dad's older brother. Yousef and two others had been killed over a philosophical discussion that had turned into an argument years ago. Dad told us that Yousef and a group of coworkers had been studying the Quran and Islam. They all worked on the oil rigs and would spend their lunchtimes discussing religion. Like most good and faithful Muslims, Uncle Yousef was very active in all his studies. One of the men in the group was from Saudi Arabia and took offense to what Yousef had been discussing. The next morning the man from Saudi Arabia showed up to work with a knife. Before the men had a chance to defend themselves, he had stabbed my uncle and two others to death. The man tried to make his escape back to Saudi Arabia. My grandfather (Mohammad Faisal Reem Al Saba) and dad, with a group of men who all loved my uncle, caught up to him before he was able to cross the Saudi Kuwait border. Kuwait was a very liberal country when it comes to religion. Women there didn't even have to wear the Hijab if they didn't want to. Saudi Arabia, on the other hand, was much more devout and extreme. If the man had made it to Saudi Arabia, not only would he not have been punished, but he would have more than likely been praised for the murders. Upon their return to Kuwait with their prisoner, they were met just outside the city by the families of the other two men who had been stabbed to death. The men surrounded my grandfather's truck. My father and grandfather tried to convince the twenty plus men to bring him back for trial. The Saudi Arabian prisoner started yelling at the mob of men.

"I'm glad I killed them, they are now fuel for the hellfire! That's where they belong – in hell to fuel the fire!"

They grabbed the prisoner out of the truck and my father said it was the most violent thing he'd ever witnessed with his own two eyes. You could tell he didn't like to talk about that day. But he was almost relieved to get the story over with because he knew he'd have to tell us one day what had happened to our Uncle Yousef.

Aunt Carol smiled at me and kept petting my head softly.

"Organized religion? That's a big use of words for you, son. It sounds like you're listening to your father. What do you think about it? You don't have to think the same way your father does, you know," she said.

"I guess you're right. But to be honest, I don't think about it at all. I see my classmates and friends studying and going to the mosque, but it never comes up at home. I think Mom tries to avoid the subject altogether."

Aunt Carol squeezes me tighter.

"I love you, Reem. You're my favorite," she said.

We waited for about two more hours in that chapel. Uncle Dennis finally came in and said we could both come back to see June. We must have gone through four or five sets of double doors before we made it to where she was lying comfortably. The air smelled sanitized and the white tile floors sparkled with color inlays. There were different colors that created different pathways throughout the hospital; I surmised that they were coded for the different departments of the hospital. We seemed to be following an orange line, which led us to the ICU. Uncle Dennis looked back at me and smiled while he opened a big sliding glass door to a room. My little sister June was awake and sitting up. She had a stuffed teddy bear under her arm and was looking at it.

"Mom, what should I name him?" she asked. Then she looked over at me with a worried look. To see June, awake and sitting up, was such a relief. I wanted to cry. I was frozen in place and couldn't believe how good June looked.

"June, you're okay?" I said.

Mom immediately motioned to Uncle Dennis to bring me into the room. She'd put down a magazine she had been reading. I sat on the side of the bed with June. Mom got up and closed the sliding glass door for privacy.

"Of course I'm okay, Reem, why wouldn't I be?" June said.

June was enjoying her new teddy bear and all the attention from Mom.

"Reem, she doesn't remember anything," Uncle Dennis said in a whisper.

Mom gave me her handkerchief to clean my face.

"It's okay, Reem. Everything is going to be okay. Uncle Jim called from the airport, and we gave him an update. Your brother and father should be landing soon. Everything's going to be okay."

Mom leaned over the bed and kissed both of us on the tops of our heads. I had already put June in a bear hug. I could smell her hair and her breath. My little sister was back.

"Stop it, Reem, you're squishing my teddy bear."

It was so good to hear June complain about something I was doing. Aunt Carol and Mom were trying not to show the tears welling up in their eyes. A nurse had opened the sliding glass door to June's room and was changing out the bottle of IV fluid next to the bed.

"Dr. Joy said that we could move you to the medical ward upstairs since all your scans came back clear. June is responding to the meds positively.

So, we should have you out of here in about twenty minutes."

The nurse had a funny penguin print on her scrubs. She was pretty and seemed to be doing five tasks all at the same time. I thought Aunt Carol and Mom felt like they were in her way.

CHAPTER 6

Uncle Dennis wouldn't leave June's side, not until my dad got there. We were asked to wait in the main lobby again until June's new room was ready. So, Aunt Carol and I went to where we first entered the hospital and waited, but before we left the room Mom whispered to me.

"Reem, try not to scare your dad and Rico when they arrive. Hold it together, son, June is in good hands," she said.

Her toughness and bravery had returned to her once again. I had to admit that mine had too – being able to see June sitting up, talking, and playing with her teddy bear, that was the best medicine for me. The trauma of this experience would haunt me throughout my life, especially whenever I saw a Mary Kay sticker or a pink Cadillac. I would get a rush of bad feelings as if transported back to that day and time.

When my Dad and Rico made it to the hospital with Uncle Jim and Robert, I was in the gift shop looking for puzzle books or anything that would give me something to do. Dad gave me a quick hug hello and immediately went upstairs with Aunt Carol to see June. Uncle Jim and Robert waited with me in the lobby. BJ was on the payphone next to the bathrooms arranging for us to extend our stay in Los Angeles, because the doctor said that they'd need to carry out more tests on her. My brother Rico looked exhausted from his trip with Dad. I had found a word puzzle book in the gift shop, but I just kept it in my hand. I just sat there staring into space, going over all that had happened that day.

"What the hell's wrong with you?" Rico asked after staring at me for a while.

"Rico, leave him alone," my Uncle Jim snapped at Rico quickly.

I couldn't tell if Rico was mad at me for something I'd done. Maybe he was just upset because he wasn't in the pool swimming, I thought.

"You have no idea what the hell we've been through today, so keep your damn comments to yourself!" Uncle Jim said.

Rico looked like he'd been slapped across the face. Uncle Jim's words had never been that abrasive, not ever. BJ came over and sat down next to Rico. He could see that Rico was upset about whatever Jim had said to him.

"Is everything okay, Mr. Green? Is there anything I can do?" BJ inquired.

Uncle Jim ignored BJ and turned to Rico.

"Look, son, I know I told you and your dad at the airport that June was fine. That she had an episode, and we brought her to the hospital. But I didn't want to alarm you or your dad. A few hours ago, your brother and I thought June wasn't going to make it," Uncle Jim said.

BJ quickly stood up.

"What do you mean you didn't think she was going to make it? What is wrong with her? What exactly happened?" BJ demanded.

Boy, Uncle Jim must have downplayed what had happened, I thought to myself.

"Reem and June were in the theater when we believe June had an epileptic seizure. Dennis got to her right away. The paramedics transported her to the hospital, and she barely achieved consciousness two hours ago. Dennis hasn't left her side the whole time," Uncle Jim said.

BJ ran back over to the bank of payphones by the bathrooms.

"What the hell is he doing? That guy gets weirder and weirder every time I see him," Uncle Jim said.

BJ had a habit of walking away from you if whatever thought hit his mind seemed to be urgent. I think that's why my dad liked him right from the start. Dad never had to finish explaining what he wanted done because BJ was already doing it, fixing it, calling it, mailing it, scheduling it, or reminding you of it.

BJ was like an uncle to me, but he could get kind of weird sometimes. What was he doing? Who was he calling?

"Uncle Jim, I'm sorry, I didn't know," Rico said. "I thought June was getting attention again. Plus, I was mad at my dad. This business trip was so boring, and he barely spent any time with me."

Uncle Jim stopped looking over at BJ.

"It's okay, Rico, you should be apologizing to your brother. He got the worst of it. He was with June when it happened. That's why I snapped at you. I should have realized I hadn't given you a full picture of what happened. I'm sorry too."

Rico came over and sat down next to me. He could see I was fighting back the tears, so he just put his arm over my shoulder, and we both sat there quietly. BJ walked back over to us with a somber look on his face.

"Okay, everything has been arranged. I need to talk to your dad. I want to let him know that June needs to see a specialist named Dr. Joy," BJ said.

Uncle Jim and I looked at each other and started laughing. We needed that one.

BJ tries to explain. "No, Joy is the name. He's board-certified, studied at Stanford…"

Uncle Jim interrupted. "No, BJ, we're laughing because Dr. Joy is with June right now. That *is* her doctor."

That even tickled Rico, who gave a small giggle. BJ just nodded and smiled. After a while, Uncle Dennis came down from the elevators. He walked over to BJ and hugged him. BJ looked surprised.

"I don't know who you called, but June is being moved into her private suite as we speak. I just came down here to get you guys and bring you up," Uncle Dennis said.

A huge smile came over BJ's face as he glanced at us. BJ always liked to be underestimated.

"Well, Mr. Al Saba enjoys full diplomatic status with the United States. So, I called the State Department and let them know our predicament. The

Mayor and the Governor are both on their way to the hospital to check on us," BJ said.

Uncle Dennis was guiding us to the elevators while BJ was bragging and explaining how he got things done.

June's private suite was lovely and had a private sleeping area to the left for the patient, and a living room area with television and refrigerator for guests. BJ had done quite a number. The Governor of California, Jerry Brown, showed up to check on how June was doing. Dr. Joy came into the room with the Governor and assured him that June was in the best hands possible. Most of the handshaking and greeting commenced in the living room area. Mom was next to June in the private bedroom area keeping June company. Finally, after almost everyone had left, my dad came and sat down next to me.

"So, I hear you had quite a day, son? Are you okay?"

I just looked up at my dad and smiled. I didn't respond to him. I thought if I did, I would start crying. It was so good to hug my dad. I felt safe.

Mom came out of the bedroom area and sat on the couch next to us.

"Is she finally asleep, sweetheart?" Dad asked while kissing her on the forehead.

"No, she's still on the phone with Grandma and Grandpa Green. Grandpa is quite upset that he isn't here," Mom said.

Everybody went back to the hotel that night, except Mom and me. Dad was going to shower and sleep a little bit. But he would be back in the middle of the night. Mom let me sleep next to June in the hospital bed. The bed was huge, and June was so tiny there was plenty of room for the both of us, and of course her damn teddy bear. Later that night, when Dad came back, I could hear my parents talking.

"Dr. Joy thinks that it's epilepsy, and if so, we can control it by medication," Mom said.

Mom was getting something out of the refrigerator.

"I got off the plane and saw Jim there waiting for us. I didn't know what to think. He said that June had got sick and that you brought her to the hospital, but she was doing good and was playing," Dad said.

Dad opened the bottle of soda in Mom's hand with a bottle opener.

"Jim had called the hospital before you landed, and I was able to update him on June's condition. She had opened her eyes and was talking in the middle of the CT scan. Dennis was there to reassure her that everything was fine. I didn't want Jim to scare you. I just wanted you here as soon as possible," Mom said.

She took a drink of her soda pop.

"I'm worried about Reem," Dad said.

Dad took a drink of soda pop from Mom. He was waiting for a response from her.

"Do you think Reem was that traumatized by all this?" Mom asked.

Mom was now waiting for a response from my dad, but he just looked at her and shrugged.

"Maybe, I'm not quite sure. I don't think it would hurt to ask the doctor," he said.

My parents both agreed and finished their soda pop together.

The next morning Dr. Joy came into the room as part of his morning rounds.

"And how is my important patient this morning?" he asked.

June sat up in her hospital bed and giggled.

"Me and Cleveland are hungry," June said.

"Cleveland and I," Mom said. She loved to correct our grammar.

"Breakfast is on the way, my Arab Princess," Dr. Joy said as he leaned over her bed and put his forehead on June's, letting their noses touch.

He had a way of being funny with kids, and completely serious with the parents. June laughed and went back to playing with her teddy bear, which she'd named Cleveland. I didn't know where she got this stuff from – Cleveland, I thought.

"We'll need to keep June for a few more days for tests and evaluation. The medication seems to be working well. We haven't had any seizures since yesterday, but I would like to continue evaluating her to be sure," Dr. Joy said.

Mom and Dad quickly agreed that it was the best for June. They didn't care about a couple more days in Los Angeles. After Dr. Joy had left the room with his entourage of student doctors, Mom and Dad looked relieved.

"So, are you ready to entertain my family for a couple more days?" Mom said to Dad with a smile on her face.

"Are you kidding me? After what Dennis and Jim did for us, I'm going to spoil the shit out of them both," Dad said.

Mom looked disappointed.

"Ahmed, you better not embarrass them!" Mom said.

The two days went by quickly. Dad took us ev-erywhere while Mom and sometimes Aunt Carol stayed at the hospital with June. Dad took us to San Juan Capistrano to tour an old Spanish mission. We had Mexican food almost every day. Dad had also chartered a fishing boat out of Dana Point, where he presented Dennis and Jim with two brand new Rolex watches.

"Ahmed, this is too much. I can't take this."

Uncle Jim was trying to give back the box.

Uncle Dennis already had the watch on his wrist and was admiring it.

"Go head, Jim. He's rich."

Dad and Uncle Dennis started laughing over the inside joke. Uncle Jim looked confused.

CHAPTER 7

We returned home a couple of weeks before we went back to school. Mom and Dad were still a little guarded when it came to June and her epilepsy. June had to see a new doctor that first week we were back. I remember feeling sorry for June, that she needed to keep going to the doctors. For the next couple of years, every time June and I went somewhere by ourselves, I had a little anxiety. Is it going to happen again? What will I do if she has a seizure? These questions and thoughts would occupy my mind. By the time June was about 11 or 12, she was highly active and healthy. She did have a couple of minor seizures from time to time, but the medication seemed to help.

I received about four letters back-and-forth between myself and Juan that first year. Juan was my compass that first year of junior high.

Dear Reem, thank you for your correspondence. I was so happy you are thinking about me. You are a good friend. As your friend I will give you a warning about having too much fun with the new video games you and your friend are playing. You should be like that salmon swimming upstream. Whatever your classmates are into you need to do the opposite. The salmon you write about in the nature video is swimming upstream for a reason, to spawn. Focus your mind on time management and grades. You need to be one or two years ahead of your class. If your class is going to cover Of Mice and Men *and* Jonathan Livingston Seagull *next year you should have already read them by now. That will be your spawn.*

I do not know if I would have been so far ahead my freshman year of high school if it hadn't been for Juan's letters of direction and encouragement.

My high school years were insanely busy. I had the road map to USC. Juan had been incredibly detailed on what I needed to do. I completed my sophomore year and started my junior year of high school and maintained a perfect 4.5 GPA, and I was on the tennis team and the swim team. I also served on the student council, organized a blood drive for the tennis team, and while on the student council, I helped to organize donations for hunger relief in Africa and AIDS research.

Dear Juan, thanks for your letter and pictures. I loved the one with your cap and gown. It was very inspirational to me. I still cannot believe you got hired on at Webb and Martin. You didn't even intern there. It is a little funny to me knowing that they are sending you back to school, it must be exciting to get to learn about computers and software. Especially if what you say is true and the future of architecture will be through computers.

I sent you the photos you asked for. I like the photo of the palace the best.

"Reem, Mom and Dad are looking for you," June yelled down my hallway towards my bedroom.

"I'm putting my clothes away!" I yelled back. Damn, what do they want, I thought to myself.

"June, if I wanted to yell for your brother, I could have done that myself. Next time just ask your brother to come into the living room. We don't shout at each other," I heard Mom say to June on her way to my bedroom.

"Reem, your dad needs your help in the garage," Mom said softly while standing in the doorway.

"Okay, Mom, I'm just putting away some clothes." I had put some towels over my mail, so Mom didn't ask any questions. Mom and Dad never picked up the mail. The mail was picked up by Bella, our maid, and sorted. Bella would always put my clothes at the foot of my bed, and my mail on my desk. By my junior year, I was receiving architectural magazines and letters from Juan in addition to a bunch of other correspondence with Uncle Dennis, Grandma, and Grandpa Green.

Mom and Dad had no idea what I was doing. My brother Rico had already sent his college application to the University of Kuwait. Dad was so proud and anxious for him to receive a degree in business from Kuwait University. I knew he felt the same about me, but I had no intention of attending university in Kuwait. It was only USC or somewhere else in California I wanted. I loved Kuwait, but from the moment I stepped on the campus at USC, I'd felt this hunger inside of me, almost like I had a connection to USC and California. Destiny or some force was pulling me back to that place. I had to figure a way of convincing my dad to let me attend USC. My time was running out. I needed to apply soon. Uncle Dennis was going to pay for my schooling, that was what my dad had reluctantly agreed to allow. I'd told Uncle Dennis how serious I was about attending USC. He'd given me tips on how I could bring the subject up with my mom.

Dear Reem, Robert is doing very well. He's attending school at his mother's house in Colorado. We felt that it was in his best interest to go with her. I have been so busy with my new job and new wife, Nicole. We're all looking forward to spending Christmas in Kuwait. Robert and your Aunt Valerie will fly out first. Nicole and I will be there two days later. Is there anything you want from Chicago? Ever since I moved to Chicago, I cannot get enough of the food here. As for your question about telling your dad. I think you should first get your mom on your side. That will help, but time is running out. Remember, USC does not allow early applications. So, do not hit your dad over the head with this. Just tell your mom what you want to do, and then lay out your reasons for going to USC. I am impressed you kept in contact with Juan. He will be a big help to you. We can talk more when I get there. We all are proud of your Father. I do not understand the award he is to receive, but I know it is a big deal. Your Mom is on the phone almost twice a day with Grandma getting ready for this dinner. If Grandpa were not having health issues, Grandma would be there. Jim and Carol are doing well also. Ever since Jim took over the excavation business from Grandpa, he has turned things around. I didn't know the company could get as big as it has. We're all impressed and proud of Jim and Carol. What they have been able to accomplish with Green Excavation. Like I told your mom on the telephone, I am happy here in Chicago. My new job here is where I want my career to go, more money and less time. Being a newlywed seems to take up more of my time than being a doctor. I guess that is a good thing. I am sorry you couldn't come out for the wedding, but Nicole and I were pleased to see your Mom and Dad. Well, son, I must make my rounds this morning. I will leave it here. I love you and miss you and will see you soon.

Your favorite Uncle
Dennis

Robert and Aunt Valerie arrived in the middle of the afternoon. It was almost Christmas time, and the weather could not have been more beautiful. I was not sure why Uncle Dennis had gotten divorced. I'd hear Aunt Valerie sometimes in conversations with my mom talking about the old days. They'd both met at college and struggled through medical school. It must have been hard since Uncle Dennis was a Doctor of Medicine, and Aunt Valerie was a psychologist. We all talked for a few hours. Robert and Aunt Valerie needed some sleep, so they went to bed early.

Dad got home late, at about 7:30pm. Mom had put dinner in the oven for him.

"How was your day, Reem?" he asked while stuffing his face with coconut cake.

"It was good, some of the guys from the swim team and I were practicing on the high dive at the pool today, it was fun," I said.

I tried stealing a piece of cake from the table.

"Reem, you already had one today." Mom slapped my hand while putting Dad's dinner plate down in front of him. The big slice of coconut cake stayed in my hand. I quickly sat down and started eating it from my palm.

"You're a pig, Reem," June said while standing behind Dad's chair with her arms around Dad's neck.

"June, your father is trying to eat. You're going to make him choke," Mom said.

Mom was still trying to clean pieces of coconut off the table from when she'd slapped my hand.

Dad had put down his fork and sat back in his chair. He was looking past me with anticipation on his face. "Well, do you have something to tell me?" he asked. His eyebrows lifted straight up.

I thought he was talking to me for a moment.

"Yes, I submitted my application," Rico's voice came from behind me. He was waiting for Mom to sit down, so he could grab a piece of cake too. Dad went back to eating his dinner.

"Now that you finished your college application, you can focus back on your grades, son," Dad said.

Rico had had a tough time with some of his studies, but there was no way Kuwait University was not going to accept him.

"Rico, I swear you and Reem eat up the food faster than Bella and I can make it," Mom said.

She got up and brought the cake it into the kitchen.

"You know that's not going to stop the boys, Mom. They're such pigs," June said while sitting next to Dad.

"I want you boys to save some for Robert and Valerie. I mean it!" Mom said.

She looked at us and tried to appear threatening.

"Oh, that's right, Valerie's here. What time did they get in, sweetheart?" Dad asked.

"Around 4:30. They looked worn out. Valerie is going to meet a friend in Spain. She's leaving the day after tomorrow. Dennis and Nicole will be here that night, and Robert will go back with them after Christmas."

Mom started cleaning the kitchen, so I waited for Dad to finish his dinner. He would go to his office and work before bed each night. That would be a good time to start talking to Mom about USC, I thought. I sat on the barstool across from the sink. The barstools were on the other side of the marble countertop. Okay, here we go, I said to myself.

"Mom, remember when we took our vacation to Disneyland, and Dad took me with him to USC?" I asked.

Mom was unloading the dishes out of the dishwasher, but she always was able to multitask.

"Of course, sweetheart, Dad said you had a fun time on campus with Uncle Dennis," Mom replied.

I was trying not to look directly at her, so I kept folding a napkin in front of me into different shapes. That was my way of being lowkey.

"Did you know that USC has one of the top ten architectural programs in the United States?" I asked.

I knew if I looked up, she would see in my eyes and down into my soul, pulling out all my dark and hidden secrets.

"Oh really, I didn't know that," she said, very slowly.

I shifted uncomfortably in my chair as I could feel my mom coming closer to me. I wanted to say something to throw her off the trail, but I couldn't think of anything. Every second that went by with no words coming out of my mouth felt like ten minutes. Mom was wearing a blue and white dress straight out of the '50s. She had one hand on the island bar and the other was holding a kitchen towel. She bent at the waist to make me look at her. Her eyes did their job, and I could see her reading me like a book.

"Reem, why are you talking about an architectural program at USC?" she asked.

I pretended to sneeze in the napkin that I was folding.

"No reason, I just remembered how much fun it was on that trip," I said.

Mom sat down on the barstool next to me. She grabbed the napkin out of my hand and threw it in the sink. She didn't believe my fake excuse or my fake sneezing to buy time.

"Reem… If your dad hears that you're thinking about going to another school other than Kuwait University, he will start a holy war in this house. Do you understand? I do not need this right now, Reem! We have a lot of company coming for your dad's award, and the dinner with the Emir. Christmas is right around the corner, and all the family will be here. So, whatever you're up to, stop!"

Mom was practically leaning into me by the time she was done yelling at me. Then she pulled herself together and started cleaning again.

"I'm sorry, Mom, I'm going to be an architect, and I will go to the absolute best school for it. Even if I have to live with Uncle Dennis," I said.

I walked out of the kitchen. I knew mentioning Uncle Dennis's name would give Mom a lot to think about and would ensure she wouldn't say anything to Dad right now.

CHAPTER 8

The family arrived in Kuwait before the big dinner at the palace. Dad took everybody to a large shopping mall. All the men got brand new tailored outfits for the dinner. I was extremely impressed by how we all looked in our new clothing. Dad looked especially nice that evening in his bisht, a kind of cloak worn over a thobe.

Dasman Palace was wonderful. From the outside, you could see the tower with a clock in it. The building was large and tannish with a touch of red. Like all architecture in Kuwait, the stone and brick buildings looked the same color as the sand. I couldn't wait to become a famous architect and change the landscape of my country. I loved thinking about new buildings and structures I could design to improve Kuwait's skyline.

Dad accepted his award and a new position with the government of Kuwait. BJ was so happy he practically cried when Dad received the ceremonial ribbon. Dad's new position was all he'd talked about ever since the Prime Minister had called and offered it to him. We all congratulated Dad as he came back from the podium. The new job meant that he would no longer have to travel to different oil fields. He was finally behind an important desk, he kept saying. Dad always worried about his position in Kuwait because my mom was Canadian.

Jaber Al-Ahmad Al-Sabah, the Prime Minister of Kuwait, left the room almost as fast as he entered it. The award ceremony was over quickly, and my dad was one of three people receiving an award: a doctor, an actor, and my dad, an oil engineer. I forgot not only the name of the award they gave him, but also what his new official title was. The Emir didn't attend the ceremony because he was sick that day. I'd overheard my mom speaking with Uncle Dennis that the Prime Minister was set to become the next Emir of Kuwait and how it had been an honor to meet him.

The ride home that evening was a bit uncomfortable. I caught my mom looking at me. I had a feeling she was going to confront my Uncle Dennis since I'd invoked Uncle Dennis's name. I needed to get Uncle Dennis in private and forewarn him that Mom was going to interrogate him about what I'd said. I continued playing with my cousin Robert in the limousine, pretending that I didn't catch my mom's glance from time to time. Robert wasn't used to wearing Arab clothing. Mom had us in our absolute best ghudtra and egal (headscarf) thobes and jalabiya. Robert was in a thobe and headscarf, but Rico liked to pull on it to see if Robert knew how to put it back on. Robert's thobe went down past his knees, so Rico and I died laughing when Robert tried getting in or out of the car.

"Boys, leave your cousin alone," Mom said as she hit the back of Rico's head with her hand. Rico was the closest one to her in the limousine.

"Mom!" Rico shouted while rubbing the back of his head.

"You're lucky it was your mother and not me," Dad said with a half-smirk on his face.

"I knew it! That imbecile waiter did spill something on my dress," June said.

She was trying to clean something off her dress by her knees. June was about to turn fourteen, and she was coming into her looks. Boys had started acting quite differently around her. Rico and I would try to keep an eye on her at school. If we saw a boy talking to her or trying to get a message or a date with our little sister, we would bring him into the stairwell and threaten to beat the shit out of him. Boy, did Rico and I get in trouble! June had come home from school the previous month crying, and told our mom that no boys in school talked or looked at her because of Rico and me. Our parents had sat us down and let us have it.

"I'm sure the waiter didn't mean to spill anything on you. He was just smitten with your beauty, my dear," Mom said, handing June a handkerchief to clean her dress.

"Boys are just dumb," June said. "Just look at my two brothers. I asked this kid in my chemistry class if he wanted to be my lab partner on our next project.

He just stared at me and mumbled something for three minutes."

June gave up on her dress and sat back in her seat with a look of frustration on her face.

"The poor kid, you can't blame him, sweetheart," Mom said.

My mom, of course, thought it was cute or sweet when a boy was in love with June. Me, on the other hand, I didn't like it at all. She was my little sister and shouldn't like boys yet. She should still be playing with her Barbies.

We arrived back home, and even though it was late, Nicole and Aunt Carol wanted to continue taking pictures of all of us. As soon as my mom had taken June inside the house to fix the stain on her dress, I walked over to my Uncle Dennis and whispered, "I need to talk to you."

Uncle Dennis could see that my dad was in a conversation with BJ about the evening's events. He grabbed me by my elbow and led me to the front of the limousine.

"I told Mom about USC. She flipped out on me, Uncle Dennis," I said.

I tried to calm down the panic in my voice. I knew that at any moment this whole issue was going to come up again, and that made me incredibly nervous. I'd never gone up against my mom or dad before, especially when it came to my education.

"It's okay. Calm down. What exactly did your mom say?" Uncle Dennis asked, positioning himself directly in front of me.

"Mom said I can't do this to her right now, not with all the different events happening with my dad, and Christmas with the family," I replied.

I looked over at my dad to make sure my voice wasn't too loud. All I needed was for him to overhear this, I thought.

"So, she didn't tell you no. She didn't go directly to your father and tell him. I think you have a chance at pulling her in on your side, Reem. Don't worry, let me handle it. I know how to get through to my sister."

Uncle Dennis pulled out a pack of chewing gum and offered me a stick. As I pulled the package apart and popped the gum in my mouth, something caught my eye. It was my mom standing in the doorway looking directly at Uncle Dennis and me. How long had she been standing there? The look on her face said it all. Yep, Uncle Dennis was in trouble.

"Dennis, can you and Reem come and help me with something?" Mom yelled out before I had a chance to motion or warn Uncle Dennis that she was standing in the doorway.

Uncle Dennis looked surprised at first, but when he looked back at me, he winked and smiled. "We'll be right there, sis," he replied.

We walked to the front of the house together. Uncle Dennis whispered to me, "She's going to bring us into the bedroom. Stay outside and listen by the door. Don't come in until you hear me call you."

Uncle Dennis and I walked into the house and straight back to my parents' room. I did what Uncle Dennis had told me and stayed outside by the door and listened. Down the hall, I could hear Uncle Jim and June discussing where he could find something for his stomach. Uncle Jim had a hard time with all the new spices and food in Kuwait. But he'd always had a sensitive stomach; I'd never known a time he didn't have a pack of Rolaids on him. It was about this time that the conversation in my mom's bedroom was at a level where it was easy to overhear it through the closed door. Mom's voice was muffled, but I could hear what Uncle Dennis was saying.

"What the hell are you talking about, Sue? That boy out there needs you on his side!"

"You want to talk about interfering in someone's business? Let's talk about interfering. Who the hell paid my student loan debt off?"

I felt a little sorry for my mom. I had heard this argument already with my dad in the limousine on our family vacation.

"You need to get a grip, sister. That boy out there is going to have the fight of his life with his father, and he needs you. You know what's best for him. Rico is all set for the University of Kuwait. You know how it works here. The firstborn gets everything, and the second-born son gets shit on. Reem is just looking out for his future, and he needs you on his side. Okay?"

My love for Uncle Dennis grew at that moment. He understood my dilemma. He also knew how to get my mom to look at it through my eyes and not my dad's. After a couple more minutes, Uncle Dennis opened the bedroom door and told me to come in. Mom looked a little defeated, like someone had handed her a bag of shredded paper that she needed to put back together. Uncle Dennis put me in front of my mom.

"Okay, Reem, tell your mom exactly what you want to do with your life," Uncle Dennis said.

I took a big breath and started to form my words carefully. Just before I started, the bedroom door opened, and my dad was standing in the doorway, looking at the three of us.

"Do I want to know what he did?" Dad said with a smile, thinking I might have done something wrong.

Mom quickly stood in front of me and Uncle Dennis.

"We… we were asking Dennis for some advice on how to bring up a very sensitive subject with you," Mom said, without missing a beat.

You could see Dad's curiosity had been more than piqued. He walked in and closed the bedroom door. Dad sat on the edge of the bed and kicked off his brand-new dress shoes.

"What sensitive subject?"

"Go ahead, Reem, there's no getting around this. Tell your dad what we've been discussing," Mom said.

A feeling of calm come over me, knowing that my mom was on my side. Uncle Dennis was correct; he knew how to talk to my mom.

"Dad, I've decided that I'm going to study to become an architect. It's something I enjoy. I think I can be good at it, given the right education. So I've told Mom, and now Uncle Dennis knows that I'm going to apply for the University of Southern California. They have one of the top ten architectural programs in the United States. I think I can make a name for myself in this field," I said.

I looked straight at my dad the whole time I was explaining to him what I wanted. Even when BJ opened the bedroom door to put some luggage away, I didn't break eye contact or stop talking. BJ just stood in the doorway and listened. Dad's face was unreadable, and he just sat there for a few moments before he spoke.

"Okay, I can see that you have chosen a career that you think you would enjoy. I do not doubt that you would be a great architect. You and I have talked about electrical engineering, what happened to that?"

"The boy wants to be an architect, Ahmed, not an electrical engineer," Mom said abruptly.

"Dad, June is going to be your electrical engineer, not me. I love architecture, and USC has the best program for it," I said quickly.

I could see my dad's engineering mind going 100 miles an hour.

"You can study architecture, but you're going to do it here at the University of Kuwait, not in some foreign country!" Dad said.

He stood up from the edge of the bed and walked over to his dresser and started taking off his watch and the metal ribbon. "Kuwait needs its youth to be educated in Kuwait and stay and work in Kuwait!" he started shouting at me in Arabic, so no one else would understand him in the room except me. "Do you not love your country, son? Do you not care about your family and all that they had to go through to make a name for us? Your grandfather fought in the Kuwait-Najd war. This country needs its youth to stay in Kuwait!" Dad finished in Arabic.

Mom looked concerned, because she did not understand Arabic.

"What the hell are you talking about, Dad!" I replied in Arabic. "Of course I love my country. I'm going to come back after I complete my degree. Just like you did. How can you sit there and say all that when you went to school in Canada!"

I could feel my emotions starting to get the best of me. My Arabic wasn't as good as my dad's, but I got my point across. Mom yelled at both of us to use "English" or else. Dad turned away from the dresser and faced me. He looked very intimidating. He was still in his new tailored clothes and looked more distinguished than I had ever seen him before.

"What the hell am I talking about? I'm talking about a compromise. You want to go to study architecture at USC. I'm willing to let you study architecture, but you will do so at the University of Kuwait. See, we each had to go halfway. I had to go to study in Canada because I had no choice, but you do thanks to your country that has built a world-class university. Oh, and by the way, you ever talk to me like that again, Reem, I will kick your little ass, young man! Now go to your room and change. You're grounded for a week!"

My emotions did get the better of me. I stormed out of my parents' bedroom down the hallway and past all who were listening. Rico looked stunned and confused. June was right on my heels, following me into my bedroom. She shut the door and sat beside me on my bed, not saying anything at first. She had one of my decorative bed pillows in her lap. I was so angry at my dad. What he had said to me was not a compromise. Tears started to swell in my eyes. I fought them back with my anger.

"Reem, I wouldn't worry about this so much right now. Dad's first reaction will be the harshest. Mom will work on him. She has more than a year to get him to agree, right?" June said.

June was right, I thought. I just tore off the band-aid. Now my dad knows what I want to do and where

I want to go. I'll just let that simmer for a month or two and keep bringing it up every chance I get. Between myself and my mom, we'll wear Dad down. Wow, I thought to myself. I know I've been hitting the books hard for the last three years, but could June still be smarter than me? She didn't read as much as she had when she was little. She was more interested in her hair and makeup than books these days. But that was some excellent insight she had on my dad. I was able to calm down and pull myself together. I gave June a big hug and smiled.

"Thanks, June. Will you help me convince Dad to let me go to USC for school?"

I opened my dresser drawer and took out my pajamas. June got up and walked over to me.

"Okay, I'll help you. But you must do it respectfully. Pretend you're a lawyer, come up with a good argument to go to USC versus staying here. You need to stay away from being confrontational," June said.

She got up and threw the pillow at me as she walked out of the room. Her smile said it all. She was incredibly pleased with herself.

"I'm going to go spy on Mom and Dad. I'll talk to you later," she said.

After June had closed my bedroom door, I quickly got into my pajamas. I wanted to go into the kitchen to show everyone that I wasn't worried. I was going to get what I wanted regardless of what my dad said. My parents had not heard the last of me or my decision to go to USC. I needed to figure out how to present it in the best light. This year would be critical. I had to maintain my grade point average and my extracurricular activities.

When I entered the kitchen, my Uncle Dennis was rummaging around in the refrigerator. He looked a little surprised to see me reappear so quickly.

"Did you find my ticket to USC in there?" I asked.

I grabbed the refrigerator door before Uncle Dennis was able to close it. I guess I was getting hungry too. I didn't usually eat this late at night but all the contention and arguing had made me hungry.

"Don't joke about that right now. Your parents are still in there arguing. Your mom stepped up and came to your defense. She's laying the groundwork for you," Uncle Dennis said.

He must have got out of there quick, I thought. I decided to make myself a sandwich. By the time I was done, I'd made a masterpiece. Grandpa Green had taught me how to make the best baloney sandwich. He started with mustard on both sides. Then two slices of baloney, one slice of Swiss cheese, tomatoes, lettuce, pickles, and avocado. Add salt and pepper, and you had a masterpiece. I cut my sandwich in half so it would be easier to manage. I grabbed two paper towels and a glass of milk and sat down next to Uncle Dennis at the kitchen table. He was eating some chicken from the night before.

My dad opened his bedroom door and walked straight into the kitchen. Our eyes met; Dad was trying not to look surprised that I was in the kitchen and not in my bedroom sulking. He sat down across the table from me. He took one of my napkins and half of my sandwich. We just stared at each other, eating our sandwiches. Uncle Dennis kept his eyes and attention on his plate of food. The intensity was mounting. I wasn't going to look away, and neither was my dad.

"Holy crap, this is a fantastic sandwich!" Dad broke first, putting a massive smile on my face.

"That's what Grandpa Green calls a Dogwood sandwich," I said.

Uncle Dennis and my dad busted out laughing and almost spit out their food.

"What's so funny?" I said.

I was confused. I had no idea what they were laughing so hard about.

"It's called a Dagwood sandwich, son. Not a Dogwood," Dad said.

Everybody who'd been eavesdropping in their respective safe corners of the house started funneling into the kitchen, to see why we were laughing so hard.

"Son, it's a comic strip from the 1930s where the character would make a sandwich so big that it would try to eat him," Dad explained.

So, I'd messed up the name Dagwood, Dogwood. I didn't think it was that funny. But of course, in this family, a mistake like that could haunt you for the rest of your life. My cousin Robert told a joke to everybody during our Disneyland vacation and messed it up. To this day, we all teased him about the punchline. Keep in mind, Robert was only ten or eleven years old when he told this joke. The punchline he gave was "Remember the gravy train." When my Uncle Dennis corrected him, "Son, you mean 'Remember the Alamo'."

Robert made it worse by saying, "Oh, that's right. I knew it was one of those dog foods."

I had never seen my grandparents laugh so hard before in my life. Grandma being such an educator tried to explain to Robert what the Alamo was. She knew that Robert thought that Uncle Dennis had said "Alpo," as in the dog food.

Even to this date, when Robert left to go somewhere, Uncle Jim or Aunt Carol, my mom or dad would tell my cousin Robert to "Remember the gravy train."

So, I guessed, I'd be stuck with Dogwood every time I made a sandwich.

CHAPTER 9

The week of Rico's graduation from high school was momentous for our family. My dad was appointed Minister of Oil Production for Kuwait. Prime Minister Jaber Al-Ahmad Al-Jaber Al-Sabah was announced to be the next Emir of Kuwait. Although my grandparents on Dad's side died before I was born, the Emir knew my grandfather and considered him a close friend. Dad's role in the government took up a lot of his time. So, I'd bring up USC every chance I could. But my opportunities diminishing the more time my dad spent at work.

My plan was simple: after Rico's graduation, I'd travel to Chicago and spend part of my summer with Uncle Dennis. That way, I could take a quick summer class at one of the thousands of colleges there. Juan got me in touch with a couple of professors at USC; he told me it would be a good idea to keep in touch with them. Professor Cornell suggested that I take a summer class in English studies to add to my admission application. Uncle Dennis had everything set up for me. All I needed to do was convince my dad to let me visit. My timing could not have been better. Before we left for the graduation ceremony, I walked into my parents' room and sat down on their bed. Mom and Dad's bedroom was enormous. Their bed could sleep twenty people comfortably. Mom had a beautiful sitting area off to the left of the bed, and Dad had an entertainment center in the center of the room so he could watch TV. Mom was sitting on a beautiful blue and gold couch that was part of her sitting area, playing with a new polaroid camera. Dad was finishing a phone call with BJ.

"Did you pick up the gift? Okay, great! We'll meet you over at the school at 6pm – talk to you then. Bye, BJ."

Dad put down the phone and walked over to my mom and sat next to her. He picked up his copy of the *Wall Street Journal* and went back to drinking his tea. I guess that was what he was doing before BJ had called. I decided that this was my opportunity to ask about going to Uncle Dennis's. I got up and walked over to the armchair in front of my dad. It was yellow and light red and had no business being next to the couch, it was so ugly.

My dad looked up from his newspaper. "What is it, Reem?"

My dad was staring at me like he was busy. It only took a second or two before I realized he was thinking of twenty different things all at once.

"Robert and I wanted to hang out for a few weeks

this summer, and Uncle Dennis said it was okay with him. So, can I go to Uncle Dennis's this summer?"

My dad hadn't heard a word I'd said. The newspaper had all his attention.

"Reem, your Uncle Dennis and I talked this morning, and we made plans to go to Chicago. All of us. Well, except for your dad," Mom said.

I took the polaroid camera away from my mom and showed her how to load the film.

"Okay, cool, Mom. When are we leaving?" I asked.

I handed the camera back to her while pressing the photo button, and the flash and film shot out abruptly, scaring my mom.

"Dammit, Reem! You're wasting the film."

The flash caught my dad's attention, and we both found it equally funny.

"We leave in two days, you little asshole!" Mom said, trying to get her vision back from the flash.

Mom using cuss words just made Dad and I laugh a little bit more.

Mom went back to fiddling with her new camera. She had it back in its new carrying case when the photo I took started to emerge. It had fallen on the coffee table in front of the couch. It was a picture of my mom's face from below her chin and up towards her nose. Dad immediately grabbed the photo and started shaking it. Every time we looked at it, we laughed even harder.

"Ahmed, give it back to me!"

My mom started chasing my dad around the bedroom. June ran into the room to see what was going on.

"Get him, Mom!"

June jumped on Dad's back and started laughing. "Get him, Mom. Get him!" she said.

My mom's athletic ability helped her jump into action. She was on Dad's back quick. They all fell on the bed. June got the picture away from Dad. She'd give it back to Mom later. Mom and Dad started kissing, so June and I ran out of the room completely grossed out.

My brother Rico's future was all decided for him. He would get a business degree from the University of Kuwait, and then Dad would put him in the right position with the right people. Rico would inherit all my dad's wealth upon his passing. He was the first-born son and was entitled to everything. Mom didn't like that, but that was the way things worked in Kuwait. Dad had put a lot of money in a trust for June and me, but it wasn't anything close to what Rico would inherit. That was why Dad expected a lot from Rico.

Mom had two other siblings, but Uncle Jack had been killed in a car accident in 1974 while coming home from a date. My Aunt Alice was born with palsy and needed care around the clock, so she lived in a home. She was just a year or two older than Uncle Jim. I knew that it was hard on my grandparents emotionally and financially. Each time we travelled to Canada with my mom, we would go and visit Aunt Alice. The home in Québec was quite lovely, staffed with doctors and nurses to take care of all her needs. Mom and Grandma always took turns holding my Aunt Alice. I always wondered what she would be like if she were healthy. I had this idea in my mind that she would have been the opposite of my mom. More wild and unpredictable.

We arrived at the ceremony just before six. Rico was already there with his friends, showing off his new car. Mom and Dad had bought him a new Toyota 4x4 truck. It wasn't a surprise. Dad had made Rico earn two thousand dollars from working the oil rigs the previous summer. Rico had been using Dad's old truck ever since he'd started driving. Dad knew if he made Rico earn part of the money, he'd appreciate it more. Mom and Dad had another big surprise to give Rico after graduation. BJ handed my dad a white envelope and whispered, "Everything is in there."

Dad placed the huge envelope in his jacket pocket. With a big grin on his face, he looked towards my mom and winked. They had already taken their seats with June in between them. I sat next to BJ, who was more excited about Rico graduating than my dad, it seemed.

"Hey BJ, what did my brother get for graduation?" I whispered.

"Your dad and mom are going to let him select three of his friends to go backpacking around Europe for six weeks, all expenses paid," BJ whispered back to me.

I don't think he was supposed to let me know, but it seemed like he was excited for Rico and couldn't hold back anymore. I giggled at first because with BJ's accent mixed in with his excitement and whispering, it sounded so funny. I wanted BJ to repeat it, but I didn't ask him to. Dad always told me how rude it was to make fun of his accent. Besides, I started getting mad.

"What the hell, BJ, Mom and Dad won't even let me go four blocks over without being interrogated.

Are they going to let Rico travel by himself to Europe? This is such bullshit!" I said.

I sat up in the chair with my arms folded.

"Don't say anything. It's going to be a surprise. You should be happy for Rico," BJ said.

BJ put his arm around me and kept squeezing me throughout the ceremony. He was so happy for Rico. I was too, I guess. I was just jealous that he got to have six weeks of freedom without Mom or Dad, June, or myself. When the ceremony had concluded, Rico was speaking to one of the valedictorians.

"Go and get your brother, Reem. We'll be over by the exit," my dad said while putting his coat over his arm and helping my mom out of her chair.

I pushed my way through the crowd and up by the stage. Rico was talking with Donna Dunn.

"Hi Donna, loved your speech. Rico, we got to go, Dad's waiting!" I said.

I was very irritated I'd even had to go and get Rico.

"Okay, Reem, I'm right behind you. Okay, Donna, I'll call you later."

I started pushing my way through the crowd again, thinking to myself, why is he going to call Donna later? I'd introduced Rico to Donna because Donna was in my advanced algebra class; she was a junior and I was a sophomore that year. We were both exceptionally good with math. How had they become friends, I wondered. As we got to the exit, I could see Mom already had the polaroid camera out and tears in her eyes.

"Mom, don't start that. You promised no crying," Rico said.

Rico wrapped his arms around Mom and gave her a big hug. Dad was brushing off some of the confetti that had landed on Rico's shoulder.

"It's not your mom's fault, son. BJ got her going," Dad said.

BJ was standing there, blubbering.

"You used to be so little. Now look at you, all grown up," BJ said.

I don't ever remember a time where BJ wasn't there for us. Since the day Rico and I had come into this world, he'd been there. If you looked at our family pictures, he was always there. My dad loved him like a brother and treated him with the utmost reverence and respect. Since my dad had been promoted, BJ had taken more of a role in the family and away from my dad's business; Kuwait had given my dad a new assistant to help him manage his office in the government. If it bothered BJ, you wouldn't have known it. He always seemed happy and willing to do anything. But truth be told, Dad did just about as much work at home as he did in the office. And of course, BJ always managed Dad's home office.

"Congratulations, son."

Dad took out the envelope from his coat pocket and handed it to Rico.

Rico smiled and just stared at the envelope.

"Open it, stupid!" June hit Rico in the arm with impatience. She wanted to see what was in the envelope too. She had on a beautiful black dress and looked so mature.

"Okay! Okay!" Rico said.

Rico opened the envelope with anticipation. He pulled out a thick letter, passport, and a credit card.

The letter had two pages to it. One from my dad, and one from my mom. The letter was written on beautiful stationery. That was why the envelope was so thick. Rico started to look a little confused.

"The letters from your dad and I and are personal," Mom explained. "The credit card and passport are for you. Take three of your best friends for six weeks to Europe. We'll pay for it."

Mom gave Rico a soft tearful kiss on the cheek. Rico's expression turned to surprise and excitement.

"You mean like Dad did when he went hiking through Europe before college?"

Rico jumped on our dad, hugging him and thanking him.

I couldn't tell you how many times as kids we'd had to sit there and listen to my dad's stories about when he'd gone backpacking through Europe before college. All the fun and trouble he'd got into with his friend Ali. Mom had told us that was when Dad found himself, backpacking through Europe. It had helped my dad come to terms with the loss of his brother Yousef.

After everything had settled down, we were all walking to our car when I discovered something about Rico.

"So how long have you and Donna been going out?" I said sarcastically.

I didn't even believe it myself, until my brother quickly turned around and shot daggers through his eyes at me. I discovered that Rico had secrets bigger than me.

"Shut up, Reem! You know we're not going out," he said.

He quickly got into the limousine. I followed in right behind him and sat between him and BJ in the car.

"Who is Donna, sweetheart?"

Mom had pulled out a compact mirror and was fixing her lipstick.

"She's just a friend, Mom. One of the valedictorians that spoke tonight. Ask Reem. He knows her more than I do," Rico replied.

Rico's elbow was cutting into my rib. He wasn't happy with the comment I'd made outside the car. He knew Mom's interrogation had only just started, and it would not end.

"She's one of the smartest kids in our school. She speaks four different languages and is in my advanced calculus class. When Rico needed help with statistics, I suggested he talk to Donna. She aced that part of the math class. I invited her to the graduation party last week so you can eviscerate her there," I announced with sarcasm.

Rico and I busted out laughing.

Mom slammed her compact mirror shut and stuffed it in her purse with her lipstick.

"That's not funny, boys! I just wanted to know who she is," Mom said.

She was looking at Rico, trying to read him.

"Who she is? Where she grew up? Who her parents are? How many teeth she has? Does she brush or floss? Does she walk to school or take the bus?" Rico was moving his head up and down with every sentence. That even made our dad laugh.

"You're not funny, Rico." Mom wasn't happy with Dad joining in on the laughter.

"Oh, come on, Mom. Every time we bring some-one new over, or you see us talking to someone you don't know, we get interrogated," Rico said.

I realized that June wasn't coming to Mom's defense in this discussion. Probably because she got the same interrogations when she was just talking to a friend herself.

"I'm just trying to take an interest in your life as a good mother should," Mom replied.

Mom started fluffing up the bottom of her dress, trying to play the martyr. Rico and I looked at each other and smiled.

"We love you, Mom! You're the best Mom in the whole world. We couldn't live without you, Mom!"

We both kept chanting as we climbed over people to get to our mom and smother her with hugs and kisses all over her face while she pretended to scream as if she didn't love all the attention. Not only did we mess up her makeup, but she had to fix her hair.

"I swear to everything holy, having three teenage children is going to be the death of me."

We got back to the house so everybody could change. Dad had rented a small room at a hotel so Rico could have a graduation party with a bunch of his friends. Mom and BJ would be the chaperones to make sure nothing got out of control. The party started at 9pm and would go to 1am. Dad had to go to Geneva in the morning, so he stayed home with June. She was on a new medication for her epilepsy, and it made her tired.

The party was a lot of fun. I had a few of my friends come and hang out with me. Word got around about Rico's graduation gift, so all his friends were wondering who he would take with him. I caught him talking with Donna a couple of times, and that was when I knew she wasn't just a friend. I decided not to push the issue. I'd leave that for another day, I thought to myself. Rico and I talked about girls we liked all the time, but Rico had never said a word about Donna.

"Are you having fun, Reem?" my mom asked as she walked closer to me. I gave her a kiss on the cheek and put my arm around her shoulder.

"This is a great party, Mom, but the one you and Dad are going to throw for me will be twice as big," I declared.

Mom laughed. "Why would we throw you a bigger party than Rico's?" she asked mockingly.

"Well for starters I'm going to have a band, not a DJ, and the food will be a lot better, with shrimp and crab. And as for why? Because I have a lot more friends than Rico, twice the people. The bigger the hall the better the amenities, that will give you more options from the hotel brochure Dad had. The next size up from this hall includes a live band and a seafood buffet," I said with a smile.

Mom looked speechless for a moment. "So, can you show me what one is Donna?" she asked as she scanned the hall with her laser beam eyes.

I quickly walked away.

CHAPTER 10

I found Rico in his room packing the morning he was to leave on his trip.

"Is there anything I can do to help?" I asked as I walked in and sat down on his bed.

"No, I'm good to go." Rico shut his bedroom door so no one could hear us. I sat up quickly. He must have something to share with me privately, I thought to myself.

"Thanks for helping me at the party. BJ told me that Mom was looking to talk with Donna, and you wouldn't point her out," Rico said with a look of gratitude.

I stood up and held out my hand. "You would have done the same for me, brother."

Rico moved my hand out of his way and hugged me. I think this was the first real hug we had given one another. I immediately became emotional but tried not to show it.

"I guess I'll see you when I get back from Europe," Rico said, moving his face away from me so as not to show his emotions. I realized that our sibling rivalry had ended, and the affection we both felt for one another that morning was real and had brought us closer together.

I arrived in Chicago in the middle of June with my mom and sister. "Wow, Uncle Dennis, this is where you live?" I was overwhelmed. Uncle Dennis and Nicole had a new place on Michigan Ave in downtown Chicago. A three-bedroom three-and-a-half-bath condo on the 59th floor. It was about 2,600 square feet. "Do you like it, Reem?" Uncle Dennis asked as he grabbed a suitcase from June.

I didn't respond to Uncle Dennis as I ran down the hall with June to see the bedrooms. I threw my little suitcase on my bed and walked back out to the living room. I hadn't packed much for this trip, just a few clothes and a pair of shoes and sandals. Uncle Dennis's new place was very modern: brand-new hardwood floors, white walls, white countertops, and black cabinets with an open floor plan. I thought this must be the way to live – way up in the clouds.

"Have Mom and Dad seen this place yet?" Mom asked Dennis while June was running around the new condo.

"Mom, we have a bathroom in our own bedroom. It's like living in a hotel!" June said.

"They came out last year for a few weeks. Dad liked the open floor plan. I don't think Mom cared for the height. You know she's always been afraid of heights," Uncle Dennis replied.

Whatever Uncle Dennis was doing in his career, it seemed to be making him a lot of money. Mom said it was rude to talk about such things but I couldn't help but wonder how much money Uncle Dennis made. I knew this place must cost an awful lot even for a doctor.

"Come on, Reem. I have something to show you in your room." Uncle Dennis put his hand on my shoulder and directed me down the hallway and into my room.

"I have some bad news, Reem. Robert decided to stay with his mom for the summer. He has a new girlfriend and I guess they made plans with her," he said.

"So Robert's not coming at all?"

I couldn't help feeling disappointed. I'd thought it was going to be great to have Robert around to explore the city.

A beautiful queen-size bed and two nightstands with a tall dresser filled the space. The bedroom set looked and smelled brand new, as if it had been brought in that week from a furniture store. I'll be extremely comfortable here, I thought to myself.

"Nicole couldn't help herself. She bought you a few things." Uncle Dennis had opened the closet door, and there before me was a full wardrobe. Even the dresser had everything I would need. She must have gone a little crazy shopping, I thought to myself. I had shirts, pants, windbreakers, an entire wardrobe hanging in the closet.

"Uncle Dennis, this is too much. You didn't have

to do this for me. I don't have a wardrobe that big at home," I insisted.

I kept looking through the clothes in the closet. I turned around to see Uncle Dennis holding my small suitcase.

"You're not going to wear these clothes here, Reem. Just let people think that you're Mexican. I don't want to worry about you getting into a fight here in Chicago."

That was what my mom had done when we'd had an issue with a waiter on our Disneyland trip – Mom and Grandma had bought us jeans and T-shirts to wear. Grandpa had laughed when he looked at us. "You look like Mexicans!" he'd said, laughing. I remembered the awful feeling I'd had when people would stare at us in our Arab clothing.

Nicole had good taste in clothing. There wasn't one thing in the closet that I disapproved of. I liked Nicole. She was always kind to me, but I couldn't bring myself to call her aunt. Uncle Dennis slid my suitcase under the bed. He opened the drawer to the nightstand; he'd already bought me my textbooks for my English class.

"Have you said anything to your mom yet?" Uncle Dennis asked.

He sat on the side of the bed and pulled out my textbook. My class schedule was folded up and sticking out the top. I looked over my schedule and the location I was to go to on my first day.

"I'm going to talk to Mom tonight after we get rid of some jet lag," I said.

I opened my textbook and started thumbing through some of the pages.

"Here's a new wallet," Uncle Dennis said. "I put a credit card and some cash in it. Keep your passport with you, and tomorrow we'll get your student ID. If you need to go anywhere, always take a taxi. In the wallet, you'll find a card with my numbers on it. If you have any trouble, page me. I'll call you. Learn to start carrying a wallet around with you everywhere you go, son. Put it in your front pocket and don't forget it or leave it anywhere."

He handed me a blue cloth-looking wallet with a velcro strip to close it and a visa card with my name on it inside plus four hundred in cash. There was also a business card with Uncle Dennis's name and phone numbers on it. I folded it up and stuck it in my shirt pocket.

"Uncle Dennis, I can't tell you how much I appreciate all you've done for me," I said.

"You can thank me by becoming the world's greatest architect," he replied.

"Is Nicole going to be okay with me staying here?"

"Nicole is happy that you're staying with us, son. You should try and call her Aunt Nicole. That would make her feel more accepted in the family," he said.

I gave Uncle Dennis a big hug before he left the room. Mom and June had already settled into their bedroom; they'd mapped out their assault on Chicago. June wanted to see the Sears Tower. Mom wanted to go shopping with Nicole and get some deep-dish pizza.

The next day Uncle Dennis and I came back to the apartment after getting my student ID. I was wearing a green polo shirt tucked into a brand-new pair of Levi 501 blue jeans, a pair of Converse shoes and a black leather belt. My hair was combed back, and I felt like a new person. Mom and June weren't even home yet. They'd gone sight-seeing, probably down to Navy Pier. Uncle Dennis had to get back to work after that weekend, so I would be on my own. My schedule wasn't too bad, it was just a summer class in English. My schedule was Monday through Friday for an hour and a half in the morning with homework and papers to write.

When Mom got back that evening, I let her know I was taking a summer course in English to add to my application for USC next year. She just looked at me, in my new clothes with my backpack over my shoulder.

"Judas Priest, Reem, you are going to kill your father!" Mom put down the bags that she was carrying.

I'd told Uncle Dennis and Nicole that I wanted to do this by myself. I didn't need him to run interference with my mom. I needed to take control of my destiny, I thought to myself. So, they went out to dinner, and Mom and I had the place to ourselves.

"I already started classes, and they're only for six weeks," I said.

"Your father is in Geneva right now. Then he travels to Brussels. I'm supposed to meet him in Spain in three and a half weeks. So, if you're not with me, he's going to want to know where you're at, Reem, and I won't lie to him," Mom said.

"That's okay, Mom. I don't mind telling Dad. I'll be almost done with the course before you even make it to Spain anyway," I said.

I started helping her with her shopping bags.

"I have to say, son, I'm a little impressed that you were able to pull this off without us knowing," she said.

The first week went by quickly. Mom and June went on their outings together. Uncle Dennis and Nicole were always at work. Nicole managed an art gallery downtown and was gone most of the day, getting home just after Uncle Dennis. I couldn't help but think, would Mom even know I was taking a college class if I hadn't told her? My class started at 9:40am and only lasted for a little more than an hour. I'd take a taxi over to Taylor Street and grab an Italian beef sandwich from Al's, then have the cab driver take me back downtown. I loved to explore the city by walking up and down different streets. I'd get back to the apartment in the afternoon and start my insanely easy homework. My mom and June would spend each day together, going on adventures. They were having a fun time with each other. I guessed that was what girls called bonding time together.

After Mom and June had left for Spain, I started cooking for Nicole and Uncle Dennis; you could set your clocks by them. Uncle Dennis would arrive home at 4:20pm each day, and Nicole would follow a half-hour later. I'd make easy dinners like spaghetti, or tacos, or salad, and salmon with rice and green beans. Nicole explained to me how I could order groceries from the store.

"Write down all the things you need on this order form and give it to the front desk. The store will send it over later," Nicole instructed.

I ordered just the things I needed to replace from the week before.

I'd just gotten out of the shower and was drying off when I heard the doorbell. I thought to myself, "It's got to be the groceries." I quickly threw on a T-shirt and a pair of shorts. I'd gone skateboarding with some friends after class that morning and needed a shower when I got back to the apartment.

"Hello, I have an order for Nicole?"

The delivery girl looked surprised that I was the one who had answered the door. She kept looking at the order form and the number on our door. The strawberry blond goddess standing right in front of me struck me dumb with her beauty. I was trying to concentrate on a voice I was hearing. I suddenly realized the sound I was trying to understand was the one in my head, shouting at me! "Say something, you idiot!! She's standing in front of you!"

"Oh... yeah... Nicole. That's right. That's my aunt, but I'm the one that put in the order." I'd held hands with and kissed the girls back home a little, but I realized I had no real experience even talking with a girl who looked like something out of a beauty magazine. My height advantage over her gave me no confidence at all.

The delivery girl was trying to look unamused and sort of bored waiting for me to do something. But I didn't know what it was that I was supposed to do... Did I take the groceries from her? Sign something?

"Look, I don't have all day. I have other deliveries." The delivery girl tried to hand me the two bags of groceries when they slipped right through my arms and onto the ground, busting open. We both bent over and started picking up the groceries.

"Oh my gosh, I'm so sorry! I'm so sorry!" I said.

I quickly gathered the groceries as the delivery girl stopped and looked at me.

"You're not from around here, are you?" she asked.

She finished helping me gather the groceries but didn't lose eye contact. We both stood up, and I placed the bags on the entrance credenza.

"No, I'm not, this is my first time in Chicago," I said, trying to compose myself.

"You're just supposed to check the list and sign here at the bottom," she explained.

I looked down. The list at the bottom said "Signature" next to the amount and there was a space that said "tip". I ran back to my room and grabbed my wallet out of my pants. I took out some money from my wallet and handed it to her.

"You're funny," she said.

She wrote "$5" in the white box next to my signature and handed me back my money. As the door closed, I looked down and saw that I had given her a $100 bill for a tip. When I looked up, I could see my reflection on the front door. My hair was standing straight up. I had just towel dried it when I got out of the shower.

"I'm such an idiot!!" I said.

It might have been a little too loud. I hoped she hadn't heard me.

It was taco Tuesday. I had dinner prepared and ready for when Nicole got home from work. I explained to her what had happened and how much of an idiot I was.

"Don't worry about it, Reem. I'm sure you weren't that bad. Penny is a nice girl and probably thought you were cute," Nicole said.

She was adding sour cream to the tacos that I'd made. Uncle Dennis was still laughing at me.

"Cute! Cute! She thinks I'm an idiot," I replied. I was so upset I couldn't even eat dinner.

"Look, place another order tomorrow, and try not to be a train wreck. Now try and eat a taco," Uncle Dennis said.

That was Uncle Dennis's sage advice. Place another order. I thought about it for a while. Maybe if I did place another order, I could be more prepared.

"Uncle Dennis, you're right! Give me a list of things you need from the store, and I'll place another order. This time I'll be ready and looking nice," I said.

The awful feeling I had in the pit of my stomach immediately went away and was replaced by enthusiasm. Yeah! I'd look my best tomorrow when I open that door.

"You know, Reem, if you want to ask Penny out on a date, you might want to think about wearing the clothes you came with. A lot of American girls like Penny have never been with someone like you. Girls find Arab men exotic and mysterious. But just remember if you get a date with her, wear nice regular clothes," Nicole said.

Nicole had good idea. But I was a little worried that it might backfire on me. What if she hates Arabs, I thought to myself. I'd begun to see Nicole differently the more I got to know her. Nicole's curly blond hair and blue eyes had taken my Uncle Dennis prisoner. He was helpless under her charms. All she needed to do was stand in front of him and look up and smile. Nicole was from Israel and had lost her husband in the Israeli Army. She said that he'd been in training and been electrocuted while working on a big electric generator. I felt bad for Nicole being a widow at such a young age.

That night I couldn't decide what to wear. I finally settled on my thobe, ghutra, with a black rope and white headdress. I figured I'd be more comfortable in my Arab clothes. I might be more myself if I was wearing them.

That morning as I headed out of the building to catch a cab, I gave the new grocery list to the bellman.

"Hi David, just a few more items I forgot to get on yesterday's grocery list. Have a good day," I said.

I jumped into the yellow taxicab that was always waiting for me in the morning. The driver was from Ethiopia, and his name was Omaha.

"Are you ready for school, little girl?"

Omaha liked to tease me about my name. Reem was a girl's name in my country. A lot of kids in Kuwait chose to use their middle names because so many of them had the name Mohammed. If any of the kids at school teased me about my name, Rico would beat them up. Reem was my grandfather's middle name, so my dad was passing the name down to the next generation. He would tell the other kids that it was a family name. I'd only met one other person named Reem through all my years in school. I think it was in the first grade. Her family had moved away before I was old enough to care.

"Shut up, Cleopatra, and drive," I said.

Omaha started laughing as he pulled away like a bat out of hell.

"Have you been to a White Sox or a Cubs game yet, my little prince?" he asked as he came to an abrupt stop. It was just a matter of time before he was going to hit another car. He must have been the worst cab driver in the whole city. But I liked him. He was hilarious and always had a joke to tell. But above all, he got me to school on time even through traffic.

"My uncle is going to take me next week to a Cubs game. I'm not sure about the White Sox."

I couldn't believe how slow the day was going. It seemed like time had stood still. I couldn't wait to get back to the apartment and set everything up. Penny was so beautiful. She had that girl next door look to her, so much natural beauty, hardly any makeup. I wondered what it would be like to kiss her beautiful strawberry lips or put my hands in her beautiful, slightly wavy hair. To place my hand on her milky white shoulder and let it slowly fall down the length of her body.

"Reem, what do you think about the sum of the abstract argument?"

I had no idea what Mrs. Wilcox was discussing. I now had a new issue. The Eiffel Tower had taken up residency in my jeans.

"I'm sorry, Mrs. Wilcox, I wasn't paying attention," I confessed.

I knew Mrs. Wilcox would let me slide on that one. I was a straight-A student in her class and never missed an assignment. My embarrassment finally shrank down to size, and I got through the next twenty minutes of class. I arrived back at the apartment and quickly got changed. I'd had my clothes dry cleaned and pressed. I was looking good and feeling confident. I had my English textbook open and was finishing a paper when the doorbell rang. I give myself one last look in the mirror before I opened the door.

"Oh, hello again. Did Nicole place another order?" I said.

I did my best to look surprised to see her again. I don't think I was very convincing. Penny was about to hand me the bag, but when she looked up from her clipboard, she held on to it.

"Boy, you were not joking when you said you weren't from around here," she said.

Penny's surprise wasn't an act. She just kept on looking at me like I'd just fallen off a magic carpet. I invited her in and shut the door. My backpack was on the island bar. I walked over to it and pulled out a five-dollar bill.

"I'm from Kuwait; it's in the Persian Gulf," I said with a smile as I gave her the five-dollar bill. Penny took the money but didn't give me the bag or have me sign her list yet.

"Oh, wow, I never heard of that place before. What are you doing in Chicago?"

Penny readjusted the bag in her arms.

"I'm just taking a summer class here to pad my college application to USC. Why don't you let me take that back from you? It looks heavy?" I said.

Penny let go of the bag full of groceries. Our forearms touched, and our eyes met as I leaned down to get the bag from her. She smelled so good, like a river with wildflowers on each side. Penny suddenly and without warning started kissing me. Her lips enveloped mine immediately. We kissed for a while until she pulled away, and I was out of breath.

"Oh my God, I'm so sorry!" she said.

I could see that her aggressiveness had shocked even her. I knew if I let her continue speaking, I would miss my moment. I grabbed her into my arms firmly but softly and went back to our passionate kiss. I had never kissed a girl like that before. Since I didn't have the experience, I let her lead me in the kiss, but the embrace was all mine. Before I knew it, the groceries were on the ground, along with her clipboard and part of our clothing. Her small frame was very light and wrapped around me in seconds as I tried to make my way down the hallway. I somehow managed to shut my bedroom door without breaking our kiss.

"I've never done that before," I confessed.

I was out of breath. As I lay there under the sheets, I could feel Penny's soft warm, naked body up against me. It was the most amazing thing I had ever felt in my entire life. It was making me aroused again. I couldn't believe what had just happened. Penny started kissing me again.

"You could have fooled me." She started laughing as she grabbed my "brave soldier" – that's what she called it.

"He feels like he's ready for action again," she said, giggling.

That afternoon in my bedroom taught me so much about women. We pulled ourselves away from each other long enough to get dressed. Penny's white lacey bra was on the floor next to my nightstand. She was leaving it there on purpose. I surmised this was a girl that knew what she was doing. I couldn't figure out what the tag inside it meant – 32C? 32 cubic centimeters?

"Hey, I have to go. Come and walk me out. I'm in so much trouble! So late!" Penny said.

I gave her my number, and she said she'd call me that night. Then she finished tying her shoelaces and rushed out. I started putting the groceries away when suddenly, I heard a sound coming from my uncle's room. Fear came over me and the euphoric feeling I had shot out of my body. Had Nicole got home early? Had I not heard someone come home? Just then, my Uncle Dennis walked out of his room. His eyes were bigger than I'd ever seen.

"Reem, what the hell!? If you get that girl pregnant, your mom and dad will kill me and then you." He didn't look mad, just genuinely concerned.

"Don't worry, Uncle Dennis, I used protection," I said.

Uncle Dennis's concern turned into relief. I'd bought some condoms a year ago. I'd thought it made me look like a lady's man with the cashier.

"Not a word of this to Nicole! Okay?" Uncle Dennis demanded.

Uncle Dennis and I had an understanding from that day on. The rest of the summer was the best of my life. I understood why Robert stayed in Colorado with his girlfriend. Penny and I hung out as much as we could until I had to go back home.

"What time does your flight leave tomorrow?" Penny asked reluctantly. I could tell she was trying not to ask that question. Just thinking about leaving her and going back home hurt. Like a punch to the gut.

"Ten o'clock, but I have to get there about nine." I was looking at her fingernail polish. We held hands and interlocked our fingers. The fingernail polish match the soft pink lip gloss she had on.

"Reem, I enjoyed our time together this summer so please write to me when you can," she said.

"Of course I will! You bust your butt in school and set goals for your career. Don't let anything get in your way," I replied.

We said our goodbyes that night, but I think it was harder for me than her. I felt this emptiness inside me knowing I'd probably not see her again. The most I could hope for was to have a friend to write to from time to time. Penny had her sights on an East Coast school and I was determined to go to USC.

CHAPTER 11

Lieutenant Kleinsmith was the first to be taken off the helicopter after we landed at the CSH (combat support hospital). There were three teams of doctors and nurses waiting for us to land. They all looked extremely excited to have wounded Marines to take care of.

"Have a seat on the bed, Corporal," the doctor said while pointing at a well-made bed. The hospital was set up to handle a lot of wounded, but the major battle hadn't started yet. So the doctor stitched up my arm while the nurse assisted. I thought the doctor was happy to be doing something.

"So, you recon guys really slugged it out over there today, huh?" the nurse asked. I looked up to see the curiosity written all over her face.

"You better get used to the questions, Corporal. There are a lot of staff here wanting to ask you about the battle. Remember not to say anything that might be classified," the doctor said while writing in my chart.

"We handled our business out there," I said.

I didn't want to talk about it. I was still trying to process it myself. Even with all my training and even my anger for the Iraqis, when you killed a person it changed you forever and not in a good way.

"Where are you from, Corporal?" the doctor asked. My name on the chart must have triggered his curiosity, I thought.

"I'm from Kuwait, Major," I replied.

"You got to be kidding me," the nurse interrupted.

"I was at USC in my junior year when this shit started. So, I joined up," I replied.

"Good for you, Corporal Al-Sabah," the major said as he directed me to a waiting area. In the military everything was hurry up and wait. Corporal Brown sat next to me about an hour later. His ear was all stitched up. We were both waiting to find out the answer to the same question – when would we get to go back to our unit?

"So, after you lost your virginity in Chicago what happened?" Corporal Brown asked. He was now trying to kill some time. We both knew it was going to take a long time to get an answer from command.

I'd arrived back in Kuwait just in time to see all hell breaking loose with Rico and my parents. I had a few weeks to get ready for my senior year. Rico returned home from his trip to Europe a day before me. On the day I returned, Mom and Dad had to sign a travel slip. The private jet company that our family used to travel with had been bought out by another carrier. The policy of this new company was now to show the name of everybody that had gone on the flight. Yep! Everyone! There it was on the travel slip: DONNA DUNN. Rico had taken her with him on his trip. I arrived in front of our home, and my dad's security detail let me in the front door.

"Hey! Everybody, I'm home!" I yelled out with enthusiasm and excitement.

I was traveling with two large suitcases now. Not only did I have a lot of new clothes from Nicole, but June and Mom had made me bring back some items they'd bought in Chicago. I walked into our kitchen and dining area, and I could see Rico sitting there with both of our parents standing over him. June was in the living room, hiding behind a chair, trying to listen.

"Hi, sweetheart, welcome back. Go ahead and unpack in your room, and your dad and I'll be in there in a minute. We need some privacy right now," Mom said.

She turned her attention back to Rico. My dad didn't even turn and acknowledge that I was there. Something was up. Without saying anything more, I walked back to my room. I could hear June following behind me. She shut my bedroom door and helped me throw my suitcases on my bed.

"Okay, June, what the hell did Rico do?" I said.

I thought Rico might have broken something or got in trouble in some other country. June went on to explain about how Donna Dunn's name had been on the travel voucher that Dad had had to sign.

"I knew it! I saw them together at the graduation party. I could tell they liked each other. I didn't know that they were boyfriend and girlfriend, though," I said.

June and I left my bags on my bed and snuck out of my bedroom and into the living room so that we could listen to Mom and Dad yell at Rico.

"Rico, you're the oldest!" Mom was shouting. "You're here to set an example for your brother and sister. You must be more responsible than that and think about your future son!"

Mom almost put her hand on her hip. She shifted left, resting her hand on the chair instead.

"Rico!" Dad took over. "You have betrayed my trust and the trust of your mother! I'm disappointed in you, son. You are the future of this family! I won't tolerate this type of behavior from you! This girl, I'm sure, is nice but she is not for you. You know what is expected of you and what you need to do! So, stop fucking around and do it!"

I could tell Dad wanted to continue yelling at him in Arabic, but Mom would have gotten incredibly angry and yelled at Dad to speak English.

"I'm sorry that 'Donna' doesn't fit in your perfect plans that you laid out for me, Dad! She's my girlfriend. I'm not going to stop seeing her!"

Rico was trying to stand up to Dad and his master plan for his life. I felt sorry for my brother. It must have been hard being the oldest and having so many expectations put upon you by your parents. The fighting continued for more than an hour, back and forth between my parents and Rico. I went back into my room and called my Uncle Dennis, not only to let him know what was going on, but to let him know I'd arrived home safely. I was able to reach him at his office.

"Reem, if what you're telling me is true, then you need to go in there and push for them to let you go to

USC. Don't wait for them to stop arguing with Rico! Your issue is small compared with Rico's. Put down the phone and go!"

He had never steered me wrong before so I dropped the phone and walked quickly into the kitchen where my parents and Rico were still arguing.

"Dad! Mom! I know you're upset with Rico right now, but you need to know that I'll be attending USC next year for college. I'll be accepted to the architectural program as a freshman! Dad, I'll return to Kuwait, but not until I complete my education," I said forcefully.

Everyone went silent. My dad just looked at me and slowly sat down. I could see tears forming in his eyes. Mom's were visible. The pain inside me was hard to bear, knowing that I had made my dad emotional. I needed to stand firm and not show any weakness when it came to this subject. Suddenly and without warning, June's soft little teenage voice came from the living room.

"I think I want to be a lawyer and help people," she said.

Rico and I had tears forming instantly. June had caught us off guard. An uncontrolled giggle came out of both of us because of our tears and instant emotions. Dad got up and walked to his bedroom. Rico and I started wiping our eyes so as not to show our emotions. Our mom was crying and laughing along with us. June's sweet little voice had driven us all over the edge.

"That's nice, sweetheart, you'll be a great lawyer," Mom said.

Mom kissed Rico and me on the tops of our heads and walked back to her bedroom to comfort our dad.

Rico and I composed ourselves. Rico looked at me and smiled.

"You saved my life, Reem. If you hadn't come out and deflected Dad's anger away from me, it would have gotten a lot worse. Donna and I have been together for a year now. We understand each other. This summer was so amazing; I have so much to tell you."

Rico was calm. June had joined us in the kitchen with three glasses and opened a bottle of pop and poured out equal parts in each glass and handed them to us.

"I want to propose a toast! To Mom and Dad! May they live through our teenage years!" June said.

Rico and I chuckled a little over June's attempt at humor. My brother's fight with my parents wasn't over. For the next two weeks, my dad and Rico went head to head over the Donna Dunn issue. Dad made it clear that he had an obligation and duty to this family. Rico made it equally clear that he wasn't going to stop seeing her. Living that month in my house wasn't fun. Dad threatened to cut off Rico and take away his car. Rico, in turn, threatened not to attend college. Dad and Rico went on forever, it seemed. At least Dad wasn't focusing on me and USC.

I had my Uncle Dennis to fall back on for counseling and advice. Rico relied on BJ for the same. So, BJ suggested to Rico, "Have your parents invite Donna and her family to dinner. That way, Rico, your dad might like her. She might change his mind on you seeing her."

The idea was not a good one, I thought when Rico told me. I knew Donna from school, she was a sweet and smart girl. But her family came from the wrong side of town in my parents' eyes. My parents' idea for Rico was for him to follow in my dad's footsteps. Rico would get his business degree and become a staff member in my dad's office and that way he could one day be Minister of Oil Production. Dad was eager to teach Rico the business, so he would have a solid background in oil and business. Dad also wanted Rico to marry a Kuwaiti girl; that way he wouldn't have to face all the prejudices my dad had.

The dinner was on Saturday, and Mom and Bella had made a ton of food. Rico had taken BJ's advice. Mom, of course, loved the idea. Dad wasn't so sure about having an oil rig worker in his home. Rico practically dared Dad to do it.

The Dunns arrived in an old beat-up Toyota 4runner. They had on their best dress, which were the same clothes they'd had on for Donna's graduation ceremony. Donna's mom Lulu (an Arabic name meaning "pearl") brought a basket of bath salts, oil, and soaps. The formal introductions began.

"Mom, Dad, let me introduce you to Mr. Kevin Dunn and his wife Lulu, with their two children Donna and Kevin junior," Rico said.

I knew how nervous Rico was. He needed tonight to go without any hiccups. June and I had promised to help if anything went wrong.

"This is my dad Ahmed and my mom, Sue, with my brother Reem and sister June," Rico said.

My mom thanked Lulu for the basket and handed it off to Bella. Then she invited everyone to come into the living room so we could get more acquainted. My dad, of course, had already done some checking into Kevin Dunn. It turned out that Mr. Dunn had been born and raised in South Texas, where he'd lost his fortune in the oil fields and owed the IRS a small fortune. Mr. Dunn had been offered a job in Kuwait, so he'd taken it. He took the money saved by not having to pay Kuwaiti tax and with it he'd been able to pay off his IRS debt. He'd met his wife through a friend and decided to stay and live in Kuwait.

"You have a very nice home, Mr. Al Saba," Mr. Dunn said.

Mr. Dunn took his seat across from my dad. Our living area was big but cozy. The rugs and cushions we all sat on had been picked out by my mom. The designs and colors were therefore not guided by an Arab woman's taste, but my Canadian Mom's. I could always see some confusion in the eyes of any Arab visitor who looked in our home.

"Please call me, Ahmed," Dad said.

Bella and June brought in a couple of trays of drinks.

"What do you do for work, Ahmed?" Mr. Dunn asked while taking a drink of his iced tea, and thanking Bella for it.

"I work over at the government offices," Dad replied, realizing that Mr. Dunn had no idea who he was. "Rico said that you're in the oil rigs?" Dad squeezed some more lemon in his iced tea.

"That's right," Mr. Dunn said. "I'm a tool runner over on the Ajax side. I've been with this group for about five years now. I got my start with the Bowman group about twenty years ago."

My dad understood everything Mr. Dunn had said. Mr. Dunn had started at the bottom and worked his way up to a tool runner, a prestigious job. A tool runner would eventually become a rig supervisor, and they were paid a fair wage. I could tell my dad liked Mr. Dunn right from the start. Rico's plan was working; he just needed Mom on his side. Lulu had a small shop at a street market, where she sold scented oils and soaps, perfume, and bath things for women. Lulu looked intimidated by her surroundings. My mom was doing her best to make her feel welcome.

"Ahmed, you have a call, sir," BJ said, entering the room briefly.

My dad excused himself and walked back to his office. Bella gave my mom a look and hand gesture.

"Bella is ready for us," Mom said.

The food was excellent, and the Dunns seemed to relax. I noticed that Dad's conversation with Mr. Dunn was just vague enough not to let on what he did for a living. When my dad's knowledge of oil rigs crossed over too far, he would ask a question about Donna.

"So, Rico tells me that your daughter Donna can speak four languages?" he said.

He had to deflect again over the conversation covering different oil valves, which Dad was an expert in and had patents on.

"Oh yes, Donna can speak Arabic, Farsi, English, and some German. Donna is going to be a scientist – or is it chemist? She's changed her mind a few times," Mr. Dunn said.

You could see the pride come out when Mr. Dunn talked about Junior or Donna.

"It must be nice knowing that you're going to have someone as educated as Donna in your home."

As soon as my dad said those words, he immediately regretted it. I looked at Rico, who looked like he wanted to die. His face was beet red with anger at our dad.

"I didn't mean that you're not educated or anybody in your home…"

Mr. Dunn interrupted my dad. "It's okay. I understood what you meant, Ahmed. There is no need to apologize. I'm very proud that Donna will be the first in our family to graduate college. My children will give my grandchildren more opportunities, and so on. That's why we work so hard, isn't it?"

Mr. Dunn and my dad went back into the living room after dinner. They both looked to be enjoying their visit together. Junior was in love with June and followed her around everywhere, it was cute. Rico and Donna stayed in the dining room with Lulu and Mom. At the end of the evening, the conversation was still going on in the foyer before the Dunns had to leave, just long enough for Mr. Dunn to notice a few things on our walls that only the Minister of Oil Production for Kuwait would have in his home. Pictures of my dad accepting his award with the Emir of Kuwait. A photo of the ceremony when he'd become the Minister of Oil Production. I could see a small change in Mr. Dunn as they left and his realization of exactly who my father was.

Rico's excitement and curiosity was too much for him to handle so as soon as he closed the door. Rico turned to them. "So, Mom! Dad! What did you think? I told you they're nice people. And Donna is amazing."

He was eager to get more feedback from Dad. Dad and Mr. Dunn had seemed to hit it off that evening. But Rico had set his hopes too high, I thought.

"Son, Mr. Dunn is a very nice man, but you should be with a nice Kuwaiti girl, not with someone from Texas," Dad said.

Rico looked like Dad had just kicked him in the stomach. He sat down next to Dad at the kitchen table and took Dad's hand in his.

"Dad, I love you, and I know you want the best for me, but I'll always be a half breed here in Kuwait. I'm okay with that because my dad is an important man. You have gone as high as you can go. The men with the great pedigree you look up to, don't have your job or status in the government. With all the trouble this country has seen, from the Iran-Iraq war, pushing us around and almost shutting down oil production to Iraq now accusing Kuwait of stealing oil through cross-border slant drilling, you're the one the Emir trusts, not them. You're a self-made man, Dad! No one gave you anything. You designed those production valves, not BP or Kuwait. You hold the patents on thirty different inventions, no one else – Reem, June, and me, we want to be like you, Dad! Self-made!"

My mom and Dad sat there for a while, just thinking about what Rico had said. Mom's hand was on her hip – that was a good sign. Dad looked up at Rico.

"BJ, get out here!" Dad barked out.

"I'm right here, Ahmed." BJ had been standing off to the side the whole time.

"Did you have anything to do with this?" Dad asked.

He looked at BJ with suspicious eyes.

"Rico only asked me how many patents you now own. So I told him. Everything else is all Rico's true thoughts. I just happen to agree with him, Ahmed."

Dad shifted in his chair back to Rico.

"Son, I can appreciate everything you said, but this girl comes from a working-class family. Your

Mom and I want more for you. Education and social status. This girl will hold you back, son."

My mom stood up and pushed her chair in.

"That is exactly what your family said to you, Ahmed, when you brought me home to meet all of the Al Saba's." Mom walked away and into her bedroom. You couldn't get a harder working-class family than the Greens. Dad had put his foot in it this time.

"See, Dad, I'm following in your footsteps," Rico said.

Dad looked in the direction of our mom.

"You're just dating her. No plans on getting married?" Dad asked.

He stood up and put his plate and cup in the sink.

"Dad, I just started college. I don't want to even think about marriage and a family for at least five years."

Dad was walking back to his room when he suddenly stopped and looked back at the three of us.

"Okay, Rico, you can date her, but no talk of marriage for five years! June, you can be a lawyer if you want to. Reem, it looks like you're going to go to USC."

The three of us were high fiving and hugging as Dad walked into his bedroom. I could hear BJ in the background saying, "Well done, Rico. Well done."

CHAPTER 12

My senior year was a blur. So many activities and sports. Not to mention, I had to have my application submitted to USC by December. Kuwait was having a lot of anxiety over the stepped-up fighting in Iran's six-and-a-half-year war with Iraq. The thought of an Iran victory scared all the Arab and Gulf countries, but especially Kuwait. The Kuwait-Iraq border was just five miles from the main front, the desert was flat and empty, and you could see the smoke from the battle and hear the thud of artillery explosions. At one point, it almost shut down oil production. We pretty much never saw my father; he worked all the time. He'd come home and within an hour he would be in his office and on the phone fixing problems. The Iran-Iraq war was rumored to be coming to an end. I'd believe it when I saw it, I thought to myself.

My mom was trying to keep everything as healthy as possible for June. Things were different at home. Dad had work, Rico had school and Donna, and I was busier than all of them put together. I had school, swimming, two or sometimes three clubs with meetings, SAT, and ACT. Oh, and I'd put together a business.

Donna was helping a friend with enough English to work as a maid for a Kuwaiti family on the north side of the city. That night I was working on a report for geography class. I had on my TV in the background and a commercial came on promising to teach you Spanish in just a short time. The idea for the business hit me like a ton of bricks. Why can't I put something like that together? I bet there are enough people out there who need this service, I thought. I rented a small classroom down by the outdoor shopping mall and offered English classes to people who were interested in speaking English. I posted a sign with my number on it; "Learn to speak everyday English in six weeks. Classes are Tuesdays and Thursdays."

My first class I'll never forget. The students were so eager to learn. Most of them had ten to fifteen years on me. But they could care less. They just wanted to learn and get higher paying jobs. I must admit seeing the love they had for something I was building tapped into my character. It made me feel so good to help people fulfill their dreams. The demand overwhelmed me immediately. I had tapped into something that people wanted. An informal course on everyday English that workers could take after their shift. I had to solicit my mom's help, and even June pitched in with scheduling. Before I knew it, I had four instructors teaching seven days a week. The money started pouring in.

My mom quickly took over the business for me. She reinvested the money back into the school and made it a legitimate language school with accredited learning materials and supplies. All this happened in two months. I couldn't believe how much my mom was able to do so quickly. But you can bet that I added that on to my college application. The Al-Saba School for Language was small, but the people loved it.

With my father too busy with work, it was agreed that the holidays would be held in Kuwait this year. So we all made time out of our busy schedules. We all unplugged from the insanity that had become our lives. My grandparents arrived first, and then Uncle Dennis. Nicole and Robert came later that night with Uncle Jim and Aunt Carol. I was so excited to see Uncle Dennis that when he got off the plane, I started waving like an idiot.

"How was your flight, Uncle Dennis?"

He handed me his overnight bag to carry for him while we walked to the car.

"It wasn't bad. I flew out of DC and slept most of the way," he said.

We got into the car, and the driver took care of Uncle Dennis's luggage. On the drive home, it seemed like I talked the whole way.

"A lot has happened, Uncle Dennis, since you told me to go in and confront my dad while he was dealing with Rico. That was the best advice you've ever given me. It was the straw that broke the camel's back."

Uncle Dennis looked a little concerned. "I hope you didn't tell your father that I put you up to anything."

I looked at my Uncle Dennis and rolled my eyes. "Don't worry, Uncle Dennis, I'm not stupid. Can you look at my application? I'm about ready to submit to USC. Everything is filled out; all the questions have been answered. My test scores, my transcripts, and four essays. Two for the admissions board, and two more essays for the architectural program president."

Uncle Dennis looked pleased. "Okay, Reem show it to me later. I heard that you opened a language school for migrant workers there in the marketplace of Kuwait?"

My excitement must have taken over. I started explaining in detail how I'd come up with the idea. I went on to tell him how quickly it had grown bigger and bigger.

"Rico's girlfriend Donna Dunn speaks four different languages, and I thought to myself, I know a lot of kids that would be happy just to know basic English. So I negotiated for a space to have a classroom and put up a simple sign down by the street market with my phone number on it. The rest as they, say is history. Donna is a big help. She works and helps at the school as much as she can. I think one day she'll be the one who takes it over from Mom," I said.

Uncle Dennis just sat there quietly. I could see a lot of sadness on his face. I wondered if I'd said something wrong. The pain in his eyes confused me.

"You started a language school in the middle of a desert and are helping hundreds of people in their lives." Uncle Dennis looked up at me with tears filling his eyes. "Reem, I'm so proud of you. I have no words to express the pride in me. My sadness comes from my failings with Robert. Nicole just picked him up from rehab. Don't tell your parents, but Robert is struggling with life and some addiction. I hope that you'll rub off on him a little bit and maybe give him more direction in his life."

The pain in Uncle Dennis's eyes was more real than I could ever imagine.

"I'm so sorry. I had no idea. Robert always seemed engaged and focused on his relationship with his girlfriend," I said.

I put my hand on top of my Uncle Dennis's and squeezed it.

We arrived at my parents' house, and I helped Uncle Dennis get settled into one of the guest rooms. I planned to grab my USC application package right away and present it to him for his review. But knowing about Robert now, I thought it would be best to wait. I didn't want my ambition to cast a magnifying glass onto Robert's failures. When Uncle Jim and Aunt Carol arrived, Robert was with them. I almost didn't recognize him. He was taller and thinner. He had a little facial hair and a couple of tattoos on his arms. What a difference a year made. That was about how long it had been since I'd last seen Robert.

"Hey cousin, how are you?" I asked.

Everybody had gathered by the front of our entrance. Hugging and kissing hello. Robert was the first one I got to greet.

"I'm doing good, Reem. Uncle Jim is talking about letting me come and work with him at Greens Excavations," Robert explained.

Before I could respond, I noticed my grandparents were standing off in the distance videotaping our reunion. I thought that was odd of my grandfather, but not my grandmother. She loved pictures and home movies, but Grandpa would typically be sitting down somewhere, waiting for all the greeting to be over and complaining there was no couch to sit on. Instead, he was right next to Grandma, smiling and whispering something to her. I felt Robert touching me on the shoulder to get my attention.

"I know what you're thinking. Just wait for it," Robert said with a smile on his face. Something was up. Robert looked like he knew what it was. It was at that point my mom started screaming.

"Are you kidding me! Oh, my goodness! Oh, my goodness! Ahmed! Ahmed! Oh, my goodness!"

I was trying to look through all the aunts and uncles to see what was going on. I realized that June and my mom were hugging my Aunt Carol.

"Aunt Carol and Uncle Jim are expecting," Robert said with happiness in his voice.

I could feel the little boy inside me that was totally in love with my Aunt Carol die a little bit. I remembered thinking that Aunt Carol and I were so close and that I was her favorite. One day she would realize this, and somehow, we would be married. I couldn't help but laugh and smile a little bit to myself, remembering those childhood feelings and thoughts. I embraced my Aunt Carol and congratulated her and my Uncle Jim on the fantastic news. The conversation continued longer in the entrance, with my parents and my aunts and uncles.

"How many weeks are you?" Mom asked as she touched Aunt Carol's belly, with no regard for her personal space. June still had a death lock around Aunt Carol's arm, hugging whatever part of her body she could.

"I'm ten weeks now, but it feels like twenty. It's okay, June, I'm not going anywhere," Aunt Carol said to June.

June let go of her arm and started to giggle a little bit at herself. She was just so excited and happy for Aunt Carol.

"This is truly a happy day. If we had known, we could have changed our plans, and all met in Québec so you wouldn't have had to travel. I'm so sorry."

My dad leaned in and kissed Aunt Carol on the cheek and gave her a big congratulatory hug.

"Don't give it a second thought, Ahmed. Mom and Dad were dying to get out of town anyway," Aunt Carol said.

My grandparents had stopped videotaping and joined in on the conversation.

The smell of fresh coffee cake was making its way down the hallway and into my bedroom. Bella made the greatest coffee cake for my dad. Dad said it was like a slice of heaven. Very few smells could pull me out of bed in the morning. Bella's coffee cake was one and Grandma making cookies for Grandpa was the other. June was already in the kitchen as I walked over to the cutting board to get a plate.

"I guess Aunt Carol is going to have a new favorite. Someone that she'll love the most, more than me or you," June said.

We both laughed at ourselves for a little bit and talked about how nice it had been to feel like we were her favorite when we were younger.

"I'm going to tell all your children that, Reem," June said with a giggle in her voice.

A feeling of happiness came over me when I realized that June was going to be the Aunt Carol to my kids. As for Rico, he was an excellent choice for an uncle because he was so playful with kids. I could see him being a fun uncle.

"Is there any tea in this place?" Robert asked, looking jet lagged.

"I got to tell you, Robert, you look taller and thinner… and not in a good way. What's up with the tattoos?" June said.

June had no idea what Uncle Dennis had revealed to me about Robert.

"I've had a rough eighteen months, June. My girlfriend dumped me. And the recreational drugs I was taking turned into a full-blown habit. My dad stuck me into a rehab center in Canada. That's why I came up here with Uncle Jim," Robert said.

June helped Robert make the tea with a stunned look on her face. I could tell she had no idea what to say. The three of us sat at the kitchen table and enjoyed our tea.

"Tell us how we can support you, cousin."

June's sincerity was very touching. She wanted to know what she could do to help and was willing to do just about anything for Robert. I just sat there and listened. Robert explained that he had fallen in love with a girl in his sophomore year of high school. His girlfriend liked to go to parties and get high. Robert said that it helped with the stress of the expectations his dad had placed upon him about his future. June and I were both able to relate to that. Our parents both had extremely high expectations over our prospects, as well. I told the story to Robert about the fight between me and my dad, and what direction I wanted to take my future.

"That's nice, Reem, but you don't understand.

I've had a big roadblock in my way. I've had a learning disability my entire life. My dad thinks that I can just overcome it and still become a doctor like him, or lawyer, something professional. It was just becoming a little too difficult dealing with all that pressure. I didn't realize it until it was too late. My addiction had taken hold of me, and I needed help. So, I got out of my mom's house and ended up with Uncle Jim. He got me into rehab and said that I could learn the excavation business. I like that because it's mechanical and hands-on. It's something I think I would enjoy doing."

I drank some more of my tea as I thought about what Robert had just said.

"So did rehab work for you?" June asked.

"Yes, that whole thing was so stupid of me. I couldn't believe I'd let myself go that far. I was disappointed in myself, and rehab was the mirror in front of my face that I needed. I never want to go back to Colorado or stay with my mom. My friends there in Colorado are just users. They didn't care about me – all they wanted was to party and get high. I was just a kid who had the money."

"Okay, Robert, but you remember that family is everything. That we'll always be here for you no matter what!"

I remembered those exact words from my mom after my fifth-grade kickball win: "Family is everything."

BJ had arranged for a photographer to come in and take our family pictures. Before the evening had started, BJ wasn't feeling particularly good, and Dad had told him to go ahead and go home. BJ had reluctantly agreed.

"Okay, doctor... Yes, please let me know... It doesn't matter whatever he needs, whatever it takes... I don't care if he won't let you! Tell him he doesn't have a choice... Okay, I'll see you soon. Thank you again."

Dad hung up the phone and turned to all of us. We'd been waiting eagerly on the news about BJ. He had called our father that evening and let him know that he was okay, but he'd had a touch of appendicitis and would need an appendectomy. He was calling to let my dad know that he might be out for a day or two. Dad called the hospital and made some arrangements for BJ's comfort.

"BJ is doing good and resting comfortably. He will be alright. He's just pissed off because the hospital put him in a private room, and the doctors and nurses are fussing over him a lot. Because of my call."

My father looked very relieved after speaking with the doctor. BJ was a part of all our lives, and we were all relieved to hear that he'd be okay.

The next day Dad had us all in the car and headed to the hospital to visit BJ. Mom insisted on stopping at the market to get BJ some flowers and his favorite chocolates.

"Do you think BJ will like what I got him, Dad?" June asked.

June was holding a Bonsai tree and a get-well card. I just had a couple of puzzle books to give him. Maybe that would help him pass the time, I thought.

"I think BJ will like it a lot, sweetheart," Dad said.

My dad was right; June did have an excellent gift. BJ enjoyed things like Bonsai trees and puzzles, books, and those fancy thermometers with colored bubbles that go up and down depending on the temperature.

Rico and I were thinking of things to say that were sarcastic – "Is Your Royal Highness comfortable? Can we get Your Holiness any water? What kind of royal fluids do you put in that bedpan?"

BJ always loved sarcasm and anytime we were sick at home or injured, BJ would always tease us by calling us Prince or Your Royal Highness or Your Most Holiness. So, now it was our turn to exercise our revenge upon him. Our entire family had come, even my grandfather, to see BJ.

"You all should not have come to see me. I'll be up and back at it in a day or two," BJ said.

I think BJ was surprised to see that we had all come. He'd probably expected my dad and Mom to show up, but he looked a little embarrassed when we all were standing in his private hospital room.

"You need to hush up! Because of your help and all your hard work making our lives easier and better. We're a close family because of you and all your efforts. That makes you not only a part of this family but an important part! Of course, we're going to come and make sure you're okay," Grampa said.

Grampa let BJ have it. Everyone in the room was stunned. I'd never heard Grandpa talk like that. But he was right, everything he said to BJ we all felt. He was part of this family – an essential part.

"Yes, sir, of course," BJ responded to my grandpa.

BJ had a hold of my dad's hand. He was reassuring him that everything was okay and that they should go home already. That was when Rico and I started in on BJ.

"How is Your Most Holiness feeling today, Sir? Can we get Your Royal Highness a beer or a glass of wine? Reem, make sure that the bedpan gets secured.

We don't want anybody to try and rob BJ of his precious bodily fluids."

Rico and I could tell right away that BJ was in pain every time we made him laugh, so we kept it up. When Rico threatened to fart in his IV tube, our mother kicked us out of the room.

After we got back to the house, I sat down with my Uncle Dennis.

"I don't think you have anything to worry about with Robert, Uncle Dennis. I talked with him about all that's been going on for the last two years. It seems to me that his girlfriend was poison for him," I said.

Uncle Dennis appreciated the Cliff Notes of mine and Roberts's conversations. He said that he liked the changes he was starting to see in his son and would be grateful for anything I could do or advice I could give Robert. The day before they all had to leave, Uncle Dennis looked at my USC application. He was impressed with my scores, but the best part, he said, was the essays that I had written.

"Reem, not only have you expressed yourself in these essays, but you have given them a look into how you will fit into their program and benefit their student body. You have educated them on your background and your achievements, but you have also demonstrated that you're already a USC graduate. You just haven't gone to school yet. I enjoyed all your essays, and I think that you have as good a chance of getting in as anyone."

That statement made me feel a little uncomfortable. Only because I didn't have a backup school – all my eggs were in one basket. The thought of not getting in had never occurred to me.

I submitted my application and went back to my day-to-day routine, which consisted of swimming, school, club meetings, meetings with my mom over the language school, household chores, senior parties, and of course fixing my dad's old Toyota that had been handed down to me when Rico got a new truck. I wished Dad had just bought me a new car. Dad liked helping me fix the old Toyota when it needed brakes or oil changes, but he was so busy now that I was doing it myself. I'd ordered some new parts for the old truck, and Dad was going to help me put them in. A leveling kit would add two more inches to the height of my vehicle. The truck parts and instruction books arrived the same day. The four boxes from Toyota that came were white and had the round Toyota symbol in red on the packages. I grabbed the air freight bag that I thought had the instructions in them. I pulled it open and took out the automotive manual and opened it. It was red and looked like a trifold. This doesn't look like the automotive manual, I thought to myself. I opened the Velcro flap and looked down at some gold lettering:

WELCOME TO THE TROJAN FAMILY

The shock and surprise that came over my entire body filled my eyes with tears immediately as I started to realize what I had in my hand was not an automotive manual but my acceptance package to USC.

"I did it. I got accepted," I said to myself out loud. I didn't think anyone was home. It was late morning and Dad was at work and Mom wasn't home for lunch yet. The overwhelming feeling of happiness consumed me. I had set a long-term goal for myself and achieved it. I thought about all the hard work and studying I'd done to get here. I wanted to remember this feeling forever.

"Reem, I need you to pick up some supplies and bring them to Donna today," Mom said as she entered the living room from the kitchen. I could hear her keys hit the credenza where she always threw them when she got home.

"Okay, Mom," I replied.

Mom could see me standing in the middle of four boxes with tears in my eyes.

"What's wrong, son?" She was closing the gap between us with her arms reaching for me.

"I got into USC. I've been accepted to the architectural school," I said while opening the red USC trifold. Mom wrapped her arms around me, and we both sat down on the rug next to the boxes. Mom read my letter out loud.

"You need to call your dad right now, son," she whispered.

My graduating class had decided to throw water balloons at each other after graduation. This made for lousy family photos with our diplomas. My mom and dad were not amused. For my graduation gift, my dad bought me an acre of land on the moon, as a joke. That way, he said every time he looked up at the moon, he could see where I would live one day. My mom presented me with a beautiful, engraved pen and pencil set.

That summer, I worked on the business with my mom and Donna. I had to get everything organized before I left for USC. Mom opened three more locations, all next to shopping malls and outdoor markets. The people that did all the shopping, it seemed, were our target customers. Our students would take a class and then go shopping for food for the week.

The convenience of the locations wasn't lost on my mom.

"Reem, we've more than doubled in size and profit since last quarter. I'm looking at the numbers, and I think we can add three more instructors this month," Mom said.

She had a ton of financial papers all over the kitchen table where we were sitting. She looked up at me through the tops of her glasses. I could see the hunger and fire in her eyes over this business. She loved having a purpose and building something that helped others. We could have increased our classroom fees and made a more significant profit, but my mom didn't want me to get greedy.

"Okay, Mom, if you say so. I don't have a problem with that. Let's talk about that next month. You and Donna are going to need someone to help with the new languages. I'm not going to be here, so you need to pull Donna in more, or hire someone to do the course outlines. I'm okay with Donna's request for 20% of the business. But if she's not able to give more of her time, then 20% is off the table. I don't care what Rico said about her time at the university."

I started closing the binders in front of me and putting them back in their boxes. Each class and schedule had to be checked against the curriculum to make sure they were on track for what the student was learning.

"I completely agree with you, Reem. I want to wait and see what direction she takes. Donna has been invaluable and a fantastic school manager. I don't think we need to rush our decision. 20% is a lot, and I don't want to make the wrong choice," Mom said.

My mom had a good point. I just wanted to ensure the business would be successful while I was gone. Donna was supervising most of our instructors and becoming a fantastic counselor for our students. Since we had such a wide variety of backgrounds and abilities in our students, Donna was able to put them in categories to be taught differently. Some had learning disabilities, and some had scheduling problems that would interfere with other students'. That decision had made our business even more successful, and I felt that she deserved to own part of our company in return.

By the time I left for college, the money was pouring in. Demand kept growing, and even though Mom would reinvest some of the profits back into the business, the money just kept coming. Dad had to give up a lot of BJ's time to help Mom that first year. Eventually, we would hire a law firm and an accounting firm to take some of the burden off our shoulders. Mom and Donna worked very well together. My brother Rico couldn't have been happier. Donna made some changes to her class schedule, giving her more time for the business so I signed over 20% to Rico and Donna. Mom had 30% and my 50% ownership in a proxy; she loved the business so much. She had a marketing degree and enjoyed helping others. It also gave June a look into corporate law.

We arrived in California the first week of August. My parents seemed to be excited for me, but I could tell they didn't like the distance. Registration and move-in was the week of the 8th. My schedule as a freshman started the week of the 15th. Time seemed to be moving too quickly. We had three days before I was to move into school housing. Dad had us at the Huntington Beach hotel. Mom loved the views from the coast.

"Reem, open the door," Rico said as he knocked on my door. We had adjoining rooms at the hotel. Mom and Dad thought it wasn't appropriate for us to share a room now that Rico and I were older.

"Okay, stop knocking!" I shouted. I had just got out of bed and was brushing my teeth. It felt good to sleep in. I had got rid of my jet lag.

"You're not dressed yet? Mom and Dad are waiting for us in the lobby," Rico said.

"I need to put on a shirt, and I'll be down in five minutes," I replied. I rushed out the door with my room key in my mouth and one hand slipping on my last shoe.

"Reem, here is the valet ticket – have them bring up our car," Dad said. BJ smiled at me and went back to talking to my dad – about work, I guessed. I grabbed the ticket out of Dad's hand and walked outside to the valet stand. The valet worker took the ticket and tore it in two pieces and handed me one back. While I was waiting for my dad I started to wonder where Rico and Mom were. The valet pulled up next to me in a Jeep Wrangler and got out and handed me the key. He must have made a mistake, I thought – we'd come in a Buick.

"Way to go, brother," Rico yelled.

"We love you, Reem," Mom and Dad yelled; they were all standing off to the side just out of my immediate sight.

My parents had bought me a brand-new orange Jeep Wrangler with black rims. The 4x4 emblem on the side was black like the interior.

You could spot that Jeep from a block away; the orange was so bright. As for me, I think it was love at first sight. I went through every nook and cranny, from the engine to the interior. I had to wait a few more days to take my driver's test at the DMV because I didn't have my student housing address yet.

"This is the best present ever! Thank you, guys, so much, I love it!" I said.

I put the keys in my front pocket when I was done hugging my dad.

"BJ has lined up a garage just two blocks off of campus where you can keep it," Dad said.

We took the Jeep out for a drive. Dad and BJ had diplomatic driver's licenses. They drove Rico and I up and down the PCH for over an hour, while Mom and June stayed back at the hotel. BJ took over driving and pulled into a Dairy Queen.

"Reem, in this envelope, you'll find two credit cards and your permanent resident card here in the United States. If anyone gives you any problems, contact this man on this business card." *Department of State Jeremy Cook United States of America* was the name on the business card. Dad motioned to BJ to give me the envelope with all the items in it. I stood up and put the envelope in my back pocket and sat back down. The small table sat four of us, Dad and Rico on one side and BJ and I on the other.

"Okay, Dad, I'll make sure to keep them safe. What's with the resident card? I didn't think I needed anything other than my passport," I asked.

"If you're going to spend more than four years here attending school, it's simply better for you legally if you have permanent resident status. So, I called in a diplomatic favor from a friend, and he got it done."

My brother Rico brought the food and ice cream over to our table, and we ate. My dad wanted to drive back. He loved driving the Jeep. Before we got back to the hotel, Dad stopped at the beach. He pulled up to a spot overlooking the ocean. We all jumped out and ran to the water. Rico ran faster than all of us. He got to the edge of the water, where a wave had just hit. He turned around and was yelling at us, "Come on, ladies! You all run like girls!"

I was the first one to notice that Rico had his back to the next wave, and it was a big one. If Rico didn't turn around, it was going to hit and knock him down. BJ and dad were a little behind me, waving their arms and pointing and yelling.

"Turn around, son! Watch out, Rico!"

I, on the other hand, decided to let it play out. Just as Rico turned to see what dad and BJ were yelling about, the big wave hit him right in the face. The next thing I saw was Rico's two feet straight up in the air. It had to be the funniest thing I'd ever seen. I helped Rico up onto his feet with my dad. He was still coughing up seawater.

"Are you okay, Rico? I tried to warn you," BJ said.

BJ was concerned but I couldn't help but smile and hold back my laughter. Rico had got what he deserved, I thought. I knew his competitive nature would one day come back and bite him. Rico was soaked; there wasn't a spot on him that didn't have saltwater dripping off.

"If you think you're getting into my new Jeep, you're crazy!" I said.

Rico looked up at me and could see my amusement. Before I could run, Rico grabbed me with the help of my dad and threw me into the water. So, I decided to chase down my dad and give him a bear hug. Dad wasn't as wet as I was after the hug, but it would do.

"Okay, that's enough, men! You're going to overdo it," BJ said.

Over to our left I could see two young men walking toward us. They'd been playing volleyball with one another. BJ went right into protection mode.

"Hey, you four want to play some beach volleyball with us?"

This guy was huge, his arms and chest looked like he came from a fitness magazine. The other guy could have been his twin brother.

Rico yelled, "Sure," before we had a chance to even think about it. He didn't even check with us. There goes Rico's competitiveness, I thought to myself. We played for a while. After Rico and I had dried out enough, I ran over to our new friends and introduced myself.

"Hey, I'm Reem, and that's my brother Rico."

I tossed the volleyball back to one of them.

"I'm Danny, and that's my squad leader Ben. We drove up from San Diego to see Ben's sister. We got bored sitting around the house, so we decided to come out here to play some beach ball," Danny said.

He kept tossing the ball up in the air and catching it.

"Oh, you're in the military?" I asked.

"We're Marines," Danny said.

We had all gathered round by this time. Ben and Danny were cool and funny. Dad and BJ seemed to enjoy asking them about life in the military. My dad even invited them to eat dinner with us.

"You two must come. Bring your sister. Dinner is on me. It's the least I can do," Dad said.

We told them to meet us at Rick's Steakhouse at 6:30pm.

"Sir, we're Marines! We don't turn down free food!" Ben said.

Ben Gibbs and Danny Sutcliffe ran off to get ready for dinner. We got back to the hotel in one piece. We must have looked bad. Mom was shocked.

"What the hell happened to you guys? You look like you've been in a fight," she said.

Rico and I had sand everywhere. It was in my ears, my nose, and possibly my teeth.

Dinner that night was a lot of fun. Ben and Danny showed up with Ben's sister Carrie. She had just finished school at UCSF and taken a job in Huntington Beach with the city. Danny had joined the Marines to help pay for school with the GI Bill. He had one more year before he would be in the reserves and could complete his education. Ben was making the military his career. Danny and I hit it off right away. We both had our minds on our future goals. He was so interested in how I got into USC. After dinner, we made plans to stay in touch. I hadn't noticed, but on the way home, Rico was teasing June about the way she'd been looking at Ben all night.

"You're so in love with him. It was obvious how you hung onto every word he said," Rico teased.

June was trying to ignore Rico, but she was blushing hard.

"I think he was very handsome; June would be crazy not to have a crush on him," Mom said, trying to stick up for June.

"Can we just change the subject, please!" June snapped.

She was starting to get mad. Dad was the one that changed the subject.

"That was a nice dinner. They were very impressive young men."

We'd all enjoyed their company. The two Marines had a lot of funny stories to share.

"Yes, hun, they were," Mom said.

"Did you see how much they could eat?" June said. I looked back at June, who was smiling. She'd liked Ben's sister Carrie and had talked to her throughout the dinner.

The next day was my registration day. I received my dorm assignment, student mailbox, and ID. Uncle Dennis had paid my semesters' tuition and my dad wasn't all that happy about it. A deal is a deal, Uncle Dennis said.

"What did you do, Mom, buy one of everything at the student store?" I asked.

It was too much. Hats, shirts, sweaters – you name it, my mom had got it.

"I just want you to have whatever you need, son," she said.

I could see that my mom was going to have a hard time saying goodbye. I tried not to think about it. I took a snapshot in my head of the four of us on the beach playing in the ocean. That was my happy place.

Move-in day had arrived! Most of the Arab clothing I kept in a small plaid suitcase that I would leave at the bottom of my dorm closet. There was still a lot of prejudice against Arab people. All the news in America about the middle east was negative. Besides, I was getting used to wearing my western-style clothing. Not cowboy western but my go-to outfit, like my 501 blue jeans and a nice comfortable Ralph Lauren Polo shirt. Nicole had taken me shopping a few more times while I was in Chicago. I'd caught a glimpse of myself in the mirror when I was trying on my first Ralph Lauren polo shirt. It was at that time I'd noticed I wasn't a little kid anymore. My arms were bigger. My chest was more substantial, and I see that even my head was more prominent. My jawline looked more distinguished and chiseled. I kept that image in my mind every time I put on a Ralph Lauren polo.

My dorm room was nice and a lot bigger than I'd thought it would be. My parents had to fly back home to get Rico and June ready for school. They only had a few hours to help me move in before they had to leave for the airport. It was still early in the morning, and I was the first student to check into my room. June and Mom had gone to Target a few times to pick up some items and decorations they wanted to put on the wall. My mom loved to decorate. Dad had bought me a Macintosh SE computer for my desk. I'd never used one before, but I knew I needed to learn computers. Mom started crying on the way to the car, where we would say our goodbyes.

"I'm sorry we're going to miss meeting your roommates. You'll have to tell us all about them. We love you, so please be careful over here and stay in touch every week."

My dad kissed me softly on both my cheeks. He waited to be the last one to say goodbye before they got in the car to leave.

"Reem, do your best and remember who you are and what you represent," Dad said.

As the limousine pulled away, I could still feel my father's embrace, my mom's tears, and June and Rico's love all over me. My mom was looking through the back window at me, waving goodbye. I knew she was looking at a five-year-old Reem waving goodbye, not the college freshman I was now. I found the nearest public bathroom, walked into a stall, and cried my eyes out.

I got back to my dorm room and surveyed what my mom and June had done with my area. I had new sheets and blankets on my bed with a beautiful white comforter, and colored decorative throw pillows strategically placed. (Although I thought my mom still had a lot to learn about matching colors.) My desk was all set up with my brand-new state of the art Macintosh SE computer and plenty of stationery, pencils, rulers, colored markers, colored pencils – the list went on and on. June had found a couple of concert posters for my wall. Bands she knew I loved: Van Halen, Bon Jovi, U2, and Huey Lewis and the News. I needed to buy some more clothes. I wanted to see what the new fashion was in Los Angeles before I completed my wardrobe. Freshman orientation wasn't until tomorrow, so I had pretty much the rest of the day to myself.

Some rooms had two to a room, and some had four with a common living area and a kitchenette. We had a resident advisor down the hall, a large bulletin board next to the elevators and access to a full gym. We even had a fantastic dining hall area, awfully close to our dorm room. My roommates were Juanito Sison from New York, Scott Harrison from Indiana, and John Hollingsworth II from right here, Dana Point, California. Juan and Scotty arrived just after lunch. John came in late just after 3pm. I got to meet all their parents and Scotty's brother Derrick.

That night Scotty and I ran out to get dinner for everyone. We found a great Mexican restaurant called Ponchos. I ordered five dinner specials, a tray of enchiladas, tacos and burritos. Enough for everyone, with chips, salsa, and rice and beans. The waitress came out with four large paper bags full of food. Scotty checked everything while I paid. It came out to $70, so I gave her a $10 tip. I signed the credit card slip, and we were on our way.

"How much do I owe you for dinner, bro?" Scotty asked as we entered the elevator to go up.

"My hands are full – push number five. It came out to about seven dollars each."

Seven dollars was enough, I thought. We got up to the dorm room and put the food on one of the desks. The parents were still helping to organize their students' spaces, just like Mom and June had done for me that morning.

"Reem, tell me where you're from again," Mrs. Sison ask.

"I'm from Kuwait, by Saudi Arabia and the Persian Gulf," I said.

I grabbed a taco and a napkin out of the bag.

"That's where we get most of our diesel and gasoline from," John said.

"Really? Your family must be doing well then. We buy a lot of gas," Scotty's Mom added.

"No, my dad has a government job. My uncle Dennis is a doctor in Chicago, and he helps me with my tuition."

I didn't want them to think I came from money. Juan had a full-ride engineering scholarship, and Scotty had a partial one with some financial aid. John was the wealthiest one in our group, everyone assumed. He was the all-American looking kid in his high school. Blond hair and blue eyes, just like Danny. Does California have a factory where they make guys like them? I thought to myself. The girls also: I couldn't go two blocks without seeing a bronze goddess with gorgeous long blonde hair and blue eyes walking or jogging down the street.

They were everywhere here. It wasn't long before all the tearful goodbyes had started, and we were all in our dorms ready for the following day's freshman orientation.

CHAPTER 14

My fall semester had ended, and I was already back at USC and in classes for the spring. That first semester was everything I thought it would be. Time management was crucial for me. Classwork, friends, social activity, and the distance from my family combined was almost too much to bear. I could feel the empty spot in my life where my family had been. To deal with the homesickness I ran up a big long-distance bill with the phone company. My dad never complained about it. I think not only did he miss me too, but he could relate to the home-sickness because he'd left home and gone to Canada.

We had Christmas in Canada that year. Dad only stayed for four days and had to go back home early. Work was keeping him going all the time, BJ told me. My roommate John's family was spending time in Europe for the holidays, so I invited John to come with me and get out of California for a couple of weeks.

"Québec? Sure, it might be nice to get the hell out of California for a while. I've never been to Canada before. Is there anything to do out there?" he asked.

He looked a little surprised when I invited him. We weren't the closest out of the four roommates, but I enjoyed hanging out with him. John was one of the fraternity guys in our dorm. He had access to all the best parties that year.

"We're probably going to do some fishing and hunting with my uncles and maybe my grandfather," I said.

I'd already packed my suitcase and was ready.

"Cool, we're going to blow some shit up!" John said.

Not only was John the loudest person in our building, but he was so gung-ho about everything. He threw a gym bag over his shoulder and looked at me as if he was ready to leave.

"You know you need a passport and probably a few more clothes other than a gym bag, numb nuts," I said.

We had a lot of names for each other in our room. Numb nuts was just one of several: mama's boy, dumb ass, peewee, and everybody's favorite, fag! John would wake up early and be so loud in the morning. We all wanted to kill John but no one more than "Juanito burrito" who was an engineering student and trying to sleep. He was having trouble in his first year.

John jumped over his desk chair and stood over his bed. He grabbed a suitcase from under the bed, opened his gym bag and dumped the contents into the suitcase along with a few other items from his dresser drawer.

"Oh crap, I need to swing by the bank and get some cash! What time is the flight? Should I call the airline from here? Or do I have enough time to buy my ticket at the airport?" John asked.

The idea of leaving LA for a couple of weeks was getting John more excited. He was talking a mile a minute.

"We have plenty of time to swing by the bank, and don't worry about the airline ticket, I have an extra one," I said.

"Are we doing a shuttle or a taxi?"

John looked at his watch to see what time it was.

"Yes, our car is already here. So, we'll go to the bank first, and I need to stop at the store to grab a few things," I said.

I liked to have a bag of snacks on the plane. John was looking for a shuttle or taxi waiting for us. I didn't say anything but kept walking down Orchard Street, to my garage. I removed the padlock from the door and grabbed the handle. I lifted the garage door, and John couldn't believe his eyes: a brand-new orange Jeep Wrangler with Huntington Beach stickers on the bumper.

"This is your car, Reem?" John asked.

I nodded my head.

"A graduation gift from my parents," I said.

John let out a "Nice!!" and threw his suitcase in the back. He jumped into the passenger seat and started playing with the radio. The fact that I had a car just off campus seemed to make his whole day.

I came out of the 7-Eleven with two bags of snacks. Some chips, candy bars, beef jerky and of course some soda pop. John was putting away the cash he'd withdrawn from the bank.

"Holy crap, Reem, did you buy the whole store?"

John grabbed the two bags from me and looked inside them before he put them on the back seat.

"Hey, do we have the same professor for math?" I asked.

"Professor Clifford? Yeah, I think so why?"

John was now going through my glove box in the Jeep, and I had to get over about three different lanes to be in the one I needed for the airport exit. John was trying to get my suitcase from the back seat.

"John, what the hell are you trying to do?" I asked.

John was distracting me from driving. He was halfway in the front and halfway in the back.

"I was trying to put your snacks away in your suitcase before we went through security. I don't think they'll let you have all this food on the plane, Reem."

I couldn't help but laugh.

"John, don't worry about it. I know a guy who lets me on the plane with all the food," I replied.

John figured I knew what I was doing. He pulled his money back out of his wallet and started counting it again. He believed the bank teller had shorted him by $20. We arrived on the edge of Los Angeles International Airport. I pulled into the Jennifer Noel office building and flight school. I parked the Jeep in the first space next to the entrance door.

"What are we doing at an office complex?" John asked.

"Come on, grab your shit, we're here," I said.

I jumped out of the Jeep. I was pulling my suit-case and snack bags from the back when Gilbert, my flight concierge, came out to greet me.

"Good morning, Mr. Al-Saba; everything is ready for you. Is there anything you need?"

Gilbert relieved me of my luggage and snack bags. He had a flight porter come and take the items and get them on the plane.

"Yes, Gilbert, thank you. I'll be flying with a companion today, and I didn't bring the top for my Jeep. Can you have it put in the hangar while I'm gone? Also, I need to make a phone call before we leave the terminal," I said as we walked quickly into the terminal entrance.

John wasn't far behind us. Gilbert clicked his fingers twice at the receptionist. She knew right away to rotate her desk phone so that I could make a call. Gilbert was highly efficient. He had a porter manage the luggage while another agent took my keys to my Jeep. They would keep it safe for me. The flight center was nice, with a lounge area with TVs and a floating staircase to the left made from dark wood and iron.

"We're flying private – fucking cool!" John's voice echoed loudly through the small office terminal. I just shook my head in disbelief.

Steve, the Gulfstream pilot, greeted me with our approximate arrival time. John settled in and started enjoying our snacks.

"You know what, man? I understand. If I had access to all this, I don't think I would advertise it to my friends either," John said.

John was considered one of the wealthy students on campus. John's mom and dad had both gone to

USC and joined a fraternity. So that was what his parents expected John to do. His family was wealthy but would only fly private on special occasions and significant family events.

"Thanks, John, I knew that you would understand," I said.

I settled in and tried to take a nap. After we arrived Uncle Jim picked us up and brought us to my grandparents' house. My family enjoyed having John for the holidays. We packed in a lot of fishing and hunting and got kicked out of the Tacklebox, a bar my cousin Robert said would have a lot of college girls. We had a lot of fun that night. Robert left early, and John and I got lucky. The next night John walked over to the girl he had been with the night before. But this time she was with her boyfriend. There was a little pushing and shoving but no fists. The owner threw John and I out and we slept it off. He was now my best friend after this trip. John and I had each other's back.

"College roommate's: check. Best friends: check. Getting kicked out of a bar in Canada: check." John liked to say check to things he thought were an accomplishment.

Classes started back on January 7th, and I was getting used to the routine of college life. Lectures, labs, and collaborations were just a part of my schedule. At USC, there were so many things to do and see. It forced you to get out and meet people. Each day's schedule of events was posted on the cork board. You needed to choose what fit your schedule. Not to mention all the parties that were going on all week long.

My friend Jeff Frame from my study group needed to use my Apple computer for a new idea he'd had. We walked back to my dorm, and on the way, I spotted Danny Sutcliffe, the Marine I'd met on the beach the previous year.

"Hey, Reem!"

Danny was waving his arm, but I had already spotted him and was walking over to him.

"Danny, how's it going?" I said.

I walked up and gave him the bro hug – you know, the one where you lock hands thumbs first and hit your shoulders together.

"I'm out! I got discharged last week."

Jeff shook Danny's hand as I introduced them.

"Holy crap, so you're no longer a Marine. So, what are you going to do?" I asked.

Jeff walked over to my right side because the sun was hitting him in the face. Jeff wasn't tall, but he was called scrappy by some of his friends, including me. Jeff moved his brown hair out of his face, and you could see the definition in his forearm.

"I'm in the reserves now. And what did I tell you, once a Marine, always a Marine," Danny said as he gave me that million-dollar smile of his.

"Where are you based out of?" Jeff asked.

"Twentynine Palms, 7th Marine!" Danny almost snapped to attention.

"Why, Jeff, do you know anything about the military?" I asked.

Jeff laughed. "My dad was the base commander for eight years at Twentynine Palms when I was born," Jeff said.

Danny was paying attention now.

"Who is your dad?" Danny asked.

"Brigadier General Frame," said Jeff.

"Wow, that must be cool to have a dad like Frame. Sorry to hear about him," Danny said.

"Why? What happened to your dad, Jeff?" I inquired respectfully.

"Cancer four years ago," he replied. You could see that Jeff didn't like to talk about it.

"Hey Danny, you want to go to a frat party tonight?" I changed the subject quickly.

"I can't. I'm meeting up with Ben and Carrie tonight. I just wanted to see if you had time this weekend to come out with us. We're going skydiving and drinking."

Danny wasn't kidding. They loved doing crazy shit like that. I knew I wouldn't get a chance to go skydiving again.

"Hell, yeah! Why the hell not! I'm in, Danny!" I said.

Jeff just looked at me like I was crazy. Danny wrote down Carrie's address.

"Meet us here tomorrow at 8am," Danny said.

I also gave Danny my new student phone number.

When Jeff and I got to my dorm room, he started working on my Apple computer while I started thinking about what I'd need for the following day. I might be with Danny and Ben for a couple of days. I needed to buy some more clothes – as I was going through my stuff, there weren't a lot of options. Danny and Ben were your All-American California Boys. Then there was me: tall, dark, and handsome. I pulled out my suitcase and opened it. Then I saw John in the hall outside my room.

"John! John! Come in here!" I yelled to get John's attention.

"Dude, what the fuck are you doing?" he asked, seeing my suitcase out. We were going to a party in three hours.

"Have you seen my white Adidas shirt? Did it come back with us from Canada? I think I left too much stuff at my grandparents' house," I said.

I put what I had in the suitcase and pushed it to the edge of my bed.

"Do you have to leave town again? Where are you going this weekend?" John asked.

He sat in Scotty's desk chair and was spinning around.

"I don't know about you, little girl, but I'm going skydiving tomorrow," I said.

John rose to his feet with excitement. "Don't tease me, Reem. Are you really going skydiving? I've always wanted to do that. Is this for real? Are you just fucking with me?" John asked.

I gave John the "look." It was the same look I'd given him when a girl at the Tacklebox had told me that she and her friend wanted to get to know us better.

"We're meeting up with Danny and Ben tomorrow, my two Marine friends who are probably experts in skydiving. But I need new clothes, so forget the party tonight," I said.

John walked over to me and investigated my suitcase. He started pulling stuff out with a look of disbelief at what I'd picked out.

"Nobody wears this, Reem! Are you going to play Polo today, fag? Enough with all the Ralph Lauren shit. Come on, let's go shopping," he said.

He picked out all my new clothes. A lot of shorts, white, green, and khakis. My shirts fit loose and had a seaport style to them. Yep, I looked like a Dana Point douche bag, just like John, I thought to myself. A new pair of Ray Bans, hat, and shoes topped me off.

I picked up Danny and Ben at Carrie's house in Huntington Beach at 8am. Ben had a nice car, but we took my Jeep for the openness it provided. John sat in the back with Ben. Danny helped me with directions to the airport where the jump school was.

"Since you two have never jumped before, you'll have to go tandem until you have enough jumps to go solo," Ben shouted from the back seat.

The airport was getting closer, and I was getting nervous. John was in my rear-view mirror and looked happy and ready. We got to this little field that didn't even look like an airport. The shack they called an office wasn't helping with my nerves. In the back was a large room that looked like a school cafeteria. The floors were cement, and the tables were picnic benches. I didn't say anything at first, I just watched. The airplane must have been out taking jumpers because the only plane visible had no wheels.

"Are you guys sure about this place?" I said, trying not to sound nervous.

"Don't worry, Reem. This place knows what they're doing. They get the job done," Danny said, putting on a jumpsuit.

"It's not the fall that kills you, Reem. It's the sudden stop at the end," Ben added. He handed me a jumpsuit while all three were laughing at me. John fit right in with the two Marines.

"Laugh it up assholes if I go splat. Which one of you is going to explain it to my brother Rico?" I said.

I opened the zipper to the suit.

"Well, not me, that's one big fucking Arab," Danny said, his eyebrows raised.

"Did you see the arms on the fucking guy when we played volleyball?" Ben asked Danny.

"Yeah, I wouldn't mess with him either. Don't worry, Reem, we got your back on this jump," Ben said.

The laughing was over. Two airplanes touched down on a small landing strip behind our building. It was almost time for us to jump. I walked up to the front counter to pay my fee and saw they had a couple more options if you wanted to buy them. If I spent extra, one of the staff members would also jump with a camcorder and record my skydive.

"How much extra to do that?" I pointed at the flyer on the counter that showed a picture of someone recording a jump.

"Seventy-five dollars extra," the lady said without even looking up at me. They must not have had a lot of people pay that much for a recording.

"What about if there are four of us?"

The lady looked up from her paper with a surprised look on her face.

"Four? You want four?" Shelly asked. Shelly was the name on her badge.

"Can you do it?" I asked.

"Hey Mike, can we do four recordings?"

An older man came out from an office with a hero sandwich in his hand and mayonnaise on his face. She had interrupted his meal, apparently. He looked at me and smiled.

"What four guys are we talking about here, son?" he asked.

I pointed over to my three friends.

"Ben and Danny are here all the time," he said. "I would only charge you for two. Does that sound like a deal, son?"

I gave Shelly my American Express card and thought, my parents are going to die when they see this charge.

"Reem, come on! Get over here," John said.

He was standing with a group of jumpers.

"Reem, this is Dave, your instructor," Ben said.

Dave was helpful and calming. He gave me all my instructions on what to do and how to do it. He'd made hundreds of tandem jumps with this company. Mike came over and greeted Ben and Danny like they were family.

"Hey men, your jump is going to be recorded today courtesy of this young man," he said.

He squeezed the top of my shoulder.

"Oh yeah, way to go, Reem!" John belted out with excitement. We had all the info we needed, and the time had come to jump. The pilot motioned us that we had hit the necessary altitude. John and I were first; Ben and Danny would be jumping at a higher altitude. The sensation that went through me as I fell back to the earth was something I'll never forget. I felt like I had entered a new world and in this world I could fly.

John and I loved the tandem experience but looking at Ben and Danny and what they did solo, I knew I had to do a solo jump.

"What do I need to do to jump solo?" I asked my tandem instructor as we were gathering up our parachute.

"We have to assign you a certified instructor and you'll have to pass all the school's requirements. It's a bit costly, but it's worth it," he said.

After our jump, John had an idea to take all the videotapes to a friend in the Cinema Department at USC to edit them all together. This was a great idea. John's friend did a fantastic job, even entering it as one of his editing projects and getting an A on the assignment. Danny and Ben showed the tape to Mike, the owner of the jump school. He asked if it would be okay to play it on a TV in the office. He said that the response was immediate – the school had almost doubled its sales for videos. After John and I got our solo certifications, we made it part of our weekly routine to find new places to go skydiving. This new world of skydiving had brought me more perspective about my life and what I wanted out of it.

CHAPTER 15

My environmental studies class was keeping me up at night, and this class covered big architectural mistakes. The class went on to cover the 1973 Standard Oil Building, a $80 million-dollar architectural mistake. Then there was the 1940 Tacoma Narrows Bridge that collapsed spectacularly. If I wanted to pull a good grade out of this class, I was going to need a tutor.

My roommate Juanito was a flamboyant Filipino. He had a picture of Marilyn Monroe above his bed in a frame. Juanito's side of the room was always neat and tidy. He had little knick-knacks that reminded me of my mom all over the place. I remember thinking to myself he must be gay. Long black Filipino hair parted in the middle and feathered back. He always shook his head as he combed it straight back. Look at this guy, I thought, he thinks he's Travolta.

"Hey, Juanito, where did you find that tutor for your engineering class?" I asked.

Juanito was going through his morning ritual of grooming and picking out the clothes he was going to wear that day.

"You're such an asshole, Reem, what are you bringing that up for?" Juanito said while looking at a vintage Grateful Dead t-shirt. I didn't know why he was so offended so quickly.

"I need to get one for my environmental studies class. The teacher is killing me with some of these assignments, and I need a tutor," I replied.

"Look here, my little Arab Prince. The TA in that class will have a list of tutors that will help you – ask him for the list."

Swear to God; I bet when I leave the room he puts on his mother's clothes and sashays around our dorm room, I thought to myself as I left.

The TA in my environmental studies class was a complete asshole. I couldn't ask Ivan Goldberg to give me a tutor referral list. This guy blamed me for the Holocaust with his eyes every time I had to talk to him. The first day of class I dropped a can of soda off my table and it fell right into Ivan's backpack. I apologized and offered to pay for any of his stuff that had been damaged. But my lack of sincerity offended him, I think.

"Hey, Jeff, what class do you have next?" I asked.

Jeff and I were getting ready to leave the project studio after other students had reviewed two of our projects.

"I have to go talk to my architectural engineering professor and see if I can get an extension on one of my papers," Jeff said.

He was putting away some papers in his portfolio case.

"Hey, can you ask Goldberg for a tutor referral? I need a little help in my environmental studies, and he's got it in for me," I said.

I gave Jeff a concerned look. Maybe he would have sympathy for me and help me out, I thought.

"Yeah, no problem, let's go now. Ivan is such a dickhead, so stay behind me a few feet," he said.

He knocked on the TA's door, and I stayed down the hallway and out of view.

"Hey, Goldberg, can I get a copy of the tutor list?"

I could hear Ivan's voice down the hallway because the door was still open.

"Who needs the list? You've already taken this class, Jeff."

"I'm going to suggest it to one of my friends who is having a little trouble. Now give me the fucking list, Ivan!"

Jeff 's voice was very intimidating, even for me. I could hear a file drawer open, and a piece of paper in someone's hand. Jeff Frame's shoes squeaked as he turned to walk away from the door.

"The only one of your friends I know of having trouble with environmental studies is Reem. You can tell that guy it will be a cold day in hell before he gets a good grade in this class," Ivan yelled.

Jeff stopped abruptly and turned around.

"You know what, Goldberg! You're an asshole! You were an asshole when I took this class, and you're an asshole now!"

Jeff walked away; Ivan slammed the door.

"Hey, Reem, here's the list. I don't know how

much it will help, though. I think you're fucked in this class," Jeff said.

He was right. I didn't know how I was going to achieve a better grade, with Goldberg hating on me. There were five names on the list. I went down and called them all. The only one that had availability and returned my call was Sarah Long. We agreed to meet for lunch on Saturday. I'd sat down in one of the booths with a window overlooking the parking lot. Coco's wasn't that busy, but it was just before the lunch rush. I was trying to get Judy the waitress's attention behind me. I had ordered a refill of my pop a while ago, and she was taking the people behind me's order.

"You must be Reem. Hi, I'm Sarah."

I quickly turned my head and body around. Sitting in front of me was the most beautiful woman I had ever seen. I just sat there staring, not saying a word. I was practically holding my breath and didn't know why. She had very dark black hair, and big beautiful brown eyes that just saw right through me.

"This is when you respond and say something," Sarah said with a touch of sarcasm in her voice.

Her beautiful voice, like angels singing to me. I could even smell her perfume. Could people look like this? I thought.

"Are you okay? Do you need a doctor?" Sarah leaned closer to me with concern in her eyes.

Her beautiful brown eyes. I could look at her all day and not get bored or tired. That was the only way I could describe it. She had to be the most beautiful feminine woman I had ever seen.

"Miss, is he okay?" Sarah asked Judy, the waitress, as she walked past.

"Well, he looks better than most that come in here, sweetheart. We get some real losers in here sometimes. What can I get you?"

Sarah looked back at me. The waitress Judy had helped me snap out of my trance, and I had my hand already extended to Sarah.

"Yes, I'm Reem. I'm sorry about that, Sarah. It's good to meet you. I'll have a refill on my pop, Judy. Sarah, would you like anything?"

I shook Sarah's hand. Her soft, gentle, loving hand. Seriously, pull yourself together, Reem! I thought to myself.

"Yes, let me have a club sandwich and an iced tea, please," Sarah said.

Even the way she ordered her food made me want to listen to her order food all day.

"So, you need a little help in your environmental studies class? I can help you with that. Here are my open availabilities and my prices."

Sarah handed me a 3x5 card decorated with her name, information and prices. It was, indeed, the most adorable thing I'd ever seen. Damn, what was that? You got to cut it out! Snap out of it! Get back into the game. You're looking like an asshole, I thought to myself.

"Okay, you show here that you have only two slots left, an afternoon, and a late afternoon." I was pointing to her schedule on the 3x5 card.

"Yes, you only need one of the slots, though. I can take up to five students a semester, and I have two openings, an afternoon, and the morning. The late afternoon is a misprint," Sarah said, looking confused, like it was self-explanatory on the card.

"I'd like to buy both times slots. Tuesday morning and afternoon and Thursday morning and afternoon. I'm up against a big roadblock that I'll tell you about later. For me to get a good grade out of this class, I'll have to know more than the professor," I said, trying to sound as sincere as I could.

Tuesday would be okay; my schedule was clear. Thursday afternoon was going to be a problem – I had a history and a math lecture. That's okay, I thought to myself. I'll drop out of school and pay Sarah to lecture me for the next four years. That will be my entire education, Sarah's lectures.

"Wow, I've never had anyone buy two slots before. Are you sure? Two slots are a lot of time and money. Environmental studies, when you apply it to architecture, isn't that hard," Sarah said.

She was working on her degrees with environmental studies and had her sights set on a doctorate. The waitress, Judy, brought our food. I had also ordered a club sandwich, turkey only, earlier, and of course, still didn't get my refill on my soda.

"There you go. You two enjoy now."

Judy was about to turn and leave.

"Excuse me, Judy, is it?" Sarah said. "Can I get some ketchup for my fries and some napkins? Oh yeah, my companion here would like a refill on his pop."

Wow, Sarah could be feisty, I thought to myself. Judy squinted her eyes and smiled.

"Right away, dear."

Sarah didn't even wait for her to walk away

before she turned to me and said, "Can you believe how some people hate their own lives? I mean, if I were doing something I hated I would stop doing it. Life is too short to be doing something that you hate. Don't you think so, Reem?"

To my astonishment, Judy sat down in the booth next to us.

"You know what, sweetheart! Some people must work hard because nothing is given to them; they must work for it," she said.

Sarah sat up straight and looked directly at Judy.

"If you could be anywhere in this world and do anything right now, this very minute, where would you be and what would you be doing?"

Judy thought about it for a couple of minutes.

"I would be back home with my sister in Chicago. She opened a bakery and is doing very well," Judy said.

"Judy, then why aren't you there? You should be in Chicago, doing what makes you happy. Not working at a Coco's in Los Angeles," Sarah said.

She leaned back and put a French fry in her mouth. Judy just sat there thinking about what Sarah had just said.

"I guess I could tell my roommate to find someone… I would have to wait till the end of the week to get my paycheck… I don't need to bring anything." Judy was now mumbling things to herself. Suddenly, Judy looked up and smiled at Sarah. "You know, I told myself several times, pack up and leave. I gave acting two and a half years, and it didn't work out. When you hear it come from a stranger's mouth at a Coco's, it hits home," she said.

We could tell Judy had been having a bad day before Sarah let into her. But Judy jumped up like she had a purpose and walked back into the kitchen. Sarah and I looked at each other and started laughing.

"Holy crap, you are something else, Sarah!" I said.

I took a bite of my sandwich.

"I think you should be doing what you genuinely enjoy. Sometimes we set goals for ourselves and then when we achieve them, we realize that we were lying to ourselves and doing what others expected of us," Sarah said.

"Holy crap, I think I'm in love!"

Sarah started giggling.

"Holy shit! Did I say that out loud?"

Fear, panic, and embarrassment enveloped my entire body.

Sarah was now laughing and nodding her head, yes.

"You're so sweet, Reem," she said.

Judy came back with my refill ketchup and napkins.

"What's so funny?" Judy asked Sarah.

I was drinking my pop, so I couldn't answer. Sarah was still laughing and pointing at me.

"Well, I did it. I called my sister and told her I wanted to come home. She said that it couldn't have come at a better time. She needs my help with her new bakery," Judy said, sitting in the booth next to me again.

"So, when do you leave for Chicago?" I inquired.

"I'll get about three hundred dollars on my next check, and I'll use that for my flight home," Judy said.

"I can't sit here and watch you waste another week of your life," I said.

I reached down and pulled out my wallet. I put four hundred dollars on the table and pushed them over to Judy.

"The first hundred is a tip, and you can pay me back the other three after you get back on your feet," I said.

Judy and Sarah both looked astonished.

"Are you serious, why would you do that?" Judy asked.

"Sarah here was born to give great advice, and I was born to finance it," I said.

Sarah was stirring a hole straight through my soul, trying to figure me out. I wrote down my Uncle Dennis's address in Chicago with my name on it and gave it to Judy.

"This is my address in Chicago. When you're back on your feet, you can send it here, but there's no hurry," I said.

I had plenty of cash on me because my parents had completely flipped out after seeing Michael's jump school on my American Express bill. My mom had gone so far as to threaten to come up and pull me out of school if I ever did something like that again. So now I took cash out of my savings account to pay for skydiving, so Mom and Dad didn't see what I was doing. My mom deposited my share of the profits from the language school each month into my savings. John and I had about fifteen jumps now, and I had just bought a new rig that morning.

I was thinking that I needed to keep myself mysterious to Sarah. It seemed to me that she was trying to put me in a box or label me with something that made sense to her.

"JOE, I QUIT!" Judy yelled, putting the money in her pocket and kissing me on the cheek as she got up and walked out.

"Okay!" someone yelled from the back kitchen. We assumed it was someone named Joe.

Sarah kept looking at me with her beautiful eyes. I knew she was trying to figure me out. But I wasn't going to let that happen. Not right now, at least.

"Wow, that was nice of you," she said.

She had finished the last of her fries and was eye-balling my plate.

"No, that was nice of you to give her advice like that. I think you made a difference in her life," I replied.

I'd finished my sandwich and put my plate in the middle of the table so we could share my fries. A man with a shirt and tie on came from the back. He grabbed an apron and a pencil. I guessed this wasn't the first time the manager had had a waitress quit on him.

"I don't know about that. I was about ready to give you a discount for buying both time slots. But now that I know your parents are rich, I might have to charge a little more," Sarah said, playfully.

"My parents? What if I'm the one who is rich? What about you? Is that a Volvo I see in the parking lot?" I said.

I gave Sarah my one eyebrow up with a half-smirk on my face. It was my go-to look when I was trying to look flirty.

"Is there something wrong with your face?" Sarah smiled at me. "Oh, so you're the millionaire, and just how did you come about this mountain of wealth?" she said, seeming pleased with herself.

I must have gotten the car wrong; she was feeling superior. But we were bantering back and forth playfully. This was awesome, I thought to myself.

"I may own my own business that pays me a royalty each month," I said smugly.

I was trying to keep the back and forth going.

"No, really, you started your own business and became wealthy?" Sarah asked.

The playful banter ended abruptly. Sarah's smile left her face and she wanted to know now. I blew it! I thought to myself.

"I own a school that teaches basic English to foreign workers," I said.

I reached over to grab a French fry, but there were no more.

"You hoovered my fries!" I said.

"I didn't! There weren't very many left," she said with a little embarrassment.

"Hey Joe, can I get an order of fries? Some mystical force came and took mine," I yelled.

"Stop it. You're so mean." Sarah playfully hit my arm.

Let the flirting commence, I thought to myself.

"Where is your school? Mexico City? Tijuana?" Sarah asked.

"Mexico? Why would you think of Mexico?" I asked.

Sometimes I forgot that to others I might look Hispanic.

"No, I just assumed. Like me, my heritage is from Mexico. Only I was adopted, that's why my name sounds Caucasian," Sarah said, laying more information about herself on the table.

"Sarah, my name is Mohammed Reem Al-Sabah Al-Saba. I'm from Kuwait. I have a language school that teaches foreign workers how to speak English, Arabic, French, Farsi, and some German. I can speak three different languages myself," I said.

I felt that might be impressive to her. Sarah just looked at me as though she'd put a puzzle piece together.

"That's cool, Reem. And what would be very impressive would be if you could only pass your environmental studies program," she said.

Damn, she got me good on that one. The rest of the time, we ate fries and talked. I hoped that the more we talked, the easier it would be not to gaze at her. Sarah was so beautiful. It was hard not to think of what it would be like to go swimming in her eyes.

"Did I lose you again?" she asked.

"No! I thought it was dinner time. We should eat again," I said.

"What? No! We've been here that long?" Sarah asked.

Time had just stood still for us, and we'd been sitting there for five hours. I wasn't sure, but I thought that was a good thing.

CHAPTER 16

The spring semester ended, and I did my absolute best during finals. The D I received in environmental studies was going to be painful to see on my transcript, Goldberg saw to that. It didn't help my case when Goldberg and I almost started fighting in front of the professor's office during finals. I only had myself to blame. Sarah and I had started dating the first week we met. She'd helped me the best she could but to be honest, I'd been distracted, and my grade reflected it. I would now have to do a summer course somewhere in my junior or senior year. I couldn't have anything other than "A" on my transcript.

Mom needed me to sign a bunch of papers for the business, so I had to go home for summer break. Mom and Donna had expanded the language school.

We now taught classes in hotels, hospitality, kitchen services, maid services, and personal assistants. Mom and Donna were done renting out rooms from bad building owners. Mom wanted to build three separate and new structures around town and own our building. The financing was already in place and the bank just wanted my signature on the contracts. I rented a storage unit for all my stuff just off campus. Sarah couldn't come out with me; she had a lot of students that had signed up for the summer class schedule. So, after a tearful goodbye, I found myself on a plane heading back home.

The door to the aircraft opened, and I stepped out on the first step. I was greeted by what I can only say was a blast furnace of air. It was 10am Kuwait time, I had my Ray-bans on and my Arab clothes. I hadn't put them on for what seemed like a lifetime. I was starting to grow out of my thobe and keffiyeh head scarf. But I knew I looked good; Sarah hadn't been able to stop staring at me as I'd left with John. John had dropped me off at the airport, and I'd let him use my Jeep for the summer. I knew John would take good care of it; besides, I didn't want the Jeep to sit unused for a long time.

A black Mercedes pulled up to my jet, and I thought I was so cool. The back door opened, and my sister June got out.

"Hey June! You look amazing!" I said.

I walked down the steps quickly to embrace my little sister.

"It's so good to see you, Reem."

We finished our embrace and quickly got into the car, where it was fifty degrees cooler.

"Did we get a new car?" I asked.

The driver was loading my luggage into the back.

"This is part of our protection detail. Dad didn't want to move us into a judicial compound, so they made us accept a bigger protection detail," June said.

Our Mercedes picked up speed as it went through the main gate exiting the private terminal. I could see another black Mercedes pick up right behind us and follow us very closely on the way home.

"Well, that's kind of cool, I guess. At least I know you guys will be safe from all those ninjas," I said with a laugh.

I gave June another hug and sat back and looked at how beautiful she was becoming.

"It's not okay! I have two of these guys with me at school. It can be a little embarrassing. I don't like it," she said.

"You mean you have two guys following you around all day at school?" I asked.

June changed the subject and the thirty-eight-minute drive from the airport to my parents' house only took twenty-five and June wasn't forthcoming with any more about what I'd been missing out on.

The car pulled up to our house. It had a brand-new security gate in front. A heavily armed guard walked up to the driver. They spoke for a second, then June lowered her window.

"Hello, Yousef, just coming back from picking up my brother," June said.

The man looked at me.

"Welcome home, sir. Gate open!" he said to his wrist.

"Well, this sure is different. Good grief, it's like a fortress around here. June, you want to tell me what's going on?" I asked once we were inside.

June looked at me and just shrugged.

"You think Mom and Dad tell me anything, Reem? You know I'm treated like a mushroom in this family, kept in the dark and fed shit," she said.

In the kitchen, she took off her headdress and threw it on the table, then stood with a glass of iced tea in her hand. Sweat was pouring down the side of her cheek. I couldn't help but laugh at her statement. I never heard that expression before.

"Where is everybody? Are we the only ones at home?" I asked.

I decided that June's iced tea looked good and had to pour myself a glass.

"Dad and Rico are at work. Mom is roaming around with Donna. It's usually just me around here until about dinner time. BJ will show up first then pretty much everybody else after that."

June started fanning herself because she wasn't cooling down quick enough apparently.

"Rico's working with dad? Doesn't he still have school and finals before his summer break starts?" I asked.

I took another big, long drink from my iced tea.

"Are you kidding me? Even during the regular school year, he's usually with Dad. He only goes to class occasionally, and yet he still gets good grades. It's bullshit if you ask me. Come and look at my new TV in my bedroom. It's huge," she said.

As June walked down the hallway, I noticed that she had the posture of a woman and no longer a little girl. That made me sad inside. Times were changing, and so was June.

"I can't believe how big you've gotten, June," I said.

I walked over to June's new TV and turned it on.

"How big *I've* gotten? You're way taller and bigger. Look at the size of your arms. You need to stop working out so much," June said.

June picked up her remote control and started changing the channel.

"You should come out to California and visit me next year. We'll have some fun and get into some trouble," I said.

I took the remote out of June's hand and started searching the channel.

"I'd really like that, Reem. You'll have to convince Mom and Dad. I got in trouble with Mom last week. Remember your friend Raza? His younger brother Mohammed and some of my friends were hanging out here at the house, and it became a small party. Well, Mohammed kissed me, and Mom and Dad saw it on the surveillance cameras."

June was looking at me for some reaction to the fact that Raza's little brother Mohammed had kissed her.

"Surveillance cameras? When the hell did they put surveillance cameras in the backyard? It's like a fortress around here. I'm glad I'm living in California. I don't know about having every part of my life under surveillance," I said.

June put her hand on my arm. "Reem, Mom, and Dad know what you've been doing and how many times you were going to that jump school. I think you're in big trouble but don't let them know I told you. Okay?"

I quickly stood up from the bed and turned to face June.

"How would they know that? How do you know that? Are they spying on me?"

June looked like she regretted telling me. "All I know is that someone is keeping an eye on you for security purposes. At least you don't have them following you around at school where everybody can see them. Dad said it's for our protection," June said.

I didn't even hear what June was saying. My mind was going 100 miles an hour. What else had I done that my parents might know?

My brother Rico came home. I could hear him putting stuff away in his bedroom.

"Hey big brother, how are you doing?" I barged into his room.

"Reem! You're home!"

Rico's hug and excitement were good, but he smelled so bad – like an oil field and sweat.

"Damn Rico, you smell like crap," I said.

"Yeah, I'm helping Dad with some issues out in the fields. Damn, little brother, you're looking big. You been pumping some iron, huh?"

Rico was grabbing my bicep to see how big my muscles were getting.

"We have a state-of-the-art gym right next to my housing unit. John and I try to hit it three times a week," I said.

I started flexing more so Rico could see how big I was getting.

"Oh, yes, your friend John. Mom is going to kill him and then you for the new hobby Ben and Danny got you into. Why would you want to jump out of a plane? Are you stupid?"

He was taking off his clothes to get into the shower. I walked over to his desk to give him some privacy.

"What's up with all the surveillance, Rico? And all the security? Is that how Mom and Dad found out that I was skydiving?" I asked.

I had to raise my voice a little bit so Rico could hear me over the water in the shower.

"Reem, they know everything. Dad has a copy of that videotape you made with your friends. But don't worry, Dad thinks it's cool that you're skydiving. Mom is the one you must watch out for. She's determined to put a stop to it."

Rico had his arms over the small pony wall to the walk-in shower. He was letting the cold water hit his back.

"I'm not worried. I can handle Mom. I want to know what's going on. There's something you're not telling me, isn't there, Rico?" I said.

I could hear BJ in the background opening my dad's office. He always liked to arrive home before my dad and prepare his office for the evening. I turned and walked away from Rico. I wanted to confront BJ. The door to my dad's office was open, and BJ was standing next to a silver machine by my dad's desk.

"Hello, BJ, how are you?" I asked.

BJ was reviewing papers in each of his hands, trying to decide which ones to put into the shredder.

"Hi Reem, how was your flight? I see you decided to land with the plane this time," BJ said with sarcasm.

BJ set down the papers he was reviewing to give me a welcome hug and more sarcasm.

"Ha ha, very funny. I only jump out of planes that are traveling under 200 knots," I said.

BJ went back to his stack of papers.

"So, are you behind all the spying my parents have been doing on me? What's with all these new security measures?"

BJ looked at me without answering. June walked into the office with a small bag of the day's mail.

"Oh, thank you, June, just set the mail down, I'll get it."

BJ turned his attention back onto the papers he was shredding.

"So that's it, no one's going to tell me why we have the Terminator securing the front gate."

June looked at me with big eyes and turned and walked away. It was apparent that she had been told not to say anything to me. I looked back over at BJ and could see that, whatever it was that they were holding back, I'd have to wait for my parents to get home to find out.

My mom arrived home first, then my dad an hour later. I avoided my mom on purpose until my father arrived.

"Reem's home!" my dad said with enthusiasm.

I had just come back from a quick visit with my friend Raza. My mom was in the kitchen with Bella.

"Hello Dad, hello Mom, I'm home!" I said.

My dad kissed both my cheeks and gave me an embrace.

"You got home a few hours ago. Where were you?" Mom asked.

My mom was already starting to pick a fight with me. Her laser-focused attention on the vegetable she was chopping was a good indication that she was maneuvering for the kill.

"Well, why don't you tell me, Mom? You have your spies following me around. It seems that everybody has been sworn to secrecy about all the security that has now entered all our lives."

"*Vous regardez votre bouche et me montrez un peu de respect!*" my mom snapped at me in French.

"Yes, I'm sorry, Mom. I'll watch my mouth and show you some respect. But someone needs to tell me what is going on. The wall of secrecy needs to come down."

I walked over to my mom and kissed her on her cheek softly and whispered, "*Je suis désolé que je vous aime*" – "I'm sorry, I love you."

"As for the security, you can take that up with your damn father. But listen to me now, Reem! You and I are going to go the rounds over the sky diving crap! I didn't go through fourteen hours of labor having you so that you could kill yourself by doing something stupid!"

Mom grabbed the top of my hair and pulled my head down and kissed me on the forehead then shoved me back. "Now, get out of the kitchen so Bella and I can make dinner."

Before leaving the kitchen, Bella stretched up to hug me hello. I bent down and put my hand in her apron pocket. She always had a chocolate chip cookie for me. I didn't know Bella kept a cookie on her in case her blood sugar went down too much. As a kid, I just thought it was there for me because she loved me so much. One day I caught Bella eating the cookie. She told me that when I was little, I felt the cookie in her pocket after hugging her, so she gave the cookie to me so, Bella decided to keep doing it.

"Come into my office, Reem."

My dad led me down the hallway and into his office. I sat at the chair next to his desk, which had been crafted out of a beautiful walnut.

"Alright, son, I have a lot to tell you. I don't want you to get alarmed or be scared. I want to take certain precautionary measures just in case. Our government leaders are doing a fantastic job, always keeping us safe. We have one of the world's best intelligence programs. Our allies help us with interpreting all those bits of intelligence. A few months ago, we caught wind of some forces that were working against Kuwait. We have been reassured by several governments, including Iraq and Saddam Hussein himself, that all of Kuwait's issues will be handled diplomatically. That is true! That is what is happening right now, but as your father, I want to prepare for the what ifs. So, don't be alarmed about extra security. The gentleman in California that has been watching you, however, will be taking a more visible role in your life. Just for a little while, my intelligence analyst has told me. It's a good thing you're in the US."

My dad was trying to put me at ease, but I could see the concern in his eyes for the future. I wanted to ask him a lot of questions, but I knew my dad would not talk about state issues.

"What do you mean the gentleman will be taking a more visible role?" I asked.

BJ had walked into the room and continued with his reading of documents.

"I mean just that, Reem. He's going to be closer to you and a part of your daily life for a while," Dad said.

I sat back in my chair and was giving that a little bit of thought. BJ started asking my dad about specific documents that were in a pile when it occurred to me, I might know who this bodyguard was. The Volvo! Outside the diner! When Sarah and I had left, she'd got into her Honda Civic. I knew I was wrong about the car she was driving. It must have been his car, I thought. He's been following me since the day I met Sarah. I thought I'd seen that car in my rear view mirror a couple of times.

"Other than the fact that I know this guy drives a Volvo, is there anything else I should know about this guy?" I asked.

My father ignored the question and continued working at his desk. BJ came over to me and put his hand on my shoulder.

"Yes, Reem, you need to realize that Cash is there for your safety. He's one of the best, and you need to respect certain boundaries."

I looked up at BJ's unibrow.

"His name is Cash? Are you kidding me?"

"Yes, Reem, his name is Cash Alan Cooper!" said Dad. "He was a Navy SEAL and knows what he's doing. So don't act like a spoiled brat around him. Be respectful and helpful always. This man doesn't play around, son! He comes highly recommended, and his résumé is one of the best I've ever seen."

My dad had that look in his eyes, and I wasn't about to mess with him. So I just excused myself and sought out Rico. If I could corner him alone, I'd be able to get more information. Just the way June had taught me when we were younger.

"So, what did Dad tell you?" June asked.

I was back in my bedroom and unpacking my suitcase. June had decided to come into my room and corner me for information the same way I intended to do with Rico.

"I just got a bunch of BS about being careful and taking precautions. That everything was okay. I know there's more to what's going on. I was going to confront Rico and trick him into telling me," I said.

June was digging around in my closet. She pulled out one of my old suitcases and placed it on my bed.

"That's an excellent idea. Rico is easy to trick. Just tell him that Dad told you everything. Say, 'Can you believe what's going on?' If he asks you what you know, say something outrageous – that way whatever is going on won't seem as bad in his mind, and he'll spill his guts. Do you mind if I have this suitcase? I've always liked it."

June had opened the suitcase. She was going through the pockets when she pulled out a woman's bra and looked at me.

"What the hell were you doing?" June said.

Oh crap, it was Penny's bra. One of my souvenirs.

I heard Rico's voice yell for me, "Reem, come out here, I have something to show you!"

June and I immediately looked at each other. Now was my chance to question Rico.

"I don't know how that got in there. It might be Nicole's when she did my laundry in Chicago. Put it back, June," I said.

Out of the corner of my eye, I could see June looking at the tag on the bra as I left the room to see what Rico wanted. That excuse would only fly if Nicole wore the same size bra. I didn't know what size she wore or if my reason held any water with June.

Rico led me to the laundry room, where the garage door was. When he opened it, I could see my Jeep inside the garage. I immediately thought that my mom was taking away my Jeep because of my skydiving. Before I started freaking out about my orange Jeep being in our garage in Kuwait, Rico turned on the light, and I could see a few subtle differences. This Jeep had a lot more stickers and badges on the side. It wasn't my Jeep.

"What the hell is this?" I asked.

Rico could see how shocked I was.

"Dad loved that damn Jeep so much he had one shipped out here for himself. He's only taken it out on weekends," Rico said.

We walked over to the far side of the garage and looked at some more decal's dad had put on it.

"I can't believe what's going on with Dad, can you?" I said.

Rico looked at me suspiciously. "Why what did he tell you?"

I kept my attention on the Jeep and acted like I knew everything.

"Just that we've been receiving a lot of death threats against all of us," I said.

That was the most outrageous thing I could think of to say.

"Death threats against us? No, it's against all the Kuwaiti leadership," Rico said.

I looked at Rico. "Tell me everything!" My facial expression must have looked intense. He shut the door to the Jeep, and although he knew that I'd tricked him, it took just a couple more seconds for him to decide to bring me up to speed on dad's BS.

"With the war winding down, Iraq has been harassing some of the oil fields. Iraq has asked for the Emir to forgive all the debt they owe Kuwait. They look at Kuwait as a piggy bank that they can steal from, Dad told me. They're trying to work things out diplomatically. Dad is just trying to prepare for a worst-case scenario with Iraq. He wanted June and Mom to stay in Canada for a while. Mom refused to leave without him. So that's why they hired more security."

Rico had finished speaking, but I still had a feeling he wasn't telling me everything. June opened the door from the laundry room and softly closed it. She quietly walked over to Rico. She didn't want Mom to know she was in the garage. She leaned against the Jeep and looked at Rico with questioning eyes.

"Did you tell him?" June asked.

"No, he didn't tell me anything yet. He's still holding back," I said quickly.

Rico looked at June and nodded. June turned her attention back to me.

"Three days after Mom and Dad sat us down and told us everything was alright, that it was 'being handled diplomatically' and there was nothing to worry about, Dad's executive assistant Ali…"

She stopped for a second and looked at Rico again.

"Go ahead June, tell him."

"Ali was sent out to get dinner for the office. Dad and a couple of members of his office were working late and had gotten hungry. Ali got attacked by two gunmen and shot dead in the street."

She had finished talking and Rico hugged her. Rico looked back at the laundry door.

"That's not all, Reem," Rico said. "BJ was the one who normally gets dinner for the office. Ali went instead because Dad needed some state documents and BJ isn't allowed to do that. If Dad didn't need those docs, BJ would have been the one to get attacked."

I just stood there, absorbing the information, and trying to think about what it meant.

"Tell him what happened next, Rico," June said.

Rico stepped closer to me. "News reports said that the two gunmen got away. But when I was in Dad's office two days after it happened, I needed to find the standard temperature levels on a pipeline test and when I was looking through Dad's desk I came across a blue and white file. It was a state intelligence briefing for Dad. Reem, they have the two gunmen!"

Rico was whispering, full of concern.

"There were a lot of things in that intelligence report! Things like Dad's name being one of the highest value targets for execution. Things like Iraq wanting to take over Kuwait's oil fields and border disputes. I didn't get to read it all because Dad interrupted me. He quickly closed the door and was yelling at me because it was classified material, and I'd go to jail if they knew I'd seen it," Rico said.

I couldn't get rid of my astonishment. I needed to find out exactly what was in that report. I decided to wait for a time when Dad and BJ would be out of the house. I'd try to find that file and get to the bottom of all this crazy shit.

"Reem, you have a phone call!" Mom yelled.

"Okay, thanks," I replied. I knew Sarah had been going to call and I was looking forward to hearing her voice.

We all walked out talking about Dad's Jeep so anyone would think that was what we'd been doing in the garage.

I opened my dad's office door at about 6:45am. Dad always left the house with BJ at 6:30am to start work each morning. The house was quiet, and I knew my mom wouldn't be up until 8 o'clock so I had time to find that file. Dad had three desk drawers with locks on them, but I knew there were copies of all of Dad's keys in Mom's jewelry box. The first drawer was all family papers and documents, the second was completely empty, and the third only had one, file of interest about Dad's new security company, Front Sight. The file was thick and heavy with contracts, disclosures, and life insurance policies. Each security officer was named, and all their credentials were listed. As I read through the file on Mr. Cooper my mom was standing in the doorway to the office.

"Mom, what the heck are you doing?" I said, startled.

"The empty drawer you opened triggers an alarm," she said, rubbing her eyes. She was just waking up. I guess Dad's alarm had alerted his security and they'd asked my mom to deal with me.

"Your dad is going to kill you when he gets home," Mom said as she walked back to bed.

CHAPTER 17

Cash Alan Cooper was standing on the flight line waiting for me as my jet taxied to the hangar at LAX. I guessed this was what my dad had meant by a more visible role. Cash introduced himself to me after I got off the aircraft, informed me that my Jeep was now back in my garage, and that he would be driving me back to my hotel. I had come back early to California to spend time with Sarah before the semester started.

"So, what would you like me to call you?" I inquired.

"Mr. Cooper or Cooper will be fine, sir. You?"

"Reem. Please call me Reem."

"Reem, you have three hours before you're scheduled to see Sarah. I want to go over some details with you since you have time," Cooper said.

That was a good idea, I thought to myself. I wanted to know what his thoughts were on the role that he'd be playing that semester. Cooper, an African American man, was very impressive-looking and very physically fit. His black t-shirt couldn't hide his arms and pecs. They were in competition to see which were going to tear the shirt first. He handed me a small bag containing the keys to my Jeep, my hotel room, and a card with a schedule of that week's events on it.

"What happened to the Volvo?" I asked Cooper on the way to the hotel. He was now driving a black BMW and looked at me in the rearview mirror with a smile.

"Very good. Yes, that was my car. I'm surprised you noticed that," he said.

I tried not to look too happy with myself.

When we arrived at the hotel, Cooper and I walked into the lounge and talked for a bit. It was very plush and a great place to meet people and do business, I thought. It was just after dinner time and not that many people were in the lounge yet.

"I don't want you to worry about me being too close. I'll be in the background. I'll try and stay out of view but close enough to handle anything if something pops off," Cooper said.

He ordered an Arnold Palmer; I quickly told the waiter to make it two. It sounded like it would be a stiff drink, and I needed some alcohol.

"Thanks, Cooper, I was a little worried about having you around. Most of my classmates don't know too much about me. I want to keep it that way."

I decided to let Cooper know what I'd found out

while I was home. He said that he'd already been briefed on everything.

"I'm an expert in surveillance, assassination tactics, and terrorism. The rest of my team is in Kuwait with your family. They're in good hands," he said.

Our drinks arrived. I sat up and prepared myself for the shock of alcohol. What I got was something unexpected, a little sweet and bitter taste. My surprise and enjoyment came over my face.

"I see you like your drink." Cooper raised his glass to me.

"Wow, that is good. I've never had one of these before. What is it?"

"Lemonade and iced tea," Cooper said.

He set his drink down in front of him.

"I thought it would have alcohol in it," I said.

I continued drinking.

"Some people put alcohol in it, but I don't drink."

Cooper and I spoke for a while that evening, I'd found out that he was staying across the street from my garage, and if anything ever happened, I should get to that location. Cooper would be with me during the day and sometimes at night. If he were going to go back to the apartment, he would let me know that he wasn't around.

Sarah arrived about an hour later. I was in my hotel room when she knocked on my door. The moment I opened the door, Sarah pinned me up against the wall with her lips and her arms. She looked so amazing. The way she smelled drove me crazy with lust. Her mouth tasted so good I couldn't have described it. I lifted her off the ground. We continued kissing when out of the corner of my eye, I saw what looked to be a little girl.

"Who's that?" I asked without breaking away from our kiss.

"My bodyguard," Sarah said while she was giggling and kissing me.

"That's what I thought. She looks dangerous," I replied.

The little girl reached out and shoved me from behind with her tiny hands.

"Cut it out, Sarah!" the little one said.

I let go of Sarah. Both her feet hit the ground at the same time, and Sarah's beautiful breasts bounced. I could tell she wasn't wearing a bra. That was one of the things I loved about Sarah, her natural beauty. She oozed femininity.

"This is my little Sis, Heather… Say hello," Sarah demanded of Heather.

"Hello," Heather said, reluctantly.

Hi, I'm sorry, I didn't know that Sarah had brought someone with her. It's lovely to meet you, Heather," I said.

It seemed like my passionate greeting with Sarah was one big sister showing off to a little sister. Heather was about ten years old. She had straight, shoulder-length blonde hair and blue eyes, and she looked to be scrappy. She didn't like the way Sarah was acting around me and let her know it several times that evening. I knew that Sarah had brought her little sister as an insurance policy so that we wouldn't go too far. Sarah's adoption had been in Mexico City to a wealthy Mormon family from Los Angeles, and she wanted to wait until we were married to have sex. I felt it my job to convince her otherwise.

Sarah introduced me to her family later that

week. Her mom and dad looked young, too young to have a twenty-one-year-old daughter. They seemed happy with Sarah's choice of boyfriend, and I guess I was okay with them. Sarah and her sister didn't look anything like their parents. I guess you get used to that when you adopt children, I thought to myself.

Being back at school was a little hectic. My classes were getting more complicated. Sarah and I saw less of each other because of our schedules. We would fight from time to time, but every time she looked at me with those beautiful brown eyes, I would cave like a house of cards. I could tell I was falling in love with her. The thought of not being with her bothered me. I decided to ask her to come home with me for Christmas. Donna and Rico broke their promise of waiting to get married and scheduled a December wedding. My entire family would be in attendance. Rico hadn't asked me to be his best man – that role had fallen to his best friend since grammar school. The decision I had to make was if I brought Sarah with me, she would know my real wealth. So far, I had been doing a good job keeping a lot of my resources hidden from her. She knew I had some money and that I did alright with my business back home. She knew my dad worked for the government, probably in some mundane job, and that my rich doctor uncle had paid for my college. If I decided to bring Sarah on this trip, there would be a lot more questions. I would have to come clean. I'd always told myself I would tell Sarah the truth, if she was someone that I wanted to marry. But I had to be sure she was the one before I took that step.

<u>Sarah's pros and cons:</u>

Cons:

1. Sarah's religion is devout, and we have not had sex yet, which bothers me a lot being a man in my 20s.

2. Upon discovering that I wasn't Hispanic, her parents seemed to discourage Sarah away from me.

3. If I do decide that I want to marry Sarah, I'd want to ask her before I brought her home. I wouldn't want her to make that decision based on my wealth.

4. Her goal to get a doctorate in environmental studies would pretty much make her a career student.

5. She might tell me no.

Pros:

1. Every single stereotype about her Mormon religion has proven false. Yes, she lives her life in a dedicated way, but she never forces it on me. She always respects my viewpoint, which is usually anti- organized religion.

2. Her parents are good people who took in children that were not their own and showered them with love and affection their whole life. So, I think they have the right to influence who Sarah marries.

3. Our children would look as beautiful as she does.

4. My body physically aches with pain when we spend too much time apart. My heart feels heavy in my chest when I'm without her. Fuck! I'm in love with her!

I ripped the sheet of paper out of my notebook, crumpled it into a ball and threw it into the trash can next to my desk. I was back in my dorm room, sitting in my chair with my feet on my bed, planning my future.

"Juanito, are you planning on getting married someday?" I said.

He'd had his face stuck in a textbook for the past three days. He was struggling with a lot of his classes.

"Oh heck, no, not for a long time. I'm too young and I want to have fun before I settle down," Juanito said, taking his head out of the textbook. "Why? Are you thinking of marrying Sarah? Are you crazy, Reem?"

I got up from my chair and jumped onto my bed. "I think about my future and what goals I need to make for myself. Do you ever do that?"

Juanito was back into his textbook and hadn't heard a word I'd said.

Sarah and I went to see a movie that night. Sarah had wanted to see a chick flick. I found myself liking the movie as much as Sarah did. After the movie, we got a bite to eat at Coco's. Sarah loved their chicken and rice dinner special. I just looked at her, wishing I'd taken her to a better place to eat.

"Did you like the movie, sweetheart?" I asked.

I thought that would be an excellent opening to the questions I wanted to ask her.

"Oh, my goodness, I never cried so hard in a movie before. Wasn't that movie fantastic and sad at the same time? I love Sally Fields," she replied.

She was almost done with her dinner and had moved on to stealing my French fries again. We liked to sit in the same booth we'd met in. I would always try to sit next to her, but she loved sitting across from me in the same seats. She said it was sweet.

"It seemed like everybody was getting married in that film," I said with three French fries in my mouth.

I didn't want Sarah to pick up on what I was trying to ask. She put down her fork and looked at me with devious eyes.

"You know, I've had a few boyfriends in my past and every time they brought up the subject of marriage, it was because they were trying to convince me to have sex with them. So, you'll have to forgive me if I think you have ulterior motives, Reem."

Her beautiful brown eyes were continuously sizing me up and waiting for a response.

"Do you think I'm talking about sex? You should know me better than that now. I respect your beliefs and I respect you. I'm just asking you what your thoughts about marriage are. I'm not sure when I want to get married." I thought I sounded very convincing.

"Well, ever since I was a little girl, I've always thought I would be married to a return missionary who would marry me in our temple for time and all eternity. That is what my religion believes. But now that I'm older, I know that life is not exactly how you always plan it to be. A lot of my friends have married outside our religion in civil ceremonies. With the hopes of one day converting their spouse to their beliefs."

That was why her parents were discouraging her away from me. It wasn't a racial thing; it was a religious thing, I thought to myself. Sarah went on...

"I think it's okay to marry outside your religion as long as the two people respect each other's beliefs and don't belittle them."

Sarah went back to hoovering my French fries. I think she just told me that she would be okay with marrying me, I thought to myself.

"What are your thoughts on marriage, Reem? What would your parents do to you if you didn't marry a Muslim girl?"

That's it! That's the question I wanted her to ask me, I said to myself.

"That's a good question, Sarah. Your concern with someone wanting to marry you just to get you into bed. I would be more concerned about someone wanting to marry me for the wrong reasons also. You know I make a little bit of money from my business and that I live in a different country. Would money make a difference in your decision if I ever asked you to marry me?"

I pushed my French fries closer to her and then sat back.

"I would never let money make any decision for me. I wouldn't like anyone who made a good living to waste it on bad choices. Money is hard to come by. My parents do okay because they plan and invest wisely. They've taught me that money is just a tool that you must respect. Learn how to make it work for you," Sarah said.

Repeating her dad's words. I presumed. She seemed surprised that I'd bring up the subject of money.

"About your business and your life in another country. I thought you were planning on staying in the United States after college?" Sarah asked me with a little concern in her voice.

"Well, I chose the field of architecture because I can do that pretty much anywhere. I have a knack for business. So, I see myself owning an architectural firm and hiring talented architects to do the work. Which brings me to another subject – I'd like you to come home with me for Christmas and meet my family," I said.

Sarah stopped eating my fries and sat up. She was looking for a napkin, so I gave her mine.

"I'll have to talk to my parents because we had planned on going to Salt Lake City this Christmas, but I would love to meet your family and get to know them."

CHAPTER 18

Penny was kissing my ear slowly. I could feel her breath on my neck, and her hand was moving down my stomach. I was nude. I started kissing her back when I felt Sarah's hand grab the back of my hair and pull my head back. She started kissing me. The two women were all over me. Wait! Wait! Is this a dream? Oh shit! It is a dream! Try and keep it going, I said to my half-conscious brain.

It didn't work. I wasn't dreaming anymore and was fully awake now. Damn, this sucks, I keep having sex dreams because I'm not getting any sex from Sarah, I thought. I turned over to my right side. I could see my frustration pointing straight up. Holy crap! Sarah was asleep right next to me. We must have fallen asleep before separating as we usually did – we'd never spent the night in the same bed before.

I pretended I was still sleeping and slowly began spooning her. Sarah started to move her bottom back and forth against me.

"Are you awake, Reem?" she asked me softly.

She didn't stop moving her hips. I started to clean the sleep out of my eyes.

"Yes, I'm awake, sexy."

I started to kiss her and press my erection harder against her leg.

"Can we stay here all day? And order room service?" Sarah asked.

She reached into my pajama bottoms and grabbed hold of my erection. We'd done a lot of kissing and rubbing before but nothing like this. For starters, we'd never slept next to each other. I would fall asleep, and she would get up and go back to her dorm, which was always a disappointment for me. I wanted to wake up next to her, so bad. It was just as I thought it would be. Her beautiful face, her soft voice, the way she smelled, were all over my blankets and pillows.

"Sweetheart, we can stay here for the rest of the school year if that's what you want," I said.

Sarah jumped out of bed and walked to the bathroom. She had on my white dress shirt that needed cufflinks. She must have gotten it from my closet. I could see that she had just her panties on and nothing else.

"Did you go through my closet last night?" I asked.

Sarah stopped and turned to me with a body that could stop a war.

"Well, I needed something to sleep in," she said.

She had a look of seduction in her eyes.

"So, you planned on spending the night and didn't tell me?" I asked.

"Didn't tell you? Reem, you heard me tell my parents that I wasn't going to be home until tomorrow when I called them," she said.

I had been watching TV and hadn't listened to what Sarah had told her parents because the news about a semi-truck driving off an overpass had taken away my attention. I was so glad I'd decided to get a hotel room. Sarah and I had needed more privacy, and my dorm room was getting crazy with college life. So I'd started to check in at the Marriott almost every weekend.

"You can wash my back if you want to?" Sarah let my dress shirt fall to the floor as she walked into the bathroom.

Holy crap! Was this happening? I thought. Was that a real offer of sex? Sarah was in the shower by the time I had undressed. I was standing there with the shower door open. We just looked at each other. I can honestly say I'd never seen a woman more beautiful in my life.

"Are you sure, sweetheart? We can hold each other if you don't want to go through with this," I said.

I hated myself for even suggesting the idea of not making love in the shower right then and there.

"I'm not going to wait anymore to share myself with you. I was watching you sleep last night. It was then I realized that I've fallen in love with you, Reem," she said softly.

I closed the shower door and let the warm steamy water hit me. Sarah was in my arms, and our kiss was as if for the first time. It was apparent to me that Sarah had never gone this far before. Her love and trust in me made me feel like I was the luckiest man on earth. This wasn't like my time with Penny. I knew this meant more to the both of us than just a college fling or a on again off again relationship of the kind John always seemed to get himself into. I'd never known love like this before. As the bodywash and water started cleaning us both, I was surprised how much that turned me on.

I didn't know that sex could be so intimate and special. The love I felt for Sarah was more than anyone could describe. I'd never felt this vulnerable before. After our shower, I sat on the bed looking at the small of Sarah's back. There were soft black tiny hairs.

"God, you're the most feminine woman I've ever seen in my life, Sarah. That was incredible. It was like a gift of yourself to me. I've never had that before," I said.

Sarah started kissing me again. She looked like she could fall asleep in a second.

"Well, I figured I'm not ready to get married yet, but I want to know about sex. I trust and love you. So last night I figured why not just go for it, but then you fell asleep on me," Sarah said.

She hit me playfully.

"You wanted to have sex last night! That's the last time I ever watch TV again," I replied.

We both fell asleep. Cooper woke us up by knocking on our hotel door.

"Hi Cooper, how's it going?" I asked as I invited him into the room.

"Hi Cooper, what up?" Sarah said as she was stretching.

I'd introduced Cooper as a family friend to Sarah a while ago.

We only had one more week of classes before winter break. I still hadn't told Sarah everything about me. Now that we'd taken our relationship to the next level, I wasn't sure how Sarah was going to react about me keeping some things about myself and family from her.

"I can't believe you have to take summer classes this year. You're going to hate that," Cooper said.

He handed me a note from my mom telling me to call her the next day. She wouldn't be home today, the note said, so I put the note in my wallet and checked out of the hotel room. We headed back to our dorm rooms because I had a class in two hours, and Sarah had a student aid class that afternoon.

"Did you give the front desk your rewards number?" Sarah asked. She wanted me to get a discount on our room. She was starting to worry about how much I was spending on hotel, food, and entertainment.

"Yes, sweetheart I gave the nice lady my rewards number," I replied.

"Reem, are you going to get into trouble over all the money you've been spending?" she asked. I think she'd caught a glimpse of the note Cooper had given me.

I locked the Jeep up in the garage and put the keys in my pocket as Sarah and I walked onto campus.

"No, not at all, sweetheart. Please don't worry about that. I'll go over my finances with you while we're traveling next week, okay?" I said.

That seemed to put Sarah's worry to rest for the time being, but I knew she was still thinking about it. Sarah's dad hadn't told her it was okay for her to go yet, but she told me to buy the tickets anyway. I called Gilbert at the Jennifer Noel executive flight center to let him know I'd be traveling home with a guest.

The fact her dad needed to give his approval rubbed me wrong. Sarah's old enough to make her own decisions, I thought to myself. Maybe it's me he has a problem with. I could feel myself starting to get angry. I had to remind myself that it might be the way Sarah showed respect to her dad.

"My dad wants us to come over to the house tonight. I think he's going to give me permission," Sarah said.

"Or he'll tell you not to go and test your loyalty to the family. That way I'll be the bad guy pulling you away from the family. I don't think your dad likes the fact that I'm an Arab," I said with some confidence.

Sarah looked at me with amazement. "Yes, my dad is not happy that I picked an Arab to date. But not because of the reasons you think. Maybe he's familiar with all the risk involved in me going over there. My dad's just trying to look out for his daughter. You must be the savior himself, Reem, to be so perfect not to judge anyone based on their race. We all do it! Judge a book by its cover. We all come from our own perspective, and we all have our own biases, even you, Reem, so don't judge my dad for looking out for me," Sarah said angrily.

Wow, Sarah is right, I thought to myself. How does she do it? She called me out on all my stuff, and I loved her for it.

"Are you going to be this protective over me if we ever get married?" I said with laughter in my voice. Sarah could see by my smile that she'd won the argument.

"I've been protecting you from the start. That's why my dad didn't kill you the first day." Sarah smiled.

The day of our trip had finally arrived. Sarah called me before leaving her dorm. The last two days I'd started dropping hints to Sarah. Things like, "I need to get our maid Bella a USC sweatshirt before we leave" and "My dad is going to send a car for us when we arrive."

Not very subtle, but I knew Sarah thought I was kidding around.

"Reem, my dad wants to come and see me off at the airport. What airline are we taking?"

The RA was at my dorm room door with a large box from Federal Express.

"Just set it on my bed, Brian. Sarah, tell your dad that we're taking Hijacker's Airline. Oh no, wait, I think it's Bomber's Express."

Brian and I started laughing. I opened the box my mom had sent me that had just arrived, only a week late.

It was my new tailored Arab clothing I'd ordered last time I was home. The best material and craftsmanship had gone into making my outfit. A lot of my clothes hadn't fit me the last time I'd gone back because I'd outgrown them.

"Knock it off, Reem, I'm serious! My dad is going to give me a lot of shit over this," Sarah said.

I started pulling out my new thobe and was looking at it.

"Okay, give him this address: 5252 Sky Dream Avenue. It's the Jennifer Noel office building. We go right through there on our way to the plane. He can say goodbye there," I said.

I gave Sarah the address again so she could write it down.

"Sarah, you know I'll be wearing my Arab clothes. Your mom and dad might not like you going overseas with some Arab-looking dude," I said.

I was a little worried about Sarah's mom seeing me like that. She could seem a bit judgmental at times.

"I'm sure you'll look sexy as hell. My parents will have to get used to it," Sarah said.

"Alright, then I'll see you over at Cooper's apartment in an hour. He'll drive us over to the airport. Please! Please! Wear something amazing! When we get off the plane, my parents will be there, and I want you to look stunning."

I used Cooper's place to get dressed because I hadn't wanted to walk across campus wearing a thobe. Cooper and Sarah arrived; she was stunning, alright. She had a form-fitting black dress that cut off just before her knees and a silk shammy that was backward across her neck and down her back.

"Holy crap, you look like a goddess," I said.

Sarah didn't say anything. She just stared at me like I wasn't real. Cooper broke our silence.

"Wow, you two look like movie stars, like you're at the Oscars. Let me take a picture of you. You'll thank me later for this memory."

After our photoshoot with Cooper, we left for the airport. Cooper drove past the office building and through the guard gate at the executive terminal. He parked the car twenty feet away from our aircraft. The door and stairs to the private plane were opened and ready for us. There was a lovely Los Angeles breeze going across the flight line as we exited Cooper's vehicle. The sun was starting to set, and the lights inside the aircraft were glowing brightly. Sarah's dress and silk shammy were gently waving in the breeze. I could feel my bisht (a cloak worn over my thobe) and headdress flapping in the breeze as well. Sarah was looking towards the office complex for her family. Before she started walking back to the offices, Heather popped her head out of the aircraft.

"Mom, Dad, they're here!" Heather said.

Sarah's Mom and Dad were on the plane, getting a tour from Gilbert.

Sarah didn't say anything. She just looked like this was normal.

"Don't worry, Sarah, my parents don't own it. It's just a rental," I said.

I took Sarah by the hand as her parents and Heather walked down the ladder and off the plane.

"Sarah, you look like a movie star! That dress! Reem, Mr. Lawrence of Arabia. You look different in those. What do you even call it?" Mrs. Long said, at a loss for words.

As I greeted Sarah's parents and Heather, Cooper was loading our bags onto the plane.

"My parents will be at the airport to greet us when we arrive. So I'm wearing my traditional Arab clothing. Can you believe how gorgeous Sarah looks tonight?" I said.

I wanted to shift the focus off me and back onto Sarah. Sarah's father gave me the "take care of my daughter or else" talk before we boarded the plane. The cabin door shut, and the plane lifted off. We had a long flight ahead of us. It was at this time Sarah sat down across from me in the beautiful white leather chair. She looked like there was something on her mind.

"What the hell was all that back there, Reem? You know I don't like surprises, and I hate it when people try to impress me. You couldn't tell me we were flying private last week when I asked you what airline we were taking?" She looked like she was trying to be angry.

"Look, sweetheart," I said softly, "I thought if I told you, you wouldn't want to go with me. I know how much you hate being spoiled with nice things and showered with love. So I'll stop! I'll learn to beat you and kick you. I'll shove you down from time to time. I'll learn to be more abusive to you, my love, if that's what you want."

My sarcasm was not lost on Sarah. She turned her head to the left so as not to look at me at all. A small hint of a smirk began to appear on her face. "Good! That's all I'm asking for, now be gone with you! Out of my presence!" she commanded.

She couldn't hold back her smile anymore, as I grabbed her and pulled her on top of me. Sarah's laughter could light up an entire room. After our little argument, we sat down to the business of explaining my family's history. By the time we landed in Kuwait, Sarah knew almost everything about my life.

Rico and Donna greeted us at the airport. After the introductions, we all got into one of the limousines. Rico talked about the wedding most of the drive to our house. They were going to move in with Mom and Dad while their home was under construction. It was supposed to be a wedding gift from Dad, but it would take a while to build.

"You must see the blueprints to the house, Reem! You'll love it with your eye for architecture. You can give me some pointers on any changes I need to make," Rico said.

Once again, Rico's competitive streak came between the two of us. Rico hadn't told me about his house until after it was designed and engineered. The drawings were done, a friend of a friend had done the work. As if I wouldn't have been able to help him with that process. I could have used it for one of my projects in school, and Rico knew that. We talked at least twice a week on the phone, and I'd always give him a rundown on what was happening at school with me.

"Yeah, Rico, that sounds good. I'd love to look at the blueprints. Whatever I can do and help with, let me know, brother," I said with no sincerity.

We arrived home, which was bustling with activity. The introductions with my parents, grandparents, aunts and uncles, cousins, dogs, hamsters and whoever else took what seemed like several hours but in reality, was probably more like 15 to 20 minutes.

"Sarah, what are you studying in school, dear?" my mom asked.

I could see she'd taken a shine to Sarah right away. Sarah knew how to hold herself in social situations. I was so proud of her.

"I'm working on an environmental studies degree. Your house is lovely, Mrs. Al-Saba."

Sarah took a drink of her Arnold Palmer. I had made a whole pitcher in the kitchen to introduce my parents to the drink. But it was only new to me – my parents had had it before.

"Please, Sarah, call me Sue," my mom insisted.

She locked arms with Sarah. Mom brought Sarah around the house to introduce her once again to each of the family members. That's how I knew my mom approved of Sarah. It seemed to me that Donna was a little jealous of the mother-in-law attention Sarah was getting.

"That's quite a young lady you brought with you, son," Dad said.

My dad startled me. I'd had no idea he was standing right next to me when he started talking.

"Hello, crap! Sorry, Dad! Yeah, she's quite a woman. We're not too serious, though. We still have a lot of school to finish before we can think about marriage," I quickly said.

Dad put his hand on my shoulder.

"Glad to hear it, son. Your education is essential."

Dad looked pleased with himself. After all, Rico was getting married. His first-born son would be providing grandchildren any year now, I thought to myself.

"Hey, Dad, I need to talk to you about my flight. I upgraded to a different aircraft that cost a little bit more. I'll cover it out of my account – just let me know what the difference is," I said.

Dad looked over at Mom and Sarah, having a conversation with the Al-Saba side of the family.

"Don't worry about it. I'll take care of it."

I grabbed my dad's cup and smelled it to make sure he wasn't drinking. My dad laughed at what I was doing. He leaned over to whisper in my ear.

"It's okay. 3M just purchased three of my patents. I'm what your Uncle Dennis calls indecently wealthy now," Dad said.

I laughed and looked at my dad. He seemed to be happy and carefree, but I could tell something was bothering him under the surface.

"That's awesome. I'm so proud of you, Dad."

I raised my glass of tea and lemonade to his victory.

"Hey son, after the wedding, I need to sit down and talk to you about a few logistics items. It won't take long," Dad said.

I nodded and went to go rescue Sarah from my mom. Most everybody was staying at the hotel where the wedding reception was to be, but I'd insisted that Sarah remain with me in my room. I knew we'd be more comfortable with my family than in some hotel room and I wanted my parents to get to know her. Mom wasn't the only one that appeared to fall in love with Sarah; June wouldn't leave her side. The two of them were instant BFFs. Teen girls enjoyed being around Sarah; I could tell Sarah made them feel important and they loved being around her natural beauty.

The next evening while in my room, I could hear Rico and Donna arguing. The words were muffled but what I could make out was that it was her wedding, and our mom and sister seemed to love Sarah more than her. Rico was responding, "That's not true, my family adores you."

The wedding went off without a hitch. It was beautiful, the way they exchanged their vows. Rico and Donna left the next day on their honeymoon to India. Most of my family had traveled back home already. I was preparing to leave at the end of the week for school. It had felt like a long two weeks, but we'd got through it. Sarah had called her family every night before bed. That made her happy and I'm sure it made her parents happy too.

My dad called me into his office. "Hi, Reem, shut the door."

He was looking for something on his desk. After the wedding, BJ had left on a trip, and hadn't even said goodbye to me.

"Okay, Dad, what's up?" I said.

Whatever Dad was looking for, he'd found it.

"I need to tell you a few things that have changed already, and there are some other things that are going to change," Dad said. "When I made a deal with 3M, BJ owned a part of it. He will clear about six million dollars. He plans on buying the house down the street so he can live close to us. It's just going to take him some time to remodel it. BJ would like your help on the blueprints."

Wow, Dad was telling me a lot about his business, I thought. I was happy for BJ. He'd always been like a third parent to me.

"Your trust fund has been transferred to Wells Fargo bank in America and has been unlocked and made available to you immediately, but son, I don't want you to touch that money. I did it so you'd be able to access it in case of an emergency. Promise me you won't touch that money," he said forcefully.

I looked very puzzled. It just didn't make any sense to me and was out of character for my dad to do this. He never liked to discuss finances with me and had always kept me in the dark when it came to our family's wealth.

"Okay Dad, I promise I won't touch that money unless it's an emergency," I said.

My dad handed me a brand-new leather wallet.

"All the information and accounts with the credit cards are in your new wallet. People within my office seem to think there is going to be a deal with Iraq and Saddam Hussein. I disagree but I've been censored and prevented from talking to the Emir," Dad said.

I could feel a wave of dread and a little fear wash over my body as my dad spoke those words to me.

"You should leave for a while then, Dad, if you think that. Just get out of town for a while and see how it plays out," I said.

My dad moved closer to me.

"I wish it were that simple, son, but it's not. Rico and I both play an important role in the amount of oil produced and shipped overseas. If we were to leave right now, it would look terrible for our family. But don't worry, I've put certain things in place, so if we have to leave Kuwait we can do so quickly and without detection."

My dad had a file in his hand.

"This is an intelligence report. It says that it would be suicide for Iraq to stop the flow of oil. That, given time, Saddam Hussein will realize that there is nothing to be gained by military action. But I'm looking at their revenue from oil productions and I don't see how Iraq can sustain itself without military action. The second thing I noticed in the report was the copy of the United States State Department summary is no longer there. I think someone is keeping information from his Highness, and I'm just trying to prepare in case something happens."

My level of worrying had gone off the chart by this point. I trusted my dad and his insights. I had to pack my suitcase and head to the airport by late morning. Our house was eerily quiet. Mom and Dad had to leave early in the morning for work and June was gone before seven for school. I started asking Sarah questions so I could keep my mind off my worries about my family. I couldn't shake a feeling of doom.

CHAPTER 19

Classes resumed the first week of January, and I found myself in a familiar routine of classes, studying, Sarah, skydiving, and roommates. But no matter what I did, I couldn't shake this bad feeling that had been following me ever since that conversation with my dad back home. He'd said that he'd made plans to get out if something happened, but my mind kept me overthinking all the what ifs, keeping me up some nights.

I was taking more units this semester; my classes were a lot of fun. I enjoyed working in the studios with classmates and projects. I quickly became one of the leaders in my group. My opinion mattered a lot to my peers. The competitiveness surprised me, though. Specific books that we needed in the library were being checked out and not brought back. I noticed a lot of students trying to peek at each other's architectural model projects before they had been submitted for review.

My roommates, Scotty and Juanito, had become close. John would hang out with me sometimes, but we both had girlfriends. The only time I had to do anything with John was Saturdays when we would skydive.

"Hey, Reem, that creepy guy that follows you around everywhere is at the door," Juanito said as he walked past me brushing his hair back like a girl. I jumped up and went to the door.

"Hey, Cooper," I said.

Cooper was already walking away from the door and looking back at me.

"June's on the phone. She said that your mom is driving her crazy," Cooper said.

He didn't seem to like what Juanito had said. I threw on a USC shirt and body-slammed Scotty against his closet door. It had become a funny thing to do. If you walked by your dormmate and they weren't paying attention, slamming them was a way of knocking them down a notch or two. I was the worst at it. Scotty would always pick the time when I was distracted and slam me against the wall or my door going into the bathroom.

I had to run across campus to Cooper's apartment. My family were calling at two.

"June, can you hear me? Are you there?"

The long-distance connection was staticky.

"Hi Reem, it's June, can you hear me?" June's voice sounded just like Mom's to me.

"Yes, that's much better, June. What's going on? Is everything okay?"

But I could already hear the tone in June's voice,

that this call was going to be her complaining to me about Mom. I was getting a little anxious every time my family called. I still had a small black cloud of dread that kept following me around in the back of my mind. The distance between my family and me was something I could feel more now than ever.

"Yes, we're all fine, Reem. How's everything going for you? Are you in finals yet?"

Cooper was in the kitchen, making a grilled cheese sandwich. He banged on the stove with a spatula to get my attention and motioned towards the skillet to ask me if I wanted one. I gave him a thumbs-up and he went back to cooking in his well-organized apartment's kitchen. No personal item around or pictures on the wall. It looked like the place was already decorated before he moved in but in fact, this was all Cooper's handy work. The bathroom had pictures of a lighthouse on the wall, along with seashells, starfish, and sand dollars to finish it off.

"Not yet, classes have ended but we're in study days. Exams are the first week of May. I'll roll right into summer classes just after exams," I said.

Cooper was right. I didn't like the idea of redoing environmental studies over the summer. I'd been able to pick two study classes that I needed for my junior year and switch them for environmental studies. The two study classes were not going to be a walk in the park. I'd have to put the work in over the summer.

Cooper put a plate with the sandwich in front of me. I realized Cooper had screwed up making the sandwich and that's why he'd wanted to give it to me. So he could make a better-looking one for himself.

"I'm not going to be coming out to see you this

summer. I'm on a new medication, and the doctor wants to monitor me this summer. I had another small seizure again so he's trying something new. But keep your worries to your finals, I'm good," June said.

I instantly became sick to my stomach. Just the thought of my little sister having a seizure and what that must have looked like. There was no way I could eat this crappy sandwich in front of me, I had no appetite.

"That's okay, June, I'm glad you're doing good and that they're going to fix your medication. I was going to be busy this summer anyways. But don't worry, I'll have you come out when you're feeling better. We'll spend some time together then, okay," I said.

Cooper could tell my conversation had turned a little personal. He turned off the stove and took his sandwich in a paper napkin and walked into his bedroom to give me some privacy.

"I'm wonderful, Reem. I don't want you to worry." June sounded determined.

"Okay, June, I believe you. Is Mom with you?"

"No, just Dad." I could hear June giving the phone to my dad. "Here, Dad. Reem doesn't believe me so he wants to talk to you," she said sarcastically.

"Hi son, how are finals going?"

My dad sounded upbeat. I was a little surprised my mom wasn't there, but I figured June must be telling the truth about not worrying about her.

"Hi Dad, classes ended, and we're in the study days right now. Exams aren't until the first week of May so I'll just be hitting the books until next week. You sound good, how's Mom?"

I could almost hear my dad putting down the *Wall Street Journal* to have a conversation with me.

"Mom is good; she was here earlier but had to go do some errands. I've been able to spend more time at home lately. Things have been easing up at work. Negotiations are going very well and we should have this drama with Iraq over within a few weeks."

My dad's optimism came through the phone and hit me square between the eyes, almost like a pressure valve relieving some of the tension that had been building up in my head.

"I've been taking my Jeep out and doing some four-wheeling," Dad said.

"That's fantastic, Dad. I was hoping you would get that thing out there and make it dirty. I pretty much take mine to the beach and around town now, but traffic is getting terrible the closer we get to summer," I said.

It was hard even to imagine my dad driving the Jeep around. The picture of him with his briefcase in hand coming and going to and from the office was the only image I could muster. June, my dad and I spoke on the phone for at least another hour. Rico showed up towards the end. He told me that next year for June's graduation we needed to do something big. I agreed, and we made plans to talk more about it.

"Everything okay at home?" Cooper asked. He was washing dishes, and the smell of burnt cheese still filled his apartment.

"Yeah, Dad seemed upbeat, and June had another seizure, but they're readjusting her medication. My brother and I are going to try and think of something special for her graduation next year. Dad said that negotiations were going well with Baghdad and that Iraqi business," I said.

It felt good to say that out loud. The dark cloud that had been following me around seemed to be gone.

"So you didn't tell him about your spring break at Zion, and the wedding proposal to Sarah," Cooper said.

He looked disappointed in me. Sarah and I had driven to Zion National Park to spend the spring break with her parents so I could get to know them a little bit better. I'd thought it would be a good idea to ask her father if he'd allow me the honor to take his daughter's hand in marriage.

"No, I thought it best to wait. I didn't want to add any more drama onto his plate. He's dealing with my sister June and her issues," I said.

Cooper sat down in the chair across from me. His front room had a modern look with a Roman touch. The couches were of this period, but Cooper liked these white columns with a glass bowl on top that stood about waist high. He would throw his keys and change in them. I found them to be helpful and not out of place for a bachelor like Cooper.

"Reem, I need to tell you about my thoughts on this business with Iraq. I have a lot of military experience. When it comes to a dog like this, Saddam Hussein, it has me concerned because when you corner a dog its only option is to strike. Iraq is like a cornered dog. They can't sell their oil for the price they want and are willing to start trouble with their neighbors to get what they need."

A feeling of dread and anxiousness had come over me and my entire body with every word Cooper was telling me. The dark cloud was back but bigger.

"I appreciate you telling me your thoughts, Cooper. My dad is a good man and if he thinks they're working it out, well then, I'll have to accept it. I don't mind telling you that it does keep me up at night thinking about it," I said.

I let my back hit the soft cushion of Cooper's couch. I had a defeated look on my face.

"To be honest with you, Reem, I don't know what's going to happen or if anything would happen, I just know I don't like what I'm seeing."

Cooper removed a 45-caliber pistol from underneath his garment top. He placed it on the coffee table and started disassembling and cleaning it.

"You have time to help me with some cleaning? Grab the two guns under my pillows in my room and get started," Cooper said.

He knew how much I like helping him clean his guns. He would take me to the gun range at least once every other week. Basically, the weekends that I didn't go skydiving I would be at the gun range with Cooper. I enjoyed learning about different weapons, how they operated and how to clean them. Cooper had finally got on board with us and started skydiving too. I think he loved the fact his client was adventurous. If I didn't know any better, I'd have said we'd become good friends. I did value his advice and opinion.

"So, tell me how you did it," Cooper said.

"Did what?" I replied, as I leaned over to get a new shop towel for the S&W 38 revolver I was cleaning.

"How did you ask her to marry you? I could see you from a distance, but I couldn't hear the words you used."

Cooper passed me the gun oil can.

"Well, I was going to wait but Sarah's dad and I had a moment alone that next day. So, I just said, I want to marry your daughter, Mr. Long."

I gave Cooper the can of oil back.

"And her father said okay? Just like that?"

"Hell, no, he didn't say okay. He tried to discourage me with everything he had. He told me that Sarah has goals set for herself in her life. That marrying me would mean that she would be giving up on her goals. Ever since she was a little girl, she wanted to marry in the Temple to a boy that belonged to their religion – hopefully, a return missionary. Sarah would be giving up on that dream by agreeing to marry me. Not to mention the fact I would probably take her out of this country and away from her family."

Cooper sat back and looked at me and let out a big gasp of air. "Holy shit man, that's a lot to lay on you. But I know her God is a big part of who she is, right?"

I got up and was washing my hands in the kitchen sink when Sarah rang the doorbell.

"Cooper, it's Sarah, put away the guns!"

Cooper took out a plastic box from under the sink and placed all his guns and supplies in it. Cooper was washing his hands when I opened the door. "Hi, Sarah," he shouted over the water faucet.

"Hi, Cooper, just came by to grab Reem for a special date," she said.

She was wearing a captain's hat with a paper cutout of an airline on it. It read "Long Airlines."

"What are you up to, Sarah?" I asked with hope of sex on my mind.

"You'll just have to come and see for yourself," she said.

"I'll tell you later the rest of the story Cooper," I shouted at Cooper as Sarah pulled me out of the apartment.

Sarah had a big date planned, alright. She'd decorated the back seat of her car to look like an airplane interior. She told me that we were going to be flying at 32,000 feet and would land in Hawaii in approximately 25 minutes. Which meant she drove to her house with me as the passenger. Her parents' backyard was all decorated in a tropical Hawaiian theme. She even had a small table on the ground decorated like a luau.

"What do you think of your Hawaiian trip?" Sarah asked.

She could see that I was blown away by all the decorations. The Tiki hut items were a nice touch. I mean, she had the entire backyard looking exactly like I'd just arrived in Hawaii. It must have taken her all day to set up.

"I don't know what to say! You're so amazing. How did you even do all of this?" I asked.

Sarah laughed and led me over to a cushion to sit down. The Hawaiian luau music played in the background as she put on what she called a feast. She made sure not to use or serve pork, but lots of chicken and fish and other things. Sarah was so creative with the leis she put on my neck and the different food. Her role-playing as if I was on a plane and in Hawaii was so sweet. I had asked Sarah to marry me the same day her dad told me that he couldn't give me his approval. Mr. Long had said that just because he wouldn't approve, this should not stop me from asking his daughter. He'd never got his own father-in-law's approval, and he and Sarah's mom had been happily married for thirty-one years.

So, when we were in Zion National Park as the sun was setting and lighting up the sky with purples and reds, I'd turned to Sarah, and knelt and proposed to her with a modest solitaire diamond ring in my hand. Sarah immediately said yes but asked me if we could have a long engagement. She also asked if I would keep an open mind towards her beliefs and her goals. With that, I'd agreed, and we were engaged.

CHAPTER 20

was watching so much news every day that Sarah would leave me and go hang out with her friends. "YOU'RE WATCHING CNN" – the sound came from a TV by the front desk of the Arizona jump school. John and Cooper and I were going up to 14,000 feet, I'd been looking forward to it all week. John and I had learned of some certifications we could receive in Arizona at a jump school there. So, on Memorial Day weekend, we planned to go up and get a lot of jumps in and qualifications signed off. My Marine buddies were supposed to meet us in Arizona that weekend, but Ben and Danny weren't going to be able to make the trip. Ben's sister Carrie was getting married in Alaska.

I loved this sport. Skydiving had become a part of who I was. But for some reason I didn't feel the exhilaration and excitement I usually got just before a jump. Instead, my focus was on the news all the time.

"In other news, the leader of Iraq, Saddam Hussein accuses Kuwait and the United Arab Emirates of economic warfare against Iraq."

I ran back into the office area where the TV was.

"What did he say? Turn that up, turn that up!"

The manager turned the volume up on the TV for me. There before my eyes, I could see the Emir of Kuwait headed into the Arab League summit in Baghdad, Iraq, with my dad four steps behind him and his entourage. The news went on to say Iraq was accusing Kuwait of stealing oil from the Rumaila oil field, an Iraqi oil field near the Iraq-Kuwaiti border.

"That's BS! We don't need to steal your oil, Iraq! We have more than you in our own country! You and your lying leaders can go fuck yourselves!" I started to shout at the TV.

"Hey, calm down, man. It's okay. The TV can't hear you," the old hippy in the office said.

"I'm sorry," I replied.

I sat down on the little wooden chair in the office. I needed to gather my thoughts and take a moment. I was bewildered about why Iraq was saying those things about my country. Was Cooper right about backing a dog into a corner? My thoughts started to go away from me. I didn't know Dad was going to be part of the conference. Seeing Dad on TV was unreal.

"Hey kid, are you going to be, okay?" the old hippie asked. Before I'd interrupted him, he'd been looking over what seemed to be the employees' schedules for the week.

"Yeah, I need a moment. That's my dad on the TV. Thanks."

I continued staring at my altimeter wristband, with thoughts of what the worst-case scenario for my family would be. If the Emir was in Iraq with my dad, they were probably negotiating their way out of the situation. I could feel the old man staring at me hard, but I didn't care. I needed to gather my thoughts.

"Was that your dad on the news?" The old man put down his paperwork and leaned forward across the desk to engage me in conversation.

"Yes, he was one of the men walking behind the Kuwaiti Emir," I replied.

"Hey, look man. I don't know what the hell is going on in the Middle East half the time, but I can tell you one thing. America loves its oil. We will do anything to protect it," he said.

The old hippie sat back in his chair and picked up the schedules he was doing. Maybe the old hippie was making sense that the world needed our oil and Iraq knew it too. So maybe they were just bluffing in order to get debt relief.

"I think you're right, mister," I said. "The world won't stand by and just let Iraq take over Kuwait's oil fields."

The old man looked a little confused. "Yeah, I guess. November 5211 is on the ground if you and your crew are going to go jump."

That was the tail number of our airplane that was going to take us up today. I almost decided not to go since I felt I was too distracted with all the news. Then I figured I needed a distraction to help me take my mind off the Iraq thing.

"Alright, ladies! Who's ready to jump!" I yelled at the guys.

John and Cooper look bored, waiting there for the aircraft to pick us up. We all piled into the aircraft, which could hold about ten jumpers at a time. Today there were only five of us: an instructor with an older lady who wanted to try it for the first time, and us.

The tandem instructor jumped first at about 10,000 feet, then our pilot Archie took us up to 13,000 feet, which was actually closer to 14,000 feet. When I decided to jump, I left the aircraft with my altimeter on my wrist showing 13,795 feet. I was doing a belly jump and hoped for a long 55-second freefall. The smell of the desert air in Arizona was sweet. It brought me back home a little bit, I remembered thinking during my free fall. With a quick tug on the release handle, I could feel my main chute deploying in a rapid deceleration to my entire body. I had a beautiful red, green, and blue canopy. As I started looking at the clear desert sky, I could see John and Cooper at about 4,500 feet. I looked at my altimeter, which read 3100 – I guessed I'd pulled a little too soon. Suddenly I felt a shift to my left, and when I looked up, my canopy had collapsed. I was in freefall again with my chute creating some drag. But I knew my situation had become life-threatening within a millisecond. I was much lower than 9,000 feet. I needed to get in the breakaway position, let go of my main chute and deploy my reserve immediately. With both of my hands, I grabbed the orange breakaway handle. I pulled down on it as hard as I could. My chute had done what it was supposed to do and detached from my harness. My left foot caught one of the ropes. I was now entangled in my main parachute.

"Son of a bitch! Son of a bitch!" I screamed out, trying to reach the cord around my foot. I needed to get this off so I could deploy my reserve in seconds, or I would be done for. Even though my training was kicking in, everything in my mind slowed down. I could see Cooper had let go of his main chute and was trying to get down faster to me but I knew that there wouldn't be enough time.

As soon as I said to myself the hell with it, I reached over and with both hands grabbed the red cloth ripcord for my reserve and pulled it up. My reserve came open, spinning me around and freeing me from my main chute. I only had a few seconds with my reserve before I hit the ground, but it was enough. The next thing I knew, I was laying on my back on the ground, trying to catch my breath. I had the wind knocked out of me, and a sprained ankle.

"All right! I'm okay! I'm okay! I'm okay!" I started yelling after I got the wind back in my lungs. I could see a man off in the distance running towards me. But I was yelling at Cooper above me that I was okay.

I freed myself from my harness and jump gear and started to look for my main parachute landing so that I could inspect it. The tandem jump instructor for the school ran up to me. I knew he was going to ask me if I was okay.

"What a ride!" he said.

"What the fuck are you talking about? I almost died! That was not fun!" I said.

The realization of what had just happened was starting to hit me. My hands were shaking, and I just kept looking for my main chute.

"You must go back up and jump right now! If you don't go, you'll never jump again," the instructor said.

Off to my left, I could see Cooper had landed using his reserve chute also. Cooper wasn't running to me but looking at my main chute. He'd had a lot of time to see me and my main parachute land. I started to run over to him, but my foot was in no shape to run so I hobbled over.

"Look, all the lines are in good shape. What the hell happened?" Cooper said.

"I had a nice chute, and all of a sudden, it collapsed," I replied.

John had hit the ground next to us. He took a few minutes taking off his harness and walking over to us.

"I saw it!" John said.

"You saw what, John?" Cooper asked quickly.

"I saw what happened."

John was pulling my parachute open and was looking for something.

"It passed me by like a bullet. What was it?" John said.

He was still looking through my chute.

"I found it!!" John yelled.

He held up a green Stanley thermos.

"What the fuck is that!" I yelled.

"That is a fucking thermos that our asshole pilot must have taken with him."

I later learned that the thermos had jumped out of the pilot's bag when John and Cooper had jumped. The pilot had turned quickly to the left and headed back to the airport. The thermos had rolled out the open door and hit my chute, collapsing it. A one in a million shot that the thermos even comes close to me, a freak accident, that's what this is, I said to myself.

"Come on, let's go!" Cooper said.

"Where are you going?" the instructor asked as Cooper marched right past him.

Cooper was walking straight to the van that was there to bring us back to the airport.

"To give this back to the pilot," Cooper said as he held up the thermos.

"We'll be back! Round up all our gear!" I said to the instructor.

John was right next to me and just as concerned that Cooper was going to kill the pilot. We got to the van, and the driver was talking to the lady that jumped.

"I'm sorry, what's your name, I didn't catch it earlier?" Cooper asked the lady sitting in the van.

"It's Joyce. What's your name?"

Joyce held out her hand to do a formal greeting. She had no idea what had just happened.

"Joyce, I'm Cooper. I'm going to need you to please get out of the van for just a minute," Cooper said.

John and I jumped in the back and waited for Cooper to get in. Cooper was standing next to the side van door. The driver looked concerned that Cooper had just asked the lady to get out.

"Hey, I have to wait for everyone before I can head back to the airport," the driver said.

Cooper didn't want to argue with the driver, so he opened the driver's door and grabbed the driver's shirt, and with one hand threw him out of the driver's seat. This was the first real sign that Cooper was going to kill the pilot, I thought.

"Hey Cooper, it was just a freak accident," I said.

Cooper was driving like a bat out of hell back to the airport.

"I know! I want to return this thermos to its rightful owner," he said.

"Dude, that doesn't sound good at all. I think Cooper has lost it," John whispered to me.

John was loving every moment of this. He wanted to see Cooper kick the pilot's ass. I guessed there was a part of me that wanted the same thing. I was still shaking and there was no way I was ever going skydiving again, I admitted to myself. The instructor hadn't been unsympathetic. He knew that with a close call like the one I'd just had, if I didn't jump again soon, I would give it all up.

We arrived back at the airport, and Cooper jumped out of the van and walked over to the flight line, but the Cessna 208 wasn't back yet. Cooper just stood there with the thermos in his hand. I could see the pilot was on his final approach, and the plane landed and rolled up to the fueling area. Cooper walked over to the aircraft and yelled something at the pilot. He then threw the thermos at the prop of the Cessna, hitting it with great force. The thermos exploded into pieces, and the Cessna engine sputtered. The pilot became angry and shut off the engine quickly. You could see the damage to the propeller.

"What the fuck is your problem, asshole!" the pilot yelled as he got out of the airplane to confront Cooper.

He was an average-looking guy in his late twenties or early thirties. The sound of the thermos hitting the propeller was so loud that the old hippie and some of the staff had come running out of the jump school.

"Where's your thermos?" Cooper shouted at the pilot.

"My what?" the pilot asked.

He had got right in the face of Cooper.

"I said, where is your fucking thermos, asshole?"

Cooper shoved the pilot back with both hands. I could tell this was going to get physical right away. The staff members and the old hippie were running toward us. I turned back around to see Cooper smacking around the pilot. He tried to fight back but Cooper was too good of a fighter. Three of the staff members got to John and me first. We held them back for a second or two, but we went to blows with all three. I turned my fear into anger and started hitting anything I could.

"STOP! STOP!" the old hippie shouted.

We all stopped and looked at him.

"What the hell is going on!?" he yelled.

The pilot was out cold. Cooper had hit him with a left and down he went. Cooper had the shirt of the third staff member and was about to hit him when the old hippie had started shouting.

"Your fucking pilot almost killed me!" I said.

I pointed to the pieces of the thermos on the ground. Two Arizona sheriff's cars drove up with Joyce and the instructor inside.

"What's going on here, Douglas?" a beached whale of a sheriff's officer got out of his car and asked the old hippie. This cop was so fat it took him two tries to get out of the vehicle.

"These three assholes just damaged my Cessna with a thermos bottle," Douglas, the old hippie, said.

"Is that right?" the sheriff said.

John quickly explained what had happened to us. He didn't want Cooper or me to open our mouths. I was a foreigner, and Cooper was black, and this sheriff looked to be what John called a good old boy. He probably lined the seats of his patrol car with the Confederate flag. We got all our gear and headed out. We came to an agreement that I wouldn't make a big deal out of what had happened, and Douglas would pay for the damage to his airplane. The sheriff was nice. He told Douglas that if it were him that had had to use a reserve chute because of a thermos, he would have kicked the shit out of the pilot too. So much for stereotypes, I thought to myself.

CHAPTER 21

R ico! Dewpoint! Dewpoint!" my dad said to me as he passed my office door. My brother Reem was still in California because he had summer school. He had been on the phone to me every day since we'd learned of Iraq's troop movements on our border. It had started July 22nd, and now I heard rumors that Iraq had about 100,000 troops on the border. Today was the 24th.

"Dewpoint? Why did he say that to you, Rico?" Nasser, one of my annoying coworkers, asked.

"Nothing, he just gave me the answer to a cross-word puzzle I've been working on," I said.

Nasser was always at my desk, bugging me.

"Don't you have a report to write? What are you doing here? Go bug someone else," I said, trying not to show him the concern that had come over my body with that word coming from my dad.

Dewpoint, the temperature to which air must be cooled to become saturated with water vapor. The codeword that my dad and I had set up to let the other one know that we needed to get our family out of the country. Dewpoint! Damn, that wasn't good. What had Dad found out that had scared him enough to give me the codeword? My thoughts were in overdrive. I needed to leave work without anyone knowing. I was scheduled to check on an oil rig the following day. Maybe I could use that as an excuse, I thought.

"Saad, I'm heading out for the day. I need to see Saleh about the tooling for number 8. I'll be back on Thursday, call my house if you need anything," I said calmly as I started to leave.

Saad just nodded at me. He must not have realized what day it was. We were all getting a little concerned about Iraq. Usually, it would be hard to get out of the office with that crappy excuse, but Saad was too busy reading the newspaper.

When I arrived home, BJ was standing outside waiting for me.

"Rico, open the back of your car so that I can put some boxes in," he said with a look of panic on his face.

"Where's my mom and June?" I snapped back at him.

"Your mom is in there packing, and June is lying down. She doesn't feel good today. Come on and help me. We must hurry and get this over to the Dunns' apartment."

I ignored BJ and walked into the house to see my mom. She had a very calming presence about her and was deciding what to pack and what not to. As if we were putting stuff in storage.

"Dad… Did you talk to Dad?" I asked her. I was a little out of breath for some reason.

"Yes, he said to get over to the Dunns', and that we're going to Saudi Arabia from there," she said, calmly and sounding annoyed that she had to leave at all.

"Rico, your dad is here!" I heard BJ yell.

"On my way!" I yelled back.

Dad left his car parked outside the driveway so anyone could see it. I walked out the front door to meet him halfway.

"What happened that made you give me the codeword, Dad?"

I waited for my dad's response. Probably to tell me that Iraq had already moved in, and the army was on their way, or some version of that, I thought. I was angry these days ever since the accusations Iraq kept making in the media. Telling other countries that Kuwait was conspiring against them and manipulating oil prices was a big lie. My anger grew each day; I wanted to take a gun and join the army and fight any son of a bitch that thought to come in my country.

"Iraq's army was posturing as if to invade this morning. It seems a couple of divisions have pulled back now. I guess I've jumped the gun by giving you the codeword. We need to move over to Dunns' house and at the same time, make it look like we're still here in our own home. I'm going to drive the Jeep into work from now on and leave my car in the front. People will think I'm still at home."

BJ had a van loaded up with a bunch of our parents' valuables, and was going to drive it over to a warehouse and hide it.

"Call me when you get to Dunns' house," Dad shouted at BJ as he drove away. BJ gave him a thumbs up through the open window.

"Hey, sweetheart, is everything done?"

Dad had walked up to Mom in the kitchen and greeted her with a kiss and a hug. I realized that Dad already spoke to Mom on the phone about jumping the gun on leaving. That was why my mom seemed so relaxed and unhurried.

"Yes, everything is ready to go sweetheart. June is in the back lying down. She doesn't feel well. I'm a little worried about taking her on this trip. I wish we could fly out of here," Mom said.

She didn't like the idea of driving across the desert into Saudi Arabia. But the Emir had already put a plan to leave Kuwait in place. All family and government officials would, on his word, go to Saudi Arabia. If Mom or Dad left before the word was given, it would look bad on our family. Our house was in an area of town close to Dasman Palace, so Dad had had an idea to make the Dunns' apartment a backup plan. My wife Donna's family lived in an apartment closer to the Saudi Arabia border. It was still miles away but a lot closer than our home was. If there was a rush to get out of Kuwait, my dad knew the traffic would be so bad that we might not get out if we were at our house. The Dunns' place was just off Highway 50, King Faisal Road. Donna and her family had left a week previously as soon as the United States State Department had issued a travel warning over the tensions in the Gulf. Donna's father had made immediate plans to travel back to the United States until tensions cooled, or the situation got better.

"I know, I wish we could fly too, sweetheart. We must keep a level head and try to stay one step ahead of the situation. Rico, take your mom and June to the Dunns' place. I'll meet you there tonight. I'm going back to work for a few hours," Dad said.

Dad went and checked on June in her room. Mom just smiled, and we left as Dad told us.

The next few days were unreal. I would travel back and forth to work and the Dunns' apartment. June had another epileptic seizure, probably due to the stress. We had no choice but to take her to the hospital. Mom and Dad stayed with June there. It was located on Arabian Gulf Street, overlooking the Persian Gulf. June was doing good, but her doctor wanted to keep an eye on her for a few more days. I needed to get to a phone and call Reem. I'd been doing an excellent job of informing him of everything, but ever since Dad had called out Dewpoint, I'd been too busy to call. The drive was so much longer to the hospital from Dunns' apartment that by the time I got to June's room, I had five calls from work and two from Reem.

"Hi Dad, how's June doing?" I whispered because June and Mom were still asleep.

"June's doing fine, son," he said, although I could tell he was worried. "You have a lot of calls from the office. They need you to go in and help them right away. Don't worry, I'll tell June you were here, just go to work and find out what's going on for me. I've gotten no word yet from the government. Everything is calming down, hopefully."

When I arrived at my office, almost everybody was shredding documents on the off chance that Iraq would invade. The government didn't want them to get their hands on any sensitive oil production documents. I thought this was ridiculous – who cared if someone knew what the standards for production were? I fell asleep around 11pm that night on the couch next to the shredder in my boss's office.

"Rico! Rico! Wake up, your dad is on the phone for you," someone said. I didn't know who, I was still trying to get my wits about me.

"Rico are you there? It's Dad," a voice said as I put the phone to my ear.

"Oh, hi, Dad, what time is it?"

I was still rubbing the sleep out of my eyes. I was feeling a little disoriented, and the couch was so small it had left me with a pain in my neck.

"Shut up and listen! I just got the word we're evacuating now! The presidential palace and all forms of government are to make their way to Saudi Arabia immediately. Your Mom and I have taken June and are on our way to the Dunns' place. Meet us there right away. The Iraqis have broken the border and are moving quickly into Kuwait. This is for real, son. I need you to do exactly what I taught you. I've not been able to get a hold of BJ or your brother. Just run out of your office and meet us at…" Dad's voice cut out, and the phone went dead. I could hear people shouting down the hallway.

"Everyone out! Iraq has started a war with us! Everyone out!"

I could hear people starting to panic. I grabbed my car keys and ran down the stairwell and out to the street. It was more chaotic outside than inside. The thought of Iraq invading my country was making my blood boil. I was so angry, I wanted to kill and hurt any Iraqi I saw. I could hear explosions in the distance. People were running everywhere. It must be 2 or 3 in the morning, I thought to myself.

"Rico, is that you?"

I turned around to see who'd said my name. My old friend from school, Jasem, with a bunch of other men from the government center, ran up to me.

"Yes, what's going on, Jasem?"

Jasem and his group of men ran past me to a military truck that had pulled up.

"They're trying to take over the palace! Come on, Rico! Help us defend our homeland."

Without even thinking, I ran towards them and jumped into the truck. Someone handed me a gun and a box of ammunition and Jasem was trying to show me how to use it. The Toyota pickup that we all crammed into was very uncomfortable. Whoever was driving the truck wasn't thinking about us in the back, and I had a hard time staying put. Then we came to a quick stop, jumped out and ran towards Dasman Palace. Two more vehicles pulled up, and more men got out. I could hear something above our heads. That was when all hell broke out. Iraqi Special Forces were coming in overhead from the helicopters. I just started shooting up in the direction everybody else was shooting. I could see the concrete around me being chopped up and realized it was Iraqi rounds coming at me. Jasem ran over to a spot of fencing where there was a cement pillar to hide behind and I followed him. This was a good vantage point for us. We could now see the enemy.

Jasem and I started shooting as many as we could. It only lasted for ten or twenty minutes before the Iraqis caught on to our location. I could see that the Kuwaitis who hadn't taken cover had been shot to death or severely injured. Most everybody had taken some form of shelter, and we put up one hell of a fight. We shot so many Iraqis that it gave us time to regroup and organize a better defense of the palace. The fighting became fierce when the Iraqis were reinforced a few hours later by the Republican Guard elements that had come in on Highway 80. The younger brother of the Emir, Fahd Al-Ahmad, fought with us. I had to get out of my sheltered area because the enemy had moved to our left, exposing us to more rounds.

"Are you hit?" Fahd asked as I ran into his covered position to help.

"No, I'm good! I need more rounds for my gun," I said.

Fahd's men gave me a box of ammunition. We had a great vantage point of the enemy. They needed to run down ten steps and into a courtyard to get into the heart of the palace. Fahd and I shot anything that moved down those steps.

"You're Rico Al-Sabah, Ahmed's son, right?" Fahd asked me.

I nodded my head as I let out a ten-round blast at the enemy.

"Good shot, Rico! You got three of them," Fahd yelled.

We both felt good about our chances of defending the Palace. But it wasn't to be. Later that day, he would die in my arms. Fahd represented what was best about Kuwait. Jasem and I could see that the Iraqis had us outgunned and outnumbered. The palace army had fallen and by mid-afternoon, we decided that we'd done all we could do. So, we left the palace to the enemy.

CHAPTER 22

made my way to the Dunns' apartment, thinking my family would already be in Saudi Arabia by now.

"Rico, you're alive! Are you okay, son?"

My dad and my mom had their arms around me and were both crying with joy to see me alive.

"Yes, I'm alive! Why are you still here? Why haven't you left across the border?"

"Rico, June is too sick to travel. We must hide here until she's better. The stress is too much for her. Even making our way to the Dunns' apartment almost killed your sister," Dad explained.

"You never mind that, Ahmed. Rico, where were you? Why didn't you come home last night? What have you been doing?" my mom asked as she pushed my dad out of the way to get closer to my face.

She must have seen it in my eyes. I could feel a

change in me that was never going to leave me. After you kill someone for the first time, even if you are justified, it leaves a scar on your soul. For me, I was still able to see the Iraqi soldiers go down from each shot I'd taken. Later, after I was making my way to the Dunns' place, I'd thought about each of the men in my sights. Somewhere there was a family that would learn of his death. They would be devastated by the news. A wife, mother, some family that knew him as a baby, not just a soldier invading a country. A person that had hopes and dreams, with likes and dislikes. A person that was alive and now was not because of my bullet.

"I helped defend the palace last night. We failed and now they have control of all of Kuwait. You should have got across the border; I don't know what's going to happen now," I said, feeling defeated.

"Rico, tell me everything that happened last night. Moment by moment. Did anyone follow you here? Where did you park your car?"

My dad's engineering brain was hard at work. Dad wanted to know what happened at the palace so he could make sure it didn't come back to our family. I told my dad what had happened. I even told him about the Emir's little brother being killed during the battle. I'd been the one holding him in my arms as he died. I'd kissed him softly on the forehead and whispered to him. The men fighting with me had watched as Fahd passed away in my arms. That was hard for my parents to hear because they'd been very fond of Fahd. After speaking with my parents for a while, I walked back to June's room and checked on her. Dad was right; she didn't look good. The medication the doctor had given her wasn't helping.

June smiled and hugged me. "I can't tell you how nice it is to see that you've not been captured or killed," she said half-jokingly.

"No, I'm your big brother. I'm indestructible and I always will be. Bullets bounce off me," I said.

June and I hugged again, and I kissed her on her forehead. She needed her rest, so I left her to sleep. Mom and Dad were sitting at the kitchen table talking about their plans.

"Rico, were you able to get hold of Reem before all this started?" Mom asked.

"No, I'd been trying to get hold of him for a couple of days now and with all the craziness going on, I never found time to do it," I said as I sat down next to my dad.

"What do you think will happen now, Ahmed?" Mom asked.

"Well, I don't think the world will let this go on. Someone like the Americans will stop this madness. I'll bet you we'll have an American hero come through that door and save us."

Dad had been saying all along that Iraq would do this. We needed to find a way out of Kuwait.

I hope Reem is okay, I thought to myself.

CHAPTER 23

REEM! I'm on the next plane to LA, take it easy, son! We'll figure this out together. When was the last time you spoke to your father or Rico?" Uncle Dennis asked over the crackle of the long-distance call from Chicago.

"I spoke to Rico two days ago, but I've not heard from anyone since. Rico said that everything seemed to be fine. June was back in the hospital and Mom and Dad were with her. Uncle Dennis, wouldn't they have called us by now if they'd gotten out of Kuwait?" I said with panic rising in my body.

I'd been sitting in my class, getting ready to turn in my final assignment when the news had broken of the invasion. Iraq had invaded Kuwait at around 2am local time. John came running into my class to get me. He'd been lying in the multipurpose room watching TV when the news had come of the invasion. He'd run clear across campus to be with me. My first instinct was to call, but of course, none of the phone lines were working in Kuwait. It had taken me four hours to get Uncle Dennis on the phone and now that I had, the news seemed to be getting worse by the hour.

"Reem, we don't know anything yet! Don't let your imagination run away with you! Keep it together. I'll see you in five hours and we'll probably find that they got out and are okay. Your dad is brilliant and put in safeguards for this very thing. Don't panic!" Uncle Dennis said.

His voice was very reassuring to me. He was my mom's brother and my only connection to the ground. I went back to my dorm after the phone call. Cooper was already out of the state and his apartment was locked up. Dad had ended our security two weeks previously and told me that things were back to normal. So my only lifeline became a payphone in our multipurpose, downstairs dorm room. John and Juanito stayed with me downstairs in the TV room. I was glued to CNN and ABC News. Sarah had come to be by my side. I didn't want to miss a moment of the news. Every hour and a half or so, I'd attempt to call my family to no avail. The story kept getting worse.

"ABC News is reporting that the country of Kuwait no longer exists. In one fell swoop, Saddam Hussein has gambled and won on this invasion." Each word out of the newscaster's mouth felt like a knife stabbing me in the heart, opening my stomach and ripping out my guts. I would take breaks and go to the bathroom, but it was only to cry in private. I couldn't take the pain of not knowing and the ugly thoughts going on in my head. I'd felt this pain before, the not knowing what was going to happen next, like when my sister had started having seizures and I'd thought she was going to die. This time it was far worse; not only was it all of my family members but with every hour of not hearing from them it was like I couldn't wake up from a nightmare.

When Uncle Dennis arrived, I picked him up in my Jeep. We drove to the Four Seasons so he could check into his room. The hotel had a sound communication system that Uncle Dennis could use to continue gathering information for the family and me. He told me Grandma and Grandpa hadn't stopped crying since the news broke. Uncle Jim and Aunt Carol sent their best wishes and prayers.

By the time I got up to the room, Uncle Dennis had already gotten off the phone with someone. I couldn't tell who it was. Uncle Dennis looked up at me with a look of frustration on his face.

"Where did you go, Reem?" he asked while not looking in my eyes.

"I was just downstairs saying goodbye to Sarah. She had come to give me some comfort, but I was in no condition to be around her right then. "Who was that on the phone, Uncle Dennis?" I asked.

"That was your dad's contact at the State Department. I've met with him two or three times. I figured since he was close to your father, he might have some information for us. He only said that the fighting seems to be ongoing, and we'll know more in the next 48 hours."

I could tell Uncle Dennis was now moving into the same lane I'd been in, which was panic, fear, and anger. If my parents had made their way into Saudi

Arabia, we would have heard something by now. I knew it and Uncle Dennis knew it, but we didn't say it to each other.

"Okay, good! If the fighting is still going on, I'm going to take the next flight over and help fight. I can't sit here for two days waiting to hear the fucking phone ring, and some asshole on the other line telling me my family has been killed! Uncle Dennis! I'm booking a flight right now!"

I grabbed the phone and started to call Jennifer Noel's flight services. Uncle Dennis didn't stop me, he walked over to me and put his hand on my arm.

"I'm sorry, son. No flights are going anywhere near there. The air space is restricted now. You can't just hop on a plane and go slug it out with the Iraqis."

I could see the pain and sadness in Uncle Dennis' eyes as the tears hit his cheek.

"I don't give a fuck about the airspace, Uncle Dennis! I'll fly the fucking plane myself if I have to, but I need to get over there and fight!" I said.

I grabbed the phone and threw it across the hotel room, breaking a lamp on a table. I looked at Uncle Dennis for a reaction. But all I saw was his back. Uncle Dennis grabbed the credenza by the couch. He picked it up and dropped it, breaking it into a thousand pieces. We both just looked at each other.

"Damn, that felt good!" Uncle Dennis said.

I smiled at him and grabbed a drawer out of the dresser and smashed it on the ground. By the time Uncle Dennis and I were done, that hotel room was severely trashed. Hotel security arrived just in time to see us walking to the elevators. Uncle Dennis told them that two guys were running down the stairs. We casually walked into the hotel's excellent dining area. We sat down and ordered the most expensive bottle of wine. By the time our steak and lobster arrived, the hotel management approached us about the room.

"Mr. Green, can we have a word with you in private?" the manager said with a touch of anger in his voice.

"In private? My nephew is the one you're looking for – he came up with the idea! Whatever you need. You can talk in front of him too, Mr… Glenn? Glenn. You know, you look like a Glenn. A little hotel manager."

Uncle Dennis was drunk and started laughing.

"Sir, I'm going to call the police. The damage to the room is extensive, and your behavior is outrageous."

I jumped up. "No, there's no need for the police, sir," I said. "Come with me, please."

I walked over to the next table and put my arm around Glenn, the manager.

"Look, Mr. Green is a surgeon, and he just lost a critical patient tonight. He's just blowing off steam. Here's my American Express black card – whatever it takes, just double it," I said.

The manager looked at me as to see if I was drunk too. He tilted his head back a bit to look in my eyes better.

"Okay, but the room is yours for as long as he stays with us. We won't give him another one. The damage will be paid for in full today! And you get him out of here before he starts a fight."

"I will! I promise."

Uncle Dennis and I got back to our room and passed out on the floor next to the minibar, the only thing we hadn't destroyed. We drank all night long, talking about Mom, June and my dad, wondering where they were. Were they okay? And what was going to happen next? We got up the next day at about 10:30am. Nothing had changed. My country had been invaded and no one knew anything about my family.

"Look, it's going on three days now, Uncle Dennis," I said. "I need to go to my dorm and transfer my stuff to Cooper's apartment. Summer classes have ended and they're getting ready for the fall semester. So I'll be back in a few hours. Call the number I gave you if you hear anything. I called Sarah to meet me at the dorm in an hour. She's been waiting for my call all morning."

I arrived at my dorm at about 2pm. Sarah wasn't there yet. I thought she must be mad at me for not calling her earlier.

The TV room, which usually only had five to eight students in it all day, was full of students watching CNN.

"Reem, over here!" John said, waving his hand.

"What's up, John?" I gave him the bro hand grab and shoulder pat.

"Bush! That's what's up! He just ordered like 20,000 US troops and 32 destroyers to the Gulf, man!"

John and all the students in our building were interested in what was going on with Iraq now.

"Dude, you got a lot of messages from your friends. I left them on your desk. What are you going to do? Are you coming back for the fall semester?" John asked.

He was a good friend, but he was asking a lot of painful questions. Sarah's beautiful face appeared in the crowd. I just stared directly at her, fighting back the tears. The smell of her hair and the warmth of her embrace felt amazing, it gave me more fuel to burn in my heart.

"Oh Reem, I'm just sick for you over all this. Have you been able to talk to your family?" Sarah asked in my ear as we hugged.

"No, not a word. I just came to move my stuff into Cooper's place. He'll be there in an hour. Can you and John help?"

I looked at John and back to Sarah.

"Whatever you need, Reem," John said, Sarah just smiled.

I opened the door to the dorm room. Scotty and Juanito were standing over Juanito's desk. They had three more days of summer schedule then they were going to rent a place off-campus in two weeks. That was what I thought they were discussing when out of the corner of my eye, I noticed Juanito was trying to hide a white posterboard sign. I continued to my side of the room and started to look at the messages on my desk. John was still in the doorway staring at Scotty and Juanito.

"What the fuck is that, Scott!" John said, with a tone of accusation in his voice.

Scotty stood in front of Juanito, blocking his view of what he had.

"That's none of your business, John! Just leave him alone!" Scotty said, as if protecting Juanito from John. But why would Scotty need to protect Juanito from John? I wondered.

"John, are you okay? What's going on?" I asked.

"Yeah, what's going on, Scott? Juanito? Tell him! Tell your fucking roommate who you've spent two

years living with! What you've both been up to!"
John demanded as Sarah came into the room.

"Go fuck yourself, John! We can have our opinion
if we want to," Scotty snapped back at John.

"Alright then, tell him. You're a fucking coward!
Tell him about your opinion, you piece of shit!"

"Wow, come on John, that's a little bit too much,"
I said, trying to make peace.

I wasn't sure why John was so mad at them.

Scotty just looked at me, then Juanito stepped in
front of Scotty and showed me the sign he'd made. It
was a white posterboard with red letters on it spelling out *NO BLOOD FOR OIL*.

That was when it hit me. Some students thought
it was cool and hip to protest even if they had no idea
what the hell they were saying. I just looked at them
both without saying a word. I thought it was best to
let them see the pain in my eyes instead.

"Yup, while you've been trying to reach your
family, two of your so-called friends have been organizing a protest against your country," John said as
he grabbed the sign out of Juanito's hand and ripped
it up.

Scotty jumped on John. They both scuffled on
the ground, hitting and wrestling until John sat on
Scotty.

"Okay John, let him up!" I demanded.

"TRAITOR," John said as he got off Scotty.

"You're an asshole, John!" Scotty said as he tried
to compose himself.

I walked up to Juanito. "You could have just asked
me what was happening over there. But you're in
love with the idea of protesting anything. You have
no clue what people are going through over there, do

you?" I got close to Juanito's face. "My family isn't able to call and tell me they're okay. They might be the Kuwaitis you see on the news channels being killed in the streets and in front of their homes. The Iraqis are raping my women and killing my brothers, so that they don't have to pay back all the money they borrowed from us. But you don't want to see that. You want to think this is just like the sixties again and protest the evil government."

Juanito's small mind hadn't heard a word I said. "Reem, I'm sorry. But this is something I believe in," he said, with a look of arrogance on his face.

That look set me off instantly. I grabbed him by his jean jacket and threw him across his desk. I started hitting him with everything I had. I could hear Sarah screaming at me to stop, but it felt so good to hit him. My quiet desperation and helplessness over my family had turned into rage. I didn't think I was hitting Juanito. I was hitting what he represented: lies, ignorance, and students protesting something they had no idea about.

CHAPTER 24

Cooper put down some eggs and toast on the table. He moved the plate closer to me. The kitchen table in his apartment was made from Formica and chrome bars. The yellow floral design on the top of the table matched the wallpaper in the kitchen. It was kind of him to make me some food, but I had no appetite. Why has no one heard from my family, I thought to myself. I had trouble concentrating on anything these days, and my thoughts about what was going on with my family consumed me. Had they been taken prisoner? Had they been killed right away? Were they in hiding? I'd been waiting for a phone call for almost a week. Sarah, John, and Cooper were the only ones who seemed to have my back. Scotty and Juanito, with a lot of other so-called friends, were out protesting US involvement.

"Come on, Reem, try and eat something. You need to do something to take your mind off all this," Cooper said, sitting next to me, shoveling down his food.

If they captured my family, were they torturing my brother or my father? I needed to do something. I needed to get up off this chair and make my way back home. These were all the thoughts that were going through my head every second.

Cooper's doorbell rang out. Shit, I thought, I bet it's campus security coming to arrest me for hitting Juanito. John had jumped on top of me before I'd hurt Juanito too severely and brought me over to Cooper's to let me cool down.

"Cooper, there's a guy out there looking for you and your friend. He says he knows you," the voice from the hallway said. Cooper's downstairs neighbor must have seen someone outside Cooper's place. To get into the apartment building, you needed a key or to be buzzed in by a resident. Cooper stepped out and into the hall where he could see the man standing at the bottom of the steps.

"Hey! Ben, come on in!" Cooper said, with a tone of a pleasant surprise.

Cooper nodded at his neighbor as he walked down to open the door leading up to Cooper's apartment.

"Reem, it's Ben!" Cooper said.

I got up from the table and walked over to greet Ben. Ben was right at the door by the time I got there.

"Ben! How are you? Where's Danny?" I asked while giving Ben my skydiving, football playing partner in crime a big hug.

Ben was dressed in his Marine camouflage uniform.

"That's why I'm here. I'm picking Danny up and we're heading over to Twentynine Palms. We just got called up. We're heading to your neck of the woods. Saudi Arabia, buddy. I just wanted to check on you and see how your dad and brother were doing."

He slammed his hat on the coffee table next to the couch as we all sat down in the living room. I sat across from him in a cushioned chair. Cooper just stood next to me.

"I've not heard a word from anyone except Donna Dunn. She and her family left weeks before all this went down. She calls me ten times a day. Rico and Dad had a plan in place, but June had a seizure and needed to be hospitalized," I said while feeling the pain grow in my heart. But seeing Ben in his uniform and him telling me they were going over there had also lit a fire in my stomach.

"Oh, Reem, I'm sorry to hear that. I'm sure they're okay. Your dad and brother are smart, I'm sure they'll get out of there." Ben was trying to say something comforting, but I was so tired of people trying to comfort me. It had gotten to the point I'd had to tell Sarah to give me some space. That hadn't gone over very well. Sarah was so angry with me. I was fighting and pushing her away during my moment of greatest need, according to her. I was going to have to fix that fence later, I thought.

"Thank you, buddy, for your reassurances, but it doesn't help at all. I need to get over there. I need to get into the fight."

I turned my head to the side so Ben couldn't see my eyes tearing up with anger. Ben got up and walked over to me. He put his hand on my shoulder, looking down at me. When I lifted my head, I saw him smiling. The look of confusion on my face made him laugh.

"Reem, if you want to get into the fight, just join the Marines!"

The look on his face said to me that he knew something. But what?

"I'm not a citizen. The Marines won't take me!"

Was that the case, I thought, or did I just assume it?

"You're right, Reem, you must be a citizen to join the military. Naturalized citizenship or regular. Oh yeah, and for those that have a permanent residency," Ben said with a massive grin on his face.

"Are you fucking with me!? I can join!?" I asked as I busted out of my chair.

Standing in front of Ben looking astonished, I felt that my prayers had been answered. An uneasy feeling came over my body as if Ben were going to say "Just kidding" or we'd find out we were both wrong. This was my one chance to do something for my family. I couldn't sit around and watch it all on TV.

"Hey man, the protesters are right! No blood for oil! But I'll go over there and kill me a bunch of Iraqis to save my friends in Kuwait. And if I'm going to go get my ass shot off for your country, your ass is coming too!" Ben said.

"Ben, are you sure about this?" Cooper asked. He was apprehensive for me. He didn't want me to get my hopes up to have them smashed.

"Yes, I already talked to my commanding officer. I told him the situation that Reem was in. Captain Hickam said that if Reem was willing to join and had a permanent residency card, the Marines would be glad to take him, especially since he can speak Arabic.

Shit, he said that alone would make him valuable to the Corps! Not many of us can speak Arabic," Ben said.

He was trying to finish talking to Cooper, but I was hugging him so hard he stopped.

"I'm just waiting for Danny to get here. We're both going to take you to the recruiter's office. Do you have all your documents and ID?" Ben asked after pushing me away.

I opened the box that had all my papers in it. I looked down, and there it was. The paperwork Dad and BJ had put together for me. Jeremy Cook US State Department – I still had the business card and my permanent residency card.

"I got it!" I professed as I held my papers in the air.

Then I noticed Danny, standing in the front doorway. My hand fell and I was immediately overcome with emotion. Seeing Danny and Ben in their uniforms gave me an overwhelming sense of hope.

"If you're going to get this emotional seeing another guy, maybe boot camp isn't right for you," Danny said.

We all started laughing. Danny gave me a hug and a punch in the arm.

"I thought you left the Marines and started school. They're going to let you back in?" I asked him.

"Reem, once you're a Marine, you're always a Marine! HOO RA!!" Danny and Ben yelled together.

"Reem, you're not going anywhere until you talk to Sarah. You can't just make this choice without her," Cooper said.

Cooper looked sad about something, but I didn't want to ask. He was always thinking five steps ahead of any situation. I didn't want to hear him give me a reason why not to join the Marines.

"You're right, Cooper," I said. "Can you give me some time, guys?"

Danny looked at his watch. "I don't know… Ben, what time did you say we needed to get Reem's vagina over to MEPS?"

Ben started laughing again and grabbed his hat. "We'll be over at Joe's having one last cold one with Cooper when you're done."

Ben and Danny loved hanging out with Cooper. He was a lot older and outranked them by a lot. Cooper had been a Navy Seal for eight years before getting out and starting his security firm. Most people would see Cooper as young, but in fact, he was forty-two. He loved telling his friends, "I'm black; that's why I don't crack."

I thought about asking Sarah to come over to Cooper's to talk, but what I needed to say should be heard by all of her family. I'd gotten to know them over the last few semesters. We'd crossed over the line of just acquaintances and started building a real relationship.

The phone only rang once before Sarah answered it. "Hi, it's me," I said as I realized she'd been waiting for my phone call. What an asshole I am, I thought to myself.

"What's going on? Is everything okay? Have you contacted your family yet?"

Sarah's questions hit me fast and hard.

"No, nothing yet. But something else has come up. I want to come over and talk to you and your family about it."

The tone in my voice was calm and serious, which

was a significant change from the last few days, and probably confused Sarah.

"Okay, we're all here. Just come over," Sarah said softly, probably sensing she wasn't going to like what I had to tell all of them.

I was at her parents' place in ten minutes, even though they lived twenty minutes away. My engine smelled like burning oil, I thought as I walked up to the door. Sarah, her mom and dad invited me in. We sat down in the kitchen. I explained that I was leaving school and joining the Marines right away. I continued about how I needed to do this not only for my family, but because it was who I was as a person. That I couldn't just sit and do nothing. After I was finished with my speech, I looked over at Sarah. She had tears running down her cheeks.

"Reem, these past few days have taken my feet out from me. All the pain and anguish you've been going through, I can see in your eyes and feel in your touch. That's why I'm so scared for you and our future. If you need to join the Marines, then do it! I'll support you in anything you choose..."

"We...We support you!" Mr. and Mrs. Long said abruptly.

I looked at all of them and felt for the first time that everything was going to be okay. I said my goodbyes to them, and Sarah insisted on coming to the recruiters with me. We jumped into my Jeep and headed for Joe's Bar to get the guys. On the drive over Sarah laid down the law.

"One, you must write to me every week even if you can't mail it. I want a comprehensive journal of your time away from me. Two, don't do anything stupid or overly risky. And three, come home to me so we can start our lives together."

Sarah placed her head on my right arm and wrapped her soft hand around my arm while I was driving. We pulled into the bar. I looked at Sarah for a moment…

"I love you, Sarah. I'm sorry for hurting you with my stupidity. I'll try to work on that. Keeping you happy and safe is my biggest quest. I want to marry you as soon as we can. Please be patient with me. I'm still trying to learn how to be a good man," I said.

Sarah just sat there for a minute and kissed me.

"You're a good man, Reem. You just haven't figured that out yet," she said.

CHAPTER 25

First Sergeant Santiago Coats sat behind his desk looking over my Armed Services Vocational Aptitude Battery test, also known as the ASVAB test. Sergeant Coats' face, arms, body, and uniform looked like they were chiseled out of marble. The look on his face dictated the mood in the office, it seemed. He had a sense of humor; after looking at me very skeptically and then back at the papers in his hand, he finally said, "You made that test your bitch, didn't you?"

He cracked a smile that was so out of character, it was a little off-putting. But I nervously laughed just the same.

"Why do you want to be a Marine?" Sergeant Coats asked.

It was obvious why I wanted to join, but Ben had told me what to say and how to say it.

"I know that I can be a better person and like my best friend Ben, I want to be a good example to all that know me. I believe the Marines can help me be more than I am."

Sergeant Coats sat back in his leather armchair, the newest piece of furniture in the office, as he considered my answer. I could feel my heart beating through my chest as this man held my fate in his hands. If he didn't let me join the Marines, I didn't know what I could do. Sarah and Danny sat in the lobby of the recruiter's office. Ben and I sat side by side in front of the gray metal desk. The place smelled like boiled chicken from the Chinese restaurant next door. There was also a donut shop and dry cleaners nearby, so it didn't surprise me when I saw Danny eating a donut.

"Sorry, I'm not buying it. If you don't tell me the real reason you want to join, I'll kick your ass out on the street. I don't care how high you scored on the ASVAB!" Sergeant Coats said, looking very intimidating.

I could feel my heart breaking. This asshole isn't going to let me join, I thought. My emotions began to take over, and I stood up from my chair and leaned over Sergeant Coats' desk.

"You're right!! That's not the reason I want to join!! I want to kill every fucking Iraqi standing in Kuwait right now!!! I want to rain down so much fire and shit on them that their great-grandchildren can feel it in their DNA!! I want to go scorch earth on the whole fucking country and shove my fist down Hussein's lying piece of shit throat and pull out his beating heart!!" I could feel my eyes filling with tears, my hands shaking with anger.

"Well, okay then, I can help you with that, son! They'll be looking at you in boot camp, Reem. The Marines will want to know where your loyalties lie. You need to put aside any patriotism toward any country other than the United States of America. Only then will you be allowed to graduate and call yourself a Marine. They'll wash you out of boot camp if you're not one hundred percent committed to God and Country."

I pushed my feelings aside and thanked the Sergeant.

"Let's get you processed," he said.

Ben had his arms folded sitting there listening with a smirk on his face. After my paperwork had been completed, he stood up. "Come on, Reem, I need to get you over to MEPS for a job," he said.

"When do you ship out, Sergeant?" Sergeant Coats asked Ben.

"Tomorrow evening," Ben answered while giving him a fist bump, hand slap, knuckle-flap. Son of a bitch!!! They know each other!! Ben's just breaking my balls, I thought to myself as he walked quickly to the door.

I caught up to Ben in the parking lot with Sarah and Danny behind me. "You're an asshole!" I said as I jumped into the driver's seat.

Danny and Ben started laughing.

"What? What did Ben do now?" Danny asked, still laughing.

"You both know the Sergeant, don't you?" I asked.

I looked in my rearview mirror to see Ben telling Danny what I'd said to Sergeant Coats. Danny, of course, laughed it up. Sarah just sat there holding on to every precious second, we had left together.

"You both can go…"

"Careful there, Reem, in about eight hours we're going to outrank you. You better watch your step, recruit. I'll call someone I know and have you doing calisthenics till you drop," Ben said, interrupting my profanity.

We got to the processing station in El Segundo right on time. As I was looking for a job -a MOD, they called it – I came across what seemed like a sign from fate.

0326 Reconnaissance Marine, Parachute Diver Qualified

MGySgt-Pvt

It took all of two seconds to pick my job, as if someone had put that Rate in front of me. My ASVAB score opened a lot of jobs to me, but when I looked down and saw Recon Parachute, I knew that was what I wanted.

I realized I was being fast-tracked into the Marine system. It would take two more days to get my lab results back from my physical. Exam tests were usually given to an auditorium of people, not just one person in a classroom. I'd already sworn in and signed my contract. Ben and Danny shipped out the next day to Saudi Arabia. They told me they would keep an eye out for me when I was finished with boot camp.

"I need to say something to the two of you before you leave." I turned and faced Ben and Danny. "I'm trying to find the right words to express my gratitude to the both of you for all you've done for me and my family," I said, trying not to get too emotional.

"Reem, thank you for saying that and the next time we see you, you'll be one of our brothers. You'll be a Marine and have new brothers who you'll trust with your life," Ben said.

"Make us proud, Marine!" Danny said while shaking my hand. The emotional weight of the moment wasn't lost on us. They were headed to war, and I was on my way to boot camp.

Sarah was going to take me to the recruiter's office in two days. I had to report for basic training on that Monday, the 20th. The recruiter told me my division had already started their processing, but they were going to have me process and join my division by the 24th. That gave them two days to process me in before I joined my squad. It turned out that Sergeant Coats was a nice guy once you got to know him. They were excited to have someone who could speak not only Arabic but French as well. Sarah had John and some of her friends come over for a goodbye party for me on the 19th. She was happy that I didn't have to leave that Friday. I guessed Sarah thought they took you the same day, but Danny had explained it was a long process to even get to the point of leaving for boot camp. I was lucky, not having to wait.

"Reem, you have a phone call," Heather, Sarah's little sister, yelled out the back door. We had a barbecue going in the backyard, and John had brought over some horseshoes. We were playing with Sarah's dad and uncles. I couldn't hear Heather yelling because they were being so loud.

"What?" I motioned to her with my hands and shoulders.

"You have a call on the phone! I think it's Cooper."

I ran into the kitchen. Heather pointed at the phone on the kitchen bar.

"Yes! This is Reem," I said into the phone.

"Hey, it's Cooper! Some guy named Cook from the State Department called and said he's coming over at three! He has some info on your family! You need to get your ass over here!" Cooper sounded out of breath.

"Holy shit! I'm on my way!" I said, looking at the time. It was five to three! Shit! "Did you talk to him?" I asked.

"No, he left a message on the machine," Cooper replied.

I arrived at Cooper's apartment, not realizing I'd just run out of Sarah's house without saying anything to anyone. Mr. Cook was sitting on the couch waiting for me when I entered the apartment. He was an older white guy with bad taste in suits. I think it was polyester, but I couldn't be sure. I shook his hand and sat across from him.

"Your message said that you might have some info on my family?" I quickly inquired.

"Well, I have some news, but the situation is very volatile and changing constantly. What we know is that your family is alive and in hiding. Your brother Rico, we have confirmed, was part of the resistance at Dasman Palace. Our sources confirmed he was with Fahd Al-Ahmad when he was killed. Fahd, not your brother."

I didn't feel the tears on my face the whole time we talked.

"Rico was fighting at Dasman Palace?" I asked.

"Yes, that's why Saddam's Ba'ath party wants your brother and father. They're trying to round up all members of the government and anybody associated with the Kuwaiti resistance. We'd kept in contact with your father, but I lost touch four days ago. That's why we know he's hiding with your mother and brother. We don't know where in the city he's hiding – I was hoping you might have some information on the location."

Before I could even respond, Cooper had pulled out his weapon from the back of his Hawaiian print shirt and aimed it at Mr. Cook. He ordered him to get on the ground.

"Don't you fucking move a muscle!! Reem, grab his identification now! Get it from his jacket!!" Cooper demanded.

He wasn't kidding around. His arm and forearm were flexed, holding the weapon on Mr. Cook while barking orders.

"Don't shoot me!! I'm just trying to get some information!!" Mr. Cook said as Cooper threw him to the floor, not moving the gun away from his head.

"If you're not who you say you are, I'm going to pull the fucking trigger myself!!" I said as I rifled through his wallet and some papers in his side pocket.

"Reem, fuck that! Look in the white pages for the State Department's phone number and call them. Let's try to verify this son of a bitch!!" Cooper said, thinking on his feet.

He didn't want to trust any information Mr. Cook had on him. I found a local number for the State Department in Los Angeles, but I didn't know what agency to call for. There must have been twenty-five numbers. I got the phone and started dialing.

"Oh wait, I have his card in my room!" I remembered; my dad had given it to me. I knew exactly where I'd left it. When I emerged from the room, Cooper was face to face with Mr. Cook.

"Okay, Mr. Cook, what's your office number?" I asked, looking at the business card.

The number on the card had a DC area code, so if he gave me one from LA, I'd know he was lying. Mr. Cook told me the correct number. He told us to call it and ask for his immediate supervisor, which we did. Everything checked out.

"Sorry, man, I just needed to check out everything before giving you info like that," Cooper said.

Mr. Cook stood up and was brushing off some dirt and straightening his suit.

"Dear Lord, man! I was trying to get a little information. I didn't know you had Robocop here ready to kill!" Mr. Cook said, very agitated over the manhandling.

"Hey, look man! I'm sorry! But if you're going to ask questions like that, you should call me into your office where I can see it's a government building. How would I know that you're not someone out to get my family? You shouldn't be asking questions like that if you're not in an office," I said, with Cooper nodding in agreement.

"Well, I thought it was a long shot that you would know anything. I wanted to come out to meet you to tell you we had some information about your family," Mr. Cook said.

He was putting his wallet back together and not looking at me.

"Well, it's a good thing because I do know where they would be hiding."

Both Cooper and Cook looked at me in shock.

"Really? Are you serious?" Cook asked.

They both huddled up next to me and we spoke in low voices.

"A few months before the invasion, my dad was the only one trying to sound the alarm about the potential of an Iraq invasion. So, Dad had a carpenter seal off the back two rooms of the Dunns' apartment house with sheetrock and paint. You couldn't even tell there were two more rooms back there by going into the hallway," I said.

"Your dad contacted me at the same time. He couldn't get anybody to listen to him in his office. NSA sent him a satellite phone, but it must have malfunctioned or stopped working four days ago. The communication was terrible; they could only make out certain things your dad was telling them," Mr. Cook said. "We have people on the ground loyal to us. Now that we know approximately where your family is, we can try to get him a new phone."

"Look, don't take any risks. My little sister is sick, she has epilepsy. You can't take any chances. Only use people you trust with your life! Nobody else! I'll be over there soon. I leave on Monday," I said, looking right at Mr. Cook.

"What are you talking about? You're going over there? You can't go, they'll catch you," Cook said, confused by my statement.

"No, I joined the United States Marine Corps. I ship out for boot camp on Monday," I said with a sense of purpose.

"I thought foreigners weren't allowed to join the military," Mr. Cook said, questioning my statement.

"I agree, foreigners aren't allowed to join the military, but permanent residents can," I replied.

"Holy shit!" A look came over Mr. Cook's face. "You used your residency card? And you joined the military? Do you know how much shit is going to rain down on me for pulling those strings for your dad? I'm in big fucking trouble," he said in a panic.

"Relax, Cook. They didn't even give it a second thought. No one's going to find out how I got my residency card. You're just freaking out for no reason," I said.

Just then, Sarah showed up with my Uncle Dennis. She, of course, was worried after I'd run out of the party.

Uncle Dennis was there to help see me off the following day. I'd called him after getting back that evening from the recruiter's office and told him about joining up. He was incredibly supportive and happy for me, but he was still drunk from the day before. I guessed that was how he was dealing with the situation.

"Reem, they're going to investigate how you got a residency card. If you go for a top-secret clearance, they'll investigate your status and how you got your residency. My ass will be on the chopping block," Cook said.

"Look, you got nothing to worry about. If anybody at the State Department says anything to you, just let them know you were doing a personal favor for me," Uncle Dennis said.

"I'm sorry, you must forgive me. Who are you?" Mr. Cook asked.

"I'm sorry, let me introduce myself. I'm Dr. Dennis Gabriel Green, Richard Cheney's physician. If Reem hadn't been able to get into the military on his own, I would have just made one phone call and it would have been done. I can't tell you how proud I am of my nephew for taking up arms against our common enemy. He is a great American."

Uncle Dennis seemed to be completely sober now and in control of his anger.

He was lying about Cheney, though. He'd met Dick Cheney in an elevator in Washington DC. Cheney had a bad cough and Uncle Dennis had told him that he should have it looked at. Afterwards he'd called everyone he knew and said that by giving Dick Cheney medical advice technically he'd treated him. It felt good to hear Uncle Dennis say words like that to someone else about me. I couldn't express the closeness I felt to a person who was supposed to just be an uncle and not a best friend, mentor, and father figure.

CHAPTER 26

Ahmed, Kuwait City

Life in Kuwait after the initial invasion was hard. You always lived in fear that they were going to find you and torture or even kill you, like they'd done to so many others. Every time Rico went out to pick up some food or find June some medicine, I said a prayer that he would return home safely. The Kuwaiti resistance movement had formed quickly after the invasion. My wife Sue had begged our son Rico not to get involved in the movement. She said it was too dangerous and the family needed him. I couldn't help disagreeing with her.

"Rico, is that you?" I asked.

I could hear Rico drag his feet as he entered the apartment. It was kind of a signal, the sound of foot-dragging.

"Yes, it's me, Dad," he replied.

I opened the big styrofoam flap at the bottom of the wall, and Rico slid his body into our room.

"I was able to find some more stuff. Hold the door open and let me drag it in."

Rico dragged a blanket in with food and some boxes on it. When it was in the room, I shut the flap.

"What is all this stuff, son? Where did you get it?" I asked.

I was looking at what seemed to be a treasure trove of supplies.

"Dad, you wouldn't believe how big the resistance movement has become. People are printing up pamphlets in their own homes and distributing them. Some of my friends have taken up sniper positions. There are certain areas of town that the Iraqi soldiers don't dare go into because they know we will shoot and kill them," Rico said.

He was excited to be a part of the resistance, but my wife and I were so afraid it would get him killed.

"Rico, what do you think they're going to do in retaliation for the sniper attacks? Son, you must be more careful. Stay out of the main resistance. We need you to keep us going with supplies. Every day it gets more and more dangerous. You can't be taking chances like this," I said while June and my wife started going through all the items Rico had brought home.

"Dad, you don't have to worry! They don't even need a leader; it's more of a horizontal leadership. Everybody is doing their part. No one person is the face of the resistance. Besides, they still have pictures of you and me at the checkpoints. I'm not stupid; I'm not going to walk into their hands and let them torture or kill me," Rico said.

My attention turned back towards the items Rico had brought in. The food was in good supply for now. But he had also brought with him a small suitcase that looked like a satellite phone.

"Is that what I think it is?" I asked, as I opened the case and discovered one of the most beautiful looking satellite phones I'd ever seen. This thing must have been costly. I had no idea how Rico was able to get hold of one. The phone Mr. Cook had sent me was a piece of junk. It had only worked a little and then stopped after the fourth day.

"That's right, Dad, this is a state-of-the-art satellite phone. Courtesy of the CIA. They've been able to sneak in a handful of them. The next two boxes are full of money. We all got two boxes full of cash to bribe Iraqi soldiers to look the other way. I've moved a family to live in front of the apartment. They're going to help us with food and info in exchange for a place to stay," Rico said, looking incredibly pleased with himself.

We had talked about it several times. We needed to find a trustworthy family to live in the apartment house. Sue was cooking in the kitchen and preparing meals for us, but if someone were to enter the house where no one lived and find the kitchen was being used, that might give us away.

"Rico, they might be able to track a satellite phone and discover us. We need to do something with it. Maybe we can put it in a secret location and use it when we need it. What do you think, son?" I asked.

"I could hide it in the building next door. It's been damaged heavily, and no one lives in it. One of the air conditioning systems has a big hollow spot. I can hide it inside one of the vents. It's surrounded by metal and hard to detect," Rico said.

We agreed, and he set out to hide the satellite phone. Inside the case was a letter from the CIA informing us not to use the phone unless we had information, we found to be significant and pressing. The phone would be hard for anyone to track, but we shouldn't take any chances.

After about two weeks, my predictions of Iraqi revenge played out.

"Are you okay, son? What's wrong?" I'd just woken up that morning and saw Rico sitting in the corner of the room crying.

"They shot and killed all of them. Then they placed their bodies in front of their families' homes," Rico said in a low voice.

I walked over and sat down next to him. He smelled like gasoline and smoke. Whatever had happened had scared Rico. I wanted to help, but at what cost? Whatever the retaliation was going to be, I knew it would be painful for us all.

"I know I've not raised you with a strong religious background because of my anger and hatred for organized religion, but the people that are doing this have a special place in hell waiting for them. They are not human, son. They are animals. Like every bloodthirsty animal, they will be put down. One day soon, you will see an American hero, come through that door and liberate our great country," I said, trying to comfort Rico from the horrors that he'd just witnessed in the streets of his own country. The Iraqis had kidnapped, tortured and were now killing our citizens. Word was spreading like wildfire. The resistance emboldened itself and started attacking Iraqi army bases and stepped-up sniper attacks. Rico wouldn't go out to help the resistance anymore. The Iraqis had placed a more significant price on his head; a Kuwaiti being tortured had given Rico's name to the Iraqis as one of the resistance organizers. Luckily, Rico had never let anyone know where he was staying. Not even his best friends knew of our location.

"I sure hope you're right, Dad. I wish they would hurry up and do it. At least Reem is safe. I wish we could use the phone and talk to him. It will only call out to a CIA number," Rico said reflectively.

In October, the Iraqi government had opened the Kuwaiti border to let anyone exit the country. This presented a problem because there were rumors, they were doing it to locate people who had been in hiding. But it was our chance to get the women and children out.

"This is our chance, Rico! We can get the girls out of here and into Saudi Arabia now," I insisted.

"What if it's a trap, Dad! What if they're using this to get us out of our hiding spot – capture the girls to get to you or me? There are a lot of Kuwaitis missing or unaccounted for; are you willing to take that chance with their lives? No! We need to stay here and wait for the Americans!" Rico argued.

"How are they going to screen that many people crossing the border all at the same time, Rico? I'm telling you this is our chance to get the girls out to safety! I know the things you've seen have scared you. But sometimes you must take a chance, son!" I argued back.

"What the hell are you two arguing about? This family is going to stay together! If you're staying, we're staying! If you're going, we're all going, Ahmed!" Sue said, visibly angry.

"You don't understand, Sue! It's too risky for Rico and me to leave across the border, but we can disguise you and June to get you both into Saudi Arabia," I explained.

"Ahmed, you're my life, and I won't leave your side. So, if you're not going to cross the border, neither am I," my wife said, making her decision clear.

Life in Kuwait City was anything but routine. All the people who had left the city when the border had been opened had taken manpower away from the resistance. Rico was playing it smart and staying out of the riskier situations the resistance was trying to pull off. With his name and picture out there, he would only go out to get food and supplies when we needed them.

"Dad, you ready to go?" Rico asked.

"Yes, I need to get my sandals on, then we can leave, son," I replied.

Every Friday morning Rico and I would go down to block 17 where we would have tea and conversation with our countrymen. A lot of the older men loved to hear Rico's account of the battle he'd fought at Dasman Palace. I was happy to finally get out of the apartment. It seemed that the Iraqis had more important things to do than keep looking for us. Block 17 was too far to walk, about three miles, so we would drive. I would get up and kiss the girl's goodbye. We would say a prayer as a family, then Rico and I would leave for about four hours.

"It's okay, son, just leave the car there, I don't want to get too close to the building," I said.

I liked to park two blocks away from the tea house and walk the rest of the way just in case there was a checkpoint on the other side of the street. Sometimes they would have it and sometimes they would not.

"Hey Dad, look! They're taking down the billboard over there."

Rico was right, the billboard that always gave us some information about the resistance had been destroyed. Rico and I walked carefully behind the building in case Iraqis were waiting for us by the tea house.

"It's my good friends Sami and Abdul!" I proclaimed as we walked into the tea house.

I had a lot of friends that would meet us and discuss the occupation. We would also talk about the US, and the coalition that would start the ground campaign.

"You know that George Bush knows what he is doing. He will come in and destroy all these motherless assholes, they will all go to hellfire where they belong," my friend Sami said.

"Have you heard any news?" I asked.

"Nothing has changed. The UN has given them until January 15th to leave or face the consequences. The forces being sent to Saudi Arabia are in the hundreds of thousands. Saddam can't win – he'll have to leave soon," Abdul said. Abdul was Sami's brother.

"We're still getting a lot of support from the United States," Rico said. "Most of my friends in the resistance have left for Saudi Arabia. There is only a small part of us now."

"We must be careful more than ever now. The Palestinians that are loyal to the Ba'ath party betrayed block five. Rumor is a lot of Kuwaitis were killed because of it. I don't trust any Palestinian at all," Rico said.

His eyes teared up a little at the thought of Kuwaitis being killed by a traitor. I looked over at Abdul and Sami; before I could say anything, Sami held up his hand to stop me.

"Palestinians? Do you know which Palestinians it was, Rico?" Sami asked, with a high level of stress in his voice.

"No! But you can't trust any Palestinian, half of them side with Saddam Hussein, and the other half are for sale," Rico said.

"What's wrong, Sami?" I quickly asked, seeing the fear in his eyes.

"The owners of this place left to Saudi Arabia during the border crossing; a Palestinian family now runs the tea house."

Fear immediately gripped Rico and me. I started looking around at the people inside the tea house. They were all Kuwaitis.

"Look outside!!" Rico said under his breath.

Sami just looked straight at me; his back was to the door of the tea house. I was facing forward and could see four men in uniform sitting in a Toyota. They looked like they were waiting for a signal. Behind the makeshift bar were two Palestinians serving tea. They looked to be in their twenties or thirties. I could tell they were no friends of ours.

"Let's just slowly get up and go to the back of the house," Abdul said. But I could see it was too late. The two men behind the bar had just waved at the door. The men from outside were out of the car and running toward the tea house. The Palestinians looked to be grabbing something from underneath the bar.

"It's too late!! Rico!!" I yelled, grabbing Rico's arm. Both of us ran to the back of the tea house. I heard the shooting start: five or six shots rang out as we went for the back door. When I looked behind me, Sami was on the ground, and Abdul had his hands up in the air while being shot by one of the Palestinians. The four Iraqi soldiers were shooting all the men that were seated in the front of the tea house. One of the rounds grazed my leg and tore part of my kneecap. As we reached the back of the house, I fell on my hands and face.

"Dad!!"

Rico lifted me off the ground, but my weight caught him off balance and we both fell over some milk crates in the backyard. The stack of crates landed on both of us, which gave us enough camouflage when the Iraqi ran out the back door in pursuit – they ran right past us.

Rico had rolled into a cubbyhole against the house. We both laid in it with a tarp over us for a day and a half. We dared not move a muscle or breathe too heavily.

"Dad, you have to keep that cloth tighter on your leg," Rico said. He was more concerned about my leg than I was. There wasn't that much bleeding. The bullet had only cut my leg open a bit, but I thought it might have been knocked out of joint, which was why I couldn't walk on it.

The next evening, we both agreed Rico would crawl out and see if all was clear. Rico came back quickly.

"The Palestinian family is in the tea house celebrating. There are no soldiers around anymore. Here, Dad, they left two guns on the back porch. Let's get out of here."

Rico handed me one of the guns he'd stolen. As I stood up, one of the milk crates that had been leaning against the house almost fell but Rico caught it, so it didn't make a sound. I slowly put my weight on my damaged leg. I could feel the knee popping back in place, but I held in the pain. It felt so good to stand on it. We started to walk quickly away from the house toward our car. I suddenly stopped; I could hear laughter coming from the tea house. The image of Sami on the floor and Abdul shot with his hands up sparked a rage inside me. Rico was five feet in front of me when he realized I'd stopped walking. When he turned around and saw me, he knew exactly what I had in mind.

"You're damn right, Dad! I'm in!"

I couldn't even feel the pain in my leg anymore. My anger had taken hold of all my senses. It wasn't just the fact that my friends had been betrayed and killed by these people at the tea house. The PLO and their leader Yasser Arafat's support for Saddam's invasion brought my anger over the top. Rico investigated the window from the side of the tea house to see if there were any Iraqis around. He calmly walked up to me.

"They're completely off guard. It looks like they just had dinner and started their celebration. I can't see any soldiers at all. We can calmly walk in there and shoot everyone. I think you should let me do it, Dad. I've killed before. You've never killed a living thing."

I smiled at Rico and checked my ammunition level in the magazine.

"Son, there comes a time in a man's life when he must do the unthinkable; this is one of those times," I said.

Rico and I walked calmly in through the back door. In the front parlor sat a father and three sons with the mother and daughter in law. The family had just eaten dinner. There was still blood on the floor that had not been cleaned up yet. What kind of people eat dinner with blood still on the floor, I thought, while Rico yelled for them to lie down on the ground.

"Get down on the floor, and don't say a fucking word!!! I'll shoot you in the fucking head!! Say one word and I'll do it!! Get down and shut up!!" Rico yelled.

I walked over to the youngest, who was about 28 or 29 years old, and without saying a word, shot him in the head. Cries rang out, I could hear the father begging us to take him and spare his family. I walked calmly over to the father and chambered another round.

"What has your religious ideology got you? You're a big piece of shit to allow your family and your children to believe that you're better than any other of God's creations!!!" I shouted as Rico and I both started shooting all of them until our ammo ran out.

"Come on, Dad, we got to get the fuck out of this place!!" Rico said.

We finally made it back to our apartment house extremely late that night. We decided to get rid of the car just in case someone had spotted it at the scene of our crime. I sat there in the car with Rico, and we both agreed never to discuss what we had done with anybody, ever. It hadn't made me feel good to murder that family the way I'd thought it would. I'd have the stain of their blood on my hands for the rest of my life. I kept looking at my hands. It was incredible to me the evil men could do to one another. What you didn't hear, and they never talked about, was the smell. Blood and death had a scent to them. My decision for vengeance hadn't come with the reality of the smell of blood or gunpowder.

Sue and June would be asleep when we walked into the apartment, I'd thought. But Sue had been up crying with June. They'd heard that the tea house had been ambushed the day before, but the soldiers didn't have our bodies.

"Ahmed, I can't take this anymore! You have to promise me, no more going out," Sue said as she kissed all over my face. She hadn't noticed my knee yet.

June had Rico in a bear hug. They were so scared we'd been shot and killed.

"What happened?" June asked.

We told them that we'd barely escaped with our lives and had had to hide for a day and a half.

The next day word got out about the Palestinian family being shot to death for collaborating with the Iraqis.

"Are you okay, Rico?" I asked.

"I've not been this good since I was at Dasman Palace," Rico said.

He loved killing Iraqis. But our days of running around gathering information were over. The Iraqi special services were hunting us down. Block by block. They knew it was us who had killed the Palestinians. Rico and I needed to concentrate on June and Sue. Keeping them safe was our priority.

CHAPTER 27

My dearest nephew,

It's with a heavy heart and a broken spirit that I need to inform you of the passing of my beloved father, your grandfather. He was a great man, Reem. Your uncle Jim was working on an excavator with your grandfather when he suddenly fell ill. Jim rushed him to the hospital where later that evening, grandpa passed away. Your letters and phone calls to him from boot camp meant the world to him. Knowing that his grandson had joined the Marines. To go and fight for your family was all anyone could ever talk about, especially your grandfather. He had ordered a Marine Corps flag and an American flag to put in his study alongside your picture.

Jim and grandmother assured me and everyone that grandpa didn't suffer much. He said he was tired and wanted the nurses to leave him alone so he could get some sleep. Grandma said it happened in the middle of the night while she sat next to him. Mom said that he opened his eyes and smiled at her then he was gone. Grandma will not make any arrangements until Susie Q is home. Since Dad wanted to be cremated, we will wait until that special time when we can all be together as a family once again. I'm sorry to report that I have no news about your family other than what you see on TV. We all love you and are so proud of you. When we heard that you made E3 in boot camp as a divisional scribe grandpa said, "that's my boy!"

I'm here in California. I delivered this letter to your commanding officer but asked not to see you, as I want you to concentrate 100% on your task at hand. When you complete your boot camp before you deploy, we'll get together then.

Just know of our love for you and how proud you made your grandfather in his last days. The stress on grandma and grandpa has been too much, and they want their daughter home and this whole thing to end.

I'll be honest, it was a little surprising to me to see you fit into the Marine Corps as well as you have. Your letters home to us are like pure gold. We love to hear what you're doing in boot camp and are incredibly surprised how easy it has been for you. I've never seen you as a soldier. I always think of you as Rico's younger brother,

*but you always have surprised me. We will all
be there at your graduation in three weeks. Be
strong for your grandma and me.*

Dennis

Marine Corps boot camp was one of the best experiences of my life until I received my uncle's letter. I'd learned everything I needed to know about myself during this period of my life. I'd also learned a thousand ways to destroy America's enemy. I'd also learned how to rely on myself and my fellow Marines. I understood my actions had consequences, and those consequences could hurt others. God, Family, Country, Devil Dogs, First to Fight, Once a Marine Always a Marine, Ooh Rah, Semper Fi – Marine Corps jargon is a unique language all of its own. My drill instructor gave me an hour to sit on my bunk and reflect on my grandfather. I did just that. I sat there and remembered all the times I had with him. Even when he let me drive the backhoe all by myself. When I would listen to his memories of WWII and how he'd asked Grandma to marry him. I remembered sitting on his lap when I was about five or six years old, smelling his Old Spice aftershave and feeling his unconditional love towards me.

"How are we doing in here, recruit?" Sergeant Villanueva asked.

The tone of his voice was foreign to me. I only heard the drill sergeant yelling orders.

"Ready, Sergeant!!" I snapped to attention and yelled.

"Recruit Al-Saba, join your unit! They're on the parade ground!"

I shoved my uncle's letter under my pillow and ran out to join Bravo company.

The rest of the day was rough. Most of the guys in Bravo company wanted to know what had happened. A few of them thought I was in trouble because the drill instructor had pulled me out of formation. When I informed them that I'd had lost a family member, the word quickly spread through my unit. Every hour or so, I would get condolences from one or two of my guys – I say my guys because I was the divisional yeoman; I took care of most of the paperwork for my division. If you've ever been in the military, you know you have to put your name on every single item they give you. Since I had the best penmanship in the division, the drill instructor had decided that I would be the one to complete the division's paperwork each week. That was why I'd been promoted to E3 while in boot camp.

"Can you believe it? It's finally here! Graduation day!" Pfc. Marks said.

"Did you get your phone call in?" Pfc. Jones asked Marks.

Marks replied with a thumbs up.

"You two dipshits better get your stuff off my rack," I said while pointing at them both.

"If DI Miller or Villanueva come in and see that we're not ready, they're going to recycle our asses!"

I wasn't going to have them screw up my graduation day by letting them make me late. Marks and Jones, better known as Kevin and Randy to the outside world, were two of the biggest fuckups in Bravo company. Not because they didn't know what to do or how to do it. No, no, it was because they liked to screw around so much and get us all in trouble. Thus, DI Miller and DI Girly had decided to put them both next to me so I could give them proper motivation. I'd completely failed. It was like watching an Abbott and Costello movie – you couldn't help but like them. But when someone made you laugh when your drill instructor was around, you'd do more pushups than you ever imagined you could. We all had Marks and Jones to thank for that.

"Will we be able to go with our family directly after graduation, Corporal?" Pfc. Marks asked.

"Yes, after the ceremony they'll dismiss our division. Then we can go be with our families," I replied.

Suddenly I heard DI Villanueva entering the barracks. I quickly turned around to yell at Marks and Jones, but Marks was slowly saluting a barracks wall, and Jones was doing pushups. I stood there between the two of them stunned. How did they know what to do? It looked like I was disciplining both of them.

DI Villanueva walked past me. "Good job," he said, then yelled "ORDERS ARE UP!" as he stapled four sheets of paper to the bulletin board. Our entire division ran to the boards to see what orders they'd received. I decided to wait until the line of recruits had thinned out. After about five minutes, I walked over and saw my orders: *LCpL Al-Saba, Mohammed First Marine Division Camp Pendleton.*

A wave of relief came over me. I'd done it. I'd completed my boot camp and been assigned to First Marine. The First Marine Division was already deployed to Saudi Arabia. I knew that my chances of going to fight for the liberation of Kuwait had just got a boost; for weeks now, my biggest fear had been that I would get picked for a division that wasn't going to Saudi.

Kevin and Randy, or should I say Marks and Jones, were at my bunk waiting for me. That could only mean one thing. They'd seen my orders and were in the same squad as me, First Marine. I'm never going to get away from these two knuckleheads, I thought. Pfc Randy Marks was the shorter of the two, Kevin Jones had to be almost four inches taller. They'd been friends since junior high and joined the Marines through the buddy system. Kevin was good looking and had a medium build with black hair. Randy was kind of ugly and had red hair. In any comedy routine, you always had a straight man and the one who would be goofy. You would have thought Kevin would be the straight guy, but that was Randy and Kevin was the goofy one.

"Let me guess. You two assholes are coming to First Marine division," I said.

Marks just smiled; Jones batted his eyes at me as if to say he loved me.

DI Miller yelled for us to report on the parade ground for graduation.

"I'm going to end up shooting the both of you," I said as I started running for the parade ground. I can honestly say never in my entire life had I ever looked so good and in such good shape. My uniform was perfect after marching and inspection. We listened to a quick speech given by our general, then we were dismissed and reunited with our families.

"Reem, I can't believe how big your arms and chest have gotten," Uncle Dennis said.

We were standing outside the base exchange while Grandma and Uncle Jim were picking up the photos they'd ordered of me.

"Yeah, I'm in the best shape of my life," I said.

When I'd walked up to meet my family after we'd all got our leave, Sarah's face had been the first I could make out. Wow, I thought, she said yes to me. We're going to get married just as soon as my family is all back together. I walked up to her, and we embraced and kissed. She looked amazing; I'd almost forgotten how beautiful she was. Sarah had a death grip on my arm ever since we'd been reunited. Uncle Jim and Dennis also hugged me and started making fun of my uniform.

"Come here, Reem," Grandma said.

When I saw my grandma's face, I lost it. I knew Uncle Dennis had told me to be strong in his letter, but the pain of seeing my grandma without my grandpa was too much.

Later that night we all went out to a steak house for dinner.

"Grandpa wanted to take you out for a steak dinner," Grandma said.

She looked so happy to be carrying out Grandpa's wishes.

"Grandma, I don't have any words. I only have my love and memories to take back to my mom. That will be the hardest thing I'll do over there, telling Mom about Grandpa," I said.

The tears filled my eyes again.

"So, Reem, tell us all about your basic training. Did you get to do anything fun?" Uncle Jim asked as he tried to change the topic. He was by himself; Aunt

Carole was pregnant again and wasn't allowed to fly out for the graduation. I'd get to talk to her on the phone later the next day. Cooper had also met us at the restaurant with John.

"I can honestly say it was one of the best experiences of my life. Of course, I was a little older than most of the guys in boot camp. But for some reason, I just seemed to fit into the Marine Corps. I love everything about it. I can't get enough of it; they're looking for educated people to do so many things. I'm thinking of completing college so I can request Officer Training School, but I'll have to talk with Sarah more about that," I said.

Sarah looked happy that I'd included her. It was about our future, after all.

"Did you have to go through the gas chamber?" Robert asked.

He'd come out with Grandma and brought his new girlfriend with him. Uncle Dennis didn't seem to like that he'd brought her, but Robert was happier than I'd seen him in a while.

"Oh yeah, the gas chamber sucked. You had to hold your hand under your chin and catch all the goop coming out of your face. By the time you get out into the open air, you want to die."

I laughed.

"How long do you get to stay with us, son?" Grandma asked.

"Two days, Grandma. I have to report to Camp Pendleton on Monday."

"Do you know if they're going to send you over there?" Grandma said.

I got up from my chair and walked to the head

of the table and sat next to her. I held her hand and looked into her eyes. It seemed that the whole restaurant fell silent.

"Grandma, I'm so much like my mom. I'm tough as nails. I'll get orders to go to Saudi Arabia, and I'll bring my family home."

The determination in my eyes gave my grandma hope that she would see my mom again. Grandma and I had a long talk that night. She was having some medical problems; Uncle Dennis had moved her to LA for the next six months for some treatments at UCLA. Uncle Dennis said that Grandma was going to be okay, but Canada's health system sucked for getting a diagnosis. "If they don't diagnose you then they don't have to treat you," Uncle Dennis said.

Back at the hotel, Sarah had the hotel suite decorated for Christmas. It was late, and my family had gone to their rooms. I opened the door, and there in the corner of the room was a tree with lights and ornaments on it.

"What have you done?" I asked.

Sarah just smiled and kissed me.

"We're going to miss Thanksgiving and Christmas. So tonight's dinner with all your family was Thanksgiving and tonight in our room, we're going to celebrate Christmas together," she said.

"You know you're lucky my mom is a Christian. I wouldn't know Christmas and the joy of having it otherwise," I replied.

"Shut up and open your present."

Sarah giggled while grabbing my hand and rushing me to the Christmas tree. There were several gifts under it, all addressed to me. A lot were travel items. My favorite, by far, was a small wooden box with a silk napkin doused in her perfume. The wooden box had a bold design on the top, so as not to look feminine. Sarah had also laminated a picture of the two of us that I could carry in my shirt pocket all the time. On the back of the photo, she had printed out the lord's prayer. She said it would keep me safe from any bad guys.

Sunday night, I said my goodbyes to everyone. Cooper was going to drive me to Camp Pendleton, and John was taking Sarah home. I was feeling very anxious. I knew I had a big job to do, and I wanted to get to it. Every day that went by without contact from my parents was one more day of living in hell. On the way to my barracks, Cooper told me that I'd be fine. He could see the fire burning inside me. He wanted me to use that fire.

"Be focused and professional, Reem. You're a team leader, always remember there are some things worth fighting for, and this is one."

I told Cooper how much I appreciated his friendship and advice. We shook hands, and Cooper drove away.

CHAPTER 28

Rico, Kuwait City

My day started as usual with Mom and June getting my dad mad. They were taking forever in the bathroom. Dad needed to use the restroom, but Mom and June had got in there before he could relieve himself. Living in a small apartment with only one bathroom sucked. But it was a lot better than the last place we'd had. We needed to keep moving around so the Iraqi special unit wouldn't find us. News of my dad and me escaping the tea house had gotten around, as had the killing of the Palestinian family. They were conducting searches block by block for Rico Al-Saba and Ahmed Al-Saba. By the time the Iraqi army got to our neighborhood, we'd moved to the inside of an abandoned building next to our apartment house. I had stashed the satellite phone inside a big opening in the air conditioning ductwork. The apartment was tiny, but we all fit with a little room to spare. That worked for just a little while, but it wasn't a permanent solution. So, during the day, I would go hunting for a new place for us to hide; Dad would always stay back with Mom and June. The new apartment felt safe enough to stay in for about a week. But I was always trying to stay one step ahead of the Iraqis.

"What do you think Reem is doing, Rico?" June asked.

It was late, and we were all just cuddled up together in the main room of an apartment that had been left by someone who'd loved the bagpipes; the place had pictures of people playing the bagpipes and two sets of them in the one-bedroom closet.

"I like to think that he's in Québec, or maybe he went to stay with Uncle Dennis in Chicago. I wish there were a way we could get a message to our family," June said.

We were all looking at the lit candles in the center of the room. The night was quiet, and we all knew it wasn't going to last. The sounds of bombs hitting their targets would be unnerving, and yet we loved to think that the Americans were coming to liberate us. Dad would tell us every night that the American heroes were just outside our borders and would be with us soon to save us from this hell.

"Oh honey, Reem is surrounded by family and friends. I'm sure he's back at school with his studies, dreaming of the day he can come back home to be with us," Mom said.

"Dad, what do you think Reem is doing right now?" I asked, trying to bring him into the conversation.

Dad had been quiet the last day and a half. He had found out the Iraqis had BJ and were holding him in Iraq. We'd all assumed BJ had gotten out of Kuwait in time.

"I think my beautiful little boy is safe and free. I wish I hadn't argued with him so much about his choices. I think he's sick with worry about us. He's so sensitive and always worried about being more like you, Rico. He just wanted to beat you at any sport."

We all started laughing. Reem hated losing to me in any game.

"You got that right, Ahmed. Reem was so happy the day the fifth grade won in kickball. I can remember his face like it was yesterday. He practiced every day for two or three weeks before the game. He was so proud to have won," Mom said, reflectively.

"He was terrific that day. I couldn't win. I didn't know that he'd been practicing, I just thought he was good. I was happy for him," I said.

The bombing had started; you could hear the planes flying by in the distance. Our conversation turned to what we should do next. Move to a new place? Or stay here for a few more days?

"Is the house you saw safer than where we're at right now, son?" Dad asked me.

"It has its pros and cons. It has a lot more exits to it, but it's closer to the freeway," I replied.

"Sue, do you think we should go to the new place?" he asked Mom.

"I don't care, Ahmed. June seems to like it here," she said. That was about all the input we could expect from my mom.

"Okay, two more days. Then we'll move," I said, looking at my dad for approval. He just smiled.

We started to get word that the Iraqis had taken the city of Khafji. Khafji was a lightly defended city in Saudi Arabia just below Kuwait. Dad used to take us there. Our father's biggest customer, Arabian Oil Company, which was later turned into a joint Kuwait and Saudi venture, wasn't that demanding of Dad's time. He would do some business and let us run around the streets. Dad loved to fly kites; it was one of Dad's favorite hobbies. I think it appealed to his engineering brain. He bought some kites that took both hands to operate, and even bought some box kites. Mom would pack some food and we would make a day out of it. Reem and I loved going with Dad to Khafji. It was like the wild west for us. Running up and down the streets and getting into trouble with our mom.

January 17, 1991, US and Coalition forces had begun air and missile attacks on targets in Iraq and Kuwait. The bombing of Iraqi positions had been going on day and night now. I had no idea how anyone could live through that kind of continual bombing. It was to the point that I didn't need to worry about the Iraqis looking for me. They seemed to be in hiding themselves. I could come and go as I pleased. The Iraqi soldiers were more concerned about the US troops that might be coming down into Kuwait.

"Dad, have you heard about Khafji?" I asked.

My dad and mom had a nice comfortable spot in the living room. We had just moved in with Sami and Abdul's widows. They were so grateful to us for killing the Palestinians. Sami's widow said that the only thing that let her sleep at night was knowing that they'd died like the dogs they were.

"Yes, just what's on the news. Rico, can you get some more medicine for June before they shut down the hospitals?" Dad asked.

He thought that with the war starting to heat up, the Iraqis would take all the medicine.

"My friend isn't there anymore, Dad. I'll have to go in myself," I replied.

I'd been getting June meds from a friend who worked at the hospital, but she'd left when they'd opened the border. June was doing well if she kept on taking her anti-seizure medicine. I would have to go. The only thing was, the Iraqis ran the hospital.

"I don't need the medicine that bad Dad," June protested.

She didn't want us to risk getting caught.

"It's okay, sweetheart I'm going to slip in and bribe one of the doctors and slip out. Rico will watch for soldiers."

Dad was trying to put a happy face on the fact we were going to do something risky and not smart.

"If you need someone to pick up some medicine. I can go; no one is looking for me," Sami's widow Emma said. I looked at my dad and shrugged my shoulders.

"You don't mind, Emma?" Dad asked.

"Tell me what to do, Ahmed," Emma said.

My dad explained to Emma that she needed as much of the medicine Dilantin as they would give her. Hopefully, three months' worth if they had it.

"Just say your little sister is having issues with all the bombing," Dad said.

He gave Emma some money in case she had to bribe anyone. Emma was gone for only about six hours. But she had done it. Three months' supply of

June's medicine was in a little white paper bag. But that was not all – she had a lot more information on the war.

"I only had to go through a couple of checkpoints to get to the hospital. It looks like the Iraqi army is getting ready to leave or go somewhere. I got into the hospital through an exit stairwell on the side of the building. I walked up to about the fourth floor when I saw a nurse, and she took me to see one of the doctors for the medication. They made me sit and wait for a couple of hours, but then the doctor came to me with the medicine. He told me to be careful, the Iraqis were getting ready to leave and they want to take prisoners with them. He said for everybody to stay off the streets. The Iraqis will run back to their country, and they will kill as many as they can before they go."

We all sat there trying to take in what Emma had discovered.

"We need to try and get some guns, Dad," I said, after thinking about all the possibilities. The Iraqis were looking more and more confused. Getting just one or two handguns might help if things got desperate.

Dad just looked at me and got up from his seat. "Okay, Rico, let's go," he said.

We started down the street looking for one of our friends who we knew could point us in the right area to get a few guns. Dad was willing to spend the rest of our money on them. Just as we came to the edge of the block, we walked up on two Iraqi police with their guns already drawn on us. They yelled, "Get down! Hands up!" and I immediately ran across the street between the two buildings. I could hear shots being fired but could tell they were shooting straight up in the air and not at me. By the time I got to the edge of the second building, I noticed my father was nowhere near me. He couldn't run; his leg was still healing.

"Son of a bitch! They got my father," I yelled out loud. "Son of a bitch!"

I kept saying that over and over out loud on my way back to my apartment. What was I going to do? I couldn't go in there and tell Mom and June. That would just upset everybody. I sat down on the ground with my back against the building. My emotions started to emerge from inside me. I felt like a little boy, scared and all alone. They had taken my dad. My dad, my best friend. The head of my household. What was I going to do? I couldn't help but wish my brother Reem was there to shoulder some of the burdens.

"Where's Ahmed, Rico?" Emma asked as I walked into the apartment and shut the door. I'd been sitting outside for about an hour. I needed to be a man and tell my mom.

"He's not with me," I said in a somber tone.

My mom came out from one of the back bedrooms and saw me sitting with my head down.

"Is he dead!? Is your father dead, Rico!?"

Mom ran up to me and started yelling at me with tears running down her face. She had my head in her hands. June was down the hallway crying so loudly that Mom couldn't understand me.

"No, they just took him," I said softly.

"What! What! June, please! I can't hear!" Mom snapped at June.

"No, he's not dead! They just took him. Dad couldn't run. I left him behind; I just ran!" I started crying.

The guilt had come over me; I'd abandoned my own father. What kind of son did that make me, that I would just leave him behind and worry about myself?

"Good, that's what you're supposed to do! Otherwise, I would be missing both of my men! You know we have been through too much, Rico! When you and your father disappeared for two days, not knowing if you were dead or alive… Why didn't you tell me right away that you'd killed the Palestinians? Did you think I couldn't handle the fact that you guys killed them all? We're going to get your father back, and you two assholes are going to stop keeping stuff from me!"

She was scared and lashing out at me. She walked back over to console June, who was still crying uncontrollably. Emma and two of her sisters put on their sandals and told me to come with them and point out the soldiers that had taken my father.

"You can't go out there, they'll kill us," I said.

"Good, then we will all die together! Come on!" Mom said.

The hatred and anger in Emma's eyes matched that in my mom's. Even June got ready, and we marched outside. I took them to the place where Dad and I had been confronted. They'd moved the roadblock down the street. The six of us started marching down the road towards the barricade. Some of the residents could see that we intended to confront the Iraqi soldiers. Emma had picked up a stick off the sidewalk to hit someone with. Emma and Mom pushed me away and said to stay back. The five Iraqi soldiers didn't see my mom and the others until they were half a block in front of them.

"You, there! Get back or I'll shoot you!" the Iraqi soldier with the most emblems on his uniform yelled out to my mom's group.

"You give me back my brother! Or you will deal with me! He has a family to feed! Who do you think you are, taking people off the streets who are hard-working and just trying to take care of their families! Shame on you! You're going to be in the hellfire if you don't give me my brother back!" Emma yelled while waving her stick at them. The yelling and commotion had brought out the residents on that block to see how the confrontation would go down.

"You listen here, you bag of shit, if you don't all leave, I'll shoot you in the fucking face. Who do you think you are, telling me what to do," the soldier yelled back at Emma and Mom; this outraged some of the women who'd come out from their homes to see the confrontation. They started telling him that his ancestors were watching, that hell was preparing a place for him for talking to a Muslim woman that way. Before I knew it, about thirty women were standing in front of those five soldiers yelling at all of them. The cries got very loud when June screamed,

"That's my daddy in the back of the car! They're going to kill my daddy!"

June could see my dad in the back of their transport truck. They had him handcuffed. Her little girl voice screaming about her daddy enraged the entire crowd that had now formed in front of the soldiers. Emma started whacking some of the Iraqis with her stick. None of the soldiers dared fire a shot. It was apparent that they all had mothers themselves and had a problem disobeying good Muslim women. Most, if not all, of the men on the street had stayed in the shadows so as not to be seen by the Iraqis. The women were in charge of this confrontation. If the men had been there, the Iraqis could have justified shooting.

"Why do you want to kill my daddy? He's not a soldier! He's a good Muslim man, who wants to take care of us. He's never hurt anyone!" June cried out.

"We're not killing him. We were asking him some questions," the head soldier replied.

"Now you've had your questions! Let him go home with his daughter!" Emma demanded.

"We will, as soon as we're done!"

The Iraqi soldier next to the truck only heard his senior officer say "we will" and started to free my dad. When the head Iraqi soldier realized that my father was halfway free from his handcuffs and re-straints, he looked for a moment at the other soldier as if to say "What are you doing?" but quickly motioned to the soldier to go ahead and let him go as if it had been his own idea.

Mom and June grabbed my father's arms and helped him. They took him to the house nearest the street. We didn't know anybody there, but the women from that block whisked them away. Emma and her sisters, with a small group of other ladies, stayed behind; they were talking to the soldiers, reassuring them that my father was just a quiet man who wasn't part of any resistance.

After they'd gotten my father out of sight and into the house, some of the other men took him out the back and we made our way quickly back to our apartment without being seen. Mom and June were right behind us. I couldn't believe a group of older women had been able to beat down five heavily armed Iraqi soldiers. Don't get me wrong; I didn't blame the soldiers. If it had been me, I would have been peeing in my pants seeing all those women ready to whack me with a stick. Sometimes we should just let the women be in charge, I thought to myself.

"Ahmed, are you okay? Did they hurt you?" Mom asked.

I had Dad propped up on some cushions in the living room. He looked like he'd been beaten up, but for the most part, it was superficial, and he was in good spirits.

"I'm fine, my sweetheart," he replied with June sobbing on his shoulder.

June was quite a woman at this point, but when it came to our dad, she always sounded like a little girl still.

"I'm okay sweetheart, they didn't hurt me too badly," Dad tried to calm her.

Emma and her sisters entered our apartment with a few of the other women to check on my dad. My mom practically collapsed with gratitude in the arms of Emma and her sisters. The women helped her up. June joined my mother in hugging and kissing the women and expressing their love and appreciation for everyone.

CHAPTER 29

Another care package, Lance Corporal? Holy crap, how big is this family of yours?" Sergeant Rudolph said.

I had just come from "mail call." I had two new care packages and four letters. The care packages were from Sarah and one letter. The other three letters were from Uncle Dennis, Grandma, and Sarah's Mom.

"You wouldn't believe me if I told you, sergeant, but it's a big family," I replied.

I'd arrived in Saudi Arabia at the end of November and been immediately put to work. I loved doing Recon. We practiced and drilled constantly. Having Jones and Marks in my squad was just God's way of torturing me. Our squad leader, Sergeant Rudolph, was a badass in a sea of badasses. At Camp Pendleton, we'd hit it off quick. The Marines that had been over there were giving the new guy's advice about living in the desert. Since I'd been born and raised in the desert, I should have been giving the class on desert life, Sergeant Rudolph also relied on me to remind everybody what to expect and take with them. He loved the fact that I could speak Arabic and had a good knowledge of what we were going to get ourselves into. Rudolph made sure I had the bunk next to him in our tent.

"Holy fuck, Sergeant! You got to come out here and see this! You're not going to believe it!" Jones said as he busted into our tent.

I threw my mail on my bunk and ran outside with everyone. Just outside our tent and down a little way by the water spigot was one of the biggest, blackest, scorpions any of these guys had ever seen in their life. But as a kid from Kuwait, I used to have one as a pet. I thought it would be a good idea to impress everyone by picking it up.

"Holy shit, Corporal, what are you doing?" Pfc Marks exclaimed. I could hear the sergeant laughing behind me.

"That big black scorpion is going to sting you, Corporal," Sergeant Rudolph said, with a little worry for my safety.

"Haven't you guys seen a household pet before?" I said as I grabbed the stinger of the scorpion and raised him in the air to show everyone.

"Holy shit, he's got him!" Jones said.

We had a 155mm Howitzer shell casing in the middle of our tent, so I decided to place the scorpion in there so the guys could look at it.

"Did you have a scorpion as a pet, Corporal?" the Sergeant asked.

"Of course, I did. But I had an aquarium to keep all my critters in," I replied.

We all woke up the next morning and looked inside the empty shell. It was gone! All hell broke loose. Most of the guys were standing on the tops of their bunks as if they were afraid of a mouse.

"Where the hell is it, Corporal?" Marks asked.

They all looked at me.

"How the hell should I know? There's no way he could have gotten out of that shell casing. Scorpions can't go up a wall like that," I said.

That day it took everybody an extra forty-five minutes to get ready. Jones and Marks picked up each article of their clothing with a stick and looked at it before putting it on. "What are you guys doing up there?" Sterling asked as he dropped his ammo bag onto his cot.

"We can't find the scorpion! So, watch out, Sterling," Marks said while standing on his cot.

"I couldn't sleep last night so I said fuck it. I got up and got rid of it," Sterling said.

"You didn't think to tell one of us? Asshole!" Sergeant Rudolph said while hitting the back of Sterling's head.

"See, this is what I'm talking about, men! Communication! We don't communicate as a unit, we're fucked out there. This is just a small example of poor communication! Sterling! Get your shit together!" Sergeant Rudolph said.

A couple of guys chuckled a little bit, but the sergeant wasn't kidding around.

"Well, I just figured I would tell you when I saw you, Sergeant. I wasn't going to keep it from anybody. I didn't think it was that important. I didn't want the scorpion in our tent," Sterling said, concerned that the sergeant was mad.

"Corporal, how long does it take our squad to get ready in the morning?" Rudolph asked me without looking away from Sterling.

"No more than ten minutes, Sergeant," I quickly responded.

"How long did it take us to get ready this morning, Corporal?" Sergeant barked.

"Little more than an hour, Sergeant!" I again quickly replied.

"More than an hour! That's fifty minutes we wasted. We could have been training or doing something to prepare ourselves for war, gentlemen! It's the little things that will fuck us up. We must be better, faster, and more vigilant. What's our motto?!"

"SWIFT, SILENT, DEADLY!!" we all yelled.

First Recon was all about deadly. We didn't stop training. Not ever. Later that night, we had a squad meeting with our Lieutenant. Lieutenant Kleinsmith entered the command tent, where we were all seated. "As you were!" he said so that we stayed in our seats.

Kleinsmith grabbed a chair from the back row and sat in front of us. He pulled out some maps from his leg pocket.

"What's up, Lieutenant?" Rudolph asked him.

We all had bubble guts. The papers in the Lieutenant's hand contained our fate. We knew that it was time for us all to move out of the tent and deploy to the frontline. The excitement for me must have been visible on my face. I needed to be out there, and I was ready to go. Ever since we'd arrived in Saudi Arabia, I'd step outside my tent in the middle of the night and breathe in the desert air. The memories, good and bad, were too much sometimes. I wanted to grab my rifle and run into Kuwait.

"Sergeant, I want you to take your squad along this line. Hit OP 7, then OP 8. Give the OP the list of encryptions. Then make your way left. Turn straight up into the area of town to the north side. Third Recon will be there to your south," Lieutenant Kleinsmith said.

"Khafji, sir? We're going to Khafji?" I asked.

Looking on the map, the line Kleinsmith was pointing out was the border of Kuwait and Saudi Arabia. OP 7 and 8 were observation posts, and if we were to take a left after OP 8, we would end up in Khafji.

"That's right, Corporal, is that a problem?" Kleinsmith asked.

"No sir!" I said.

My Lieutenant was very gung-ho and loved it when we were too.

"Corporal, there's a Kuwaiti mechanized unit in that area, is that going to be a problem for you?" Kleinsmith asked as he stood up and put the map back in his pocket. I realized that he wasn't happy with my status as a permanent resident and not a citizen. Maybe he thought I intended to free Kuwait and not serve my country. I could feel everybody's eyes on me. So, I took a chapter out of his book.

"Well, sir, I woke up this morning and pulled out my American-sized cock and started peeing red, white, and blue. Then I ate an apple pie and said the Pledge of Allegiance," I replied.

"OORAH!" my squad yelled.

"Very good, Corporal, carry on!" Lieutenant Kleinsmith said.

We all saluted as we walked out of the tent. Our Sergeant stayed behind to discuss more details of our deployment. I knew our Lieutenant liked gung-ho Marines, but that had had some sarcasm with it. Kleinsmith had a hint of a smile on his face that I knew everyone in my squad had taken note of. What my team didn't know was that while I'd been on the gun range the previous week, Kleinsmith had shot a perfect score and when Sergeant Rudolph had asked him, "How do you do it?" he'd responded, "I just piss excellence." The Sergeant had then asked, "What does that look like, sir?" and Kleinsmith and responded. "Like red, white, and blue."

"Damn, Corporal! I thought the Lieutenant was going to light you up," Marks said.

"No, he just wanted to make sure that I was mission ready. I told him I was more than ready. Damn, Marks, you got to learn to speak Lieutenant. They have their own language."

"Yeah, Marks! Corporal here speaks Arabic, English, French, and Lieutenant!" Jones said.

We all laughed at Jones's remark. We were all back in the tent, packing our gear as we waited for Sergeant Rudolph. Looking around the tent I thought our squad was a mix of young and uneducated men from around the country. Rudolph was originally from Nebraska but had moved to Fresno, California, as a kid. Marks and Jones had grown up in Portland, Oregon. We also had men from Nevada, Arizona, Idaho, and Texas. Me, Marks, and Jones were the new additions to First Recon.

"Room Ten-Hut!!" Sergeant Rudolph said as he entered the tent.

Everyone in the room immediately stood to attention, except for Hayes and Brown, who'd had their backs to the door and must have thought it was Jones playing around again. At Camp Pendleton during training, Marks and Jones liked to enter a room of enlisted men and yell, "Room 10!" and watch everybody snap to attention. "Does anyone know where room 10 is?" they would then say as a joke.

"I said attention, damnit!!" Sergeant yelled.

Corporal Hayes and Brown quickly came to attention. Right behind the Sergeant was none other than Lieutenant Colonel Robert Carry, commander of the forward headquarters of the First Recon intelligence group.

"That's okay, Sergeant, they probably didn't hear you the first time. Hello, Marines, I just wanted to come and shake your hands before you left. Corporal, Corporal, Private." Commander Carry started shaking our hands as he looked us over.

"You must be Corporal Al-Saba," he said while shaking my hand.

"Sir, yes, sir!" was my quick response.

"Tell me, Corporal, why didn't you join the Kuwaiti military?"

With that question from the Commander, I realized that my situation had gone up the flagpole a lot higher than I'd ever imagined.

"Sir?" I questioned.

"I'm just surprised a young man from Kuwait like yourself chose to join the Marines," the Commander responded.

"Sir, I've spent a lot of time in America. I knew from an early age that I wanted to live in America and become an American. There was no other choice for me. I was going to join the Marines or not go at all," I said.

"Well, I'm glad to hear it, Corporal. We're damn glad to have young men like you serving in our Marine Corps. Tell me, Corporal, are you familiar with this area you will be operating in?"

"Khafji? I know Khafji like I know the items in my duffel bag, Sir. My brother and I would go with my father to Khafji and run all over that town. My dad worked at the refinery for several hours; I know every inch of Khafji, Sir," I said.

"Excellent, Corporal. As you were," Commander Carry said. As he left the tent with Sergeant Rudolph, they gave each other a quick salute.

After we got our gear packed and, on the Humvee, Sergeant Rudolph led us in prayer. Corporal Brown and the Sergeant were the most religious out of our squad. I thought it was kind of them to say a prayer. I think it helped with all our nerves and put some humor into our mission.

"Dear almighty, please watch over the First Recon as we go out and seek our enemy to destroy them. Bless our equipment that will work properly. Help us go out and accomplish the things that we need to accomplish this day. Keep us safe from our enemies and friendly fire. If someone must get it in our squadron, please let it be Marks and Jones. They're just a couple of dip shits anyways, and no one would mind."

"Amen!!" we all yelled.

As I got in the M60 machine gun seat I could hear Marks and Jones saying, "Damn, that's fucked up!"

Sergeant Rudolph sat in the front with Corporal Horn. Roy Horn was an excellent driver and an expert at the radios. Horn was from Nevada and joined right out of high school. He was the one I thought should have been a sergeant by now. Horn liked doing all the crap assignments. Then there was Corporal Jason Brown from Arizona. He was good with people and weapons. The heat and humidity were something that Brown was okay with. PFC Sterling was a good Marine, but we all wondered in the back of our minds what Sterling would do in battle. Staff Sergeant Brad Oz was our team leader and the guy you wanted next to you if anything went down. Oz was from Texas and had spent the most time in Saudi Arabia. Lance Corporal Eric Hayes was African American and loved boxing.

"Let's head out, Marines!" Master Sergeant Rudolph ordered.

CHAPTER 30

We arrived at OP 7 just after 2pm on January 17th, 1991. My squad got out of our vehicles and gathered for a quick meeting before we headed over to OP 8.

"Okay, we know that the deadline has come and gone for Iraq to withdraw. Come on, guys, stop screwing around. Listen up!"

Some of us were still talking to each other as we walked up to Sergeant Rudolph's Humvee.

"Like I was saying, Marines! Things are starting to get dicey out there. The word is that we're in the Operation Desert Storm phase of this campaign. That's the name given to indicate the offensive campaign of this coalition," Rudolph said.

"Desert Storm? Not Desert Shield, Sergeant?" Private Sterling asked.

Ever since we could remember, we'd been training for an offensive fight. I think we'd all become comfortable with training and putting on the chemical suits and masks. Trying to think about fighting a war with this gear wasn't what anyone of us wanted to do. It was harder to see and move around with the chemical suits on.

"Yes, Desert Storm, Private! The air campaign has started," Rudolph said.

It was one thing to hear the air campaign had started, but an entirely different thing when you saw it. We all looked up at the same time. A fast-moving jet was coming our way.

"What the fuck is that?" Jones said.

"That's no jet I've ever seen," Marks replied.

"That's a Tomahawk cruise missile fired from one of our frigates, more than likely," Rudolph said.

The hair on the back of my neck stood straight up when I saw that missile about 100 feet off the ground and hauling ass to somewhere in Iraq. It was long like a pencil and had small wing-like flaps in the middle. I saw that cruise missile on its way to kill its target. It gave me the biggest thrill I think I'd ever had. To be a part of a military that had that type of technology and weaponry solidified in my mind and heart that I wanted more time in the Marines and more knowledge and skills to be the best.

"We're wasting daylight, Marines. Come on, let's move out!" Rudolph ordered.

I'd received letters from Sarah and my family, but I had not sent any to them since arriving in Saudi Arabia. I hadn't wanted to share my thoughts and feelings with anyone while I was here. This whole experience was changing me. Becoming a United States Marine, it was like nothing else you could ever experience. We'd said things like Semper Fi, Adapt or Die, Honor and Country while I was at Camp Pendleton for training. I'd noticed my fellow Marines came from every walk of life. We were Marines, and we were all Americans. I knew at that moment I was no longer the little boy trying to beat my brother in a sport. I was like all Americans. I came from somewhere else first, but now I was an American.

The excitement our entire squad was feeling after seeing a tomahawk cruise missile on its way to Iraq was terrific. We reached OP 8, and heard that they'd seen the cruise missile through the forward-looking scopes. I couldn't help but feel anxious and excited. I wanted to drive into Kuwait right then and there. The road we were going to take into Khafji was the same one from Kuwait.

"Reem, you okay?" Rudolph asked.

We had just left OP 8 and connected with the highway into Khafji.

"Yes, I'm good, Rudolph. I'm just thinking about all the times my dad and I traveled this road. It's funny, the last time I was on this road I was a little boy from Kuwait City and now I'm a US Marine," I said.

Sitting beside Master Sergeant Rudolph was always a treat. He liked to ask me questions about my life, and I loved asking him questions about his life. You could say we were good friends on and off base.

"I can't even imagine what it would be like to have my country invaded by an enemy force. This must be very surreal for you," Rudolph said.

"It is, Sergeant," I said.

"Will your family give you grief for not joining the Kuwaiti army?" Sergeant asked.

"No, most of my family already knows that I'm a Marine. My family in Kuwait probably thinks I'm still in school. My brother Rico is the oldest and toughest in our family. If he's still alive, he probably thinks that I'm with my Uncle Dennis and waiting for the outcome in Chicago," I said.

"So, your family in Kuwait has no idea what you're doing?" Rudolph asked.

"We haven't had contact with any of them," I replied.

"Damn, that must be so hard, not knowing," Rudolph said.

Our vehicles entered the town of Khafji the next day. We said hi to some friends from the Third Recon and then took positions on the north side of the city. Khafji seemed abandoned, not as I remembered it.

After about ten days of living out of a Humvee and going on recon patrols, I'd had enough of the air campaign. I wanted to start killing Iraqis. I met up with Staff Sergeant Oz and Private Marks on the west side of a brick wall. Some Marines from Second Marine were listening to a radio.

"Corporal, you have to listen to this," Sergeant Oz said.

He handed me the headset. I put one side of the earpiece next to my right ear.

It was a broken speech, like the mic wasn't working part of the time.

"I don't think this mic is working," I said.

"No, it works. The guy has the hiccups," Marks said, laughing.

"What if that fire mission was coming in over your position, Private? Would you think it was so funny then?" I said to Marks.

Three Marines from the Second stopped laughing and looked at me for a moment, then started laughing again all together.

"You're all a bunch of dumbasses," I said while turning back to my truck.

"Dumbasses! You think my boys are dumbasses?" Two Marines from the Second were walking up to me quickly. I recognized their faces immediately: my old friends Danny and Ben.

"Hey, guys!!" I ran up to them both and hugged them like they were family.

"Last time we saw you, Corporal, you were just a shitbag recruit," Ben said.

"Yeah, and thanks to you, I'm now a US Marine," I said.

Danny just kept looking at me with amazement.

"You okay there, Danny?" I asked.

"Holy shit, Reem, your arms are huge. I can't believe how well you're doing in the Marines. I thought for sure you would bell out after the first month."

"Look, no one is more surprised than I am at how well I'm doing in the Marines. But I love it! I can't believe I get to wake up in the morning and do this for a living. Getting paid to scuba and sky dive is the best career," I said.

Ben and Danny just looked at one another.

"Corporal, we're just glad to see you," Danny said.

"Reem," Ben said, "we got a letter from Sarah asking us if we've seen you. Come on, man, you can't just sit back and not write to her. It's not fair to her.

We all get it. It's hard to write a letter over here with so much going on. But you must find the time and send something."

"Okay, alright. I'll send one out today," I said.

That night we had about eight hours together. We talked about Rico and my dad and the day we all met. We spoke about Carrie, Ben's sister, and her new husband. But mostly we talked about how funny life was and how we missed our families.

The next day was historic. January 29th, 1991. The Iraqis had moved into Khafji. Coalition forces held back the bulk of the Iraqi advancement into Saudi Arabia but since Khafji was lightly defended the Iraqis had been able to capture it easily. The sound of hundreds of Iraqi armored vehicles moving into Khafji was terrifying, to say the least.

"Sir, are we bugging out?" Horn asked.

"No, we're going to hold our position to the north, call in artillery fire if possible," Sergeant Rudolph said.

"Horn, tell Oz to spread the word we're staying!" I said.

Rudolph liked that I took the initiative on sharing his orders.

"Corporal, what's the word on Third Recon to our south?" he asked Brown.

"Sergeant! Third Recon is moving to a different building to get a better view," Corporal Brown said.

It was clear that Khafji had fallen into the hands of the Iraqis. A bold move by Saddam, I thought to myself.

"First Recon, gather up!" Rudolph ordered. "This is the situation. Third Recon is to the south of us on top of the center building. We're over here to the north. Between both Recon units, we should be able to rain down hell on earth. This is what any Recon soldier lives for. Moments like this only come once in a lifetime, Marines. Let's do our job. Swift, silent, deadly."

That night, listening to the radio chatter, a picture started to emerge of the situation. Iraqis had control of Khafji, but the Third Recon had eyes on some of the tanks and Armored Personnel Carriers. I had a good view of what looked like two tanks, three APCs. I had a block wall obstructing part of my view of the tanks. I could see about twenty to thirty soldiers standing outside their APCs, looking for us. My squad had divided into two areas; four of us had stayed behind a block wall next to a store parking lot and Rudolph had taken Marks, Hayes, and Sterling a half click to the south for a secondary view. I was with Oz, Jones, and Brown. Horn was with the Humvee in case we needed to bug out. The enemy was getting closer to our position, which was why I knew they were looking for us. I kept looking through my thermal scope at the enemy, marking their location.

"Bulldogs online," Oz whispered.

I looked at Oz and thought to myself, remember your training, Reem. Bulldog was the US artillery we'd been waiting for. Now was the time to kill the enemy.

CHAPTER 31

B ulldog 9, 6, this is Benji 3, 4, adjust fire, over!"
I let go of the mic, waiting for a response.

"Benji 3, 4, this is Bulldog 9, 6, out."

FDC – The Fire Direction Center – came back.

Me: "Enemy grid November Delta 0116 5244 break… direction 1800."

FDC: "Benji 3, 4, enemy grid November Delta 0116 5244 break direction 1800."

Me: "One tank three times APC ten times enemy dismount DPICM, over."

Dual Purpose Individual Cluster Munition was a cluster bomb that could devastate your enemy's day.

FDC: "One tank three times APC 10 times enemy dismounts DPICM, out."

FDC: "Delta 4 rounds, target number Alpha Echo 1800, over."

Me: "Delta 4 rounds, target number Alpha Echo 1800, out."

FDC: "Shot, over."

Me: "Shot, out."

FDC: "Splash, over."

Oz turned to the rest of the squad after hearing FDC call out splash over the mic and yelled, "Incoming!"

We all crouched down a little. I kept my eye in the viewfinder of my thermal scope to witness what our squad had done. This would be our first-ever shot fired in this war. First Recon had been building up to this moment. We'd trained for this ever since we'd put on the uniform. I looked up and over to our squad leader Rudolph's position. Sergeant Rudolph was looking directly at me with a sense of hope and anxiety in his eyes. Suddenly I heard the crackle of the munition above our heads. The crackle was the shell bursting open. Cluster munition travels to a certain altitude and breaks apart into hundreds of explosive grenades that can pierce an armored personnel carrier, drop-down destroying everything. It was genuinely like raining down hell upon your enemy. Bulldog was dead on target. As soon as I put my eye back into the thermal scope, all I could see was utter destruction – a direct hit.

Me: "Splash, out."

Me: "Fire for effect, over."

FDC: "Fire for effect, out."

After I called out "fire for effect," the artillery battery bulldog started shelling the enemy's location with everything they had. The day went on much the same. We would find the enemy and call in the fire missions. Third Recon to the south was also calling out fire missions, but they were dangerously close. I could only imagine what they were going through, having that cluster munitions exploding so close to their position. We all kept an eye out for each other. We needed to get a better view of the enemy's location, so our squad relocated two clicks to the south.

"Sergeant Rudolph, that Saudi battalion is moving in quick," I cried out.

"That's a pretty bold move! He's going to get his men killed. Corporal, take Horn with you, drive over to the command Qatar and Kuwaitis, find out what the fuck is going on!"

A Saudi Arabia National Guard battalion had moved into Khafji but was being repelled by heavy fighting with the Iraqis. Just getting back to the Humvee wasn't going to be easy. It seemed like the Iraqis were everywhere and ready for a fight. I needed to dash past two large buildings to get to the outskirts of town. The pavement stopped, and the desert began behind the last building. That was where I would find Horn and the Humvee. I sprinted over to the first building, but Oz, Jones, and Brown got cut off by rifle fire down the street.

"Oz, is Brown okay?" I yelled back at them.

The street that separated the two buildings was small but long. I knew it well. Rico and I used to run down this way to get in the side of a store that sold flavored Pop. The shots could only be coming from the stairs leading down into the building.

"We're okay, but we're cut off from you! Can you see anything?" Oz yelled.

"Yes, I can see they're hiding in a concrete stairwell leading down into the building next to you.

Throw a frag in there, I'll get them as they run out. On the count of three."

Jones threw the frag, hitting the stairwell perfectly. All three Iraqis ran out of the stairs and into the street. I was looking right at them as I pulled the trigger of my M16. I remembered they looked surprised as all three bodies fell to the ground. Didn't they know I was right there? I thought as I yelled, "CLEAR!" They'd just shot at me when I'd run by; were they so confused that they couldn't remember a minute ago that I was behind the second building?

"Damn, Corporal, you smoked all three of those motherfuckers!" Brown said.

"I did? Are they all dead?" I asked.

Oz and Brown were checking the bodies for intelligence and injuries. I was on one knee looking down the street with my rifle. Jones was across from me on one knee looking up the road with his rifle so we could provide cover if any enemies were spotted.

"These two are dead. This one is just fucked up," Oz said.

I knew that Brown was putting a dressing on the wounded Iraqi, but my training wouldn't let me take my eyes off the street.

"Corporal, you shot him, you carry him," Brown said, dressing the enemy's wounds.

"You're an asshole, Brown!" Oz said, picking up the Iraqi and carrying him over his shoulder. We got to Horn and the Humvee. Oz and a medic from Second Marine were providing medical assistance to the Iraqi until someone could take him to a field hospital.

"Are you okay, Corporal?" Brown asked, seeing me over by the ammo boxes. I was getting some more magazines. He was probably concerned that I might have trouble dealing with killing the Iraqis.

"I've never felt better in my life, Corporal," I said, to put his worries to rest and with a look of confidence on my face.

"Good, I'm glad to hear it, Corporal! What was it like? Did it feel the same as the airstrikes we called in?" Corporal Brown asked as Oz approached us.

A sense of realization came over the entire squad. Spotting the enemy's location and then watching through a thermal scope as men and equipment were destroyed; we'd all been responsible for the carnage that the cluster bombs had created.

"No, it felt personal, much more personal. But the result was the same: dead enemies, who had no business in this country," I said.

I could see the enemy I'd shot was awake now and asking for help in Arabic. He was pleading for us not to kill him.

"Hey, Corporal, can you come over here and calm this guy down," the medic from Second Marine asked me.

I walked over to the Iraqi. I must have looked like a Marine that was ready to kill him. He started shouting in Arabic. I yelled at him in Arabic to shut up and calm down, no one was going to kill him. The look on his face when he realized I was from Kuwait was priceless.

"What are you doing here with these infidels?" he asked.

"We're exterminating cockroaches that have invaded my home," I snapped at him. He tried to tell me his name and rank, but I cut him off.

"I don't care what your name is! Your name is cockroach! That's all I need to know, Mr. Cockroach!" I said.

"I'm Muslim, you're Muslim – do you know what the holy Quran says about the Hellfire?" the cockroach asked.

"I'm an American! Look!" I pointed at the flag on my shoulder. "We kill cockroaches! I was the one who shot you and the other two cockroaches," I said with so much anger for him.

"Sergeant! Load the prisoner up for transport before Corporal here commits a war crime," the medic said. The Marines from the Second Division took the Iraqi away.

"What did you say to him, Corporal?" Oz asked.

"He was just spouting propaganda his superiors taught him," I replied.

We met up with some Saudis and some Kuwait tanks that were moving in to help the Saudi National Guard. They were so surprised to see me in a Marine uniform. At first, I would get a lot of criticism from all of them, I thought, but I was like a rock star. The Kuwaitis wanted to take a picture with me. So I did. We talked about Khafji and the Saudi national guardsmen that were being repelled.

Qatar and Saudi forces, with help from the US and others, started slugging it out house to house until Khafji was back under Saudi control. The Saudi Arabian government was so pissed off over the invasion of the city, they wanted to be the ones to free it. We arrived back at First Recon's rally point; Lieutenant Kleinsmith was there with the rest of the First Recon.

"You Marines and Third Recon have done an outstanding job over here, Sergeant. Things are starting to wind down. I want you to move your squad further north by the end of tomorrow. We're getting word that the ground war will start soon," Lieutenant Kleinsmith said.

"Any word on the intelligence we got off the Iraqi bodies Corporal smoked earlier today?" Sergeant Rudolph asked.

"Nothing yet, but I doubt they'll let me know anything for a while," Lieutenant Kleinsmith said. "We've been successful playing this cat and mouse game with the Iraqis. We've destroyed most of their equipment. I don't see any Saudi Arabian forces yet. They're coming from the south. I want to get eyes over there so we can let Third Recon know when it's safe to get off the roof of that fucking building."

We could hear the fighting inside the city going off constantly.

"They've dug in and they're putting up a fight," Sergeant Rudolph said.

CHAPTER 32

e need to..." Lieutenant Kleinsmith didn't finish because Marks and Sterling started shooting and yelling. They both had point and had made contact with the enemy. Our rally point was just outside the city – we didn't realize it, but the Saudi forces had begun pushing the enemy toward us. I ran around to the other side of the Humvee to take cover and started shooting at where Marks was aiming. The Iraqis were pinned between the Saudi forces and us; they'd have to fight their way through us if they were to retreat. They start returning fire immediately. Bullets were ricocheting off the Humvee and the ground. Someone had popped smoke, which made it difficult for us to see their position.

"Stay there, Lieutenant! Stay down, sir!" Jones yelled. He was the one who'd popped the smoke shell.

The Lieutenant took a round in the leg and went down. The only things keeping him from the onslaught of bullets were two truck tires lying on the ground where someone had left them behind. Jones crawled over to Lieutenant Kleinsmith and grabbed him by the collar and dragged him under the Humvee for cover. We all rose and started shooting to give him cover fire. I got hit in the left arm, but kept shooting.

"Give me cover!" Jones yelled. He was still trying to get Lieutenant Kleinsmith away from the open area. The fighting intensified until a Saudi V-150 Armored Car rolled up behind the Iraqis and cut down all those that didn't surrender.

"Give me a dressing," Jones said. He was helping Lieutenant Kleinsmith with his leg. Over to my left, I started hearing Brown and Hayes talking on the radio about a quick medevac. The Lieutenant wasn't that badly hit, I thought to myself. Then I looked over to Hayes and saw that Horn was down. He'd got hit in the neck and chest. Brown was over him, putting pressure on his wounds.

"Niner seven one-two Hotel November!" Hayes said, yelling into the mic.

I noticed part of Brown's ear was missing as he leaned over Horn. I looked at my left arm. I'd taken a round just below my shoulder. Marines from the Second Division and the Saudis descended upon us with their medics.

"Someone get me a litter!" the medic cried out.

They scooped up Corporal Horn and put him on the stretcher. One of the armored vehicles came and took him away.

"Looks like you got one in the arm, Corporal,"

Brown said. We both looked at one another, holding back tears. Corporal Horn hadn't looked good. Brown and the medic from Second had had to perform a tracheotomy on him to let him breathe.

"I can't feel it. It doesn't even hurt," I said as Brown put a pressure bandage on my arm.

"Well, it doesn't look like it hit the bone. So, I think the adrenaline is helping with the pain," Brown said.

"Is that why you haven't noticed half your ear is missing?" I replied.

"What!! Damn it!! My ear is gone?" Brown said, surprised. He started to move his hand to feel for his ear, but I stopped him.

"Don't touch it. You might get it infected," I said, moving his hand away.

"Here, just put this directly on my ear and wrap the bandage around my head to hold it in place," Brown said.

I did what he said, and that was when I felt the pain in my arm. We drove to a spot where the Saudis had a camp set up. Lieutenant Kleinsmith, Brown, and I all said that we would see them soon when the squad members left us at the helicopter pad, on our way to the field hospital. The pilot informed us that Horn was in surgery. How in the hell did he get there so fast? I thought. He'd been taken just about twenty minutes before us. I couldn't help but feel relieved. At least he's being looked after by surgeons, I thought.

I looked over at Lieutenant Kleinsmith. He seemed to be happy and full of drugs. Brown and I sat in a daze. Corporal Brown kept asking me questions about my childhood in Kuwait. I started telling him all about Kuwait and my family. It was nice to take my mind off the pain in my arm.

CHAPTER 33

2/12/1991
Dear Sarah,

I'm sorry for not writing sooner. I was informed that a notice was sent to my family about my injury. Please don't worry, I'm fine. I was hit in the shoulder and received ten stitches. I have been working out, and I'm back with my squad already. So please tell everyone that I'm doing well.

My time over here has had a significant effect on me ever since I graduated boot camp. I started to notice small changes in my thinking. Now that I'm over here, those small changes are now undeniably evident to me. The Marine Corps pounds it into you from the start. Family, God and country. My love, I need to free my family from this evil. But at the same time, I feel like a foreigner in this land of my birth. When I think of you and our future together, I can only see us in America. Starting a family and a future together is where my country is, and that country is America. Please don't get me wrong, I still love Kuwait. It's just not the same anymore for me.

Sarah, I've been thinking of staying in the Marine Corps and making it my career. I love everything about it: the structure, the opportunities. The men in my squad are like family to me. It's hard to put into words, the trust and love you have for the guy next to you when you're in battle. I think the men and women of the Marines are some of the best in the world. I know that I am from Kuwait and not used to seeing America in action, but the pride I feel being a part of something so big and powerful appeals to me.

Please don't worry. I won't make any decision without you. Just know that I love you, and we will be together soon. The commanders make us wear our chemical suits all the time. We are ready for this to be over so we can all go home. We have a little more to do.

Until then, my love, you are always on my mind and heart. Tell John and Cooper to take you out occasionally.

Always yours
Reem!

"Just tell me in your own words, Lance Corporal Al-Saba, what happened on January 31st, 1991," Major Garry McClintock asked.

"Yes, sir. I had just come back to our rally point from being out of pocket with Oz, Jones, and Brown. I could hear the fighting going on in the city but didn't think the Iraqis were going to retreat in our direction," I said.

"You were out of pocket?" the Major interrupted.

"Yes sir, Sergeant Rudolph ordered me to go talk with the Saudi commander because it looked like their push into Khafji had been stalled. By the time I got to a Kuwaiti tank commander, they were aware of the situation and had reinforcements on the way. I gave Commander Ippis our rally point. He just said the fighting was house to house, and he didn't see an issue with our location," I explained.

"Okay, continue," the Major said.

"Well, like I said. We got to the rally point. Lieutenant Kleinsmith was there briefing our squadron on our next assignment. Since the fighting was going house to house, we were going to move further to the north. That was when Marks and Sterling started firing. They had positioned themselves in front of our equipment and were keeping watch as the Lieutenant was briefing us. The Saudi soldiers had entered one of the houses on the street directly in front of us, and apparently, the enemy came out the back to avoid them, only to run right directly into our rally point. The Lieutenant went down immediately with a shot to the leg. I got hit in the arm as I ran for cover. At that time, I was returning fire on the enemy's location, but I had a hard time seeing where they were."

"Why is that, Corporal?" the Major interrupted again.

"Because that's when Jones opened a smoke grenade to give the Lieutenant cover. He was down behind some tractor tires upfront and in a bad position. Jones had crawled over to the Lieutenant and dragged him under the Humvee as we all laid down cover fire. That's when the V-150 showed up and killed the remaining enemy forces, sir."

"Did you see Horn go down?"

"No, I didn't know he was hit until Hayes was calling for a medevac on the radio. I looked over to see Brown working on Horn."

"Very good, Corporal. That should do it for now," the Major said.

I snapped to attention and gave the Major a salute as I turned to leave. Then I stopped abruptly. "Sir, are they going to do anything for Jones? It was pretty damn brave what he did," I asked.

"I'm not sure, Corporal, but it looks good. I wouldn't be surprised if your unit receives some recognition for what went on here."

The Major smiled. I headed back to the First Recon's tent. We were all waiting for someone to tell us how Horn was doing. He was scheduled for another surgery that day. The doctors had had to remove part of his left lung, and he was still using the tracheotomy.

Sergeant Rudolph entered our squadron tent and sat down on his bunk. "Did everything go okay with the Major, Corporal?" he asked me.

I gave him a thumbs up and sat down on the rack next to him.

"Have you heard anything about Corporal Horn, Sergeant? I said.

The sergeant didn't look at me for a minute. I could see he was about to lose it. Was Horn dead? I put my hand on his back. The sergeant lifted his head and looked at me for a minute. Then he let his head fall back down so I couldn't see his face.

"Horn is out of surgery and in recovery, but there were some complications. They lost him a couple of times on the table. They were able to bring him back. The doctors weren't sure how long he was gone without oxygen to his brain. The surgeon told me that it doesn't look good even though he's still with us. The doctors think he won't make it past today," Rudolph said.

I could see tears hitting his knees.

"Horn is a Marine, Sir! He's going to make it! Hoo, Rahh!" Brown yelled.

"He's a badass, Sir! He's just fighting a new battle! Hoo, Rahh!" Marks said.

"Thanks, First Squad," Rudolph said.

He got up and shucked off the bad news the docs had given him. We all started packing up our gear. First Marine was moving out and up to the Kuwaiti border. We all knew the ground war was about to begin soon. Thousands of US Marines were on the move, and we had received orders to head out in front of the First Marine Division. We needed to help identify the trenches and minefields so we could clear them for First Marine. Knowing what we were going to do and sitting there waiting to get orders to do it sucked. I found myself sitting next to a gas tanker. It was providing me with some shade and a tire to lean up against. I sat there thinking about June's face and Rico's smile. Mom was hard as a rock, but Dad, he might have been having a hard time. I wondered if they were being held prisoners by the Iraqis. Maybe they'd gotten out and didn't know how to notify me. The thoughts in my head always started to occupy my time when I found myself alone.

"Hey, Corporal! Rudolph is calling a squad meeting. It looks like we're going. Our orders are to advance," Staff Sergeant Oz said.

"On my way, Sergeant," I said.

"Marines, we are this day making history! All of you are standing up to a bully named Iraq and Saddam! If the world fails to act against a tyrant like Saddam, we'll just be asking for trouble! This is not about oil! Let me say that again! THIS IS NOT ABOUT OIL!! It's about not letting a country like Iraq just come in and destroy a small, peace-loving people and country like Kuwait! If the world decided to run and hide and not stand up to Saddam and Iraq, we would have murderous dictators ruling the world! Make no doubt about it, soldiers! You are what stands between right and wrong! Between good and evil! I have the reports right here! Kuwaiti citizens being tortured and shot in the streets, women sexually assaulted and killed! Saddam is dumping oil into the gulf and burning all oil wells. Saddam and the Iraqis are committing acts of unprecedented environmental damage! The estimated cost of the ground war comes in at one in three Marines dead or wounded! One in three!! That is unacceptable to me as your commander! First Marine Division, we are trained and ready to go! We will all wear our chemical suits with no exceptions! They hope we can make five kilometers our first day. I say we double that! Let's do our jobs and be our best! I won't let you down, and I know you won't let your country down!"

I ran over to my Humvee and got into the passenger's seat. Hayes drove, and Brown was on the scope looking for any sign of the enemy. We broke through the border into Kuwait. I was finally home with half a million friends to help me kill my family's captors. To be a part of First Marine, cutting through sandhills and ditches, was fun. The minefield seemed to go for miles, but we got through them quickly. Kuwait City was ours for the taking, I thought. I could see the others felt the same way. Sergeant Rudolph was with Marks and Sterling. Sergeant Oz had the third Humvee with Jones.

By the next day, First Marine had gone so far with zero losses. You could hear the Marines starting to get overly ambitious on the radio.

"Benji 3, this is Eagle 1, over."

"Eagle 1, this is Benji 3, go ahead."

"Can you and Benji 4 come over to my area and help me with some Iraqis soldiers, over."

"Copy."

"Hey, Oz! Rudolph needs help with some more Iraqis!" I yelled.

Sergeant Oz and Brown had driven a little to our right flank to see if they could get a glimpse of the Iraqi counteroffensive.

"Did Eagle 1 say where he was at?" Brown asked.

"Yes, he's just over this sand berm to the left," I replied.

"Is it strange to be back in your home country?" Brown asked. He must have been wanting to ask me that for a while now, I thought.

"Yes, to be honest with you, Corporal. It feels extraordinary to be back in my country. I feel as if I'm now a foreigner. It doesn't feel the same to me anymore."

I looked out across the desert, reflecting on my childhood.

"That's because you're a United States Marine! No going back now, Corporal!" Brown yelled.

"You're so right, Brown. The Marines have become a part of my identity. There's no going back now," I said. We high fived.

Sergeant Rudolph had about fifty enemy soldiers that had surrendered. I got out and started checking them for weapons, at the same time yelling at them, "We will not kill you, obey our orders!" in Arabic. Most of the Iraqis wanted the shelling to stop. They were hungry and thirsty and were in no condition to fight.

"Did you see anything to the west?" Sergeant Rudolph asked.

He'd heard on the radio that the Iraqis had started mounting a counterattack on our right flank.

"We didn't see the Iraqi positions, Sergeant, but they're there," I told him.

We had all three Humvees lined up next to each other. We were waiting for orders to press forward. About an hour later, a squad of Army Apache helicopters flew over us. They were low to the ground and hauling ass to our right flank; we could see far off in the distance plumes of smoke. The Apaches were kicking ass out there. It wasn't long after that we were told to move forward. By the end of the third day, I was lying on top of my Humvee's hood just outside Kuwait City.

"Are you going to be able to see your family when we go in there, Corporal?" Sergeant Rudolph asked.

"I don't think so, Sergeant. My family's home is on the other side of town. If we go to the center of the city, I hope they're there and I'll hopefully get to see them."

"We'll go anywhere you want, Corporal. You have my word on it," Rudolph said.

The excitement and anxiety that had risen in me several times had come and gone like waves in the ocean, had made me numb to what I was feeling. Across a few bridges and some roads lay the city, and hopefully my family. I think I was trying to prepare myself for the worst. I knew whatever the case, I wouldn't find out sitting on this Humvee. Like much of this ordeal, waiting had become the standard practice. The rest of the First Marine Division had rallied next to us. We were poised to take over the city of Kuwait on both sides. Word had come down to let the Arab forces go into the city first, whenever that was going to be. I kept telling myself to have patience, rely on my brothers next to me for support and inspiration. Concentrate on your job, I said to myself.

The next day we decided to move into the city. As we started driving in, thousands of Kuwaitis filled the streets. People were celebrating and waving American and Kuwaiti flags, screaming, "Thank you, America. Thank you, President Bush!" I jumped out of my Humvee and grabbed an American flag a Kuwaiti citizen gave me. I got on the hood and joined in the celebration with the rest of the Marines hanging off the APC. It was going to take forever to get to the center of Kuwait, I thought. People were on scooters and in cars driving up and down the roads waving flags and cheering. The celebration was truly overwhelming for all of us in the First Recon. I just kept yelling, "USA!"

CHAPTER 34

Rico, Kuwait City

R ico, can you see what is happening?" June asked.

"It looks like there are three of them this time. Don't come over here! You don't want to see this," I said.

We'd moved into a high-rise apartment building. It was a three-bedroom apartment that had a back-service elevator to it for a quick getaway and a trash chute for an emergency backup. We were on the ninth floor, and the window in the main room overlooked the front of the building. Across the street I could see the Iraqi soldiers tying up three more Kuwaitis for execution. Torture and executions happened more frequently now. The resistance was still alive and inflicting some damage to the Iraqi soldiers but the retaliations were brutal.

"It's okay, Rico. I've already seen it three or four

times this week. I'm not some weak little girl any-more," June replied.

She had looked out our window to see the view from our new apartment the first time they'd executed Kuwaitis. At first, she'd thought the Iraqis were going to whip them with sticks, but then the sticks had started shooting and killing all who had been tied up.

I moved away from the window and motioned for her to come and see. The shots from the rifles echoed between the tall apartment buildings. The quiet, almost peaceful morning was once again abruptly ended by gunshots. That was what my parents woke up to. It was getting to be routine.

"Good morning, you two," Dad said. He was very cheerful for some reason.

"Morning, Daddy," June said, kissing him on the cheek. "Why are you so happy this morning?" she asked.

"Because we're one more day closer to freedom," Dad replied. He poured out his cup and cleaned it. "Is there any tea made?"

"Maybe one day closer to death," I said.

I was not in the best of moods. I'd had the night shift last night, and it was hard to keep from falling asleep.

"We only have coffee left, Dad, it's on the table," June said.

"Why so gloomy, Rico? I'm telling you, any day now the American heroes will be coming down that road to free us," Dad said.

"Dad is still so happy about Khafji. He thinks the Americans can do the same for Kuwait," June said.

Mom walked into the kitchen, her hair a mess and her clothes looking slept in. We had to be ready at any moment, so we all slept in our clothes from the day before.

"Don't listen to Rico, sweetheart. He hasn't gotten any sleep yet. He's always been grumpy when he's tired, ever since he was a little boy. My grumpy little boy."

June and Dad laughed at Mom's teasing. I was tired, but my attitude was more residual anger from the day before. The Iraqis had set fire to our oil wells and started dumping oil into the Gulf. There was just no end to what these bastards were going to do to our country, I thought to myself.

"I'm going to bed. Wake me if the pipe alarm goes off," I said.

I'd found that at each corner of the building, there was a vent pipe that went the entire length of the building. If you cut open a section of the wall and exposed the pipe, you could hit it with a hammer or something metal. Three to four floors above could hear it, and they would then hit the pipe and so on until you had the people all the way up to the top floor aware that the Iraqis were coming. The Iraqis always used the front elevators and stairs to enter a building. This place had two back stairwells and a freight elevator.

If that wasn't good enough, the little boy from Germany who was bored and playing with the trash chute one day had fallen down the entire length of the building. That was when we'd discovered that the trash chute had a gradual curve to it. All the apartments had a trash chute in the back-freight area which came out behind the far-left corner of the building where the dumpsters were. That was where I was standing with a friend who was talking about the vent pipes when the little boy had shot out of the trash chute, scaring the hell out of us. He was okay, no broken bones, just a couple of scratches. Mohammed was the one who realized we could use the trash chute for an emergency escape plan.

The next night I was up all night again watching out for any Iraqis.

"Mom! Dad! Get up, something is going on!" I said, shaking my parents awake.

"What is it, son!" Dad asked. He was awake instantly.

"June, wake up, dear," Mom said. She was getting June up without startling her.

"Dad, something is going on outside, I can't tell what," I said.

I was so confused. It was early morning, and I had been up all night on watch. I was watching the Iraqis moving in and out of our area.

"Did anyone tap on the pipes?" Dad asked.

"No, not a sound!" I replied. Mom and Dad ran over to the window to see what I was talking about. June stood next to me, holding my hand and wiping her face on my shoulder. She was trying to wake herself up. The meds she was on made her a heavy sleeper.

"What the hell is all this? Are they preparing for battle?" Dad said, looking at me. I just nodded my head.

"Rico, get the lights!!" Mom ordered. I quickly shut off the lights.

"Should I hit the pipes twice?" I asked my dad. One hit meant the Iraqis were in front of our building, two hits meant get ready, something was going on. Five quick hits meant get the hell out of the building.

"Yes!! Why isn't that done already?" Dad replied.

"Maybe the first floor fell asleep," I said.

I had the hammer in my hand when someone tapped on our front door.

"Rico, it's us. Don't hit the pipe!" The voice sounded familiar. My dad opened the door a crack and talked to someone in the hallway. They whispered, but I couldn't hear from the living room. Dad quickly shut the door.

"What is it? Who was that?" I asked.

I was on my way to the front door to see for myself.

"No, Rico, it's just if we all wake up and turn on the lights, the Iraqis will know that we've seen them," Dad explained.

We all went back to the window. There were thousands of soldiers going up and down the street. Some looked confused. Some seemed to be out of place. The commanders looked to be having a hard time with the other commanders. A group of about four soldiers got out of line and started running. The commander in the back area opened fire, killing the four of them. That was when things got more out of hand. One of the soldiers shot the commander who'd killed the four deserters. Something was going on. I slowly backed away from the window.

"What's wrong, Dad?" June asked.

Dad had a look in his eyes as if he had just come up with a great idea.

"It's the Americans! The heroes are on their way!" he said.

"Dad, you're crazy! The Americans would have announced it over the radio," I said.

"Rico! Look, this is the main road into Kuwait from the south! If the Americans start our liberation, they'll have to come right through here!" he yelled with excitement.

"Ahmed, look!" my mom said.

We both went back to see what Mom wanted. Two Iraqi tanks had come down the street, which seemed to put the soldiers into a panic. The commanders on the ground got everyone back into line and started moving south to the edge of town. Suddenly a quick knock hit our front door.

"Rico, come on! Open up!"

The quick knock scared us, but we quickly realized it was Mohammed's voice in the hallway.

I opened the door. "What are you doing, Mohammed? What's going on?" I asked.

Mohammed gave a quick smile to June. "Come on! Let's go to the roof! I have my binoculars! I think the Americans are coming!" Mohammed said.

"Okay, let me grab a blanket," I replied.

It was not going to be fun climbing up the stairwell to the roof. We'd disabled the elevators because the Iraqis wouldn't want to climb the stairs, especially those of a twenty-three-story building.

"Can you see anything?" I asked. We got to the roof and put the blanket over us so no one could see us.

"Just the Iraqis. It looks like they're moving to the Saudi border," Mohammed said. He let me take a look with his binoculars; they were old but did the job. I could see about eight tanks and some more armored vehicles moving out into the desert.

"I'm going to tell my dad what's going on. I'll be back soon. Just keep looking at what they're up to." I ran back down the stairs to my apartment to tell my dad what I'd seen. Could it be the Americans, I thought to myself? I was so stressed out, I'd started to feel something strange in my chest. Was I having a heart attack from climbing the damn stairs? No, it felt more like nerve pain. I reached for the handle of my apartment door. I stopped and looked down at my hand. It was shaking.

"Pull yourself together, Rico!" I said out loud. My hand was shaking even more now. June opened the door and motioned me to come in.

"What the hell is wrong with you?" she said. She had a toothbrush in her mouth. My dad was on the chair in the kitchen, trying to use the satellite phone again. That fucking phone is not worth the trouble, I thought. But dad seemed to be talking to someone.

"What's Dad doing on the phone?" I asked.

Mom waved June and me over to them with some urgency. "Your dad is talking to a General. A real-life American General!" Mom said.

"Okay. What should we be doing to help, General?" Dad asked. The mic on the sat phone was loud enough for us to hear what the General was saying. Dad pointed it up so we all could listen to it better.

"Ground offenses have started. What we're looking for is any sign of a counterattack from the Iraqis. If you see anything that looks like they're organizing their efforts, we need to know," the General said.

"Okay, General. We saw the soldiers this morning gathered up, about a hundred of them moving to the south," Dad replied.

"Yes, we saw that too, Mr. Al-Saba. Just hold tight and stay off the streets. We should have your country back to you very soon."

Dad looked up at Mom, June, and me. Tears started to stream down his face like I'd never seen before.

"God bless you, Sir! God bless the United States! God bless Mr. Bush!"

Dad was crying right into the phone.

"Well, thank you for that, Sir. We're doing our jobs the best we know how. I hope and pray for you and your family's safety and prosperity," the General said.

I could hear the General starting to get a little emotional at the other end. That was when I realized the pain in my chest was hope. Hope that this was the start of the ground campaign. We might make it out of this hell after all. I started to cry with the rest of my family.

The next forty-eight hours were intense. We could hear the shelling of the American artillery; the Iraqis had lost all control of the battlefield. We'd seen them try to mount a counterattack and my father had called and talked to someone about it after the first day. Then the Iraqis started running for their lives, which was extremely dangerous for us. They were grabbing anything that would drive, and there were rumors that Iraqis were kidnapping Kuwaitis to use as human shields. We all stayed inside and kept a lookout for each other.

"Rico! Are you okay?" Mohammad asked.

He was starting to get scared because I was making weird sounds out of my mouth as I looked through the binoculars. We had been on the roof for a few days. I was looking for any signs of the Americans; it was the third day now. I'd decided to take one more look before going back to our apartment.

"Yes, I'm good, Mohammad!! It's the Americans! I can see column after column of American soldiers down the road," I said. My breathing was excited and rapid. I was making a funny sound out of my mouth again.

"Let me see, Rico!!" Mohammad said. He grabbed the binoculars out of my hands and stood up to look clearly.

"Holy shit!! It's the entire American army!" Mohammad said.

I just looked at Mohammad and smiled. We both ran downstairs to give our families the news.

"Dad! Dad!" I yelled.

I was out of breath from running. My mom and dad jumped out of their seats; June came running down the hall from her bedroom to see what I was yelling about.

"What is it, Rico?" Dad asked.

"The Americans…! The Americans…!" I tried to catch my breath. "The Americans are right down the street!!"

Dad ran over to the window. "I don't see anything, son! Where are they?"

He thought they might be right outside our building.

"No, no! About five kilometers down the highway. You can see them just sitting there in their tanks and trucks. Thousands of them!" I said.

"Look!! Look!! There's nobody out there!" Dad said.

He was excited for some reason; we just looked at him, puzzled.

"Don't you see! They're all gone! They're all gone!!" Dad started yelling.

We all moved to the window to see what Dad was trying to say. I could see a couple of men looking around but no more soldiers. We just kept looking out the window until it was clear to us that the Iraqis had left. More and more people started to go into the street. By the time we decided to make our way outside, the road was full of people.

"Rico! Rico! My brother! Please, Allah! Praise him! Praise him every day!" Mohammad said.

He was dancing with his aunt and father in the street. I looked back at my mom and June. They were sitting on the steps of our building, watching everyone celebrate. Thousands of Kuwaitis had taken to the streets.

"We're free, Mohammad; we're free, my brother!"

I started celebrating with everyone, Mohammad and I walked up and down the street, yelling blessings on America. Dad was sitting next to Mom and June, waving at me to go.

"Go! Go! Have fun! We will be right here!" he said. He was encouraging me to go with Mohammed up the street to meet the soldiers as they came in. Kuwaiti soldiers, Saudi Arabian soldiers, Qatari soldiers, and American Marines. The Marines came down the street, and everyone started chanting "USA! USA! USA!"

I'd stopped yelling my chant as the first Marine armored vehicles started their way down the street. I could see some Marines sitting on top of their armored vehicles. As they got closer, I was taken aback by their appearance. The uniform was very impressive looking; I don't think I'd ever seen a Marine in uniform up close before. I liked the way one Marine had his sleeve folded up, it was intimidating-looking, I thought. Just above his folded sleeve was the American flag and, on the shoulder, a First Recon patch. The Marine's forearm had the same birthmark Reem had on it, I thought to myself. I pulled my focus out and instantly saw my brother sitting on the hood of that armored vehicle, in a Marine uniform, chanting "USA!" along with the crowd.

"Rico, what's wrong?" Mohammad asked.

"That Marine is my brother Reem!" I said.

Is my mind playing tricks on me? I thought to myself. But the closer he got, the more he looked like Reem. His arms were like cannons, his jawline looked chiseled out of marble.

"Your brother's on the Marine vehicle?" Mohammad asked.

Just as the armored vehicle got right next to me, it stopped. I looked up at the Marine on top of the hood. He was still chanting "USA!" His arm was in the air with his index finger pointing to the sky. And there was his birthmark. I started shaking.

"The American Hero" we had all been waiting for was my little brother Reem. I climbed on top of the hood and wrapped my arms around his neck.

I started kissing his face with my lips and feeling tears running down my cheeks. Reem was still yelling "USA!" He hadn't realized it was me, his older brother Rico. One of the Marines on the top of the cab grabbed my arm and was trying to take it off Reem's neck.

"Thank you, sir, thank you!" The Marine was trying to be polite but was worried that I might be hurting Reem.

"No, this is my brother! Reem!" I said.

I pulled my arm away from the Marine. Reem finally looked at me and realized who I was. We both embraced each other at once.

"What are you doing here?" Reem asked.

"Me? What are *you* doing here!" I replied.

Reem laughed at that.

"No, I mean what are you doing on this side of town? Where are Mom and Dad? Where's June? Are they okay?"

His men stopped the truck, and they all gathered around us.

"Reem, we had to hide. The Iraqis were trying to kill us. We're all alive. Mom and Dad are just up the street, about a mile," I said.

The men around us went nuts after I said that. They picked Reem up off his feet and threw him on top of the vehicle. Then they grabbed me and put me next to him. Before I knew it, we were driving up the street to all the cheering and yelling.

"USA! USA! USA!"

I looked at Reem's face. I couldn't believe it was him. I didn't want this moment to end. The feeling of overwhelming joy had enveloped me. I didn't even know what had happened to Mohammed. The mile-long drive back to the apartment complex seemed to last forever. I couldn't wait to see my mother's face and enjoy this unexpected family reunion.

Ahmed, Kuwait City

"Ahmed, can you believe all of this?" Sue said.

"Yes, I can, my love. I knew the Americans would stand up to Saddam," I replied. June was sitting on the step just below me with her arms on my knees. I squeezed her tight. Sue had her head on my shoulder and her soft little arm around mine.

"What are we going to do now, Dad?" June asked. It was hard to hear her amidst all the celebrating. I thought about it for a second. I knew my wife needed time away from Kuwait. She needed to be back home with her family.

"We're going to do whatever your mom wants to do," I said.

Sue laughed out loud. "That's a good answer, sweetheart. But for now, we need to keep an eye out for your brother. He's wearing a green thobe and hanging out with Mohammad," Sue said to June. We all squeezed tight and enjoyed the celebration.

"Look! There's Rico on top of that truck," I said.

I noticed Rico's green thobe. He was cheering on top of a truck with some US soldiers. They had their arms around him like he was one of them. I started clapping my hands and cheering. June shot up and started screaming as she ran toward the truck. Sue just looked at me, confused.

"What the heck?" she started to say.

One of the soldiers jumped down from the truck and scooped June up into his arms, and this gave Sue and me a shock. We both jumped to our feet. Then Sue started screaming too.

"It's Reem! It's Reem!" she yelled. She was already on the road and putting her arms around the soldier. I just stood there trying to figure out what the hell was going on. Reem, I thought! Reem is in America… Rico and Sue moved to the side, and between them stood my beautiful son Reem. They all approached me with Reem in the middle. I could hardly stand; my knee was giving out.

"You were right, Dad. The American hero did come and save us," Rico said.

Reem was standing right in front of me. He was so much bigger than I'd ever imagined him. His battle dress uniform was dusty but still pristine. His rifle was slung behind his back, and the name on his uniform said Al-Saba US Marine. I couldn't take it anymore and fell into his embrace. I'd sent my son off to school in America; America had sent me back a hero.

"Dad, are you okay?" Reem asked as he knelt next to me. I was sitting on the step again as my knees had no strength.

"I'm so happy! I'm so happy!" Those were the only words I could get out of my mouth.

Reem introduced all of his Marine unit. We got to spend an hour with him before they had to go. We sat on the steps of the apartment building just looking at Reem and what a change we could see in him. June had a death-grip on his arm.

"I thought I was going to have to go to our home to find all of you. I didn't expect to run into my family in the first mile of Kuwait," Reem said, and we all laughed.

"No, we had to hide and move around to stay safe from the Iraqis," Rico said.

I noticed Reem wasn't making eye contact with Sue. Sue's smile slowly left her face as she realized that Reem was having a hard time looking at her.

"What is it, son?" she asked as she put her hand on Reem's face, forcing Reem to look right at her.

"Mom, I can't be the one to tell you this," Reem said with tears welling up in his eyes. He pulled a piece of paper from inside his uniform and handed it to his mother. Sue opened the letter, taking her hand off Reem's face.

"What is it, Mom?" June asked with trepidation in her voice.

"It's a letter from Dennis to Reem telling him that my father has passed." Sue didn't show any emotions at first. She just kept looking at the letter Reem had given her.

"Grandpa Green is gone?" June repeated.

Rico pulled June into his arms and they both started to cry. I took Sue's hand and asked if she was okay.

"Ahmed, I need to go home now," she said softly.

I put my arms around her and kissed her forehead. "We will go right away, my love." I just held her in my arms.

Reem's unit returned to collect him. We all agreed to meet in Canada as soon as possible.

Book Two

AN AMERICAN HERO
Home Coming

John Lawrence is writer and author
of the novel *"An American Hero."*

A professionally trained low voltage engineer. He has spent the last two decades reading and writing historical fiction. He loves developing complex characters that incite you to emotion. His debut novel An American Hero is just the first in a series of three. His love for family and country are evident in his six children and twelve grandchildren. A proud certified veteran advocate for more then a decade John has continued helping veterans navigate the veteran's administration system. He is a great storyteller that will take you on his journeys, learning history through a fictional tale.

WWW.JOHNLAWRENCEAUTHOR.COM